PENGUIN CLASSICS

THE TALE OF OLD MORTALITY

WALTER SCOTT was born in Edinburgh in 1771, educated at the High
School and University there and admitted to the Scottish Bar in 1792.
From 1799 until his death he was Sheriff-Depute of Selkirkshire, and
from 1806 to 1830 he held a well-paid office as a principal clerk to
the Court of Session in Edinburgh, the supreme Scottish civil court.
From 1805, too, Scott was secretly an investor in, and increasingly
controller of, the printing and publishing businesses of his associates,
the Ballantyne brothers.

Despite suffering crippling polio in infancy, conflict with his
Calvinist lawyer father in adolescence, rejection by the woman he
loved in his twenties and financial ruin in his fifties, Scott displayed an
amazingly productive energy and his personal warmth was attested by
almost everybody who met him. His first literary efforts, in the late
1790s, were translations of romantic and historical German poems and
plays. In 1805 Scott's first considerable original work, *The Lay of the
Last Minstrel*, began a series of narrative poems that popularized key
incidents and settings of early Scottish history and brought him fame
and fortune.

In 1813 Scott, having declined the poet laureateship and recommended Southey instead, turned towards fiction and devised a new
form that was to dominate the early-nineteenth-century novel.
Waverley (1814) and its successors draw on the social and cultural
contrasts and the religious and political conflicts of recent Scottish
history to illustrate the nature and cost of political and cultural change
and the relationship between the historical process and the individual.
Waverley was published anonymously and, although many people
guessed, Scott did not acknowledge authorship of the Waverley novels
until 1827. Many of the novels from *Ivanhoe* (1819) on extended their
range to the England and Europe of the Middle Ages and Renaissance.
Across the English-speaking world, and by means of innumerable
translations throughout Europe, The Waverley novels changed forever
the way people constructed their personal and national identities.

Scott was created a baronet in 1820. During the financial crisis of
1825–6 Scott, his print   ble and

the ▬▬▬▬rtner became insolvent. Scott chose not to be declared bankrupt, determining instead to work to generate funds to pay his creditors. Despite his failing health he continued to write new novels, to revise and annotate the earlier ones for a new edition, and to write a nine-volume *Life of Napoleon* and a history of Scotland under the title *Tales of a Grandfather*. His private thoughts during and after his financial crash are set down in a revealing and moving *Journal*. Scott died in September 1832; his creditors were finally paid in full in 1833 from the proceeds of his writing.

DOUGLAS S. MACK is a native of Lanarkshire and grew up in Bothwell, where several of the events of *The Tale of Old Mortality* take place. He has held posts in the National Library of Scotland and other libraries, and is now a Reader in the Department of English Studies at the University of Stirling. He is General Editor of the Stirling/South Carolina Research Edition of the works of James Hogg.

CLAIRE LAMONT is a graduate of the universities of Edinburgh and Oxford and is currently a Senior Lecturer in English at the University of Newcastle. She specializes in late-eighteenth-century and early-nineteenth-century English and Scottish literature. She has published editions of Scott's *Waverley* (1981) and *The Heart of Midlothian* (1982), and is editing *Chronicles of the Canongate* for the Edinburgh Edition of the Waverley novels. She is Advisory Editor for the Waverley Novels in Penguin and the Textual Adviser for the new Penguin edition of the novels of Jane Austen.

WALTER SCOTT

THE TALE OF OLD MORTALITY

Edited with an introduction by
DOUGLAS S. MACK

PENGUIN BOOKS

PENGUIN BOOKS

Published by the Penguin Group
Penguin Books Ltd, 27 Wrights Lane, London w8 5tz
Penguin Putnam Inc., 375 Hudson Street, New York, New York 10014, USA
Penguin Books Australia Ltd, Ringwood, Victoria, Australia
Penguin Books Canada Ltd, 10 Alcorn Avenue, Toronto, Ontario, Canada m4v 3b2
Penguin Books (NZ) Ltd, 182–190 Wairau Road, Auckland 10, New Zealand

Penguin Books Ltd, Registered Offices· Harmondsworth, Middlesex, England

First published 1816
Published in the Edinburgh Edition of the Waverley Novels by Edinburgh University Press 1993
Published with revised critical apparatus in Penguin Classics 1999
1 3 5 7 9 10 8 6 4 2

Text, historical note, explanatory notes and glossary
copyright © The University Court of the University of Edinburgh 1993
Editor-in-chief's preface and chronology copyright © David Hewitt, 1999
Introduction and note on the text copyright © Douglas S. Mack, 1999
All rights reserved

The moral right of the editors has been asserted

Typeset in Linotype Ehrhardt
Typeset by Speedspools, Edinburgh, and
Rowland Phototypesetting Ltd, Bury St Edmunds, Suffolk
Printed in England by Clays Ltd, St Ives plc

CONTENTS

ACKNOWLEDGEMENTS

The editors of a critical edition incur many debts, but the indebtedness of the editors of the Edinburgh Edition of the Waverley Novels and of its paperback progeny in the Penguin Scott is particularly heavy. The universities which employ the editors (in this case the University of Stirling) have, in practice, provided the most substantial assistance, but in addition the Universities of Edinburgh and of Aberdeen have been particularly generous with their grants towards the costs of editorial preparation, and it has been the support of the Humanities Research Board of the British Academy that has allowed the Edition to employ a research fellow.

The Edinburgh Edition of the Waverley Novels has been most fortunate in having as its principal financial sponsor the Bank of Scotland, which has continued its long and fruitful involvement with the affairs of Walter Scott. In addition the P. F. Charitable Trust and the Robertson Trust have given generous grants, and the Carnegie Trust for the Universities of Scotland has been most helpful.

Scott's manuscripts are widely distributed, but the greatest concentrations are in the National Library of Scotland in Edinburgh, and the Pierpont Morgan Library in New York. Without their preparedness to make manuscripts readily accessible, and to provide support beyond the ordinary, this edition would not have been feasible.

The editors have, perforce, had to seek specialist advice on many matters, and they are most grateful to their consultants Dr John Cairns, Professor Thomas Craik, Caroline Jackson-Houlston, Professor David Nordloh, Roy Pinkerton, and Professor David Stevenson. They owe much to their research fellows, Mairi Robinson, Dr Alison Lumsden, and Gerard Carruthers. They have asked many colleagues far and wide for information. They have continuously sought advice from the members of the Scott Advisory Board, and are particularly grateful for the support of Sir Kenneth Alexander, Professor David Daiches, Professor Jane Millgate, and Dr Archie Turnbull.

In particular the editor of *The Tale of Old Mortality* would like to thank Mairi Robinson for her excellent work in preparing the Glossary of the present edition. Dr Peter Davidson and Dr Janey Stevenson, who have recently prepared an edition of *Old Mortality* for the Oxford University Press, have generously provided much valuable advice and information. For various kinds of assistance and advice, warm thanks are due to Dr Ian Clark, Professor David Daiches, Dr Gillian Hughes, Professor William Johnstone, Dr Alison Lumsden, Patricia Marshall, Professor Jane Millgate, Mairi Robinson, Dr Henry Sefton and Dr A. R. Turnbull.

To all of these the editors express their thanks, and acknowledge that the production of the Edinburgh Edition of the Waverley Novels and the Penguin Scott has involved a collective effort to which all those mentioned by name, and very many others, have contributed generously and with enthusiasm.

David Hewitt
Editor-in-chief

Claire Lamont
Advisory editor, the Penguin Scott

J. H. Alexander,
P. D. Garside,
G. A. M. Wood
General editors

The novels of Walter Scott published in Penguin are based on the volumes of the Edinburgh Edition of the Waverley Novels (EEWN). This series, which started publication in 1993 and which when complete will run to thirty volumes, is published in hardback by Edinburgh University Press. The Penguin edition of *The Tale of Old Mortality* reproduces the text of the novel, Historical Note, Explanatory Notes and Glossary unaltered from the EEWN volume. It does not reproduce the substantial amount of textual information in the Edinburgh Edition but instead provides, in the following paragraphs, a summary of general issues common to all Scott's novels and, in the Note on the Text, a succinct statement of the textual history of *The Tale of Old Mortality*. A new critical Introduction has been written specifically for the paperback, as well as a Chronology of Scott's life and a list of recommended Further Reading.

The most important aspect of the EEWN is that the text of the novels is based on the first editions, corrected so as to present what may be termed an 'ideal first edition'. Normally Scott's novels gestated over a long period: for instance, the historical works on which he drew for *The Tale of Old Mortality* (1816) had all been read by 1800. By contrast the process of committing a novel to paper, and of converting the manuscript into print, was in most cases extremely rapid. Scott wrote on only one side of his paper, and he used the blank back of the preceding leaf for additions and corrections, made both as he wrote and as he read over what he had written the previous day. Scott's novels were published anonymously—hence the title 'the Waverley Novels', named after the first of them—which meant that only a few people could be allowed to see his handwritten manuscript. Before delivery to the printing-house, therefore, the manuscript was copied and it was the copy that went to the compositor. The person who oversaw the printing of Scott's novels was his friend and business partner James Ballantyne, with whom he jointly owned the printing firm of James Ballantyne & Co. from 1805 (except for the period 1816–22 when Scott was sole partner) until they both became insolvent in 1826.

The compositors in the printing-house set the novels as copy arrived, and while doing so they inserted the great majority of the punctuation marks, normalised and regularised the spelling without standardising it, and corrected many small errors. It was in the printing-house that the presentation of the texts of the novels was changed from the conventions appropriate to manuscript to those of a printed novel of the early nineteenth century. Proofs were corrected in-house, and then a new set of proofs was given to Ballantyne who annotated them prior to sending them to the author. Scott did not read his proofs against his manuscript or against the printer's copy; he read for sense and, making full use of the prerogatives of ownership, he took the opportunity of revising, amplifying, and even introducing new ideas. Thus for Scott reading proofs was a creative rather than just a corrective engagement with his texts. The proofs went back to Ballantyne who oversaw the copying of Scott's new material on to a clean set of proofs and its incorporation into the printed text. Only occasionally did Scott see revised proofs. Two points in particular might be noted about the above procedures. First, Scott delivered his manuscript in batches as he wrote it, and the result was that the first part of a novel was set in type, and proofs corrected, before the end was written. And secondly, in the business of turning a rapidly written text from manuscript to print Scott was indebted to a series of people, copyist, printer, proof-reader, whom Scott editors have come to refer to as 'the intermediaries'.

The business of producing a Waverley novel was so pressurised that mistakes were inevitable. The manuscript was sometimes misread or misunderstood (Scott's handwriting is neat but his letters poorly differentiated); punctuation was often inserted in a mechanical way and the implication of Scott's light manuscript punctuation lost; period words were sometimes not recognised and more obvious, modern terms were substituted for them. The EEWN has examined every aspect of the first-edition texts in the light of the manuscript and the full textual history of the novel. This has enabled the editors to correct the text where Scott's intentions were clearly not fulfilled in the first edition. The EEWN corrects errors, but it does so conservatively bearing in mind that the production of the printed text was a collective effort to which Scott had given his sanction.

Most of the Waverley Novels went through many editions in Scott's lifetime; Scott was not normally involved in the later editions although very occasionally he did see proofs. But in 1827, after his insolvency the previous year, it was decided to issue the first full collected edition of the Waverley Novels, and much of Scott's time in the last years of his life was committed to writing introductions and notes, and to reviewing his text for what he called his 'Magnum Opus' ('Great Work'), or Magnum for short. Scott had acknowledged his authorship of the novels in 1827, and this enabled him to describe the origins of his novels in the introductions to the Magnum edition in a way which was impossible to an author seeking anonymity. The Magnum has formed the basis of every edition of the Waverley Novels published from Scott's death in 1832 until the EEWN chose the first editions as its base-text. In the EEWN the additions made for the Magnum will be published in two volumes at the end of the series. In the volumes published in Penguin passages from the Magnum Introduction relating to the genesis of the novel are included in the new editorial material produced for the paperback edition.

This edition of Scott in Penguin offers the reader a text which is not only closer to what the author actually wrote and intended but is also new in that it uses for the first time material recovered from the manuscripts, revealing to fuller view the flair and precision of Scott's writing. In addition it supplies the editorial assistance necessary for a modern reader to interpret and enjoy the novel.

David Hewitt
Editor-in-chief
The Edinburgh Edition of the Waverley Novels

INTRODUCTION

The Solemn League and Covenant
Now brings a smile, now brings a tear.
But sacred Freedom, too, was theirs;
If thou 'rt a slave, indulge thy sneer.
(BURNS,
'The Solemn League and Covenant')

Since the early 1830s, it has been natural to think of *Old Mortality* as part of an imposing row of volumes called the 'Waverley Novels'. This was by no means the case, however, when Scott's tale of the Covenanters was first published in December 1816. At that time, Scott was known as a poet rather than a novelist, and his literary reputation seemed to be entering a decline. His most recent major poem, *The Lord of the Isles* of 1815, had received a markedly less enthusiastic welcome than its predecessors. Scott's poems had long been favourites, and they were still much liked; but they were beginning to seem tame in comparison with the excitements offered by the writings of two more recent arrivals on the literary scene.

One of these recent arrivals was Lord Byron; and the other was that intriguing figure, the 'Great Unknown'. The Unknown was the anonymous author of *Waverley*, a novel that had created a sensation on its publication in 1814; and the mysterious 'Author of *Waverley*' quickly followed up his initial success with two other well-received fictions: *Guy Mannering* (1815), and *The Antiquary* (1816). Speculation about the identity of the Unknown was intense, as Henry Cockburn records in *Memorials of his Time*:

> The unexpected newness of the thing, the profusion of original characters, the Scotch language, Scotch scenery, Scotch men and women, the simplicity of the writing, and the graphic force of the descriptions, all struck us with an electric shock of delight. ... If the concealment of the authorship of the novels was intended to make mystery heighten their effect, it completely succeeded. The speculations and conjectures, and nods and winks, and predictions and assertions were endless, and occupied every company, and almost every two men who met and spoke in the street.[1]

As we now know, of course, Scott was the mysterious Unknown. His desire to remain anonymous may seem strange to us; but in 1816 he had various reasons for 'the concealment of the authorship', as Cockburn puts it. As a respected professional lawyer, Scott enjoyed a position of great prestige in Scottish society. While such a man might further enhance his prestige by writing poetry for publication, the writing of novels was a much less acceptable activity. Furthermore, as Cockburn suggests, the mystery created interest. This interest stimulated sales; sales created wealth; and Scott, like many other people before and since, enjoyed making money.

It would be unfair to suggest, however, that Scott's motives for anonymity were entirely prudential and mercenary. He undoubtedly enjoyed the fun of the thing; and it was in this spirit that he decided to do something unexpected. *The Antiquary* was not to be followed by a fourth novel by 'the Author of *Waverley*'. Instead, Scott would create a rival for the Great Unknown; and in doing so he sought to strike out into a new path, into a new kind of fiction. The new plan was to create a framework within which various speakers could tell their tales; and the various tales would build up into a complex picture of Scottish manners, and of Scottish society.

This audacious and spirited plan bore its first fruits in *Tales of my Landlord*, a set of four volumes published in December 1816. When he began work on this project, Scott's plan was to write four separate tales, each occupying one volume. Each tale was to be devoted to a different province of Scotland: the Borders, the Highlands, the West, and Fife.[2] These stories from every corner of the country were to be presented as having been told by various travellers at 'my landlord's' Wallace Inn, in the village of Gandercleuch.

The Wallace Inn is named after Scotland's national hero, Sir William Wallace (1272?–1305); and it is situated at the very heart of the country, at a place where, as it were, all paths meet. Gandercleuch's new rival to 'the Author of *Waverley*' is one Peter Pattieson, a young assistant schoolmaster struggling with an illness that will bring him to an early grave. Pattieson's role is to listen to the travellers at the Wallace Inn, and to set their tales down in writing. After his early and expected death, the tales are prepared for the press from his surviving papers by his patron Jedidiah Cleishbotham (that is to say, 'Solomon Smackbottom'), the local schoolmaster and Session Clerk.

In the event, this plan was somewhat modified in *Tales of my Landlord* as published. The framing narrative of Pattieson and Cleishbotham remains intact; and, as planned, the first volume of the 1816 *Tales* is devoted to the projected tale of the Borders. This tale, *The Black Dwarf*, is followed by *Old Mortality*, the tale of the West.

According to Scott's original plan *Old Mortality* ought, like *The Black Dwarf*, to have been confined to a single volume. As it took shape, however, this particular story so powerfully caught hold of Scott's imagination that it expanded to fill the remaining three volumes of the first series of *Tales of my Landlord*.

In spite of its development into a three-volume novel, *Old Mortality* remains very much a story of the West of Scotland. More specifically, it is a story of Lanarkshire, and in particular of that stretch of the Clyde valley lying between the small county town of Lanark and the village of Bothwell several miles downstream.

Scott's links to the Bothwell area can be traced back to the autumn of 1799, as we learn from his son-in-law and biographer, J. G. Lockhart.

> It was also in the course of this autumn that he first visited Bothwell Castle, the seat of Archibald Lord Douglas, who had married the Lady Frances Scott, sister to Henry, Duke of Buccleuch; a woman whose many amiable virtues were combined with extraordinary strength of mind, and who had, from the first introduction of the young poet at Dalkeith, formed high anticipations of his future career. Lady Douglas was one of his dearest friends through life; and now, under her roof, he met with one whose abilities and accomplishments not less qualified her to estimate him . . . the Lady Louisa Stuart, daughter of the celebrated John, Earl of Bute.[3]

Scott, then, was in congenial company during his visit to Bothwell in 1799. The surrounding countryside was also congenial, as there was a great deal in the Bothwell area to stimulate his life-long interest in places evocative of the past. One such place was Bothwell Bridge, where, in 1679, a popular insurrection by the Covenanters of the West of Scotland had been bloodily defeated by a powerful royal army acting on behalf of Charles II. Covenanters were supporters of the 'National Covenant' of 1638 and the 'Solemn League and Covenant' of 1643. They enjoyed particularly strong support in the West of Scotland; and the development of their movement is described in the present edition's Historical Note (354–58). In brief, however, Covenanters were deeply opposed to attempts by the State to control the affairs of the Scottish Church; and by the late 1670s they had become a religiously-motivated popular movement, ready to assert the rights of the people by means of open rebellion against the forces of the Crown. Much of the action of *Old Mortality* is concerned with the flaring up of a rebellion of the Covenanters in the West of Scotland during the summer of 1679.

The defeat of the Covenanters at Bothwell Bridge figures promi-

nently in Scott's novel; and, as we shall see, another Bothwell land-
mark, the medieval Bothwell Castle, also makes its presence felt.
During his visit to Bothwell in the autumn of 1799, Scott's base was
the Douglas family's seventeenth-century mansion of the same name.
This building was completed in the eighteenth century and demolished some two hundred years later; but the beautifully situated and
extensive earlier castle stood near by, on steep banks above the windings of the Clyde. The medieval Bothwell Castle still survives; and
W. Douglas Simpson takes the view that 'the noble castle of Bothwell
... takes rank among the foremost secular structures of the Middle
Ages in Scotland'.[4]

Scott could not fail to be aware of the adjacent medieval castle
while he was a guest of the Douglas family in the autumn of 1799. At
that period his hosts also owned the ruins of Craignethan Castle,
situated a few miles up-river from Bothwell; and Scott's visit to
Lanarkshire included a morning excursion to Craignethan.
According to Lockhart,

> the poet expressed such rapture with the scenery, that his hosts
> urged him to accept, for his lifetime, the use of a small habitable
> house, enclosed within the circuit of the ancient walls. This offer
> was not at once declined; but circumstances occurred before the
> end of the year, which rendered it impossible for him to estab-
> lish his summer residence in Lanarkshire. The castle of
> Craignethan is the original of his "Tillietudlem."[5]

Craignethan is a ruined sixteenth-century tower standing above
the Clyde's tributary, the Nethan. Protected on three sides by
steep ravines and equipped with elaborate defensive fortifications, it
played its part on the royalist side in the armed conflicts of sixteenth-
century Scotland. Because of the persevering loyalty of its owners the
Hamiltons to the cause of the deposed Mary Queen of Scots,
Craignethan was partly demolished when the Reformers gained control of the kingdom for a period. This work of demolition began in
1579, during the second period in power of the Regent Morton, one
of sixteenth-century Scotland's leading Reformers.

The history of Craignethan did not end with its partial demolition
in the sixteenth century. In the seventeenth century it was purchased
by the Covenanter Andrew Hay, who built a high and narrow house
in a corner of the walled courtyard, using stone from the ruined
tower. This was the house offered to Scott in 1799 by the Douglas
family; and it still remains in use as a dwelling-house, being the home
of the custodian of the ancient monument.[6]

Andrew Hay's house is a decent, modest, unflamboyant, and somewhat austere structure: in short, it gives the impression of being an

appropriate house for a puritanical Covenanter. No doubt it would have been greatly extended and altered if it, rather than Abbotsford, had indeed become Scott's summer residence. However that may be, the courtyard of Craignethan now contains a tower, aristocratic and imposing, which has sustained assault and ruin in the cause of the royal Stuarts; and it also contains a Covenanter's house, comparatively modest and mean, but still intact and habitable. It is possible to see in this a manifestation in stone of the conflicts described in *Old Mortality*.

The Tillietudlem of Scott's novel has much in common with Craignethan, as the following description indicates:

> The Tower of Tillietudlem, having very thick walls, and very narrow windows, having also a strong court-yard wall, with flanking turrets on the only accessible side, and rising on the other three from the very verge of a precipice, was fully capable of defence against any thing but a train of heavy artillery. (161)

Tillietudlem is the home of Lady Margaret Bellenden and her beautiful granddaughter Edith. Lady Margaret is an enthusiastic royalist who treasures the memory of a visit made to the tower by Charles II; and the chair on which the King sat on that occasion becomes, for Lady Margaret, a throne to be revered and carefully preserved. Thanks in part to Lady Margaret's enthusiasm for the royal cause, the Tillietudlem of the novel becomes a rallying point for the old loyalties to the King; and one of *Old Mortality*'s most significant moments comes when Tillietudlem is captured by forces led by the moderate Covenanter Henry Morton. The Covenanters of the seventeenth century were the inheritors of the cause of the Reformers of the sixteenth century; and when *Old Mortality*'s fictional Henry Morton captures Tillietudlem for the cause of the Covenant, he is in a sense echoing the work of the historical Regent Morton at Craignethan.

The parallels between Craignethan and Tillietudlem were too obvious to be missed by Scott's Scottish readers; and Craignethan quickly became identified in the public mind with the tower of the novel. Indeed, in the 1860s the Caledonian Railway, ever anxious to encourage day trippers, established a passenger station called Tillietudlem on a new branch line that passed nearby. The station is long closed, but a cluster of houses grew up around it and this hamlet, called Tillietudlem, still exists.

The Tillietudlem of *Old Mortality* is, of course, Scott's fictional creation. Situated on the banks of the Clyde rather than the Nethan, and being much older than the sixteenth century, the tower of the novel seems to draw elements from the medieval Bothwell Castle as well as from Craignethan. Nevertheless, it is clear that Craignethan was strongly present in Scott's mind in writing about Tillietudlem; and it may be suggested that Andrew Hay's house made a similar contribution to the creation of Milnewood, the Morton family home in the novel. Equally clear is the influence on the novel of the landscape of the upper Clyde valley, with its fertile land and fruit trees lying below barren and bleak moors. In *Old Mortality*, the fanaticism, violence, and sterile divisions of the past are associated with the moorland; while the fertile, cultivated, and well-ordered valley is associated with a future that will bring the calm, civilised rationality of the eighteenth-century Scottish Enlightenment. Significantly, the Tower of Tillietudlem commands the pass from the moorland to the valley; and the struggle in the novel to gain control of Tillietudlem is in effect a struggle to gain control of the direction the future will take.

Scott spent the Christmas of 1801 as a guest at Hamilton Palace, the seat of the Dukes of Hamilton. This involved a return to Lanarkshire, as Hamilton is situated on the opposite bank of the Clyde from Bothwell, and a little up-river. Over the years political differences began to cloud Scott's initially cordial relations with the Hamilton family. Alexander Hamilton Douglas (1767–1852), a man of Scott's generation, was the eldest son of the ninth Duke, and himself became tenth Duke in 1819. The ninth Duke's heir was a prominent Whig; in 1802 he was appointed colonel of the Lanarkshire militia and lord-lieutenant of Lanarkshire—a role that calls to mind the Duke of the early chapters of *Old Mortality*. The Duke of the novel is likewise lord-lieutenant of Lanarkshire, and when the narrative opens he proves to be a somewhat absurd and ineffectual figure at the wappen-schaw organised to rally support for the royal cause.

Scott's feelings about the Lanarkshire landscape, and about the Hamilton family, emerge strongly in *The Visionary*, a political squib which he contributed under the name 'Somnambulus' to the *Edinburgh Weekly Journal*, and which was quickly reprinted as a pamphlet. *The Visionary* was published in 1819, three years after *Old Mortality*, and it attacks the tenth Duke of Hamilton, who had enraged Scott and other Tories in the aftermath of the Peterloo massacre by publicly donating £50 'in aid of those who have suffered in Manchester'.⁷ Somnambulus has a dream in the Duke's park: 'the rocks, the sky, the rivers of Evan and of Clyde were the same, but every vestige of beauty and plenty, once the distinctive marks of the landscape, were vanished and gone'. The dreamer learns that he is in 'the Land of the Radicals', and he is confronted by a

half naked ruffian, who approached me with a huge club in his hand. He was unshaved and uncombed; the matted locks of his hair and his beard obscuring a physiognomy, which, from the unbridled indulgence of every passion as it awaked in its turn, was rather brutal than human.[8]

In 'the Land of the Radicals' the fabric of society has disintegrated, leaving famine and desolation to inherit the ruins. As Peter Garside points out, *The Visionary* is clearly intended as 'a warning against erratic behaviour such as Hamilton's in high circles'. Garside further suggests that, for Scott, the Duke of Buccleuch was a model aristocrat, binding together and sustaining his local community; but 'Scott apparently saw an obverse in the Duke of Hamilton'.[9]

Habakkuk Meiklewrath, one of the prominent Covenanters in *Old Mortality*, has much in common with the 'half naked ruffian' who presides over 'the Land of the Radicals' in *The Visionary*. The rebellion of the Covenanters in *Old Mortality* begins with a victory over Government forces at Loudoun-hill; and Meiklewrath is described as follows, as he addresses the victorious Covenanters after the battle:

> The rags of a dress which had once been black, added to the tattered fragments of a shepherd's plaid, composed a covering scarce fit for the purposes of decency, much less for those of warmth or comfort. A long beard, as white as snow, hung down on his bosom, and mingled with bushy, uncombed, grizzled hair, which hung in elf-locks around his wild and staring visage. The features seemed to be extenuated by penury and famine, until they hardly retained the likeness of a human aspect. The eyes, grey, wild, and wandering, evidently betokened a bewildered imagination. He held in his hand a rusty sword, clotted with blood, as were his long lean hands, which were garnished at the extremity with nails like eagle's claws. (180)

The moderate Covenanter Henry Morton is 'surprised, shocked, and even startled' at the appearance of Meiklewrath, as well he might be. Nevertheless, Meiklewrath has the support of the more extreme wing of the Covenanters, who believe that 'he speaketh of the spirit', and who believe that they 'fructify by his pouring forth' (181). Meiklewrath duly proceeds to pour forth, and, with the approval of the more extreme Covenanters, he makes the following proposal for dealing with Lady Margaret and her family at Tillietudlem:

> "Who talks of peace and safe-conduct? who speaks of mercy to the bloody house of the malignants? I say, take the infants and dash them against the stones; take the daughters and the mothers of the house and hurl them from the battlements of their trust, that the dogs may fatten on their blood as they did on that of Jezebel the spouse of Ahab, and that their carcases may

be dung to the face of the field even in the portion of their
fathers!" (181)

Old Mortality seems to suggest that its Duke of Hamilton carries a
heavy responsibility for allowing the nightmare figure of Meiklewrath
to gain a position from which he can pose a real threat of death and
devastation. The novel is set in a district Scott would see as the natural sphere of influence of the Duke of Hamilton. Nevertheless, the
Duke of the novel vanishes from its pages after his initial appearance
at the wappen-schaw, during which his grotesque coach narrowly
escapes being transfixed by the lance of the hapless Goose Gibby,
when that deeply incompetent cavalier is carried away by a horse
which acts 'as if in league with the disaffected' (25). In the novel, the
absence and ineffectiveness of the Duke is highly significant. A rebel
army is trained in his park, and a crucial battle is fought on his territory, but while all this is going on, the Duke is nowhere to be seen.
He has failed to bind society together; and things begin to fall apart.
In this the Duke reflects another failure to bind society together: the
absent King is far away and out of touch in London while his ancient
kingdom tears itself to pieces.

It appears that the composition of the manuscript of *Old Mortality*
began in September 1816; a few weeks earlier Scott had renewed his
association with Hamilton and Bothwell by making a journey via
'Bothwell Banks and the Falls to Clyde-side'.[10] The decision to focus
the planned tale of the West on the events surrounding the Battle of
Bothwell Bridge gave Scott an opportunity to explore some of his
deepest interests. When he was a young man, the French Revolution
(1789) had been the political event of overwhelming importance and
significance throughout Europe; and when, in his forties, he was
writing *Old Mortality*, fear of revolution at home was one of his live-
liest concerns. A novel on the violent upheavals in the West of
Scotland in 1679 made it possible for Scott to confront nightmarish
visions of the chaos and horror engendered by civil war and violent
revolution, and in *Old Mortality* extreme Covenanters like
Meiklewrath and Balfour of Burley are radical revolutionaries capable
of releasing atrocities as terrible as anything thrown up by the French
Revolution. By facing up to these disturbing possibilities of human
behaviour, *Old Mortality* articulates some of the most troubling fears
of the gentlemanly elite of Scott's generation; fears which also animate the dream of Somnambulus about the conversion of the Duke of
Hamilton's prosperous and well-ordered park into the desolation and
famine of 'the Land of the Radicals'.

This is not to suggest that *Old Mortality* takes a wholly negative
view of the extreme wing of the Covenanters. For example, the young

preacher Macbriar endures torture with an admirable fortitude and
loyalty when on trial for rebellion after Bothwell Bridge:

> "Will you yet say," repeated the Duke of Lauderdale, "where
> and when you last parted from Balfour of Burley?"
> "You have my answer," said the sufferer resolutely, and the
> second blow fell. The third and fourth succeeded, but at the
> fifth, when a larger wedge was introduced, the prisoner set up a
> scream of agony. (281)

In *Old Mortality*, Macbriar is a prominent figure on the extreme
wing of the Covenanters; here, in spite of excruciating torture, he
heroically refuses to betray his principles or his friend. A few pages
earlier in this complex and subtle novel, however, Macbriar had
joined forces with Meiklewrath in a decision to kill Morton in cold
blood. Macbriar says:

> "His blood be on his head, the deceiver,—let him go down to
> Tophet with the ill-mumbled mass which he calls a prayer-book
> in his right hand." (264–65)

Meiklewrath then prepares for the immediate killing of Morton, so
that 'the wicked may be taken away from among the people, and the
Covenant established in its purity'. (265) It is clear that Macbriar has
loyalty and heroism; but in spite of this it appears that he also has
something in common with the guilt of his own persecutor, the Duke
of Lauderdale.

Fear of the instability generated by rebellion runs powerfully
through *Old Mortality*. Men of Scott's generation and class tended to
see themselves as pivotal figures in the task of defending society
against such dangers. On this view, each land-owning gentleman had
the task of binding society together in his own district, and it fell to
the King to undertake this task on a national scale, thus establishing
the orderly organisation of society as a whole. Such arrangements
meant that everyone knew his or her place; but people of Scott's circle feared that this satisfactory and safe state of affairs was threatened
by the Radicals, with their newfangled and dangerous desire to experiment with the mob rule of democracy. Such fears are given powerful
expression in *Old Mortality*.

It appears that a conversation with Joseph Train, an exciseman and
antiquary from Galloway in the south-west of Scotland, helped Scott
to focus his ideas for his tale of the West. Train, who had supplied
information used in *The Lord of the Isles* and *Guy Mannering*, visited
Scott's Edinburgh home in May 1816. During this visit, by his own
account, Train commented favourably on a portrait, owned by Scott,
of the seventeenth-century Royalist and scourge of the Covenanters,
John Grahame of Claverhouse.

"No man", replied Sir Walter—"has been more traduced by his Historians, by following out the superstitious belief that he rode a Goblin Galloway, was proof against shot, and in league with the Devil."—I asked Sir Walter if he might not in good hands be made the hero of a national romance as interesting as either Wallace or the Pretender?—"He might—" was the reply—"but your Western zealots would require to be faithfully pourtrayed to make the picture complete."—Seeing that the subject pleased Sir Walter I added—"And if the story was delivered as if from the mouth of Old Mortality, in a manner somewhat similar to the "Lay of the last Minstrel" it would certainly heighten the effect of the tale."—"Old Mortality! Man! who was he?" said Sir Walter hastily, his eye brightening . . . whilst I related briefly all the particulars of that singular individual I could then recollect.—

I promised immediately on my return to Galloway to make every possible enquiry respecting him and to forward the same . . . without the least delay.—He said he would look most anxiously for my communication.[11]

Scott, in this conversation with Train, calls the Covenanters 'your western zealots'. Robert Paterson, nicknamed 'Old Mortality', was a latter-day 'western zealot' who lived towards the end of the eighteenth century, and who devoted the final years of his life to travelling around Scotland repairing the century-old gravestones of Covenanters executed for insisting (as they saw it) on obeying God rather than the King. As will be seen from the present edition's Explanatory Notes (at 9.18), Scott had in fact met Old Mortality in Dunnottar churchyard many years earlier; the conversation with Train reminded him of this meeting.

In the framing narrative of the novel that bears his name, Old Mortality visits Gandercleuch to repair the gravestones of Covenanters killed there 'by a small detachment of the King's troops' (7). While at work on this task, he is met by Peter Pattieson; and their subsequent conversations form the basis for the novel which Scott, in his manuscript, calls *The Tale of Old Mortality* (a form of the title restored in the present edition).

Peter Pattieson makes it clear that he has imposed his own perspective on the material supplied by Old Mortality:

My readers will of course understand, that, in embodying into one compressed narrative many of the anecdotes which I had the advantage of deriving from Old Mortality, I have been far from adopting either his style, his opinions, or even his facts, so far as they appear to have been distorted by party prejudice. I have endeavoured to correct or verify them from the most authentic

>   sources of tradition, afforded by the representatives of either
>   party. (13)

Pattieson claims that this process has allowed him 'to present an
unbiassed picture of the manners of that unhappy period' (13); and
he asserts that his own 'unbiassed' picture differs significantly from
Old Mortality's strongly pro-Covenanter account. Nevertheless,
Pattieson makes it clear that what he calls the 'peasantry' share the
reverence felt by Old Mortality for the tombs of the Covenanters:

> The peasantry continue to attach to the tombs of these victims
> of prelacy an honour which they do not render to more splendid
> mausoleums; and, when they point them out to their sons, and
> narrate the fate of the sufferers, usually conclude, by exhorting
> them to be ready, should times call for it, to resist to the death
> in the cause of civil and religious liberty, like their brave fore-
> fathers. (7)

In Scott's novel, extreme Covenanters like Burley, Macbriar, and
Meiklewrath release the nightmarish energies of Revolution. The
moderate Covenanter Henry Morton, in contrast, is a man who helps
create a better future by being ready to resist to the death in the cause
of civil and religious liberty, when the times do indeed call for it.

The conversation between Scott and Train, quoted above, was
prompted by a portrait of the royalist leader John Grahame of
Claverhouse; and it is Claverhouse that Morton is called upon to
resist. In Scott's generation, the popular tradition of the 'peasantry'
remembered Claverhouse as a demonic figure, the merciless aristocratic persecutor of the heroic defenders of God's cause. Scott's novel
of the Covenanters offers a different perspective: *The Tale of Old
Mortality* presents Claverhouse as one of Scott's complex Jacobites, a
man of heroic but flawed loyalty to an outdated cause.

After the Union of Scotland and England in 1707, the Jacobites of
the eighteenth century sought to restore the exiled Stuart royal family to power in the new multi-nation state of Britain. Scott's fictions
approach the Jacobite story in various ways. In *Waverley*, for example, we see the Jacobite movement at its high-water mark in 1745;
while in *Redgauntlet* we encounter it as it dwindles away a generation
later. *The Tale of Old Mortality* offers still another perspective. This
novel goes back to the events of 1679 to explore the build-up of the
pressures that eventually led to a major change of direction in the
political life of Scotland. Things finally began to come to a head when
England's 'Glorious Revolution' of 1688 created a situation in which
the Scottish Parliament deposed the absent James VII in the spring of
1689. This brought to an end the rule of the Stuarts in the male line:
a disturbing and significant change, as it represented the deposition of

a dynasty that had ruled Scotland since 1371. As a result of this profound change, Scotland began in 1689 to move towards a new kind of
future.

Appropriately, the final chapters of *The Tale of Old Mortality* are
set in 1689; this allows the novel to explore the background of the
first Jacobite rising—a campaign of that year which sought to restore
James VII to the throne of Scotland, and which expired after its
leader Claverhouse's death in victory at the Battle of Killiecrankie.

As a loyal Jacobite, the Claverhouse of *The Tale of Old Mortality*
exhibits both the virtues and the flaws which the novel suggests were
characteristic of the rule of the Stuarts. This Claverhouse is a cultivated gentleman, elegant and civilised; but he is also despotic and
arbitrary, with a frightening disregard of the rights of the King's
subjects. The rule of law has little meaning for him; the King's will
is what matters. At one point Henry Morton, being unjustly held
captive by Claverhouse's troops, demands to be taken before a civil
magistrate. Claverhouse, however, replies 'coolly' that Morton

> "is one of those scrupulous gentlemen, who, like the madman in
> the play, will not tie his cravat without the warrant of Mr Justice
> Overdo; but I will let him see, before we part, that my shoulder-
> knot is as legal a badge of authority as the mace of the
> Justiciary." (114)

Fears about the arbitrary abuse of royal power emerge in *The Tale
of Old Mortality* when Milnewood, the home of Henry Morton's
uncle, is invaded by a party of royal troops led by Serjeant Bothwell.
Bothwell represents Charles II partly because he is a soldier in the
King's army, and partly because he is a close blood relation. Bothwell,
it appears, is the great-grandson of an illegitimate child of James V, a
monarch from whom Charles II was likewise descended. In spite of
his royal blood, however, Bothwell does not prove to be a welcome
guest at Milnewood.

> "What is your pleasure here, gentlemen?" said Milnewood,
> humbling himself before the satellites of power.
> "We come in behalf of the king," answered Bothwell; "why
> the devil did you keep us so long standing at the door?" (63)

The miserly old Morton of Milnewood reluctantly tries to placate
the troopers by offering a drink, and the offer is accepted with
alacrity.

> "Brandy, ale, and wine, sack, and claret,—we'll try them all,"
> said Bothwell, "and stick to that which is best. There's good
> sense in that, if the damn'dest whig in Scotland had said it." (63)

And so Bothwell and his men begin, in effect, to loot the house, taking young Henry Morton prisoner in the process. This outrage forces Henry into open rebellion against the government; and it thus gives concrete expression to the reasons why the arbitrary rule of the Stuarts will prove to be unsustainable in the long term. Scott's novel takes the view that political stability requires that able gentlemen like Henry Morton should support the political status quo. Such men have an essential role in binding society together. If and when they turn to rebellion, the old order's days are numbered.

In taking this line, *Old Mortality* reflects the assumptions and concerns of property-owning gentlemen of Scott's generation. Clearly, such people would feel more secure if their continued possession of their wealth depended, not on the whims of arbitrary royal power, but on due legal process. For this reason they would be likely to regard the limitation of royal power that had been imposed at the 'Glorious Revolution' as a benign development. After the Revolution and the Union, real power in Britain came to lie with Parliament rather than the Monarch, and the owners of property were the only people who could vote at British Parliamentary elections. So long as that situation could be maintained, neither the mob rule of democracy nor the arbitrary rule of the Monarch could seriously threaten the wealth of property-owning gentlemen. The looting of Milnewood gives expression to deep fears about the dangers of departing from this satisfactory situation by returning to the bad old days before the Union and the Revolution.

In *Old Mortality*, characters like Lady Margaret Bellenden, or Mause Headrigg, or Ephraim Macbriar seem completely at home in the world of late-seventeenth-century Scotland. Indeed, in their debate in Chapter Seven of the first volume of the novel, Lady Margaret and Mause lucidly give expression to the nature of the forces driving the conflicts of the period, as these forces are experienced from their own (very different) female points of view. Lady Margaret speaks out of the assumptions and the experience of life of a seventeenth-century royalist aristocrat; while Mause (one of Peter Pattieson's 'peasantry') speaks out of the assumptions and the experience of life of a seventeenth-century woman loyal to the principles of the Covenant. Other aspects of the lives of women in seventeenth-century Scotland emerge through the experiences of the younger female characters, notably the enterprising Jenny Dennison, who (like her mistress Edith Bellenden) has to choose between two lovers, one a Covenanter and the other a Royalist.

Unlike these characters, however, Henry Morton does not seem to belong naturally to late-seventeenth-century Scotland. Rather, he emerges from the page as someone who lives by the gentlemanly values of the Britain of the 1810s, the Britain of the Regency period. No doubt he exhibits the Covenanters' cardinal virtue, the brave defence of freedom, as he energetically opposes the differing but equally dangerous despotisms of Claverhouse on the one hand and Burley on the other. Nevertheless, Morton can be seen as an idealised embodiment of the virtues of the British officer class, who, a few months before the publication of *Old Mortality*, had faced down the tyrant Napoleon at Waterloo. Morton, in Scott's novel, is a man who represents the future. He acts on behalf of the forces that will move Scotland from a dark past of despotic violence into a happy, law-abiding, fertile, and domestic world; the world, that is to say, of the Britain of Scott's own Regency period. As the man who embodies the future, Morton wins a bride from the defeated side, a bride through whom something of value is rescued from the dark old dying world of the Jacobite past. Morton's bride is Edith Bellenden, and, like Rose Bradwardine in *Waverley*, Edith is a bride who is docile, quiet, unthreatening. These meek women represent a Jacobitism tamed and made acceptable for a new world of domesticity.

The British political settlement ushered in by the 'Glorious Revolution' of 1688 and the Union of 1707 remained in place in all its essentials when Scott was writing *The Tale of Old Mortality* in 1816. Indeed, it remained in place until the Reform Bill of 1832 introduced major changes by extending the right to vote; and Scott, by then sinking into illness and old age, bitterly opposed these changes. Indeed, it is possible to read Scott's novel of the Covenanters as an eloquent defence of the political status quo of the Scotland of his own day, a status quo to which he was deeply committed. This novel, that is to say, celebrates the 'Glorious Revolution' and the Union as the precursors of a rational, stable British settlement that secured the rights of men of property by establishing freedom, under the law, from arbitrary power.

The virtues of this new world are given expression in the concluding chapters of *Old Mortality*. These chapters are set in 1689, the year of the decisive step by which the new world replaced the old: the year of the opening out of 'a new æra', as the narrator of *Old Mortality* puts it (286). Significantly, many of the events of these chapters take place in the immediate vicinity of Bothwell Bridge, the place where the pressures that would help to create the new world had so memorably manifested themselves.

The new post-Revolution world has dawned over Bothwell Bridge, as Henry Morton, in 1689, returns from exile to seek Edith Bellenden as his bride.

The opposite field, once the scene of slaughter and conflict, now lay as placid and quiet as the surface of a summer lake. The trees and bushes, which grew around in romantic variety of shade, were hardly seen to stir under the influence of the evening breeze. The very murmur of the river seemed to soften itself into unison with the stillness of the scene around. The path, through which the traveller descended, was occasionally shaded by detached trees of great size, and elsewhere by the hedges and boughs of flourishing orchards, now loaden with summer fruit. (288)

All, it appears, is peace, plenty, and fertility in the post-Revolution world; and this is reflected in the fate of the major characters, both male and female, who are in tune with the new world. Marriage, happiness, and many children await them; but death is the fate of those characters who remain enmeshed in the ways of the old world.

Old Mortality, then, is a text that celebrates the legacy of the 'Glorious Revolution'; but it is also a text that warns of the horrors that await if revolutionary Radicals, heirs of the extreme Covenanters, are allowed to rise up and overthrow the benign political settlement established by the 'Glorious Revolution'. However, Scott's view of the threat posed by revolutionary Radicals was not universally shared in the Scotland of his day. Indeed, as the Historical Note in the present edition suggests (at 357–58), many people outside the gentlemanly elite hoped for precisely the developments that Scott dreaded. A few months before Scott began to write *The Tale of Old Mortality*, thousands of 'democrats' (mainly textile workers from the West of Scotland) assembled on the battlefield of Loudoun-hill to celebrate the escape of Napoleon from Elba; and also to celebrate the victory at Loudon-hill in 1679 of their ancestors the Covenanters against the established government of the day.[12]

The folk-memory of events like the battle at Loudoun-hill remained a potent force in the Scotland of the 1810s and the 1820s, because the Covenanters symbolised the possibility of a heroic, principled, and ultimately successful armed defence of the rights of the people against an unjust aristocratic government. This potentially dangerous folk-memory was the tiger that *The Tale of Old Mortality* sought to tame, by demonstrating not only what was valuable, but also what was dangerous, in the legacy of those revered national heroes the Covenanters. Scott's attempt to tame the tiger provoked an outraged reaction from many people who were deeply in sympathy with the cause of the Covenanters. For example, Dr Thomas McCrie (the biographer of John Knox) responded to the publication of *Old Mortality* with an influential attack on the presentation of the Covenanters in Scott's novel.[13] Similarly, John Galt was provoked into writing his strongly pro-Covenanter novel, *Ringan Gilhaize* (1823) as a reply to *Old Mortality*.[14]

The framing narrative of Scott's novel seeks to contain and make safe the revolutionary energies of the past by placing them firmly within the old moss-covered tombs tended by Old Mortality. In a sense Old Mortality is the last Covenanter, but in Scott's novel he is an eccentric figure, out of touch with the modern world. His one remaining task is to repair mouldering gravestones in a vain attempt to keep alive the fading memory of his heroes. All this suggests that the dangerous violence of the old days of the Covenanters has now been left behind. We have arrived in a new, well-ordered world in which the old conflicts have been happily resolved. All is now well, and there is no need to re-fight old wars.

This deft device for neutering the legacy of the Covenanters is referred to and subverted in one of the most sophisticated replies to *Old Mortality*, James Hogg's novel *The Private Memoirs and Confessions of a Justified Sinner* (1824). Hogg, who had been on friendly terms with Scott since 1802, was a 'peasant' (to follow Peter Pattieson's terminology) by birth and by upbringing. He had already given a sympathetic account of the Covenanters in *The Brownie of Bodsbeck* (1818); this novel offers a deeply hostile account of Claverhouse and the atrocities for which he was held responsible in popular tradition, and the publication of *The Brownie* provoked a quarrel between Hogg and Scott. What follows is an extract from Hogg's manuscript account of their angry conversation on this subject:

> "I have read through your new work Mr Hogg" said he "and must tell you downright and plainly as I always do that I like it very ill—very ill indeed."
>
> "What for Mr Scott?"
>
> "Because it is a false and unfair picture of the times and the existing characters altogether. An exhaggerated and unfair picture!"
>
> "I dinna ken Mr Scott. It is the picture I hae been bred up in the belief o' sin' ever I was born and I had it frae them whom I was most bound to honour and believe."[15]

Hogg, a self-educated shepherd, had an instinctive sympathy with the Covenanters, and indeed with all figures on the margins of society. In the *Justified Sinner*, an 'Editor' who seems to share Scott's attitudes and assumptions presents an account of the life of one Robert Wringhim. This Editor, like Peter Pattieson in *Old Mortality*, draws on various traditional sources in preparing what he believes to be an unbiased version of the story he is telling. According to the

Editor, Wringhim is a fanatic of the party of the Covenanters; and this young man is even more chillingly bloodthirsty than Balfour of Burley in *Old Mortality*. 'We have heard much of the rage of fanaticism in former days,' writes the Editor, 'but nothing to this.'[16]

After telling Robert's story in a narrative that has a good deal of the outlook and flavour of a Waverley novel, the Editor goes on to present Robert's own 'Private Memoirs and Confessions of a Justified Sinner', printed from a document recovered from Robert's grave. This dark and troubling narrative increasingly unsettles the reader's trust in the Editor's account of Robert's life and times. The reader continues to see and to deplore Robert's manifest faults; but gradually Robert ceases to seem to be the mere monster depicted by the Editor. He begins to emerge as a human being, capable of winning the reader's sympathy.

Hogg's novel concludes with the Editor's account of his expedition to the Sinner's grave with some literary friends from Scott's circle. In this expedition, the Editor and his fellow grave-robbers are obstructed by a surly local shepherd called James Hogg; but Hogg's efforts to protect the grave prove in vain. When the Editor and his cronies dig up the body, they find part of it has been startlingly well preserved; and they also find Robert's disturbing manuscript.

The opening chapter of Scott's novel is concerned with Peter Pattieson's meeting with 'Old Mortality'. This chapter ends with a reference to the Covenanters and their opponents:

> Peace to their memory! Let us think of them as the heroine of our only Scottish tragedy entreats her lord to think of her departed sire,
>> "O, rake not up the ashes of our fathers!
>> Implacable resentment was their crime,
>> And grievous has the expiation been." (14)

The conclusion of Hogg's novel suggests that Scott in *Old Mortality*, in spite of protestations to the contrary, did in fact rake up 'the ashes of our fathers' by giving an unsympathetic and imperfect account of the Covenanters. Hogg's novel also suggests, in contradiction to *Old Mortality*, that the disturbing energies of the Covenanters cannot ultimately be comfortably sealed away in a moss-covered tomb.

In seeking to make sense of the Scotland of their own time, Scots of the generation of Scott and Hogg engaged in eloquent and passionate debate about the Scotland of the time of the Covenanters. This debate produced, in *Old Mortality* and the *Justified Sinner*, two of the outstanding novels of the nineteenth century.

NOTES

1 Henry Cockburn, *Memorials of his Time* (Edinburgh, 1856), 281.

2 See the volume of the EEWN devoted to *The Black Dwarf*, ed. P. D. Garside (Edinburgh, 1993), 125, 128–30, for a detailed account of the original plans for *Tales of my Landlord*.

3 J. G. Lockhart, *Memoirs of the Life of Sir Walter Scott, Bart.*, 7 vols (Edinburgh, 1837–38), 1.304–05.

4 W. Douglas Simpson, *Bothwell Castle* (Edinburgh, 1958), 3.

5 Lockhart, *Life*, 1.306–07.

6 See Iain MacIvor, *Craignethan Castle* (Edinburgh, 1978).

7 Scott, *The Visionary*, ed. Peter Garside (Cardiff, 1984), vii.

8 *The Visionary*, ed. Garside, 33.

9 *The Visionary*, ed. Garside, viii.

10 See the volume of the EEWN devoted to *The Tale of Old Mortality*, ed. Douglas Mack (Edinburgh, 1993), 362–66; and *The Letters of Sir Walter Scott*, ed. H. J. C. Grierson and others, 12 vols (London, 1932–37), 4.264.

11 Joseph Train, 'Brief Sketch of a Correspondence with Sir Walter Scott, Commencing in the Year 1814', National Library of Scotland MS 3277, ff. 66–68. Robert Paterson, known as 'Old Mortality', is discussed in the note to 9.18.

12 This incident is discussed in David Stevenson, *The Covenanters: The National Covenant and Scotland* (Edinburgh, 1988), 76–77.

13 McCrie's attack and Scott's reaction to it are discussed in Edgar Johnson, *Sir Walter Scott: The Great Unknown*, 2 vols (London, 1970), 1.561–62.

14 For Galt's discussion of this, see his *Literary Life and Miscellanies*, 3 vols (Edinburgh, 1834), 1.254.

15 James Hogg, *Memoir of the Author's Life; and Familiar Anecdotes of Sir Walter Scott*, ed. Douglas Mack (Edinburgh, 1972), 106.

16 James Hogg, *The Private Memoirs and Confessions of a Justified Sinner*, ed. John Carey (London, 1969), 93.

1771   *15 August.* Born in College Wynd, Edinburgh. His
            father, Walter (1729–99), son of a sheep-farmer at
            Sandyknowe, near Smailholm Tower, Roxburghshire,
            was a lawyer. His mother, Anne Rutherford (1732–
            1819), was daughter of Dr John Rutherford, Professor of
            Medicine in the University of Edinburgh. His parents
            married in April 1758; Walter was their ninth child. The
            siblings who survived were Robert (1767–87), John
            (1769–1816), Anne (1772–1801), Thomas (1774–1823),
            and Daniel (?1776–1806).

1772–73   *Winter.* Contracted what is now termed poliomyelitis,
            and became permanently lame in his right leg. His
            grandfather Rutherford advised that he be sent to
            Sandyknowe to benefit from country air, and, apart from
            a period of 'about a year' in 1775 spent in Bath, a spell in
            1776 with his family in their new home on the west side
            of George Square, Edinburgh, and a time in 1777 at
            Prestonpans, near Edinburgh, he lived there until 1778.
            From his grandmother and his aunt Janet he heard many
            ballads and stories of the Border past, and these narra-
            tives were crucial to his intellectual and imaginative
            development.

1779–83   Attended the High School of Edinburgh; he was partic-
            ularly influenced by the Rector, Dr Alexander Adam,
            and his teaching of literature in Latin. After the High
            School, he spent 'half a year' with his aunt Janet in
            Kelso, where he attended the grammar school, and read
            for the first time Thomas Percy's *Reliques of Ancient
            English Poetry.*

1783–86   Attended classes in Edinburgh University, including
            Humanity (Latin), Greek, Logic and Metaphysics, and
            Moral Philosophy.

1786   Studies terminated by serious illness; convalescence in
            Kelso. Apprenticed as a lawyer to his father.

1787   Met Robert Burns at the house of the historian and
            philosopher, Adam Ferguson.

1789   Decided to prepare for the Bar.

1789–92	Attended classes at Edinburgh University, including History, Moral Philosophy, Scots Law, and Civil Law.
1792	*11 July*. Admitted to the Faculty of Advocates.
	Autumn. First visit to Liddesdale, in the extreme south of Scotland, with Robert Shortreed, in search of ballads and ballad-singers. Seven such 'raids' followed over seven years. Shortreed later commented: 'He was makin' himsell a' the time'. His tours took him into many parts of Scotland and the north of England: e.g. in 1793 to Perthshire and the Trossachs; in 1796 to the north-east of Scotland; and in 1797 to Cumberland and the Lake District.
1794	In April involved in a brawl with some political radicals and bound to keep the peace. In September attended the trials of the radicals Watt and Downie, and in November Watt's execution.
c.1794–96	In love with Williamina Belsches, culminating in April 1796 with an invitation to her home, Fettercairn House, Kincardineshire.
1796	Anonymous publication of *The Chase and William and Helen*, Scott's translations of two of Bürger's poems.
	October. Announcement of the engagement of Williamina Belsches to William Forbes.
1797	Volunteered for the new volunteer cavalry regiment, the Royal Edinburgh Light Dragoons, and appointed quartermaster.
	September. Met Charlotte Carpenter (1770–1826), at Gilsland, Cumberland, and within three weeks proposed marriage. Charlotte's parents were Jean François Charpentier and Margaret Charlotte Volère (d. 1788), of Lyons. Sometime after the break-up of the marriage around 1780, her mother brought Charlotte and her brother Charles (1772–1818) to England; Charlotte and Charles later became the wards of the 2nd Marquess of Downshire, and changed their name to Carpenter.
	24 December. Married Charlotte in Carlisle, and set up house at 50 George St, Edinburgh.
1798	Met Matthew Gregory ('Monk') Lewis, and agreed to contribute to *Tales of Wonder* (published 1801).
	Rented cottage in Lasswade near Edinburgh for the summer, and made many political and literary contacts, including Lady Louisa Stuart, who proved to be one of the most acute and trusted of his friends and critics.

Moved to 19 Castle Street, Edinburgh.

October. Birth and death of first son.

1799   Publication of *Goetz of Berlichingen*, Scott's translation of Goethe's tragedy.

April. Death of Scott's father.

Met John Leyden and the publisher Archibald Constable, and had his first discussion with the printer James Ballantyne about undertaking book-printing: Ballantyne brought out Scott's anthology *An Apology for Tales of Terror* in 1800.

October. Birth of daughter, Charlotte Sophia Scott.

December. Appointed Sheriff-Depute of Selkirkshire.

1801   *October*. Birth of son, Walter Scott.

Moved to 39 Castle Street, Edinburgh.

1802   Publication of *Minstrelsy of the Scottish Border*, Vols 1 and 2. The *Minstrelsy* was the first publication in a life-time of scholarly editing, and it shows both the strengths and weaknesses of Scott as editor. He found new texts (of the 72 ballads he published, 38 had not appeared in print before), and his literary, historical, and anthropological essays and notes are always illuminating; but, following the editorial practice of the time, he had no settled methods or principles for choosing or establishing a text. Met James Hogg.

1803   *February*. Birth of daughter, Anne Scott.

Second edition of *Minstrelsy of the Scottish Border*, Vols 1 and 2, and first edition of Vol. 3.

Began to contribute reviews to the *Edinburgh Review*. Scott was an acute reviewer, in the expansive manner characteristic of heavyweight reviews in the early nine-teenth century, and was particularly perceptive about such contemporaries as Jane Austen, Byron, and Mary Shelley.

September. Visit from William and Dorothy Words-worth.

1804   Took the lease of Ashestiel near Selkirk as his country house in place of the cottage in Lasswade.

Publication of Scott's edition of the medieval romance, *Sir Tristrem*.

1805   Publication of *The Lay of the Last Minstrel*, the first of a series of verse romances which established his fame as a poet.

Entered into partnership with James Ballantyne in the

printing business of James Ballantyne & Co. Until the financial crash in 1826, the partnership was not just a financial arrangement, but a unique collaboration: Ballantyne managed the business, but also acted as Scott's editor; Scott seems to have been responsible for much of the financial planning, and it was a standard part of his contracts with publishers that his works should be printed by James Ballantyne & Co.

December. Birth of son, Charles Scott.

1806   Hurried to London to secure his appointment as one of the Principal Clerks to the Court of Session, a position which had been under negotiation for much of the previous year but which was imperilled by the advent of a new government after the death of William Pitt on 23 January. The appointment was announced on 8 March. Scott took the place of an elderly Clerk, but, as there was no retirement and pension scheme, allowed his predecessor to keep the salary of £800 per annum for life. While in London Scott was 'taken up' by high society.

1807   Brother Tom bankrupt. It also emerged that Tom, a lawyer who had inherited his father's practice, and who had been retained as agent for the Duddingston estate of the Marquess of Abercorn, had misappropriated some of his client's money. Scott felt financially and morally endangered by his brother's breach of trust, and extended efforts were required over several years to protect his own financial credit and provide for his brother and his family.

1808   Publication of poem *Marmion* (the rights of which the publisher Archibald Constable had bought for £1050 in 1807).

Appointed secretary to the Parliamentary Commission to Inquire into the Administration of Justice in Scotland. The Commission ended its work in 1810.

Publication of *The Works of John Dryden . . . with Notes . . . and a Life of the Author*, 18 vols.

Cancelled his subscription to the *Edinburgh Review* because of its 'defeatist' view of the war in Spain, and began (with others) planning the *Quarterly Review* and the *Edinburgh Annual Register*, both launched in 1810. The political disagreement developed into a quarrel with Archibald Constable & Co., and Scott and the Ballantyne brothers, James and John, set up and became the partners in a rival publishing business, John Ballantyne & Co. Scott entrusted his own works to the new business and whenever possible directed other writers and new ventures to it, but Constable withdrew printing work from James Ballantyne & Co., and the printing firm stopped making significant profits.

1809   Publication of *A Collection of Scarce and Valuable Tracts* (Somers' Tracts), Vols 1–3; completed in 13 vols 1812.

1810   Publication of *The Lady of the Lake*, his most commercially successful poem.

1811   Scott's predecessor as Clerk of Session agreed to apply for a pension, and from 1812 Scott was paid a salary of £1300 per annum.
Publication of poem *The Vision of Don Roderick*.
Purchase of Cartley Hole, the nucleus of the Abbotsford Estate, between Galashiels and Melrose.

1812   Byron began correspondence with Scott.
Removal from Ashestiel to Abbotsford, and plans for rebuilding the small farmhouse there.

1813   Publication of poems *Rokeby* and *The Bridal of Triermain*.
First financial crisis. It became apparent in 1812 that the publishing firm of John Ballantyne and Co. was making losses on every publication except Scott's poetry, and that the *Edinburgh Annual Register* was losing £1000 per issue. The firm was undercapitalised, and depended overmuch on bank credit. The national financial crisis of 1812–14 led to reduced orders for books from retailers, late payments, and to the bankruptcy of many companies whose debts to John Ballantyne & Co. were either not paid or paid in part. John Ballantyne & Co. found itself unable to pay its own bills and repay the banks on time, and *Rokeby*, greatly profitable though it was, failed to generate enough ready money to meet obligations. Protracted negotiations with Constable over much of 1813 led to the purchase of Ballantyne stock, on the condition that John Ballantyne & Co. ceased to be an active publisher, to the sale of a share in *Rokeby*, and later to the advance sale to Constable of rights for the publication of the long poem *The Lord of the Isles*. Scott had to ask the Duke of Buccleuch to guarantee a bank loan of £4000, and many friends gave small loans. All the personal loans were repaid in 1814, and the publishing business was

eventually wound up profitably in 1817, largely through Scott's efforts. As part of the reconciliation Constable commissioned essays on Chivalry and the Drama for the Supplement to the *Encyclopaedia Britannica* (published 1818 and 1819 respectively).

Offered and declined the Poet Laureateship.

1814   Publication of his first novel, *Waverley*. The novel was probably begun in 1808 (the date '1st November, 1805' in the first chapter is part of the fiction), continued in 1810, and completed 1813–14; it was first advertised in 1810, and again in January 1814. The early parts (up to the beginning of Chapter 5, and Chapters 5–7) were probably written in parallel with Scott's autobiography (first published at the beginning of Lockhart's *Life of Scott* in 1837).

Publication of *The Works of Jonathan Swift ... with Notes and a Life of the Author*, 19 vols.

Toured the northern and western isles of Scotland with the Lighthouse Commissioners. His diary of the voyage is published in Lockhart's *Life of Scott* (1837).

1815   Publication of poem *The Lord of the Isles*, and *Guy Mannering*, his second novel.

First visit to the Continent, including Waterloo and Paris, where he was lionised.

1816   Publication of *Paul's Letters to His Kinsfolk*, *The Antiquary*, and *Tales of my Landlord* (*The Black Dwarf* and *The Tale of Old Mortality*).

1817   Publication of *Harold the Dauntless* (Scott's last long poem), and *Rob Roy* (1818 on title page).

1817–19   First phase of the building of Abbotsford.

1818   Publication of *Tales of my Landlord*, second series (*The Heart of Mid-Lothian*).

Offered and accepted a baronetcy (announced March 1820).

1819   Seriously ill, probably from gall-stones. From 1817 Scott had been suffering stomach cramps, but in the spring and early summer of 1819 he was thought to be dying. Nonetheless he continued to work, dictating to an amanuensis when he was too ill to write. He completed *The Bride of Lammermoor* in April (the greater part of the manuscript is in his own hand) but the latter part of the novel and most of *A Legend of the Wars of Montrose* must have been dictated. The two tales constitute *Tales of my*

Landlord, third series, and were published in June 1819. Purchase by Constable of the copyrights of the 'Scotch novels' and publication of the first collection of Scott's fiction as *Novels and Tales of the Author of Waverley*, 16 vols. All the novels eventually appeared in collected editions in three formats: 8vo, 12mo and 18mo. Publication of three articles in the *Edinburgh Weekly Journal*, later issued as a pamphlet entitled *The Visionary*, which was in essence political propaganda for the constitutional status quo in the period after Peterloo, when there was a real possibility of a radical rising in the west of Scotland.
December. Death of Scott's mother.
Publication of *Ivanhoe* (1820 on title-page).

1820   Publication of *The Monastery*, and *The Abbot*.
Marriage of daughter Sophia to John Gibson Lockhart.
Elected president of the Royal Society of Edinburgh.

1821   Publication of *Kenilworth*, and *The Pirate* (1822 on title-page).

1821–24 Publication of *Ballantyne's Novelist's Library*, for which Scott wrote the lives of the novelists.

1822   Publication of *The Fortunes of Nigel*, and *Peveril of the Peak* (1823 on title-page).
Visit of King George IV to Edinburgh.

1822–25 Demolition of the original house and second phase of the building of Abbotsford.

1823   Bannatyne Club founded and Scott made first president.
Publication of *Quentin Durward*, and *St Ronan's Well* (1824 on title-page).

1824   Publication of *Redgauntlet*.

1825   Marriage of son Walter to Jane Jobson.
Publication of *Tales of the Crusaders* (*The Betrothed* and *The Talisman*).
Began his Journal.

1826   *January*. Scott insolvent. There was a severe economic recession in the winter of 1825–26 and many companies and individuals became bankrupt. Scott's principal publishers, Archibald Constable & Co., and the printers James Ballantyne & Co. in which he was co-partner, had always been undercapitalised, and relied on bank borrowings for working capital. In paying for goods and services, including such things as paper, printing, and publication rights, all parties used promissory bills, a system in which the drawer promised to pay stated

sums on stated dates, and which the acceptor 'dis-
counted' at the banks, i.e. got the money in advance of
the date less the amount the banks charged in interest for
what was in fact a loan. Both Constable's and
Ballantyne's hoped that the money coming in from the
sale of books when they were published would be sufficient to pay off the money due to the banks, but in practice both firms too often borrowed more money to pay
off debts when they were due, and acted as guarantors
for each other's loans. In December 1825 it was realised
that they were unable to get further credit from the
banks; and in January the bankruptcy of the London
publishers of Scott's works, Hurst, Robinson & Co., precipitated the collapse of Constable's, then Ballantyne's,
and the ruin of all the partners. Scott, the only one of
those involved with a capacity to generate a large income,
signed a trust deed undertaking to repay his own private
debts (£35,000), all the debts of the printing business for
which he and James Ballantyne were jointly liable
(£41,000), the debts of Archibald Constable & Co. for
which he was legally liable (£40,000), and a mortgage on
Abbotsford (£10,000), amounting in all to over
£126,000. Such were the profits from works like
Woodstock, *The Life of Napoleon Buonaparte*, and above
all the Magnum Opus, the collected edition of the
Waverley Novels with introductions and notes specially
written by Scott, and issued in monthly parts from
1829–33, that by Scott's death in 1832 more than
£53,000 had been repaid, and the remaining debts were
paid in 1833.

Publication of three letters in the *Edinburgh Weekly
Journal*, later issued as *The Letters of Malachi
Malagrowther*, in which Scott attacked a government
proposal to restrict the rights of the Scottish banks to
issue their own banknotes; Scott was so effective that the
government withdrew its proposal.

Sale of 39 Castle Street, Edinburgh, on behalf of creditors.

15 May. Death of wife, Charlotte Scott.

Publication of *Woodstock*.

Autumn. Visit to Paris.

1827   Public acknowledgement of the authorship of the
Waverley Novels.

Publication of *The Life of Napoleon Buonaparte*, 9 vols, *Chronicles of the Canongate* (Chrystal Croftangry's Narrative, 'The Highland Widow', 'The Two Drovers', and 'The Surgeon's Daughter'), and *Tales of a Grandfather* (Scotland to 1603).

1828   Publication of *Chronicles of the Canongate*, second series (*The Fair Maid of Perth*), and *Tales of a Grandfather*, second series (Scotland 1603–1707).

1829   Publication of *Anne of Geierstein*, *History of Scotland*, Vol. 1, and *Tales of a Grandfather*, third series (Scotland 1707–45). The first volume of the Magnum Opus, completed in 48 vols in 1833, appeared on 1 June.

1830   *February*. First stroke.
November. Retired as Clerk to the Court of Session with pension of £864 per annum. Second stroke.
Publication of *Letters on Demonology and Witchcraft*, *Tales of a Grandfather* (France), and *History of Scotland*, Vol. 2.

1831   *April*. Third stroke.
Publication of *Tales of my Landlord*, fourth series (*Count Robert of Paris* and *Castle Dangerous*).
October. Departure on HMS *Barham* to the Mediterranean, Malta and Naples.

1832   Overland journey home, via Rome, Florence, Venice, Verona, the Brenner Pass, Augsburg, Mainz, and down the Rhine, but had his fourth stroke at Nijmegen. Travelling by sea to London and then Edinburgh, he reached Abbotsford on 11 July.
21 September. Death at Abbotsford.

FURTHER READING

THE WORKS OF SCOTT

The Journal of Sir Walter Scott, ed. W. E. K. Anderson (Oxford, 1972).

The Letters of Sir Walter Scott, ed. H. J. C. Grierson and others, 12 vols (London, 1932–37). The index to this edition is by James C. Corson, *Notes and Index to Sir Herbert Grierson's Edition of the Letters of Sir Walter Scott* (Oxford, 1979).

'Memoirs', in *Scott on Himself: A Selection of the Autobiographical Writings of Sir Walter Scott*, ed. David Hewitt (Edinburgh, 1981).

The Poetical Works of Sir Walter Scott, ed. J. Logie Robertson (Oxford, 1904; frequently reprinted).

The Poetical Works of Sir Walter Scott, Bart., [ed. J. G. Lockhart], 12 vols (Edinburgh, 1833–34).

The Prose Works of Sir Walter Scott, Bart., 28 vols (Edinburgh, 1834–36).

Waverley Novels, 48 vols (Edinburgh, 1829–33), known as the 'Magnum Opus'.

The Waverley Novels were among the most frequently reprinted works of the nineteenth century, and all editions after Scott's death were based upon the edition of 1829–33. Of these, the best are the Centenary Edition, 25 vols (London, 1871), the Dryburgh Edition, 25 vols (London, 1892–94), and the Border Edition, ed. Andrew Lang, 48 vols (London, 1892–94). The first critical edition is the Edinburgh Edition of the Waverley Novels (1993–) on which the volumes of the new Penguin Scott are based.

There is no comprehensive listing of the works of Scott; the best currently available are:

J. G. Lockhart, 'Chronological List of the Publications of Sir Walter Scott' in *Memoirs of the Life of Sir Walter Scott, Bart.*, 7 vols (Edinburgh, 1837; many times republished), 7.433–39.

James C. Corson, 'Sir Walter Scott', in *The New Cambridge Bibliography of English Literature*, ed. George Watson, 5 vols (Cambridge, 1969–77), 3.670–79.

BIOGRAPHY

There are many biographies of Scott. The most important is still by J. G. Lockhart for although it is unreliable in much of its detail it is

the work of a writer and an intimate. The most comprehensive of the
modern works is by Edgar Johnson; it is generally reliable. John
Buchan's one-volume life is the most sympathetic of all the studies of
Scott, while John Sutherland takes a harsher view of the way in which
Scott used those in his circle for his own advantage.

James Hogg, *Memoir of the Author's Life; and Familiar Anecdotes of
  Sir Walter Scott*, ed. Douglas S. Mack (Edinburgh, 1972).
James Hogg, *Anecdotes of Sir W. Scott*, ed. Douglas S. Mack
  (Edinburgh, 1983).
J. G. Lockhart, *Memoirs of the Life of Sir Walter Scott, Bart.*, 7 vols
  (Edinburgh, 1837–38; many times republished).
John Buchan, *Sir Walter Scott* (London, 1932).
Sir Herbert Grierson, *Sir Walter Scott, Bart.: A New Life supplemen-
  tary to, and corrective of, Lockhart's Biography* (London, 1938).
Arthur Melville Clark, *Sir Walter Scott: The Formative Years*
  (Edinburgh, 1969).
Edgar Johnson, *Sir Walter Scott: The Great Unknown*, 2 vols
  (London, 1970).
Joan Sutherland, *The Life of Walter Scott* (Oxford, 1995).

CRITICISM

Complete listings of critical works on Scott are to be found in:
James C. Corson, *A Bibliography of Sir Walter Scott: A Classified and
  Annotated List of Books and Articles relating to his Life and Works
  1797–1940* (Edinburgh, 1943).
Jill Rubenstein, *Sir Walter Scott: A Reference Guide* (Boston, MA,
  1978) [covers the period 1932–77].
Jill Rubenstein, *Sir Walter Scott: An Annotated Bibliography of
  Scholarship and Criticism 1975–1990* (Aberdeen, 1994).

THE FOLLOWING ARE USEFUL FOR THE STUDY OF
THE TALE OF OLD MORTALITY:

Francis R. Hart, *Scott's Novels: The Plotting of Historic Survival*
  (Charlottesville, VA, 1960).
David Craig, *Scottish Literature and the Scottish People* (London,
  1961).
Alexander Welsh, *The Hero of the Waverley Novels* (New Haven, CT,
  1963).
A. O. J. Cockshut, *The Achievement of Walter Scott* (London,
  1969).
Robert Gordon, *Under Which King?* (Edinburgh, 1969).
Douglas S. Mack, '"The Rage of Fanaticism in Former Days": James
  Hogg's *Confessions of a Justified Sinner* and the Controversy over

Old Mortality', in Ian Campbell (ed.), *Nineteenth-Century Scottish Fiction* (Manchester, 1979).

Peter D. Garside, '*Old Mortality*'s Silent Minority', *Scottish Literary Journal*, 7 (May 1980), 127–44.

Graham Tulloch, *The Language of Walter Scott: A Study of his Scottish Period Language* (London, 1980).

H. B. de Groot, 'Scott and Galt: *Old Mortality* and *Ringan Gilhaize*', in J. H. Alexander and David Hewitt (eds), *Scott and his Influence: The Papers of the Aberdeen Scott Conference 1982* (Aberdeen, 1983).

Emma Letley, *From Galt to Douglas Brown: Nineteenth-Century Fiction and Scots Language* (Edinburgh, 1988).

Gary Kelly, *English Fiction of the Romantic Period, 1789–1830* (London, 1989).

John MacQueen, *The Rise of the Historical Novel* (Edinburgh, 1989).

Ina Ferris, *The Achievement of Literary Authority* (Ithaca, NY, 1991).

Bruce Beiderwell, *Power and Punishment in Scott's Novels* (Athens, GA, 1992).

Martina Hacker, 'Literary Dialects and Communication in *The Tale of Old Mortality* and *The Brownie of Bodsbeck*', *Studies in Hogg and his World*, 8 (1997), 1–11.

For reasons set out above in 'The Waverley Novels in Penguin', the text of the present volume is based on the first edition of *Old Mortality*, which was published in December 1816 by William Blackwood in Edinburgh and by John Murray in London. Scott's manuscript of the novel survives in its entirety in the Pierpont Morgan Library, New York; and the evidence of the manuscript has enabled the present edition to correct many errors in the original 1816 printing.[1]

When it first appeared, *Old Mortality* was published along with Scott's *The Black Dwarf* in a four-volume set entitled *Tales of my Landlord*. In this set, *The Black Dwarf* occupies volume 1, and *Old Mortality* occupies volumes 2–4. This is reflected in the running headlines of the present edition, which give the original *Tales of my Landlord* volume and chapter numbers, as well as giving a continuous chapter numbering for ease of cross-reference to one-volume printings of the novel.

Scott did not begin to compose the manuscript of *The Tale of Old Mortality* until September 1816, and the novel was in the shops, ready for purchase, before the end of December in the same year.[2] This was a prodigious feat, not least because of the slow and laborious methods of hand typesetting and hand printing then used in book production. Speed was important, because of financial pressures; and, in getting the books ready for sale so quickly, Scott was ably assisted by the workforce of James Ballantyne & Company, an Edinburgh printing firm in which he had a major financial stake. Nevertheless, and in spite of the professionalism and élan with which all concerned worked together, the sheer speed of the operation was such that the first edition could not be expected to be a triumph of polished consistency in spelling, punctuation, and other matters of presentation.

Because of the rush in which it was produced, the first edition contains mistakes as well as inconsistencies. Many of these mistakes result from misreadings. At one point, for example, Scott's manuscript's 'wherever' becomes 'whenever' in the first edition; and the manuscript's 'idiots' becomes 'idiot' at another point (268.11 and 269.28 in the present edition). Some of the mistakes involved matters of greater substance, however: indeed, it appears that one printing-house mistake altered the title of the novel. In Scott's manuscript, the title is twice given as *The Tale of Old Mortality*.³ In printing-house conversations about the urgent job in hand, this was no doubt informally shortened to *Old Mortality*; and it was the shortened form of the title that appeared in the first edition. Famously, Scott anonymously reviewed *The Black Dwarf* and *Old Mortality* in the *Quarterly Review* for January 1817; and in this review he remarks that the latter novel 'is entitled "Old Mortality," but should have been called the Tale of Old Mortality, for the personage so named is only quoted as the authority for the incidents'.⁴

This seems to be an indication of displeasure at the change of title; and it appears that the first edition also strays from Scott's wishes with regard to volume breaks. Scott's manuscript marks the intended volume breaks clearly: but what Scott indicated was be the last chapter of the second volume becomes, in the published version, the first chapter of the final volume. The present edition restores Scott's desired volume breaks, as indicated in the manuscript. This is potentially a matter of some significance. In nineteenth-century novels, volume divisions can perform the same shaping function as act breaks in a play: and volumes, like acts, normally end at a moment of particular importance and dramatic tension.

Scott's feelings on this matter emerge in an entry in his *Journal* for 28 December 1827, in which he discusses a 'demand' from his publisher Robert Cadell 'to prepare a revised copy of the *Tales of my Grandfather* for the press':

> The two first volumes of these little tales are shorter than the third by 70 or 80 pages. Cadell proposes to equalise them by adding part of Vol II to vol I and of vol III to vol II. But then vol I ends with the reign of Robert Bruce, vol II with the defeat of Flodden. Happy points of pause which I cannot think of disturbing; the first in particular for surely we ought to close one volume at least of Scottish history at a point which leaves the Kingdom triumphant and happy, and alas! where do her annals present us with such an aera excepting after Bannockburn? So I will set about to fill up the volumes which are too short with some additional matter and so diminish at least if we cannot altogether remove the unsightly inequality in the size of volumes.⁵

In the first edition of *Tales of my Landlord*, the first of the volumes containing *Old Mortality* runs to 340 pages, the second to 349, and the third to 347. If the volume divisions indicated in the manuscript had been followed, the figures would have been 340, 383, and 313; and it seems clear that the final break has been moved to avoid 'unsightly inequality in the size of volumes'.

In the manuscript, the first two 'volumes' appear to be of equal length: the first section of the manuscript runs to 106 folios, and the second to 105. Scott must therefore have been unpleasantly surprised when he discovered that the second section, when converted into print, turned out to be significantly longer than the first. The volume breaks marked in the manuscript are richly significant, and were no doubt carefully planned. Scott places the first break at the point at which Claverhouse and his troops march from Tillietudlem to encounter the Covenanters at Loudoun-hill; and the concluding words of the volume tell us that 'it was supposed they would come in sight of the enemy in not more than two hours'. (118) The second volume break appears in Scott's manuscript at a similarly dramatic point. We are once again in the company of Claverhouse, this time immediately before the battle of Bothwell Bridge; and Scott ends the volume with these words: 'So saying, he addressed himself to the task of preparation for instant battle' (247).

The volume breaks of the manuscript thus provide 'happy points of pause', as Scott puts it: the pauses come immediately before crucial battles. A coherent pattern thus emerges in which the role of the first volume is to explain the reasons for the rising of the Covenanters in 1679, by showing the state of the country in that year. The second volume then presents the initial victory of the Covenanters when their resistance erupts into open violence at Loudoun-hill; and it also presents their failure to achieve all their objectives in the aftermath of that victory. Loudoun-hill and its consequences having been considered, the final volume presents the battle of Bothwell Bridge and *its* consequences. The short-term consequences are shown in the first half of the volume; while the second half of the volume, set in 1689, shows the long-term consequences. Significantly, much of the action of the 1689 portion of the novel takes place in the immediate vicinity of Bothwell Bridge.

The present edition of *The Tale of Old Mortality* follows the text of the Edinburgh Edition of 1993. In doing so it restores Scott's manuscript volume breaks; it restores Scott's manuscript title; and it restores hundreds of manuscript readings lost or distorted in the rushed preparation of the first edition.

Many reprintings followed the first edition of 1816. In the early reprintings, James Ballantyne and his employees attempted numerous small corrections and improvements; and they also made numerous small errors. In addition, these early reprintings contain a very few alterations that appear to be authorial.[6] Scott, however, did not undertake any extensive revision of *Old Mortality* until, late in life, he began work on what he called his 'Magnum Opus'. This was a new collected edition of the Waverley Novels, annotated by the author; it played an important part in Scott's attempts to repay his debts after his ruin in the financial crash of 1826. In the Magnum, Scott provided new introductions for his novels; and he also made a number of revisions to the texts in matters of detail. Almost all editions of Scott since the early 1830s derive ultimately from the Magnum Opus.

In effect, Scott produced two main versions of *Old Mortality*. One of these was created in the final months of 1816, and frequently reprinted over the next half-dozen years. The other was prepared in the late 1820s, and was first published (as part of the Magnum Opus) in the early months of 1830. The later version does not make structural changes to the text: the events of the narrative remain the same, and their significance is not altered. Nevertheless, the Magnum's Introduction and Notes, together with its extensive textual revisions in matters of detail, combine to produce an experience for the reader significantly different from that provided by one of the earlier editions. Scott's editorial presence in the Magnum is powerful, and inevitably the reader is influenced by it.

The original and Magnum Opus versions of *Old Mortality* were products of different stages of Scott's career, and were designed for different audiences: the world of 1830 was very different from the world of 1816. The author, too, had changed; by the late 1820s the stresses of financial ruin and declining health had taken a heavy toll. One might almost say that each version of the novel is the product of a different Scott.

The present text is an edition of the original version of Scott's tale of the Covenanters, a version now much less familiar than the later Magnum Opus version. There is a good case for saying that the original version, unencumbered by the mass of new material Scott produced for the Magnum, is more accessible for a modern audience than the later version. That is not to suggest, however, that the reappearance of the original version renders Magnum-based editions obsolete. Recent writers on editorial theory have increasingly stressed the existence and legitimacy of multiple versions of literary texts.[7] These modern insights tend to confirm that each version of Scott's novel has its own coherence, integrity, and value: and many readers will wish to have on their shelves both versions of one of the major novels of the nineteenth century.

NOTES

1 These emendations are listed in Walter Scott, *The Tale of Old Mortality*, ed. Douglas Mack, EEWN 4b (Edinburgh: Edinburgh University Press, and New York: Columbia University Press, 1993), 392–427.

2 There is a detailed discussion of the genesis and composition of the novel in *The Tale of Old Mortality*, ed. Mack (EEWN) 355–72.

3 The details are discussed in *The Tale of Old Mortality*, ed. Mack (EEWN) 363–64.

4 *Quarterly Review*, 16 (January 1817), 446.

5 *The Journal of Sir Walter Scott*, ed. W. E. K. Anderson (Oxford, 1972), 405–06.

6 These are discussed in the Essay on the Text in *The Tale of Old Mortality*, ed. Mack (EEWN) 374–75 and 378–79.

7 A particularly valuable discussion is to be found in Jack Stillinger, *Coleridge and Textual Instability: The Multiple Versions of the Major Poems* (New York and Oxford, 1994).

TALES OF MY LANDLORD,

COLLECTED AND REPORTED

BY

JEDIDIAH CLEISHBOTHAM,

PARISH-CLERK AND SCHOOLMASTER OF GANDERCLEUGH.

> Hear, Land o' Cakes and brither Scots,
> Frae Maidenkirk to Jonny Groats',
> If there's a hole in a' your coats,
>   I rede ye tent it,
> A chiel's amang you takin' notes,
>   An' faith he'll prent it.

> BURNS.

IN FOUR VOLUMES.

VOLS. II, III & IV.

EDINBURGH:

PRINTED FOR WILLIAM BLACKWOOD, PRINCE'S STREET:
AND JOHN MURRAY, ALBEMARLE STREET, LONDON.

1816.

Ahora bien, dixo el Cura, traedme, senor huésped, aquesos libros, que los quiero ver. Que me place, respondió el, y entrando, en su aposento, sacó dél una maletilla vieja cerrada con una cadenilla, y abriéndola, halló en ella tres libros grandes y unos papeles de muy buena letra escritos de mano.—DON QUIXOTE, Parte I. Capitulo 32.

It is mighty well, said the priest; pray, landlord, bring me those books, for I have a mind to see them. With all my heart, answered the host; and, going to his chamber, he brought out a little old cloke-bag, with a padlock and chain to it, and opening it, he took out three large volumes, and some manuscript papers written in a fine character.—JARVIS's *Translation*.

TO

HIS LOVING COUNTRYMEN,

WHETHER THEY ARE DENOMINATED

MEN OF THE SOUTH,

GENTLEMEN OF THE NORTH,

PEOPLE OF THE WEST,

OR

FOLK OF FIFE;

THESE TALES,

ILLUSTRATIVE OF ANCIENT SCOTTISH MANNERS,

AND

OF THE TRADITIONS OF THEIR RESPECTIVE DISTRICTS,

ARE RESPECTFULLY INSCRIBED,

BY THEIR FRIEND AND LIEGE FELLOW-SUBJECT,

JEDIDIAH CLEISHBOTHAM.

THE TALE OF
OLD MORTALITY

Chapter One

PRELIMINARY

Why seeks he with unwearied toil
Through death's dim walks to urge his way;
Reclaim his long-asserted spoil,
And lead oblivion into day?
LANGHORNE

"MOST READERS," says the Manuscript of Mr Pattieson, "must have witnessed with delight the joyous burst which attends the dismissing of a village-school on a fine summer evening. The buoyant spirits of childhood, repressed with so much difficulty during the tedious hours of discipline, may then be seen to explode, as it were, in shout, and song, and frolic, as the little urchins join in groups on their play-ground, and arrange their matches of sport for the evening. But there is an individual who partakes of the relief afforded by the moment of dismission, whose feelings are not so obvious to the eye of the spectator, or so apt to receive his sympathy. I mean the teacher himself, who, stunned with the hum, and suffocated with the closeness of his school-room, has spent the whole day (himself against a host) in controuling petulance, exciting indifference to action, striving to enlighten stupidity, and labouring to soften obstinacy; and whose very powers of intellect have been confounded by hearing the same dull lesson repeated a hundred times by rote, and only varied by the various blunders of the reciters. Even the flowers of classic genius, with which his solitary fancy is most gratified, have been rendered degraded, in his imagination, by their connection with tears, with errors, and with punishment; so that the Eclogues of Virgil and Odes of Horace are each inseparably allied in association with the sullen figure and monotonous recitation of some blubbering school-boy. If to these mental distresses are added a delicate frame of body, and a mind ambitious of some higher distinction than that of being the tyrant of childhood, the reader may have some slight conception of the relief which a solitary walk, in the cool of a fine summer evening, affords to the head which has ached, and the nerves which have been shattered, for so many hours, in plying the irksome task of public instruction.

"To me these evening strolls have been the happiest hours of an unhappy life; and if any gentle reader shall hereafter find pleasure in perusing these lucubrations, I am not unwilling he should know, that the plan of them has been usually traced in those moments, when relief from toil and clamour, combined with the quiet scenery around me, has disposed my mind to the task of composition.

"My chief haunt in these hours of golden leisure, is the banks of that small stream, which, winding through a 'lone vale of green bracken,' passes in front of the village school-house of Gandercleugh. For the first quarter of a mile, perhaps, I may be disturbed from my meditations, in order to return the scrape, or doffed bonnet, of such stragglers among my pupils as fish for trouts or minnows in the little brook, or are seeking rushes and wild-flowers by its margin. But, beyond the space I have mentioned, the juvenile anglers do not, after sun-set, voluntarily extend their excursions. The cause is, that farther up the narrow valley, and in a recess which seems scooped out of the side of the steep heathy bank, there is a deserted burial-ground which the little cowards are fearful of approaching in the twilight. To me, however, the place has an inexpressible charm. It has been long the favourite termination of my walks, and, if my kind patron forgets not his promise, will (and probably at no very distant day) be my final resting-place after my mortal pilgrimage.*

"It is a spot which possesses all the solemnity of feeling attached to a burial-ground, without exciting those of a more unpleasing description. Having been very little used for many years, the few hillocks which rise above the level plain are covered with the same short velvet turf that covers it. The monuments, of which there are not above seven or eight, are half sunk in the ground and overgrown with moss. No newly-erected tomb disturbs the sober serenity of our reflections by reminding us of recent calamity, and no rank-springing grass

* Note by Mr Jedidiah Cleishbotham.—That I kept my plight in this melancholy matter with my deceased and lamented friend, appeareth from a handsome head-stone, erected at my proper charges in this spot, bearing the name and calling of Peter Pattieson, with the date of his nativity and sepulture, with a testimony of his merits, attested by myself, as his superior and patron.

forces upon our imagination the recollection, that it owes its dark luxuriance to the foul and festering remnants of mortality which ferment beneath. The daisy which sprinkles the sod, and the hare-bell which hangs over it, derive their pure nourishment from the dew of Heaven, and their growth impresses us with no degrading or disgusting recollections. Death has indeed been here, and its traces are before us; but they are softened and deprived of their horror by our distance from the period when they have been first impressed. Those who sleep beneath are only connected with us by the reflection that they have once been what we now are, and that, as their reliques are now identified with their mother earth, ours shall, at some future period, undergo the same transformation.

"Yet, although the moss has been collected on the most modern of these humble tombs during four generations of mankind, the memory of some of those who sleep beneath them is still held in reverend remembrance. It is true, that, upon the largest, and, to an antiquary, the most interesting monument of the group, which bears the effigies of a doughty knight in his hood of mail, with his shield hanging on his breast, the armorial bearings are defaced by time, and a few worn-out letters may be read at the pleasure of the decypherer, *Dns. Johan de Hamel*, or *Johan de Lamel*. And it is also true, that of another tomb richly sculptured with an ornamented cross, mitre, and pastoral staff, tradition only can aver, that a certain nameless Bishop lies interred there. But upon other two stones which lie beside, may still be read in rude prose, and ruder rhyme, the history of those who lie beneath them. They belong, we are assured by the epitaph, to the class of persecuted Presbyterians who afforded a melancholy subject for history in the times of Charles II. and his successor.* In returning from the battle of Pentland Hills, a party of the insurgents had been attacked in this glen by a small detachment of the King's troops, and three or four either killed in the skirmish, or shot after being made prisoners, as rebels taken with arms in their hands. The peasantry continue to attach to the tombs of these victims of prelacy an honour which they do not render to more splendid mausoleums; and, when they point them out to their sons, and narrate the fate of the sufferers, usually conclude, by exhorting them to be ready, should times call for it, to resist to the death in the cause of civil and religious liberty, like their brave forefathers.

"Although I am far from venerating the peculiar tenets asserted by those who call themselves the followers of these men, and whose intolerance and narrow-minded bigotry are at least as conspicuous as

* Foot Note. James, Seventh King of Scotland of that name, and Second according to the numeration of the Kings of England.—J.C.

their devotional zeal, yet it is without depreciating the memory of those sufferers, many of whom united the independent sentiments of a Hampden with the suffering zeal of an Hooper or Latimer. On the other hand it would be unjust to forget, that many even of those who had been most active in crushing what they conceived the rebellious and seditious spirit of these unhappy wanderers, displayed, when called upon themselves to suffer for their political and religious opinions, the same daring and devoted zeal, tinctured, in their case, with chivalrous loyalty, as in the former with republican enthusiasm. It has often been remarked of the Scottish character, that the stubbornness with which it is moulded shews most to advantage in adversity, when it seems akin to the native sycamore of their hills, which scorns to be biassed in its mode of growth even by the influence of the prevailing wind, but, shooting its branches with equal boldness in every direction, shews no weather-side to the storm, and may be broken, but can never be bended. It must be understood that I speak of my countrymen as they fall under my own observation. When in foreign countries, I have been informed that they are more docile. But it is time to return from this digression.

"One summer evening, as in a stroll, such as I have described, I approached this deserted mansion of the dead, I was somewhat surprised to hear sounds distinct from those which usually sooth its solitude, the gentle chiding, namely, of the brook, and the sighing of the wind in the boughs of three gigantic ash trees, which mark the cemetery. The clink of a hammer was now distinctly heard, and I entertained some alarm that a march-dike, long meditated by the two proprietors whose estates were divided by my favourite brook, was about to be drawn up the glen, in order to substitute its rectilinear deformity for the graceful winding of the natural boundary.* As I approached I was agreeably undeceived. An old man was seated upon the monument of the slaughtered presbyterians, and busily employed in deepening, with his chisel, the letters of the inscription, which, announcing, in scriptural language, the promised blessings of futurity to be the lot of the slain, anathematized the murderers with corresponding violence. A blue bonnet of unusual dimensions covered the

*Foot Note. I deem it fitting that the reader should be apprised, that this limitary boundary between the conterminous heritable property of his honour the Laird of Gandercleugh, and his honour the Laird of Gussdub, was to have been in fashion an *agger*, or rather *murus* of uncemented granite, called, by the vulgar, a *dry-stane-dike*, surmounted, or coped, *cespite viridi*, i.e. with a sod-turf. Truly their honours fell into discord concerning two roods of marshy ground, near the cove called the Bedral's Beild; and the controversy, having some years by-gone been removed from before the Judges of the Land, (with whom it abode long,) even unto the Great City of London and the Assembly of the Nobles therein, is, as I may say, *adhuc in pendente.*—J.C.

grey hairs of the pious workman. His dress was a large old-fashioned coat, of the coarse cloth called *hoddin-grey*, usually worn by the elder peasants, with waistcoat and breeches of the same; and the whole suit, though still in decent repair, had obviously seen a long train of hard service. Strong clouted shoes, studded with hob-nails, and *gramoches*, or *leggins*, made of thick black cloth, completed his equipment. Beside him, fed among the graves a poney, the companion of his journey, whose extreme whiteness, as well as its projecting bones and hollow eyes, indicated its antiquity. It was harnessed in the most simple manner, with a pair of branks, and hair tether, or halter, and a *sunk*, or cushion of straw, instead of bridle and saddle. A canvas pouch hung around the neck of the animal, for the purpose, probably, of containing the rider's tools, and any thing else he might have occasion to carry with him. Although I had never seen this old man before, yet, from the singularity of his employment, and the style of his equipage, I had no difficulty in recognizing a religious itinerant whom I had often heard talked of, and who was known in various parts of Scotland by the title of Old Mortality.

"Where this man was born, or what was his real name, I have never been able to learn, nor are the motives which made him desert his home, and adopt the erratic mode of life which he pursued, known to me except very generally. According to the belief of most people, he was a native of either the county of Dumfries or Galloway, and lineally descended from some of those champions of the Covenant whose deeds and sufferings were his favourite theme. He is said to have held, at one period of his life, a small moorland farm; but, whether from pecuniary losses, or domestic misfortune, he had long renounced that and every other gainful calling. In the language of Scripture, he left his house, his home, and his kindred, and wandered about until the day of his death, a period, it is said, of nearly thirty years.

"During this long pilgrimage, the pious enthusiast regulated his circuit so as annually to visit the graves of the unfortunate Covenanters who suffered by the sword, or by the executioner, during the reigns of the two last monarchs of the Stuart line. These are most numerous in the western districts of Ayr, Galloway, and Dumfries; but they are also to be found in other parts of Scotland, wherever the fugitives had fought, or fallen, or suffered by military or civil executions. Their tombs are often apart from all human habitation, in the remote moors and wilds to which the wanderers had fled for concealment. But wherever they existed, Old Mortality was sure to visit them when his annual round brought them within his reach. In the most lonely recesses of the mountains, the moor-fowl shooter has been often surprised to find him busied in cleansing the moss from the grey stones, renewing with his chisel the half-defaced inscriptions, and repairing the emblems of death with which these simple monuments are usually adorned. Motives of the most sincere, though fanciful devotion, induced the old man to dedicate so many years of existence to perform this tribute to the memory of the deceased warriors of the church. He considered himself as fulfilling a sacred duty, while renewing to the eyes of posterity the decaying emblems of the zeal and sufferings of their forefathers, and thereby trimming, as it were, the beacon-light which was to warn future generations to defend their religion even unto blood.

"In all his wanderings, the old pilgrim never seemed to need, or was known to accept, pecuniary assistance. It is true his wants were very few, for wherever he went, he found ready quarters in the house of some Cameronian of his own sect, or of some other religious person. The hospitality which was reverentially paid to him he always acknowledged, by repairing the gravestones (if there existed any) belonging to the family or ancestors of his host. As the Wanderer was usually to be seen bent on this pious task within the precincts of some country church-yard, or reclined on the solitary tombstone among the heath, disturbing the plover and the black-cock with the clink of his chisel and mallet, with his old white poney grazing by his side, he acquired, from his converse among the dead, his popular appellation of Old Mortality.

"The character of such a man could have in it little connection even with innocent gaiety. Yet, among those of his own religious persuasion, he is reported to have been chearful. The descendants of persecutors, or those whom he supposed guilty of entertaining similar tenets, and the scoffers at religion by whom he was sometimes assailed, he usually termed the generation of vipers. Conversing with others, he was grave and sententious, not without a cast of severity. But he is said never to have been observed to give way to violent passion, excepting upon one occasion, when a mischievous truant-boy defaced with a stone the nose of a cherub's face which the old man was engaged in re-touching. I am in general a sparer of the rod, notwithstanding the maxim of Solomon, for which school-boys have little reason to thank his memory; but on this occasion I deemed it proper to shew that I did not hate the child. But I must return to the circumstances attending my first interview with this interesting enthusiast.

"In accosting Old Mortality, I did not fail to pay respect to his years and his principles, beginning my address by a respectful apology for interrupting his labours. The old man intermitted the operation of the chisel, took off his spectacles and wiped them, then replacing them on his nose, acknowledged my courtesy by a suitable return. Encouraged

by his affability, I intruded upon him some questions concerning the
sufferers upon whose monument he was now employed. To talk of the
exploits of the Covenanters was the delight, as to repair their monuments was the business, of his life. He was profuse in the communication of all the minute information which he had collected concerning
them, their wars, their woes, and their wanderings. One would almost
have supposed he must have been their contemporary, and have
actually beheld the passages which he related, so much had he identified his feelings and opinions with theirs, and so much had his narratives the minute circumstantiality of an eye-witness.

"'We,' said he, in a tone of exultation, 'are the only true whigs.
Carnal men have assumed that triumphant appellation, following him
whose kingdom is of this world. Which of them would sit six hours on
a wet hill side to hear a godly sermon? I trow an hour o't wad staw
them. They are ne'er a hair better than them that shame na to tak upon
themsels the persecuting name of blude-thirsty tories. Self-seekers all
of them, strivers after wealth, power, and worldly ambition, and forgetting alike what has been dree'd and done by the mighty men who
stood in the gap in the great day of wrath. Nae wonder they dread the
accomplishment of what was spoken by the mouth of the worthy
Mr Peden, (that precious servant of the Lord, none of whose words
fell to the ground) that the French monzies* sall rise as fast in the
Glens of Ayr, and the Kenns of Galloway, as ever the Highlandmen did in 1678. And now they are gripping to the bow and to the
spear, when they suld be mourning for a sinfu' land and a broken
covenant.'

"Soothing the old man by letting his peculiar opinions pass without
contradiction, and anxious to prolong conversation with so singular a
character, I prevailed upon him to accept that hospitality which Mr
Cleishbotham is always willing to extend to those who need it. In our
way to the schoolmaster's house, we called at the Wallace Inn, where I
was pretty certain I could find my patron about that hour of the
evening. After a courteous interchange of civilities, Old Mortality
was, with difficulty, prevailed upon to join his host in a single glass of
liquor, and that on condition that he should be permitted to name the
pledge, which he prefaced with a grace of about five minutes length,
and then, with bonnet doffed and eyes uplifted, drank to the Memory
of those Heroes of the Kirk who had first uplifted her banner upon the
mountains. As no persuasion could prevail on him to extend his conviviality to a second cup, my patron accompanied him home, and
accommodated him in the prophet's chamber, as it is his pleasure to

*Foot Note. Probably monsieurs. It would seem this was spoken during the apprehen-
sions of invasion from France.—*Publishers*.

call the closet which holds his spare bed, and which is frequently a place of retreat for the poor traveller.*

"The next day I took leave of Old Mortality, who seemed affected by the unusual attention with which I had cultivated his acquaintance and listened to his conversation. After he had mounted, not without difficulty, the old white poney, he took me by the hand and said, 'The blessing of our Master be with you, young man. My hours are like the ears of the latter harvest, and your days are yet in the spring; and yet you may be gathered into the garner of mortality before me, for the sickle of death cuts down the green as oft as the ripe, and there is a colour in your cheek, that, like the bud of the rose, serveth oft to hide the worm of corruption. Wherefore labour as one who knoweth not when his master calleth. And if it be my lot to return to this village after ye are gane hame to your ain place, these auld withered hands will frame a stane of memorial, that your name may not perish from among the people.'

"I thanked Old Mortality for his kind intentions in my behalf, and heaved a sigh, not, I think, of regret so much as of resignation, to think of the chance that I might soon require his good offices. But though, in all human probability, he did not err in supposing, that my span of life may be abridged in youth, he had over-estimated the period of his own pilgrimage on earth. It is now some years since he has been missed in all his usual haunts, while moss, lichen, and deers-hair, are fast covering those stones to cleanse which was the business of his life. About the beginning of this century he closed his mortal toils, being found on the high-road near Lockerby, in Dumfries-shire, exhausted and just expiring. The old white poney, the companion of all his wanderings, was standing by the side of his dying master. There was found about his person a sum of money sufficient for his decent inter- ment, which serves to shew that his death was in no ways hastened by violence or by want. The common people still regard his memory with great respect; and many are of opinion, that the stones which he repaired will not again require the assistance of the chisel. They even assert, that on the tombs where the manner of the martyrs' murder is recorded, their names have remained indelibly legible since the death of Old Mortality, while those of persecutors, sculptured on the same monuments, have been entirely defaced. It is hardly necessary to say

* Foot Note. He might have added, and for the *rich* also, since, I laud my stars, the great of the earth have taken herborage in my poor domicile. And, during the service of my hand-maiden, Dorothy, who was buxom and comely of aspect, his Honour the Laird of Smackawa, in his peregrinations to and from the metropolis, was wont to prefer my prophet's chamber even to the sanded chamber of dais in the Wallace Inn, and to bestow a mutchkin, as he would jocosely say, to obtain the freedom of the house, but in reality to assure himself of my company during the evening.—J.C.

that this is a fond imagination, and that, since the time of the pious
pilgrim, the monuments which were the objects of his care are hastening, like all earthly memorials, to fall into ruin or decay.

"My readers will of course understand, that, in embodying into one
compressed narrative many of the anecdotes which I had the advantage of deriving from Old Mortality, I have been far from adopting
either his style, his opinions, or even his facts, so far as they appear to
have been distorted by party prejudice. I have endeavoured to correct
or verify them from the most authentic sources of tradition, afforded
by the representatives of either party.

"On the part of the presbyterians, I have consulted such moorland
farmers from the western districts, as, by the kindness of their land-
lords, or otherwise, have been able, during the late general change of
property, to retain possession of the grazings on which their grand-
sires fed their flocks and herds. I must own, that, of late days, I have
found this a limited source of information. I have, therefore, called in
the supplementary aid of those modest itinerants, whom the scrupulous civility of our ancestors denominated travelling-merchants, and
whom, of late, accommodating ourselves in this as in more material
particulars to the feelings and sentiments of our more wealthy neighbours, we have learned to call packmen, or pedlars. To country
weavers travelling in hopes to get rid of their winter web, but more
especially to tailors, who, from their sedentary profession, and the
necessity, in our country, of exercising it by temporary residence in
the families by whom they are employed, may be considered as possessing a complete register of rural traditions, I have been indebted
for many illustrations of the narratives of Old Mortality, much in the
taste and spirit of the original.

"I had more difficulty in finding materials for correcting the tone of
partiality which evidently pervaded these stores of traditional learning, in order that I might be enabled to present an unbiassed picture of
the manners of that unhappy period, and, at the same time, to do
justice to the merits of both parties. But I have been enabled to qualify
the narratives of Old Mortality and his Cameronian friends, by the
reports of more than one descendant of ancient and honourable families, who, themselves decayed into the humble vale of life, yet look
proudly back on the period when their ancestors fought and fell in
behalf of the exiled house of Stuart. I may even boast right reverend
authority on the same score; for more than one non-juring bishop,
whose authority and income was upon as apostolical a scale as the
greatest abominator of Episcopacy could well desire, have deigned,
while partaking of the humble cheer of the Wallace Inn, to furnish me
with information corrective of the facts which I learned from others.

There is also here and there a laird or two, who, though they shrug their shoulders, profess no great shame in their fathers having served in the persecuting squadrons of Earlshall and Claverhouse. From the gamekeepers of these gentlemen, an office the most apt of any other to become hereditary in such families, I have contrived to collect much valuable information.

"Upon the whole, I can hardly fear, that, at this time, in describing the operation which their opposite principles produced upon the good and bad of both parties, I can be suspected of meaning insult or injustice to either. If recollection of former injuries, extra-loyalty, and contempt and hatred of their adversaries, produced rigour and tyranny in the one party, it will hardly be denied, on the other hand, that, if the zeal for God's house did not eat up the conventiclers' reason entirely, it devoured, at least, to imitate the phrase of Dryden, no small portion of their loyalty, sober sense, and good breeding. We may safely hope, that the souls of the brave and sincere on either side have long looked down with surprise and pity upon the ill-appreciated motives which caused their mutual hatred and hostility while in this valley of darkness, blood, and tears. Peace to their memory! Let us think of them as the heroine of our only Scottish tragedy entreats her lord to think of her departed sire,

> "O, rake not up the ashes of our fathers!
> Implacable resentment was their crime,
> And grievous has the expiation been."

Chapter Two

> Summon an hundred horse by break of day
> To wait our pleasure at the castle gates.
> *Douglas*

UNDER the reign of the last Stuarts, there was an anxious wish on the part of the government to counteract, by every means in their power, the strict or puritanical spirit which had been the chief characteristic of the republicans, and to revive those feudal institutions which united the vassal to the liege-lord, and both to the crown. Frequent musters and assemblies of the people, for sports and pastimes, were appointed by authority. The interference was impolitic, to say the least; for, as usual upon such occasions, the consciences which were at first only scrupulous, became confirmed in their opinion instead of giving way to the terrors of authority; and the youth of both sexes, to whom the pipe and tabor in England, or the bagpipe in Scotland, would have been by themselves an irresistible temptation, were enabled to set them at defiance, from the proud consciousness that they were, at the

same time, resisting an act of Council. To compel men to dance and
be merry by authority has rarely succeeded, even on board of slave-
ships, where it was formerly sometimes attempted by way of inducing
the wretched captives to agitate their limbs, and restore the circula-
tion, during the few minutes they were permitted to enjoy the fresh air
upon deck. The rigour of the strict Calvinists increased in proportion
to the wishes of the government that it should be relaxed. A Judaical
observance of the Sabbath—a supercilious condemnation of all manly
pastimes and harmless recreations, as well as of the profane custom of
promiscuous dancing, that is, of men and women dancing together in
the same party, (for I believe they admitted that the exercise might be
inoffensive if practised by the parties separately)—distinguished
those who professed a more than ordinary share of sanctity. They
discouraged, as far as lay in their power, even the ancient *wappen-
schaws*, as they were called, when the feudal array of the county was
called out, and each crown vassal was required to appear with such
muster of men and armour as he was bound to make by his fief, and
that under high statutory penalties. The Covenanters were the more
jealous of these assemblages, as the lord-lieutenants and sheriffs
under whom they were held had instructions from the government to
spare no pains which might render them agreeable to the young men
who were thus summoned together, upon whom the military exercise
of the morning, and the sports which usually closed the evening, might
naturally be supposed to have a seductive effect.

The preachers and proselytes of the more rigid presbyterians
laboured, therefore, by every means of caution, remonstrance, and
authority, to diminish the attendance upon these summonses, conscious that in doing so, they lessened not only the apparent, but the
actual strength of the government, by impeding the extension of that
esprit de corps which soon unites young men who are in the habit of
meeting together for manly sport, or military exercise. They, therefore, exerted themselves earnestly to prevent attendance upon these
occasions by those who could find any possible excuse for absence,
and were especially severe upon such of their hearers as mere curiosity led to be spectators, or love of exercise to be partakers, of the array
and the sports which took place. Such of the gentry as acceded to
these doctrines were not always, however, in a situation to be ruled by
them. The commands of the law were imperative; and the Privy
Council, who administered the executive power in Scotland, were
severe in enforcing the statutory penalties against the crown vassals
who did not appear at the periodical wappen-schaw. The landholders
were compelled, therefore, to send their sons, tenants, and vassals to
the rendezvous, to the number of horse, men, and spears, at which

they were rated; and it frequently happened, that, notwithstanding the strict charge of their elders to return as soon as the formal inspection was over, the young men-at-arms were unable to resist the temptation of sharing in the sports which succeeded the muster, or to avoid listening to the prayers read in the churches on these occasions, and thus, in the opinion of their repining parents, meddling with the accursed thing which is an abomination in the sight of the Lord.

The sheriff of the county of Lanark was holding the wappen-schaw of a wild district, called the Upper Ward of Clydesdale, on a haugh, or level plain, near to a royal borough, the name of which is no way essential to my story, upon the morning of the 5th of May, 1679, when our narrative commences. When the musters had been made, and duly reported, the young men, as was usual, were to mix in various sports, of which the chief was to shoot at the popinjay, an ancient game formerly practised with archery, and then with fire-arms. This was the figure of a bird, decked with party-coloured feathers, so as to res-emble a popinjay, or parrot. It was suspended to a pole, and served for a mark, at which the competitors discharged their fusees and cara-bines in rotation, at the distance of sixty or seventy paces. He whose ball brought down the mark, held the proud title of Captain of the Popinjay for the remainder of the day, and was usually escorted in triumph to the most reputable change-house in the neighbourhood, where the evening was closed with conviviality, conducted under his auspices.

It will, of course, be supposed that the ladies of the country assembled to witness this gallant strife, those excepted who held the stricter tenets of puritanism, and would therefore have deemed it criminal to afford countenance to the profane gambols of the malig-nants. Landaus, barouches, or tilburies, there were none in those simple days. The lord-lieutenant of the county (a personage of ducal rank) alone pretended to the magnificence of a wheel-carriage, a thing covered with tarnished gilding and sculpture, in shape like the vulgar picture of Noah's ark, dragged by eight long-tailed Flanders mares, bearing eight *insides* and six *outsides*. The insides were their graces in person, two maids of honour, two children, a chaplain, stuffed into a sort of lateral recess, formed by a projection at the door of the vehicle, and called, from its appearance, the boot, and an equery to his Grace ensconced in the corresponding convenience on the opposite side. A coachman, and three postillions, who wore short swords, and tie-wigs with three tails, had blunderbusses slung behind them, and pistols at their saddle-bow, conducted the equipage. On the foot-board, behind this moving mansion-house, stood, or rather hung, in triple file, six lacquies, in rich liveries, armed up to the teeth.

The rest of the gentry, men and women, old and young, were upon horseback, followed by their servants; but the company, for the reasons already assigned, was rather select than numerous.

Near to the enormous leathern vehicle which we have attempted to describe, vindicating her title to precedence over the untitled gentry of the country, might be seen the sober palfrey of Lady Margaret Bellenden, bearing the erect and primitive form of Lady Margaret herself, decked in those widow's weeds which the good lady had never laid aside since the execution of her husband for his adherence to Montrose.

Her grand-daughter, and only earthly care, the fair-haired Edith, who was generally allowed to be the prettiest lass in the Upper Ward, appeared beside her aged relative like Spring placed close to Winter. Her black Spanish jennet, which she managed with great grace, her gay riding-dress, and laced side-saddle, had been anxiously prepared to set her forth to the best advantage. But the clustering profusion of ringlets, which, escaping from under her cap, were only confined by a green ribband from wantoning over her shoulders; her cast of features, soft and feminine, yet not without a certain expression of playful archness, which redeemed their sweetness from the charge of insipidity, sometimes brought against *blondes* and blue-eyed beauties,— these attracted more admiration from the western youth than either the splendour of her equipments or the figure of her palfrey.

The attendance of these distinguished ladies was rather inferior to their birth and fashion in these times, as it consisted only of two servants on horseback. The truth was, that the good old lady had been obliged to make all her domestic servants turn out in arms to complete the quota which her barony ought to furnish for the muster, and in which she would not for the universe have been found deficient. The old steward, who, in steel cap and jack-boots, led forth her array, had sweated, as he said, blood and water in his efforts to overcome the scruples and evasions of the moorland farmers who ought to have furnished men, horse, and harness on these occasions. At last, their dispute came near to an open declaration of hostilities, the incensed episcopalian bestowing on the recusants the whole thunders of the commination, and receiving from them, in return, the denunciations of a Calvinistic excommunication. What was to be done? To punish the refractory tenants would have been easy enough. The Privy Council would readily have imposed fines, and sent a troop of horse to collect them. But this would have been calling in the huntsman and hounds into the garden to kill the hare: "For," said Harrison to himself, "the carles have little eneugh gear at ony rate, and if I call in the red-coats to take away what little they have, how is my worshipful lady to get her rents paid at Candlemas, which is but a difficult matter to bring round even in the best of times?"

So he armed the fowler, and falconer, the footman, and the plough-man at the home farm, with an old drunken cavaliering butler, who had served with the late Sir Richard under Montrose, and stunned the family nightly with his exploits at Kilsythe and Tippermoor, and who was the only man in the party that had the smallest zeal for the work in hand. In this manner, and by recruiting one or two latitudinarian poachers and black-fishers, Mr Harrison completed the quota of men which fell to the share of Lady Margaret Bellenden, as life-rentrix of the barony of Tillietudlem and others. But when the steward, on the morning of the eventful day, had mustered his *troupe doree* before the iron grate of the tower, the mother of Cuddie the ploughman appeared, loaded with the jack-boots, buff coat, and other accoutre-ments which had been issued forth for the service of the day, and laid them in a heap before the steward; demurely assuring him, that whether it were the cholic, or a qualm of conscience, she couldna take upon her to decide, but sure it was, Cuddie had been in sair straits a' night, and she couldna say he was muckle better this morning. The finger of Heaven, she said, was in it, and her bairn should gang on nae sic errands. Pains, penalties, and threats of dismission were denounced in vain; the mother was obstinate, and Cuddie, who underwent a domiciliary visitation for the purpose of verifying his state of body, could, or would, answer only by deep groans. Mause, who had been an ancient domestic in the family, was a sort of favourite with Lady Margaret, and presumed accordingly. Lady Margaret had her-self set forth, and her authority could not be appealed to. In this dilemma, the good genius of the old butler suggested an expedient.

"He had seen mony a braw callant, far less than Goose Gibbie, fight brawly under Montrose. What for no take Goose Gibbie?"

This was a half-witted lad, of very small stature, who had a kind of charge of the poultry under the old hen-wife; for in a Scottish man-sion of that day there was a wonderful substitution of labour. This urchin being sent for from the stubble-field, was hastily muffled in the buff coat, and girded rather *to* than *with* the sword of a full-grown man, his little legs plunged into jack-boots, and a steel cap put upon his head, which seemed, from its size, as if they were going to extin-guish him. Thus accoutred, he was hoisted, at his own earnest request, upon the tamest horse of the party; and prompted and sup-ported by old Gudyill the butler, as his front file, he passed muster tolerably enough; the sheriff not caring to examine too closely the recruits of so well-affected a person as Lady Margaret Bellenden.

To the above cause it was owing that the personal retinue of Lady

Margaret, on this eventful day, amounted only to two lacqueys, with which diminished train she would, upon any other occasion, have been much ashamed to appear in public. But, for the cause of royalty, she was ready at any time to have made the most unreserved personal sacrifices. She had lost her husband and two promising sons in the civil wars of that unhappy period; but she had received her reward, for, upon his route through the west of Scotland to meet Cromwell in the unfortunate field of Worcester, Charles the Second had actually breakfasted in the Tower of Tillietudlem, an incident which formed, from that moment, an important æra in the life of Lady Margaret, who seldom afterwards partook of that meal, either at home or abroad, without detailing the whole circumstances of the royal visit, not forgetting the salutation which his majesty conferred on each side of her face, though she sometimes omitted to notice that he bestowed the same favour on two buxom serving-wenches who appeared at her back, elevated for the day into the capacity of waiting gentlewomen.

These instances of royal favour were decisive; and if Lady Margaret had not been a confirmed royalist already, from sense of high birth, influence of education, and hatred to the opposite party, through whom she had suffered such domestic calamity, the having given a breakfast to majesty, and received the royal salute in return, were honours enough of themselves to unite her exclusively to the fortunes of the Stuarts. These were now, in all appearance, triumphant; but Lady Margaret's zeal had adhered to them through the worst of times, and was ready to sustain the same severities of fortune should their scale once more kick the beam. At present she enjoyed, in full extent, the military display of the force which stood ready to support the crown, and stifled, as well as she could, the mortification she felt at the defalcation of her own retainers.

Many civilities passed between her ladyship and the representatives of sundry ancient loyal families who were upon the ground, by whom she was held in high reverence; and not a young man of rank passed by them in the course of the muster but he carried his body more erect in the saddle, and threw his horse upon his haunches, to display his own horsemanship and the complete bitting of his steed to the best advantage in the eyes of Miss Edith Bellenden. But the young cavaliers, distinguished by high descent and undoubted loyalty, attracted no more attention from Edith than the laws of courtesy peremptorily demand; and she turned an indifferent ear to the various compliments with which she was addressed, most of which were little the worse for the wear, though borrowed for the nonce from the laborious and long-winded romances of Calprenede and Scuderi, the mirrors in which the youth of that age delighted to dress themselves, ere Folly had thrown her ballast overboard, and cut down her vessels of the first rate, such as the romances of Cyrus, Cleopatra, and others, into small-craft, drawing as little water, or, to speak more plainly, consuming as little time as the little cock-boat in which the gentle reader has deigned to embark. It was, however, the decree of fate that Miss Bellenden should not continue to evince the same equanimity till the conclusion of the day.

Chapter Three

Horseman and horse confessed the bitter pang,
And arms and warrior fell with heavy clang.
Pleasures of Hope

WHEN the military evolutions had been gone through tolerably well, allowing for the awkwardness of men and of horses, a loud shout announced that the competitors were about to step forth for the game of the popinjay already described. The mast or pole, from a yard extended across which the mark was displayed, was raised amid the acclamations of the assembly; and even the more vulgar part who had eyed the evolutions of the feudal militia with a sort of malignant and sarcastic sneer, from disinclination to the royal cause in which they were professedly embodied, could not refrain from taking considerable interest in the strife which was now approaching. They crowded towards the goal, and criticized the appearance of each competitor as, in succession, they advanced, discharged their pieces at the mark, and had their good or bad address rewarded by the laughter or applause of the spectators. But when a slender young man, dressed with great simplicity, yet not without a certain air of pretension to elegance and gentility, approached the station with his fusee in his hand, his dark-green cloak thrown back over his shoulder, his laced ruff and feathered cap, indicating a superior rank to the vulgar, there was a murmur of interest among the spectators, whether altogether favourable to the young adventurer, it was difficult to discover.

"Ewhow, sirs, to see his father's son at the like o' these fearless follies!" was the ejaculation of the elder and more rigid puritans, whose curiosity had so far overcome their bigotry as to bring them to the play-ground. But the generality viewed the strife less morosely, and were contented to wish success to the son of a deceased presbyterian leader, without strictly examining the propriety of his being a competitor for the present prize.

Their wishes were gratified. At the first discharge of his piece the green adventurer struck the popinjay, being the first palpable hit of the day, though several balls had passed very near the mark. A loud shout of applause ensued. But the success was not decisive, it being necessary that each who followed should have his chance, and that those who succeeded in hitting the mark should renew the strife among themselves, till one displayed a decided superiority over the others. Two only of those who followed in order succeeded in hitting the popinjay. The first was a young man of low rank, heavily built, and who kept his face muffled in his grey cloak; the second a gallant young cavalier, remarkable for a handsome exterior, sedulously decorated for the day. He had been since the muster in close attendance on Lady Margaret and Miss Bellenden, and had left them with an air of indifference, when Lady Margaret had asked whether there was no young man of family and loyal principles who would dispute the prize with those two lads who had been successful. In half a minute, young Lord Evandale threw himself from his horse, borrowed a gun from a servant, and, as we have already noticed, hit the mark. Great was the interest excited by the contest between the three candidates who had been hitherto successful. The state equipage of the Duke was, with some difficulty, put in motion, and approached more near to the scene of action. The riders, both male and female, turned their horses' heads in the same direction, and all eyes were bent upon the issue of the trial of skill.

It was the etiquette in the second contest that the competitors should take their turns of firing after drawing lots. The first fell upon the young plebeian, who, as he took his stand, half uncloaked his rustic countenance, and said to the gallant in green, "Ye see, Mr Harry, if it were ony other day, I could hae wished to miss for your sake; but Jenny Dennison is looking at us, sae I maun do my best."

He took his aim, and his bullet whistled past the mark so nearly, that the pendulous object at which it was directed was seen to shiver. Still, however, he had not hit it, and, with a downcast look, he withdrew himself from further competition, and hastened to disappear from the assembly, as if fearful of being recognized. The green chasseur next advanced, and his ball, a second time, struck the popinjay. All shouted; and from the outskirts of the assembly arose a cry of, "The good old cause for ever!"

While the dignitaries bent their brows at these exulting shouts of the disaffected, the young Lord Evandale advanced again to the hazard, and again was successful. The shouts and congratulations of the well-affected and aristocratic part of the audience attended his success, but still a subsequent trial of skill remained.

The green marksman, as if determined to bring the affair to a decision, took his horse from a person who held him, having previously looked carefully to the security of his girths and the setting of his saddle, vaulted on his back, and motioning with his hand for the by-standers to make way, set spurs, passed the place from which he was to fire at a gallop, and, as he passed, threw up the reins, turned sideways upon his seat, discharged his carabine, and brought down the popinjay. Lord Evandale imitated his example, although many around him said it was an innovation on the established practice, which he was not obliged to follow. But his skill was not so perfect, or his horse was not so well trained. The animal swerved at the moment his master fired, and the ball missed the popinjay. Those who had been surprised by the address of the green marksman were now equally pleased by his courtesy. He disclaimed all merit from the last shot, and proposed to his antagonist that it should not be counted as a hit, and that they should renew the contest on foot.

"I would prefer horseback if I had a horse as well bitted, and, probably, as well broken to the exercise as yours," said the young Lord, addressing his antagonist.

"Will you do me the honour to use him for the next trial, on condition you will lend me yours?" said the young gentleman.

Lord Evandale was ashamed to accept this courtesy, as conscious how much it would diminish the value of victory; and yet unable to suppress his wish to redeem his reputation as a marksman, he added, "that although he renounced all pretensions to the honours of the day," (which he said somewhat scornfully,) "yet, if the victor had no particular objection, he would willingly embrace his obliging offer, and change horses with him for the purpose of trying a shot for love."

As he said so, he looked boldly towards Miss Bellenden, and tradition says, that the eyes of the young tirailleur travelled, though more covertly, in the same direction. The young Lord's last trial was as unsuccessful as the former, and it was with difficulty that he preserved the tone of scornful indifference which he had hitherto assumed. But, conscious of the ridicule which attaches itself to the resentment of a losing party, he returned to his antagonist the horse on which he had made his last unsuccessful attempt, and received back his own; paying, at the same time, thanks to his competitor, who, he said, had re-established his favourite horse in his good opinion, for he had been in great danger of transferring to the poor nag the blame of an inferiority which every one, as well as himself, must now be satisfied remained with the rider. Having made this speech in a tone in which mortification assumed the veil of indifference, he mounted his horse and rode off the ground.

As is the usual way of the world, the applause and attention even of those whose wishes had favoured Lord Evandale, were, upon his decisive discomfiture, transferred to his triumphant rival.

"Who is he? what is his name?" ran from mouth to mouth among the gentry who were present, to few of whom he was personally known. His style and title having soon transpired, and being within that class whom a great man might notice without derogation, four of the Duke's friends, with the obedient start which poor Malvolio ascribes to his imaginary retinue, made out to lead the victor to his presence. As they conducted him in triumph through the crowd of spectators, and stunned him at the same time with their compliments on his success, he chanced to pass, or rather to be led, immediately in front of Lady Margaret and her grand-daughter. The Captain of the popinjay and Miss Bellenden coloured like crimson, as the latter returned, with embarrassed courtesy, the low inclination which the victor made even to his saddle-bow in passing her.

"So you know that young person?" said Lady Margaret.

"I—I—have seen him, Madam, at my uncle's, and—and elsewhere occasionally," stammered Miss Edith Bellenden.

"I hear them say around me," said Lady Margaret, "that the young spark is the nephew of old Milnewood."

"The son of the late Colonel Morton of Milnewood, who commanded a regiment of horse with great courage at Dunbar and Inverkeithing," said a gentleman who sate on horseback beside Lady Margaret.

"Ay, and who, before that, fought for the Covenanters both at Marston-Moor and Philiphaugh," said Lady Margaret, sighing as she pronounced the last fatal word, which her husband's death gave her such sad reason to remember.

"Your ladyship's memory is just," said the gentleman, smiling, "but it were well all that were forgot now."

"He ought to remember it, Gilbertscleugh," returned Lady Margaret, "and dispense with intruding himself into the company of those to whom his name must bring unpleasing recollections."

"You forget, my dear lady," said her nomenclator, "that the young gentleman comes here to discharge suit and service in name of his uncle. I would every estate in the county sent out as pretty a fellow."

"His uncle, as well as his umquhile father, is a round-head, I presume," said Lady Margaret.

"He is an old miser," said Gilbertscleugh, "with whom a broad piece would at any time weigh down political opinions, and, therefore, although probably somewhat against the grain, he sends this young gentleman to attend the musters to save pecuniary pains and penalties. As for the rest, I suppose the youngster is happy enough to escape here for a day from the dulness of the old house at Milnewood, where he sees nobody but his hypochondriac uncle and the favourite house-keeper."

"Do you know how many men and horse the lands of Milnewood are rated at?" said the old lady, continuing her enquiry.

"Two horsemen with complete harness," answered Gilberts-cleugh.

"Our land," said Lady Margaret, drawing herself up with dignity, "has always furnished to the muster eight men, cousin Gilberts-cleugh, and often a voluntary aid of thrice the number. I remember his sacred Majesty King Charles, when he took his disjune at Tillie-tudlem, was particular in enquiring"——

"I see the Duke's carriage in motion," said Gilbertscleugh, partak-ing at the moment an alarm common to all Lady Margaret's friends, when she touched upon the topic of the royal visit at her family mansion,—"I see the Duke's carriage in motion; I presume your ladyship will take your right of rank in leaving the field. May I be permitted to convey your ladyship and Miss Bellenden home?—Par-ties of the wild whigs have been abroad, and are said to insult and disarm the well-affected who travel in small numbers."

"We thank you, cousin Gilbertscleugh," said Lady Margaret; "but, as we shall have the escort of my own people, I trust we have less need than others to be troublesome to our friends. Will you have the good-ness to order Harrison to bring up our people somewhat briskly; he rides there towards us as if he were leading a funeral procession."

The gentleman in attendance communicated his lady's orders to the trusty steward.

Honest Harrison had his own reasons for doubting the prudence of this command; but, once issued and received, there was a necessity of obeying it. He set off, therefore, at a hand gallop, followed by the butler, in such a military attitude as became one who had served under Montrose, and with a look of defiance rendered sterner and fiercer by the inspiring fumes of a gill of brandy, which he had snatched a moment to bolt to the king's health and confusion to the Covenant, during the intervals of military duty. Unhappily this potent refresh-ment wiped away from the tablets of his memory the necessity of paying some attention to the distresses and difficulties of his rear file, Goose Gibbie. No sooner had the horses struck a canter than Gibbie's jack-boots, which the poor boy's legs were incapable of steadying, began to play alternately against the horse's flanks, and being armed with long-rowelled spurs, totally overcame the patience of the animal, which bounded and plunged, while poor Gibbie's entreaties for aid never reached the ears of the too heedless butler, being drowned, partly in the concave of the steel cap in which his head was immersed, and partly in the martial tune of the Gallant Græmes, which Mr Gudyill whistled with all his power of lungs.

The upshot was, that the steed speedily took the matter into his own hands, and having gambolled hither and thither to the great amusement of all spectators, set off at speed towards the huge family-coach already described. Gibbie's pike, escaping from its sling, had fallen to a level direction across his hands, which, I grieve to say, were seeking dishonourable safety in as strong a grasp of the mane as their muscles could manage. His casque, too, had slipped completely over his face, so that he saw as little in front as he did in rear. Indeed, if he could, it would have availed him little in the circumstances; for his horse, as if in league with the disaffected, ran full tilt towards the solemn equipage of the Duke, which the projecting lance threatened to perforate from window to window, at the risk of transfixing as many in its passage as the celebrated thrust of Orlando, which, according to the Italian epic poet, broached as many Moors as a Frenchman spits frogs.

On beholding the bent of this misdirected career, a panic shout of mingled terror and wrath was set up by the whole equipage, insides and outsides, at once, which had the blessed effect of averting the threatened misfortune. The capricious horse of Goose Gibbie was terrified by the noise, and, stumbling as he turned short round, kicked and plunged violently so soon as he recovered. The jack-boots, the original cause of the disaster, maintaining the reputation they had acquired when worn by better cavaliers, answered every plunge by a fresh prick of the spurs, and, by their ponderous weight, kept their place in the stirrups. Not so Goose Gibbie, who was fairly spurned out of those wide and ponderous greaves, and precipitated over the horse's head, to the infinite amusement of all the spectators. His lance and helmet had forsaken him in his fall, and, for the completion of his disgrace, Lady Margaret Bellenden, not perfectly aware that it was one of her warriors who was furnishing so much entertainment, came up in time to see her diminutive man-at-arms stripped of his lion's hide, of the buff coat, that is, in which he was muffled.

As she had not been made acquainted with this metamorphosis, and could not even guess its cause, her surprise and resentment were extreme, nor were they much modified by the excuses and explanations of her steward and butler. She made a hasty retreat homeward, extremely indignant at the shouts and laughter of the company, and much disposed to vent her displeasure on the refractory agriculturist whose place Goose Gibbie had so unhappily supplied. The greater part of the gentry now dispersed, the whimsical misfortune which had befallen the gens d'armerie of Tillietudlem furnishing them with huge entertainment on their road homeward. The horsemen also, in little parties, as their road lay together, dispersed from the place of rendez-vous, excepting such as, having tried their dexterity at the popinjay, were, by ancient custom, obliged to partake of a grace-cup with their captain before their departure.

Chapter Four

At fairs he play'd before the spearmen,
And gaily graithed in their gear then,
Steel bonnets, pikes, and swords shone clear then
        As ony bead;
Now wha sall play before sic wier-men,
        Since Habbie's dead?
        Elegy on Habbie Simson

THE CAVALCADE of horsemen on their road to the little borrow-town were preceded by Niel Blane, the town-piper, mounted on his white galloway, armed with his dirk and broad-sword, and bearing a chanter streaming with as many ribbands as would deck out six country belles for a fair or preaching. Niel, a clean, tight, well-timbered, long-winded fellow, had gained the official situation of town-piper of ―― by his merit, with all the emoluments thereof; namely, the Piper's Croft, as it is still called, a field of about an acre in extent, five merks and a new livery-coat of the town's colours, yearly; some hopes of a dollar upon the day of the election of magistrates, providing the provost was able and willing to afford such a gratuity; and the privilege of paying, at all the respectable houses in the neighbourhood, an annual visit at spring-time, to rejoice their hearts with his music, to comfort his own with their ale and brandy, and to beg from each a modicum of seed-corn.

In addition to these inestimable advantages, Niel's personal, or professional, accomplishments won the heart of a jolly widow, who then kept the principal change-house in the borough. Her former husband having been a strict presbyterian of such note that he usually went among his sect by the name of Gaius the publican, many of the more rigid were scandalized by the profession of the successor whom his relict had chosen for a second help-mate. As the *browst* (or brew-ing) of the Howff retained, nevertheless, its unrivalled reputation, most of the old customers continued to give it a preference. The character of the new landlord, indeed, was of that accommodating kind, which enabled him, by close attention to the helm, to keep his little vessel pretty steady amid the contending tides of faction. He was a good-humoured, shrewd, selfish sort of fellow, indifferent alike to the disputes about church and state, and only anxious to secure the good-will of customers of every description. But his character, as well as the state of the country, will be best understood by giving the reader an account of the instructions which he issued to his daughter, a girl about eighteen, whom he was initiating in those cares which had been faithfully discharged by his wife, until about six months before our story commences, when the honest woman had been carried to the kirk-yard.

"Jenny," said Niel Blane, as the girl assisted to disencumber him of his bagpipes, "this is the first day that you are to take the place of your worthy mither in attending to the public; a douce woman she was, civil to the customers, and had a gude name wi' whig and tory, baith up the street and doun the street. It will be hard for you to fill her place, especially on sic a thrang day as this, but Heaven's will maun be obeyed.—Jenny, whatever young Milnewood ca's for be sure he maun hae't, for he's the Captain o' the Papinjay, and auld customs maun be supported; if he canna pay the lawing himsel, as I ken he's keepit unco short by the head, I'll find a way to shame it out o' his uncle.—The curate is playing at dice wi' Cornet Grahame. Be eident and civil to them baith—clergy and captains can gi'e an unco deal o' fash in thae times, where they take an ill-will.—The dragoons will be crying for ale, and they winna want it, and mauna want it—they are unruly chields, but they pay ane some gate or other. I gat the humle-cow, that's the best in the byre, frae black Frank Inglis and Serjeant Bothwell, for ten pund Scots, and they drank out the price at ae downsitting."

"But father," interrupted Jenny, "they say the twa reiving loons drave the cow frae the gudewife o' Bell's-moor, just because she gaed to hear a field-preaching ae Sabbath afternoon."

"Whisht! ye silly taupie," said her father, "we have naething to do how they come by the bestial they sell—be that atween them and their consciences.—Aweel—Take notice, Jenny, of that dour, stour-looking carle that sits by the cheek o' the ingle, and turns his back on a' men. He looks like ane o' the hill-folk, for I saw him start awee when he saw the red-coats, and I jalouse he wad hae liked to hae ridden bye, but his horse (it's a gude gelding) was ower sair travailed; he behoved to stop whether he wad or no. Serve him cannily, Jenny, and wi' little din, and dinna bring the sodgers on him by speering ony questions at him; but let na him hae a room to himsel, they wad say we were hiding him.—For yoursel, Jenny, ye'll be civil to a' the folk, and take nae heed o' ony nonsense daffing the young lads may say t'ye. Folk in the hostler line maun pit up wi' muckle. Your mother, rest her saul, could pit up wi' as muckle as maist women—but aff hands is fair play; and if

ony body be uncivil ye may gi'e me a cry.—Aweel—When the malt
gets aboon the meal, they'll begin to speak about government in kirk
and state, and then, Jenny, they are like to quarrel—let them be doing
—anger's a drouthy passion, and the mair they dispute, the mair ale
they'll drink; but ye were best serve them wi' a jute of the sma browst,
it will heat them less, and they'll never ken the difference."

"But, father," said Jenny, "if they come to lounder ilk ither as they
did last time, suld na I cry on you?"

"At no hand, Jenny; the redder gets aye the warst lick in the fray. If
the sodgers draw their swords, ye'll cry on the corporal and the guard.
If the countra folk tak the tangs and poker, ye'll cry on the baillie and
town-officers. But in nae event cry on me, for I am wearied wi'
doudling the bag o' wind a' day, and I am ganging to eat my dinner
quietly in the spence.—And, now I think on't, the Laird of Lickitup
(that's him that *was* the laird) was speering for sma' drink and a saut
herring—gi'e him a pu' be the sleeve, and sound into his lug I wad be
blyth o' his company to dine wi' me; he was a gude customer anes in a
day, and wants naething but means to be a gude ane agane—he likes
drink as weel as e'er he did. And if ye see ony poor body o' our
acquaintance that's blate for want o' siller, and has far to gang hame,
ye needna stick to gi'e them a waught o' drink and a bannock—we'll
ne'er miss't, and it looks creditable in a house like ours. And now,
hinny, gang awa', and serve the folk, but first bring me my dinner and
twa choppin o' yill and the mutchkin stoup o' brandy."

Having thus devolved his whole cares on Jenny as prime minister,
Niel Blane and the *ci-devant* laird, once his patron, but now glad to be
his trencher-companion, sate down to enjoy themselves for the
remainder of the evening, remote from the bustle of the public room.

All in Jenny's department was in full activity. The knights of the
popinjay received and requited the hospitable entertainment of their
captain, who, though he spared the cup himself, took care it should go
round with due celerity among the rest, who might not have otherwise
deemed themselves handsomely treated. Their numbers melted away
by degrees, and were at length diminished to four or five, who began
to talk of breaking up their party. At another table, at some distance,
sat two of the dragoons whom Niel Blane had mentioned, a serjeant
and a private in Claverhouse's regiment of life-guards. Even the non-
commissioned officers and privates in these corps were not considered as ordinary mercenaries, but rather approached to the rank of the
French mousquetaires, being regarded in the light of cadets, who
performed the duties of rank-and-file with the prospect of obtaining
commissions in case of distinguishing themselves.

Many young men of good family were to be found in the ranks, a circumstance which added to the pride and self-consequence of these troops. A remarkable instance of this occurred in the person of the non-commissioned officer in question. His real name was Francis Stuart, but he was universally known by the appellation of Bothwell, being lineally descended from the last Earl of that name; not the infamous lover of the unfortunate Queen Mary, but Francis Stuart, Earl of Bothwell, whose turbulence and repeated conspiracies embarrassed the early part of James Sixth's reign, and who at length died in exile in great poverty. The son of this earl had sued to Charles I. for the restitution of part of his father's forfeited estates, but the grasp of the nobles to whom they had been allotted was too tenacious to be unclenched. The breaking out of the civil wars utterly ruined him, by intercepting a small pension which Charles I. had allowed him, and he died in the utmost indigence. His son, after having served as a soldier abroad and in Britain, and passed through several vicissitudes of fortune, was fain to content himself with the situation of a non-commissioned officer in the life-guards, although lineally descended from the royal family, the father of the forfeited Earl of Bothwell having been a natural son of James V. Great personal strength, and dexterity in the use of his arms, as well as the remarkable circumstances of his descent, had recommended this man to the attention of his officers. But he partook in a great degree of the licentious and oppressive disposition, which the habit of acting as agents for government in levying fines, exacting free quarters, and otherwise oppressing the presbyterian recusants, had rendered too general among these soldiers. They were so much accustomed to these missions, that they conceived themselves at liberty to commit all manner of license with impunity, as if totally exempted from all law and authority, excepting the command of their officers. On such occasions Bothwell was usually the most forward.

It is probable that Bothwell and his companion would not so long have remained quiet, but for respect to the presence of their cornet, who commanded the small party quartered in the borough, and who was engaged in a game at dice with the curate of the place. But both of these being suddenly called from their amusement to speak with the chief magistrate upon some urgent business, Bothwell was not long of evincing his contempt for the rest of the company.

"Is it not a strange thing, Halliday," he said to his comrade, "to see a set of bumpkins sit carousing here this whole evening without having drunk the king's health?"

"They have drank the king's health," said Halliday. "I heard that green kail-worm of a lad name his majesty's health."

"Did he?" said Bothwell. "Then, Tom, we'll have them drink the Archbishop of St Andrews' health, and do it on their knees too."

"So we will, by G—," said Halliday, "and he that refuses it, we'll have him to the guard-house, and teach him to ride the colt foaled of an acorn, with a brace of carabines at each foot to keep him steady."

"Right, Tom," continued Bothwell; "and, to do all things in order, I'll begin with that sulky blue-bonnet in the ingle-nook."

He rose accordingly, and taking his sheathed broad-sword under his arm to support the insolence which he meditated, placed himself in front of the stranger noticed by Niel Blane, in his admonitions to his daughter, as being, in all probability, one of the hill-folk, or refractory presbyterians.

"I make so bold as to request of your precision, beloved," said the trooper in a tone of affected solemnity, and assuming the snuffle of a country preacher, "that you will arise from your seat, beloved, and, having bent your hams until your knees do rest upon the floor, beloved, that you will turn over this measure (called by the profane a gill) of the comfortable creature, which the carnal denominate brandy, to the health and glorification of his Grace the Archbishop of St Andrews, the worthy primate of all Scotland."

All waited for the stranger's answer.—His features, austere even to ferocity, with a cast of eye which, without being actually oblique, approached nearly to a squint, and which gave a very sinister expression to his countenance, joined to a frame, square, strong, and muscular, though something under the middle size, seemed to announce a man unlikely to understand rude jesting, or to receive insults with impunity.

"And what is the consequence," said he, "if I should not be disposed to comply with your uncivil request?"

"The consequence thereof, beloved," said Bothwell, in the same tone of raillery, "will be, first, that I will tweak thy proboscis, or nose. Secondly, beloved, that I will apply my fist to thy distorted visual optics; and will conclude, beloved, with a practical application of the flat of my sword to the shoulders of the recusant."

"Is it even so?" said the stranger, "then give me the cup;" and, taking it in his hand, said, with a peculiar expression of voice and manner, "The Archbishop of St Andrews, and the place he now worthily holds;—may each prelate in Scotland soon be as the Right Reverend James Sharpe!"

"He has taken the test," said Halliday exultingly.

"But with a qualification," said Bothwell; "I don't understand what the devil the crop-eared whig means."

"Come, gentlemen," said Morton, who became impatient of their insolence, "we are here met as good subjects, and on a merry occasion; and we have a right to expect we shall not be troubled with this sort of discussion."

Bothwell was about to make a surly answer, but Halliday reminded him in a whisper, that there were strict injunctions that the soldiers should give no offence to the men who were sent out to the musters, agreeably to the Council's orders. So, after honouring Morton with a broad and fierce stare, he said, "Well, Mr Popinjay, I shall not disturb your reign; I reckon it will be out by twelve at night.—Is it not an odd thing, Halliday," he continued, addressing his companion, "that they should make such a fuss about cracking off their birding-pieces at a mark which any woman or boy could hit with a day's practice? If Captain Popinjay now, or any of his court, would try a bout, either with the broadsword, backsword, single rapier, or rapier and dagger, for a gold noble, the first drawn blood, there would be some soul in it—or, zounds, would the bumpkins but wrestle, or pitch the bar, or putt the stone, or throw the axle-tree, if (touching the end of Morton's sword scornfully with his toe,) they carry things about them that they are afraid to draw."

Morton's patience and prudence now gave way entirely, and he was about to make a very angry answer to Bothwell's insolent observation, when the stranger stepped forward.

"This is my quarrel," he said, "and in the name of the good cause, I will see it out myself.—Hark thee, friend," (to Bothwell,) "wilt thou wrestle a fall with me?"

"With my whole spirit, beloved," answered Bothwell; "yea I will strive with thee, even to the downfall of one or both."

"Then, as my trust is in Him that can help," retorted his antagonist, "I will forthwith make thee an example to all such railing Rabshekahs."

With that he dropped his coarse grey horseman's coat from his shoulders, and extending his strong brawny arms with a look of determined resolution, he offered himself to the contest. The soldier was nothing abashed by the muscular frame, broad chest, square shoulders, and hardy look of his antagonist, but, whistling with great composure, unbuckled his belt, and laid aside his military coat. The company stood round them anxious for the event.

In the first struggle the trooper seemed to have some advantage, and also in the second, though neither could be considered as decisive. But it was plain he had put his whole strength too suddenly forth, against an antagonist possessed of great endurance, skill, vigour, and length of wind. In the third close, the countryman lifted his opponent fairly from the floor, and hurled him to the ground with such violence, that he lay for an instant stunned and motionless. His comrade, Halliday, immediately drew his sword; "You have killed my serjeant," he exclaimed to the victorious wrestler, "and by all that is sacred you shall answer it."

"Stand back!" cried Morton and his companions, "it was all fair play; your comrade sought a fall, and he has got it."

"That is true enough," said Bothwell as he slowly rose; "put up your bilbo, Tom. I did not think there was a crop-ear of them all could have laid the best cap and feather in the King's Life Guards on the floor of a rascally change-house.—Hark ye, friend, give me your hand." The stranger held out his hand. "I promise you," said Bothwell, squeezing his hand very hard, "that the time shall come when we will meet again, and try this game over in a more earnest manner."

"And I'll promise you," said the stranger, returning the grasp with equal firmness, "that, when we next meet, I will lay your head as low as it lay even now, and you shall lack the power to lift it up again."

"Well, beloved," answered Bothwell, "if thou be'st a whig, thou art a stout and a brave one, and so good even to thee—Had'st best take thy nag before the cornet make the rounds, for, I promise thee, he has stay'd less suspicious-looking persons."

The stranger seemed to think that the hint was not to be neglected; he flung down his reckoning, and, going into the stable, saddled and brought out a powerful black horse, now recruited by rest and forage, and turning to Morton, observed, "I ride towards Milnewood, which I hear is your home; will you give me the advantage and protection of your company?"

"Certainly," said Morton, although there was something of gloomy and relentless severity in the man's manner from which his mind recoiled. His companions, after a courteous good-night, broke up and went off in different directions, some keeping them company for about a mile, until they dropped off one by one, and the travellers were left alone.

The company had not long left the Howff, as Blane's public-house was called, when the trumpets and kettle-drums sounded. The troopers got under arms in the market-place at this unexpected summons, while, with faces of anxiety and earnestness, Cornet Grahame, and the Provost of the borough, followed by half a dozen soldiers, and town-officers with halberts, entered the apartment of Niel Blane.

"Guard the doors," were the first words which the cornet spoke; "let no man leave the house.—So, Bothwell, how comes this? Did you not hear them sound boot and saddle?"

"He was just going to quarters, sir," said his comrade; "he has had a bad fall."

"In a fray, I suppose?" said Grahame. "If you neglect duty in this way, your royal blood will hardly protect you."

"How have I neglected duty?" said Bothwell, sulkily.

"You should have been at quarters, Serjeant Bothwell; you have lost a golden opportunity. Here are news come that the Archbishop of St Andrews has been strangely and foully assassinated by a body of the rebel whigs, who pursued and stopped his carriage on Magus-Muir, near the town of St Andrews, dragged him out, and dispatched him with their swords and daggers."

All stood aghast at the intelligence.

"Here are their descriptions," continued the cornet, pulling out a proclamation, "the reward of a thousand merks is on each of their heads."

"The test, the test, and the qualification!" said Bothwell to Halliday; "I know the meaning now—Zounds that we should not have stopt him! Go saddle our horses, Halliday.—Was there one of the men, cornet, very stout and square-made, double-chested, thin in the flanks, hawk-nosed?"

"Stay, stay," said Cornet Grahame, "let me look at the paper.—Haxtoun of Rathillet, tall, thin, black-haired."

"That is not my man," said Bothwell.

"John Balfour, called Burley, aquiline nose, red-haired, five feet eight inches in height"——

"It is he—it is the very man," said Bothwell, "skellies fearfully with one eye?"

"Right," continued Grahame, "rode a strong black horse taken from the primate at the time of the murder."

"The very man," exclaimed Bothwell, "and the very horse! he was in this room not a quarter of an hour since."

A few hasty enquiries tended still more to confirm the opinion, that the reserved and stern stranger was Balfour of Burley, the actual commander of the band of assassins, who, in the fury of misguided zeal, had murdered the primate, whom they accidentally met, as they were searching for another person at whom they bore enmity. In their excited imaginations the casual rencounter had the appearance of a providential interference, and they put to death the archbishop, with circumstances of great and cool-blooded cruelty, under the belief, that the Lord, as they expressed it, had delivered him into their hand.

"Horse, horse, and pursue, my lads," exclaimed Cornet Grahame; "the murdering dog's head is worth its weight in gold."

Chapter Five

Arouse thee, youth!—it is no human call—
God's church is leaguered—haste to man the wall;
Haste where the Redcross banners wave on high,
Signal of honoured death, or victory.
                                    JAMES DUFF

MORTON and his companion had attained some distance from the town before either of them addressed the other. There was something, as we have observed, repulsive in the manner of the stranger, which prevented Morton from opening the conversation, and he himself seemed to have no desire to talk, until, on a sudden, he abruptly demanded, "What has your father's son to do with such profane mummeries as I find you engaged in?"

"I do my duty as a subject, and pursue my harmless recreations according to my own pleasure," replied Morton, somewhat offended.

"Is it your duty, think you, or that of any Christian young man, to bear arms in their cause who have poured out the blood of God's saints in the wilderness as if it had been water? or is it a lawful recreation to waste time in shooting at a bunch of feathers, and close your evening with wine-bibbing in public-houses and market-towns, when He that is mighty is come into the land with his fan in his hand, to purge the wheat from the chaff?"

"I suppose, from your style of conversation," said Morton, "that you are one of those who have thought proper to stand out against the government. I must remind you that you are unnecessarily using dangerous language in the presence of a mere stranger, and that times do not render it safe for me to listen to it."

"Thou can'st not help it, Henry Morton," said his companion; "thy master has his uses for thee, and when he calls thou must obey. Well wot I thou hast not heard the call of a true preacher, or thou hadst ere now been what thou wilt assuredly one day become."

"We are of the presbyterian persuasion," said Morton, "like yourself"—for his uncle's family attended the ministry of one of those numerous presbyterian clergymen, who, complying with certain regulations, were licensed to preach without interruption from the government. This *Indulgence*, as it was called, made a great schism among the presbyterians, and those who accepted of it were severely censured by the more rigid sect, who refused the proffered terms. The stranger, therefore, answered with great disdain to Morton's profession of faith.

"That is but an equivocation—a poor equivocation. Ye listen on the Sabbath to a cold, worldly, time-serving discourse, from one who forgets his high commission so much as to hold his apostleship by the favour of the courtiers and the false prelates, and ye call that hearing the word! Of all the baits with which the devil has fished for souls in these days of blood and darkness, that Black Indulgence has been the most destructive. An awful dispensation it has been, a smiting of the shepherd and a scattering of the sheep upon the mountains—an uplifting of one Christian banner against another, and a fighting of the wars of darkness with the swords of the children of light."

"My uncle," said Morton, "is of opinion, that we enjoy a reasonable freedom of conscience under the indulged clergymen, and I must necessarily be guided by his sentiments respecting the choice of a place of worship for his family."

"Your uncle," said the horseman, "is one of those to whom the least lamb in his own folds at Milnewood is dearer than the whole Christian flock. He is one that would willingly bend down to the golden calf of Bethel, and would have fished for the dust thereof when it was ground to powder and cast upon the waters. Thy father was a man of other stamp."

"My father," replied Morton, "was indeed a brave and gallant man. And you may have heard, sir, that he fought for that royal family in whose name I was this day carrying arms."

"Ay; and had he lived to see these days, he would have cursed the hour he ever drew sword in their cause. But more of this hereafter—I promise thee full surely that thy hour will come, and then the words thou hast now heard will stick in thy bosom like barbed arrows. My road lies there."

He pointed towards a pass leading up into a wild extent of dreary and desolate hills; but as he was about to turn his horse's head into a rugged path, which led from the high road in that direction, an old woman, wrapped in a red cloak, who was sitting by the cross way, arose, and approaching him, said in a mysterious tone of voice, "If ye be of our ain folk, gang na up the pass the night for your lives. There is a lion in the path, that is there. The curate of Brotherstane and ten soldiers hae beset the pass, to hae the lives of ony of our puir wanderers that venture that gate to join wi' Hamilton and Dingwall."

"Have the persecuted folk drawn to any head among themselves?" demanded the stranger.

"About sixty or seventy horse and foot," said the old dame; "but, ewhow! they are puirly armed, and warse fended."

"God will help his own," said the horseman. "Which way shall I take to join them?"

"It's a mere impossibility this night," said the woman, "the troopers keep sae strick a guard; and they say there's strange news come frae the east, that makes them rage in their cruelty mair fierce than ever— Ye maun take shelter somegate for the night before ye get to the muirs, and keep yoursel in hiding till the grey o' the morning, and then ye may find your way through the Drake Moss. When I heard the awfu' threatenings o' the oppressors, I e'en took my cloak about me, and sate down by the way-side, to warn ony of our poor scattered remnant that chanced to come this gate, before they fell into the nets of the spoilers."

"Have you a house near this?" said the stranger; "and can you give me hiding there?"

"I have," said the old woman, "a hut by the way-side, it may be a mile from hence; but four men of Belial, called dragoons, are lodged therein, to spoil my household goods at their pleasure, because I will not wait upon the thowless, thriftless, fissenless ministry of that carnal man, John Halftext, the curate."

"Good night, good woman, and thanks for thy council," said the stranger, as he rode away.

"The blessings of the promise upon you," returned the old dame; "may He keep you that can keep you."

"Amen!" said the traveller; "for where to hide my head this night, mortal skill cannot direct me."

"I am very sorry for your distress," said Morton; "and had I a house or place of shelter that could be called my own, I almost think I would risk the utmost rigour of the law rather than leave you in such a strait. But my uncle is so frightened at the pains and penalties denounced by the laws against such as comfort, receive, or consort with inter-communed persons, that he has strictly forbidden all of us to hold any intercourse with them."

"It is no less than I expected," said the stranger; "nevertheless, I might be received without his knowledge;—a barn, a hay-loft, a cart-shed,—any place where I could stretch me down, would be to my habits like a tabernacle of silver set about with planks of cedar."

"I assure you," said Morton, much embarrassed, "that I have not the means of receiving you at Milnewood without my uncle's consent and knowledge; nor, if I could do so, would I think myself justifiable in engaging him unconsciously in a danger which, most of all others, he fears and deprecates."

"Well," said the traveller, "I have but one word to say. Did you ever hear your father mention John Balfour of Burley?"

"His ancient friend and comrade, who saved his life, with almost the loss of his own, in the battle of Longmarston-Moor?—Often, very often."

"I am that Balfour. Yonder stands thy uncle's house; I see the light among the trees. The Avenger of Blood is behind me, and my death certain unless I have refuge there. Now, make thy choice, young man, to shrink from the side of thy father's friend, like a thief in the night, and to leave him exposed to the bloody death from which he rescued thy father, or to expose thine uncle's worldly goods to such peril as, in this perverse generation, attends those who give a morsel of bread or a draught of cold water to a Christian man, when perishing for lack of refreshment!"

A thousand recollections thronged on the mind of Morton at once. His father, whose memory he idolized, had often enlarged upon his obligations to this man, and regretted, that, after having been long comrades, they had parted in some unkindness at the time when the kingdom of Scotland was divided into Resolutioners and Protesters; the former of whom adhered to Charles II. after his father's death upon the scaffold, while the Protesters inclined rather to an union with the triumphant republicans. The stern fanaticism of Burley had attached him to this latter party, and the comrades had parted in displeasure, never, as it happened, to meet again. These circumstances the deceased Colonel Morton had often mentioned to his son, and always with an expression of deep regret, that he had never, in any manner, been enabled to repay the assistance, which, on more than one occasion, he had received from Burley.

To hasten Morton's decision, the night-wind, as it swept along, brought from a distance the sullen sound of a kettle-drum, which, seeming to approach nearer, intimated that a body of horse were upon their march towards them.

"It must be Claverhouse, with the rest of his regiment. What can have occasioned this night-march? If you go on, you fall into their hands—if you turn back towards the borrow-town, you are in no less danger from Cornet Grahame's party.—The path to the hills is beset. I must shelter you at Milnewood, or expose you to instant death;—but the punishment of the law shall fall upon myself, as in justice it should, not upon my uncle.—Follow me."

Burley, who had awaited his resolution with great composure, now followed him in silence.

The house of Milnewood, built by the father of the present proprietor, was a decent mansion, suitable to the size of the estate, but, since the accession of this owner, it had been suffered to go considerably into disrepair. At some little distance from the house stood the court of offices. Here Morton paused.

"I must leave you here for a little while," he whispered, "until I can provide a bed for you in the house."

"I care little for such delicacy," said Burley; "for thirty years this head has rested oftener on the turf, or on the next grey stone, than upon either wool or down. A draught of ale, a morsel of bread, to say my prayers, and to streak me down upon dry hay, were to me as good as a painted chamber and a prince's table."

It occurred to Morton at the same moment, that to attempt to introduce the fugitive within the house, would materially increase the danger of detection. Accordingly, having struck a light with implements left in the stable for that purpose, and having fastened up their horses, he assigned Burley, for his place of repose, a wooden bed, placed in a loft half full of hay, which an out-of-doors domestic had occupied until dismissed by his uncle in one of those fits of parsimony which became more rigid from day to day. In this untenanted loft Morton left his companion, with a caution to shade his light so that no reflection could be seen from the windows, and a promise that he would presently return with such refreshments as he might be able to procure at that late hour. This last, indeed, was a subject on which he felt by no means confident, for the power of obtaining even the most ordinary provisions depended entirely upon the humour in which he might happen to find his uncle's sole confidante, the old housekeeper. If she chanced to be a-bed, which was very likely, or out of humour, which was not less so, Morton well knew the case to be at least problematical.

Cursing in his heart the sordid parsimony which pervaded every part of his uncle's establishment, he gave the usual gentle knock at the bolted door, by which he was accustomed to seek admittance, when accident had detained him abroad beyond the early and established hour of rest at the house of Milnewood. It was a sort of hesitating tap, which carried an acknowledgment of transgression in its very sound, and seemed rather to solicit than to command attention. After it had been repeated again and again, the housekeeper, grumbling betwixt her teeth as she rose from the chimney corner in the hall, and wrapping her checked handkerchief round her head to secure her from the cold air, paced across the stone passage, and repeated a careful "Whae's there at this time o' night?" more than once before she undid bolt and bar, and cautiously opened the door.

"This is a fine time o' night, Mr Harry," said the old dame, with the tyrannic insolence of a spoilt and favourite domestic;—"a braw time o' night and a bonnie, to disturb a peaceful house in, and to keep quiet folk out o' their beds waiting for ye. Your uncle's been in his amaist three hours syne, and Robin's ill o' the rheumatize, and he's to his bed too, and sae I hae had to sit up for ye mysel, for as sair a hoast as I hae."

Here she coughed once or twice, in further evidence of the inconvenience which she had sustained.

"Much obliged to you, Alison, and many kind thanks."

"Hegh, sirs, sae fair-fashioned as we are! Mony folk ca' me Mistress Wilson, and Milnewood himsel is the only ane about the town thinks o' ca'ing me Alison, and indeed he as aften says Mistress Alison as ony other thing."

"Well, then, Mistress Alison," said Morton, "I really am sorry to have kept you up waiting till I came in."

"And now that ye are come in, Mr Harry, what for do ye no tak up your candle and gang to your bed? and mind ye dinna let the candle sweal as ye gang alang the wainscot parlour, and haud a' the house scouring to get out the grease again."

"But, Alison, I really must have something to eat, and a draught of ale, before I go to bed."

"Eat?—and ale, Mr Harry?—My certie, ye're ill to serve! Do ye think we have na heard o' your grand papinjay-wark yonder, and how ye bleezed away as muckle pouther as wad hae shot a' the wild-fowl that we'll want atween and Candlemas—and than ganging majoring to the piper's Howff wi' a' the idle loons in the country, and sitting there birling, at your poor uncle's cost nae doubt, wi' a' the scaff and raff o' the water-side, till sun-down, and then coming hame and crying for ale, as if ye were maister and mair?"

Extremely vexed, yet anxious, on account of his guest, to procure refreshments if possible, Morton suppressed his resentment, and good-humouredly assured Mrs Wilson that he was really both hungry and thirsty; "and as for the shooting at the popinjay, I have heard you say you have been there yourself, Mrs Wilson—I wish you had come to look at us."

"Ah, Maister Harry," said the old dame, "I wish ye binna beginning to learn the way of blawing in a woman's lug, wi' a' your whilly-wha's! —Aweel, sae ye dinna practise them but on auld wives like me, there's the less matter. But tak heed o' the young queans, lad.—Popinjay—ye think yersell a bra' fellow enow; and troth!" (surveying him with the candle,) "there's nae fault to find wi' your outside, if the inside be conforming. But I mind, when I was a gilpey of a lassock, seeing the Duke, that was him that lost his head at London—folk said it was na a very gude ane, but it was aye a sair loss to him, puir gentleman— Aweel, he wan the popinjay, for few cared to win it ower his Grace's head—Weel, he had a comely presence, and when a' the gentles mounted to show their capers, his Grace was as near me as I am to you; and he said to me, 'Take tent o' yoursel, my bonnie lassie, (these were his very words) for my horse is not very chancy.'—And now, as ye say ye have had sae little to eat or drink, I'll let you see that I have na been sae unmindfu' o' you, for I dinna think it safe for young folks to gang to bed on an empty stamach."

To do Mrs Wilson justice, her nocturnal harangues upon such occasions not unfrequently terminated with this sage apothegm, which always prefaced the producing of some provision a little better than ordinary, such as she now placed before him. In fact, the principal object of her *maundering* being to display her consequence and love of power, Mrs Wilson was not, at the bottom, an ill-tempered woman, and certainly loved her old and young master (both of whom she frequently tormented extremely) better than any one else in the world. She now eyed Mr Harry, as she called him, with great complacency as he partook of her good cheer.

"Muckle gude may it do ye, my bonny man. I trow ye didna eat siccan a skirl-in-the-pan as that at Niel Blane's. His wife was a canny body, and could dress things very weel for ane in her line o' business, but no like a gentleman's housekeeper, to be sure. But I doubt the daughter's a silly thing—an unco cockernony she had busked on her head at the kirk last Sunday. I am doubting there will be news o' a' thae braws. But my auld een's drawing thegither—dinna hurry yoursel, my bonny man, and see ye mind about the putting out the candle, and there's a horn of ale, and a glass of clow-gillieflower water; I dinna gi'e ilka body that; I keep it for a pain I whiles hae in my ain stamach, and it's better for your young blood than brandy. Sae, gude-night to ye, Mr Harry, and see that ye take a gude care o' the candle."

Morton promised to attend punctually to her caution, and requested her not to be alarmed if she heard the door opened, as she knew he must again, as usual, look to his horse, and arrange him for the night. Mrs Wilson then retreated, and Morton, folding up his provisions, was about to hasten to his guest, when the noddling head of the old housekeeper was again thrust in at the door, with an admonition, to remember to take an account of his ways before he laid himself down to rest, and to pray for protection during the hours of darkness. Such were the manners of a certain class of domestics, once common in Scotland, and perhaps still to be found in some old manor houses in its remote counties. They were fixtures in the family they belonged to; and as they never conceived the possibility of such a thing as dismission to be within the chances of their lives, they were, of course, sincerely attached to every member of it. On the other hand, when spoiled by the indulgence or indolence of their superiors, they were very apt to become ill-tempered, self-sufficient, and tyrannical;

so much so, that a mistress or master would sometimes almost have wished to exchange their cross-grained fidelity for the smooth and accommodating duplicity of a modern menial.

Chapter Six

Yea, this man's brow, like to a tragic leaf,
Foretels the nature of a tragic volume.
SHAKSPEARE

BEING at length rid of the housekeeper's presence, Morton made a collection of what he had reserved from the provisions set before him, and prepared to carry them to his concealed guest. He did not think it necessary to take a light, being perfectly acquainted with every turn of the road; and it was lucky he did not do so, for he had hardly stepped beyond the threshold ere a heavy trampling of horse announced, that the body of cavalry, whose kettle-drums they had before heard, were in the act of passing upon the high-road which winded along the foot of the bank on which the house of Milnewood was placed. He heard the commanding officer distinctly give the word *halt*. A pause of silence followed, interrupted only by the occasional neighing or pawing of an impatient charger.

"Whose house is this?" said one voice in a tone of authority and command.

"Milnewood, if it like your honour," was the reply.

"Is the owner well affected?" said the enquirer.

"He complies with the orders of government, and frequents an indulged minister," was the response.

"Hum! ay! Indulged? a mere mask for treason, very impolitically allowed to those who are too great cowards to wear their principles barefaced. Had we not better send up a party and search the house, in case some of the bloody villains concerned in this heathenish butchery may be concealed in it?"

Ere Morton could recover from the alarm into which this proposal had thrown him, a third speaker rejoined, "I cannot think it is at all necessary; Milnewood is an infirm, hypochondriac old man, who never meddles with politics, and loves his money-bags and bonds better than any thing else in the world. His nephew, I hear, was at the wappin-schaw to-day, and gained the popinjay, which does not look like a fanatic. I should think they are all gone to bed long since, and an alarm at this time of night might kill the poor old man."

"Well," rejoined the leader, "if that be so, to search the house would be lost time, of which we have but little to lose. Gentlemen of the Life Guards, forward—March."

A few notes on the trumpets, mingled with the occasional boom of the kettle-drum, to mark the cadence, joined with the tramp of hoofs and clash of arms to announce that the troop had resumed its march. The moon broke out as the leading files of the column attained a hill up which the road winded, and shewed indistinctly the glittering of their steel-caps; and the dark figures of the horses and riders might be imperfectly traced through the gloom. They continued to advance up the hill, and sweep over the top of it in such long succession, as intimated a considerable numerical force.

When the last of them had disappeared, young Morton resumed his purpose of visiting his guest. Upon entering the place of refuge, he found him seated on his humble couch with a pocket-bible open in his hand, which he seemed to study with intense meditation. His broadsword, which he had unsheathed on the first alarm of the arrival of the dragoons, lay naked across his knees, and the little taper that stood beside him upon the old chest, which served the purpose of a table, threw a partial and imperfect light upon those stern and harsh features, in which ferocity was rendered more solemn and dignified by a wild cast of tragic enthusiasm. His brow was that of one in whom some strong o'er-mastering principle has overwhelmed all other passions and feeling, like the swell of a high spring-tide, when the usual cliffs and breakers vanish from the eye, and their existence is only indicated by the chafing fume of the waves that burst and wheel over them. He raised his head, after Morton had contemplated him for about a minute.

"I perceive," said Morton, looking at his drawn sword, "that you heard the horsemen ride by; their passage delayed me for some minutes."

"I hardly heeded them," said Balfour; "my hour is not yet come. That I shall one day fall into their hands, and be honourably associated with the saints whom they have slaughtered, I am full well aware. And I would, young man, that the hour were come; it should be as welcome to me as ever wedding hour to bridegroom. But if my Master has more work for me on earth, I must not do his labour grudgingly."

"Eat and refresh yourself," said Morton; "to-morrow your safety requires you should leave this place with day-break, in order to gain the hills, so soon as you can see to distinguish the tract through the morasses."

"Young man," returned Balfour, "you are already weary of me, and would be yet more so, perchance, did you know the task upon which I have been lately put. And I wonder not that it should be so, for there are times when I am weary of myself. Think you not it is a sore trial for flesh and blood to be called upon to execute the righteous judgments of Heaven while we are yet in the body, and retain that blinded sense and sympathy for carnal suffering which makes our own flesh thrill when we strike a gash upon the body of another? And think you, that when some prime tyrant has been removed from his place, that the instruments of his punishment can at all times alike look back on their share in his downfall with firm and unshaken nerves? Must they not sometimes question even the truth of that inspiration which they have felt and acted under? Must they not sometimes doubt the origin of that strong impulse with which their prayers for heavenly direction under difficulties have been inwardly answered and confirmed, and confuse, in their disturbed apprehensions, the responses of Truth himself with some strong delusion of the enemy?"

"These are subjects, Mr Balfour, on which I am ill qualified to converse with you," answered Morton; "but I own I should strongly doubt the origin of any inspiration which seemed to dictate a line of conduct contrary to those feelings of natural humanity, which Heaven has assigned to us as the general law of our conduct."

Balfour seemed somewhat disturbed, and drew himself hastily up, but immediately composed himself, and answered coolly, "It is natural you should think so; you are yet in the dungeon-house of the Law, a pit darker than that into which Jeremiah was plunged, even the dungeon of Malcaiah the son of Hamelmelech, where there was no water but mire. Yet is the seal of the covenant upon your forehead, and the son of the righteous, who resisted to blood when the banner was spread on the mountains, shall not be utterly lost as one of the children of darkness. Trow ye, that in this day of bitterness and calamity, nothing is required at our hands but to keep the moral law as far as our carnal frailty will permit?—think ye our conquests must be only over our corrupt and evil affections and passions?—no—we are called upon when we have girded up our loins to run the race boldly, and when we have drawn the sword to smite the ungodly with the edge, though he be our neighbour, and the man of power and cruelty, though he were of our own kindred and the friend of our bosom."

"These are the sentiments," said Morton, "that your enemies impute to you, and which palliate, if they do not exculpate, the cruel measures which the Council have directed against you. They affirm, that you pretend to inward light, and reject the restraint of legal magistracy, and national law, and even of common humanity, when in opposition to what you call the spirit within you."

"They do us wrong," answered the Covenanter; "it is they, perjured as they are, who have rejected all law, both divine and civil, and who now persecute us for adherence to the Solemn League and Covenant between God and the kingdom of Scotland, to which all of them have sworn in former days, save a few popish malignants, and which they now burn in the market-places and tread under foot in derision. When this Charles Stuart returned to these kingdoms, did the malignants bring him back? They had tried it with the strong hand, but they failed, I trow. Could James Grahame of Montrose and his Highland catterin have put him again in the place of his father? I think their heads on the Westport told another tale for many a long day. It was the workers of the glorious work—the reformers of the beauty of the tabernacle, that called him again to the high place from which his father fell. And what has been our reward? In the words of the prophet, 'We looked for peace, but no good came; and for a time of health, and behold trouble—The snorting of his horses was heard from Dan; the whole land trembled at the sound of the neighing of his strong ones; for they are come, and have devoured the land and all that is in it.'"

"Mr Balfour," answered Morton, "I neither undertake to subscribe to or refute your complaints against this government. I have endeavoured to repay a debt due to the comrade of my father, by giving you shelter in your distress, but you will excuse my engaging myself either in your cause, or in controversy. I will leave you to repose, and heartily wish it were in my power to render your condition more comfortable."

"But I shall see you, I trust, in the morning, ere I depart?—I am not a man whose bowels yearn after kindred and friends of this world. When I put my hand to the plough, I entered into a covenant with my worldly affections that I should not look back on the things I left behind me. Yet the son of mine ancient comrade is to me as mine own, and I cannot behold him without the deep and firm belief, that I shall one day see him gird on his sword in the dear and precious cause for which his father fought and bled."

With a promise on Morton's part that he would call the refugee when it was time for him to pursue his journey, they parted for the night.

Morton retired to a few hours rest; but his imagination, disturbed by the events of the day, did not permit him to enjoy sound repose. There was a blended vision of horror before him in which his new friend seemed to be a principal actor. The fair form of Edith Bellenden also mingled in his dream, weeping, and with dishevelled hair, and appearing to call on him for comfort and assistance which he had it not in his power to render. He awoke from these unrefreshing slumbers with a feverish pulse, and a heart which foreboded disaster. There was already a tinge of dazzling lustre on the verge of the distant hills, and the dawn was abroad in all the freshness of a summer morning.

"I have slept too long," he exclaimed to himself, "and must now hasten to forward the journey of this unfortunate fugitive."

He dressed himself as fast as possible, opened the door of the house with as little noise as he could, and hastened to the place of refuge occupied by the Covenanter. Morton entered on tiptoe, for the determined tone and manner, as well as the unusual language and sentiments of this singular individual, had struck him with a sensation approaching to awe. Balfour was still asleep. A ray of light streamed on his uncurtained couch, and shewed to Morton the working of his harsh features, which seemed agitated by some strong internal cause of disturbance. He had not undressed. Both his arms were above the bed-cover, the right hand strongly clenched, and occasionally making that abortive attempt to strike which usually attends dreams of violence; the left was extended, and agitated, from time to time, by a movement as if repulsing some one. The perspiration stood on his brow, "like bubbles in a late disturbed stream," and these marks of emotion were accompanied with broken words which escaped from him at intervals—"Thou art taken, Judas—thou art taken—Cling not to my knees—cling not to my knees—hew him down—a priest? Ay, a priest of Baal to be bound and slain, even at the brook Kishon—Fire-arms will not prevail against him—Strike—thrust with the cold iron— put him out of pain—put him out of pain, were it but for the sake of his grey hair."

Much alarmed at the import of these expressions, which seemed to burst from him even in sleep with the stern energy accompanying the perpetration of some act of violence, Morton shook his guest by the shoulder in order to awake him. The first words he uttered were, "Bear me where ye will, I will avouch the deed."

His glance around having then fully awakened him, he at once assumed all the stern and gloomy composure of his ordinary manner, and throwing himself on his knees before speaking to Morton, poured forth an ejaculatory prayer for the suffering Church of Scotland, entreating that the blood of her murdered saints and martyrs might be precious in the sight of Heaven, and that the shield of the Almighty might be spread over the scattered remnant, who, for His name's sake, were abiders in the wilderness. Vengeance—speedy and ample vengeance on the oppressors, was the concluding petition of his devotions, which he expressed aloud in strong and emphatic language, rendered more impressive by the orientalism of Scripture.

When he had finished his prayer he arose, and, taking Morton by the arm, they descended together to the stable, where the Wanderer, to give Burley a title which was often conferred on his sect, began to make his horse ready to pursue his journey. When the animal was saddled and bridled, Burley requested Morton to walk with him a gun-shot into the wood, and put him upon the right road for gaining the moors. Morton readily complied, and they walked for some time in silence under the shade of some fine old trees, pursuing a sort of natural path, which, after passing through woodland for about half a mile, led into the bare and wild country which extends to the foot of the hills.

At length Burley suddenly asked Morton, "Whether the words he had spoken over-night had borne fruit in his mind?"

Morton answered, "That he remained of the same opinion which he had formerly held, and was determined, at least as far and as long as possible, to unite the duties of a good Christian with those of a peaceful subject."

"In other words," replied Burley, "you are desirous to serve both God and Mammon—to be one day professing the truth with your lips, and the next day in arms, at the command of carnal and tyrannic authority, to shed the blood of those who for the truth have forsaken all things? Think ye," he continued, "to touch pitch and remain undefiled? to mix in the ranks of malignants, papists, papa-prelatists, latitudinarians, and scoffers; to partake of their sports, which are like the meals offered unto idols; to hold intercourse, perchance, with their daughters, as the sons of God with the daughters of men in the world before the flood, and yet to remain free from pollution? I say unto you, that all communication with the enemies of the Church is the accursed thing which God hateth! Touch not—taste not—handle not! And grieve not, young man, as if you alone were called upon to subdue your carnal affections, and renounce those pleasures which are a snare to your feet—I say to you, that the son of David hath denounced no better lot on the whole generation of mankind."

He then mounted his horse, and, turning to Morton, repeated the text of Scripture, "An heavy yoke was ordained for the sons of Adam from the day they go out of their mother's womb till the day that they return to the mother of all things; from him who is clothed in blue silk and weareth a crown, even to him who weareth simple linen,—wrath, envy, trouble, and unquietness, rigour, strife, and fear of death in the time of rest."

Having uttered these words he set his horse into motion, and soon disappeared among the boughs of the forest.

"Farewell, stern enthusiast," said Morton, looking after him; "in some moods of my mind, how dangerous would be the society of such a companion!" If I am unmoved by his zeal for abstract doctrines of faith, or rather for a peculiar mode of worship, (such was the purport of his reflections,) can I be a man, and a Scotchman, and look with indifference on that persecution which has made wise men mad? And is not the cause of freedom, civil and religious, that for which my father fought, and shall I do well to remain inactive, or to take the part of an oppressive government, if there should appear any rational prospect of redressing the insufferable wrongs to which my miserable country is subjected?—And yet who shall warrant me that these people, rendered wild by persecution, would not be, in the hour of victory, as cruel and as intolerant as those by whom they are now hunted down? What degree of moderation, or of mercy, can be expected from this Burley, so distinguished as one of their principal champions, and who seems even now to be reeking from some recent deed of violence, and to feel stings of remorse, which even his enthusiasm cannot altogether stifle? I am weary of seeing nothing but violence and fury around me—now assuming the mask of lawful authority, now taking that of religious zeal—I am sick of my country— of myself—of my dependent situation—of my repressed feelings—of these woods—of that river—of that house—of all but Edith—and she can never be mine. Why should I haunt her walks?—Why encourage my own delusion and perhaps hers?—she never can be mine. Her grandmother's pride—the opposite principles of our families—my wretched state of dependence—a poor miserable slave, for I have not even the wages of a servant—all circumstances give the lie to the vain hope we can ever be united. Why then protract a delusion so painful?

"But I am no slave," he said aloud, and drawing himself up to his full stature—"no slave, in one respect, surely. I can change my abode —my father's sword is mine, and Europe lies open before me, as before him and hundreds besides of my countrymen who have filled it with the fame of their exploits. Perhaps some lucky chance may raise me to a rank with our Ruthvens, our Lesleys, our Monroes, the chosen leaders of the famous Protestant champion, or, if not, a soldier's life or a soldier's grave."

When he had formed this determination, he found himself near the door of his uncle's house, and resolved to lose no time in making him acquainted with it.

"Another glance of Edith's eye, another walk by Edith's side, and my resolution would melt away. I will take an irrevocable step—and then see her—for the last time."

In this mood he entered the wainscotted parlour in which his uncle was already placed at his morning's refreshment, a huge plate of oatmeal porridge, with a corresponding allowance of butter-milk. The favourite housekeeper was in attendance, half standing half resting on the back of a chair, in a posture betwixt freedom and respect. The old gentleman had been remarkably tall in his earlier days, an advantage which he now lost by stooping to such a degree, that at a meeting, where there was some dispute concerning the sort of arch which should be thrown over a considerable brook, a facetious neighbour proposed to offer Milnewood a handsome sum for his curved backbone, alleging that he would sell any thing that belonged to him. Splay feet of unusual size, long thin hands, garnished with nails which seldom felt the steel, a wrinkled and puckered visage, the length of which corresponded with that of his person, together with a pair of little sharp bargain-making grey eyes, that seemed eternally looking out for their advantage, completed the highly unpromising exterior of Mr Morton of Milnewood. As it would have been very injurious to have lodged a liberal or benevolent disposition in such an unworthy cabinet, nature had suited his person with a mind exactly in conformity with it, that is to say, mean, selfish, and covetous.

When this amiable personage was aware of the presence of his nephew, he hastened, before addressing him, to swallow the spoonful of porridge which he was in the act of conveying to his mouth, and, as it chanced to be scalding hot, the pain occasioned by its descent down his throat and into his stomach, inflamed the ill humour with which he was already prepared to receive his kinsman.

"The de'il take them that made them," was his first ejaculation, apostrophizing his mess of porridge.

"They're gude parritch eneugh," said Mrs Wilson, "if ye wad but take time to them. I made them mysel; but if folk winna hae patience, they should get their thrapples causewayed."

"Haud your peace, Alison, I was speaking to my nevoy.—How is this, sir? And what sort o' scampering gates are these o' going on? Ye were not at hame last night till near midnight."

"Thereabouts, sir, I believe," answered Morton, in an indifferent tone.

"Thereabouts, sir?—What sort of an answer is that, sir? Why came ye na hame when other folk left the grund?"

"I suppose you know the reason very well, sir," said Morton; "I had the fortune to be the best marksman, and remained, as is usual, to give some little entertainment to the other young men."

"The deevil ye did, sir! And ye come to tell me that to my face? You pretend to gi'e entertainments, that canna come by a dinner except by sorning on a carefu' man like me? But if ye put me to charges, I'se work it out o' ye. I see na why ye shouldna haud the pleugh, now that the pleughman has left us; it wad set ye better than wearing thae green duds, and wasting your siller in powther and lead; it wad pit ye in an honest calling, and wad keep ye in bread without being uphauden to ony ane."

"I am very ambitious of learning such a calling, sir, but I don't understand driving the plough."

"And what for no? It's easier than your archery and your gunnery that ye like sae weel. Auld Davie is ca'ing it e'en now, and ye may be goadsman for the first twa or three days, and tak tent ye dinna o'er-drive the owsen, and than ye will be fit to gang between the stilts. Ye'll ne'er learn younger, I'll be your caution—Haggie-holm is heavy land, and Davie is ower auld to keep the coulter down now."

"I beg pardon for interrupting you, sir, but I have formed a scheme for myself, which will have the same effect of relieving you of the burden and charge attending my company."

"Ay? Indeed? a scheme o' yours? that must be a dennty ane!" said the uncle, with a very peculiar sneer; "let's hear about it, lad."

"It is said in two words, sir. I intend to leave this country, and serve abroad, as my father did before these unhappy troubles broke out at home. His name will not be so entirely forgotten in the countries where he served but that it will procure his son at least the opportunity of trying his fortune as a soldier."

"Gude be gracious to us!" exclaimed the housekeeper, "our young Mr Harry gang abroad?—na, na! eh, na! that maun never be."

Milnewood entertaining no thought or purpose of parting with his nephew, who was, moreover, very useful to him in many respects, was thunderstruck at this abrupt declaration of independence from a person whose deference to him had hitherto been unlimited. He recovered himself, however, immediately.

"And wha do ye think is to give ye the means, young man, for such a wild-guse chase? Not me, I am sure. I can hardly support you at hame. And ye wad be marrying, I'se warrant, as your father did afore ye, too, and sending your uncle hame a pack o' weans to be fighting and skirling through the house in my auld days, and to take wing and flee aff like yoursel, whenever they were asked to serve a turn about the town."

"I have no thoughts of ever marrying," answered Henry.

"Hear till him now!" said the housekeeper. "It's a shame to hear a douce young lad speak in that way, since a' the warld kens that they maun either marry or do waur."

"Haud your peace, Alison," said her master; "and you, Henry, put this nonsense out o' your head—this comes o' letting ye gang a sod-gering for a day—mind ye hae nae siller, lad, for ony sic nonsense plans."

"I beg your pardon, sir, my wants shall be very few; and would you please to give me the gold chain which the Margrave gave to my father after the battle of Lutzen"——

"Mercy on us! the gowd chain?" exclaimed his uncle.

"The chain of gowd!" re-echoed the housekeeper, both aghast with astonishment at the audacity of the proposal.

"I will keep a few links to remind me of him by whom it was won, and the place where he won it," continued Morton; "the rest shall furnish me the means of following the same career in which my father obtained that mark of distinction."

"Mercifu' powers!" said the governante, "my master wears it every Sunday."

"Sunday and Saturday," added old Milnewood, "whenever I put on my black velvet coat; and Wylie Mactrickit is partly of opinion it's a kind of heir-loom, that rather belangs to the head of the house than to the immediate descendant. It has three thousand links; I have counted them a thousand times. It's worth three hundred pounds sterling."

"That is more than I want, sir; if you choose to give me a third part of the money, and five links of the chain, it will amply serve my purpose, and the rest will be some slight atonement for the expence and trouble I have put you to."

"The laddie's in a creel!" exclaimed his uncle. "O, sirs, what will come o' the rigs o' Milnewood when I am dead and gane! He would fling the crown of Scotland awa, if he had it."

"Hout, sir," said the old housekeeper, "I maun e'en say it's partly your ain faut. Ye mauna curb his head ower sair in neither; and, to be sure, since he *has* gane doun to the Howff, ye maun just e'en pay the lawing."

"If it be not abune twa dollars, Ailison," said the old gentleman, very reluctantly.

"I'll settle it mysel wi' Niel Blane, the first time I gang down to the clachan," said Alison, "cheaper than your honour or Mr Harry can do;" and then whispered to Henry, "dinna vex him ony mair, I'll pay the lave out o' the butter siller, and nae mair words about it." Then proceeding aloud, "And ye mauna speak o' the young gentleman hauding the pleugh; there's puir distressed whigs enow about the country will be glad to do that turn for a bite and a sowp—it sets them far better than the like o' him."

"And than we'll hae the dragoons on us," said Milnewood, "for comforting and entertaining intercommuned rebels, a bonny stress ye wad put us in!—But take your breakfast, Harry, and then lay by your new green coat, and pit on your Raploch grey; it's a mair mensefu' and thrifty dress, and a mair seemly sight, than thae dangling slops and ribbands."

Morton left the room, perceiving plainly that he had at present no chance of gaining his purpose, and, perhaps, not altogether displeased at the obstacles which seemed to present themselves to his leaving the neighbourhood of Tillietudlem. The housekeeper followed him into the next room, patting him on the back, and bidding him be a gude bairn, and pit by his braw things.

"And I'll loop doun your hat, and lay by the band and ribband," said the officious dame; "and ye maun never, at no hand, speak o' leaving the land, or of selling the gowd chain, for your uncle has an unco pleasure in looking on you, an' in counting the links of the chainzie; and ye ken auld folk canna last for ever; sae the chain, and the lands, and a', will be your ain ae day; and ye may marry ony leddy in the country side ye like, and keep a braw house at Milnewood, for there's enow of means. And is not that worth waiting for, my dow?"

There was something in the latter part of the prognostic which sounded so agreeably in the ears of Morton, that he shook the old dame cordially by the hand, and assured her he was much obliged by her good advice, and would weigh it carefully before he proceeded to act upon his former resolution.

Chapter Seven

From seventeen years till now, almost fourscore,
Here lived I, but now live here no more.
At seventeen years many their fortunes seek,
But at fourscore it is too late a week.
                                        As You Like It

WE MUST now conduct our readers to the Tower of Tillietudlem, to which Lady Margaret Bellenden had returned, in romantic phrase, malcontent and full of heaviness, at the unexpected, and, as she deemed it, indelible affront, which had been brought upon her dignity by the public miscarriage of Goose Gibbie. That unfortunate man-at-arms was forthwith commanded to drive his feathered charge to the most remote part of the common moor, and on no account to awaken the grief or resentment of his lady, by appearing in her presence while the sense of the affront was yet recent.

The next proceeding of Lady Margaret was to hold a solemn bed of justice, to which Harrison and the butler were admitted, partly on the footing of witnesses, partly as assessors, to enquire into the recusancy of Cuddie Headrigg the ploughman, and the confort and abetment which he had received from his mother, these being regarded as the original causes of the disaster which had befallen the chivalry of Tillietudlem. The charge being fully made out and substantiated, Lady Margaret resolved to reprimand the culprits in person, and, if she found them impenitent, to extend the censure into a sentence of expulsion from the barony. Miss Bellenden alone ventured to say any thing in behalf of the accused, but her countenance did not profit them as it might have done on any other occasion. For so soon as Edith had heard it ascertained that the unfortunate cavalier had not suffered in his person, his disaster had affected her with an irresistible disposition to laugh, which, in spite of Lady Margaret's indignation, or rather irritated, as usual, by restraint, had broke out repeatedly on her return homeward, until her grandmother, in no shape imposed upon by the several fictitious causes which the young lady assigned for her ill-timed risibility, upbraided her in very bitter terms with being insensible to the honour of her family. Miss Bellenden's intercession, therefore, had, on this occasion, little chance to be listened to.

As if to evince the rigour of her disposition, Lady Margaret, upon this solemn occasion, exchanged the ivory-headed cane with which she commonly walked, for an immense gold-headed staff which had belonged to her father, the deceased Earl of Torwood, and which, like a sort of mace of office, she only made use of upon occasions of special solemnity. Her steps supported by this awful baton of command, Lady Margaret Bellenden entered the cottage of the delinquents.

There was an air of consciousness about old Mause, as she rose from her wicker chair in the chimney-nook, not with the cordial alertness of visage which used, on other occasions, to express the honour she felt in the visit of her lady, but with a certain solemnity and embarrassment, like an accused party on his first appearance in presence of his judge, before whom he is, nevertheless, determined to assert his innocence. Her arms were folded, her mouth primmed into an expression of respect, mingled with obstinacy, her whole mind apparently bent up to the solemn interview. With her best curtesy to the ground, and a mute motion of reverence, Mause pointed to the chair, which, on former occasions, Lady Margaret (for the good lady was somewhat of a gossip) had deigned to occupy for half an hour sometimes at a time, hearing the news of the village and of the borough. But at present her mistress was far too indignant for such condescension. She rejected the mute invitation with a haughty wave of her hand, and drawing herself up as she spoke, she uttered the following interrogatory in a tone calculated to overwhelm the culprit.

"Is it true, Mause, as I am informed by Harrison, Gudyill, and others of my people, that you ha'e ta'en it upon you, contrary to the faith ye awe to God and the king, and to me, your natural lady and

mistress, to keep back your son frae the wappen-schaw, held by order
of the sheriff, and to return his armour and abuilyiements at a moment
when it was impossible to find a suitable delegate in his stead, whereby
the barony of Tillietudlem, baith in the person of its mistress and
indwellers, has incurred sic a disgrace and dishonour as hasna befa'an
the family since the days of Malcolm Canmore?"

Mause's habitual respect for her mistress was extreme; she hesitated, and one or two short coughs expressed the difficulty she had in
defending herself.

"I am sure—my leddy—hem, hem!—I am sure I am sorry—very
sorry that ony cause of displeasure should hae occurred—but my
son's illness"—

"Dinna tell me of your son's illness, Mause! Had he been sincerely
unweel, ye would ha'e been at the Tower wi' daylight to get something
that wad do him gude; there are few ailments that I havena medical
recipes for, and that ye ken fu' weel."

"O ay, my leddy! I am sure ye hae wrought wonderfu' cures; the last
thing ye sent Cuddie when he had the batts, e'en wrought like a
charm."

"Why, then, woman, did ye not apply to me, if there was ony real
need?—But there was none, ye fause-hearted vassal that ye are!"

"Your leddyship never ca'd me sic a word as that before. Ohon! that
I suld live to be ca'd sae," she continued, bursting into tears, "and me a
born servant o' the house o' Tillietudlem! I am sure they belied baith
Cuddie and me sair if they said he wad na' fight ower boots in blude
for your leddyship and Miss Edith, and the auld Tower—ay suld he,
and I would rather see him buried beneath it, than he suld gi'e way—
but thir ridings and wappen-shawings, my leddy, I hae nae broo o'
them ava. I can find nae warrant for them whatsoever."

"Nae warrant for them? Do ye na ken, woman, that ye are bound to
be liege vassals in all hunting, hosting, watching, and warding, when
lawfully summoned thereto in my name? Your service is no gratuitous. I trow ye hae land for it.—Ye're kindly tenants; hae a cot-house, a
kale-yard, and a cow's grass on the common.—Few hae been brought
farther ben, and ye grudge your son suld gi'e me a day's service in the
field?"

"Na, my leddy—-na, my leddy, it's no that," exclaimed Mause,
greatly embarrassed, "but ane canna serve twa maisters; and, if the
truth maun e'en come out, there's Ane abune whase commands I
maun obey before your leddyship's. I am sure I wad put neither king's
nor kaisar's, nor ony earthly creature's, afore them."

"How mean ye by that, ye auld fule woman?—D'ye think that I
would order ony thing against conscience?"

"I dinna presume to say that, my leddy, in regard o' your leddyship's conscience, which has been brought up, as it were, in prelatic principles, but ilka ane maun walk by the light o' their ain; and mine," said Mause, waxing bolder as the conference became animated, "tells me that I suld leave a',—cot and kale-yard, cow's grass and a'—and suffer a', rather than that I or mine should put on harness in an unlawfu' cause."

"Unlawfu'?" exclaimed her mistress; "the cause to which you are called by your lawfu' leddy and mistress—by the command of the king —by the writ of the Privy Council—by the order of the lord-lieutenant —by the warrant of the sheriff!"

"Ay, my leddy, nae doubt; but, no to displeasure your leddyship, ye'll mind that there was ance a king in Scripture they ca'd Nebuchadnezzar, and he set up a golden image in the plain o' Dura, as it might be in the haugh yonder by the water-side, where the array were warned to meet yesterday; and the princes, and the governors, and the captains, and the judges themsels, forbye the treasurers, the counsellors, and the sheriffs, were warned to the dedication thereof, and commanded to fall down and worship at the sound of the cornet, flute, harp, sackbut, psaltery, and all kinds of music."

"And what o' a' this, ye fule wife? Or what has Nebuchadnezzar to do with the wappen-schaw of the Upper Ward of Clydesdale?"

"Ou, just thus far, my leddy," continued Mause, firmly, "that prelacy is like the great golden image in the plain of Dura, and that as Shadrach, Meshach, and Abednego were borne out in refusing to bow down and worship, so neither shall Cuddy Headrigg, your leddyship's poor ploughman, at least wi' his auld mither's consent, mak murgeons or jenny-flections, as they ca' them, in the house of the prelates and curates, nor gird him wi' armour to fight in their cause, either at the sound of trumpets, kettle-drums, organs, bagpipes, or ony other kind of music whatsoever."

Lady Margaret Bellenden heard this exposition of Scripture with the greatest possible indignation as well as surprise.

"I see which way the wind blaws," she exclaimed, after a pause of astonishment; "the evil spirit of the year sixteen hundred and forty-twa is at wark again as merrily as ever, and ilka auld wife in the chimley-neuck will be for knapping doctrine wi' doctors o' divinity and the godly fathers o' the church."

"If your leddyship means the bishops and curates, I'm sure they hae been but stepfathers to the Kirk o' Scotland. And, since your leddyship is pleased to speak o' parting wi' us, I am free to tell you a piece o' my mind in another article. Your leddyship and the steward hae been pleased to propose that my son Cuddy suld work in the barn wi' a newfangled machine* for dighting the corn frae the chaff, thus impiously thwarting the will of Divine Providence, by raising wind for your leddyship's ain particular use by human art, instead of soliciting it by prayer, or waiting patiently for whatever dispensation of wind Providence was pleased to send upon the sheeling-hill. Now, my leddy"——

"The woman would drive ony reasonable being daft!" said Lady Margaret; then, resuming her tone of authority and indifference, she concluded, "Weel, Mause, I'll just end whare I suld hae begun—ye're ower learned and ower godly for the like o' me to dispute wi'; sae I have just this to say—Either Cuddy maun attend musters when he's lawfully warned by the ground-officer, or the sooner him and you flit and quit my bounds the better; there's nae scarcity o' auld wives or pleughmen; but, if there were, I had rather that the rigs of Tillietudlem bare naething but windle-straes and sandy-lavrocks than they were ploughed by rebels to the king."

"Aweel, my leddy," said Mause, "I was born here, and thought to die where my father died; and your leddyship has been a kind mistress, I'll ne'er deny that, and I'se ne'er cease to pray for ye, and for Miss Edith, and that ye may be brought to see the error of your ways. But still"——

"The error of my ways?" interrupted Lady Margaret—"The error of *my* ways, ye uncivil woman?"

"Ou ay, my leddy, we are blinded that live in this valley of tears and darkness, and hae a' ower mony errors, grit folks as weel as sma—but, as I said, my puir bennison will rest wi' you and yours wherever I am. I will be wae to hear o' your affliction, and blythe to hear o' your prosperity, temporal and spiritual. But I canna prefer the commands of an earthly mistress to those of a heavenly master, and sae I am e'en ready to suffer for righteousness sake."

"It is very well," said Lady Margaret, turning her back in great displeasure; "ye ken my will, Mause, in the matter. I'll hae nae whiggery in the barony of Tillietudlem—the next thing wad be to set up a conventicle in my very withdrawing room."

Having said this, she departed with an air of great dignity; and Mause, giving way to feelings which she had suppressed during the interview,—for she, like her mistress, had her own feeling of pride,—now lifted up her voice and wept aloud.

Cuddie, whose malady, real or pretended, still detained him in bed, lay perdue during all this conference, snugly ensconced within his

---

*Probably something similar to the barn-fanners now used for winnowing corn, which were not, however, used in their present shape until about 1730. They were objected to by the more rigid sectaries on their first introduction, upon such reasoning as that of honest Mause, in the text.

boarded bedstead, and terrified to death lest Lady Margaret, whom he held in hereditary reverence, should have detected his presence, and bestowed on him personally some of those bitter reproaches with which she loaded his mother. As soon as he thought her ladyship fairly out of hearing, he bounced up in his nest.

"The foul fa' ye, that I suld say sae," he cried out to his mother, "for a lang-tongued wife, as my father, honest man, aye ca'd ye! Couldna ye let the leddy alane wi' your whiggery? And I was e'en as great a gomeril to let ye persuade me to lie up here amang the blankets like a hurcheon, instead o' ganging to the wappen-schaw like other folk. Odd, but I pat a trick on ye, for I was out at the window-bole when your auld back was turned, and awa' doun by to hae a baff at the papinjay, and I shot within twa o't. I cheated the leddy for your clavers, but I wasna ganging to cheat my joe. But she may marry whae she likes now, for I'm clean dung ower. This is a waur dirdum than we gat frae Mr Gudyill when ye garr'd me refuse to eat the plumb-damis-parridge on Yule-eve, as if it were ony matter to God or man whether a ploughman lad suppit on minched pies or on sour sowens."

"O, whisht, my bairn, whisht," replied Mause; "thou kens nae about thae things—It was forbidden meats, things dedicated to set days and holidays, which are inhibited to the use of protestant Christ-ians."

"And now," continued her son, "ye hae brought the leddy hersel on our heads!—An' I could but hae gotten some decent claes on, I wad hae spanged out o' bed, and tauld her I wad ride where she likit, night or day, an' she wad but leave us the free house and the yaird that grew the best curly kale in the hail country, and the cow's grass."

"O wow! my winsome bairn, Cuddie," continued the old dame, "murmur not at the dispensation; never grudge suffering in the gude cause."

"But what ken I if the cause is gude or no, mither," rejoined Cuddie, "for a' ye bleeze out sae muckle doctrine about it? It's clean beyond my comprehension a' thegither. I see nae sae muckle differ-ence atween the twa ways o't as a' the folk pretend. It's very true the curates read aye the same words ower again; and if they be right words, what for no? A gude tale's no the waur o' being twice tauld, I trow; and a body has aye the better chance to understand it. Every body's no sae gleg at the uptake as ye are yoursel, mither."

"O, my dear Cuddie, this is the sairest distress of a'—O, how aften hae I shewn ye the difference between a pure evangelical doctrine and ane that's corrupt wi' human inventions? O, my bairn, if no for your ain saul's sake, yet for my grey hairs"——

"Weel, mither," said Cuddie, interrupting her, "what need ye mak sae muckle din about it? I hae aye dune whate'er ye bade me, and gaed to kirk whare'er ye likit on the Sundays, and fended weel for ye on the ilka days besides. And that's what vexes me mair than a' the rest, when I think how I am to fend for you now in thae brickle times. I am no clear if I can plough ony place but the Mains and Mucklewhame, at least I never tried ony other grund, and it wadna come natural to me. And nae neighbouring heritors daur tak us after being turned aff thae bounds for non-enormity."

"Non-conformity, hinnie," sighed Mause, "is the name that thae warldly men gi'e us."

"Weel, aweel—we'll hae to gang to a far country, maybe twal or fifteen miles aff. I could be a dragoon, nae doubt; I can ride and play wi' the broadsword a bit, but ye wad be roaring about your blessing and your grey hairs." (Here Mause's exclamations became extreme.) "Weel, weel, I but spoke o't; besides ye're ower auld to be sitting cocked up on a baggage-waggon wi' Eppie Dumblane the corporal's wife. Sae what's to come o' us I canna weel see—I doubt I'll hae to tak the hills wi' the wild whigs, as they ca' them, and than it will be my lot to be shot down like a mawkin at some dykeside, or to be sent to Heaven wi' a Saint Johnstone's tippit about my hause."

"O, my bonnie Cuddie, forbear sic carnal, self-seeking language, whilk is just a misdoubting o' Providence—I have not seen the son of the righteous begging his bread, sae says the text; and your father was a douce honest man, though somewhat warldly in his dealings, and cumbered about earthly things e'en like yoursel, my jo!"

"Aweel," said Cuddie, after a little consideration, "I see but ae gate for't, and that's but a cauld coal to blaw at neither. Howsomever, mither, ye hae some guess o' a wee bit kindness that's atween Miss Edith and young Mr Henry Morton, that suld be ca'd young Milnewood, and that I hae whiles carried a bit book or maybe a bit letter quietly atween them, and made believe never to ken wha it cam frae, though I kenn'd brawly. There's whiles convenience in looking a wee stupid—and I hae aften seen them walking at e'en on the little path by Dinglewood-burn when they little wotted I saw them; but naebody ever kenn'd a word about it frae Cuddie; I ken I'm gay thick in the head, but I'm as honest as our auld fore-hand ox, puir fallow, that I'll ne'er work ony mair—I hope they'll be as kind to him that come ahint me as I hae been.—But, as I was saying, we'll awa down to Milnewood and tell Mr Harry our distress. They want a ploughman, and the grund's no unlike our ain—I am sure Mr Harry will stand my friend, for he's a kind-hearted gentleman.—I'll get but little penny-fee, for his uncle, auld Nippie Milnewood, has as close a grip as the de'il himsel. But we'll aye get a bit bread, and a drap kale, and a fire-side, and theeking ower our heads, and that's a' we'll want for a season—Sae get up, mither, and sort your things to gang away, for, since sae it is that gang we maun, I wad like ill to wait till Mr Harrison and auld Gudyill cam to pu' us out by the lug and the horn."

Chapter Eight

The devil a puritan, or any thing else, he is, but a time-server.
Twelfth Night

IT WAS evening when Mr Henry Morton perceived an old woman, wrapped in her tartan plaid or serun, supported by a stout, stupid-looking young fellow, in hoddin-grey, approach the house of Milnewood. Old Mause made her courtesy, but Cuddie took the lead in addressing Morton. Indeed he had previously stipulated with his mother that he was to manage matters his own way; for though he readily allowed his general inferiority of understanding, and submitted to the guidance of his mother on most ordinary occasions, yet he said, "For getting a service or getting forward in the warld, he could somegate gar the wee pickle sense he had gang muckle farther than hers, though she could crack like ony minister o' them a'."

Accordingly he thus opened the conversation with young Morton,—

"A braw night this for the rye, your honour; the west park will be brearing bravely the e'en."

"I do not doubt it, Cuddie; but what can have brought your mother—this is your mother, is she not?" (Cuddie nodded.) "What can have brought your mother and you down the water so late?"

"Troth, stir, just what gars the auld wives trot—neshessity, stir—I'm seeking for service, stir."

"For service, Cuddie, and at this time of the year? how comes that?"

Mause could forbear no longer. Proud alike of her cause and her sufferings, she commenced with an affected humility of tone, "It has pleased Heaven, an' it like your honour, to distinguish us by a visitation."—

"De'il's in the wife and nae gude!" whispered Cuddie to his mother; "an ye come out wi' your whiggery they'll no daur open a door to us through the haill countra!" Then aloud and addressing Morton, "My mother's auld, stir, and she has rather forgotten hersel in speaking to my leddy, that canna weel bide to be contradicted, (as I ken naebody likes it if they could help themsels,) especially by her ain folk, —and Mr Harrison the steward, and Mr Gudyill the butler, they're no very fond o' us, and it's ill sitting at Rome and striving wi' the Pope, sae I thought it best to flit before ill came to waur—and here's a wee bit line to your honour frae a friend will maybe say some mair about it."

Morton took the billet, and crimsoning up to the ears, between joy and surprise, read these words, "If you can serve these poor helpless people, you will oblige E. B."

It was a few instants before he could attain composure enough to ask, "And what is your object, Cuddie? or how can I be of use to you?"

"Wark, stir, wark, and a service is my object—a bit beild for my mither and mysel—we hae gude plenishing o' our ain, if we had the cast o' a cart to bring it down—and milk and meal, and greens enow, for I'm gay gleg at meal time, and sae is my mother, lang may it be sae —And, for the penny-fee and a' that, I'll just leave it to the laird and you. I ken ye'll no see a poor lad wranged, if ye can help it."

Morton shook his head. "For the meat and lodging, Cuddie, I think I can promise something, but the penny-fee will be a hard chapter, I doubt."

"I'll tak my chance o't, stir, rather than gang down about Hamilton, or into ony sic far country."

"Well; step into the kitchen, Cuddie, and I'll do what I can for you."

The negotiation was not without difficulties. Morton had first to bring over the housekeeper, who made a thousand objections, as usual, in order to have the pleasure of being besought and entreated; but, when she was gained over, it was comparatively easy to induce old Milnewood to accept of a servant, whose wages were to be in his own option. An outhouse was, therefore, assigned to Mause and her son for their habitation, and it was settled that they were for the time to be admitted to eat of the frugal provisions provided for the family until their own establishment should be completed. As for Morton, he exhausted his own very slender stock of money in order to make Cuddie such a present, under the name of *arles*, as might shew his sense of the value of the recommendation delivered to him.

"And now we are settled ance mair," said Cuddie to his mother, "and if we are na sae bien and comfortable as we were up yonder, yet life's life ony gate, and we're wi' decent kirk-ganging folk o' your ain persuasion, mither; there will be nae quarrelling about that."

"Of my persuasion, hinnie! waes me for thy blindness and theirs. O, Cuddie, they are but in the court of the Gentiles, and will ne'er win farther ben, I doubt; they are but little better than the prelatists themsels. They wait on the ministry of that blinded man, Peter Poundtext, ance a precious teacher of the Word, but now a backsliding pastor, that has, for the sake of stipend and family maintenance, forsaken the strait path and gone astray after the Black Indulgence. O, my son, had ye but profited by the gospel doctrines ye hae heard in the Glen o' Bengonnar from the dear Richard Rumbleberry, that sweet youth, wha suffered martyrdom in the Grassmarket, afore Candlemas! Didna ye hear him say, that Erastianism was as bad as prelacy, and that the Indulgence was as bad as Erastianism?"

"Heard ever ony body the like o' this," interrupted Cuddie, "we'll be driven out o' house and ha' agen afore we ken where to turn oursels. Weel, mither, I hae just ae word mair—An' I hear ony mair o' your din—afore folk, that is, for I dinna mind your clavers mysel, they aye set me sleeping—but if I hear ony mair din afore folk, as I was saying, about Poundtexts and Rumbleberries, and doctrines and malignants, I'se e'en turn a single sodger mysel, or maybe a serjeant or a captain if ye plague me the mair, and let Rumbleberry and you gang to the de'il thegither. I ne'er gat ony gude by his doctrine, as ye ca't, but a gude fit o' the batts wi' sitting amang the wat moss-hags for four hours at a yoking, and the leddy cured me wi' some hickery-pickery; mair be taken, an' she had kenn'd how I came by the disorder, she wadna hae been in sic a hurry to cure it."

Although groaning in spirit over the obdurate and impenitent state, as she thought it, of her son Cuddie, Mause durst neither urge him farther on the topic, nor altogether neglect the warning he had given. She knew the disposition of her deceased helpmate, whom this surviving pledge of their union greatly resembled, and remembered, that although submitting implicitly in most things to her boast of superior acuteness, he used on certain occasions, when driven to extremity, to be seized with fits of obstinacy which neither remonstrance, flattery, nor threats, were capable of overpowering. Trembling, therefore, at the very possibility of Cuddie's fulfilling his threat, she put a guard over her tongue, and even when Poundtext was commended in her presence, as an able and fructifying preacher, she had the good sense to suppress the contradiction which thrilled upon her tongue, and to express her dissent no otherwise than by deep groans, which the hearers charitably construed to flow from a vivid recollection of the more pathetic parts of his homilies. How long she could have repressed her feelings it is difficult to say. An unexpected accident relieved her from the necessity.

The Laird of Milnewood kept up all old fashions which were connected with economy. It was, therefore, still the custom in his house, as had been universal in Scotland about fifty years before, that the domestics, after having placed the dinner on the table, sate down at the lower end of the board, and partook of the share which was assigned to them, in company with their masters. Upon the day, therefore, after Cuddie's arrival, being the third from the opening of this narrative, old Robin, who was butler, valet-de-chambre, foot-man, gardener, and what not, in the house of Milnewood, placed on the table an immense charger of broth, thickened with oatmeal and colewort, in which ocean of liquid was indistinctly discovered, by close observers, two or three short ribs of lean mutton sailing to and fro. Two huge baskets, one of bread made of barley and pease-meal baked into thick cakes called bannocks, and one of oat-cakes, flanked this standing dish. A large boiled salmon would now-a-days have indic-ated more liberal housekeeping; but at that period it was caught in such plenty in all the considerable rivers in Scotland, that it was generally applied to feed the servants, who are said sometimes to have stipulated that they should not be required to eat a food so luscious and surfeiting in its quality above five times a-week. The large black-jack, filled with very small beer of Milnewood's own brewing, was indulged to the servants at discretion, as were the bannocks, cakes, and broth; but the mutton was reserved for the heads of the family, Mrs Wilson included; and a measure of ale, somewhat deserving the name, was set apart in a silver tankard for their exclusive use. A huge kebbock, (a cheese that is made of ewe milk mixed with cow's milk) and a jar of salt butter, were in common to the company.

To enjoy this exquisite cheer, was placed at the head of the table the old laird himself, with his nephew on the one side, and the favourite housekeeper on the other. At a long interval, and beneath the salt of course, sate old Robin, a meagre, half-starved serving-man, rendered cross and cripple by the rheumatism, and a dirty drab of a house-maid, whom use had rendered callous to the daily exercitations which her temper underwent at the hands of her master and Mrs Wilson; a barnsman, a white-headed cow-herd boy, and Cuddie the new ploughman and his mother, completed the party. The other labourers belonging to the property resided in their own houses, happy at least in this, that if their cheer was not more delicate than that which we have described, they could at least eat their fill, unwatched by the sharp, envious, grey eyes of Milnewood, which seemed to measure the quan-tity that each of his dependants swallowed, as closely as if their glances attended each mouthful in its progress from the lips to the stomach. This close inspection was unfavourable to Cuddie, who was much prejudiced in his new master's opinion, by the silent celerity with which he caused the victuals to disappear before him. And ever and anon Milnewood turned his eyes from the huge feeder to cast indig-nant glances upon his nephew, whose repugnance to rustic labour was the principal cause of his needing a ploughman, and who had been the direct means of his hiring this very cormorant.

"Pay thee wages, quotha?" said Milnewood to himself. "Thou wilt eat in a week the value of mair than thou canst work for in a month."

These disagreeable ruminations were interrupted by a loud knocking at the outer-gate. It was a universal custom in Scotland, that, when the family was at dinner, the outer-gate of the court-yard, if there was one, and, if not, the door of the house itself, was always shut and locked, and only guests of importance, or persons upon urgent business, sought or received admittance at that time. The family of Milnewood were therefore surprised, and, in the unsettled state of the times, something alarmed, at the earnest and repeated knocking with which the gate was now assailed. Mrs Wilson ran in person to the door, and, having reconnoitred those who were so clamorous for admittance, through some secret aperture with which most Scottish door-ways were furnished for the express purpose, she returned wringing her hands in great dismay, exclaiming, "The red-coats! the red-coats!"

"Robin—ploughman, what ca' they ye—Benny—Nevoy Harry— open the door, open the door," exclaimed old Milnewood, snatching up and slipping into his pocket the two or three silver spoons with which the upper end of the table was garnished, those beneath the salt being of goodly horn. "Speak them fair, sirs—Lord love ye, speak them fair—they winna bide thrawing—we are a' harried—we are a' harried!"

While the servants admitted the troopers, whose oaths and threats already indicated their resentment at the delay they had been put to, Cuddie took the opportunity to whisper to his mother, "Now, ye daft auld carline, mak yoursel deaf—ye hae made us a' deaf ere now—and let me speak for ye. I wad like ill to get my neck raxed for an auld wife's clashes, though ye be our mither."

"O, hinny, ay; I'se be silent or thou sall come to ill," was the corresponding whisper of Mause; "but bethink ye, my dear, them that deny the Word, the Word will deny."—

Her admonition was cut short by the entrance of the Life Guard's-men, a party of four troopers commanded by Bothwell.

In they tramped, making a tremendous clatter upon the stone-floor with the high iron-shod heels of their large jack-boots, and the clash and clang of their long, heavy, basket-hilted broadswords. Milnewood and his housekeeper trembled from well-grounded apprehension of the system of exaction and plunder carried on during these domiciliary visits. Henry Morton was discomposed with more special cause, for he remembered that he stood amenable to the laws for having harboured Burley. The widow Mause Headrigg, between fear for her son's life and an overstrained and enthusiastic zeal, which

reproached her for consenting even tacitly to belie her religious sentiments, was in a strange quandary. The other servants quaked for they
knew not well what. Cuddie alone, with the look of supreme indifference and stupidity which a Scottish peasant can at times assume as a
masque for considerable shrewdness and craft, continued to swallow
large spoonfuls of his broth, to command which, he had drawn within
his sphere the large vessel that contained it, and helped himself, amid
the confusion, to a sevenfold portion.

"What is your pleasure here, gentlemen?" said Milnewood, hum-
bling himself before the satellites of power.

"We come in behalf of the king," answered Bothwell; "why the
devil did you keep us so long standing at the door?"

"We were at dinner," answered Milnewood, "and the door was
locked, as it is usual in landward towns in this country. I am sure,
gentlemen, if I had kenn'd ony servants of our gude king had stood at
the door—But wad ye please to drink some ale—or some brandy—or
a cup of canary sack, or clairet wine?" making a pause between each
offer as long as a stingy bidder at an auction, who is loth to advance his
offer for a favourite lot.

"Claret for me," said one fellow.

"I like ale better," said another, "provided it is right juice of John
Barleycorn."

"Better never was malted," said Milnewood; "I can hardly say sae
muckle for the claret. It's thin and cauld jut, gentlemen."

"Brandy will cure that," said a third fellow; "a glass of brandy to
three glasses of wine prevents the curmurring in the stomach."

"Brandy, ale, and wine, sack, and claret,—we'll try them all," said
Bothwell, "and stick to that which is best. There's good sense in that,
if the damn'dest whig in Scotland had said it."

Hastily, yet with a reluctant quiver of his muscles, Milnewood
lugged out two ponderous keys, and delivered them to the governante.

"The housekeeper," said Bothwell, taking a seat and throwing himself upon it, "is neither so young nor so bonny as to tempt a man to
follow her to the gauntrees, and devil a one here is there worth sending in her place.—What's this?—meat?" (searching with a fork
among the broth, and fishing up a cutlet of mutton)—"I think I could
eat a bit—it's as tough as if the devil's dam had hatched it."

"If there is any thing better in the house, sir," said Milnewood,
alarmed at these symptoms of disapprobation——

"No, no," said Bothwell, "it's not worth while, I must proceed to
business.—You attend Poundtext, the presbyterian parson, I understand, Mr Morton?"

Mr Morton hastened to slide in a confession and apology.

"By the Indulgence of his gracious majesty and the government, for I wad do nothing out of law—I hae nae objection whatever to the establishment of a moderate episcopacy, but only that I am a country-bred man, and the ministers are a hamelier kind of folk, and I can follow their doctrine better; and, with reverence, sir, it's a mair frugal establishment for the country."

"Well, I care nothing about that," said Bothwell; "they are indulged, and there's an end of it; but, for my part, if I were to give the law, never a crop-eared cur of the whole pack should bark in a Scotch pulpit. However, I am to obey commands—Here comes the liquor; put it down, my good old lady."

He decanted about one half of a quart bottle of claret into a wooden quaigh or bicker, and took it off at a draught.

"You did your good wine injustice, my friend;—it's better than your brandy, though that's good too. Will you pledge me to the king's health?"

"With pleasure," said Milnewood, "in ale,—but I never drink claret, and keep only a very little for some honoured friends."

"Like me, I suppose," said Bothwell; and then, pushing the bottle to Henry, he said, "Here, young man, pledge you the king's health."

Henry filled a moderate glass in silence, regardless of the hints and pushes of his uncle, which seemed to indicate that he ought to have followed his example in preferring beer to wine.

"Well," said Bothwell, "have ye all drank the toast?—What is that old wife about? Give her a glass of brandy, she shall drink the king's health, by ——."

"If your honour pleases," said Cuddie, with great stolidity of aspect, "she's my mither, sir; and she's as deaf as Corra-linn; we canna make her hear day nor door; but, if your honour pleases, I am ready to drink the king's health for her in as mony glasses of brandy as ye think necessary."

"I dare swear you are," answered Bothwell, "you look like a fellow that would stick to brandy—help thyself, man; all's free where'er I come.—Tom, help the maid to a comfortable cup, though she's but a dirty jilt neither. Fill round once more—Here's to our noble commander, Colonel Grahame of Claverhouse!—What the devil is the old woman groaning for? She looks as very a whig as ever sate on a hill side.—Do you renounce the Covenant, good woman?"

"Whilk Covenant is your honour meaning? Is it the Covenant of Works, or the Covenant of Grace?" said Cuddie, interposing.

"Any covenant; all covenants that ever were hatched," answered the trooper.

"Mither," cried Cuddie, affecting to speak as to a deaf person, "the gentleman wants to ken if ye will renunce the Covenant of Works."

"With a' my heart, Cuddie," said Mause, "and pray that my feet may be delivered from the snare thereof."

"Come," said Bothwell, "the old dame has come more frankly off than I expected. Another cup round, and then we'll proceed to business.—You have all heard, I suppose, of the horrid and barbarous murder committed upon the person of the Archbishop of St Andrews, by ten or eleven armed fanatics?"

All started and looked at each other; at length Milnewood himself answered, "They had heard of some such misfortune, but they were in hopes it had not been true."

"There is the relation published by government, old gentleman; what do you think of it?"

"Think, sir? Wh—wh—whatever the Council please to think of it," stammered Milnewood.

"I desire to have your opinion more explicitly, my friend," said the dragoon authoritatively.

Milnewood's eyes hastily glanced through the paper to pick out the strongest expressions of censure with which it abounded, in gleaning which he was greatly aided by their being printed in italics.

"I think it a—bloody and execrable—murder and parricide—devised by hellish and implacable cruelty—utterly abominable, and a scandal to the land."

"Well said, old gentleman," said the querist—"Here's to thee, and I wish you joy of your good principles. You owe me a cup of thanks for having taught you them; nay, thou shalt pledge me in thine own sack —sour ale sits ill upon a loyal stomach.—Now comes your turn, young man; what think you of the matter in hand?"

"I should have little objection to answer you," said Henry, "if I knew what right you had to put the question."

"The Lord preserve us!" said the old housekeeper, "to ask the like o' that at a trooper, when a' folk ken they do whatever they like through the hail country wi' man and woman, beast and body."

The old gentleman exclaimed in the same horror at his nephew's audacity, "Hold your peace, sir, or answer the gentleman discreetly. Do ye mean to affront the king's authority in the person of a serjeant of the life-guards?"

"Silence, all of you," exclaimed Bothwell, striking his hand fiercely on the table—"Silence, every one of you, and hear me!—You ask me for my right to examine you, sir; (to Henry) my cockade and my broadsword are my commission, and a better one than ever Old Nol gave to his round-heads; and if you want to know more about it, you may look at the Act of Council empowering his majesty's officers and soldiers to search for, examine, and apprehend suspected persons; and, therefore, once more I ask you your opinion of the death of Archbishop Sharpe—it's a new touchstone we have got for trying people's metal."

Henry had, by this time, reflected upon the useless risk to which he would expose the family by resisting the tyrannical power which was delegated to such rude hands; he therefore read the narrative over, and replied, composedly, "I have no hesitation to say, that the perpetrators of this assassination have committed, in my opinion, a rash and wicked action, which I regret the more, as I foresee it will be made the cause of proceedings against many who are both innocent of the deed, and as far from approving it as myself."

While Henry thus expressed himself, Bothwell, who bent his eyes keenly upon him, seemed suddenly to recollect his features.

"Aha! my friend Captain Popinjay, I think I have seen you before, and in very suspicious company."

"I saw you once," answered Henry, "in the public-house at the town of ——."

"And with whom did you leave that public-house, youngster?—Was it not with John Balfour of Burley, one of the murderers of the Archbishop?"

"I did leave the house with the person you have named," answered Henry, "I scorn to deny it; but, so far from knowing him to be a murderer of the primate, I did not even know at the time that such a crime had been committed."

"Lord have mercy on me, I am ruined!—utterly ruined and undone!" exclaimed Milnewood. "That callan's tongue will rin the head aff his ain shoulders, and waste my gudes to the very grey cloak aff my back."

"But you know Burley," continued Bothwell, still addressing Henry, and regardless of his uncle's interruption, "to be an intercommuned rebel and traitor, and you know the prohibition to deal with such persons. You know, that, as a loyal subject, you were prohibited to reset, supply, or intercommune with this attaint traitor, to correspond with him by word, writ, or message, or to supply him with meat, drink, house, harbour, or victual, under the highest pains—You know all this, and yet you broke the law." (Henry was silent.) "Where did you part from him?" continued Bothwell; "was it in the highway, or did you give him herbourage in this very house?"

"In this house!" said his uncle, "he dared not for his neck bring ony traitor into a house of mine."

"Dare he deny that he did so?" said Bothwell.

"As you charge it to me as a crime," said Henry, "you will excuse my saying any thing that will criminate myself."

"O, the lands of Milnewood!—the bonny lands of Milnewood, that have been in the name of Morton twa hundred years!" exclaimed his uncle; "they are barking and fleeing, outfield and infield, heugh and holme!"

"No, sir," said Henry, "you shall not suffer on my account—I own," he continued, addressing Bothwell, "I did give this man a night's lodging, as to an old military comrade of my father. But it was not only without my uncle's knowledge, but contrary to his express general orders. I trust, if my evidence is considered as good against myself, it will have some weight in proving my uncle's innocence."

"Come, young man," said the soldier, in somewhat a milder tone, "you're a smart spark enough, and I am sorry for you; and your uncle here is a fine old Trojan, kinder, I see, to his guests than himself, for he gives us wine and drinks his own thin ale—tell me all you know about this Burley, what he said, when you parted from him, where he went, and where he is likely now to be found; and, d—n it, I'll wink as hard on your share of the business as my duty will permit. There's a thousand merks on the murdering whigamore's head, an' I could but light on it—Come, out with it—where did you part with him?"

"You will excuse my answering that question, sir," said Morton; "the same cogent reasons which induced me to afford him hospitality at considerable risk to myself and my friends, would command me to respect his secret, if indeed he had trusted me with any."

"So you refuse to give me an answer?" said Bothwell.

"I have none to give," returned Henry.

"Perhaps I could teach you to find one, by tying a piece of lighted match betwixt your fingers," answered Bothwell.

"O, for pity's sake, sir," said old Alison apart to her master, "gi'e them siller—it's siller they're seeking—they'll murder Mr Harry, and yoursel next."

Milnewood groaned in perplexity and bitterness of spirit, and with a tone, as if he was giving up the ghost, exclaimed, "If twenty p—p— punds wad make up this unhappy matter"——

"My master," insinuated Alison to the serjeant, "would gi'e twenty punds sterling."

"Punds Scotch, you b—h," interrupted Milnewood, for the agony of his avarice overcame alike his puritanic precision and the habitual respect he entertained for his housekeeper.

"Punds sterling," insisted the housekeeper, "if ye wad hae the gudeness to look ower the lad's misconduct; he's that dour ye might tear him to pieces, and ye wad ne'er get a word out on him; and it wad do ye little gude to burn his bonny finger ends."

"Why," said Bothwell, hesitating, "I don't know—most of my cloth would have the money, and take off the prisoner too; but I bear a conscience, and if your master will stand to your offer, and enter into bond to produce his nephew, and if all in the house will take the test-oath, I do not know but"——

"O ay, ay, sir," cried Mrs Wilson, "ony test, ony oaths you please!" And then aside to her master, "Haste ye away, sir, and get the money, or they will burn the house about our lugs."

Old Milnewood cast a rueful look upon his adviser, and moved off, like a piece of Dutch clock-work, to set at liberty his imprisoned angels in this dire emergency. Meanwhile, Serjeant Bothwell began to put the Test with such a degree of solemn reverence as might have been expected, being just about the same which is used to this day in his majesty's custom-house.

"You—what's your name, woman?"

"Alison Wilson, sir."

"You, Alison Wilson, solemnly swear, certify, and declare, that you judge it unlawful for subjects under pretext of reformation, or any other pretext whatsoever, to enter into Leagues and Covenants"——

Here the ceremony was interrupted by a strife between Cuddie and his mother, which, long conducted in whispers, now became audible.

"O, whisht, mither, whisht! they're upon a communing—Oh! whisht, and they'll agree weel e'enow."

"I will not whisht, Cuddie," replied his mother, "I will uplift my voice and spare not—I will confound the man of sin, even the scarlet man, and through my voice shall Mr Henry be freed from the net of the fowler."

"She has her leg ower the harrows now," said Cuddie, "stop her wha can—I see her cocked up behint a dragoon on her way to the Tolbooth—I find my ain legs tied below a horse's belly—Ay—she has just mustered up her sermon, and there—wi' that grane—out it comes, and we are a' ruined, horse and foot!"

"And div ye think to come here," said Mause, her withered hand shaking in concert with her keen, though wrinkled visage, animated by zealous wrath, and emancipated, by the very mention of the test, from the restraints of her own prudence and of Cuddie's admonition—"div ye think to come here, wi' your soul-killing, saint-seducing, con-science-confounding oaths, and tests, and bands—your snares, and your traps, and your gins?—Surely it is in vain that a net is spread in the sight of any bird."

"Eh! what, good dame?" said the soldier. "Here's a whig miracle, egad! the old wife has got both her ears and tongue, and we are like to be driven deaf in our turn.—Go to, hold your peace, and remember whom you talk to, you old idiot."

"Whae do I talk to? Eh, sirs, ower weel may the sorrowing land ken what ye are. Malignant adherents ye are to the prelates, foul props to a feeble and filthy cause, bloody beasts of prey, and burdens to the earth."

"Upon my soul," said Bothwell, astonished as a mastiff-dog might be should a hen-partridge fly at him in defence of her young, "this is the finest language I ever heard! Can't you give us some more of it?"

"Gie ye some mair o't?" said Mause, clearing her voice with a preliminary cough, "I will take up my testimony against you ance and again.—Philistines ye are, and Edomites—leopards are ye, and foxes—evening-wolves, that gnaw not the bones till the morrow—wicked dogs, that compass about the chosen—crushing kine, and pushing bulls of Bashan—piercing serpents ye are, and allied baith in name and nature with the great Red Dragon, Revelations, twalfth chapter, third and fourth verses."

Here the old lady stopped, apparently much more from lack of breath than of matter.

"Curse the old hag," said one of the dragoons, "gag her, and take her to head-quarters."

"For shame, Andrews," said Bothwell; "remember the good lady belongs to the fair sex, and uses only the privilege of her long tongue. —But, hark ye, good woman, every Bull of Bashan and Red Dragon will not be so civil as I am, or be contented to leave you to the charge of the constable and ducking-stool. In the mean time, I must necessarily carry off this young man to head-quarters. I cannot answer it to my commanding-officer to leave him in a house where I have heard so much treason and fanaticism."

"See now, mither, what ye hae dune," whispered Cuddie; "there's the Philistines, as ye whiles ca' them, are ganging to whirry awa' Mr Harry, and a' wi' your nash-gab, de'il be on't!"

"Haud your tongue, ye cowardly loon," said the mother, "and lay na the wyte on me; if you and thae dowless gluttons that are sitting staring like cows bursting on clover, wad testify wi' your hands as I have testified wi' my tongue, they suld never harle the precious young lad awa' to captivity."

While this dialogue passed, the soldiers had already bound and secured their prisoner. Milnewood returned at this instant, and, alarmed at the preparations he beheld, hastened to proffer to Bothwell, though with many a grievous groan, the purse of gold which he had been obliged to rummage out as ransom for his nephew. The trooper took the purse with an air of indifference, weighed it in his hand, chucked it up into the air, and caught it as it fell, then shook his head, and said, "There's many a merry night in this nest of yellow boys, but d—n me if I dare venture for them—that old woman has spoke too loud, and before all the men too.—Hark ye, old gentleman," to Milnewood, "I must take your nephew to head-quarters, so I cannot, in conscience, keep more than is my due as civility-money;" then opening the purse, he gave a gold piece to each of the soldiers, and took three to himself. "Now," said he, "you have the comfort to know that your kinsman, young Captain Popinjay, will be carefully looked after and civilly used, and the rest of the money I return to you."

Milnewood eagerly extended his hand.

"Only you know," said Bothwell, still playing with the purse, "that every land-holder is answerable for the conformity and loyalty of his household, and that these fellows of mine are not obliged to be silent on the subject of the fine sermon we have had from that old puritan in the tartan plaid there; and I presume you are aware that the consequences of delation will be a heavy fine before the Council."

"Good serjeant,—worthy captain!" exclaimed the terrified miser, "I am sure there is no person in my house, to my knowledge, would give cause of offence."

"Nay," answered Bothwell, "you shall hear her give her testimony, as she calls it, herself.—You fellow," (to Cuddie) "stand back, and let your mother speak her mind. I see she's primed and loaded again since her first discharge."

"Lord! noble sir," said Cuddie, "an auld wife's tongue's but a feckless matter to mak sic a fash about. Neither my father nor me ever minded muckle what our mither said."

"Hold your peace, my lad, while you are well," said Bothwell; "I promise you I think you are slyer than you would like to be supposed. —Come, good dame, you see your master will not believe that you can give us so tight a testimony."

Mause's zeal did not require this spur to set her again on full career.

"Woe to the carnal self-seekers," she said, "that daubs over and drowns their conscience by complying with wicked exactions, and giving mammon of unrighteousness to the sons of Belial, that it may make their peace with them! It is a sinful compliance, a base confederacy with the enemy. It is the evil that Menahem did in the sight of the Lord, when he gave a thousand talents to Peel, King of Assyria, that his hand might be with him, Second Kings, feifteenth chapter, aughteenth verse. It is the evil deed of Ahab, when he sent money to Tiglath-pileser. See the saame Second Kings, saxteenth and aught. And it was accounted a backsliding even in godly Hezekiah, that he

complied with Sennacherib, giving him money and offering to bear
that which was put upon him. See the saame Second Kings aughteenth, fourteenth and feifteenth verses. Even so it is with them that in
this contumacious and backsliding generation pays localities and fees,
and cess and fines, to greedy and unrighteous publicans and extor-
tioners, and stipends to hireling curates, (dumb dogs which bark not,
sleeping, lying down, loving to slumber) and gives gifts to be helps and
hires to our oppressors and destroyers. They all are like the casters of
a lot with them—like the preparing of a table for the troop, and the
furnishing a drink-offering to the number."

"There's a fine sound of doctrine for you, Mr Morton! How like
you that?" said Bothwell; "or how do you think the Council will like it?
I think we can carry the greatest part of it in our heads without a
kylevine pen and a pair of tablets, such as you bring to conventicles.
She denies paying cess, I think, Andrews?"

"Yes, by G—," said Andrews; "and she swore it was a sin to give a
trooper a pot of ale, or ask him to sit down at a table."

"You hear," said Bothwell, addressing Milnewood, "but it's your
own affair," and he proffered back the purse with its diminished
contents, with an air of indifference.

Milnewood, whose head seemed stunned by the accumulation of
his misfortunes, extended his hand mechanically to take the purse.

"Are ye mad?" said his housekeeper, in a whisper; "tell them to
keep it;—they *will* do it either by fair means or foul, and it's our only
chance to make them quiet."

"I canna do it, Alie—I canna do it," said Milnewood, in the bitterness of his heart. "I canna part wi' the siller I hae counted sae often
ower, to thae blackguards."

"Then I maun do't mysel, Milnewood," said the housekeeper, "or
see a' gang wrang thegither.—My master, sir," she said, addressing
Bothwell, "canna think o' taking back ony thing at the hand of an
honourable gentleman like you; he implores ye ti pit up the siller,
and be as kind to his nephew as ye can, and be favourable in reporting
our dispositions to government, and let us tak nae wrang for the daft
speeches of an auld jaud," (here she turned fiercely upon Mause, to
indulge herself for the effort which it cost her to assume a mild
demeanour to the soldiers,) "a daft auld whig randie, that ne'er was in
the house (foul fa' her) till yesterday afternoon, and that sall ne'er
cross the door-stane again an' anes I had her out o't."

"Ay, ay," said Cuddie, "e'en sae. I kenn'd we wad be put to our
travels again whene'er you suld get three words spoken to an end. I
was sure that wad be the upshot on't, mither."

"Whisht, my bairn," said she, "and dinna murmur at the cross

—cross their door-stane? weel I wot I'll cross their door-stane. There's nae mark on their threshold for a signal that the destroying angel should pass by. They'll get a back cast o' his hand yet, that think sae muckle o' the creature, and sae little o' the Creator—sae muckle o' warld's gear and sae little o' a broken covenant—sae muckle about thae wheen pieces o' yellow muck, and sae little about the pure gold o' the Scripture—sae muckle about their ain friend and kinsman, and sae little about the elect that are tried wi' hornings, harassings, huntings, searchings, chasings, catchings, imprisonments, torturings, banishments, headings, hangings, dismemberings, and quarterings quick, forbye the hundreds forced from their ain habitations to the deserts, mountains, muirs, mosses, moss-flows, and peat-hags, there to hear the covenanted word like bread eaten in secret."

"She's at the Covenant now, serjeant, shall we not have her away?" said one of the soldiers.

"You be d—d," said Bothwell, aside to him; "cannot you see she's better where she is, so long as there is a respectable, sponsible, money-broking heritor, like Mr Morton of Milnewood, who has the means of atoning her trespasses? Let the old mother fly to raise another brood, she's too tough to be made any thing of herself— Here," he cried, "one other round to Milnetown and his roof-tree, and to our next merry meeting with him!—which I think will not be far distant, if he keeps such a fanatical family."

He then ordered his party to take their horses, and pressed the best in Milnewood's stable into the king's service to carry the prisoner. Mrs Wilson, with weeping eyes, made up a small parcel of necessaries for Henry's compelled journey, and, as she bustled about, took an opportunity, unseen by the party, to slip into his hand a small sum of money. Bothwell and his troopers, in other respects, kept their promise, and were civil. They did not bind their prisoner, but contented themselves with leading his horse between a file of men. They then mounted, and marched off with much mirth and laughter among themselves, leaving the Milnewood family in great confusion. The old laird himself, overpowered by the loss of his nephew, and the unavailing outlay of twenty pounds sterling, did nothing the whole evening but rock himself backwards and forwards in his great leathern easy-chair, repeating the same lamentation, of "Ruined on a' sides, ruined on a' sides—body and gudes, body and gudes!"

Mrs Alison Wilson's grief was partly indulged and partly relieved by the torrent of invectives with which she accompanied Mause and Cuddie's expulsion from Milnewood.

"Ill luck be in the graning corse o' thee! the prettiest lad this day on Clydeside maun be a sufferer, and a' for you and your daft whiggery."

"Gae wa'," replied Mause; "I trow ye are yet in the bonds of sin, and in the gall of iniquity, to grudge your bonniest and best in the cause of Him that gave ye a' ye hae—I promise you I hae dune as muckle for Mr Harry as I wad do for my ain; for, if Cuddie was found worthy to bear testimony in the Grassmarket"——

"And there's gude hope o't," said Alison, "unless you and he change your courses."

"And if," continued Mause, disregarding the interruption, "the bloody Doegs and the flattering Ziphites were to seek to insnare me with a proffer of his remission upon sinful compliances, I wad persevere, natheless, in lifting my testimony against Popery, Prelacy, Antinomianism, Erastianism, Lapsarianism, Sublapsarianism, and the sins and snares of the times—I wad cry as a woman in labour against the Black Indulgence, that has been a stumbling-block to professors—I wad uplift my voice as a powerful preacher."

"Hout tout, mither," cried Cuddie, interfering, and dragging her off forcibly, "dinna deave the gentlewoman wi' your testimony; ye hae preached eneugh for sax days; ye preached us out o' our canny free-house and gude kale-yard, and out o' this new city of refuge afore our hinder-end was weel hafted in it; and ye hae preached Mr Henry awa' to the prison; and ye hae preached twenty punds out o' the laird's pocket that he likes as ill to quit wi'; and sae ye may haud sae for ae wee while without preaching me up a ladder and down a tow; sae cum awa', cum awa'; the family hae had eneugh o' your testimony to mind it for ae while."

So saying, he dragged off Mause, the words, "Testimony—Covenant—malignants—indulgence," still thrilling upon her tongue, to make preparations for instantly renewing their travels in quest of an asylum.

"Ill-fa'ard, crazy, crack-brained gowk, that she is!" exclaimed the housekeeper, as she saw them depart, "to set up to be sae muckle better than ither folk, the auld besom, and to bring sae muckle distress on a douce quiet family! If it hadna been that I am mair than half a gentlewoman by my station, I wad hae tried my ten nails in the wizen'd hide o' her."

Chapter Nine

I am a son of Mars who have been in many wars,
And shew my cuts and scars wherever I come;
This here was for a wench, and that other in a trench,
When welcoming the French at the sound of the drum.
                                                        BURNS

"DON'T be too much cast down," said Serjeant Bothwell to his prisoner as they journeyed on towards the head-quarters; "you are a smart pretty lad, and well connected; the worst will happen will be strapping up for it, and that is many an honest fellow's lot. I tell you fairly your life's within the compass of the law, unless you make submission, and get off by a round fine upon your uncle's estate; he can well afford it."

"That vexes me more than the rest," said Henry. "He parts with his money with regret; and, as he had no concern whatever with my having given this person shelter for a night, I wish to Heaven, if I escape a capital punishment, that the penalty may be of a kind I could bear in my own person."

"Why, perhaps," said Bothwell, "they will propose to you to go into one of the Scottish regiments that are serving abroad. It's no bad line of service; if your friends are active, and there are any knocks going, you may soon get a commission."

"I am by no means sure," answered Morton, "that such a sentence is not the best thing that can happen to me."

"Why, then, you are no real whig after all," said the serjeant.

"I have hitherto meddled with no party in the state," said Henry, "but have remained quietly at home, but I have had serious thoughts of joining one of our foreign regiments."

"Have you?" replied Bothwell; "why, I honour you for it—I have served in the Scotch French guard myself many a long day—it's the place for learning discipline, d—n me. They never mind what you do when you are off duty; but miss the roll-call, and see how they will arrange you— D—n me, if old Captain Montgomery didn't make me mount guard upon the arsenal in my steel back and breast, plate-sleeves and head-piece, for six hours at once, under so burning a sun, that gad I was baked like a turtle in Port Royale. I swore never to miss answering to Francis Stuart again, though I should leave my hand of cards upon the drum-head—Ah! discipline is a capital thing."

"In other respects you liked the service?" said Henry.

"*Par excellence*," said Bothwell; "woman, wine, and wassail, all to be had for little but the asking; and if you find it in your conscience to let a fat priest think he has some chance to convert you, gad he'll help you to those comforts himself just to gain a little ground in your good affection. Where will you find a crop-eared whig parson will be so civil?"

"Why, nowhere, I agree with you," said Henry; "but what was your chief duty?"

"To guard the king's person," said Bothwell, "to look after the safety of Louis le Grand, my boy: and now and then to take a turn among the Huguenots (protestants that is.) And there we had fine scope; it brought my hand pretty well in for the service in this country. But, come, as you are to be a *buon camerado*, as the Spaniards say, I must put you in cash with some of your old uncle's broad-pieces. This is cutter's law; we must not see a pretty fellow want, if we have cash ourselves."

Thus speaking, he pulled out his purse, took out some of the contents, and offered them to Henry without counting them. Young Morton declined the favour; and, not judging it prudent to acquaint the serjeant, notwithstanding his apparent generosity, that he was actually in possession of some money, he assured him he would have no difficulty in getting a supply from his uncle.

"Well," said Bothwell, "in that case these yellow rascals must serve to ballast my purse a little longer. I always make it a rule never to quit the tavern (unless ordered on duty) while my purse is so weighty that I can chuck it over the signpost. When it is so light that the wind blows it back, then, boot and saddle,—we must fall on some way of replenishing.—But what tower is that before us, rising so high upon the steep bank, out of the woods that surround it on every side?"

"It is the tower of Tillietudlem," said one of the soldiers. "Old Lady Margaret Bellenden lives there, one of the best affected women in the country, and one that's a soldier's friend. When I was hurt by one of the d—d whig dogs that shot at me from behind a fauld-dyke, I lay a month there, and I would stand such another wound to be in as good quarters again."

"If that be the case," said Bothwell, "I will pay my respects to her as we pass, and request some refreshments for men and horses; I am as thirsty already as if I had drunk nothing at Milnewood. But it is a good thing in these times," he continued, addressing himself to Henry, "that the King's soldier cannot pass a house without getting a refreshment. In such houses as Tillie—what d'ye call it, you are served for love; in the houses of the avowed fanatics you help yourself by force; and among the moderate presbyterians and other suspicious persons, you are well treated from fear; so your thirst is always quenched on some terms or other."

"And you propose," said Henry anxiously, "to go upon that errand up to the tower yonder?"

"To be sure I do," answered Bothwell. "How should I be able to report favourably to my officers of the worthy lady's sound principles, unless I know the taste of her sack, for sack she will produce—that I take for granted; it is the favourite comforter of your old dowager of quality, as small claret is the potation of your country laird."

"Then, for Heaven's sake," said Henry, "if you are determined to go there, do not mention my name, or expose me to a family that I am acquainted with. Let me be muffled up for the time in one of your soldier's cloaks, and only mention me generally as a prisoner under your charge."

"With all my heart," said Bothwell; "I promised to use you civilly, and I scorn to break my word.—Here, Andrews, wrap a cloak round the prisoner, and do not mention his name, nor where we caught him, unless you would have a trot on a horse of wood."

They were at this moment at an arched gateway, battlemented and flanked with turrets, one whereof was totally ruinous, excepting the lower story, which served as a cow-house to the peasant, whose family inhabited the turret which remained entire. The gate had been broken down by Monk's soldiers during the civil war, and had never been replaced, therefore presented no obstacle to Bothwell and his party. The avenue, very steep and narrow, and causewayed with large round stones, ascended the side of the precipitous bank in an oblique and zigzag course, now shewing now hiding a view of the tower and its exterior bulwarks, which seemed to rise almost perpendicularly above their heads. The fragments of Gothic defences which it exhibited were upon such a scale of strength as induced Bothwell to exclaim, "It's well this place is in honest and loyal hands. Egad, if the enemy had it, a dozen of old whigamore wives with their distaffs might keep it against a troop of dragoons, at least if they had half the spunk of the old girl we left at Milnewood. Upon my life," he continued, as they came in front of the large double tower and its surrounding defences and flankers, "it is a superb place—founded, says the worn inscription over the gate—unless the remnant of my Latin has given me the slip— by Sir Ralph de Bellenden in 1350—a respectable antiquity. I must greet the old lady with due honour, though it should put me to the labour of recalling some of the compliments that I used to dabble in when I kept that sort of company."

As he thus communed with himself, the butler, who had recon- noitered the soldiers from an arrow-slit in the wall, announced to his lady, that a commanded party of dragoons waited at the gate with a prisoner under their charge.

"I am certain," said Gudyill, "and positive, that the sixth man is a prisoner, for his horse is led, and the two dragoons that are before have their carabines out of their budgets and rested upon their thighs. It was aye the way we guarded prisoners in the days of the great Marquis."

"King's soldiers?" said the lady; "probably in want of refreshment. Go, Gudyill, make them welcome, and let them be accommodated with what provisions and forage the Tower can afford.—And stay, tell my gentlewoman to bring my black scarf and manteau. I will go down myself to wait upon them; one cannot shew them too much respect in times when they are doing so much for royal authority. And d'ye hear, Gudyill, let Jenny Dennison slip on her pearlins to walk before my niece and me, and the three women to walk behind; and bid my niece attend me instantly."

Fully accoutred, and attended according to her directions, Lady Margaret now sailed out into the court-yard of her tower with great courtesy and dignity. Serjeant Bothwell saluted the grave and reverend lady of the manor with an assurance which had something of the light and careless address of the dissipated men of fashion in Charles the Second's time, and did not at all savour of the awkward or rude manners of a non-commissioned officer of dragoons. His language, as well as his manner, seemed also to be refined for the time and occasion; though the truth was, that, in the fluctuations of an adventurous and profligate life, Serjeant Bothwell had sometimes kept company much better suited to his ancestry than to his present situation of life. To the lady's request to know whether she could be of service to them, he answered, with a suitable bow, "That as they had to march some miles farther that night, they would be much accommodated by permission to rest their horses for an hour before continuing their journey."

"With the greatest pleasure," answered Lady Margaret, "and I trust that my people will see that neither horse nor men want suitable refreshment."

"We are well aware, madam," continued Bothwell, "that such has always been the reception, within the walls of Tillietudlem, of those who served the King."

"We have studied to discharge our duty faithfully and loyally on all occasions, sir," answered Lady Margaret, pleased with the compliment, "both to our monarchs and to their followers, particularly their faithful soldiers. It is not long ago, and it probably has not escaped the recollection of his sacred majesty, now on the throne, since he himself honoured my poor house with his presence, and breakfasted in a room in this castle, Mr Serjeant, which my waiting-gentlewomen shall shew you; we still call it the King's room."

Bothwell had by this time dismounted his party, and committed the horses to the charge of one file, and the prisoner to that of another, so that he himself was at liberty to continue the conversation which the lady had so condescendingly opened.

"Since the King, my master, had the honour to experience your hospitality, I cannot wonder that it is extended to those that serve him, and whose principal merit is doing it with fidelity. And yet I have a nearer relation to his majesty than this coarse red coat would seem to indicate."

"Indeed, sir? Probably," said Lady Margaret, "you have belonged to his household?"

"Not exactly, madam, to his household, but rather to his *house*, a connection through which I may claim kindred with most of the best families in Scotland, not, I believe, exclusive of that of Tillietudlem."

"Sir?" said the old lady, drawing herself up with dignity at hearing what she conceived an impertinent jest, "I do not understand you."

"It's but a foolish subject for one in my situation to talk of, madam," answered the trooper, "but you must have heard of the history and the misfortunes of my grandfather, Francis Stuart, to whom James I., his cousin-german, gave the title of Bothwell, as my comrades give me the same nickname. It was not in the long run more advantageous to him than it is to me."

"Indeed?" said Lady Margaret, with much sympathy and surprise; "I have indeed always understood that the grandson of the last Earl was in necessitous circumstances, but I should never have expected to see him so low in the service. With such connections what ill fortune could have reduced you"——

"Nothing much out of the ordinary course, I believe, madam," said Bothwell, interrupting and anticipating the question. "I have had my moments of good luck like my neighbours—have drunk my bottle with Rochester, thrown a merry main with Buckingham, and fought at Tangiers side by side with Sheffield. But my luck never lasted; I could not make useful friends out of my jolly companions—Perhaps I was not sufficiently aware," he continued with some bitterness, "how much the descendant of the Scottish Stuarts was honoured by being admitted into the convivialities of Wilmot and Villiers."

"But your Scottish friends, Mr Stuart, your relations here, so numerous and so powerful?"

"Why, ay, my lady, I believe some of them might have made me their gamekeeper, for I am a tolerable shot—some of them would have entertained me as their bravo, for I can use my sword well—and here and there was one, who, when better company was not to be had, would have made me his companion, since I can drink my three bottles of wine.—But I don't know how it is—between service and service among my kinsmen, I prefer that of my cousin Charles as the most creditable of them all, though the pay is but poor and the livery far from splendid."

"It is a shame, it is a burning scandal," said Lady Margaret. "Why do you not apply to his most sacred majesty? he cannot but be surprised to learn that a scion of his august family"——

"I beg your pardon, madam," interrupted the serjeant, "I am but a blunt soldier, and I trust you will excuse me when I say, his most sacred majesty is more busy with grafting scions of his own than with nourishing those which were planted by his grandfather's grandfather."

"Well, Mr Stuart," said Lady Margaret, "one thing you must promise me—remain at Tillietudlem to-night; to-morrow I expect your commanding-officer, the gallant Claverhouse, to whom king and country are so much obliged for his exertions against those who would turn the world upside down. I will speak to him on the subject of your speedy promotion, and I am certain he feels too much, both what is due to the blood which is in your veins, and to the request of a lady so highly distinguished as myself by his most sacred majesty, not to make better provision for you than you have yet received."

"I am much obliged to your ladyship, and I certainly will remain here with my prisoner, since you request it, especially as it will be the earliest way of presenting him to Colonel Grahame, and obtaining his ultimate orders about the young spark."

"Who is your prisoner, pray you?" said Lady Margaret.

"A young fellow of rather the better class in this neighbourhood, who has been so incautious as to give countenance to one of the murderers of the primate, and to facilitate the dog's escape."

"O, fie upon him!" said Lady Margaret, "I am but too apt to forgive the injuries I have received at the hands of these rogues, though some of them, Mr Stuart, are of a kind not like to be forgotten; but those who could abet the perpetrators of so cruel and deliberate a homicide on a single man, an old man, and a man of the Archbishop's sacred profession—O fie upon him! If you wish to make him secure, with little trouble to your people, I will cause Harrison, or Gudyill, look for the keys of our pit, or principal dungeon. It has not been opened since the week after the victory of Kilsythe, when my poor Sir Arthur Bellenden put twenty whigs into it; but it is not more than two stories beneath ground, so it cannot be unwholesome, especially as I believe there is somewhere an opening to the outer air."

"I pray your pardon, madam," answered the serjeant; "I dare say the dungeon is a most admirable dungeon, but I have promised to be civil to the lad, and I will take care he is watched so as to render escape impossible. I'll set those to look after him shall keep him as fast as if his legs were in the boots, or his fingers in the thumbkins."

"Well, Mr Stuart," rejoined the lady, "you best know your own duty. I heartily wish you good evening, and commit you to the charge of my steward, Harrison. I would ask you to keep us company, but a— a—a—"

"O madam, it requires no apology; I am sensible the red rug coat of King Charles II. does and ought to annihilate the privileges of the red blood of King James V."

"Not with me, I do assure you, Mr Stuart; you do me injustice if you think so. I will speak to your officer to-morrow; you shall soon find yourself in a rank where there shall need no anomalies to be reconciled."

"I believe, madam," said Bothwell, "your goodness will find itself deceived; but I am obliged to you for your intention, and, at all events, I will have a merry night with Mr Harrison."

Lady Margaret took a ceremonious leave, with all the respect which she owed to royal blood, even when flowing in the veins of a serjeant of the life-guards, again assuring Mr Stuart, that whatever was in the Tower of Tillietudlem was heartily at his service and that of his attendants.

Serjeant Bothwell did not fail to take the lady at her word, and readily forgot the height from which his family had descended, in a joyous carousal, during which Mr Harrison exerted himself to produce the best wine in the cellar, and to excite his guest to be merry by that seducing example, which, in matters of conviviality, goes farther than precept. Old Gudyill associated himself with a party so much to his taste, pretty much as Davy in the Second Part of Henry the Fourth mingles in the revels of his master, Justice Shallow. Now he ran down to the cellar at the risk of breaking his neck, to ransack some private catacomb, known, as he boasted, only to himself, and which never either had, or should, during his superintendance, render forth a bottle of its contents to any one but a real king's friend.

"When the Duke dined here," said the butler, seating himself at a distance from the table, being somewhat overawed by Bothwell's genealogy, but yet hitching his seat half a yard nearer at every clause of his speech, "my leddy was importunate to have a bottle of that Burgundy," (here he advanced his seat a little)—"but I dinna ken how it was, Mr Stuart, I misdoubted him. I jaloused him, sir, no to be the friend to government he pretends; the family are not to lippen to. That auld Duke James lost his heart before he lost his head; and the Worcester man was but wersh parritch, neither gude to fry, boil, nor sup cauld." (With this pithy observation he completed his first parallel, and commenced a zigzag after the manner of an experienced engineer, in order to continue his approaches to the table.) "Sae, sirs, the faster my leddy cried 'Burgundy to his Grace—the auld Burgundy —the choice Burgundy—the Burgundy that cam ower in the thirty-nine'—the mair did I say to mysel, de'il a drap gangs down his hause unless I was mair sensible o' his principles; sack and claret may serve him. Na, na, gentlemen, as lang as I hae the trust o' butler in this house o' Tillietudlem, I'll tak it upon me to see that nae disloyal or doubtfu' person is the better o' our binns. But when I can find a true friend to the king and his cause, and to a moderate episcopacy; when I find a man, as I say, that will stand by church and crown as I did mysel in my master's life, and all through Montrose's time, I think there is nae-thing in the cellar ower gude to be spared on him."

By this time he had completed a lodgment in the body of the place, or, in other words, advanced his seat close to the table.

"And now, Mr Francis Stuart of Bothwell, I have the honour to drink your gude health, and a commission t'ye, and much luck may ye have in raking this country clear o' whigs and round-heads, fanatics and Covenanters."

Bothwell, who, it may well be believed, had long ceased to be very scrupulous in point of society, which he regulated more by his convenience and station in life than his ancestry, readily answered the butler's pledge, acknowledging, at the same time, the excellence of the wine; and Mr Gudyill, thus adopted a regular member of the company, continued to furnish them with the means of mirth until an early hour in the next morning.

Chapter Ten

Did I but purpose to embark with thee
On the smooth surface of a summer sea,
And would forsake the skiff and make the shore
When the winds whistle and the tempests roar?
                              PRIOR

WHILE Lady Margaret held, with the high-descended serjeant of dragoons, the conference which we have detailed in the preceding pages, her grand-daughter, partaking in a less degree her ladyship's enthusiasm for all who descended of the blood-royal, did not honour Serjeant Bothwell with more attention than by a single glance, which showed her a tall powerful person, and a set of hardy weather-beaten features, to which pride and habitual dissipation had given an air where discontent mingled with the reckless gaiety of desperation. The other soldiers offered still less to detach her consideration; but from the prisoner, muffled and disguised as he was, she found it impossible to withdraw her eyes. Yet she blamed herself for indulging a curiosity which seemed obviously to give pain to him who was its object.

"I wish," she said to Jenny Dennison, who was the immediate attendant on her person, "I wish we knew who that poor fellow is."

"I was just thinking sae mysel, Miss Edith; but it canna be Cuddie Headrigg, because he's taller and no sae stout."

"Yet," continued Miss Bellenden, "it may be some poor neighbour for whom we might have cause to interest ourselves."

"I can sune learn wha he is, if the soldiers were anes settled and at leisure, for I ken ane o' them very weel—the best-looked and the youngest o' them."

"I think you know all the idle young fellows about the country," answered her mistress.

"Na, Miss Edith, I am no sae free o' my acquaintance as a' that. To be sure, ane canna help kenning the folk by head-mark that they see aye glowring and looking at them at kirk and market; but I ken few young lads to speak to unless it be them o' the family, and the three Steinsons, and Tam Rand, and the young miller, and the five Howiesons in Nethersheils, and lang Tam Gilry, and"——

"Pray cut short a list of exceptions that threatens to be a long one, and tell me how you came to know the young soldier," said Miss Bellenden.

"Lord, Miss Edith, it's Tam Halliday, Trooper Tam, as they ca' him, that was wounded by the hill-folk at the conventicle at Outer-side-Muir, and lay here while he was under cure. I can ask him ony thing, and Tam will not refuse to answer me, I'll be caution for him."

"Try, then," said Miss Edith, "if you can find an opportunity to ask him the name of his prisoner, and come to my room and tell me what he says."

Jenny Dennison proceeded on her errand, but soon returned with such a face of surprise and dismay as evinced a deep interest in the fate of the prisoner.

"What is the matter?" said Edith, anxiously; "does it prove to be Cuddie, after all, poor fellow?"

"Cuddie, Miss Edith? Na! na! it's nae Cuddie," blubbered out the faithful fille-de-chambre, sensible of the pain which her news were about to inflict on her young mistress. "O dear, Miss Edith, it's young Milnewood himsel!"

"Young Milnewood?" exclaimed Edith, aghast in her turn; "it is impossible—totally impossible!—His uncle attends the clergyman indulged by law, and has no connection whatever with the refractory people; and he himself has never interfered in this unhappy dissention; he must be totally innocent, unless he has been standing up for some invaded right."

"O, my dear Miss Edith," said her attendant, "these are not days to ask what's right or what's wrang; if he were as innocent as the newborn infant, they would find some way of making him guilty, if they liked; but Tam Halliday says it will touch his life, for he has been resetting ane o' the Fife gentlemen that killed the auld carle of an Archbishop."

"His life!" exclaimed Edith, starting hastily up and speaking with a hasty and tremulous accent,—"they cannot—they shall not—I will speak with him—they shall not hurt him!"

"O, my dear young lady, think on your grandmother—think on the danger—and the difficulty," added Jenny; "for he's kept under close confinement till Claverhouse comes up in the morning, and if he does na gie him full satisfaction, Tam Halliday says there will be brief wark wi' him—Kneel down—mak ready—present—fire—just as they did wi' auld deaf John Macbriar, that never heard a question they pat till him, and lost his life for lack o' hearing."

"Jenny," said the young lady, "if he should die, I will die with him; this is no time to talk of danger or difficulty—I will put on a plaid, and slip down with you to the place where they have kept him—I will throw myself at the feet of the centinel, and entreat him, as he has a soul to be saved"——

"Eh guide us!" interrupted the maid, "our young leddy at the feet o' Trooper Tam, and speaking to him about his soul, when the poor chield hardly kens if he has ane or no, unless that he whiles swears by it —that will never do; but what maun be maun be, and I'll never desert a true-love cause—An' sae, if ye maun see young Milnewood, though I ken nae gude it will do, but to make baith your hearts the sairer, I'll e'en tak the risk o't, and try to manage Tam Halliday; but ye maun let me hae my ain gate and no speak ae word—he's keeping guard on Milnewood in the easter round of the tower."

"Go, go, fetch me a plaid," said Edith. "Let me but see him, and I will find some remedy for his danger—Haste ye, Jenny, as ever you hope to have a good turn at my hands."

Jenny hastened, and soon returned with a plaid, in which Edith muffled herself so as completely to screen her face, and in part to disguise her person. This was a mode of arranging the plaid very common among the ladies of that century, and the earlier part of the succeeding one; so much so, indeed, that the venerable sages of the Kirk, conceiving that the mode gave tempting facilities for intrigue, directed more than one act of Assembly against this use of the mantle. But fashion, as usual, proved too strong for authority, and while plaids continued to be worn, women of all ranks occasionally employed them as a sort of muffler or veil. Her face and figure thus concealed, Edith, holding by her attendant's arm, hastened with trembling steps to the place of Morton's confinement.

This was a small study, or closet, in one of the turrets, opening from a gallery in which the centinel was pacing to and fro; for Serjeant Bothwell, scrupulous in observing his word, and perhaps touched with some compassion for the prisoner's youth and genteel demeanour, had waived the indignity of putting his guard into the same apartment with him. Halliday, therefore, with his carabine on his arm, walked up and down the gallery, occasionally solacing himself with a draught of ale, a huge flagon of which stood upon a table at one end of the apartment, and at other times humming the lively Scottish air,

> "Between Saint Johnstone and Bonny Dundee,
> I'll gar ye be fain to follow me"——

Jenny Dennison cautioned her mistress once more to let her take her own way.

"I can manage the trooper weel eneugh," she said, "for as rough as he is—I ken their nature weel; but ye maunna say a single word."

She accordingly opened the door of the gallery just as the centinel had turned his back from it, and, taking up the tune which he hummed, she sung in a coquettish tone of rustic raillery,

> "If I were to follow a poor sodger lad,
> My friends wad be angry, my minnie be mad;
> A laird, or a lord, they were fitter for me,
> Sae I'll never be fain to follow thee."——

"A fair challenge, by Jove," cried the centinel, turning round, "and from two at once I think, but it's not easy to bang the soldier with his bandeliers;" then taking up the song where the damsel had stopt,

> "To follow me ye weel may be glad,
> A share of my supper, a share of my bed,
> To the sound of the drum to range fearless and free,
> I'll gar ye be fain to follow me."——

"Come, my pretty nurse, and kiss me for my song."

"I should not have thought of that, Mr Halliday," answered Jenny, with a look and tone expressing just the necessary degree of contempt at the proposal, "and, I'se assure ye, ye'll hae but little o' my company unless ye shew gentler havings—It was na to hear that sort o' nonsense that brought me here wi' my friend, and ye should think shame o' yoursel."

"Umph! and what sort of nonsense did bring you here then, Mrs Dennison?"

"My kinswoman has some particular business with your prisoner, young Mr Harry Morton, and I am come wi' her to speak till him."

"The devil you are," answered the centinel; "and pray, Mrs Dennison, how do your kinswoman and you propose to get in? You are rather too plump to whisk through a key-hole, and opening the door is a thing not to be spoke of."

"It's no a thing to be spoken o', but a thing to be dune," replied the persevering damsel.

"We'll see about that, my bonny Jenny," and the soldier resumed his march, humming as he walked to and fro along the gallery,

> "Keek into the draw-well,
>   Janet, Janet,
> There ye'll see your bonny sell,
>   My joe Janet."

"So ye're no thinking to let us in, Mr Halliday? Weel, weel—gude e'en to you—ye hae seen the last o' me, and o' this bonny-dye too," said Jenny, holding between her finger and thumb a silver dollar.

"Give him gold, give him gold," whispered the agitated young lady.

"Silver's e'en ower gude for the like o' him, that disna care for the blink o' a bonny lassie's e'e—and what's waur, he wad think there was something mair in't than a kinswoman o' mine. My sarty! siller's no sae plenty wi' us, let alane gowd." Having addressed this advice aside to her mistress, she raised her voice, and said, "My cousin winna stay ony langer, Mr Halliday; sae, if ye please, gude e'en t'ye."

"Halt a bit, halt a bit," said the trooper; "rein up and parley, Jenny. If I let your kinswoman in to speak to my prisoner, you must stay here and keep me company till she come out again, and then we'll be all well pleased you know."

"The fiend be in my feet then," said Jenny; "d'ye think my kinswoman and I are ganging to lose our gude name wi' cracking clavers wi' the like o' you or your prisoner either, without somebody by to see fair play? Hegh, hegh, sirs, to see sic a difference between folks promises and performance! Ye were aye willing to slight poor Cuddie; but an' I had asked him to oblige me in a thing, though it had been to cost his hanging, he wadna hae stude twice about it."

"D—n Cuddie," retorted the dragoon, "he'll be hanged in good earnest, I hope. I saw him to-day at Milnewood with his old puritanical b—— of a mother, and if I had thought I was to have him cast in my dish, I would have brought him up at my horse's tail—we had law enough to bear us out."

"Very weel, very weel—See if Cuddie winna hae a lang shot at you ane o' thae days, if ye gar him tak the muir wi' sae mony honest folk. He can hit a mark brawly; he was third at the popinjay; and he's as true of his promise as of e'e and hand, though he disna mak sic a phrase about it as some acquaintance o' yours—But it's a' ane to me— Come, cousin, we'll awa'."

"Stay, Jenny; d—n me, if I hang fire more than another when I have said a thing," said the soldier in a hesitating tone. "Where is the serjeant?"

"Drinking and driving ower," quoth Jenny, "wi' the steward and John Gudyill."

"So, so—he's safe enough—and where are my comrades?" said the centinel.

"Birling the brown bowl wi' the fowler and the falconer, and some o' the serving folk."

"Have they plenty of ale?"

"Sax gallons, as gude as e'er was masked," said the maid.

"Well, then, my pretty Jenny," said the relenting centinel, "they are fast till the hour of relieving guard, and perhaps something later; and so, if you will promise to come alone the next time"——

"Maybe I will, and maybe I winna," said Jenny; "but if ye get the dollar, ye'll like that just as weel."

"I'll be d—n'd if I do," said Halliday, taking the money however; "but it's always something for my risk; for, if Claverhouse hears what I have done, he'll build me a horse as high as the Tower of Tillietudlem. But every one in the regiment takes what they can come by; I am sure Bothwell and his blood-royal shews us a good example. And if I were trusting to you, you little jilting devil, I should lose both pains and powder; whereas this fellow," looking at the piece, "will be good as far as he goes. But come—there's the door open for you; do not stay groaning and praying with the young whig now, but be ready, when I call at the door, to start as if they were sounding, 'Horse and away.'"

So speaking, Halliday unlocked the door of the closet, admitted Jenny and her pretended kinswoman, locked it behind them, and hastily reassumed the indifferent measured step and the time-killing whistle of a centinel upon his regular duty.

The door, which slowly opened, discovered Morton with both arms reclined upon a table, and his head resting upon them in a posture of deep dejection. He raised his face as the door opened, and, perceiving the female figures which it admitted, jumped up in great surprise. Edith, as if modesty had quelled the courage which despair had bestowed, stood about a yard from the door without having either the power to speak or to advance. All the plans of aid, relief, or comfort, which she had proposed to lay before her lover, seemed at once to have vanished from her recollection, and left only a painful chaos of ideas, with which was mingled a fear that she had degraded herself in the eyes of her lover by a step which might appear precipitate and unfeminine. She hung motionless and almost powerless upon the arm of her attendant, who in vain endeavoured to reassure and inspire her with courage, by whispering, "We are in now, madam, and we maun mak the best o' our time; for, doubtless, the corporal or the serjeant will gang the rounds, and it wad be a pity to hae the poor lad Halliday punished for his civility."

Morton, in the mean time, was timidly advancing, suspecting the truth; for what other female in the house, excepting Edith herself, was like to take an interest in his misfortunes? and yet afraid, owing to the doubtful twilight and the muffled dress, of making some mistake which might be prejudicial to the object of his affections. Jenny, whose ready wit and forward manners well qualified her for such an office, hastened to break the ice.

"Mr Morton, Miss Edith's very sorry for your present situation, and"——

It was needless to say more; he was at her side, almost at her feet, pressing her unresisting hands, and loading her with a confusion of thanks and gratitude which would be hardly intelligible from the mere broken words, unless we could describe the tone, the gesture, the impassioned and hurried indications of deep and tumultuous feeling with which they were accompanied.

For two or three minutes, Edith stood as motionless as the statue of a saint which receives the adoration of a worshipper; and when she recovered herself sufficiently to withdraw her hands from Henry's grasp, she could at first only faintly articulate, "I have taken a strange step, Mr Morton—a step," she continued with more coherence, as her ideas arranged themselves in consequence of a strong effort, "that perhaps may expose me to censure even in your eyes—But I have long permitted you to use the language of friendship—perhaps I might say more—too long to leave you when the world seems to have left you. How, or why, is this imprisonment? what can be done? can my uncle who thinks so highly of you—can your own kinsman, Milnewood, be of no use? are there no means? and what is likely to be the event?"

"Be what it will," answered Henry, contriving to make himself master of the hand that had escaped from him, but which was now again abandoned to his clasp, "be what it will it is to me from this moment the most welcome incident of a weary life. To you, dearest

Edith—forgive me, I should have said Miss Bellenden, but misfortune claims strange privileges—to you I have owed the few happy moments which have gilded a gloomy existence, and if I am now to lay it down, the recollection of this honour will be my happiness in the last hour of suffering."

"But is it even thus, Mr Morton? Have you, who use to mix so little in the unhappy feuds, become so suddenly and deeply implicated, that nothing short of——"

She paused, unable to bring out the word which should have come next.

"Nothing short of my life you would say?" replied Morton, in a calm, but melancholy tone; "I believe that will be entirely in the bosoms of my judges. My guards spoke of a possibility of exchanging the penalty for entry into foreign service. I thought that I could have embraced the alternative; and yet, Miss Bellenden, since I have seen you once more, I feel that exile would be more galling than death."

"And is it then true," said Edith, "that you have been so desperately rash as to entertain communication with any of those cruel wretches who assassinated the primate?"

"I knew not even that such a crime had been committed," replied Morton, "when I gave unhappily a night's lodging and concealment to one of those rash men, the ancient friend and comrade of my father. But my ignorance will avail me little; for who, Edith, save you, will believe it? And, what is worse, I am at least uncertain whether, even if I had known the crime, I could have brought my mind, under all the circumstances, to refuse a temporary refuge to the fugitive."

"And by whom," said Edith, anxiously, "or under what authority will the investigation of your conduct take place?"

"Under that of Colonel Grahame of Claverhouse, I am given to understand," said Morton; "one of the military commission, to whom it has pleased our King, our Privy Council, and our Parliament that used to be more tenacious of our liberties, to commit the sole charge of our goods and of our lives."

"To Claverhouse?" said Edith, faintly; "merciful Heaven, you are lost ere you are tried! He wrote to my grandmother that he was to be here to-morrow morning, on his road to the head of the county, where some desperate men are said to have assembled for the purpose of making a stand, animated by the presence of two or three of the actors in the primate's murder. His expressions made me shudder, even when I could not guess that—that—a friend"——

"Do not be too much alarmed on my account, my dearest Edith," said Henry, as he supported her in his arms; "Claverhouse, though stern and relentless, is, by all accounts, brave, fair, and honourable. I am a soldier's son, and will plead my cause like a soldier. He will perhaps listen more favourably to a blunt and unvarnished defence than a tricking and time-serving judge might do. And, indeed, in a time when justice is, in all its branches, so completely corrupted, I would rather lose my life by open military violence than be conjured out of it by the *hocus-pocus* of some arbitrary lawyer, who lends the knowledge he has of the statutes made for our protection, to wrest them to our destruction."

"You are lost—you are lost, if you are to plead your cause with Claverhouse!" sighed Edith; "root and branch-work was the mildest of his expressions. The unhappy primate was his intimate friend and early patron. 'No excuse, no subterfuge,' said his letter, 'shall save either those connected with the deed, or such as have given them countenance and shelter, from the ample and bitter penalty of the law, until I shall have taken as many lives in vengeance of this atrocious murder, as the old man had grey hairs upon his venerable head.' There is neither ruth nor favour to be found with him."

Jenny Dennison, who had hitherto remained silent, now ventured, in the extremity of distress, which the lovers felt, but for which they were unable to devise a remedy, to offer her own advice.

"Wi' your leddyship's pardon, Miss Edith, and young Milnewood's, we maunna waste time. Let Milnewood take my plaid and gown; I'll slip it aff in the dark corner, if he'll promise no to look about, and he may walk past Tam Halliday, who is half blind with his ale, and I can tell him a canny way to get out o' the Tower, and your leddyship will gang quietly to your ain room, and I'll row mysel in his grey cloak, and pit on his hat, and play the prisoner till the coast's clear, and then I'll cry in Tam Halliday and gar him let me out."

"Let you out?" said Morton; "they'll make your life answer it."

"Ne'er a bit," replied Jenny; "Tam daurna tell he let ony body in, for his ain sake; and I'll gar him find some other gate to account for the escape."

"Will ye, by G——?" said the centinel, suddenly opening the door of the apartment; "if I am half blind, I am not deaf, and you should not plan an escape quite so loud, if you expect to go through with it. Come, come, Mrs Janet—march, troop—quick time—trot, d——n me!—And you, madam kinswoman,—I won't ask you your real name, though you were going to play me so rascally a trick,—but I must make a clear garrison; so beat a retreat, unless you would have me turn out the guard."

"I hope," said Morton, very anxiously, "you will not mention this circumstance, my good friend, and trust to my honour to acknowledge your civility in keeping the secret. If you overheard our conversation, you must have observed that we did not accept of, or enter into, the hasty proposal made by this good-natured girl."

"Oh, devilish good-natured, to be sure," said Halliday. "As for the rest, I guess how it is, and I scorn to bear malice, or to tell tales, as much as another; but no thanks to that little jilting devil, Jenny Dennison, who deserves a tight skelping for trying to lead an honest lad into a scrape, just because he was so silly as to like her good for little chit face."

Jenny had no better means of justification than the last apology to which her sex trust, and usually not in vain; she pressed her handkerchief to her face, sobbed with great vehemence, and either wept, or managed, as Halliday might have said, to go through the motions wonderfully well.

"And now," continued the soldier, somewhat mollified, "if you have any thing to say, say it in two minutes, and let me see your backs turned; for if Bothwell take it into his drunken head to make the rounds a half hour too soon, it will be a black business to us all."

"Farewell, Edith," whispered Morton, assuming a firmness he was far from possessing; "do not remain here—leave me to my fate—it cannot be beyond endurance since you are interested in it.—Good night, good night!—Do not remain here till you are discovered."——

Thus saying, he resigned her to her attendant, by whom she was partly led and partly supported out of the apartment.

"Every one has his taste, to be sure," said Halliday; "but d—n me if I would have vexed so sweet a girl as that is for all the whigs that ever swore the Covenant."

When Edith had regained her apartment, she gave way to a burst of grief which alarmed Jenny Dennison, who hastened to administer such scraps of consolation as occurred to her.

"Dinna vex yoursel sae muckle, Miss Edith," said that faithful attendant; "wha kens what may happen to help young Milnewood? He's a brave lad, and a bonny, and a gentleman of a good house, and they winna string the like o' him up as they do the puir whig bodies that they catch in the muirs, like straps o' onions; maybe his uncle will buy him aff, or maybe your ain granduncle Major Bellenden will speak a gude word for him—he's weel acquent wi' a' the red-coat gentlemen."

"You are right, Jenny! you are right," said Edith, recovering herself from the stupor into which she had sunk; "this is no time for despair, but for exertion. You must find some one to ride this very night to my uncle's with a letter."

"To Charnwood, madam? It's unco late, and it's sax miles an' a bittock doun the water; I doubt if we can find man an' horse the night,

mair specially as they hae mounted a centinel before the gate. Puir
Cuddie! he's gane, puir fallow, that wad hae dune aught in the warld I
bade him, and ne'er asked a reason—an' I've had nae time to draw up
wi' the new pleugh-lad yet; forby that, they say he's ganging to be
married with Meg Murdieson, ill-fa'ard cuttie as she is."

"You *must* find some one to go, Jenny; life and death depend upon
it."

"I wad gang mysel, my leddy, for I could creep out at the window o'
the pantry, and speel down by the auld yew-tree weel eneugh—I hae
played that trick ere now. But the road's unco wild, and sae mony red-
coats about, forby the whigs, that are no muckle better, (the young
lads o' them) if they meet a fraim body their lane in the muirs. I wadna
stand for the walk—I can walk ten miles by moonlight weel eneugh."

"Is there no one you can think of, that, for money or favour, would
serve me so far?" said Edith, in great anxiety.

"I dinna ken," said Jenny, after a moment's consideration, "unless
it be Guse Gibbie—and he'll maybe no ken the way—though it's no
sae difficult to hit, if he keep the horse-road, and mind the turn at the
Cappercleuch, and dinna drown himsel in Whomlekirn-pule, or fa'
ower the scaur at the De'il's Loaning, or miss ony o' the kittle staps at
the Pass o' Walkwary, or be carried to the hills by the whigs, or be ta'en
to the tolbooth by the red-coats."

"All ventures must be run," said Edith, cutting short the list of
chances against Goose Gibbie's safe arrival at the end of his pilgrimage; "all risks must be run, unless you can find a better messenger.—
Go, bid the boy get ready, and get him out of the Tower as secretly as
you can. If he meets any one, let him say he is carrying a letter to Major
Bellenden of Charnwood, but without mentioning any names."

"I understand, madam," said Jenny Dennison; "I warrant the callant will do weel aneugh, and Tib the hen-wife will tak care o' the
geese for a word o' my mouth; and I'll tell Gibbie your leddyship will
mak his peace wi' Lady Margaret, and will gie him a dollar."

"Two, if he does his errand well," said Edith.

Jenny departed to rouse Goose Gibbie out of the slumbers to which
he was usually consigned at sun-down, or shortly after, he keeping the
hours of the birds under his charge. During her absence, Edith took
her writing materials, and prepared against her return the following
letter, superscribed,

"For the hands of Major Bellenden of Charnwood, my much-
honoured uncle, These:

"My dear Uncle—These will serve to inform that I am desirous to
know how your gout is, as we did not see you at the wappin-schaw,

which made both my grandmother and myself very uneasy. And if it will permit you to travel, we will be happy to see you at our poor house to-morrow at the hour of breakfast, as Colonel Grahame of Claver-house is to pass this way on his march, and we would willingly have your assistance to receive and entertain a military man of such distinction, who, probably, will not be much delighted with the company of women. Also, my dear uncle, I pray you to let Mrs Carfort, your housekeeper, send me my double-trimmed paduasoy with the hanging sleeves, which she will find in the third drawer of the walnut press in the green room, which you are so kind as to call mine. Also, my dear uncle, I pray you to send me the second volume of the Grand Cyrus, as I have only read as far as the imprisonment of Philidaspes upon the seven hundredth and thirty-third page. But, above all, I entreat you to come to us to-morrow before eight of the clock, which, as your pacing nag is so good, you may well do without rising before your usual hour. So, praying to God to preserve your health, I rest your dutiful and loving niece,

"EDITH BELLENDEN

"*Postscriptum*. A party of soldiers have last night brought your friend, young Mr Henry Morton of Milnewood, hither as a prisoner. I conclude you will be sorry for the young gentleman, and, therefore, let you know this, in case you may think of speaking to Colonel Grahame in his behalf. I have not mentioned his name to my grandmother, knowing her prejudice to the family."

This epistle being duly sealed and delivered to Jenny, that faithful confidante hastened to put the same in the charge of Goose Gibbie, whom she found in readiness to start from the castle. She then gave him various instructions touching the road which she apprehended he was likely to mistake, not having travelled it above five or six times, and possessing only the same slender proportion of memory as of judgment. Lastly, she smuggled him out of the garrison through the pantry window into the branchy yew-tree which grew close beside it, and had the satisfaction to see him reach the bottom in safety, and take the right turn at the commencement of his journey. She then returned to persuade her young mistress to go to bed, and to lull her to rest, if possible, with assurances of Gibbie's success in his embassy, only qualified by a passing regret that the trusty Cuddie, with whom the commission might have been more safely reposed, was no longer within reach of serving her.

More fortunate as a messenger than as a cavalier, it was Gibbie's good hap, rather than his good management, which, after he had gone astray not oftener than nine times, and given his garments a taste of the variation of each bog, brook, and slough, between Tillietudlem and Charnwood, placed him about day-break before the gate of Major Bellenden's mansion, having completed a walk of ten miles (for the bittock, as usual, amounted to four) in little more than the same number of hours.

Chapter Eleven

At last comes the troop, by the word of command
Drawn up in our court, when the captain cries, Stand.
SWIFT

MAJOR BELLENDEN'S ancient valet, Gideon Pike, as he adjusted his master's clothes by his bed-side, preparatory to the worthy veteran's toilet, acquainted him, as an apology for disturbing him an hour earlier than his usual time of rising, that there was an express from Tillietudlem.

"From Tillietudlem?" said the old gentleman, rising hastily in his bed, and sitting bolt upright. "Open the shutters, Pike—I hope my sister-in-law is well—furl up the bed-curtain.—What have we all here?" (glancing at Edith's note.) "The gout?—why, she knows I have not had a fit since Candlemas.—The wappin-schaw? I told her a month since I was not to be there.—Paduasoy and hanging sleeves? why, hang the gipsey herself!—Grand Cyrus and Philipdastus—Philip Devil—is the wench gone crazy all at once? was it worth while to send an express and wake me at five in the morning for all this trash?—But what says her postscriptum? Mercy on us!" he exclaimed on perusing it,—"Pike, Pike, saddle old Kilsythe instantly, and another horse for yourself."

"I hope nae ill news frae the Tower, sir?" said Pike, astonished at his master's sudden emotion.

"Yes—no—yes—that is, I must meet Claverhouse there on some express business; so boot and saddle, Pike, as fast as you can.—O, Lord! what times are these!—the poor lad—my old cronie's son!—and the silly wench sticks it into her postscriptum, as she calls it, at the tail of all this trumpery about old gowns and new romances!"

In a few minutes the good old officer was fully equipped; and, having mounted upon his arm-gaunt charger as soberly as Mark Antony himself could have done, he paced forth his way to the Tower of Tillietudlem.

On the road he formed the prudent resolution to say nothing to the old lady, (whose dislike to presbyterians of all kinds he knew to be inveterate,) of the quality and rank of the prisoner detained within her walls, but to try his own influence with Claverhouse to obtain Morton's liberation.

"Being so loyal as he is, he must do something for so old a cavalier as I am," thought the veteran to himself, "and if he is so good a soldier as the world speaks of, why, he will be glad to serve an old soldier's son. I never knew a real soldier that was not a frank-hearted, honest fellow; and I think the execution of the laws (though it's a pity they find it necessary to make them so severe) may be a thousand times better entrusted with them than with peddling lawyers and thick-skulled country gentlemen."

Such were the ruminations of Major Miles Bellenden, which terminated by John Gudyill (not more than one-half drunk) taking hold of his bridle, and assisting him to dismount in the rough paved court of the Tower of Tillietudlem.

"Why, John," said the veteran, "what devil of a discipline is this you have been keeping? You have been reading Geneva print this morning already."

"I have been reading the Litany," said John, shaking his head with a look of drunken gravity, and having only caught one word of the major's address to him; "life is short, sir; we are flowers of the field, sir,—hiccup—and lilies of the valley."

"Flowers and lilies? why, man, such carles as thou and I can hardly be called old hemlocks, decayed nettles, or withered rag-weed; but I suppose you think that we are still worth watering."

"I am an old soldier, sir, I thank Heaven"—hiccup—

"An old skinker you mean, John. But, come, never mind, shew me the way to your mistress, old lad."

John Gudyill led the way to the stone-hall, where Lady Margaret was fidgetting about, superintending, arranging, and reforming the preparations made for the reception of the celebrated Claverhouse, whom one party honoured and extolled as a hero, and another execrated as a blood-thirsty oppressor.

"Did I not tell you," said Lady Margaret to her principal female attendant—"did I not tell you, Mysie, that it was my especial pleasure on this occasion to have every thing in the precise order wherein it was upon that famous morning when his most sacred majesty partook of his disjune at Tillietudlem?"

"Doubtless, such were your leddyship's commands, and to the best of my remembrance"——was Mysie answering, when her ladyship broke in with, "Then wherefore is the venison pasty placed on the left side of the throne, and the stoup of claret upon the right, when ye may right weel remember, Mysie, that his most sacred majesty with his ain hand shifted the pasty to the same side with the flagon, and said they were too good friends to be parted?"

"I mind that weel, madam," said Mysie; "and if I had forgot, I have heard your leddyship often speak about that grand morning sin' syne; but I thought every thing was to be placed just as it was when his majesty, God bless him, came into this room, looking mair like an angel than a man, if he hadna been sae black-a-vised."

"Then ye thought nonsense, Mysie; for in whatever way his most sacred majesty ordered the position of the trenchers and flagons, that, as weel as his royal pleasure in greater matters, should be a law to his subjects, and shall ever be to those of the house of Tillietudlem."

"Weel, madam," said Mysie, making the alteration required, "it's easy mending the error; but if every thing is to be just as his majesty left it, there should be an unco hole in the venison pasty."

At this moment the door opened.

"Who is that, John Gudyill?" exclaimed the old lady. "I can speak to no one just now.—Is't you, my dear brother?" she continued, in some surprise, as the Major entered; "this is a right early visit."

"Not more early than welcome, I hope," replied Major Bellenden, as he saluted the widow of his deceased brother; "but I heard by a note which Edith sent to Charnwood about some of her equipage and books, that you were to have Claver'se here this morning, so I thought, like an old firelock as I am, that I should like to have a chat with this rising soldier. I caused Pike saddle Kilsythe, and here we both are."

"And most kindly welcome you are," said the old lady; "it is just what I should have prayed of you, if I had thought there was time. You see I am busy in preparation. All is to be in the same order as when"——

"The king breakfasted at Tillietudlem," said the Major, who, like all Lady Margaret's friends, dreaded the commencement of that narrative, and was desirous to cut it short. "I remember it well; you know I was waiting on his majesty."

"You were, brother," said Lady Margaret; "and perhaps you can help me to remember the order of the entertainment."

"Nay, good sooth," said the Major, "the damnable dinner that Noll gave us at Worcester a few days afterwards, drove all your good cheer out of my memory.—But how's this?—you have even the great Turkey-leather elbow-chair, with the tapestry cushions, placed in state."

"The throne, brother, if you please," said Lady Margaret, gravely.

"Well, the throne be it, then," continued the Major. "Is that to be Claver'se's post in the attack upon the pasty?"

"No, brother," said the lady; "as these cushions have been once honoured by accommodating the person of our most sacred monarch, they shall never, please Heaven, during my life-time, be pressed by any less dignified weight."

"You should not put them in the way, then, of an honest old cavalier, who has ridden ten miles before breakfast; for, to confess the truth, they look very inviting. But where is Edith?"

"On the battlements of the warder's turret," answered the old lady, "looking out for the approach of our guests."

"Why, I'll go there too; and so should you, Lady Margaret, as soon as you have your line of battle properly formed in the hall here. It's a pretty thing, I can tell you, to see a regiment of horse upon the march."

Thus speaking, he offered his arm with an air of old-fashioned gallantry, which Lady Margaret accepted with such a curtesy of acknowledgment as ladies were wont to make in Holyrood-house before the year 1642, which, for one while, drove curtesies and courts alike out of fashion.

Upon the bartizan of the turret, to which they ascended by many a winding passage and uncouth staircase, they found Edith, not indeed in the attitude of a young lady who watches with fluttering curiosity the approach of a smart regiment of dragoons, but pale, downcast, and evincing, by her countenance, that sleep had not, on the preceding night, been the companion of her pillow. The good old veteran was hurt at her appearance, which, in the hurry of preparation, her grandmother had omitted to notice.

"What is come over you, you silly puss?" he said; "why, you look like an officer's wife when she opens the News-letter after an action, and expects to find her husband among the killed and wounded. But I know the reason—you will persist in reading these nonsensical romances, day and night, and whimpering for distresses that never existed. Why, how the devil can you believe that Artamenes, or what d'ye call him, fought single-handed with a whole battalion? One to three is as great odds as ever fought and won, and I never knew any body that cared to take it except old Corporal Raddlebanes. But these d—d books put all pretty men's actions out of countenance. I dare say you would think very little of Raddlebanes, alongside of Artamenes. —I would have the fellows that write such nonsense brought to the picquet for leasing-making."

Lady Margaret, herself something attached to the perusal of romances, took up the cudgels.

"Monsieur Scuderi," she said, "is a soldier, brother, and, as I have heard, a complete one, and so is the Sieur D'Urfé."

"More shame for them; they should have known better what they were writing about. For my part, I have not read a book this twenty years except my Bible, The Whole Duty of Man, and, of late days,

Turner's Pallas Armata on the ordering of the pike exercise, and I don't like *his* discipline much neither. He wants to draw up the cavalry in front of a stand of pikes, instead of being upon the wings. Sure am I, if we had done so at Kilsythe, instead of having our handful of horse on the flanks, the first discharge would have sent them back among our Highlanders.—But I hear the kettle-drums."

All heads were now bent from the battlements of the turret, which commanded a distant prospect down the vale of the river. The Tower of Tillietudlem stood, or perhaps yet stands, upon the angle of a very precipitous bank, formed by the junction of a considerable brook with the Clyde. There was a narrow bridge of one steep arch, across the brook near its mouth, over which, and along the foot of the high and broken bank, winded the public road; and the fortalice, thus commanding both bridge and pass, had been, in times of war, a post of considerable importance, the possession of which was necessary to secure the communication of the upper and wilder districts of the country with those beneath, where the valley expands, and is more capable of cultivation. The view downwards is of a grand woodland character; but the level ground and gentle slopes near the river form cultivated fields of an irregular form, interspersed with hedge-row trees and copses, the inclosures seeming as it were to have been cleared out of the forest which surrounds them and occupies, in unbroken masses, the steeper declivities and more distant banks. The noble stream, in colour a clear and sparkling brown, like the hue of the cairngorm pebbles, rushes through this romantic region in bold sweeps and curves, partly visible and partly concealed by the trees which clothe its banks. With a providence unknown in other parts of Scotland, the peasants have, in most cases, planted orchards around their cottages, and the general blossom of the apple-trees at this season of the year gave all the lower part of the view the appearance of a flower-garden.

Looking up the river, the character of the scene was varied considerably for the worse. A hilly, waste, and uncultivated country approached close to the banks; the trees were few, and limited to the neighbourhood of the stream, and the rude moors swelled at a little distance into shapeless and heavy hills, which were again surmounted in their turn by a range of lofty mountains, dimly seen on the horizon. Thus the Tower commanded two prospects, the one richly cultivated and highly adorned, the other exhibiting the monotonous and dreary character of a wild and inhospitable moorland.

The eyes of the spectators on the present occasion were attracted to the downward view, not alone by its superior beauty, but because the distant sounds of military music began to be heard from the public high road which winded up the vale, and announced the approach of the expected body of cavalry. Their glimmering files were shortly afterwards seen in the distance, appearing and disappearing as the trees and the windings of the road permitted them to be visible, and distinguished chiefly by the flashes of light which their arms occasionally reflected against the sun. The train was long and imposing, for there were about two hundred and fifty horse upon the march, and the glancing of the swords and waving of their banners, joined to the clang of their trumpets and kettle-drums, had at once a lively and an awful effect upon the imagination. As they advanced still nearer and nearer, they could distinctly see the files of these chosen troops following each other in long succession, completely equipped and superbly mounted.

"It's a sight makes me thirty years younger," said the old cavalier, "and yet I do not much like the service that these poor fellows are to be engaged in. Although I had my share of the civil war, I cannot say I had ever so much real pleasure in that sort of service as when I was in the wars on the continent, and we were hacking at fellows with foreign faces and outlandish language. It's a hard thing to hear a hamely Scotch tongue cry quarter, and be obliged to cut him down just the same as if he called out *misericordé*.—So, there they come through the Netherwood haugh; upon my word, fine-looking fellows, and capitally mounted—He that is galloping from the rear of the column must be Claver'se himself;—ay, he gets into the front as they cross the bridge, and now they will be with us in less than five minutes."

At the bridge beneath the Tower the cavalry divided, and the greater part, moving up the left bank of the brook and crossing at a ford a little above, took the road of the Grange, as it was called, a large set of farm offices belonging to the Tower, where Lady Margaret had ordered preparation to be made for their reception and suitable entertainment. The officers alone, with their colours and an escort to guard them, were seen to take the steep road up to the gate of the Tower, appearing by intervals as they gained the ascent, and again hidden by projections of the bank and of the huge old trees with which it is covered. When they emerged from this narrow path they found themselves in front of the old Tower, the gates of which were hospitably open for their reception. Lady Margaret, with Edith and her brother-in-law, having hastily descended from their post of observation, appeared to meet and to welcome their guests, with a retinue of domestics in as good order as the orgies of the preceding evening permitted. The gallant young cornet (a relation as well as namesake of Claverhouse, with whom the reader has been already made acquainted) lowered the standard amid the fanfare of the trumpets, in homage to the rank of Lady Margaret and the charms of her grand-daughter, and the old walls echoed to the flourish of the instruments and the stamp and neigh of the chargers.

Claverhouse himself alighted from a black horse, the most beautiful perhaps in Scotland. He had not a single white hair upon his whole body, a circumstance, which, joined to his spirit and fleetness, and to his being so frequently employed in pursuit of the presbyterian recusants, caused an opinion to prevail among them, that the steed had been presented to his rider by the great Enemy of mankind in order to assist him in persecuting the fugitive wanderers. When Claverhouse had paid his respects to the ladies with military politeness, had apologized for the trouble to which he was putting Lady Margaret's family, and had received the corresponding assurances that she could not think any thing an inconvenience which brought within the walls of Tillietudlem so distinguished a soldier, and so loyal a servant of his most sacred majesty; when, in short, all forms of hospitable and polite ritual had been duly complied with, the Colonel requested permission to receive the report of Bothwell, who was now in attendance, and with whom he spoke apart for a few minutes. Major Bellenden took that opportunity to say to his niece, without the hearing of her grandmother, "What a trifling foolish girl you are, Edith, to send me an express crammed with nonsense about books and gowns, and to slide the only thing I cared a marvedie about into the postscript."

"I did not know," said Edith, hesitating very much, "whether it would be quite—quite proper for me to"——

"I know what you would say—whether it would be right to take any interest in a presbyterian. But I knew this lad's father well. He was a brave soldier; and, if he was once wrong, he was once right too. I must commend your caution, Edith, for having said nothing of this young gentleman's apprehension to your grandmother—you may rely I shall not—I will take an opportunity to speak to Claver'se. Come, my love, they are going to breakfast—Let us follow them."

Chapter Twelve

Their breakfast so warm to be sure they did eat,
A custom in travellers mighty discreet.
PRIOR

THE BREAKFAST of the Lady Margaret Bellenden no more resembled a modern dejeuné, than the great stone-hall of Tillietudlem could brook comparison with a modern drawing-room. No tea, no coffee, no variety of rolls, but solid and substantial viands—the priestly ham, the knightly sirloin, the noble baron of beef, the princely venison pasty. Silver flagons, saved with difficulty from the claws of the Covenanters, now mantled, some with ale, some with mead, some with generous wine of various qualities and descriptions. The appetites of the guests were in correspondence to the magnificence and solidity of the preparation—no piddling—no boys' play, but that steady and persevering exercise of the jaws which is best learned by early morning hours, and by occasional hard commons.

Lady Margaret beheld with delight the cates which she had provided descending with such alacrity into the persons of her honoured guests, and had little occasion to exercise, with respect to any of the company saving Claverhouse himself, the compulsory urgency of pressing to eat, to which, as to the *peine forte et dure*, the ladies of that period were in the custom of subjecting their guests.

But the leader himself, more anxious to pay courtesy to Miss Bellenden, next whom he was placed, than to gratify his appetite, appeared somewhat negligent of the good cheer set before. Edith heard, without reply, many courtly speeches addressed to her, in a tone of voice of that happy modulation which could alike melt in the low tones of interesting conversation, and rise amid the din of battle, "loud as a trumpet with a silver sound." The sense that she was in presence of the dreaded chief upon whose fiat the fate of Henry Morton must depend—the recollection of the terror and awe which were attached to the very name of this commander, deprived her for some time, not only of the courage to answer, but even of the power of looking upon him. But when, emboldened by the soothing tones of his voice, she lifted her eyes to frame some reply, the person on whom she looked bore, in his appearance at least, none of the terrible attributes in which her apprehensions had arrayed him.

Grahame of Claverhouse was in the prime of life, rather low of stature, and slightly, though elegantly, formed; his gesture, language, and manners, were those of one whose life had been spent among the noble and among the gay. His features exhibited even feminine regularity. An oval face, a straight and well-formed nose, dark hazel eyes, a complexion just sufficiently tinged with brown to save it from the charge of effeminacy, a short upper-lip, curved upward like that of a Grecian statue, and slightly shaded by small mustachios of light brown, joined to a profusion of long curled locks of the same colour, which fell down on each side of his face, contributed to form such a countenance as limners love to paint and ladies to look upon.

The severity of his character, as well as the higher attributes of undaunted and enterprising valour which even his enemies were compelled to admit, lay concealed under an exterior which seemed better adapted to the court or the saloon than to the field. The same gentleness and gaiety of expression which reigned in his features seemed to inspire his actions and gestures; and, on the whole, he was generally esteemed, at first sight, rather qualified to be the votary of pleasure than of ambition. But under this soft exterior was hidden a spirit unbounded in daring and in aspiring, yet cautious and prudent as that of Machiavel himself. Profound in politics, and imbued, of course, with that disregard for individual rights which its intrigues usually generate, this leader was cool and collected in danger, fierce and ardent in pursuing success, careless of death himself, and ruthless in inflicting it upon others. Such are the characters formed in times of civil discord, when the highest qualities, perverted by party spirit, and inflamed by habitual opposition, are too often combined with vices and excesses which deprive them at once of their merit and of their lustre.

In endeavouring to reply to the polite trifles with which Claverhouse accosted her, Edith showed so much confusion, that her grandmother thought it necessary to come to her relief.

"Edith Bellenden," said the old lady, "has, from my retired mode of living, seen so little of those of her own sphere, that truly she can hardly frame her speech to suitable answers. A soldier is so rare a sight with us, Colonel Grahame, that unless it be your lieutenant, my young Lord Evandale, we have hardly had an opportunity of receiving a gentleman in uniform. And, now I talk of that excellent young nobleman, may I enquire if I was not to have had the honour of seeing him this morning with the regiment?"

"Lord Evandale, madam, was on his march with us," answered the leader, "but I was obliged to detach him with a small party to disperse a conventicle of these troublesome scoundrels who have had the impudence to assemble within five miles of my head-quarters."

"Indeed!" said the old lady; "that was a height of presumption to which I should have thought no rebellious fanatics would have ventured to aspire. But these are strange times! There is an evil spirit in the land, Colonel Grahame, that excites the vassals of persons of rank to rebel against the very house that holds and feeds them. There was ane of my able-bodied men the other day who plainly refused to attend the wappen-schaw at my bidding. Is there no law for such recusancy, Colonel Grahame?"

"I think I could find one," said Claverhouse, with great composure, "if your ladyship will inform me of the name and residence of the culprit."

"His name," said Lady Margaret, "is Cuthbert Headrigg; I can say naething of his domicile, for ye may weel believe, Colonel Grahame, he did not dwell long in Tillietudlem, but was speedily expelled for his contumacy. I wish the lad nae ill; but incarceration, or even a few stripes, would be a good example in this neighbourhood. His mother, under whose influence I doubt he acted, is an ancient domestic of this family, which makes me incline to mercy, although," continued the old lady, looking towards the pictures of her husband and her sons, with which the hall was hung, and heaving, at the same time, a deep sigh, "I, Colonel Grahame, have in my ain person but little right to compassionate that stubborn and rebellious generation. They have made me a childless widow, and, unless for the protection of our sacred sovereign and his gallant soldiers, they would soon deprive me of land and goods, of hearth and altar. Seven of my tenants, whose joint rent-mail may mount to well nigh a hundred merk, have already refused to pay either cess or rent, and had the assurance to tell my steward that they would acknowledge neither king nor landlord but who should have taken the Covenant."

"I will take a course with them—that is, with your ladyship's permission," answered Claverhouse; "it would ill become me to neglect the support of lawful authority when it is lodged in such worthy hands as that of Lady Margaret Bellenden. But I must needs say this country turns worse and worse daily, and reduces me to the necessity of taking measures with the recusants that are much more consonant with my duty than with my inclinations. And, speaking of this, I must not forget that I have to thank your ladyship for the hospitality you have been pleased to extend to a party of mine who have brought in a prisoner, charged with having resetted the murdering villain, Balfour of Burley."

"The house of Tillietudlem," answered the lady, "has ever been open to the servants of his majesty, and I hope that the stones of it will no longer rest on each other when it surceases to be as much at their command as at ours. And this reminds me, Colonel Grahame, that the gentleman who commands the party can hardly be said to be in his proper place in the army, considering whose blood flows in his veins; and if I might flatter myself that any thing would be granted to my request, I would presume to entreat that he might be promoted on some favourable opportunity."

"Your ladyship means Serjeant Francis Stuart, whom we call Bothwell?" said Claverhouse, smiling. "The truth is, he is a little too rough in the country, and has not been uniformly so amenable to discipline as the rules of the service require. But to instruct me how to oblige Lady Margaret Bellenden is to lay down the law to me—Bothwell," he continued, addressing the serjeant who just then appeared at the door, "go kiss Lady Margaret Bellenden's hand who interests herself in your promotion, and you shall have a commission the first vacancy."

Bothwell went through the salutation prescribed, but not without evident marks of haughty reluctance, and, when he had done so, said aloud, "To kiss a lady's hand can never disgrace a gentleman; but I would not kiss a man's, save the king's, to be made a general."

"You hear him," said Claverhouse, smiling, "there's the rock he splits upon; he cannot forget his pedigree."

"I know, my noble colonel," said Bothwell in the same tone, "that *you* will not forget your promise; and then, perhaps, you may permit *Cornet* Stuart to have some recollection of his grandfather, though the *serjeant* must forget him."

"Enough of this, sir," said Claverhouse, in the tone of command which was familiar to him, "and let me know what you came to report to me just now."

"My Lord Evandale and his party have halted on the high-road with some prisoners," said Bothwell.

"My Lord Evandale?" said Lady Margaret. "Surely, Colonel Grahame, you will permit him to honour me with his society, and to take his poor disjune here, especially considering, that even his most sacred majesty did not pass the Tower of Tillietudlem without halting to partake of some refreshment."

As this was the third time in the course of the conversation that Lady Margaret had adverted to this distinguished event, Colonel Grahame, as speedily as politeness would permit, took advantage of the first pause to interrupt the farther progress of the narrative, by saying, "We are already too numerous a party of guests; but as I know what Lord Evandale will suffer (looking towards Edith) if deprived of the pleasure which we enjoy, I will run the risk of overburdening your ladyship's hospitality.—Bothwell, let Lord Evandale know that Lady Margaret Bellenden requests the honour of his company."

"And let Harrison take care," added Lady Margaret, "that the people and their horses are suitably seen to."

Edith's heart sprung to her lips during this conversation, for it instantly occurred to her, that, through her influence over Lord Evandale, she might acquire some means of releasing Morton from his present state of danger, in case her uncle's intercession with Claverhouse should prove ineffectual. At any other time, she would have been much averse to exert this influence; for, however inexperienced in the world, her native delicacy taught her the advantage which a beautiful young woman gives to a young man when she permits him to lay her under an obligation. And she would have been the farther disinclined to request any favour of Lord Evandale, because the voice of the gossips in Clydeside had, for reasons hereafter to be made known, assigned him to her as a suitor, and because she could not disguise from herself that very little encouragement was necessary to realize conjectures which had hitherto no foundation. This was the more to be dreaded, that, in case of Lord Evandale making a formal declaration, he had every chance of being supported by the influence of Lady Margaret and her other friends, and that she would have nothing to oppose to their solicitations and authority, except a pre-dilection, to avow which she knew would be equally dangerous and unavailing. She determined, therefore, to wait the issue of her uncle's intercession, and, should it fail, which she conjectured she should soon learn, either from the looks or language of the open-hearted veteran, she would then, as a last effort, make use in Morton's favour of her interest with Lord Evandale. Her mind did not long remain in suspense on the subject of her uncle's application.

Major Bellenden, who had done the honours of the bottom of the table, laughing and chatting with the military guests who were at that end of the board, was now, by the conclusion of the repast, at liberty to leave his station, and accordingly took an opportunity to approach Claverhouse, requesting from his niece, at the same time, the honour of a particular introduction. As his name and character were well known, the two military men met with expressions of mutual regard, and Edith, with a beating heart, saw her aged relative withdraw from the company, together with his new acquaintance, into a recess formed by one of the arched windows of the hall. She watched their conference with eyes almost dazzled by the eagerness of suspense, and, with observation rendered more acute by the internal agony of her mind, could guess, from the pantomime of the conversation, the progress and fate of her uncle's intercession in behalf of Henry Morton.

The first expression of the countenance of Claverhouse betokened that open and willing courtesy, which, ere it requires to know the nature of the favour asked, seems to say, how happy the party will be to confer an obligation on the suppliant. But as the conversation pro-ceeded, the brow of that officer became darker and more severe, and his features, though still retaining the expression of the most perfect politeness, assumed, at least to Edith's terrified imagination, a harsh and inexorable character. His lip was now compressed as if with impatience, now curled slightly upward as if in civil contempt of the arguments urged by Major Bellenden. The language of her uncle, as far as expressed in his manner, appeared to be that of earnest interces-sion, urged with all the affectionate simplicity of his character, as well as with the weight which his age and reputation entitled him to use. But it seemed to have little impression upon Colonel Grahame, who soon changed his posture, as if about to cut short the Major's importunity, and to break up their conference with a courtly expression of regret, calculated to accompany a positive refusal of the request solicited. This movement brought them so near Edith, that she could distinctly hear Claverhouse say, "It cannot be, Major Bellenden; lenity, in his case, is altogether beyond the bounds of my commission, though in any thing else I am so heartily desirous to oblige you.—And here comes Evandale with news, as I think. What tidings do you bring us, Evandale?" he continued, addressing the young lord, who now entered in complete uniform, but with his dress disordered, and his boots spattered as if by riding hard.

"Unpleasant news, sir," was his reply. "A large body of whigs are in arms among the hills, and have broken out into actual rebellion. They have publicly burned the Act of Supremacy, that establishing episcopacy, that for observing the martyrdom of Charles I., and some others, and have declared their intention to remain together in arms for furthering the covenanted work of Reformation."

This unexpected intelligence struck a sudden and unpleasant surprise into the minds of all who heard it, excepting Claverhouse.

"Unpleasant news call you these?" replied Colonel Grahame, his dark eyes flashing fire, "they are the best I have heard this six months. Now that the scoundrels are drawn into a body we will make short work with them. When the adder crawls into daylight," he added, striking the heel of his boot upon the floor, as if in the act of crushing a noxious reptile, "I can trample him to death; he is only safe when he remains lurking in his den or morass.—Where are these knaves?" he continued, addressing Evandale.

"About ten miles off among the mountains, at a place called Loudoun-hill," was the young nobleman's reply. "I dispersed the conventicle against which you sent me, and made prisoner an old trumpeter of rebellion, who was in the act of exhorting his hearers to rise and be doing in the good cause, as well as one or two of his hearers who seemed to be particularly insolent; and from some country people and scouts I learned what I now tell you."

"What may be their strength?" asked his commander.

"Probably a thousand men, but accounts differ widely."

"Then," said Claverhouse, "it is time for us to be up and be doing also—Bothwell, bid them sound to horse."

Bothwell, who, like the war-horse of scripture, snuffed the battle afar off, hastened to give orders to six negroes, in white dresses richly laced, and having massive silver collars and armlets. These sable functionaries acted as trumpeters, and speedily made the castle and the woods around it ring with their summons.

"Must you then leave us?" said Lady Margaret, her heart sinking

under recollection of former unhappy times; "had ye no better send to
learn the force of the rebels?—O, how mony a fair face hae I heard
these fearfu' sounds call awa frae the Tower of Tillietudlem that my
auld e'en were ne'er to see return to it!"

"It is impossible for me to stop," said Claverhouse; "there are
rogues enough in this country to make the rebels five times their
strength, if they are not checked at once."

"Many," said Evandale, "are flocking to them already, and they give
out that they expect a strong body of the indulged presbyterians,
headed by young Milnewood, as they call him, the son of the famous
old round-head, Colonel Silas Morton."

This speech produced a very different effect upon the hearers.
Edith almost sunk from her seat with terror, while Claverhouse darted
a glance of sarcastic triumph at Major Bellenden, which seemed to
imply,—"You see what are the principles of the young man you were
pleading for."

"It's a lie—it is a d—d lie of these rascally fanatics," said the Major,
hastily. "I will answer for Harry Morton as I would for my own son. He
is a lad of as good church-principles as any gentleman in the life-
guards. I mean no offence to any one. He has gone to church service
with me fifty times, and I never heard him miss one of the responses in
my life. Edith Bellenden can bear witness to it as well as I. He always
read on the same Prayer book with her, and could look out the lessons
as well as the curate himself. Call him up; let him be heard for
himself."

"There can be no harm in that," said Claverhouse, "whether he be
innocent or guilty.—Major Allan," he said, turning to the officer next
in command, "take a guide, and lead the regiment forward to
Loudoun-hill by the best and shortest road. Move steadily, and do not
blow the horses; Lord Evandale and I will overtake you in a quarter of
an hour. Leave Bothwell with a party to bring up the prisoners."

Allan bowed, and left the apartment, with all the officers, excepting
Claverhouse and the young nobleman. In a few minutes the sound of
the military music and the clattering of hoofs announced that the
horsemen were leaving the Castle. The sounds were presently heard
only at intervals, and soon died away entirely.

While Claverhouse endeavoured to sooth the terrors of Lady Margaret, and to reconcile the veteran Major to his opinion of Morton,
Evandale, getting the better of that conscious shyness which renders
ingenuous youth diffident in approaching the object of his affections,
drew near to Miss Bellenden, and accosted her in a tone of mingled
respect and interest.

"We are to leave you," he said, taking her hand, which he pressed with much emotion—"to leave you for a scene which is not without its dangers. Farewell, dear Miss Bellenden;—let me say for the first, and perhaps the last time, dear Edith. We part in circumstances so singular as may excuse some solemnity in bidding farewell to one, whom I have known so long and whom I—respect so highly."

The manner differing from the words, seemed to express a feeling much deeper and more agitating than was conveyed in the phrase he made use of. It was not in woman to be utterly insensible to his modest and deep-felt expression of tenderness. Although borne down by the misfortunes and imminent danger of the man she loved, Edith was touched by the hopeless and reverential passion of the gallant youth, who now took leave of her to rush into dangers of no ordinary description.

"I hope—I sincerely trust," she said, "there is no danger. I hope there is no occasion for this solemn ceremonial—that these hasty insurgents will be dispersed rather by fear than force, and that Lord Evandale will speedily return to be what he must always be, the dear and valued friend of all in this castle."

"Of *all?*" he repeated, with a melancholy emphasis upon the word. "But be it so—whatever is near you is dear and valued to me, and I value their approbation accordingly. Of our success I am not sanguine. Our numbers are so few, that I dare not hope for so speedy, so bloodless, or so safe an end of this unhappy disturbance. These men are enthusiastic, resolute, and desperate, and have leaders not altogether unskilled in military matters. I cannot help thinking that the impetuosity of our Colonel is hurrying us against them rather prematurely. But there are few that have less reason to shun danger than I have."

Edith had now the opportunity she wished to bespeak the young nobleman's intercession and protection for Henry Morton, and it seemed the only remaining channel of interest by which he could be rescued from impending destruction. Yet she felt at that moment as if, in doing so, she was abusing the partiality and confidence of the lover, whose heart was as open before her as if his tongue had made an express declaration. Could she with honour engage Lord Evandale in the service of a rival? or could she with prudence make him any request, or lay herself under any obligation to him, without affording ground for hopes which she could never realize? But the moment was too urgent for hesitation, or even for those explanations with which her request might otherwise have been qualified.

"I will but dispose of this young fellow," said Claverhouse, from the other side of the hall, "and then, Lord Evandale—I am sorry to interrupt agreeable conversation—but then we must mount.—Bothwell, why do you not bring up the prisoner? and, hark ye, let two files load their carabines."

In these words, Edith conceived she heard the death-warrant of her lover. She instantly broke through the restraint which had hitherto kept her silent.

"My Lord Evandale," she said, "this young gentleman is a particular friend of my uncle's—your interest must be great with your colonel —let me request your intercession in his favour—it will confer on my uncle a lasting obligation."

"You over-rate my interest, Miss Bellenden," said Lord Evandale, "I have been often unsuccessful in such applications when I have made them on the mere score of humanity."

"Yet try once again for my uncle's sake."

"And why not for your own?" said Lord Evandale. "Will you not allow me to think I am obliging *you* personally in this matter?—Are you so diffident of an old friend that you will not allow him even the satisfaction of thinking that he is gratifying your wishes?"

"Surely—surely," replied Edith; "you will oblige me infinitely—I am interested in the young gentleman on my uncle's account—Lose no time, for God's sake!"

She became bolder and more urgent in her entreaties, for she heard the steps of the soldiers who were entering with their prisoner.

"By Heaven! then," said Evandale, "he shall not die, if I should die in his place!—But will you not," said he, resuming the hand, which, in the hurry of her spirits, she had not courage to withdraw, "will you not grant me one suit, in return for my zeal in your service?"

"Any thing you can ask, my Lord Evandale, that sisterly affection can give."

"And is this all," he continued, "all you can grant to my affection living, or my memory when dead?"

"Do not speak thus, my lord," said Edith, "you distress me, and do injustice to yourself. There is no friend I esteem more highly, or to whom I would more readily grant every mark of regard—providing—But"——

A deep sigh made her turn her head suddenly, ere she had well uttered the last word; and, as she hesitated how to frame the exception with which she meant to close the sentence, she became instantly aware she had been overheard by Morton, who, heavily ironed and guarded by soldiers, was now passing behind her in order to be presented to Claverhouse. As their eyes met each other, the sad and reproachful expression of Morton's glance seemed to imply that he had partially heard, and altogether misinterpreted, the conversation which had just passed. There wanted but this to complete Edith's

distress and confusion. Her blood, which rushed to her brow, made a
sudden revulsion to her heart, and left her as pale as death. This
change did not escape the attention of Evandale, whose quick glance
easily discovered that there was between the prisoner and the object of
his own attachment, some singular and uncommon connection. He
resigned the hand of Miss Bellenden, again surveyed the prisoner
with more attention, again looked at Edith, and plainly observed the
confusion which she could no longer conceal.

"This," he said, after a moment's gloomy silence, "is, I believe, the
young gentleman who gained the prize at the shooting-match."

"I am not sure," hesitated Edith—"yet—I rather think not," scarce
knowing what she replied.

"It *is* he," said Evandale, decidedly; "I know him well. A victor," he
continued, somewhat haughtily, "ought to have interested a fair spectator more deeply."

He then turned from Edith, and advancing towards the table at
which Claverhouse now placed himself, stood at a little distance,
resting on his sheathed broadsword, a silent, but not an unconcerned
spectator of that which passed.

Chapter Thirteen

O, my Lord, beware of jealousy.
Othello

TO EXPLAIN the deep effect which the few broken passages of the
conversation we have detailed, made upon the unfortunate prisoner
by whom they were overheard, it is necessary to say something of his
previous state of mind, and of the origin of his connection with Edith.

Henry Morton was one of those gifted characters which possess a
force of talent unsuspected by the owner himself. He had inherited
from his father an undaunted courage, much personal dexterity in the
use of arms, and a firm and uncompromising detestation of oppression, whether in politics or religion. But his enthusiasm was unsullied
by fanatical zeal, and unleavened by the sourness of the puritanical
spirit. From these his mind had been freed, partly by the active exertion of his own excellent understanding, partly by frequent and long
visits at Major Bellenden's, where he had an opportunity of meeting
with many guests whose conversation taught him, that goodness or
worth were not limited to those of any single form of religious observance.

The base parsimony of his uncle had thrown many obstacles in the
way of his education; but he had so far improved the opportunities

which offered themselves, that his instructors as well as his friends were surprised at his progress under such disadvantages. Still, however, the current of his soul was frozen by a sense of dependence, of poverty, above all, of an imperfect and limited education. These feelings impressed him with a diffidence and reserve which effectually concealed from all but very intimate friends, the extent of talent and the firmness of character, which we have stated him to be possessed of. The circumstances of the times had added to this reserve an air of indecision and of indifference; for, being attached to neither of the factions which divided the kingdom, he passed for dull, insensible, and uninfluenced by the feeling of religion or of patriotism. No conclusion, however, could be more unjust; and the reasons of the neutrality which he had hitherto professed had root in very different and most praise-worthy motives. He had formed few congenial ties with those who were the objects of persecution, and was revolted alike by their narrow-minded and selfish party-spirit, their gloomy fanaticism, their abhorrent condemnation of all elegant studies or innocent exercises, and the envenomed rancour of their political hatred. But his mind was still more revolted by the tyrannical and oppressive conduct of the government, the misrule, license, and brutality of the soldiery, the executions on the scaffold, the slaughters in the open field, the free quarters and exactions imposed by military law, which placed the lives and fortunes of a free people on a level with Asiatic slaves. Condemning, therefore, each party as its excesses fell under his eyes, disgusted with the sight of evils which he had no means of alleviating, and hearing alternate complaints and exultations with which he could not sympathise, he would long ere this have left Scotland had it not been for his attachment to Edith Bellenden.

The earlier meeting of these young people had been at Charnwood, where Major Bellenden, who was as free from suspicion on such occasions as Uncle Toby himself, had encouraged their keeping each other constant company without entertaining any apprehension of the natural consequences. Love, as usual in such cases, borrowed the name of friendship, used her language, and claimed her privileges. When Edith Bellenden was recalled to her grandmother's castle, it was astonishing by what singular and recurring accidents she often met young Morton in her sequestered walks, especially considering the distance of their places of abode. Yet it somehow happened that she never expressed the surprise which the frequency of these rencontres ought naturally to have excited, and that their intercourse assumed gradually a more delicate character, and their meetings began to wear the air of appointments. Books, drawings, letters, were exchanged between them, and every trifling commission, given or

executed, gave rise to a new correspondence. Love indeed was not yet
mentioned between them by name, but each knew the situation of
their own bosom, and could not but guess at that of the other. Unable
to desist from an intercourse which possessed such charms for them
both, yet trembling for its too probable consequences, it had been
continued without specific explanation until now, when fate appeared
to have taken the conclusion into her own hands.

It followed, as a consequence of this state of things, as well as of the
diffidence of Morton's disposition at this period, that his confidence
in Edith's return of his affection had its occasional cold fits. Her
situation was in every respect so superior to his own, her worth so
eminent, her accomplishments so many, her face so beautiful, and her
manners so bewitching, that he could not but entertain fears that some
suitor more favoured than himself by fortune, and more acceptable to
Edith's family than he durst hope to be, might step in between him and
the object of his affections. Common rumour had raised up such a
rival in Lord Evandale, whom birth, fortune, connections, and political principles, as well as his frequent visits at Tillietudlem, and his
attendance upon Lady Bellenden and her niece at all public places,
naturally pointed out as a candidate for her favour. It frequently and
inevitably happened that engagements to which Lord Evandale was a
party, interfered with the meeting of the lovers, and Henry could not
but mark that Edith either studiously avoided speaking of the young
nobleman, or did so with obvious reserve and hesitation.

These symptoms, which, in fact, arose from the delicacy of her own
feelings towards Morton himself, were misconstrued by his diffident
temper, and the jealousy which they excited was fomented by the
occasional observations of Jenny Dennison. This true-bred suivante
was, in her own person, a complete country coquette, and when she
had no opportunity of teazing her own lovers, used to take some
occasional opportunity to torment her young lady's. This arose from
no ill will to Henry Morton, who, both on her mistress's account and
his own handsome form and countenance, stood high in her esteem.
But then Lord Evandale was also handsome; he was liberal far beyond
what Morton's means could afford, and he was a lord, moreover; and,
if Miss Edith Bellenden should accept his hand, she would become a
baron's lady, and what was more, little Jenny Dennison, whom the
awful housekeeper at Tillietudlem huffed about at her pleasure,
would be then Mrs Dennison, Lady Evandale's own woman, or
perhaps her ladyship's lady-in-waiting. The impartiality of Jenny
Dennison, therefore, did not, like that of Mrs Quickly, extend to a
wish that both the handsome suitors could wed her young lady; for it
must be owned that the scale of her regard depressed in favour of

Lord Evandale, and her wishes in his favour took many shapes extremely tormenting to Morton; being now expressed as a friendly caution, now as an article of intelligence, and anon as a merry jest, but always tending to confirm the idea, that, sooner or later, his romantic intercourse with her young mistress must have a close, and that Edith Bellenden would, in spite of summer walks beneath the greenwood-tree, exchange of verses, of drawings, and of books, end in becoming Lady Evandale.

These hints coincided so exactly with the very point of his own suspicions and fears, that Morton was not long of feeling that jealousy which every one has felt who has truly loved, but to which those are most liable whose love is crossed by the want of friends' consent, or some other envious impediment of fortune. Edith herself, unwittingly, and in the generosity of her own frank nature, contributed to the error into which her lover was in danger of falling. Their conversation once chanced to turn upon some late excesses committed by the soldiery on an occasion when it was said (inaccurately however) that the party was commanded by Lord Evandale. Edith, as true in friendship as in love, was somewhat hurt at the severe strictures which escaped from Morton upon this occasion, and which, perhaps, were not the less strongly expressed on account of their supposed rivalry. She entered into Lord Evandale's defence with such spirit as hurt Morton to the very soul, and afforded no small delight to Jenny Dennison, the usual companion of their walks. Edith perceived her error, and endeavoured to remedy it; but the impression was not so easily erazed, and had no small effect in inducing her lover to form the resolution of going abroad, which was disappointed in the manner we have already mentioned.

The visit which he received from Edith during his confinement, the deep and devoted interest which she had expressed in his fate, ought of themselves to have dispelled his suspicions; yet, ingenious in tormenting himself, even this he thought might be imputed to anxious friendship, or, at most, to a temporary partiality, which might soon give way to circumstances, the entreaties of her friends, the authority of Lady Margaret, and the assiduities of Lord Evandale.

"And to what do I owe it," he said, "that I cannot stand up like a man, and plead my interest in her ere I am thus cheated out of it?—to what, but to the accursed tyranny which afflicts at once our bodies, souls, estates, and affections! And is it to one of the pensioned cut-throats of this oppressive government that I must yield my pretensions to Edith Bellenden?—I will not, by Heaven!—It is a just punishment on me for being dead to public wrongs, that they have visited with their injuries where they can be least brooked or borne."

As these stormy resolutions boiled in his bosom, and while he ran over the various kinds of insult and injury which he had sustained in his own cause and in that of his country, Bothwell entered the tower, followed by two dragoons, one of whom carried handcuffs.

"You must follow me, young man," said he, "but first we must put you in trim."

"In trim!" said Morton, "What do you mean?"

"Why, we must put on these rough bracelets. I durst not—nay, d—n it I *durst* do any thing—but I *would* not for three hours plunder of a stormed town bring a whig before my colonel without his being ironed. Come, come, young man, never look sulky about it."

He advanced to put on the irons; but, seizing the oaken-seat upon which he had rested, Morton threatened to dash out the brains of the first who should approach him.

"I should manage you in a moment, my youngster," said Bothwell, "but I had rather you would strike sail quietly."

Here indeed he spoke the truth, not from either fear or reluctance to adopt force, but because he dreaded the consequences of a noisy scuffle, through which it might probably be discovered that he had, contrary to express orders, suffered his prisoner to pass the night without being properly secured.

"You had better be prudent," he continued, in a tone which he meant to be conciliatory, "and don't spoil your own sport. They say in the castle here that Lady Margaret's niece is immediately to marry our young Captain, Lord Evandale. I saw them close together in the hall yonder, and I heard her ask him to intercede for your pardon. She looked so devilish handsome and kind upon him that on my soul—but what the devil's the matter with you?—You are as pale as a sheet— Will you have some brandy?"

"Miss Bellenden ask my life of Lord Evandale?" said the prisoner, faintly.

"Ay, ay; there's no friend like the women—their interest carries all in court and camp—Come, you're reasonable now—Ay, I thought you would come round."

Here he employed himself in putting on the fetters, against which, Morton, thunderstruck by this intelligence, no longer offered the least resistance.

"My life begged of him, and by her!—ay—ay—put on the irons— my limbs shall not refuse to bear what has entered into my very soul— My life begged by Edith, and begged of Evandale!"

"Ay, and he has power to grant it too," said Bothwell—"He can do more with the Colonel than any man in the regiment."

And as he spoke he and his party led their prisoner towards the hall.

In passing behind the seat of Edith the unfortunate prisoner heard enough, as he conceived, of the broken expressions which passed between Edith and Lord Evandale to confirm all that the soldier had told him. That moment made a singular and instantaneous revolution in his character. The depth of despair to which his love and fortunes were reduced, the peril in which his life appeared to stand, the transference of Edith's affections, her intercession in his favour, which rendered her fickleness yet more galling, seemed to destroy every feeling for which he had hitherto lived, but, at the same time, awakened those which had hitherto been smothered by passions more gentle though more selfish. Desperate himself, he determined to support the rights of his country, insulted in his person. His character was for the moment as effectually changed as the appearance of a villa, which, from being the abode of domestic quiet and happiness, is, by the sudden intrusion of an armed force, converted into a formidable post of defence.

We have already said that he cast upon Edith one glance in which reproach was mingled with sorrow, as if to bid her farewell for ever; his next motion was to walk firmly to the table at which Colonel Grahame was seated.

"By what right is it, sir," said he, firmly, and without waiting until he was questioned,—"By what right is it that these soldiers have dragged me from my family, and put fetters on the limbs of a free man?"

"By my commands," answered Claverhouse; "and I now lay my commands on you to be silent and hear my questions."

"I will not," replied Morton, in a determined tone, while his boldness seemed to electrify all around him. "I will know whether I am in lawful custody, and before a civil magistrate, ere the charter of my country shall be forfeited in my person."

"A pretty springald this, upon my honour!" said Claverhouse.

"Are you mad?" said Major Bellenden to his young friend. "For God's sake, Harry Morton," he continued, in a tone between rebuke and entreaty, "remember you are speaking to one of his majesty's officers high in the service."

"It is for that very reason, sir," returned Henry, firmly, "that I desire to know what right he has to detain me without a legal warrant. Were he a civil officer of the law, I should know my duty was submission."

"Your friend, here," said Claverhouse to the veteran, coolly, "is one of those scrupulous gentlemen, who, like the madman in the play, will not tie his cravat without the warrant of Mr Justice Overdo; but I will let him see, before we part, that my shoulder-knot is as legal a badge of authority as the mace of the Justiciary. So, waiving this discussion, you will be pleased, young man, to tell me directly when you saw Balfour of Burley."

"As I know no right you have to ask me such a question, I decline replying to it."

"You confessed to my serjeant," said Claverhouse, "that you saw and entertained him, knowing him to be an intercommuned traitor; why are you not as frank with me?"

"Because," replied the prisoner, "I presume you are, from education, taught to understand the rights upon which you seem disposed to trample, and I am willing you should be aware that there are yet Scotsmen who can assert the liberties of Scotland."

"And these supposed rights you would vindicate with your sword, I presume?" said Colonel Grahame.

"Were I armed as you are, and we were alone upon a hill-side, you should not ask me the question twice."

"It is quite enough," answered Claverhouse, calmly; "your language corresponds with all I have heard of you;—but you are the son of a soldier, though a rebellious one, and you shall not die the death of a dog; I will save you that indignity."

"Die in what manner I may," replied Morton, "I will die like the son of a brave man; and the ignominy you mention will remain with those who shed innocent blood."

"Make your peace, then, with Heaven in five minutes space.— Bothwell, lead him down to the court-yard and draw up your party."

The appalling nature of this conversation, and of its result, struck the silence of horror into all but the speakers. But now those who stood round broke forth into clamour and expostulation. Old Lady Margaret, who, with all the prejudices of rank and party, had not laid aside the feelings of her sex, was loud in her intercession.

"O, Colonel Grahame," she exclaimed, "spare his young blood! Leave him to the law—do not repay my hospitality wi' shedding men's blood on the threshold of my doors!"

"Colonel Grahame," said Major Bellenden, "you must answer this violence. Don't think, though I am old and feckless, that my friend's son shall be murdered before my eyes with impunity. I can find friends that shall make you answer it."

"Be satisfied, Major Bellenden, I will answer it," replied Claverhouse, totally unmoved; "and you, madam, permit me to say, might spare me the pain of resisting this passionate intercession for a traitor, when you consider the noble blood your own house has lost by such as he is."

"Colonel Grahame," answered the lady, her aged frame trembling with anxiety, "I leave vengeance to God, who calls it his own. The shedding of this young man's blood will not call back the lives that were dear to me; and how can it comfort me to think that there has maybe been another widowed mother made childless, like mysel, by a deed done at my very door-stane?"

"This is stark madness," said Claverhouse; "I *must* do my duty to church and state. Here are a thousand villains hard by in open rebellion, and you ask me to pardon a young fanatic who is enough of himself to set a whole kingdom in a blaze! It cannot be—remove him, Bothwell."

She who was most interested in this dreadful decision, had twice strove to speak, but her voice had totally failed her; her mind refused to suggest words and her tongue to utter them. She now sprung up and attempted to rush forward, but her strength gave way, and she would have fallen flat upon the pavement had she not been caught by her attendant.

"Help," cried Jenny,—"Help for God's sake! my young lady is dying."

At this exclamation, Evandale, who, during the preceding part of the scene, had stood motionless, leaning upon his sword, now stepped forward, and said to his commanding-officer, "Colonel Grahame, before proceeding in this matter, will you speak a word with me in private?"

Claverhouse looked surprised, but instantly rose and withdrew with the young nobleman into a recess, where the following brief dialogue passed between them:

"I think I need not remind you, colonel, that when our family interest was of service to you last year in that affair in the Privy Council, you considered yourself as laid under some obligation to us?"

"Certainly, my dear Evandale," answered Claverhouse, "I am not a man who forgets such debts; you will delight me by shewing me how I can evince my gratitude."

"I will hold the debt cancelled if you will spare this young man's life."

"Evandale," replied Grahame, in great surprise, "you are mad—absolutely mad—what interest can you have in this young spawn of an old roundhead?—His father was positively the most dangerous man in all Scotland, cool, resolute, soldierly, and inflexible in his cursed principles. His son seems his very model; you cannot conceive the mischief he may do—I know mankind, Evandale—were he an insignificant, fanatical, country booby, do you think I would have refused such a trifle as his life to Lady Margaret and this family? But this is a lad of fire, zeal, and education—and these knaves want but such a leader to direct their blind enthusiastic hardiness. I mention this not as refusing your request, but to make you fully aware of the possible consequences—I will never evade a promise, or refuse to return an obligation—If you ask his life, he shall have it."

"Keep him close prisoner," answered Evandale, "but do not be surprised if I persist in requesting you will not put him to death. I have most urgent reasons for what I ask."

"Be it so then," replied Grahame;—"but, young man, should you wish through your future life to rise to eminence in the service of your king and country, let it be your first task to subject to the public interest, and to the discharge of your duty, your private passions, affections, and feelings. These are not times to sacrifice to the dotage of greybeards, or the tears of silly women, the measures of salutary severity, which the dangers around compel us to adopt. And remember that if I now yield this point, in compliance with your urgency, my present concession must exempt me from future solicitations of the same nature."

He then stepped forwards to the table, and bent his eyes keenly on Morton, as if to observe what effect the pause of awful suspense between death and life, which seemed to freeze the by-standers with horror, could produce upon the prisoner himself. Morton maintained a degree of firmness, which nothing but a mind which had nothing left on earth to love, or to hope, could have supported at such a crisis.

"You see him," said Claverhouse, in a half whisper to Lord Evandale, "he is tottering on the verge between time and eternity, a situation more appalling than the most hideous certainty; yet his is the only cheek unblenched, the only eye that is calm, the only heart that keeps its usual time, the only nerves that are not quivering. Look at him well, Evandale—If that man heads an army of rebels, you will have much to answer for on account of this morning's work." He then said aloud, "Young man, your life is for the present safe, through the intercession of your friends.—Remove him, Bothwell, and let him be properly guarded and brought along with the other prisoners."

"If my life," said Morton, stung with the idea that he owed his respite to the intercessions of a favoured rival, "if my life be granted at Lord Evandale's request"——

"Take the prisoner away, Bothwell," said Colonel Grahame, interrupting him; "I have neither time to make nor to hear fine speeches."

Bothwell forced off Morton, saying, as he conducted him into the court-yard, "Have you three lives in your pocket, besides one in your body, my lad, that you can afford to let your tongue run away with them at this rate? Come, come, I'll take care to keep you out of the Colonel's way, for egad you will not be five minutes with him before the next tree or the next ditch will be the word. So, come along to your companions in bondage."

So saying, the serjeant, who, in his rude manner, did not altogether want sympathy for a gallant young man, hurried Morton down to the court-yard, where three other prisoners (two men and a woman) who had been taken by Lord Evandale, remained under an escort of dragoons.

Mean time, Claverhouse took his leave of Lady Margaret. But it was difficult for the good lady to forgive his neglect of her intercession.

"I thought till now," she said, "that the Tower of Tillietudlem might have been a place of succour to those that are ready to perish, even if they were na sae deserving as they suld hae been—but I see auld fruit has little savour—our suffering and our services have been of an ancient date."

"They are never to be forgotten by me, let me assure your ladyship," said Claverhouse. "Nothing but what seemed my sacred duty could make me hesitate to grant a favour requested by you and the major. Come, my good lady, let me hear you say you have forgiven me, and, as I return to-night, I will bring a drove of two hundred whigs with me, and pardon fifty head of them for your sake."

"I shall be happy to hear of your success, colonel," said Major Bellenden; "but take an old soldier's advice, and spare blood when battle's over—and once more let me request to enter bail for young Morton."

"We will settle that when I return," said Claverhouse. "Meanwhile, be assured his life shall be safe."

During this conversation, Evandale looked anxiously around for Edith; but the precaution of Jenny Dennison had occasioned her mistress being transported to her own apartment.

Slowly and heavily he obeyed the impatient summons of Claverhouse, who, after taking a courteous leave of Lady Margaret and the Major, had hastened to the court-yard. The prisoners with their guard were already on their march, and the officers with their escort mounted and followed. All pressed forward to overtake the march of the main body, as it was supposed they would come in sight of the enemy in not more than two hours.

END OF VOLUME

THE TALE OF
OLD MORTALITY

Chapter One

My hounds may a' rin masterless,
  My hawks may fly frae tree to tree,
My lord may grip my vassal lands,
  For there again maun I never be!
                              Old Ballad

WE LEFT Morton, along with three companions in captivity, travelling in the custody of a small body of soldiers who formed the rearguard of the column under the command of Claverhouse, and were immediately under the charge of Serjeant Bothwell. Their route lay towards the hills in which the insurgent presbyterians were reported to be in arms. They had not prosecuted their march a quarter of a mile ere Claverhouse and Evandale galloped past them, followed by their orderly-men, in order to take their proper places in the column which preceded them. No sooner were they past than Bothwell halted the body which he commanded, and disencumbered Morton of his irons.

"King's blood must keep word," said the dragoon. "I promised you should be civilly treated so far as rested with me.—Here, Corporal Inglis, let this gentleman ride alongside of the other young fellow who is prisoner; and you may permit them to converse together at their pleasure, under their breath, but take care they are guarded by two files with loaded carabines. If they attempt an escape, blow their brains out.—You cannot call that using you uncivilly," he continued, addressing himself to Morton, "it's the rules of war, you know.—And, Inglis, couple up the parson and the old woman, they are fittest company for each other, d—n me; a single file may guard them well enough. If they speak a word of cant or fanatical nonsense, let them have a strapping with a shoulder belt. There's some hope of choking a silenced parson; if he is not allowed to hold forth, his own treason will burst him."

Having made this arrangement, Bothwell placed himself at the head of the party, and Inglis, with six dragoons, brought up the rear.

The whole then set forward at a trot, with the purpose of overtaking the main body of the regiment.

Morton, overwhelmed with a complication of feelings, was totally indifferent to the various arrangements made for his secure custody, and even to the relief afforded him by his release from the fetters. He experienced that blank and waste of the heart which follows the hurricane of passion, and, no longer supported by the pride and conscious rectitude which dictated his answers to Claverhouse, he surveyed with deep dejection the glades through which he travelled, each turning of which had something to remind him of past happiness and of disappointed hope. The eminence which they now ascended was that from which he used first and last to behold the ancient tower when approaching or retiring from it, and, it is needless to add, that there he was wont to pause, and gaze with a lover's delight on the battlements, which, rising at a distance out of the lofty wood, indicated the dwelling of her, whom he either hoped soon to meet or had recently parted from. Instinctively he turned his head back to take a last look of a scene formerly so dear to him, and no less instinctively he heaved a deep sigh. It was echoed by a loud groan from his companion in misfortune, whose eyes, moved, perchance, by similar reflections, had taken the same direction. This indication of feeling, on the part of the captive, was uttered in a tone more coarse than sentimental; it was, however, the expression of a grieved spirit, and so far corresponded with the sigh of Morton. In turning their heads their eyes met, and Morton recognised the stolid countenance of Cuddie Headrigg, bearing a rueful expression, in which sorrow under his own lot was mixed with sympathy for the situation of his companion.

"Hegh, sirs!" was the expression of the ci-devant ploughman of the Mains of Tillietudlem; "it's an unco thing that decent folk suld be harled through the country this gate, as if they were a warld's wonder."

"I am sorry to see you here, Cuddie," said Morton, who, even in his own distress, did not lose feeling for that of others.

"And sae am I, Milnewood," answered Cuddie, "baith for mysel and you; but neither of our sorrows will do muckle gude that I can see. To be sure, for me," continued the captive agriculturist, relieving his heart by talking, although he well knew it was to little purpose,—"to be sure, for my part, I hae nae right to be here ava', for I ne'er did nor said a word against either king or curate; but my mother, puir body, couldna haud the auld tongue o' her, and we maun baith pay for't, it's like."

"Your mother is their prisoner likewise?" said Morton, hardly knowing what he said.

"In troth is she, riding ahint ye there like a bride wi' that auld carle o' a minister, that they ca' Gabriel Kettledrummle—De'il that he had been in the inside of a drum or a kettle either, for my share o' him! Ye see, we were nae sooner chased out o' the doors o' Milnewood, and your uncle and the housekeeper banging them to and barring them ahint us, as if we had had the plague on our bodies, than I says to my mither, What are we to do neist, for every hole and bore in the kintra will be steekit against us, now that ye hae affronted my auld leddy, and gar't the troopers tak up young Milnewood? Sae she says to me, Binna cast doun, but gird yoursel up to the great task o' the day, and gi'e your testimony like a man upon the mount o' the Covenant."

"And so I suppose you went to a conventicle?" said Morton.

"Ye sall hear," continued Cuddie.—"Aweel, I kenn'd na muckle better what to do, sae I e'en ga'ed wi' her to an auld daft carline like hersel, and we gat some water-broo and bannocks, and mony a weary grace they said, and mony a psalm they sung, or they wad let me win to, for I was amaist famished wi' vexation. Aweel, they had me up in the grey o' the morning, and I behoved to whig awa' wi' them, reason or nane, to a grit gathering o' their folk at the Miry-sikes, and there this chield, Gabriel Kettledrummle, was blashing awa' to them on the hill-side, about lifting up their testimony, nae doubt, and ganging down to the battle to Ramoth Gilead, or some sic place. Eh, Mr Henry! but the carle gae them a screed o' doctrine! Ye might hae heard him a mile down the wind—He routed like a cow in a fremd loaning.—Weel, thinks I, there's nae place in this country they ca' Roman Gilead—it will be some gate in the west moorlands; and or we win there I'll see to slip awa' wi' this mother o' mine, for I winna rin my neck into a tether for ony Kettledrummle in the kintra-side.—Aweel," continued Cuddie, relieving himself by detailing his misfortunes, without being scrupulous concerning the degree of attention which his companion bestowed on his narrative, "but just as I was wearying for the tail o' the preaching, cam word that the dragoons were upon us—Some ran, and some cried stand, and some cried down wi' the Philistines—I was at my mither to get her awa' sting and ling or the red-coats cam up, but I might as weel hae tried to drive our auld five-a-hand ox without the goad—de'il a step wad she budge.—Weel, after a', the cleugh we were in was strait, and the mist cam thick, and there was gude hope the dragoons wad hae missed us if we could hae held our ain tongues; but, as if auld Kettledrummle himsel hadna made din aneuch to waken the very dead, they behoved a' to skirl up a psalm that ye could hae heard as far as Lanrick!—Aweel, to mak a lang tale short, up cam my young Lord Evandale, skelping as fast as his horse could trot, and twenty red-coats at his back. Twa or three chields wad needs fight, wi' the pistol and whinger in the tae hand, and the Bible in the t'other, and they got their crowns weel clowred; but there was nae muckle skaith dune, for Evandale aye cried to scatter us, but to spare life."

"And did you not resist?" said Morton, who probably felt, that, at that moment, he himself would have encountered Lord Evandale on much slighter grounds.

"Na, truly," answered Cuddie, "I keepit aye before the auld woman, and cried for mercy to life and limb; but twa o' the red-coats cam up, and ane o' them was ganging to strike my mither wi' the side o' his broadsword—And I gat up my kebbie at them, and said I wad gar them as gude. Weel, they turned on me, and clinked at me with their swords, and I garr'd my hand keep my head as weel as I could till Lord Evandale cam up, and I cried out I was a servant at Tillietudlem—ye ken yoursel he was aye judged to hae a look after the young leddy— and he bade me fling doun my kent, and sae me and my mither yielded oursels prisoners.—I'm thinking we wad hae been letten slip awa', but Kettledrummle, he was ta'en near us, for Andrew Wilson's naig that he was riding on had been a dragooner lang syne, and the sairer Kettledrummle spurred to win awa', the readier the dour beast ran to the dragoons when he saw them draw up.—Aweel, when my mother and him forgathered, they set till the sodgers, and I think they gae them their kale through the reek! Bastards o' the whore of Babylon was the best word in their wame. Sae then the kiln was in a bleeze again, and they brought us a' three on wi' them to mak us an example, as they ca' it."

"It is most infamous and intolerable oppression," said Morton, half speaking to himself; "here is a poor peaceable fellow, whose only motive for joining the conventicle was a sense of filial piety, and he is chained up like a thief or murderer, and likely to die the death of one, but without the privilege of a formal trial, which our law indulges to the worst malefactor! Even to witness such tyranny, and still more to suffer under it, is enough to make the blood of the tamest slave boil within him."

"To be sure," said Cuddie, hearing and partly understanding what had broken from Morton in resentment of his injuries, "it isna right to speak evil o' dignities—my auld leddy aye said that, as nae doubt she had a gude right to do, being in a place o' dignity hersel; and troth I listened to her very patiently, for she aye ordered a dram, or a sowp kale, or something to us, after she had gi'en us a hearing on our duties. But de'il a dram, or kale, or ony thing else—no sae muckle as a cup o' cauld water do thae lords at Edinburgh gie us; and yet they're heading and hanging amang us, and trailing us after thae blackguard troopers, and taking our goods and gear as if we were outlaws. I canna say I tak it kind at their hands."

"It would be very strange if you did," answered Morton, with suppressed emotion.

"And what I like warst o' a'," continued poor Cuddie, "is thae ranting red-coats coming amang the lassies and taking awa' our joes. I had a sair heart o' my ain when I passed the Mains down at Tillietudlem this morning about parritch-time, and saw the reek coming out at my ain lum-head, and kenn'd there was some ither body than my auld minnie sitting by the ingle-side. But I think my heart was e'en sairer when I saw that hellicat trooper, Tam Halliday, kissing Jenny Dennison afore my face. I wonder women can hae the impudence to do sic things; but they are aye for the red-coats. Whiles I hae thought o' being a trooper mysel, when I thought naething else wad gae doun wi' Jenny—and yet I'll no blame her ower muckle neither, for maybe it was a' for my sake that she loot Tam touzle her cocker nonny that gate."

"For your sake?" said Morton, unable to refrain from taking some interest in a story which seemed to bear a singular coincidence with his own.

"E'en sae, Milnewood," replied Cuddie; "for the puir quean gat leave to come near me wi' speaking the loon fair, (d—n him, that I suld say sae) and sae she bade me God speed, and she wanted to stap siller into my hand;—I'se warrant it was the tae half o' her fee and bountith, for she wared the ither half on pinners and pearlings to gang to see us shute yon day at the popinjay."

"And did you take it, Cuddie?" said Morton.

"Troth did I no, Milnewood; I was sic a fule as to fling it back to her—my heart was ower grit to be behadden to her, when I had seen that loon slavering and kissing at her. But I was a grit fule for my pains; it wad hae dune mither and me some gude, and she'll ware't a' in duds and nonsense."

There was here a deep and long pause. Cuddie was probably engaged in regretting the rejection of his mistress's bounty, and Henry Morton in considering from what motives, or upon what conditions, Miss Bellenden had succeeded in procuring the interference of Lord Evandale in his favour.

"Was it not possible," suggested his awakening hopes, "that he had construed her influence over Lord Evandale hastily and unjustly? Ought he to censure her severely, if, submitting to dissimulation for his sake, she had permitted the young nobleman to entertain hopes which she had no intention to realize? Or what if she had appealed to the generosity which Lord Evandale was supposed to possess, and had engaged his honour to interfere to protect the person of a favoured rival?"

Still, however, the words which he had overheard recurred ever and anon to his remembrance, with a pang which resembled the sting of an adder.

"Nothing that she could refuse him!—was it possible to make a more unlimited declaration of predilection? The language of affection has not, within the limits of maidenly delicacy, a stronger expression. She is lost to me wholly, and for ever; and nothing remains for me now, but vengeance for my own wrongs, and for those which are hourly inflicted on my country."

Apparently, Cuddie, though with less refinement, was following out a similar train of ideas; for he suddenly asked Morton, in a low whisper,—"Wad there be ony ill in getting out o' thae chields' hands, an' ane could compass it?"

"None in the world," said Morton; "and if an opportunity occurs of doing so, depend on it I for one will not let it slip."

"I'm blythe to hear ye say sae," answered Cuddie. "I am but a puir silly fallow, but I canna think there wad be muckle ill in breaking out by strength o' hand, if ye could mak it ony thing feasible. I am the lad that will ne'er fear to lay on, if it were come to that; but our auld leddy wad hae ca'd that a resisting o' the king's authority."

"I will resist any authority on earth," said Morton, "that invades tyrannically my chartered rights as a freeman; and I am determined I will not be unjustly dragged to a jail, or perhaps a gibbet, if I can possibly make my escape from these men either by address or force."

"Weel, that's just my mind too, aye supposing we hae a feasible opportunity o' breaking loose. But than ye speak o' a charter; now these are things that only belang to the like o' you, that are a gentleman, and it might na bear me through, that am but a husbandman."

"The charter that I speak of," said Morton, "is common to the meanest Scotchman. It is that freedom from stripes and bondage which was claimed, as you may hear in Scripture, by the Apostle Paul himself, and which every man who is free-born is called upon to defend, for his own sake and that of his countrymen."

"Hegh, sirs!" replied Cuddie, "it wad hae been lang or my Leddy Margaret, or my mither either, wad hae found out sic a wiselike doctrine in the Bible! The tane was aye graning about giving tribute to Cæsar, and the tither is as daft wi' her whiggery. I hae been clean spoilt, just wi' listening to twa bathering auld wives; but if I could get a gentleman that wad let me tak on to be his servant, I am confident I wad be a clean contrary creature; and I hope your honour will think on what I am saying, if we were ance fairly delivered out o' this house of bondage, and just tak me to be your ain wally-de-shamle."

"My valet, Cuddie?" answered Morton, "alas! that would be sorry preferment, even if we were at liberty."

"I ken what ye're thinking—that because I'm landward bred, I wad be bringing ye to disgrace afore folk; but ye maun ken I'm gay gleg at the uptak; there was never ony thing dune wi' hand but I learned gay readily, 'septing reading, and writing, and cyphering; but there's no the like o' me at the fit-ba', and I can play wi' the broadsword as weel as Corporal Inglis there. I hae broken his head or now, for as massy as he's riding ahint us.—And then—ye'll no be ganging to stay in this country?" said he, stopping and interrupting himself.

"Probably not," replied Morton.

"Weel, I care na a boddle. Ye see I wad get my mither bestowed wi' her auld graning tittie, auntie Meg, in the Gallowgate o' Glasgow, and than I trust they wad neither burn her for a witch, or let her fail for fau't o' food, or hang her up for an auld whig wife; for the provost, they say, is very regardful o' sic puir bodies. And then you and I wad gang and pouss our fortunes, like the folk i' the daft auld tales about Jock the Giant killer and Valentine and Orson; and we wad come back to merry Scotland, as the sang says, and I wad tak to the stilts again, and turn sic furs on the bonnie rigs o' Milnewood holms, that it wad be worth a pint but to look at them."

"I fear," said Morton, "there is very little chance, my good friend Cuddie, of our getting back to your old occupation."

"Hout, sir—hout, sir," replied Cuddie, "it's aye gude to keep up a hardy heart—as broken a ship's come to land.—But what's that I hear?—never stir, if my auld mither is na at the preaching again! I ken the sough o' her texts, that sound just like the wind blawing through the spence; and there's Kettledrummle setting to wark, too—Lordsake, if the sodgers anes get angry, they will murder them baith, and us for company!"

Their farther conversation was in fact interrupted by a blatant noise which arose behind them, in which the voice of the preacher emitted, in unison with that of the old woman, tones like the grumble of a bassoon combined with the screaking of a cracked fiddle. At first, the aged pair of sufferers had been contented to condole with each other in smothered expressions of complaint and indignation; but the sense of their injuries became more pungently aggravated as they communicated with each other, and they became at length unable to suppress their ire.

"Woe, woe, and a threefold woe unto you, ye bloody and violent persecutors!" exclaimed the Reverend Gabriel Kettledrummle—"Woe, and threefold woe unto you, even to the breaking of seals, the blowing of trumpets, and the pouring forth of vials!"

"Ay—ay—a black cast to a' their ill-fa'ar'd faces, and the outside o' the loof to them at the last day," echoed the shrill counter-tenor of Mause, falling in like the second part of a catch.

"I tell you," continued the divine, "that your rankings and your ridings—your neighings and your prancings—your bloody, barbarous, and inhuman cruelties—your benumbing, deadening, and debauching the consciences of poor creatures by oaths, soul-damning and self-contradictory, have risen from earth to Heaven like a foul and hideous outcry of perjury for hastening the wrath to come——hugh! hugh! hugh!"

"And I say," cried Mause, in the same tune, and nearly at the same time, "that wi' this auld breath o' mine, and it's sair ta'en doun wi' the ashtmatics and the rough trot"——

("De'il gin they wad gallop," said Cuddie, "wad it but gar her haud her tongue!")

"Wi' this auld and brief breath," continued Mause, "will I testify against the backslidings, defections, defalcations, and declinings of the land—against the grievances and the causes of wrath."

"Peace, I pr'ythee—Peace, good woman," said the preacher, who had just recovered from a violent fit of coughing, and found his own anathema borne down by Mause's better wind, "peace, and take not the words out of the mouth of a servant of the altar.—I say, I uplift my voice and tell ye, that before the play is played out—ay, before this very sun gaes down, ye sall learn that neither a desperate Judas, like your prelate Sharpe that's gone to his place; nor a sanctuary-breaking Holofernes, like bloody-minded Claverhouse; nor an ambitious Diotrephes, like the lad Evandale; nor a covetous and warld-following Demas, like him they ca' Serjeant Bothwell, that makes every wife's plack and her meal-ark his ain; neither your carabines, nor your pistols, nor your broadswords, nor your horses, nor your saddles, bridles, surcingles, nose-bags, nor martingales, shall resist the arrows that are whetted and the bow that is bent against you."

"That shall they never, I trow," echoed Mause; "castaways are they ilk ane o' them—besoms of destruction, fit only to be flung into the fire when they hae sweepit the filth out o' the Temple—whips of small cords, knotted for the chastisement of those wha like their warldly gudes and gear better than the Cross or the Covenant, but when that wark's done, only meet to mak latchets to tie the de'il's brogues."

"Fiend hae me," said Cuddie, addressing himself to Morton, "if I dinna think our mither preaches as weel as the minister!—But it's a sair pity o' his hoast, for it aye comes in just when he's at the best o't, and that lang routing he made air this morning is sair again him too—

De'il an I care if he wad roar her dumb, than he wad hae it a' to answer for himsel—It's lucky the road's rough, and the troopers are no taking muckle tent to what they say wi' the rattling o' the horses feet; but an' we were anes on saft grund, we'll hear news o' a' this."

Cuddie's conjectures were but too true. The words of the prisoners had not been much attended to while drowned by the clang of the horses hoofs on a rough and stony road; but they now entered upon the moorland, where the testimony of the two zealous captives lacked this saving accompaniment. And, accordingly, no sooner had their steeds begun to tread heath and green sward, and Gabriel Kettle-drummle had again raised his voice with, "Also I uplift my song like that of a pelican in the wilderness"——"and I mine," had issued from Mause, "like a sparrow on the house-tops"——than "hollo! ho!" cried the corporal from the rear; "rein up your tongues, the devil blister them, or I'll clap a martingale on them."

"I will not peace at the commands of the profane," said Gabriel.

"Nor I neither," said Mause, "for the bidding of no earthly pot-sherd, though it be painted as red as a brick of the Tower of Babel, and ca' itsel a corporal."

"Halliday," cried the corporal, "hast got never a gag about thee, man?—We must stop their mouths before they talk us all dead."

Ere any answer could be made, or any measure taken in consequence of the corporal's motion, a dragoon galloped towards Serjeant Bothwell, who was considerably a-head of the party he commanded. On hearing the orders which he brought, Bothwell instantly rode back to the head of his party, ordered them to close their files, to mend their pace, and to move with silence and precaution, as they would soon be in presence of the enemy.

Chapter Two

Quantum in nobis, we've thought good
To save the expence of Christian blood,
And try if we, by mediation,
Of treaty, and accommodation,
Can end the quarrel, and compose
This bloody duel without blows.
                    BUTLER

THE INCREASED PACE of the party of horsemen soon took away from their zealous captives the breath, if not the inclination, necessary for holding forth. They had now for more than a mile got free of the woodlands, whose broken glades had, for some time, accompanied them after they had left the woods of Tillietudlem. A few birches and

oaks still feathered the narrow ravines, or occupied in dwarf clusters
the hollow places of the moor. But these were gradually disappearing;
and a wide and waste country lay before them, swelling into hills of
dark heath, intersected by deep gullies; being the passages by which
torrents forced their course in winter, and, during summer, the dis-
proportioned channels for diminutive rivulets that winded their puny
way among heaps of stones and gravel, the effects and tokens of their
winter fury, like so many spendthrifts dwindled down by the consequences of former excesses and extravagance. This desolate region
seemed to extend farther than the eye could reach, without grandeur,
without even the dignity of mountain wilderness, yet striking, from the
huge proportion which it seemed to bear to such more favoured spots
of the neighbouring country as were adapted to cultivation and fitted
for the support of man; and thereby impressing irresistibly the mind
of the spectator with a sense of the omnipotence of nature, and the
comparative inefficacy of the boasted means of amelioration which
man is capable of opposing to the disadvantages of climate and soil.

It is a remarkable effect of such extensive wastes, that they impose
an idea of solitude even upon those who travel through them in considerable numbers; so much is the imagination affected by the dispro-
portion between the desert around and the party who are traversing it.
Thus the member of a caravan of a thousand souls may feel, in the
deserts of Africa or Arabia, a sense of loneliness unknown to the
individual traveller, whose solitary course is through a thriving and
cultivated country.

It was not, therefore, without a peculiar feeling of emotion, that
Morton beheld, at the distance of about half a mile, the body of cavalry
to which his escort belonged, creeping up a steep and winding path
which ascended from the level moor into the hills. Their numbers,
which appeared formidable when they crowded through narrow
roads, and seemed multiplied by appearing partially, and at different
points, among the trees, were now apparently diminished by being
exposed at once to view, and in a landscape whose waste extent bore
such immense proportion to the column of horses and men, which,
shewing more like a drove of black cattle than a body of soldiers,
crawled slowly along the face of the hill, their force and their numbers
seeming trifling and contemptible.

"Surely," said Morton to himself, "a handful of resolute men might
defend any defile in these mountains against such a force as this is,
providing that their bravery was equal to their enthusiasm."

While he made these reflections, the rapid movement of the horsemen who guarded him soon traversed the space which divided them
from their companions; and ere the front of Claverhouse's column

had gained the brow of the hill which they had been seen ascending, Bothwell, with his rear-guard and prisoners, had united himself, or nearly so, with the main body led by his commander. The extreme difficulty of the road, which was in some places steep, and in others boggy, retarded the progress of the column, especially in the rear; for the passage of the main body, in many instances, potched up the swamps through which they passed, and rendered them so deep, that the last of their followers were forced to leave the beaten path, and find safer passage where they could.

On these occasions, the distresses of the Reverend Gabriel Kettledrummle and of Mause Headrigg were considerably augmented, as the brutal troopers, by whom they were guarded, compelled them, at all risks which such inexperienced riders were likely to incur, to leap their horses over drains and gullies, or to push them through morasses and swamps.

"Through the help of the Lord I have leaped over a wall," exclaimed poor Mause, as her horse was, by her rude attendants, brought up to leap the turf inclosure of a deserted fold, in which feat her curch flew off, leaving her grey hairs uncovered.

"I am sunk in deep mire where there is no standing—I am come into deep waters where the floods overflow me," exclaimed Kettledrummle, as the charger on which he was mounted plunged up to the saddle-girths in a *well-head*, as they call the springs which supply the marshes; and the sable streams beneath spouted over the face and person of the captive preacher.

These exclamations excited shouts of laughter among their military attendants; but events soon occurred which rendered them all sufficiently serious.

The leading files of the regiment had nearly attained the brow of the steep hill we have mentioned, when two or three horsemen, speedily discovered to be a part of their own advanced-guard, who had acted as patroles, appeared returning at full gallop, their horses much blown, and the men apparently in a disordered flight. They were followed upon the spur by five or six riders, well mounted and armed with sword and pistol, who halted upon the top of the hill, on observing the approach of the Life Guards. One or two who had carabines dismounted, and, taking a leisurely and deliberate aim at the foremost rank of the regiment, discharged their pieces, by which two troopers were wounded, one severely. They then mounted their horses, and disappeared over the ridge of the hill, retreating with so much coolness as evidently shewed they were, on the one hand, undismayed by the approach of so considerable a force as was moving against them, and conscious, upon the other, that they were supported by numbers sufficient for their protection. This incident occasioned a halt through the whole body of cavalry; and while Claverhouse himself received the report of his advanced-guard, which had been thus driven back upon the main body, Lord Evandale advanced to the top of the ridge over which the enemy's horsemen had retired, and Major Allan, Cornet Grahame, and the other officers, employed themselves in extricating the regiment from the broken ground, and drawing them up upon the side of the hill in two lines, one to support the other.

The word was then given to advance; and in a few minutes the first line stood on the brow and commanded the prospect on the other side. The second line closed up on them, and also the rear-guard with the prisoners; so that Morton and his companions in captivity could, in like manner, see the form of opposition which was now offered to the further progress of their captors.

The brow of the hill, on which the royal Life Guards were now drawn up, sloped downwards (on the side opposite to that which they had ascended) with a gentle declivity, for more than a quarter of a mile, and presented ground, which, though unequal in some places, was not altogether unfavourable for the manœuvres of cavalry, until nigh the bottom, when the slope terminated in a marshy level, traversed through its whole length by what seemed either a natural gulley, or a deep artificial drain, the sides of which were broken by springs, trenches filled with water, out of which peats and turfs had been dug, and here and there by some straggling thickets of alders which loved the moisture so well, that they continued to live as bushes, although too much dwarfed by the sour soil and the stagnant bog-water to ascend into trees. Beyond this ditch, or gulley, the ground arose into a second heathy swell, or rather hill, near to the foot of which, and as if with the purpose of defending the broken ground and ditch which covered their front, the body of insurgents appeared to be drawn up with the purpose of abiding battle.

Their infantry was divided into three lines. The first, tolerably provided with fire-arms, were advanced almost close to the verge of the bog, so that their fire must necessarily annoy the royal cavalry as they descended the opposite hill, the whole front of which was exposed, and would probably be yet more fatal if they attempted to cross the morass. Behind this first line was a body of pikemen, designed for their support in case the dragoons should force the passage of the marsh. In their rear was the third line, consisting of countrymen armed with scythes set straight on the poles, hay-forks, spits, clubs, goads, fish-spears, and such other rustic implements as hasty resentment had converted into instruments of war. On each flank of the infantry, but a little backward from the bog, as if to allow themselves dry and sound ground whereon to act in case their enemies should force the pass, there was drawn up a small body of cavalry, who were, in general, but indifferently armed, and worse mounted, but full of zeal for the cause, being chiefly either land-holders of small property, or farmers of the better class, whose means enabled them to serve on horseback. A few of those who had been engaged in driving back the advanced guard of the royalists, might now be seen returning slowly towards their own squadrons. These were the only individuals of the insurgent army which seemed to be in motion. All the others stood firm and motionless, as the grey stones that lay scattered on the heath around them.

The total number of the insurgents might amount to about a thousand men; but of these there were scarce a hundred cavalry, nor were the one half of them even tolerably armed. The strength of their position, however, the sense of their having taken a desperate step, the superiority of their numbers, but, above all, the ardour of their enthusiasm, were the means on which their leaders reckoned for supplying the want of arms, equipage, and military discipline.

On the side of the hill which rose above the array of battle which they had adopted, were seen the women, and even the children, whom zeal, opposed to persecution, had driven into the wilderness. They seemed stationed there to be spectators of the engagement by which their own fate, as well as that of their parents, husbands, and sons, was to be decided. Like the females of the ancient German tribes, the shrill cries which they raised, when they beheld the glittering ranks of their enemies appear on the brow of the opposing eminence, acted as an incentive to their relatives to fight to the last in defence of that which was dearest to them. Such exhortations seemed to have their full and emphatic effect; for a wild halloo, which went from rank to rank on the appearance of the soldiers, intimated the resolution of the insurgents to fight to the uttermost.

As the horsemen halted their lines on the ridge of the hill, their trumpets and kettle-drums sounded a bold and warlike flourish of menace and defiance, that rung along the waste like the shrill summons of a destroying angel. The wanderers, in answer, united their voices, and sent forth, in solemn modulation, the two first verses of the seventy-sixth Psalm, according to the metrical version of the Scottish Kirk:

"In Judah's land God is well known,
  His name's in Israel great,
In Salem is his tabernacle,
  In Zion is his seat.
There arrows of the bow he brake,

    The shield, the sword, the war.
More glorious thou than hills of prey,
    More excellent art far."

A shout, or rather a solemn acclamation, attended the close of the stanza; and, after a dead pause, the second verse was resumed by the insurgents, who applied the destruction of the Assyrians as prophetical of the issue of their own impending contest:—

    "Those that were stout of heart were spoiled,
      They slept their sleep outright,
    And none of those their hands did find,
      That were the men of might.
    When thy rebuke, O Jacob's God,
      Had forth against them past,
    Their horses and their chariots both
      Were in a dead sleep cast."

There was another acclamation, which was followed by the most profound silence.

While these solemn sounds, accented by a thousand voices, were prolonged amongst the waste hills, Claverhouse looked with great attention on the ground, and on the order of battle which the wanderers had adopted, and in which they seemed determined to await the assault.

"The churles," he said, "must have some old soldiers with them; it was no rustic that made choice of that ground."

"Burley is said to be with them for certain," answered Lord Evandale, "and also Hackstoun of Rathillet, Paton of Meadowhead, Cleland, and some other men of military skill."

"I judged as much," said Claverhouse, "from the style in which these detached horsemen leapt their horses over the ditch, as they returned to their position. It was easy to see that there are a few roundhead troopers among them, the true spawn of the old Covenant. We must manage this matter warily as well as boldly. Evandale, let the officers come to this knoll."

He moved to a small moss-grown cairn, probably the resting-place of some Celtic chief of other times, and the call of, "Officers to the front," soon brought them around their commander.

"I did not call you round me, gentlemen," said Claverhouse, "in the formal capacity of a council of war, for I will never turn over on others the responsibility which my rank imposes on myself. I only want the benefit of your opinions, reserving to myself, as most men do when they ask advice, the liberty of following my own.—What say you, Cornet Grahame? Shall we attack these fellows who are bellowing yonder? You are youngest and hottest, and therefore will speak first whether I will or no."

"Then," said Cornet Grahame, "while I have the honour to carry the standard of the Life Guards, it shall never, with my will, retreat before rebels. I say, Charge, in God's name and the King's!"

"And what say you, Allan?" continued Claverhouse, "for Evandale is so modest we shall never get him to speak till you have said what you have to say."

"These fellows," said Major Allan, an old cavalier officer of experience, "are three or four to one—I should not mind that much upon a fair field, but they are posted in a very formidable strength, and show no inclination to quit it. I therefore think, with deference to Cornet Grahame's opinion, that we should draw back to Tillietudlem, occupy the pass between the hills and the open country, and send for reinforcements to my Lord Ross, who is lying at Glasgow with a regiment of infantry. In this way we shall cut them off from the Strath of Clyde, and either compel them to come out of their strong-hold, and give us battle on fair terms, or, if they remain here, we will attack them so soon as our infantry has joined us, and enabled us to act with effect among these ditches, bogs, and quagmires."

"Pshaw!" said the young Cornet, "what signifies strong ground, when it is only held by a crew of canting, psalm-singing old women?"

"A man may fight ne'er the worse," retorted Major Allan, "for honouring both his bible and psalter. These fellows will prove as stubborn as steel; I know them of old."

"Their nasal psalmody," said the Cornet, "reminds our major of the race of Dunbar."

"Had you been at that race, young man," retorted Allan, "you would have wanted nothing to remind you of it for the longest day you had to live."

"Hush, hush, gentlemen," said Claverhouse, "these are untimely repartees.—I should like your advice well, Major Allan, had our rascally patroles (whom I will see duly punished) brought us timely notice of the enemy's numbers and position. But having once presented ourselves before them in line, the retreat of the Life Guards would argue gross timidity, and be the general signal for insurrection through the west. In which case, so far from obtaining assistance from my Lord Ross, I promise you I should have great apprehensions of his being cut off before we could join him, or he us. A retreat would have quite the same fatal effect upon the King's cause as the loss of a battle —and as to the difference of risk or of safety it might make with respect to ourselves, that, I am sure, no gentleman thinks a moment about. There must be some gorges or passes in the morass through which we can force our way; and, were we once on firm ground, I trust there is no man in the Life Guards who supposes our squadrons, though so weak in numbers, are unable to trample into dust twice the number of these unpractised clowns.—What say you, my Lord Evandale?"

"I humbly think," said Lord Evandale, "that, go the day how it will, it must be a bloody one; and that we shall lose many brave fellows, and probably be obliged to slaughter a great number of these misguided men, who, after all, are Scotchmen and subjects of King Charles, as well as we are."

"Rebels! rebels! and undeserving the name either of Scotchmen or of subjects," said Claverhouse; "but come, my lord, what does your opinion point at?"

"To enter into a treaty with these ignorant and misled men."

"A treaty, and with rebels having arms in their hands? Never while I live," answered his commander.

"At least send a trumpet and a flag of truce, summoning them to lay down their weapons and disperse," said Lord Evandale, "upon promise of a free pardon—I have always heard that had that been done before the battle of Pentland-hills, much blood might have been saved."

"Well," said Claverhouse, "and who the devil do you think would carry a summons to these headstrong and desperate fanatics? They acknowledge no laws of war. Their leaders, who have been almost all active in the murder of the Archbishop of St Andrews, fight with a rope round their necks, and are likely to kill the messenger, were it but to dip their followers in loyal blood, and to make them as desperate of pardon as themselves."

"I will go myself," said Evandale, "if you will permit me. I have often risked my life to spill that of others, let me now do so in order to save effusion of human blood."

"You shall not go on such an errand, my lord," said Claverhouse; "your rank and situation render your safety of too much consequence to the country in an age when good principles are so rare.—Here's my brother's son, Dick Grahame, who fears shot or steel as little as if the devil had given him armour of proof against it, as the fanatics say he has given to his uncle. He shall take a flag-of-truce and a trumpet, and ride down to the edge of the morass to summon them to lay down their arms and disperse."

"With all my soul, Colonel," answered the Cornet; "and I'll tie my cravat on a pike to serve for a white flag—the rascals never saw such a pennon of Flanders lace in their lives before."

"Colonel Grahame," said Evandale, while the young officer prepared for his expedition, "this young gentleman is your nephew—your beloved nephew and your apparent heir; for God's sake, permit me to go. It was my counsel—I ought to stand the risk."

"Were he my only son," said Claverhouse, "this is no cause, no time to spare him. I hope my private affections will never interfere with my public duty. If Dick Grahame falls, the loss is chiefly mine; were your lordship to die, the King and country would be the sufferers.—Come, gentlemen, each to his post. If our summons is unfavourably received, we will instantly attack, and, as the old Scotch blazon has it, God shaw the right!"

Chapter Three

With many a stout thwack and many a bang,
Hard crab-tree and old iron rang.
Hudibras

CORNET RICHARD GRAHAME descended the hill, bearing in his hand the extemporé flag of truce, and making his managed horse keep time by bounds and curvets to the tune which he whistled. The trumpeter followed. Five or six horsemen, having something the appearance of officers, detached themselves from each flank of the presbyterian array, and, meeting in the centre, approached the ditch which divided the hollow as near as the morass would permit. Towards this group, but keeping the opposite side of the swamp, Cornet Grahame directed his horse, his motions being now the conspicuous object of attention to both armies; and, without disparagement to the courage of either, it is probable there was a general wish on both sides that this embassy might save the risks and bloodshed of the impending conflict.

When he had arrived right opposite to those, who, by their advancing to receive his message, seemed to take upon themselves as the leaders of the enemy, Cornet Grahame commanded his trumpet to sound a parley. The insurgents having no instrument of martial music wherewith to make the appropriate reply, one of their number called out with a loud, strong voice, demanding to know why he approached their leaguer.

"To summon you in the King's name, and in that of Colonel John Grahame of Claverhouse, specially commissioned by the right honourable Privy Council of Scotland," answered the Cornet, "to lay down your arms and dismiss the followers whom you have led into rebellion, contrary to the laws of God, of the King, and of the country."

"Return to them that sent thee," said the insurgent leader, "and tell them that we are this day in arms for a broken Covenant and a persecuted Kirk; tell them that we renounce the licentious and perjured Charles Stuart, whom you call King, even as he renounced the Covenant, after having once and again sworn to prosecute to the utmost of his power all the ends thereof, really, constantly, and sincerely, all the days of his life, having no enemies but the enemies of the Covenant, and no friends but its friends. Whereas, far from keeping the oath he had called God and angels to witness, his first step, after his incoming into these kingdoms, was the fearful grasping at the prerogative of the Almighty, by that hideous Act of Supremacy, together with his expulsing, without summons, libel, or process of law, hundreds of famous faithful preachers, thereby wringing the bread of life out of the mouth of hungry, poor creatures, and forcibly cramming their throats with the lifeless, saltless, foisenless, lukewarm drammock of the fourteen false prelates, and their sycophantic, formal, carnal, scandalous creature-curates."

"I did not come to hear you preach," answered the officer, "but to know in one word, if you will disperse yourselves, on condition of a free pardon to all but the murderers of the late Archbishop of St Andrews; or whether you will abide the attack of his majesty's forces, which will instantly advance upon you."

"In one word, then," answered the spokesman, "we are here with our swords on our thighs, as men that watch in the night. We will take one part and portion together, as brethren in righteousness. Whosoever assails us in our good cause, his blood be on his own head. So return to those that sent thee, and God give them and thee a sight of the evil of your ways!"

"Is not your name," said the Cornet, who began to recollect having seen the person whom he was now speaking with, "John Balfour of Burley?"

"And if it be," said the spokesman, "hast thou aught to say against it?"

"Only," said the Cornet, "that as you are excluded from pardon by your atrocious guilt, it is to these country people and not to you that I offer it; and it is not with you, or such as you, that I am sent to treat."

"Thou art a young soldier, friend," said Burley, "and scant well-learned in thy trade, or thou wouldst know that the bearer of a flag of truce cannot treat with the army but through the officers; and that if he presume to do otherwise, he forfeits his safe-conduct."

While speaking these words, Burley unslung his carabine, and held it in readiness.

"I am not to be intimidated from the discharge of my duty by the menaces of a murderer," said Cornet Grahame.—"Hear me, good people; I proclaim, in the name of the King and of my commanding officer, full and free pardon to all, excepting"——

"I give thee fair warning," said Burley, presenting his piece.

"A free pardon to all," continued the young officer, still addressing the body of the insurgents—"to all but"——

"Then the Lord grant grace to thy soul—amen," said Burley.

With these words he fired, and Cornet Richard Grahame dropped from his horse. The shot was mortal. The poor young gentleman had only strength to turn himself on the ground and mutter forth, "My poor mother!" when life forsook him in the effort. His startled horse fled back to the regiment at the gallop, as did his scarce less-affrighted attendant.

"What have ye done?" said one of Balfour's brother-officers.

"My duty," said Balfour, firmly. "Is it not written, thou shalt be zealous even to slaying? Let those who dare, NOW venture to speak of truce or pardon!"

Claverhouse saw his nephew fall. He turned his eye on Evandale, while a transitory glance of indescribable emotion disturbed, for a second's space, the serenity of his features, and briefly said, "You see the event."

"I will avenge him or die!" exclaimed Evandale; and, putting his horse into motion, rode furiously down the hill, followed by his own troop, and that of the deceased Cornet which broke down without orders, and each striving to be the foremost to revenge that young officer, their ranks soon fell into confusion. These forces formed the first line of the royalists. It was in vain that Claverhouse exclaimed, "Halt, halt! this rashness will undo us." It was all that he could accomplish by galloping along the second line, entreating, commanding, and even menacing the men with his sword, that he could restrain them from following an example so contagious.

"Allan," he said, as soon as he had rendered the men in some degree more steady, "lead them slowly down the hill to support Lord Evandale, who is about to need it very much.—Bothwell, thou art a cool and a daring fellow"——

"Ay," muttered Bothwell, "you can remember that in a moment like this."

"Lead ten file up the hollow to the right," continued his commanding officer, "and try every means to get through the bog; then form and charge the rebels in flank and rear, while they are engaged with us in front."

Bothwell made a signal of intelligence and obedience, and moved off with his party at a round pace.

Mean time, the disaster which Claverhouse had apprehended did not fail to take place. The troopers, who, with Lord Evandale, had rushed down upon the enemy, soon found their disorderly career interrupted by the impracticable character of the ground. Some stuck fast in the morass as they attempted to struggle through, some recoiled from the attempt and remained on the brink, others dispersed to seek a more favourable place to pass the swamp. In the midst of this confusion, the first line of the enemy, of which the foremost rank knelt, the second stooped, and the third stood upright, poured in a close and destructive fire that emptied at least a score of saddles, and increased tenfold the disorder into which the horsemen had fallen. Lord Evandale, in the mean time, at the head of a very few well-mounted men, had been able to clear the ditch, but was no sooner across than he was charged by the left body of the enemy's cavalry, who, encouraged by the small number of opponents that had made their way through the broken ground, set upon them with the utmost fury, crying, "Woe, woe to the uncircumcised Philistines! down with Dagon and all his adherents!"

The young nobleman fought like a lion; but most of his followers were killed, and he himself could not have escaped the same fate but for a heavy fire of carabines, which Claverhouse, who had now advanced with the second line near to the ditch, poured so effectually upon the enemy, that both horse and foot for a moment began to shrink, and Lord Evandale, disengaged from his unequal combat, and finding himself nearly alone, took the opportunity to effect his retreat through the moss. But notwithstanding the loss they had sustained by Claverhouse's first fire, the insurgents became soon aware that the advantage of numbers and of position were so decidedly theirs, that, if they could but persist in making a brief but resolute defence, the Life Guards must necessarily be defeated. Their leaders flew through their ranks, exhorting them to stand firm, and pointing out how efficacious their fire must be where both men and horse were exposed to it; for the troopers, according to the custom, fired without having dismounted. Claverhouse, more than once, when he perceived his best men dropping by a fire which they could not effectually return, made desperate efforts to pass the bog at various points, and renew the battle on firm ground and fairer terms. But the close fire of the insurgents, joined to the natural difficulties of the pass, disappointed his attempts on every point.

"We must retreat," he said to Evandale, "unless Bothwell can effect a diversion in our favour. In the mean time, draw the men out of fire, and leave skirmishers behind these patches of alder-bushes to keep the enemy in check."

These directions being accomplished, the appearance of Bothwell with his party was earnestly expected. But Bothwell had his own disadvantages to struggle with. His detour to the right had not escaped the penetrating observation of Burley, who made a corresponding movement with the left wing of the mounted insurgents, so that when Bothwell, after riding a considerable way up the valley, found a place at which the bog could be passed, though with some difficulty, he perceived he was still in front of a superior enemy. His daring character was in no degree checked by this unexpected opposition.

"Follow me, my lads," he called to his men; "never let it be said that we turned our backs before these canting round-heads!"

With that, as if inspired by the spirit of his ancestors, he shouted, "Bothwell! Bothwell!" and throwing himself into the morass, he struggled through it at the head of his party, and attacked that of Burley with such fury, that he drove them back above a pistol-shot, killing or disabling three men with his own hand. Burley, perceiving the consequences of a defeat on this point, and that his men, though more numerous, were unequal to the regulars in using their arms and managing their horses, threw himself across Bothwell's way, and attacked him hand to hand. Each of the combatants was considered as the champion of his respective party, and a result ensued more usual in romance than in real story. Their followers, on either side, instinctively paused, and looked on as if the fate of the day were to be decided by the event of the combat between these two redoubted swordsmen. The combatants themselves seemed of the same opinion; for, after two or three eager cuts and pushes had been exchanged, they paused, as if by joint consent, to recover the breath which preceding exertions had exhausted, and to prepare for a duel in which each seemed conscious he had met his match.

"You are the murdering villain, Burley," said Bothwell, griping his sword firmly, and setting his teeth close—"you escaped me once, but" —(he swore an oath too tremendous to be written down) "thy head is worth its weight of silver, and it shall go home at my saddle-bow, or my saddle shall go home empty for me."

"Yes," retorted Burley, with a stern and gloomy deliberation, "I am that John Balfour who promised to lay thy head where thou should'st never lift it again; and God do so to me, and more also, if I do not redeem my word."

"Then a bed of heather, or a thousand marks!" said Bothwell, striking at Burley with his full force.

"The sword of the Lord and of Gideon!" answered Balfour, as he parried and returned the blow.

There have seldom met two combatants more equally matched in strength of body, skill in the management of their weapons and horses, determined courage, and unrelenting hostility. After exchanging many desperate blows, each receiving and inflicting several wounds, though none of great consequence, they grappled together as if with the desperate impatience of mortal hatred, and Bothwell, seizing his enemy by the shoulder-belt, while the grasp of Balfour was upon his own collar, they came headlong to the ground. The companions of Burley hastened to his assistance, but were repelled by the dragoons, and the battle became again general. But nothing could withdraw the attention of the combatants from each other, or induce them to unloose the deadly clasp in which they rolled together on the ground, tearing, struggling, and foaming, with the inveteracy of thorough-bred bull-dogs.

Several horses passed over them in the melée without their quitting hold of each other, till the sword-arm of Bothwell was broken by the kick of a charger. He then relinquished his grasp with a deep and suppressed groan, and both combatants started to their feet. Bothwell's right hand dropped helpless by his side, but his left griped to the place where his dagger hung; it had escaped from the sheath in the struggle,—and, with a look of mingled rage and despair, he stood totally defenceless, as Balfour, with a laugh of savage joy, flourished his sword aloft, and then passed it through his adversary's body. Bothwell received the thrust without falling—it had only grazed on his ribs. He attempted no farther defence, but, looking at Burley with a grin of deadly hatred, exclaimed,—"Base peasant churl, thou hast spilt the blood of a line of kings!"

"Die, wretch!—die," said Balfour, redoubling the thrust with better aim; and, setting his foot on Bothwell's body as he fell, he a third time transfixed him with his sword.—"Die, blood-thirsty dog! die, as thou hast lived!—die, like the beasts that perish—hoping nothing—believing nothing"——

"And FEARING nothing!" said Bothwell, collecting the last effort of respiration to utter these desperate words, and expiring as soon as they were spoken.

To catch a stray horse by the bridle, throw himself upon it, and rush to the assistance of his followers, was, with Burley, the affair of a moment. And as the fall of Bothwell had given to the insurgents all the courage of which it had deprived his comrades, the issue of this partial contest did not remain a moment undecided. Several soldiers were slain, the rest driven back over the morass and dispersed, and the victorious Burley, with his party, crossed in their turn, to direct against Claverhouse the very manœuvre which he had instructed Bothwell to execute. He now put his troop into order, with the view of attacking the right wing of the royalists; and, sending news of his success to the main body, exhorted them, in the name of Heaven, to cross the marsh, and work out the glorious work of the Lord by a general attack upon the enemy.

Meanwhile, Claverhouse, who had in some degree remedied the confusion occasioned by the first irregular and unsuccessful attack, and reduced the combat in front to a distant skirmish with fire-arms, chiefly maintained by some dismounted troopers whom he had posted behind the cover of the shrubby copses of alders which, in some places, covered the edge of the morass, and whose close, cool, and well-aimed fire greatly annoyed the enemy, and concealed their own deficiency of numbers,—Claverhouse, while he maintained the contest in this manner, still expecting that a diversion by Bothwell and his party might facilitate a general attack, was accosted by one of the dragoons, whose bloody face and jaded horse bore witness he was come from hard service.

"What is the matter, Halliday?" said Claverhouse, for he knew every man in his regiment by name—"Where is Bothwell?"

"Bothwell is down," replied Halliday, "and many a pretty fellow with him."

"Then the king," said Claverhouse, with his usual composure, "has lost a stout soldier. The enemy have passed the marsh, I suppose?"

"With a strong body of horse, commanded by the devil incarnate that killed Bothwell," answered the terrified soldier.

"Hush! hush!" said Claverhouse, putting his finger on his lips; "not a word to any one but me.—Lord Evandale—we must retreat— the fates will have it so—draw together the men that are dispersed in this skirmishing work. Let Allan form the regiment, and do you two retreat up the hill in two bodies, each halting alternately as the other falls back. I'll keep the rogues in check with the rear-guard, making a stand and facing from time to time. They will be over the ditch presently, for I see their whole line in motion, and preparing to cross; therefore lose no time."

"Where is Bothwell with his party?" said Lord Evandale, astonished at the coolness of his commander.

"Fairly disposed of," said Claverhouse, in his ear—"the king has lost a servant, and the devil has got one. But away to business, Evandale—ply your spurs and get the men together. Allan and you must keep them steady. This retreating is new work for us all; but our turn will come round again another day."

Evandale and Allan betook themselves to their task; but ere they had arranged the regiment for the purpose of retreating in two alternate bodies, a considerable number of the enemy had crossed the marsh. Claverhouse, who had retained immediately around his person a few of his most active and tried men, charged those who had crossed, in person, while they were yet disordered by the broken ground. Some they killed, others they repulsed into the morass, and checked the whole so as to enable the main body, now greatly diminished, as well as disheartened by the loss they had sustained, to commence their retreat up the hill.

But the enemy's van being soon reinforced and supported, compelled Claverhouse to follow his troops. Never did man, however, better support the character of a soldier than he did that day. Conspicuous by his black horse and white feather, he was first in the repeated charges which he made at every favourable opportunity, to arrest the progress of the pursuers, and to cover the retreat of his regiment. The object of aim to every one, it seemed as if he was impassive to their shot. The superstitious fanatics, who looked upon him as a man gifted by the Evil Spirit with supernatural means of defence, averred that they saw the bullets recoil from his jack-boots and buff coat like hailstones from a rock of granite, as he gallopped to and fro amid the storm of shot. Many a whig that day loaded his musket with a dollar cut into slugs, in order that a silver bullet (such was their belief) might bring down the persecutor of the holy kirk, on whom lead had no power.

"Try him with the cold steel," was the cry at every renewed charge —"powder is wasted on him. Ye might as weel shoot at the auld enemy himsel."

But though this was loudly shouted, yet the awe on the insurgents' minds was such, that they gave way before Claverhouse as before a supernatural being, and few men ventured to cross swords with him. Still, however, he was fighting in retreat, and with all the disadvantages attending that movement. The soldiers behind him, as they beheld the increasing number of enemies who poured over the morass, became unsteady; and, at every successive movement, Major Allan and Lord Evandale found it more and more impossible to bring them to halt and form line regularly, while, on the other hand, their motion in the act of retreating became, by degrees, much more rapid than was consistent with good order. As they approached nearer to the top of the ridge, from which in so luckless an hour they had descended, the panic began to increase. Every one became impatient to place the brow of the hill between him and the continued fire of their pursuers, nor could any individual think it reasonable that he should be the last in the retreat, and thus sacrifice his own safety for that of others. In this mood, several troopers set spurs to their horses and fled outright, and the others became so unsteady in their movements and formations, that their officers every moment feared they would follow the same example.

Amid this scene of blood and confusion, the trampling of the horses, the groans of the wounded, the continued fire of the enemy, which fell in a succession of unintermitted musketry, while loud shouts accompanied each bullet which the fall of a trooper shewed to have been successfully aimed—amid all the terrors and disorder of such a scene, and when it was dubious how soon they might be totally deserted by their dispirited soldiery, Evandale could not forbear remarking the composure of his commanding officer. Not at Lady Margaret's breakfast-table that morning did his eye appear more lively, or his demeanour more composed. He had closed up to Evandale for the purpose of giving some orders, and picking out a few men to reinforce his rear-guard.

"If this rout lasts five minutes longer," he said, in a whisper, "our rogues will leave you, old Allan, and me, the honour of fighting this battle with our own hands. I must do something to disperse the musqueteers who annoy them so hard, or we will be all shamed. Don't attempt to succour me if you see me go down, but keep at the head of your men; get off as you can, in God's name, and tell the king and the Council I died in my duty."

So saying, and commanding about twenty stout men to follow him, he gave, with this small body, a charge so desperate and unexpected, that he drove the foremost of the pursuers back to some distance. In the confusion of the assault he singled out Burley, and, desirous to strike terror into his followers, he dealt him so severe a blow on the head, as cut through his steel head-piece, and threw him from his horse, stunned for the moment, though unwounded. A wonderful thing it was afterwards thought, that one so powerful as Balfour should have sunk under the blow of a man, to appearance, so slightly made as Claverhouse; and the vulgar, of course, set down to supernatural aid, the effect of that energy which a determined spirit can give to a feebler arm. Claverhouse had, in this last charge, however, involved himself too deeply among the insurgents, and was fairly surrounded.

Lord Evandale saw the danger of his commander, his body of dragoons being then halted, while that commanded by Allan was in the act of retreating. Regardless of Claverhouse's disinterested command to the contrary, he ordered the party which he headed to charge down hill and extricate their Colonel. Some advanced with him— most halted and stood uncertain—many ran away. With those who followed Evandale, he disengaged Claverhouse. His assistance came just in time, for a rustic had wounded his horse in a most ghastly manner by the blow of a scythe, and was about to repeat the stroke when Lord Evandale cut him down. As they got out of the press, they looked around them. Allan's division had ridden clear over the hill, that officer's authority having proved altogether unequal to halt them. Evandale's division was scattered and in total confusion.

"What is to be done, Colonel?" said Lord Evandale.

"We are the last men in the field, I think," said Claverhouse; "and when men fight as long as they can there is no shame in flying. Hector himself would say, 'devil take the hindmost,' when there are but twenty against a thousand.—Save yourselves, my lads, and rally as soon as you can.—Come, my Lord, we must e'en ride for it."

So saying, he put spurs to his wounded horse, and the generous animal, as if conscious that the life of his rider depended on his exertions, pressed forward with speed, unabated either by pain or loss of blood. A few officers and soldiers followed him, but in a very irregular and tumultuary manner. The flight of Claverhouse was the signal for all the stragglers, who yet offered desultory resistance, to fly as fast as they could, and yield up the field of battle to the victorious insurgents.

Chapter Four

But see! through the fast-flashing lightnings of war,
What steed to the desert flies frantic and far!
                                        CAMPBELL

DURING the severe skirmish of which we have given the details, Morton, together with Cuddie and his mother, and the Reverend Gabriel Kettledrummle, remained on the brow of the hill, near to the small cairn, or barrow, beside which Claverhouse had held his preliminary council-of-war, so that they had a commanding view of the action which took place in the bottom. They were guarded by Corporal Inglis and four soldiers, who, as may readily be supposed, were much more intent on watching the fluctuating fortunes of the battle, than in attending to what passed among the prisoners.

"If yon lads stand to their tackle," said Cuddie, "we'll hae some chance o' getting our necks out o' the brecham again; but I misdoubt them—they hae little skeel o' arms."

"Much is not necessary, Cuddie," answered Morton; "they have a strong position, and weapons in their hands, and are more than three times the number of their assailants. If they cannot fight for their freedom now, they and theirs deserve to lose it for ever."

"O, sirs," exclaimed Mause, "here's a goodly spectacle indeed! My spirit is like that of the blessed Elihu, it burns within me—my bowels are as wine which lacketh vent—they are ready to burst like new bottles. O, that He may look after his ain people in this day of judgment and deliverance!—And now, what ailest thou, precious Mr Gabriel Kettledrummle? I say, what ailest thou? thou that wert a Nazarite purer than snow, whiter than milk, more ruddy than sulphur, (meaning, perhaps, sapphires)—I say, what ails thee now, that thou art blacker than a coal, that thy beauty is departed, and thy loveliness withered like a dry potsherd? Surely it is time to up and be doing, to cry loudly, and to spare nought, and to wrestle for the safety of the puir lads that are yonder testifying with their ain blude and that of their enemies."

This expostulation implied a reproach on Mr Kettledrummle, who, though an absolute Boanerges, or son of thunder, in the pulpit, when the enemy were afar, and indeed sufficiently contumacious, as we have seen, even when in their power, had been struck dumb by the firing, shouts, and shrieks, which now arose from the valley, and,—as many an honest man might have been, in a situation where he could neither fight nor flee, was too much dismayed to take so favourable an opportunity to preach the terrors of presbytery, as the courageous Mause had expected at his hand, or even to pray for the successful event of the battle. His presence of mind was not, however, entirely lost, any more than his jealous respect for his reputation as a pure and powerful preacher of the word.

"Hold your peace, woman," he said, "and do not perturb my inward meditations and the wrestlings wherewith I wrestle—but of a verity the shooting of the foeman doth begin to increase; peradventure, some pellet may attain unto us even here. Lo! I will ensconce me behind the cairn, as behind a strong wall of defence."

"He's but a coward body after a'," said Cuddie, who was himself by no means deficient in that sort of courage which consists in insensibility to danger; "he's but a daidling coward body. He'll never fill Rumbleberry's bonnet.—Odd! Rumbleberry fought and flyted like a fleeing dragon. It was a great pity, poor man, he could na cheat the woodie. But they say he gaed singing and rejoicing till't, just as I wad gae till a bicker o' brose, supposing me hungry, as I stand a gude chance to be.—Eh, sirs! yon's an awfu' sight, and yet ane canna keep their een aff frae it!"

Accordingly, strong curiosity on the part of Morton and Cuddie, together with the heated enthusiasm of old Mause, detained them on the spot from which they could best hear and see the issue of the action, leaving to Kettledrummle to occupy alone his chosen place of security. The vicissitudes of combat, which we have already described, were witnessed by our spectators from the top of the eminence, but without their being able positively to determine to what they

tended. That the presbyterians defended themselves stoutly was evident from the heavy smoke, which, illumined by frequent flashes of fire,
now eddied along the valley, and hid the contending parties in its
sulphurous shade. On the other hand, the continued firing from the
nearer side of the morass indicated that the enemy persevered in their
attack, that the affair was fiercely disputed, and that every thing was to
be apprehended from a continued contest, in which undisciplined
rustics had to repel the assaults of regular troops so completely offi-
cered and armed.

At length horses, whose caparisons shewed they belonged to the
Life-Guards, began to fly masterless out of the confusion. Mounted
soldiers next appeared, forsaking the conflict, and straggling over the
side of the hill, in order to escape from the scene of action. As the
numbers of these fugitives increased, the fate of the day seemed no
longer doubtful. A larger body was then seen emerging from the
smoke, forming irregularly on the hill-side, and with difficulty kept
stationary by their officers, until Evandale's corps also appeared in full
retreat. The result of the conflict was then apparent, and the joy of the
prisoners was corresponding to the approaching deliverance.

"They hae done the job for anes," said Cuddie, "an' they ne'er do it
again."

"They flee!—they flee!" exclaimed Mause, in ecstasy. "O, the
truculent tyrants! they are riding now as they never rode before. O,
the false Egyptians—the proud Assyrians—the Philistines—the
Moabites—the Edomites—the Ishmaelites—The Lord has brought
sharp swords upon them, to mak them food for the fowls of heaven
and the beasts of the field. See how the clouds roll, and the fire flashes
ahint them, and goes forth before the chosen of the Covenant, e'en
like the pillar o' cloud and the pillar o' flame that led the people o'
Israel out o' the land of Egypt! This is indeed a day of deliverance to
the righteous, a day of pouring out of wrath to the persecutors and the
ungodly."

"Lord safe us," said Cuddie, "mither, haud the clavering tongue o'
ye, and lie down ahint the cairn, like Kettledrummle, honest man.
Thae whigamore bullets ken unco little discretion, and will just as
sune knock out the harns o' a psalm-singing auld wife as a swearing
dragoon."

"Fear naething for me, Cuddie," said the old dame, transported to
ecstacy by the success of her party; "fear naething for me. I will stand,
like Deborah, on the tap o' the cairn, and take up my song of reproach
against these men of Harosheth of the Gentiles, whose horse-hoofs
are broken by means of their prancings."

The enthusiastic old woman would in fact have accomplished her purpose, of mounting on the cairn, and becoming, as she said, a sign and a banner to the people, had not Cuddie, with more filial tenderness than respect, detained her by such force as his shackled arms would permit him to exert.

"Eh, sirs!" he said, having accomplished this task, "look out yonder, Milnewood; saw ye ever mortal fight like the devil Claver'se yonder?—he's been thrice doun amang them, and thrice cam free aff.—But I think we'll sune be free oursels, Milnewood. Inglis and his troopers look ower their shouther very aften, as if they liked the road ahint them better than the road afore."

Cuddie was not mistaken; for, when the main tide of fugitives passed at a little distance from the spot where they were stationed, the corporal and his party fired their carabines at random upon the advancing insurgents, and, abandoning all charge of their prisoners, joined the retreat of their comrades. Morton and the old woman, whose hands were at liberty, lost no time in undoing the bonds of Cuddie and of the clergyman, both of whom had been secured by a cord tied round their arms above the elbows. By the time this was accomplished, the rear-guard of the dragoons, which still preserved some order, passed beneath the hillock or rising ground which was surmounted by the cairn already repeatedly mentioned. They exhibited all the hurry and confusion incident to a forced retreat, but still continued in a body. Claverhouse led the van, his naked sword deeply dyed with blood, as were his face and clothes. His horse was all covered with gore, and now reeled with weakness. Lord Evandale, in not a much better plight, brought up the rear, still exhorting the soldiers to keep together and to fear nothing. Several of the men were wounded, and one or two dropped from their horses as they surmounted the hill.

Mause's zeal broke forth once more at this spectacle, while she stood on the heath with her head uncovered, and her grey hairs streaming in the wind, no bad representation of a superannuated bacchante, or a Thessalian witch in the agonies of incantation. She soon discovered Claverhouse at the head of his fugitive party, and exclaimed with bitter irony, "Tarry, tarry, ye wha were aye sae blythe to be at the meetings of the saints, and wad ride every muir in Scotland to find a conventicle. Wilt thou not tarry, now thou hast found ane? Wilt thou na stay for one word mair? Wilt thou na bide the afternoon preaching?—Wae betide ye!" she said, suddenly changing her tone, "and cut the houghs of the creature whase fleetness ye trust in!—Sheugh—Sheugh—awa' wi' ye that hae spilled sae muckle innocent blude, and now wad save your ain—awa' wi' ye for a railing Rabshekah, a cursing Shemei, a blood-thirsty Doeg—the sword's drawn now that winna be lang o' overtaking ye, ride as fast as ye will."

Claverhouse, it may be easily supposed, was too busy to attend to her reproaches, but hastened over the hill, anxious to get the remnant of his men out of gun-shot, in hopes of again collecting the fugitives round his standard. But as the rear of his followers rode over the ridge, a shot struck Lord Evandale's horse, which instantly sunk down dead beneath him. Two of the whig horsemen, who were the foremost in the pursuit, hastened up with the purpose of killing him, for hitherto there had been no quarter given. Morton, on the other hand, rushed forward to save his life, if possible, in order at once to indulge his natural generosity, and to requite the obligation which Lord Evandale had conferred on him that morning, and which circumstances had made him wince under so acutely. Just as he had assisted Evandale, who was much wounded, to extricate himself from his dying horse, and to gain his feet, the two horsemen came up, and one of them exclaiming, "Have at the red-coated tyrant!" made a blow at the young nobleman, which Morton parried with difficulty, exclaiming to the rider, who was no other than Burley himself, "Give quarter to this gentleman, for my sake—for the sake," he added, observing that Burley did not immediately recognize him, "of Henry Morton, who so lately sheltered you."

"Henry Morton?" replied Burley, wiping his bloody brow with his bloodier hand, "did I not say that the son of Silas Morton would come forth out of the land of bondage, nor be long an indweller in the tents of Ham? Thou art a brand snatched out of the burning—But for this booted apostle of prelacy, he shall die the death!—We must smite them hip and thigh, even from the rising to the going down of the sun. It is our commission to slay them like Amalek, and utterly destroy all they have, and spare neither man nor woman, infant or suckling; therefore, hinder me not," he continued, endeavouring again to cut down Lord Evandale, "for this work must not be wrought negligently."

"You must not, and you shall not, slay him, more especially while incapable of defence," said Morton, planting himself before Lord Evandale so as to intercept any blow that should be aimed at him; "I owed my life to him this morning—my life, which was endangered solely by my having sheltered you; and to shed his blood when he can offer no effectual resistance, were not only a cruelty abhorrent to God and man, but detestable ingratitude both to him and to me."

Burley paused—"Thou art yet," he said, "in the court of the Gentiles, and I compassionate thy human blindness and frailty. Strong meat is not fit for babes, nor the mighty and grinding dispensation under which I draw my sword, for those whose hearts are yet dwelling

in huts of clay, whose footsteps are tangled in the mesh of mortal
sympathies, and who clothe themselves in the righteousness that is as
filthy rags. But to gain a soul to the truth is better than to send one to
Tophet; therefore I give quarter to this youth, providing the grant is
confirmed by the general council of God's army, whom he hath this
day blessed with so signal a deliverance.—Thou art unarmed—Abide
my return here. I must yet pursue these sinners, the Amalekites, and
destroy them till they be utterly consumed from the face of the land,
even from Havilah unto Shur."

So saying, he set spurs to his horse, and continued to pursue the
chase.

"Cuddie," said Morton, "for God's sake catch a horse as quickly as
you can. I will not trust Lord Evandale's life with these obdurate men.
—You are wounded, my Lord. Are you able to continue your retreat?"
he continued, addressing himself to his prisoner, who, half stunned by
the fall, was but beginning to recover himself.

"I think so," replied Lord Evandale. "But is it possible?—Do I owe
my life to Mr Morton?"

"My interference would have been the same from common humanity," replied Morton; "to your Lordship it was a sacred debt of gratitude."

Cuddie at this instant returned with a horse.

"God-sake, mount—mount, and ride like a fleeing hawk, my
Lord," said the good-natured fellow, "for ne'er be in me, if they are na
killing every ane o' the wounded and prisoners."

Lord Evandale mounted the horse, while Cuddie officiously held
the stirrup.

"Stand off, good fellow, thy courtesy may cost thy life.—Mr Morton," he continued, addressing Henry, "this makes us more than even
—rely on it I will never forget your generosity—Farewell."

He turned his horse, and rode swiftly away in the direction which
seemed least exposed to pursuit.

Lord Evandale had just rode off, when several of the insurgents,
who were in the front of the pursuit, came up, denouncing vengeance
on Henry Morton and Cuddie for having aided the escape of a Philistine, as they called the young nobleman.

"What wad ye hae had us do?" cried Cuddie. "Had we aught to stop
a man wi', that had twa pistols and a sword? suldna ye hae come faster
up yoursels, instead of flyting at huz?"

This excuse would hardly have passed current; but Kettledrummle, who now awakened from his trance of terror, and was
known to, and reverenced by, most of the wanderers, together with
Mause, who possessed their appropriate language, as well as the

preacher himself, proved active and effectual intercessors.

"Touch them not, harm them not," exclaimed Kettledrummle, in his very best double-bass tones; "this is the son of the famous Silas Morton, by whom the Lord wrought great things in this land at the breaking forth of the reformation from prelacy, when there was a plentiful pouring forth of the Word and a renewing of the Covenant; a hero and champion of those blessed days, when there was power, and efficacy, and convincing, and converting of sinners, and heart-exercises, and fellowship of saints, and a plentiful flowing forth of the spices of the garden of Eden."

"And this is my son, Cuddie," exclaimed Mause in her turn, "the son of his father, Judden Headrigg, wha was a douse honest man, and of me, Mause Middlemas, an unworthy professor and follower of the pure gospel, and ane o' your ain folk. Is it not written, 'Cut ye not off the tribes of the families of the Kothathites from among the Levites?' Numbers, fourth and seventh—O, sirs! dinna be standing here prattling wi' honest folk, when ye suld be following forth your victory with which Providence has blessed ye."

This party having passed on, they were immediately beset by another, to whom it was necessary to give the same explanation. Kettledrummle, whose fear was much dissipated since the firing had ceased, again took upon him to be interpreter, and, grown bold, as he felt his good word necessary for the protection of his late fellow-captives, he laid claim to no small share of the merit of the victory, appealing to Morton and Cuddie, whether the tide of battle had not turned while he prayed on the Mount of Jehovah Nisi, like Moses, that Israel might prevail over Amalek; but granting them, at the same time, the credit of holding up his hands when they waxed heavy, as those of the prophet were supported by Aaron and Hur. It seems probable that Kettledrummle allotted this part in the success to his companions in adversity, lest they should be tempted to disclose his carnal and self-seeking falling away, in regarding too closely his own personal safety. These strong testimonies in favour of the liberated captives quickly flew abroad with many exaggerations among the victorious army. The reports on the subject were various; but it was universally agreed, that young Morton of Milnewood, the son of the stout soldier of the Covenant, Silas Morton, together with the precious Gabriel Kettle-drummle, and a singular devout Christian old woman, whom many thought as good as himself at extracting a doctrine or an use, whether of terror or consolation, had arrived to support the good old cause, with a reinforcement of a hundred well-armed men from the Middle Ward.

Chapter Five

When pulpit, drum ecclesiastic,
Was beat with fist instead of a stick.
Hudibras

IN the mean time, the insurgent cavalry returned from the pursuit, jaded and worn out with their unwonted efforts, and the infantry assembled on the ground which they had won, fatigued with toil and hunger. Their success, however, was a cordial to every bosom, and seemed even to serve in the stead of food and refreshment. It was, indeed, much more brilliant than they durst have ventured to anticipate; for, with no great loss on their own part, they had totally routed a regiment of picked men, commanded by the best officer in Scotland, and one whose very name had long been a terror to them. Their success seemed even to have upon their spirits the effect of a sudden and violent surprise, so much had their taking up arms been a measure rather of desperation than of hope. Their meeting was also casual, and they had hastily arranged themselves under such commanders as were remarkable for zeal and courage, without much respect to any other qualities. It followed, from this state of disorganization, that the whole army appeared at once to resolve itself into a general committee for considering what steps were to be taken in consequence of their success, and no opinion could be started so wild that it had not some favourers and advocates. Some proposed they should march to Glasgow, some to Hamilton, some to Edinburgh, some to London. Some were for sending a deputation of their number to London to convert Charles II. to a sense of the error of his ways, and others, less charitable, proposed either to call a new successor to the crown, or to declare Scotland a free republic. A free parliament of the nation, and a free Assembly of the Kirk, were the objects of the most sensible and moderate of the party. In the meanwhile, a clamour arose among the soldiers for bread and other necessaries, and while all complained of hardship and hunger, none took the necessary measures to procure supplies. In short, the camp of the Covenanters, even in the very moment of success, seemed about to dissolve like a rope of sand, from want of the original principles of combination and union.

Burley, who had now returned from the pursuit, found his fellows in arms in this distracted state. With the ready talent of one accustomed to encounter exigencies, he proposed, that one hundred of the freshest men should be drawn out for duty—that a small number of those who had hitherto acted as leaders, should constitute a committee of direction until officers should be regularly chosen—and that, to crown the victory, Gabriel Kettledrummle should be called upon to improve the providential success which they had obtained by a word in season addressed to the army. He reckoned very much, and not without reason, on this last expedient, as a means of engaging the attention of the bulk of the insurgents, while he himself, and two or three of their leaders, held a private council-of-war, undisturbed by the discordant opinions or senseless clamour of the general body.

Kettledrummle more than answered the expectations of Burley. Two mortal hours did he preach at a breathing; and certainly no lungs, or doctrine, excepting his own, could have kept up, for so long a time, the attention of men in such precarious circumstances. But he possessed in perfection a sort of rude and familiar eloquence peculiar to the preachers of that period, which, though it would have been fastidiously rejected by an audience which possessed any proportion of taste, was a cake of the right leaven for the palates of those whom he now addressed. His text was from the forty-ninth chapter of Isaiah. "Even the captives of the mighty shall be taken away, and the prey of the terrible shall be delivered; for I will contend with them that contendeth with thee, and I will save thy children. And I will feed them that oppress thee with their own flesh, and they shall be drunken with their own blood as with sweet wine, and all flesh shall know that I the Lord am thy Saviour, and thy Redeemer, the Mighty One of Jacob."

The discourse which he pronounced upon this subject was divided into fifteen heads, each of which was garnished with seven uses of application, two of consolation, two of terror, two declaring the causes of backsliding and of wrath, and one announcing the promised and expected deliverance. The first part of his text he applied to his own deliverance and that of his companions, and took occasion to speak several words in praise of young Milnewood, of whom, as a champion of the Covenant, he augured great things. The second part he applied to the punishments which were about to fall upon the persecuting government. At times he was familiar and colloquial; at times he was loud, energetic, and boisterous;—some parts of his discourse might be called sublime, and others sunk below burlesque. Occasionally he vindicated with great animation the right of every free man to worship God according to his own conscience; and presently he charged the guilt and misery of the people on the awful negligence of their rulers, who had not only failed to establish presbytery as the national religion, but had tolerated sectaries of various descriptions, Papists, Prelatists, Erastians assuming the name of Presbyterians, Independents, Socinians, and Quakers; all of whom, Kettledrummle proposed, by one sweeping act, to expel from the land, and thus re-edify in its integrity the beauty of the sanctuary. He next handled very pithily the doctrine of defensive arms and of resistance to Charles II., observing, that, instead of a nursing father to the Kirk, that monarch had been a nursing father to none but his own bastards. He went at some length through the life and conversation of that joyous prince, few parts of which, it must be owned, were qualified to stand the rough handling of so uncourtly an orator, who conferred on him the hard names of Jeroboam, Omri, Ahab, Shallum, Pekah, and every other evil monarch recorded in the Chronicles, and concluded with a round application of the Scripture, "Tophet is ordained of old; yea, for the KING it is provided: he hath made it deep and large; the pile thereof is fire and much wood: the breath of the Lord, like a stream of brimstone, doth kindle it."

Kettledrummle had no sooner ended his sermon, and descended from the huge rock which had served him for a pulpit, than his post was occupied by a pastor of a very different description. The reverend Gabriel was advanced in years, somewhat corpulent, with a loud voice, a square face, and a set of stupid and unanimated features, in which the body seemed more to predominate over the spirit than was seemly in a sound divine. The youth who succeeded him in exhorting this extraordinary convocation, was hardly twenty years old, yet his thin features already indicated, that a constitution, naturally hectic, was worn out by vigils, by fasts, by the rigour of imprisonment, and the fatigues incident to a fugitive life. Young as he was, he had been twice imprisoned for several months, and suffered many severities, which gave him great influence with those of his own sect. He threw his faded eyes over the multitude and over the scene of battle, and a light of triumph arose in his glance, his pale yet striking features were coloured with a transient and hectic blush of joy. He folded his hands, raised his face to Heaven, and seemed lost in mental prayer and thanksgiving ere he addressed the people. When he spoke, his faint and broken voice seemed at first inadequate to express his conceptions. But the deep silence of the assembly, the eagerness with which the ear gathered every word, as the famished Israelites collected the heavenly manna, had a corresponding effect upon the preacher himself. His words became more distinct, his manner more earnest and energetic; it seemed as if religious zeal was triumphing over bodily weakness and infirmity. His natural eloquence was not altogether untainted with the coarseness of his sect, and yet, by the influence of a good natural taste, it was freed from the grosser and more ludicrous errors of his contemporaries; and the language of Scripture, which, in their mouths, was sometimes degraded by misapplication, gave, in

Macbriar's exhortations, a rich and solemn effect, like that which is produced by the beams of the sun streaming through the storied representation of saints and martyrs on the Gothic window of some ancient cathedral.

He painted the desolation of the church, during the late period of her distresses, in the most affecting colours. He described her, like Hagar watching the waning life of her infant amid the fountainless desert; like Judah, under her palm-tree, mourning for the devastation of her temple; like Rahel, weeping for her children and refusing comfort. But he chiefly rose into rough sublimity when, addressing men yet reeking from battle, he called on them to remember the great things which God had done for them, and to persevere in the career which their victory had opened.

"Your garments are dyed—but not with the juice of the wine-press; your swords are filled with blood," he exclaimed, "but not with the blood of goats or lambs; the dust of the desart on which ye stand is made fat with gore, but not with the blood of bullocks, for the Lord hath a sacrifice in Bozrah, and a great slaughter in the land of Idumea. These are not the firstlings of the flock, the small cattle of burnt-offerings, whose bodies lie like dung on the ploughed field of the husbandman; this is not the savour of myrrh, of frankincense, or of sweet herbs, that is steaming in your nostrils; but these bloody trunks are the carcases of those that held the bow and the lance, who were cruel and would shew no mercy, whose voice roared like the sea, who rode upon horses, every man in array as if to the battle—they are the carcases even of the mighty men of war that came against Jacob in the day of his deliverance, and the smoke is that of the devouring fires that have consumed them. And these wild hills that surround you are not a sanctuary planked with cedar and plated with silver; nor are ye ministering priests at the altar, with censors and with torches, but ye hold in your hands the sword, and the bow, and the weapons of death—And yet verily, I say to you, that not when the ancient Temple was in its first glory was there offered sacrifice more acceptable than that which you have this day presented, giving to the slaughter the tyrant and the oppressor, with the rocks for your altars, and the sky for your vaulted sanctuary, and your own good swords for the instruments of sacrifice. Leave not, therefore, the plough in the furrow—turn not back from the path in which you have entered, like the famous worthies of old, whom God raised up for the glorifying of his name and the deliverance of his afflicted people—halt not in the race you are running, lest the latter end should be worse than the beginning. Wherefore, set up a standard in the land; blow a trumpet upon the mountains; let not the shepherd tarry by his sheepfold, or the seedsman continue in the ploughed field, but make the watch strong, sharpen the arrows, burnish the shields, name ye the captains of thousands, and captains of hundreds, of fifties, and of tens; call the footmen like the rushing of winds, and cause the horsemen to come up like the sound of many waters, for the passages of the destroyers are stopped, their rods are burned, and the face of their men of battle hath been turned to flight. Heaven has been with you, and has broken the bow of the mighty; then let every man's heart be as the heart of the valiant Maccabeus, every man's hand as the hand of the mighty Sampson, every man's sword as that of Gideon, which turned not back from the slaughter; for the banner of Reformation is spread abroad on the mountains in its first loveliness, and the gates of hell shall not prevail against it.

"Well is he this day that shall barter his house for a helmet, and sell his garment for a sword, and cast in his lot with the children of the Covenant, even to the fulfilling of the promise; and woe, woe unto him who, for carnal ends and self-seeking, shall withhold himself from the great work, for the curse shall abide with him, even the bitter curse of Meroz, because he came not to the help of the Lord against the mighty. Up, then, and be doing; the blood of martyrs, reeking upon scaffolds, is crying for vengeance; the bones of saints, which lie whitening in the highways, are pleading for retribution; the groans of innocent captives from desolate isles of the sea, and from the dungeons of the tyrants' high places, cry for deliverance; the prayers of persecuted Christians, sheltering themselves in dens and desarts from the sword of their persecutors, famished with hunger, starving with cold, lacking fire, food, shelter, and cloathing, because they serve God rather than man—all are with you, pleading, watching, knocking, storming the gates of heaven in your behalf. Heaven itself shall fight for you, as the stars in their courses fought against Sisera. Then whoso will deserve immortal fame in this world, and eternal happiness in that which is to come, let them enter into God's service, and take arles at the hand of his servant,—even a blessing upon him and his household, and his children, to the ninth generation, even the blessing of the promise, for ever and ever! Amen."

The eloquence of the preacher was rewarded by the deep hum of stern approbation which resounded through the armed congregation at the conclusion of an exhortation so well suited to that which they had done, and that which remained for them to do. The wounded forgot their pain, the faint and hungry their fatigues and privations, as they listened to doctrines which elevated them alike above the wants and calamities of the world, and identified their cause with that of the Deity. Many crowded around the preacher, as he descended from the

eminence on which he stood, and, clasping him with hands on which
the gore was yet hardened, pledged their sacred vow that they would
play the part of Heaven's true soldiers. Exhausted by his own enthusiasm, and by the animated fervour which he had exerted in his discourse, the preacher could only reply, in broken accents,—"God bless
you, my brethren—it is HIS cause—stand strongly up and play the
men—the worst that can befal us is but a brief and bloody passage to
heaven."

Balfour, and the other leaders, had not lost the time which was
employed in these spiritual exercises. Watch-fires were lighted, centinels were posted, and arrangements were made to refresh the army
with such provisions as had been hastily collected from the nearest
farm-houses and villages. The present necessity thus provided for,
they turned their thoughts to the future. They had dispatched parties
in a wider range to spread the news of their victory, and to obtain,
either by force or favour, supplies, of which they stood much in need.
In this they had succeeded beyond their hope, having at one village
seized a small magazine of provisions, forage, and ammunition, which
had been provided for the royal forces. This success not only gave
them relief at the time, but such hopes for the future, that whereas
formerly some of their number began to slacken in their zeal, they now
unanimously resolved to abide together in arms, and commit themselves and their cause to the event of war.

And whatever may be thought of the extravagance or narrow-
minded bigotry of many of their tenets, it is impossible to deny the
praise of devoted courage to a few hundred peasants, who, without
leaders, without money, without magazines, without any fixed plan of
action, and almost without arms, borne out only by their innate zeal,
and a detestation of the oppression of their rulers, ventured to declare
open war against an established government, supported by a regular
army, and the whole force of three kingdoms.

Chapter Six

Why, then, say an old man can do somewhat.
Henry IV. Part II

WE MUST now return to the Tower of Tillietudlem, which the march
of the Life-Guards, on the morning of this eventful day, had left to
silence and anxiety. The assurances of Lord Evandale had not
succeeded in quelling the apprehensions of Edith. She knew him
generous, and faithful to his word; but it seemed too plain that he
suspected the object of her intercession to be a successful rival; and

was it not expecting from him an effort above human nature, to suppose that he was to watch over Morton's safety, and rescue him from all the dangers to which his state of imprisonment, and the suspicions which he had incurred, must repeatedly expose him? She therefore resigned herself to the most heart-rending apprehensions, without admitting, and indeed almost without listening to, the multifarious grounds of consolation which Jenny Dennison brought forward, one after another, like a skilful general, who charges with the several divisions of his troops in regular succession.

First, Jenny was morally positive that young Milnewood would come to no harm—then, if he did, there was consolation in the reflection, that Lord Evandale was the better and more appropriate match of the two—then, there was every chance of a battle in which the said Lord Evandale might be killed, and there wad be nae mair fash about that job—then, if the whigs gat the better, Milnewood and Cuddie might come to the Castle, and carry off the beloved of their hearts by the strong hand.

"For I forgot to tell ye, madam," continued the damsel, putting her handkerchief to her eyes, "that puir Cuddie's in the hands of the Philistines as weel as young Milnewood, and he was brought here a prisoner this morning, and I was fain to speak Tam Halliday fair, and fleech him, to let me near the puir creature; but Cuddie wasna sae thankfu' as he needed till hae been neither," she added, and at the same time changed her tone, and briskly withdrew the handkerchief from her face; "so I sall ne'er waste my e'en wi' greeting about the matter. There wad be aye enow o' young men left, if they were to hang the tae half o' them."

The other inhabitants of the Castle were also in a state of dissatisfaction and anxiety. Lady Margaret thought that Colonel Grahame, in commanding an execution at the door of her house, and refusing to grant a reprieve at her request, had fallen short of the deference due to her rank, and had even encroached on her seignorial rights.

"The Colonel," she said, "ought to have remembered, brother, that the barony of Tillietudlem has the baronial privilege of pit and gallows, and therefore, if the lad was to be executed on my estate, (which I consider as an unhandsome thing, seeing it is in the possession of females, to whom such tragedies cannot be acceptable) he ought, at common law, to have been delivered up to my baillie, and justified at his sight."

"Martial law, sister," answered Major Bellenden, "supersedes every other. But I must own I think Colonel Grahame rather deficient in attention to you; and I am not over and above pre-eminently flattered by his granting to young Evandale (I suppose because he is a

lord and has interest with the Privy Council) a request which he
refused to so old a servant of the king as I am. But so long as the poor
young fellow's life is saved, I can comfort myself with the fag end of a
ditty as old as myself." And therewithal, he hummed a stanza:—

> "And what though winter will pinch severe
>   Through locks of grey and a cloak that's old,
> Yet keep up thy heart, bold cavalier,
>   For a cup of sack shall fence the cold.

"I must be your guest here to-day, sister. I wish to hear the issue of
this gathering on Loudoun-hill—Though I cannot conceive their
standing a body of horse appointed like our guests this morning.—
Woes me, the time has been that I would have liked ill to have sate in
biggit wa's waiting for the news of a skirmish to be fought within ten
miles of me! But, as the old song goes,

> For time will rust the brightest blade,
>   And years will break the strongest bow;
> Was never wight so starkly made,
>   But time and years would overthrow."

"We are well pleased you will stay, brother," said Lady Margaret;
"I will take my old privilege to look after my household, whom this
collation has thrown into some disorder, although it is uncivil to leave
you alone."

"O, I hate ceremony as I hate a stumbling horse," replied the
Major. "Besides, your person would be with me, and your mind with
the cold meat and reversionary pasties.—Where is Edith?"

"Gone to her room a little evil-disposed, I am informed, and laid
down on her bed for a gliff," said her grandmother; "as soon as she
wakes, she shall take some drops."

"Pooh! pooh! she's only sick of the soldier," answered Major
Bellenden.—"She's not accustomed to see one acquaintance led out
to be shot, and another marching off to actual service with some
chance of not finding his way back again. She would soon be used to it,
if the civil war were to break out again."

"God forbid, brother!" said Lady Margaret.

"Ay, Heaven forbid, as you say—and, in the mean time, I'll take a
hit at trick-track with Harrison."

"He has ridden out, sir," said Gudyill, "to try if he can hear any
tidings of the battle."

"D—n the battle," said the Major; "it puts the family as much out
of order as if there had never been such a thing in the country before
—and yet there was such a place as Kilsythe, John."

"Ay, and as Tippermuir, your honour," replied Gudyill, "where I
was his honour, my late master's, rear-rank-man."

"And Alford, John, where I commanded the horse; and Innerlochy, where I was the great Marquis's aid-de-camp; and Auld Earn, and Brig o' Dee."

"And Philiphaugh, your honour," said John.

"Umph!" replied the Major; "the less, John, we say about that matter the better."

However, being once fairly embarked on the subject of Montrose's campaigns, the Major and John Gudyill carried on the war so stoutly, as for a considerable time to keep at bay the formidable enemy called Time, with whom retired veterans, during the quiet close of a bustling life, usually wage an unceasing hostility.

It has been frequently remarked, that the tidings of important events fly with a celerity almost beyond the power of credibility, and that reports, correct in the general point, though inaccurate in details, precede the certain intelligence, as if carried by the birds of the air. Such rumours anticipate the reality, not unlike to the "shadows of coming events" which occupy the imagination of the Highland Seer. Harrison, in his ride, encountered some such report concerning the event of the battle, and turned his horse back to Tillietudlem in great dismay. He made it his first business to seek out the Major, and interrupted him in the midst of a prolix account of the siege and storm of Dundee, with the ejaculation, "Heaven send, Major, that we do not see a siege of Tillietudlem before we are many days older."

"How is that, Harrison?—what the devil do you mean?" exclaimed the astonished veteran.

"Troth, sir, there is strong and increasing belief that Claver'se is clean broken, some say killed; that the soldiers are all dispersed, and that the rebels are hastening this way, threatening death and devastation to a' that winna take the Covenant."

"I will never believe it," said the Major, starting on his feet—"I will never believe that the Life Guards would retreat before rebels;—and yet what needs I say that," he continued, checking himself, "when I have seen such sights myself?—Send out Pike, and one or two of the servants, for intelligence, and let all the men in the Castle and in the village that can be trusted take up arms. This old tower may hold them play a bit, if it were but victualled and garrisoned, and it commands the pass between the high and low country.—It's lucky I was here.—Go, muster men, Harrison. You, Gudyill, look what provisions you have or can get brought in, and be ready, if the news be confirmed, to knock down as many bullocks as you have salt for.—The well never goes dry. —There are some old-fashioned guns on the battlements; if we had but ammunition, we should do well enough."

"The soldiers left some casks of ammunition at the Grange this morning, to bide their return," said Harrison.

"Hasten, then," said the Major, "and bring it into the Castle, with every pike, sword, pistol, or gun, that is within reach; don't leave so much as a bodkin—lucky that I was here.—I will speak to my sister instantly."

Lady Margaret Bellenden was astounded at intelligence so unexpected and so alarming. It had seemed to her that the imposing force which had that morning left her walls, was sufficient to have routed all the disaffected in Scotland, if collected in a body; and her first reflection was upon the inadequacy of their own means of resistance, to an army strong enough to have defeated Claverhouse and his select troops.

"Woes me! woes me!" said she; "what will all that we can do avail us, brother?—What will resistance do but bring sure destruction on the house, and on the bairn Edith; for, God knows, I think na on my ain auld life."

"Come, sister," said the Major, "you must not be cast down; the place is strong, the rebels ignorant and ill-provided; my brother's house shall not be made a den of thieves and rebels while old Miles Bellenden is in it. My hand is weaker than it was, but I thank God my old grey hairs thatch some knowledge of war yet. Here comes Pike with intelligence.—What news, Pike? Another Philiphaugh job, eh?"

"Ay, ay!" said Pike, composedly; "a total scattering.—I thought this morning little gude would come of their new-fangled gate of slinging their carabines."

"Whom did you see?—Who gave you the news?" asked the Major.

"O, mair than half-a-dozen dragoon fellows that are a' on the spur whilk to get first to Hamilton. They'll win the race, I warrant them, win the battle wha like."

"Continue your preparations, Harrison; get your ammunition in, and the cattle killed. Send down to the borough-town for what meal you can get in. We must not lose an instant.—Had not Edith and you, sister, better return to Charnwood, while we have the means of sending you there?"

"No, brother," said Lady Margaret, looking very pale, but speaking with the greatest composure; "since the auld house is to be held out, I will take my chance in it; I have fled twice from it in my days, and I have aye found it desolate of its bravest and its bonniest when I returned, sae that I will e'en abide now, and end my pilgrimage in it."

"It may, on the whole, be the safest course both for Edith and you," said the Major; "for the whigs will rise all the way between this and

Glasgow, and make your travelling there, or your dwelling at Charnwood, very unsafe."

"So be it, then," said Lady Margaret; "and, dear brother, as the
nearest blood-relation of my deceased husband, I deliver to you, by
this symbol,"—(here she gave into his hand the venerable gold-
headed staff of the deceased Earl of Torwood)—"the keeping and
government and seneschalship of my Tower of Tillietudlem, and the
appurtenances thereof, with full power to kill, slay, and damage those
who shall assail the same, as freely as I might do myself. And I trust
you will so defend it, as becomes a house in which his most sacred
majesty has not disdained"——

"Pshaw! sister," interrupted the Major, "we have not time to speak
about the king and his breakfast just now!"

And, hastily leaving the room, he hurried, with all the alertness of a
young man of twenty-five, to examine the state of his garrison, and
superintend the measures which were necessary for defending the
place.

The Tower of Tillietudlem, having very thick walls, and very
narrow windows, having also a strong court-yard wall, with flanking
turrets on the only accessible side, and rising on the other three from
the very verge of a precipice, was fully capable of defence against any
thing but a train of heavy artillery.

Famine or escalade was what the garrison had chiefly to fear.
For artillery, the top of the Tower was mounted with some antiquated wall-pieces, and small cannons, which bore the old-
fashioned names of culverins, sakers, demi-sakers, falcons, and
falconets. These, the Major, with the assistance of John Gudyill,
caused to be scaled and loaded, and pointed them so as to command the road over the brow of the opposite hill by which the
rebels must advance, causing, at the same time, two or three trees
to be cut down, which would have impeded the effect of the artillery when it should be necessary to use it. With the trunks of
these trees, and other materials, he directed barricades to be constructed upon the winding avenue which rose to the Tower from
the high-road, taking care that each should command the other.
The large gate of the court-yard he barricaded yet more
strongly, leaving only a wicket open for the convenience of passage. What he had most to apprehend, was the slenderness of his
garrison; for all the efforts of the steward were unable to get
more than nine men under arms, himself and Gudyill included, so
much more popular was the cause of the insurgents than that of
the government. Major Bellenden, and his trusty servant Pike,
made the garrison eleven in number, of whom one half were old

men. The round dozen might indeed have been made up, would Lady Margaret have consented that Goose Gibbie should again take up arms. But she recoiled from the proposal, when moved by Gudyill, with such abhorrent recollection of the former achievements of that luckless cavalier, that she declared she would rather the Castle were lost than that he were to be enrolled in the defence of it. With eleven men, however, himself included, Major Bellenden determined to hold out the place to the uttermost.

The arrangements for defence were not made without the degree of fracas incidental to such occasions. Women shrieked, cattle bellowed, dogs howled, men ran to and fro, cursing and swearing without inter-mission, the lumbering of the old guns backwards and forwards shook the battlements, the court resounded with the hasty gallop of messen-gers who went and returned upon errands of importance, and the din of warlike preparation was mingled with the sounds of female lam-entation.

Such a Babel of discord might have awakened the slumbers of the very dead, and, therefore, was not long ere it dispelled the abstracted reveries of Edith Bellenden. She sent out Jenny to bring her the cause of the tumult which shook the castle to its very basis; but Jenny, once engaged in the bustling tide, found so much to ask and to hear that she forgot the state of anxious uncertainty in which she had left her young mistress. Having no pigeon to dismiss in pursuit of information when her raven-messenger had failed to return with it, Edith was compelled to venture in quest of it out of the ark of her own chamber into the deluge of confusion which overflowed the rest of the castle. Six voices speaking at once, informed her, in reply to her first enquiry, that Claver'se and all his men were killed, and that ten thousand whigs were marching to besiege the castle, headed by John Balfour of Burley, young Milne-wood, and Cuddie Headrigg. This strange association of persons seemed to infer the falsehood of the whole story, and yet the gen-eral bustle in the castle intimated that danger was instantly appre-hended.

"Where is Lady Margaret?" was Edith's second question.

"In her oratory," was the reply; a cell adjoining to the old chapel in which the good old lady was wont to spend the greater part of the days destined by the rules of the Episcopal Church to special devotional observances, as also the anniversaries of those on which she lost her husband and her children, and, finally, those hours, in which a deeper and more solemn address to Heaven was called for, by national or domestic calamity.

"Where, then," said Edith, much alarmed, "is Major Bellenden?"

"On the battlements of the Tower, madam, pointing the cannon," was the reply.

To the battlements, therefore, she made her way, impeded by a thousand obstacles, and found the old gentleman, in the midst of his natural military element, commanding, rebuking, encouraging, instructing, and exercising all the numerous duties of a good governor.

"In the name of God, what is the matter, uncle?" exclaimed Edith.

"The matter, my love?" answered the Major coolly, as, with his spectacles on his nose, he examined the position of a gun—"the matter?—Why—raise her breech a thought more, John Gudyill—the matter? Why, Claver'se is routed, my dear, and the whigs are coming down upon us in force, that's all the matter."

"Gracious powers!" said Edith, whose eye at that instant caught a glance of the road which ran up the river, "and yonder they come."

"Yonder? where?" said the veteran, and, his eyes taking the same direction, beheld a large body of horsemen coming down the path. "Stand to your guns, my lads," was his first exclamation; "we'll make them pay toll as they pass the heugh.—But stay, stay, these are certainly the Life Guards."

"O no, uncle, no," replied Edith; "see how disorderly they ride, and how ill they keep their ranks; these cannot be the fine soldiers who left us this morning."

"Ah, my dear girl!" answered the Major, "you do not know the difference between men before a battle and after a defeat; but the Life Guards it is, for I see the red and blue and the King's colours. I am glad they have brought them off, however."

His opinion was confirmed as the troops approached nearer, and finally halted on the road beneath the Tower; while their commanding officer, leaving them to breathe and refresh their horses, hastily rode up the hill.

"It is Claverhouse, sure enough," said the Major; "I am glad he has escaped, but he has lost his famous black horse. Let Lady Margaret know, John Gudyill; order some refreshments; get oats for the soldiers' horses; and let us to the hall, Edith, to meet him. I surmise we shall hear but indifferent news."

Chapter Seven

With careless gesture, mind unmoved,
    On rade he north the plain,
His seem in thrang of fiercest strife,
    When winner aye the same.
                                    Hardyknute

COLONEL GRAHAME of Claverhouse met the family, assembled
in the hall of the Tower, with the same serenity and the same
courtesy which had graced his manners in the morning. He had
even had the composure to rectify in part the disorders of his dress,
to wash the signs of battle from his face and hands, and did not
appear more disordered in his exterior than if returned from a morning's ride.

"I am grieved, Colonel Grahame," said the reverend old lady, the
tears trickling down her face, "deeply grieved."

"And I am grieved, my dear Lady Margaret," replied Claverhouse,
"that this misfortune may render your remaining at Tillietudlem dangerous for you, especially considering your recent hospitality to the
King's troops, and your well-known loyalty. And I came here chiefly
to request Miss Bellenden and you to accept my escort (if you will not
scorn that of a poor runaway) to Glasgow, from whence I will see you
safely sent either to Edinburgh or to Dumbarton Castle, as you shall
think best."

"I am much obliged to you, Colonel Grahame," replied Lady Margaret, "but my brother, Major Bellenden, has taken on him the responsibility of holding out this house against the rebels; and, please
God, they shall never drive Margaret Bellenden from her ain hearth-
stane while there's a brave man that says he can defend it."

"And will Major Bellenden undertake this?" said Claverhouse
hastily, a joyful light glancing from his dark eye as he turned it on the
veteran,—"Yet why should I question it? it is of a piece with the rest of
his life.—But have you the means, Major?"

"All, but men and provisions, with which we are ill supplied,"
answered the Major.

"As to men," said Claverhouse, "I will leave you a dozen or twenty
fellows who will make good a breach against the devil. It will be of the
utmost service, if you can defend the place but a week, and by that time
you must surely be relieved."

"I will make it good three times that space, Colonel," replied the
Major, "with twenty-five good men and store of ammunition, if we

should gnaw the soles of our shoes for hunger; but I trust we will get in provisions from the country."

"And, Colonel Grahame, if I might presume a request," said Lady Margaret, "I would entreat Serjeant Francis Stuart might command the auxiliaries whom you are so good as to add to the garrison of our people; it may serve to legitimate his promotion, and I have a prejudice in favour of his noble birth."

"The serjeant's wars are ended, madam," said Grahame, in an unaltered tone, "and he now needs no promotion that an earthly master can give."

"Pardon me," said Major Bellenden, taking Claverhouse by the arm, and turning him away from the ladies, "but I am anxious for my friends; I fear you have other and more important loss. I observe another officer carries your nephew's standard."

"You are right, Major Bellenden," answered Claverhouse firmly; "my nephew is no more. He has died in his duty as became him."

"Great God!" exclaimed the Major, "how unhappy!—the handsome, gallant, high-spirited youth!"

"He was, indeed, all you say," answered Claverhouse; "poor Dick was to me as an eldest son, the apple of my eye, and my destined heir; but he died in his duty, and I—I, Major Bellenden" —(he wrung the Major's hand hard as he spoke)—I live to avenge him."

"Colonel Grahame," said the affectionate veteran, his eyes filling with tears, "I am glad to see you bear this misfortune with such fortitude."

"I am not a selfish man," replied Claverhouse, "though the world will tell you otherwise; I am not selfish either in my hopes or fears, my joys or sorrows. I have not been severe for myself, or grasping for myself, or ambitious for myself. The service of my master and the good of the country is what I have tried to aim at. I may, perhaps, have driven severity into cruelty, but I acted for the best; and now I will not yield to my own feelings a deeper sympathy than I have given to those of others."

"I am astonished at your fortitude under all the unpleasant circumstances of this affair," pursued the Major.

"Yes," replied Claverhouse, "my enemies in the Council will lay this misfortune to my charge—I despise their accusations. They will calumniate me to my sovereign—I can repel their charge. The public enemy will exult in my flight—I shall find a time to shew them that they exult too early. This youth that has fallen stood betwixt a grasping kinsman and my inheritance, for you know that my marriage-bed is barren; yet, peace be with him! the country can better spare him than your friend Lord Evandale, who, after behaving very gallantly, has, I fear, also fallen."

"What a fatal day!" ejaculated the Major. "I heard a report of this, but it was again contradicted; it was added, that the poor young noble-man's impetuosity had occasioned the loss of this unhappy field."

"Not so, Major," said Grahame; "let the living officer bear the blame, if there be any, and let the laurels flourish untarnished on the grave of the fallen. I do not, however, speak of Lord Evandale's death as certain; but killed, or prisoner, I fear he must be. Yet he was extricated from the tumult the last time we spoke together. We were then on the point of leaving the field with a rear-guard of scarce twenty men; the rest of the regiment were chiefly dispersed."

"They have rallied again soon," said the Major, looking from the window on the dragoons, who were feeding their horses and refresh-ing themselves beside the brook.

"Yes," answered Claverhouse, "my blackguards have little tempta-tion either to desert, or to straggle farther than they were driven by their first panic. There is small friendship and scant courtesy between them and the boors of this country; every village they pass is likely to rise on them, and so the scoundrels are driven back to their colours by a wholesome terror of spits, pike-staves, hay-forks, and broom-sticks. —But now let us talk about your plans and wants, and the means of corresponding with you. To tell you the truth, I doubt being able to make a long stand at Glasgow, even when I have joined my Lord Ross; for this transient and accidental success of the fanatics will raise the devil through all the western counties."

They then discussed Major Bellenden's means of defence, and settled a plan of correspondence, in case a general insurrection took place, as was to be expected. Claverhouse renewed his offer to escort the ladies to a place of safety; but, all things considered, Major Bellenden thought they would be in equal safety at Tillietudlem.

The Colonel then took a polite leave of Lady Margaret and Miss Bellenden, assuring them, that, though he was reluctantly obliged to leave them for the present in dangerous circumstances, yet his earliest means should be turned to the redemption of his character as a good knight and true, and that they might speedily rely on hearing from or seeing him.

Full of doubt and apprehension, Lady Margaret was little able to reply to a speech so much in unison with her usual expressions and feelings, but contented herself with bidding Claverhouse farewell, and thanking him for the succours which he had promised to leave them. Edith longed to enquire the fate of Henry Morton, but could find no pretext for doing so, and could only hope that it had made a subject of some part of the long private communication which her uncle had held with Claverhouse. On this subject, however, she was disappointed; for the old cavalier was so deeply immersed in the duties of his new office, that he had scarce said a single word to Claverhouse, excepting upon military matters, and most probably would have been equally forgetful had the fate of his own son, instead of his friend's, lain in the balance.

Claverhouse now descended the bank on which the castle is founded, in order to put his troops again in motion, and Major Bellenden accompanied him to receive the detachment who were to be left in the Tower.

"I shall leave Inglis with you," said Claverhouse, "for, as I am situated, I cannot spare an officer of rank; it is all we can do, by our joint efforts, to keep the men together. But should any of our missing officers make their appearance I authorise you to detain them, for my fellows can with difficulty be subjected to any other authority."

His troops being now drawn up, he picked out sixteen men by name, and committed them to the command of Corporal Inglis, whom he promoted to the rank of serjeant upon the spot.

"And hark ye, gentlemen," was his concluding harangue, "I leave you to defend the house of a lady, and under the command of her brother, Major Bellenden, a faithful servant of the King. You are to behave bravely, soberly, regularly, and obediently, and each of you shall be handsomely rewarded on my return to relieve the garrison. In case of mutiny, cowardice, neglect of duty, or the slightest excess in the family, the provost-marshal and cord—you know I keep my word for good and evil."

He touched his hat as he bade them adieu, and shook hands cordially with Major Bellenden.

"Adieu," he said, "my stout-hearted old friend! Good luck be with you, and better times to us both."

The horsemen whom he commanded had been once more reduced to tolerable order by the exertions of Major Allan, and, though shorn of their splendour, and with their gilding all besmirched, made a much more regular and military appearance in leaving, for the second time, the Tower of Tillietudlem, than when they returned to it after their rout.

Major Bellenden, now left to his own resources, sent out several videttes, both to obtain supplies of provisions, and especially of meal, and to get knowledge of the motions of the enemy. All the news he could collect on the second subject tended to prove, that the insurgents meant to remain on the field of battle for that night. But they, also, had abroad their detachments and advanced guards to collect supplies, and great was the doubt and distress of those who received contrary orders in the name of the King and in that of the Kirk; the one commanding them to send provisions to victual the castle of Tillietudlem, and the other enjoining them to forward supplies to the camp of the godly professors of true religion, now in arms for the cause of covenanted reformation, presently pitched at Drumclog, nigh to Loudoun-hill. Each summons closed with a denunciation of fire and sword if it was neglected, for neither party could so far confide in the loyalty or zeal of those whom they addressed, as to hope they would part with their property upon other terms. So that the poor people knew not which hand to turn themselves to; and, to say truth, there were some who turned themselves to more than one.

"Thir kittle times will drive the wisest o' us daft," said Niel Blane, the prudent host of the Howff; "but I'se aye keep a calm sough.— Jenny, what meal is in the girnel?"

"Four bows o' aitmeal, twa bows o' bear, and twa bows o' pease," was Jenny's reply.

"Aweel, hinny," continued Niel, sighing deeply, "let Bauldie drive the pease and bear meal to the camp at Drumclog—he's a whig, and was the auld gudewife's pleughman—the mashlum bannocks will suit their moorland stamachs weel. He maun say it's the last unce o' meal in the house, or, if he scruples to tell a lie, (as it's no likely he will when it's for the gude o' the house,) he may wait till Duncan Glen, the auld drunk trooper, drives up the aitmeal to Tillietudlem, wi' my dutifu' service to my Leddy and the Major, and I haena as muckle left as will mak my parritch; and, if Duncan manage right, I'll gi'e him a tass o' whisky shall mak the blue low come out at his mouth."

"And what are we to eat oursels then, father, when we hae sent awa' the hail meal in the ark and the girnel?"

"We maun gar wheat-flour serve us for a blink," said Niel, in a tone of resignation; "it's no that ill food, though far frae being sae hearty or kindly to a Scotsman's stamach as the curney aitmeal is; the English-ers live amaist a' upon't; but, to be sure, the pock-puddings ken nae better."

While the prudent and peaceful endeavoured, like Niel Blane, to make fair weather with both parties, those who had more public (or party) spirit, began to take arms on all sides. The loyalists in the country were not numerous, but were respectable from their fortune and influence, being chiefly landed proprietors of ancient descent, who, with their brothers, cousins, and dependants, to the ninth gen-eration, as well as their domestic servants, formed a sort of militia, capable of defending their own peel-houses against detached bodies of the insurgents, of resisting their demand of supplies, and intercepting those which were sent to the presbyterian camp by others. The news that the Tower of Tillietudlem was to be defended against the insurgents, afforded great courage and support to these feudal volunteers, who considered it as a strong-hold to which they might retreat, in case it should become impossible for them to maintain the desultory war they were now about to wage.

On the other hand, the towns, the villages, the farm-houses, the properties of smaller heritors, sent forth numerous recruits to the presbyterian interest. These men had been the principal sufferers during the oppression of the time. Their minds were fretted, soured, and driven to desperation, by the various exactions and cruelties to which they had been subjected; and, although by no means united among themselves, either concerning the end of this formidable insurrection, or the means by which that end was to be obtained, most considered it as a door opened by Providence to obtain the liberty of conscience of which they had been long deprived, and to shake themselves free of a tyranny, directed both against body and soul. Numbers of these men, therefore, took up arms, and, in the phrase of their time and party, prepared to cast in their lot with the victors at Loudoun-hill.

Chapter Eight

Ananias. I do not like the man: He is a heathen,
And speaks the language of Canaan truly.
   Tribulation. You must await his calling, and the coming
Of the good spirit. You did ill to upbraid him.
                                                   The Alchemist

WE RETURN to Henry Morton whom we left upon the field of battle. He was eating, by one of the watch-fires, his portion of the provisions which had been distributed to the army, and musing deeply on the path which he was next to pursue, when Burley suddenly came up to him, accompanied by the young minister, whose exhortation after the victory had produced such a powerful effect.

"Henry Morton," said Balfour, abruptly, "the council of the army of the Covenant, confiding that the son of Silas Morton can never prove a lukewarm Laodicean, or an indifferent Gallio, in this great day, have nominated you to be a captain of their host, with the right of a vote in their council, and all authority fitting for an officer who is to command Christian men."

"Mr Balfour," replied Morton, without hesitation, "I feel this mark of confidence, and it is not surprising that a natural sense of the injuries of my country, not to mention those I have sustained in my own person, should make me sufficiently willing to draw my sword for liberty and freedom of conscience. But I will own to you, that I must be better satisfied concerning the principles on which you bottom your cause ere I can agree to take a command amongst you."

"And can you doubt of our principles," answered Burley, "since we have stated them to be the reformation both of church and state, the rebuilding of the decayed sanctuary, the gathering of the dispersed saints, and the destruction of the man of sin?"

"I will own frankly, Mr Balfour," replied Morton, "much of this sort of language, which, I observe, is so powerful with others, is entirely lost upon me. It is proper you should be aware of this before we commune further together." (The young clergyman here groaned deeply.) "I distress you, sir," said Morton; "but, perhaps, it is because you will not hear me out. I revere the Scriptures as deeply as you or any Christian can do. I look into them with humble hope of extracting a rule of conduct and a law of salvation. But I expect to find this by an examination of their general tenor, and of the spirit which they uniformly breathe, and not by wresting particular passages from their context, or by the application of Scriptural phrases to circumstances and events with which they have often very slender relation."

The divine, whose name was Ephraim Macbriar, seemed shocked and thunderstruck with this declaration, and was about to remonstrate.

"Hush, Ephraim!" said Burley, "remember he is yet but as a babe in swaddling clothes.—Listen to me, Morton. I will speak to thee in the worldly language of that carnal reason, which is, for the present, thy blind and imperfect guide. What is the object for which thou art content to draw thy sword? Is it not that the church and state should be reformed by the free voice of a free parliament, with such laws as shall hereafter prevent the executive government from spilling the blood, torturing and imprisoning the person, exhausting the estates, and trampling upon the consciences of men at their own wicked pleasure?"

"Most certainly," said Morton; "such I esteem legitimate causes of warfare, and for such I will fight while I can wield a sword."

"Nay, but," said Macbriar, "ye handle this matter too tenderly, nor will my conscience permit me to fard or daub over the causes of divine wrath"——

"Peace, Ephraim Macbriar," again interrupted Burley.

"I will not peace," said the young man. "Is it not in the cause of my Master who has sent me? Is it not a profane and an Erastian destroying of his authority, usurpation of his power, and denial of his name, to place either King or parliament in his place as the master and governor of his household, the adulterous husband of his spouse?"

"You speak well," said Burley, dragging him aside, "but not wisely; your own ears have heard this night in council how this scattered remnant are broken and divided, and would ye now make a veil of separation between those? Would ye build a wall with unslaked mortar?—if a fox go up, it will breach it."

"I know," said the young clergyman, in reply, "that thou art faithful, honest, and zealous, even unto slaying; but, believe me, this worldly craft, this temporizing with sin and with infirmity, is in itself a falling away, and I fear me Heaven will not honour us to do much more for His glory, when we seek to carnal cunning and to a fleshly arm. The sanctified end must be wrought by sanctified means."

"I tell thee," answered Balfour, "thy zeal is too rigid in this matter; we cannot yet do without the help of the Laodiceans and the Erastians; we must endure for a space the Indulged in the midst of the council—the sons of Zeruiah are yet too strong for us."

"I tell thee I like it not," said Macbriar; "God can work deliverance by a few as well as by a multitude. The host of the faithful that was broken upon Pentland-hills, paid but the fitting penalty of acknowledging the carnal interest of that tyrant and oppressor, Charles Stuart."

"Well, then," said Balfour, "thou knowest the healing resolution that the council have adopted to make a comprehending declaration, that may suit the tender consciences of all who groan under the yoke of our present oppressors. Return to the council if thou wilt, and get them to recall it, and send forth one upon narrower grounds. But abide not here to hinder my gaining over this youth whom my soul travails for; his name alone will call forth hundreds to our banner."

"Do as thou wilt, then," said Macbriar; "but I will not assist to mislead the youth, nor to bring him into jeopardy of life, unless upon such grounds as will ensure his eternal reward."

The more artful Balfour then dismissed the impatient preacher, and returned to his proselyte.

That we may be enabled to dispense with detailing at length the arguments by which he urged Morton to join the insurgents, we shall take this opportunity to give a brief sketch of the person by whom they were used, and the motives which he had for interesting himself so deeply in the conversion of young Morton to his cause.

John Balfour of Kinloch, or Burley, for he is designated both ways in the histories and proclamations of that melancholy period, was a gentleman of some fortune, and of good family, in the county of Fife, and had been a soldier from his youth upward. In the younger part of his life he had been wild and licentious, but had early laid aside open profligacy, and embraced the strictest tenets of Calvinism. Unfortunately, habits of excess and intemperance were more easily rooted out of his dark, saturnine, and enterprising spirit, than the vices of revenge and ambition, which continued, notwithstanding his religious professions, to exercise no small sway over his mind. Daring in design, precipitate and violent in execution, and going to the very extremity of the most rigid recusancy, it was his ambition to place himself at the head of the presbyterian interest.

To attain this eminence among the whigs, he had been active in attending their conventicles, and more than once had headed them when they had appeared in arms, and beaten off the forces sent to disperse them. At length, the gratification of his own fierce enthusiasm, joined, as some say, with motives of private revenge, placed him at the head of that party who assassinated the Primate of Scotland, as the author of the sufferings of the presbyterians. The violent measures adopted by government to revenge this deed, not on the perpetrators only, but on the whole professors of the religion to which they belonged, together with long previous suffering, without any prospect of deliverance, except by force of arms, had occasioned the insurrection, which, as we have already seen, commenced by the defeat of Claverhouse in the bloody skirmish of Loudoun-hill.

But Burley, notwithstanding the share he had in the victory, was far from finding himself at the summit which his ambition aimed at. This was partly owing to the various opinions entertained among the insurgents concerning the murder of Archbishop Sharpe. The more violent party among them did indeed approve of this act as a deed of justice, executed upon a persecutor of God's church through the immediate inspiration of the Deity; but the greater part of the presbyterians disowned the deed as a crime highly culpable, although they admitted, that the Archbishop's punishment had by no means exceeded his deserts. The insurgents differed in another main point, which has been already touched upon. The more warm and extravagant fanatics condemned, as guilty of a pusillanimous abandonment of the rights of the church, those preachers and congregations who were contented, in any manner, to exercise their religion through the permission of the ruling government. This, they said, was absolute Erastianism, or subjection of the church of God to the regulations of an earthly government, and therefore but one degree better than prelacy or popery.—Again, the more moderate party were content to allow the king's title to the throne, and, in secular affairs, to acknowledge his authority, so long as it was exercised with due regard to the liberties of the subject, and in conformity to the laws of the realm. But the tenets of the wilder party, called, from their leader Richard Cameron, by the name of Cameronians, went the length of disowning the reigning monarch, and every one of his successors who should not acknowledge the Solemn League and Covenant. The seeds of disunion were, therefore, thickly sown in this ill-fated party; and Balfour, however enthusiastic, and however much attached to the most violent of those tenets which we have noticed, saw nothing but ruin to the general cause, if they were insisted on during this crisis, when unity was of so much consequence. Hence he disapproved, as we have seen, of the honest, downright, and ardent zeal of such men as Macbriar, and was extremely desirous to receive the assistance of the moderate party of presbyterians in the immediate overthrow of the government, with the hope of being hereafter able to dictate to them what should be substituted in its place.

He was, on this account, particularly anxious to secure the accession of Henry Morton to the cause of the insurgents. The memory of his father was generally esteemed among the presbyterians; and, as few persons of any decent quality had joined the insurgents, this young man's family and prospects were such as almost ensured his being chosen a leader. Through Morton's means, as being the son of his ancient comrade, Burley conceived he might exercise some influence over the more liberal part of the army, and ultimately, perhaps, ingratiate himself so far with them, as to be chosen commander-in-chief, which was the mark at which his ambition aimed. He had, therefore, without waiting till any other person took up the subject, exalted to the council the talents and disposition of Morton, and easily obtained his elevation to the painful rank of a leader in this disunited and undisciplined army.

The arguments by which Balfour pressed Morton to accept of this dangerous promotion, as soon as he had gotten rid of his less artful and more uncompromising companion, Macbriar, were sufficiently artful and urgent. He did not affect either to deny or disguise that the sentiments which he himself entertained concerning church-government, went as far as those of the preacher who had just left them. But he argued, that when the affairs of the nation were at such a desperate crisis, minute difference of opinion should not prevent those who, in general, wished well to their oppressed country, from drawing their swords in its behalf. Many of the subjects of division, as, for example, that concerning the Indulgence itself, arose, he observed, out of circumstances which would cease to exist, provided their attempt to free the country should be successful, seeing that presbytery, being in that case triumphant, would need to make no such compromise with the government, and, consequently, with the abolition of the Indulgence, all discussion of its legality would be at once ended. He insisted much and strongly upon the necessity of taking advantage of this favourable crisis, upon the certainty of their being joined by the force of the whole western shires, and upon the gross guilt which all those would incur, who, seeing the distress of the country, and the increasing tyranny with which it was governed, should, from fear or indifference, with-hold their active aid from the good cause.

Morton wanted not these arguments to induce him to join in any insurrection, which might appear to have such a feasible prospect of success as promised freedom to the country. He doubted, indeed, greatly whether the present attempt was likely to be supported by the strength sufficient to ensure success, or by the wisdom and liberality of spirit necessary to make a good use of the advantages that might be gained. Upon the whole, however, considering the wrongs he had personally endured, and those which he had seen daily inflicted on his fellow-subjects; meditating also upon the precarious and dangerous situation in which he already stood with relation to the government, he conceived himself, in every point of view, called upon to join the body of presbyterians presently in arms.

But, while he expressed to Burley his acquiescence in the vote which had named him a leader among the insurgents, and a member of their council of war, it was not without a qualification.

"I am willing," he said, "to contribute every thing within my limited power to aid the emancipation of my country. But do not mistake me. I disapprove, in the utmost degree, of the action in which this rising seems to have originated, and no arguments should induce me to join in it, if it is to be carried on by such measures as that with which it has commenced."

Burley's blood rushed to his face, giving a ruddy and dark glow to his swarthy brow.

"You mean," he said, in a voice which he designed should not betray any emotion—"You mean the death of James Sharpe?"

"Frankly," answered Morton, "such is my meaning."

"You imagine, then," said Burley, "that the Almighty, in times of difficulty, does not raise up instruments to deliver his church from her oppressors? You are of opinion that the justice of an execution con-sists, not in the extent of the sufferer's crime, or in his having merited punishment, or in the wholesome and salutary effect which that example is like to produce upon other evil-doers, but hold that it rests solely in the robe of the judge, the height of the bench, and the voice of the doomster? Is not just punishment justly inflicted, whether on the scaffold or the moor? And where constituted judges, from cowardice, or from having cast in their lot with transgressors, suffer them not only to pass at liberty through the land, but to sit in the high places, and dye their garments in the blood of the saints, is it not well done in any brave spirits who shall lend their private swords to the public cause?"

"I have no wish to judge this individual action," replied Morton, "further than is necessary to make you fully aware of my principles. I therefore repeat, that the case you have supposed does not satisfy my judgment. That the Almighty, in his mysterious providence, may bring a bloody man to an end deservedly bloody, does not vindicate those who, without authority of any kind, take upon themselves to be the instruments of execution, and presume to call themselves the executors of divine vengeance."

"And were we not so?" said Burley, in a tone of fierce enthusiasm. "Were not we—was not every one who owned the interest of the Covenanted Church of Scotland, bound by that covenant to cut off the Judas who had sold the cause of God for fifty thousand merks a-year? Had we met him by the way as he came down from London, and there smitten him with the edge of the sword, we had done but the duty of men faithful to our cause, and to our oaths recorded in heaven. Was not the execution itself a proof of our warrant? Did not the Lord deliver him into our hands, when we looked out but for one of his inferior tools of persecution? Did we not pray to be resolved how we should act, and was it not borne in on our hearts as if it had been written on them with the point of a diamond, 'Ye shall surely take him and slay him?'—Was not the tragedy full half an hour in acting ere the sacrifice was completed, and that on an open heath, and within the patroles of their garrisons, and yet who interrupted the great work?— What dog so much as bayed us during the pursuit, the taking, the slaying, and the dispersing? Then, who will say—who dare say, that a mightier arm than ours was not herein revealed?"

"You deceive yourself, Mr Balfour," said Morton; "such circum-stances of facility of execution and escape have often attended the commission of the most enormous crimes. But it is not mine to judge you. I have not forgotten that the way was opened to the former liberation of Scotland by an action of violence which no man can justify,—the slaughter of Cumming by the hand of Robert Bruce; and, therefore, condemning this action, as I do and must, I am not unwilling to suppose that you may have had motives vindicating it in your own eye, though not to mine, or to those of sober reason; and only now mention it, because I desire you to understand, that I join a cause supported by men engaged in open war, which it is proposed to carry on according to the rules of civilized nations; and do not in any respect subscribe to the act of violence which gave immediate rise to it."

Balfour bit his lip, and with difficulty suppressed a violent answer. He perceived, with disappointment, that, upon points of principle, his young brother in arms possessed a clearness of judgment, and a firmness of mind, which afforded but little hope of his being able to exert that degree of influence over him which he had expected to possess. After a moment's pause, however, he said, with coldness, "My conduct is open to men and angels; the deed was not done in a corner; I am here in arms to avow it, and care not where, or by whom, I am called on to do so, whether in the council, the field of battle, the place of execution, or the day of the last great trial. I will not now discuss it further with one who is yet on the outer side of the vail. But if you will cast in your lot with us as a brother, come with me to the council, who are still sitting, to arrange the future march of the army and the means of improving our victory."

Morton arose and followed him in silence, not greatly delighted with his associate, and better satisfied with the general justice of the cause which he had espoused, than either with the measures or motives of many of those who were embarked in it.

Chapter Nine

And look how many Grecian tents do stand
Hollow upon this plain—so many hollow factions.
                    Troilus and Cressida

IN a hollow of the hill, about a quarter of a mile from the field of battle, was a shepherd's hut, a miserable cottage, which, as the only enclosed spot within a moderate distance, the leaders of the presbyterian army had chosen for their temporary council-house. Towards this spot Burley guided Morton, who was surprised, as he approached it, at the multifarious confusion of sounds which issued from its precincts. The calm and anxious gravity which it might be supposed would have presided in councils held on such important subjects, and at a period so critical, seemed to have given place to discord wild, and loud uproar, which fell on the ear of their new ally as an evil augury of their future measures. As they approached the door, they found it open indeed, but choked up with the bodies and heads of country-men, who, though no members of the council, felt no scruple in intruding themselves upon deliberations in which they were so deeply interested. By expostulation, by threats, and even by some degree of violence, Burley, the sternness of whose character maintained a sort of superiority over these disorderly forces, compelled the intruders to retire, and, introducing Morton into the cottage, secured the door behind them against impertinent curiosity. At a less agitating moment, the young man might have been entertained with the singular scene of which he now found himself an auditor and a spectator.

The precincts of the gloomy and ruinous hut were enlightened partly by some furze which blazed on the hearth, the smoke whereof, having no legal vent, eddied around, and formed over the heads of the assembled council a cloudy canopy, as opake as their metaphysical theology, through which, like stars through mist, were dimly seen to twinkle a few blinking candles, or rather rushes dipped in tallow, the property of the poor owner of the cottage, which were stuck to the walls by patches of wet clay. This broken and dusky light shewed many a countenance elated with spiritual pride, or rendered dark by fierce enthusiasm; and some whose anxious, wandering, and uncertain looks shewed they felt themselves rashly embarked in a cause which they had neither courage nor conduct to bring to a good issue, yet knew not how to abandon, for very shame. They were, indeed, a doubtful and disunited body. The most active of their number were those concerned with Burley in the death of the Primate, four or five of whom had found the way to Loudoun-hill, together with other men of the same relentless and uncompromising zeal, who had, in various ways, given desperate and unpardonable offence to the government.

With them were mingled their preachers, men who had spurned at the Indulgence offered by government, and preferred assembling their flocks in the wilderness, to worshipping in temples built by human hands, if their doing the latter could be construed to admit any right on the part of their rulers to interfere with the supremacy of the Kirk. The other class of counsellors were such gentlemen of small fortune, and substantial farmers, as a sense of intolerable oppression had induced to take arms and join the insurgents. These also had their clergymen with them, who, having many of them taken advantage of the Indulgence, were prepared to resist the measures of the more violent, who proposed a declaration in which they should give testimony against the warrants and instructions for Indulgence as sinful and unlawful acts. This delicate question had been passed over in silence in the first draught of the manifesto which they intended to publish, of the reasons of their gathering in arms; but it had been stirred anew during Balfour's absence, and, to his great vexation, he now found that both parties had opened upon it in full cry, Macbriar, Kettledrummle, and other teachers of the wanderers, being at the very spring-tide of polemical discussion with Peter Poundtext, the indulged pastor of Milnewood's parish, who, it seems, had e'en girded himself with a broad-sword, but, ere he was called upon to fight for the good cause of presbytery in the field, was manfully defending his own dogmata in the council. It was the din of this conflict, maintained chiefly between Poundtext and Kettledrummle, together with the clamour of their adherents, which had saluted Morton's ears upon approaching the cottage. Indeed, as both the divines were men well gifted with words, breathing, and lungs, and each fierce, ardent, and intolerant in defence of his own doctrine, prompt in the recollection of texts wherewith they battered each other without mercy, and deeply impressed with the importance of the subject of discussion, the noise of the debate betwixt them fell little short of that which might have attended an actual bodily conflict.

Burley, scandalized at the disunion implied in this virulent strife of tongues, interposed between the disputants, and, by some general remarks on the unseasonableness of discord, a soothing address to the vanity of each party, and the exertion of the authority which his services in that day's victory entitled him to assume, at length succeeded in prevailing upon them to adjourn further discussion of the controversy. But although Kettledrummle and Poundtext were thus for the time silenced, they continued to eye each other like two dogs, who, having been separated while fighting, by the authority of their masters, have retreated, each one beneath the chair of his owner, still watching each other's motions, and indicate, by occasional growls, by the erected bristles of the back and ears, and by the red glance of the eye, that their discord is unappeased, and that they only wait the first opportunity afforded by any general movement or commotion in the company, to fly once more at each other's throats.

Balfour took advantage of the momentary pause to present to the council Mr Henry Morton of Milnewood, as one touched with a sense of the evils of the times, and willing to peril goods and life in the precious cause for which his father, the renowned Silas Morton, had given in his time a soul-stirring testimony. Morton was instantly received with the right hand of fellowship by his ancient pastor, Poundtext, and those among the insurgents who supported the more moderate principles. The others muttered something about Erastianism, and reminded each other in whispers, that Silas Morton, once a stout and worthy servant of the Covenant, had been a backslider in the day when the resolutioners had led the way in owning the authority of Charles Stuart, thereby making a gap whereat the present tyrant was afterward brought in, to the oppression both of Kirk and country. They added, however, that, on this great day of calling, they would not refuse society with any who should put hand to the plough; and so Morton was installed in his office of leader and counsellor, if not with the full approbation of his colleagues, at least without any formal or avowed dissent. They proceeded, on Burley's motion, to divide among themselves the command of the men who had assembled, and whose numbers were daily increasing. In this partition, the insurgents of Poundtext's parish and congregation were naturally placed under the command of Morton; an arrangement mutually agreeable to both parties, as he was recommended to their confidence, as well by his personal qualities as his having been born among them.

When this task was accomplished, it became necessary to determine what use was to be made of their victory. Morton's heart throbbed high when he heard the Tower of Tillietudlem named as one of the most important positions to be seized upon. It commanded, as we have often noticed, the pass between the more wild and the more fertile country, and must furnish, it was plausibly urged, a strong-hold and place of rendezvous to the cavaliers and malignants of the district, supposing the insurgents were to march onward and leave it uninvested. This measure was particularly urged as necessary by Poundtext and those of his immediate followers, whose habitations and families might be exposed to great severities, if this strong place was permitted to remain in possession of the royalists.

"I opine," said Poundtext,—for, like the other divines of the period, he had no hesitation in offering his advice upon military matters of which he was profoundly ignorant,—"I opine, that we should take in and raze that strong-hold of the woman Lady Margaret Bellenden, even although we should build a fort and raise a mount against it; for the race is a rebellious and a bloody race, and their hand has been heavy on the children of the Covenant, both in the former and the latter times. Their hook hath been in our noses, and their bridle betwixt our jaws."

"What are their means and men of defence?" said Burley. "The place is strong; but I conceive that two women cannot make it good against a host."

"There is also," said Poundtext, "John Gudyill, even the lady's chief butler, who boasteth himself a man of war from his youth upward, and who spread the banner against the good cause with that man of Belial, James Grahame of Montrose."

"Pshaw!" returned Balfour, scornfully, "a butler!"

"Also, there is that ancient malignant," replied Poundtext, "Miles Bellenden of Charnwood, whose hands have been dipped in the blood of the saints."

"If that," said Burley, "be Miles Bellenden, the brother of Sir Arthur, he is one whose sword will not turn back from battle; but he must now be stricken in years."

"There was word in the country as I rode along," said another of the council, "that so soon as they had heard of the victory which has been given to us, they caused shut the gates of the Tower, and called in men, and collected munition. They were ever a fierce and a malignant house."

"We will not, with my consent," said Burley, "engage in a siege which may consume time. We must rush forwards, and follow our advantages by occupying Glasgow; for I do not fear that the troops we have this day beaten, even with the assistance of my Lord Ross's regiment, will judge it safe to await our coming."

"Howbeit," said Poundtext, "we may display a banner before the Tower, and blow a trumpet, and summon them to come forth. It may be that they will give over the place unto our mercy, though they be a rebellious people. And we will summon the women to come forth of their strong-hold, that is, Lady Margaret Bellenden and her grand-daughter, and Jenny Dennison, which is a damsel of an ensnaring eye, and the other maids, and we will give them a safe-conduct, and send them in peace to the city, even the town of Edinburgh. But John Gudyill, and Hugh Harrison, and Miles Bellenden, we will restrain with fetters of iron, even as they, in times bypast, have done to the martyred saints."

"Who talks of safe-conduct and of peace?" said a shrill, broken, and overstrained voice, from the crowd.

"Peace, brother Habakkuk," said Macbriar, in a soothing tone to the speaker.

"I will not hold my peace," reiterated this strange and unnatural voice; "is this a time to speak of peace, when the earth quakes, and the mountains are rent, and the rivers are changed into blood, and the two-edged sword is drawn from the sheath to drink gore as if it were water, and devour flesh as the fire devours dry stubble?"

While he spoke thus, the orator struggled forward to the inner part of the circle, and presented to Morton's wondering eyes a figure worthy of such a voice and such language. The rags of a dress which had once been black, added to the tattered fragments of a shepherd's plaid, composed a covering scarce fit for the purposes of decency, much less for those of warmth or comfort. A long beard, as white as snow, hung down on his bosom, and mingled with bushy, uncombed, grizzled hair, which hung in elf-locks around his wild and staring visage. The features seemed to be extenuated by penury and famine, until they hardly retained the likeness of a human aspect. The eyes, grey, wild, and wandering, evidently betokened a bewildered imagina-tion. He held in his hand a rusty sword, clotted with blood, as were his long lean hands, which were garnished at the extremity with nails like eagle's claws.

"In the name of Heaven! who is he?" said Morton, in a whisper to

Poundtext, surprised, shocked, and even startled at this ghastly apparition, which looked more like the resurrection of some cannibal priest, or Druid, red from his human sacrifice, than like an earthly mortal.

"It is Habakkuk Meiklewrath," answered Poundtext, in the same tone, "whom the enemy have long detained in captivity in forts and castles, until his understanding hath departed from him, and, as I fear, an evil spirit hath possessed him. Nevertheless, our violent brethren will have it, that he speaketh of the spirit, and that they fructify by his pouring forth."

Here he was interrupted by Meiklewrath, who cried in a voice that made the very beams of the roof quiver—"Who talks of peace and safe-conduct? who speaks of mercy to the bloody house of the malignants? I say, take the infants and dash them against the stones; take the daughters and the mothers of the house and hurl them from the battlements of their trust, that the dogs may fatten on their blood as they did on that of Jezebel the spouse of Ahab, and that their carcases may be dung to the face of the field even in the portion of their fathers!"

"He speaks right," said more than one sullen voice from behind; "we will be honoured with little service in the great cause, if we already make fair weather with Heaven's enemies."

"This is utter abomination and daring impiety," said Morton, unable to contain his indignation. "What blessing can you expect in a cause, in which you listen to the mingled ravings of madness and atrocity?"

"Hush, young man!" said Kettledrummle, "and reserve thy censure for that of which thou canst render a reason. It is not for thee to judge into what vessels the spirit may be poured."

"We judge of the tree by the fruit," said Poundtext, "and allow not that to be of divine inspiration that contradicts the divine laws."

"You forget, brother Poundtext," said Macbriar, "that these are the latter days, when signs and wonders shall be multiplied."

Poundtext stood forward to reply; but, ere he could articulate a word, the insane preacher broke in with a scream that drowned all competition.

"Who talks of signs and wonders? Am I not Habakkuk Meiklewrath, whose name is changed to Magor-Missabib, because I am made a terror unto myself and unto all that are around me?—I heard it —Where did I hear it?—Was it not in the tower of the Bass, that overhangeth the wide wild sea?—And it howled in the winds, and it roared in the billows, and it screamed, and it whistled, and it clanged, with the scream and the clang and the whistle of the sea-birds, as they floated, and flew, and dropped, and dived, on the bosom of the waters.

I saw it—Where did I see it?—was it not from high peaks of Dumbarton, when I looked westward upon the fertile land, and northward on the wild Highland hills, when the clouds gathered and the tempest came, and lightnings of Heaven flashed in sheets as wide as the banners of an host?—What did I see?—Dead corpses and wounded horses, the rushing together of battle, and garments rolled in blood.—What heard I?—The voice that cried, Slay, slay—smite—slay utterly —let not your eye have pity—slay utterly, old and young, the maiden, the child, and the woman whose head is grey—Defile the house and fill the courts with the slain!"

"We receive the command," exclaimed more than one of the company. "Six days he hath not spoken nor broken bread, and now his tongue is unloosed!—We receive the command; as he hath said so will we do."

Astonished, disgusted, and horror-struck, at what he had seen and heard, Morton turned away from the circle and left the cottage. He was followed by Burley who had his eye on his motions.

"Whither are ye going," said the latter, taking him by the arm.

"Any where; I care not whither; but here I will abide no longer."

"Art thou so soon weary, young man?" answered Burley. "Thy hand is but now put to the plough, and wouldst thou already abandon it? Is this thy adherence to the cause of thy father?"

"No cause," replied Morton, indignantly—"no cause can prosper so conducted—One party declares for the ravings of a blood-thirsty madman; another leader is an old scholastic pedant; a third"—he stopped, and his companion continued the sentence—"is a desperate homicide, thou wouldst say, like John Balfour of Burley?—I can bear thy misconstruction without resentment. Thou dost not consider, that it is not men of sober and self-seeking minds, who arise in these days of wrath to execute judgment and to accomplish deliverance. Hadst thou but seen the armies of England, during her parliament of 1642, whose ranks were filled with sectarians and enthusiasts, wilder than the anabaptists of Munster, thou wouldst have had more cause to marvel; and yet these men were unconquered on the field, and their hands wrought marvellous things for the liberties of the land."

"But their affairs," replied Morton, "were wisely conducted, and the violence of their zeal expended itself in their exhortations and sermons, without bringing division into their councils, or cruelty into their conduct. I have often heard my father say so, and protest, that he wondered at nothing so much as the contrast between the extravagance of their religious tenets, and the wisdom and moderation with which they conducted their civil and military affairs. But our councils seem all one wild chaos of confusion."

"Thou must have patience, Henry Morton," answered Balfour; "thou must not leave the cause of thy religion and country either for one wild word, or one extravagant action. Hear me. I have already persuaded the wiser of our friends, that the counsellors are too numerous, and that we cannot expect that the Midianites shall, by so large a number, be delivered into our hands. They have hearkened to my voice, and our assemblies will be shortly reduced within such a number as can consult and act together, and in these thou shalt have a free voice, as well as in ordering our affairs of war, and protecting those to whom mercy should be shewn—Art thou now satisfied?"

"It will give me pleasure, doubtless," answered Morton, "to be the means of softening the horrors of civil war, and I will not leave the post I have taken, until I see measures adopted at which my conscience revolts. But to no bloody executions, after quarter asked, or slaughters without trial, will I lend countenance or sanction; and you may depend on my opposing them, with both heart and hand, as constantly and resolutely if attempted by our own followers, as when they are the work of the enemy."

Balfour waved his hand impatiently.

"Thou wilt find," he said, "that the stubborn and hard-hearted generation with whom we deal, must be chastized with scorpions ere their hearts be humbled, and ere they accept the punishment of their iniquity. The word is gone forth against them, 'I will bring a sword upon you that shall avenge the quarrel of my Covenant.' But what is done shall be done gravely, and with discretion, like that of the worthy James Melvin, who executed judgment on the tyrant and oppressor, Cardinal Beaton."

"I own to you," replied Morton, "that I feel still more abhorrent at cold-blooded and premeditated cruelty, than at that which is practised in the heat of zeal and resentment."

"Thou art yet but a youth," replied Balfour, "and hast not learned how light in the balance are a few drops of blood in comparison to the weight and importance of this great national testimony. But be not afraid; thyself shall vote and judge in these matters; it may be we shall see little cause to strive together anent them."

With this concession Morton was compelled to be satisfied for the present, and Burley left him, advising him to lie down and get some rest, as the host would probably move in the morning.

"And you?" said Morton, "do not you go to rest also?"

"No," said Burley; "my eyes must not yet know slumber. This is no work to be done lightly; I have yet to perfect the chusing of the committee of leaders, and I will call you by times in the morning to be present at their consultation."

He turned away and left Morton to his repose.

The place in which he found himself was not ill adapted for the purpose, being a sheltered nook, beneath a large rock, well protected from the prevailing wind. A quantity of moss with which the ground was overspread, made a couch soft enough for one who had suffered so much hardship and anxiety. Morton wrapped himself in the horseman's cloak which he had still retained, stretched himself on the ground, and had not long indulged in melancholy reflections on the state of the country, and upon his own condition, ere he was relieved from them by deep and sound slumber.

The rest of the army slept on the ground, dispersed in different groups, which chose their beds on the field as they could best find shelter and convenience. A few of the principal leaders held wakeful conference with Burley on the state of their affairs, and some watchmen were appointed who kept themselves on the alert by chanting psalms, or listening to the exercises of the more gifted of their number.

Chapter Ten

Got with much ease—now merrily to horse.
Henry IV. Part I

WITH the first peep of day Henry awoke, and found the faithful Cuddie standing beside him with a portmanteau in his hand.

"I hae been just putting your honour's things in readiness again ye were waking," said Cuddie, "as is my duty, seeing ye hae been sae gude as to tak me into your service."

"I take you into service, Cuddie?" said Morton, "you must be dreaming."

"Na, na, sir," answered Cuddie; "didna I say when I was tied on the horse yonder, that if ever we gat loose I wad be your servant, and ye didna say no? and if that isna hiring, I kenna what is. Ye gae me nae arles, indeed, but ye had gi'en me aneugh before at Milnewood."

"Well, Cuddie, if you insist on taking the chance of my unprosperous fortunes"——

"Ou ay, I'se warrant us a' prosper weel aneugh," answered Cuddie, cheerily, "an' anes my auld mither was weel putten up. I hae begun the campaigning trade at an end that is easy aneugh to learn."

"Pillaging, I suppose," said Morton, "for how else could you come by that portmanteau?"

"I wotna if it's pillaging, or how ye ca't," said Cuddie, "but it comes very natural to a body, and it's a profitable trade. Our folk had tirled

the dead dragoons as bare as bawbees before we were loose amaist—
But when I saw the whigs a' weel yokit by the lugs to Kettledrummle
and the other chield, I set aff at the lang trot on my ain errand and your
honour's. Sae I took up the syke a wee bit, away to the right, where I
saw the marks o' mony a horse-foot, and sure aneugh I cam to a place
where there had been some clean lathering, and a' the puir chields
were lying there buskit wi' their claiths just as they had put them on
that morning—naebody had found out that pose o' carcages—and
wha suld be in the midst thereof (as my mither says) but our auld
acquaintance, Serjeant Bothwell?"

"Ay? has that man fallen?" said Morton.

"Troth has he," answered Cuddie; "and his e'en were open, and
his brow bent, and his teeth clenched thegither, like the jaws of a trap
for foumarts when the spring's doun—I was amaist feared to look at
him; however, I thought to hae turn about wi' him, and sae I e'en riped
his pouches, as he had done mony an honester man's; and here's your
ain siller again (or your uncle's, which is the same) that he got at
Milnewood that unlucky night that made us a' sodgers thegither."

"There can be no harm, Cuddie," said Morton, "in making use of
this money, since we know how he came by it; but you must divide
with me."

"Bide a wee, bide a wee," said Cuddie. "Weel, and there's a bit ring
he had hinging in a black ribbon doun on his breast. I am thinking it
has been a love-token, puir fallow—there's naebody sae rough but
they hae aye a kind heart to the lasses—and there's a book wi' a wheen
papers, and I gat twa or three odd things that I'll keep to mysel forby."

"Upon my word you have made a very successful foray for a begin-
ner," said his new master.

"Haena I e'en now?" said Cuddie, with great exultation. "I tauld ye
I wasna that dooms stupid, if it cam to lifting things—And forby, I hae
gotten twa gude horse. A feckless loon of a Straven weaver, that had
left his loom and his bein house to sit skirling psalms on a cauld hill-
side, had catched twa dragoon naigs, and he could neither gar them
hup nor wind, sae he took a gowd noble for them baith.—I suld hae
tried him wi' half the siller, but it's an unco ill place to get change in—
Ye'll find the siller's missing out o' Bothwell's purse."

"You have made a most excellent and useful purchase, Cuddie; but
what is that portmanteau?"

"The pockmankle," answered Cuddie, "was Lord Evandale's yesterday, and it's yours the day. I fand it ahint the bush o' broom yonder
—ilka dog has its day—Ye ken what the auld sang says,

Take turn about, mither, quo Tam o' the Linn.

And speaking o' that, I maun gang and see about my mither, puir auld body, if your honour hasna ony immediate commands."

"But, Cuddie," said Morton, "I really cannot take these things from you without some recompense."

"Hout fie, sir," answered Cuddie, "ye suld aye be taking,—for recompense, ye may think of that some other time—I hae seen gay weel to mysel wi' some things that fit me better. What could I do wi' Lord Evandale's braw claiths? Serjeant Bothwell's will serve me weel aneugh."

Not being able to prevail on his self-constituted and disinterested follower to accept of any thing for himself out of these warlike spoils, Morton resolved to take the first opportunity of returning Lord Evandale's property, supposing him yet to be alive; and, in the meanwhile, did not hesitate to avail himself of Cuddie's prize, so far as to appropriate some change of linen and other trifling articles amongst those of more value which the portmanteau contained.

He then hastily looked over the papers which were found in Bothwell's pocket-book. These were of a miscellaneous description. The roll of his troop, with the names of those absent on furlough, memorandums of tavern-bills, and lists of delinquents who might be made subjects of fine and prosecution, first presented themselves, along with a copy of a warrant from the Privy Council to arrest certain persons of distinction therein named. In another pocket of the book, were one or two commissions which Bothwell had held at different times, and certificates of his services abroad, in which his courage and military talents were highly praised. But the more remarkable paper was an accurate account of his genealogy, with reference to many documents for establishment of its authenticity; subjoined was a list of the ample possessions of the forfeited Earl of Bothwell, and a particular account of the proportions in which King James VI. had bestowed them on the courtiers and nobility by whose descendants they were at present actually possessed; beneath this list was written, in red letters, in the hand of the deceased, *Haud Immemor*, F.S.E.B., the initials probably intimating Francis Stuart, Earl of Bothwell. To these documents, which strongly painted the character and feelings of the deceased proprietor of these papers, were added some which shewed it in a light greatly different from that in which we have hitherto presented it to the reader.

In a secret pocket of the book, which Morton did not discover without some trouble, were one or two letters, written in a beautiful female hand. They were dated about twenty years back, bore no address, and were subscribed only by initials. Without having time to peruse them accurately, Morton perceived that they contained the elegant yet fond expressions of female affection, directed towards an object whose jealousy they endeavoured to sooth, and of whose hasty, suspicious, and impatient temper, the writer seemed gently to complain. The ink of these manuscripts had faded by time, and notwithstanding the great care which had obviously been taken for their preservation, they were in one or two places chafed so as to be illegible.

"It matters not," these words were written on the envelope of that which had suffered most, "I have them by heart."

With these letters was a lock of hair wrapped in a copy of verses, written obviously with a feeling which atoned, in Morton's opinion, for the roughness of the poetry, and the conceits with which it abounded, according to the taste of the period :—

> Thy hue, dear pledge, is pure and bright,
> As in that well-remembered night,
> When first thy mystic braid was wove,
> And first my Agnes whispered love.
>   Since then how often hast thou pressed
> The torrid zone of this wild breast,
> Whose wrath and hate have sworn to dwell
> With the first sin which peopled hell,
> A breast whose blood's a troubled ocean,
> Each throb the earthquake's wild commotion?—
> O, if such clime thou canst endure,
> Yet keep thy hue unstained and pure,
> What conquest o'er each erring thought
> Of that fierce realm had Agnes wrought!
> I had not wandered wild and wide,
> With such an angel for my guide;
> Nor heaven nor earth could then reprove me,
> If she had lived, and lived to love me.
>   Not then this world's wild joys had been
> To me one savage hunting scene,
> My sole delight the headlong race,
> And frantic hurry of the chace,
> To start, pursue, and bring to bay,
> Rush in, drag down, and rend my prey,
> Then—from the carcase turn away!
> Mine ireful mood had sweetness tamed,
> And soothed each wound which pride inflamed;
> Yes, God and man might now approve me,
> If thou hadst lived, and lived to love me!

As he finished reading these lines, Morton could not forbear reflecting with compassion on the fate of this singular and most unhappy being, who, it appeared, while in the lowest state of desperation, and almost of contempt, had his recollections continually fixed on the high station to which his birth seemed to entitle him; and, while plunged in gross licentiousness, was in secret looking back with bitter remorse to the period of his youth, during which he had nourished a virtuous, though unfortunate attachment.

"Alas! what are we," said Morton, "that our best and most praise-worthy feelings can be thus debased and depraved—that honourable pride can sink into haughty and desperate indifference for general opinion, and the sorrow of blighted affection inhabit the same bosom which licence, revenge, and rapine have chosen for their citadel? But it is the same throughout; the liberal principles of one man sink into cold and unfeeling indifference, the religious zeal of another hurries him into frantic and savage enthusiasm. Our resolutions—our passions, are like the waves of the sea, and, without the aid of Him who formed the human breast, we cannot say to its tides, 'Thus far shall ye come, and no farther.'"

While he thus moralized, he raised his eyes, and observed that Burley stood before him.

"Already awake?" said that leader—"It is well, and shews zeal to tread the path before you. What papers are these?" he continued.

Morton gave him some brief account of Cuddie's successful marauding party, and handed him the pocket-book of Bothwell, with its contents. The Cameronian leader looked with some attention on such of the papers as related to military affairs, or public business; but when he came to the verses, he threw them from him with contempt.

"I little thought," he said, "when, by the blessing of God, I passed my sword three times through the body of that arch tool of cruelty and persecution, that a character so desperate and so dangerous could have stooped to an art as trifling as it is profane. But I see that Satan can blend the most different qualities in his well-beloved and chosen agents, and that the same hand which can wield a club or a slaughter-weapon against the godly in the valley of destruction, can touch a tinkling lute, or a gittern, to sooth the ears of the dancing daughters of perdition in this Vanity Fair."

"Your ideas of duty, then," said Morton, "exclude love of the fine arts, which have been supposed in general to purify and to elevate the mind."

"To me, young man," answered Burley, "and to those who think as I do, the pleasures of this world, under whatever name disguised, are vanity, as its grandeur and power is a snare. We have but one object on earth, and that is, to build up the temple of the Lord."

"I have heard my father observe," replied Morton, "that many who assumed power in the name of Heaven, were as severe in its exercise, and as unwilling to part with it, as if they had been solely moved by the motives of worldly ambition—But of this another time. Have you succeeded in obtaining a committee of the council to be nominated?"

"I have," answered Burley. "The number is limited to six, of which you are one, and I come to call you to their deliberations."

Morton accompanied him to a sequestered grass-plot, where their colleagues awaited them. In this delegation of authority, the two principal factions which divided the tumultuary army had each taken care to send three of their own number. On the part of the Cameronians, were Burley, Macbriar, and Kettledrummle; and on that of the moderate party, Poundtext, Henry Morton, and a small proprietor, called the Laird of Langcale. Thus the two parties were equally balanced by their representatives in the committee of management, although it seemed likely that those of the most violent opinions were, as usual in such cases, to possess and exert the greater degree of energy. Their debate, however, was conducted more like men of this world than could have been expected from their conduct on the preceding evening. After maturely considering their means and situation, and the probable increase of their numbers, they agreed that they would keep their position for that day, in order to refresh their men, and give time to reinforcements to join them, and that, on the next morning, they would direct their march towards Tillietudlem, and summon that strong-hold, as they expressed it, of malignancy. If it was not surrendered to their summons, they resolved to try the effect of a brisk assault, and, should that miscarry, it was settled that they should leave a part of their number to blockade the place, and reduce it, if possible, by famine, while their main body should march forward to drive Claverhouse and Lord Ross from the town of Glasgow. Such was the determination of the council of management; and thus Morton's first enterprize in active life was likely to be the attack of a castle belonging to the parent of his mistress, and defended by her relative, Major Bellenden, to whom he personally owed many obligations. He felt fully the embarrassment of his situation, yet consoled himself with the reflection, that his newly-acquired power in the insurgent army would give him, at all events, the means of extending to the inmates of Tillietudlem a protection which no other circumstance could have afforded them, and he was not without hope that he might be able to mediate such an accommodation betwixt them and the presbyterian army as should secure them a safe neutrality during the war which was about to ensue.

Chapter Eleven

There came a knight from the field of slain,
His steed was drench'd with blood and rain.
FINLAY

WE MUST now return to the fortress of Tillietudlem and its inhabitants. The morning, being the first after the battle of Loudoun-hill,
had dawned upon its battlements, and the defenders had already
resumed the labours by which they proposed to render the place
tenable, when the watchman, who was placed in a high turret, called
the Warder's Tower, gave the signal that a horseman was approaching. As he came nearer, his dress indicated an officer of the Life-
Guards; and the slowness of his horse's pace, as well as the manner in
which the rider stooped on the saddle-bow, plainly shewed that he was
sick or wounded. The wicket was instantly opened to receive him, and
Lord Evandale rode into the court-yard, so reduced by loss of blood,
that he was unable to dismount without assistance. As he entered the
hall, leaning upon a servant, the ladies shrieked with surprise and
terror; for, pale as death, stained with blood, his regimentals soiled
and torn, and his hair matted and disordered, he resembled rather a
spectre than a human being. But their next exclamation was that of joy
at his escape.

"Thank God!" exclaimed Lady Margaret, "that you are here, and
have escaped the hands of the bloodthirsty murderers who have cut
off so many of the king's loyal servants!"

"Thank God," added Edith, "that you are here and in safety! We
have dreaded the worst; but you are wounded, and I fear we have little
the means of assisting you."

"My wounds are only sword-cuts," answered the young nobleman,
as he reposed himself on a seat; "the pain is not worth mentioning,
and I should not even feel exhausted but for the loss of blood. But it
was not my purpose to bring my weakness to add to your danger and
distress, but to relieve them, if possible. What can I do for you?—
Permit me," he added, addressing Lady Margaret—"permit me to
think and act as your son, my dear madam—as your brother, Edith!"

He pronounced the last part of the sentence with some emphasis, as
if he feared that the apprehension of his pretensions as a suitor might
render his proffered services unacceptable to Miss Bellenden. She
was not insensible to his delicacy, but there was no time for exchange
of sentiments.

"We are preparing for our defence," said the old lady, with great dignity; "my brother has taken charge of our garrison, and, by the grace of God, we will give the rebels such a reception as they deserve."

"How gladly," said Evandale, "would I share in the defence of the Castle! But, in my present state, I should be but a burden to you, nay, something worse; for the knowledge that an officer of the Life-Guards is in the Castle would be sufficient to make these rogues more desperately earnest to possess themselves of it. If they find it defended only by the family, they may possibly march on to Glasgow rather than hazard an assault."

"And can you think so meanly of us, my Lord," said Edith, with the generous burst of feeling which Woman so often evinces, and which becomes her so well, her voice faultering through eagerness, and her brow colouring with the noble warmth which dictated her language—"Can you think so meanly of your friends, as that they would permit such considerations to interfere with their sheltering and protecting you at a moment when you are unable to defend yourself, and when the whole country is filled with the enemy? Is there a cottage in Scotland whose owners would permit a valued friend to leave it in such circumstances? And do you think we will allow you to go from a castle which we think strong enough for our own defence?"

"Lord Evandale need never think of it," said Lady Margaret. "I will dress his wounds myself; it is all an old wife is fit for in war time; but to quit the Castle of Tillietudlem when the sword of the enemy is drawn to slay him,—the meanest trooper that ever wore the king's coat on his back should not do so, much less my young Lord Evandale.—Ours is not a house that ought to brook such dishonour. The Tower of Tillietudlem has been too much distinguished by the visit of his most sacred"——

Here she was interrupted by the entrance of the Major.

"We have taken a prisoner, my dear uncle," said Edith—"a wounded prisoner, and he wants to escape from us. You must help us to keep him by force."

"Lord Evandale?" exclaimed the veteran. "I am as much pleased as when I got my first commission. Claverhouse reported you killed, or missing at least."

"I should have been slain, but for a friend of yours," said Lord Evandale, speaking with some emotion, and bending his eyes on the ground, as if he wished to avoid seeing the impression that what he was about to say would make upon Miss Bellenden. "I was unhorsed and defenceless, and the sword raised to dispatch me, when young Mr Morton, the prisoner for whom you interested yourself yesterday morning, interposed in the most generous manner, preserved my life, and furnished me with the means of escaping."

As he ended the sentence, a painful curiosity overcame his first resolution, he raised his eyes to Edith's face, and imagined he could read in the glow of her cheek and the sparkle of her eye, joy at hearing of her lover's safety and freedom, and triumph at his not having been left last in the race of generosity. Such, indeed, were her feelings, but they were also mingled with admiration of the ready frankness with which Lord Evandale had hastened to bear witness to the merit of a favoured rival, and to acknowledge an obligation which, in all probability, he would rather have owed to any other individual in the world.

Major Bellenden, who would never have observed the emotions of either party, even had they been much more markedly expressed, contented himself with saying, "Since Henry Morton has influence with these rascals, I am glad he has so exerted it; but I hope he will get clear of them as soon as he can. Indeed, I cannot doubt it. I know his principles, and that he detests their cant and hypocrisy. I have heard him laugh a thousand times at the pedantry of that old presbyterian scoundrel, Poundtext, who, after enjoying the indulgence of the government for so many years, has now, upon the very first ruffle, shewn himself in his own proper colours, and set off, with three fourths of his crop-eared congregation, to join the host of the fanatics.—But how did you escape after leaving the field, my Lord?"

"I rode for my life, as a recreant knight must," answered Lord Evandale, smiling. "I took the route where I thought I had least chance of meeting with any of the enemy, and I found shelter for several hours —you will hardly guess where."

"At Castle-Brecklan, perhaps," said Lady Margaret, "or in the house of some other loyal gentleman?"

"No, madam. I was repulsed, under one mean pretext or another, from more than one house of that description, for fear of the enemy following my traces; but I found refuge in the cottage of a poor widow, whose husband had fallen in fight, within these three months, with a party of our corps, and whose two sons had perished more cruelly still."

"Indeed?" said Lady Margaret Bellenden; "and was a fanatic woman capable of such generosity?—but she disapproved, I suppose, of the tenets of her family?"

"Far from it, madam," continued the young nobleman; "she was in principle a rigid recusant, but she saw my danger and distress, considered me as a fellow-creature, and forgot that I was a cavalier and a soldier. She bound my wounds, and permitted me to rest upon her bed, concealed me from a party of the insurgents who were seeking for stragglers, supplied me with food, and did not suffer me to leave my place of refuge until she had learned that I had every chance of getting to this tower without danger."

"It was nobly done," said Miss Bellenden; "and I trust you will have an opportunity of rewarding her generosity."

"I am running up an arrear of obligation on all sides, Miss Bellenden, during these unfortunate occurrences," replied Lord Evandale; "but when I shall attain the means of shewing my gratitude, the will shall not be awanting."

All now joined in pressing Lord Evandale to relinquish his intention of leaving the Castle; but the argument of Major Bellenden proved the most effectual.

"Your presence in the Castle will be most useful, if not absolutely necessary, my Lord, in order to maintain, by your authority, proper discipline among the fellows whom Claverhouse has left in garrison here, and who do not promise to be of the most orderly description of inmates; and, indeed, we have the Colonel's authority, for that very purpose, to detain any officer of his regiment who might pass this way."

"That," said Lord Evandale, "is an unanswerable argument, since it shews me that my residence here may be useful, even in my present disabled state."

"For your wounds, my Lord," said the Major, "if my sister, Lady Bellenden, will undertake to give battle to any feverish symptom, if such should appear, I will answer that my old campaigner, Gideon Pike, shall dress a flesh-wound with any of the incorporation of Barber Surgeons. He had enough of practice in Montrose's time, for we had few regularly-bred army chirurgeons, as you may well suppose.— You agree to stay with us, then?"

"My reasons for leaving the Castle," said Lord Evandale, glancing a look towards Edith, "though they certainly seemed weighty, must needs give way to those which infer the power of serving you. May I presume, Major, to enquire into the means and plan of defence which you have prepared? or can I attend you to examine the works?"

It did not escape Miss Bellenden, that Lord Evandale seemed much exhausted both in body and mind. "I think, sir," said she, addressing the Major, "that since Lord Evandale condescends to become an officer of our garrison, you should begin by rendering him amenable to your authority, and ordering him to his apartment, that he may take some repose ere he enters on military discussions."

"Edith is right," said the old lady; "you must go instantly to bed, my Lord, and take some febrifuge, which I will prepare with my own hand; and my lady-in-waiting, Mistress Martha Weddell, shall make some friar's chicken, or something very light. John Gudyill, let the housekeeper make ready the chamber of dais. Lord Evandale must lie down instantaneously. Pike will take off the dressings and examine the state of the wounds. I would not advise wine"—&c. &c. &c.

"These are melancholy preparations, madam," said Lord Evandale, as he returned thanks to Lady Margaret, and was about to leave the hall,—"but I must submit to your ladyship's directions; and I trust that your skill will soon make me a more able defender of your castle than I am at present. You must render my body serviceable as soon as you can, for you have no use for my head while you have Major Bellenden."

With these words he left the apartment.

"An excellent young man, and a modest," said the Major.

"None of that conceit," said Lady Margaret, "that often makes young folks suppose they know better how their complaints should be treated than people that have had experience."

"And so generous and handsome a young gentleman," said Jenny Dennison, who had entered during the latter part of this conversation, and was now left alone with her mistress in the hall, the Major returning to his military cares, and Lady Margaret to her medical preparations.

Edith only answered these encomiums with a sigh; but, although silent, she felt and knew better than any one how much they were merited by the person on whom they were bestowed. Jenny, however, failed not to follow up her blow.

"After a', it's true that my leddy says—there's nae trusting a presbyterian; they are a' faithless man-sworn loons. Whae wad hae thought that young Milnewood and Cuddie Headrigg wad hae ta'en on wi' thae rebel blackguards?"

"What do you mean by such improbable nonsense, Jenny?" said her young mistress, very much displeased.

"I ken it's no pleasing for you to hear, madam," answered Jenny, hardily; "and it's as little pleasant for me to tell it; but as gude ye suld ken a' about it soon as syne, and the haill castle's ringing wi't."

"Ringing with what, Jenny? Have you a mind to drive me mad?" answered Edith, impatiently.

"Just that Henry Morton o' Milnewood is out wi' the rebels, and ane o' their chief leaders."

"It is a falsehood," said Edith—"a most base calumny! and you are very bold to dare to repeat it to me. Henry Morton is incapable of such treachery to his king and country—such cruelty to me—to—to all the innocent and defenceless victims, I mean, who must suffer in a civil war—I tell you he is utterly incapable of it, in every sense."

"Dear! dear! Miss Edith," replied Jenny, still constant to her text; "they maun be better acquented wi' young men than I am, or ever wish to be, that can tell preceesely what they're capable and no capable o'. But there has been Trooper Tam, and another chield, out in bonnets and grey plaids, like countrymen, to recon—reconnoitre, I think John Gudyill ca'd it; and they hae been amang the rebels, and brought back word that they had seen young Milnewood, mounted on ane o' the dragoon horses that was ta'en at Loudoun-hill, and armed wi' sword and pistols, like wha but him, and hand and glove wi' a' the foremost o' them, and dreeling and commanding the men; and Cuddie at the heels o' him, in ane o' Serjeant Bothwell's laced waistcoats, and a cockit hat with a bab o' blue ribbands at it, for the auld cause o' the Covenant, (but Cuddie aye liked a blue ribband) and a ruffled sark, like ony lord o' the land—it sets the like o' him, indeed!"

"Jenny," said her young mistress, hastily, "I trust it is impossible these men's report can be true; my uncle knew nothing of it but this instant."

"Because Tam Halliday," answered the handmaiden, "came in just five minutes after Lord Evandale; and when he heard his Lordship was in the Castle, he swore (the profane loon) he would be d—d ere he would make the report, as he ca'd it, of his news to Major Bellenden, since there was an officer of his ain regiment in the garrison. Sae he wad have said naething till Lord Evandale waked in the neist morning; only he tauld me about it," (here Jenny looked a little down,) "just to vex me about Cuddie."

"Pooh, you silly girl," said Edith, assuming some courage, "it is all a trick of that fellow to teaze you."

"Na, ma'am, it canna be that, for John Gudyill took the other dragoon (he's an auld hard-favoured man, I wotna his name) into the cellar, and gae him a tass o' brandy to get the news out o' him, and he said just the same as Tam Halliday, word for word; and Mr Gudyill was in sic a rage, that he tauld it a' ower again to us, and says the haill rebellion is owing to the nonsense o' my Leddy, and the Major, and Lord Evandale, that begged off young Milnewood and Cuddie yesterday morning, for that, if they had suffered, the country wad hae been quiet—and troth I am muckle o' that opinion mysel."

This last commentary Jenny added to her tale, in resentment of her mistress's extreme and obstinate incredulity. She was instantly alarmed, however, by the effect which her news produced upon her young mistress, an effect rendered doubly violent by the High church principles and prejudices in which Miss Bellenden had been educated. Her complexion became instantly as pale as a corpse, her respiration so difficult that it was on the point of altogether failing her, and her limbs so incapable of supporting her that she sunk, rather than sat, down upon one of the seats in the hall, and seemed on the eve of fainting. Jenny tried cold water, burnt feathers, cutting of laces, and all other remedies usual in hysterical cases, but without any immediate effect.

"God forgi'e me, what hae I done?" said the repentant fille-de-chambre, "I wish my tongue had been cuttit out!—Wha wad hae thought o' her taking on that way, and a' for a young lad?—O, Miss Edith—dear Miss Edith—haud your heart up about it—it's maybe no true for a' that I hae said—O, I wish my mouth had been blistered!—A' body tells me my tongue will do me a mischief some day. What if my Leddy comes? or the Major?—and she's sitting in the throne too that naebody has sate in since that weary morning the King was here!—O, what will I do? What will become o' us?"

While Jenny Dennison thus lamented herself and her mistress, Edith slowly returned from the paroxysm into which she had been thrown by this unexpected intelligence.

"If he had been unfortunate," she said, "I never could have deserted him. I never did so, even when there was danger and disgrace in pleading his cause. If he had died, I would have mourned him—if he had been unfaithful, I would have forgiven him; but a rebel to his King,—a traitor to his country,—the associate and colleague of cut-throats and common stabbers,—the persecutor of all that is noble,—the professed and blasphemous enemy of all that is sacred,—I will tear him from my heart, if my life-blood should ebb in the effort!"

She wiped her eyes, and rose hastily from the great chair, (or throne, as Lady Margaret chose to call it,) while the terrified damsel hastened to shake up the cushion, and efface the appearance of any one having occupied that sacred seat; although King Charles himself, considering the youth and beauty as well as the affliction of the momentary usurper of his hallowed chair, would probably have thought very lightly of the profanation. She then hastened officiously to press her support on Edith, as she paced the hall apparently in deep meditation.

"Tak my arm, madam; better just tak my arm; sorrow maun hae its vent, and doubtless"——

"No, Jenny," said Edith, with firmness; "you have seen my weakness, and you shall see my strength."

"But ye leaned on me the other morning, Miss Edith, when ye were sae sair grieved."

"Misplaced and erring affection may require support, Jenny—duty can support itself; yet I will do nothing rashly. I will be aware of the reasons of his conduct—and then—cast him off for ever," was the firm and determined answer of her young lady.

Overawed by a manner of which she could neither conceive the motive, nor estimate the merit, Jenny muttered between her teeth, "Odd, when the first flight's ower, Miss Edith taks it as easy as I do, and muckle easier, and I'm sure I ne'er cared half sae muckle about Cuddie Headrigg as she did about young Milnewood. Forbye that, it's maybe as weel to hae a friend on baith sides; for, if the whigs suld cum to tak the Castle, as it's like they may, when there's sae little victual, and the dragoons wasting what's o't, ou, in that case, Milnewood and Cuddie wad hae the upper hand, and their freendship wad be worth siller—I was thinking sae this morning or I heard the news."

With this consolatory reflection the damsel went about her usual accommodations, leaving her mistress to school her mind as she best might, for eradicating the sentiments which she had hitherto entertained towards Henry Morton.

Chapter Twelve

Once more unto the breach—dear friends, once more—
Henry V.

ON the evening of this day, all the information which they could procure led them to expect that the insurgent army would be with early dawn on their march against Tillietudlem. Lord Evandale's wounds had been examined by Pike, who reported them in a very promising state. They were numerous, but none of any consequence; and the loss of blood, as much perhaps as the boasted specific of Lady Margaret, had prevented any tendency to fever; so that, notwithstanding he felt some pain and great weakness, the patient maintained that he was able to creep about with the assistance of a stick. In these circumstances, he refused to be confined to his apartment, both that he might encourage the soldiers by his presence, and suggest any necessary addition to the plan of defence, which the Major might be supposed to have arranged upon something of an antiquated fashion of warfare. Lord Evandale was well qualified to give advice on such subjects, having served, during his early youth, both in France and in the Low Countries. There was little or no occasion, however, for altering the preparations already made; and, excepting on the article of provisions, there seemed no reason to fear for the defence of so strong a place against such assailants as those by whom it was threatened.

With the peep of day, Lord Evandale and Major Bellenden were on the battlements again, viewing and reviewing the state of their preparations, and anxiously expecting the approach of the enemy. I ought to observe, that the report of the spies had now been regularly made and received. But the Major treated the report that Morton was in arms against the government, with the most scornful incredulity.

"I know the lad better," was the only reply he deigned to make; "the fellows have not dared to venture near enough, and have been deceived by some fanciful resemblance, or have picked up some idle story."

"I differ from you, Major," answered Lord Evandale; "I think you will see that young gentleman at the head of the insurgents, and, though I shall be heartily sorry for it, I will not be greatly surprised."

"You are as bad as Claverhouse," said the Major, "who contended yesterday morning down my very throat, that this young fellow, who is as high-spirited and gentleman-like a boy as I have ever known, wanted but an opportunity to place himself at the head of the rebels."

"And considering the usage which he has received, and the suspicions under which he lies," said Lord Evandale, "what other course is open to him? For my own part, I should hardly know whether he deserved most blame or pity."

"Blame, my Lord?—Pity?" echoed the Major, astonished at hearing such sentiments, "he would deserve to be hanged, that's all; and, were he my own son, I should see him strung up with pleasure— Blame indeed! But your Lordship cannot think as you are pleased to speak."

"I give you my honour, Major Bellenden, that I have been for some time of opinion, that our politicians and prelates have driven matters to a painful extremity in this country, and have alienated, by violence of various kinds, not only the lower classes, but all those in the upper ranks, whom strong party-feeling, or a desire of court-interest, does not attach to their standard."

"I am no politician," answered the Major, "and I do not understand nice distinctions. My sword is the King's, and when he commands I draw it in his cause."

"I trust," replied the young Lord, "you will not find me more backward than yourself, though I heartily wish that the enemies were foreigners. It is, however, no time to debate that matter, for yonder they come, and we must defend ourselves as well as we can."

As Lord Evandale spoke, the van of the insurgents began to make their appearance on the road where it crossed the top of the hill, and thence descended opposite to the Tower. They did not, however, move downwards, as if aware that, in doing so, their columns would be exposed to the fire of the artillery of the place. But their numbers, which at first seemed few, appeared so to deepen and concentrate themselves, that, judging of the masses which occupied the road behind the hill from the closeness of the front which they presented on the top of it, their force seemed very considerable. There was a pause of anxiety in both sides; and, while the unsteady ranks of the Covenanters were agitated, as if by pressure behind, or uncertainty as to their next movement, their arms, picturesque from their variety, glanced in the morning sun, whose beams were reflected from a grove of pikes, muskets, halberds, and battle-axes. The armed mass occupied, for a few minutes, this fluctuating position, until three or four horsemen, who seemed to be leaders, advanced from the front, and occupied a height a little nearer to the castle. John Gudyill, who was not without some skill as an artilleryman, brought a gun to bear on this detached group.

"I'll flee the falcon," (so the small cannon was called)—"I'll flee the falcon whene'er your honours gi'e command; my certie she'll ruffle their feathers for them."

The Major looked at Lord Evandale.

"Stay a moment," said the young nobleman, "they send us a flag of truce."

In fact, one of the horsemen at that instant dismounted, and, displaying a white cloth on a pike, moved forwards towards the Tower, while the Major and Lord Evandale, descending from the battlements of the main fortress, advanced to meet him as far as the first barricade, judging it unwise to admit him within the precincts which they designed to defend. At the same time that the ambassador set forth, the group of horsemen, as if they had anticipated the preparations of John Gudyill for their annoyance, withdrew from the advanced station which they had occupied, and fell back to the main body.

The envoy of the Covenanters, to judge by his mien and manner, seemed fully imbued with that spiritual pride which distinguished his sect. His features were drawn up to a contemptuous primness, and his half-shut eyes seemed to scorn to look upon the terrestrial objects around, while, at every solemn stride, his toes were pointed outwards with an air that appeared to despise the ground on which they trode. Lord Evandale could not suppress a smile at this singular figure.

"Did you ever," said he to Major Bellenden, "see such an absurd automaton? One would swear it moves upon springs—Can it speak, think you?"

"O, ay," said the Major; "that seems to be one of my old acquaintance, a genuine puritan of the right pharasaical leaven.—Stay—he coughs and hems; he is about to summon the Castle with the butt end of a sermon instead of a parley on the trumpet."

The veteran, who in his day had many an opportunity to become acquainted with the manners of these religionists, was not far mistaken in his conjecture, only that, instead of a prose exordium, the

Laird of Langcale, for it was no less a personage, uplifted, with a Stentorian voice, a verse of the twenty-fourth Psalm:

> "Ye gates lift up your heads, ye doors,
> Doors that do last for aye,
> Be lifted up"——

"I told you so," said the Major to Evandale, and then presented himself at the entrance of the barricade, demanding to know for what purpose or intent he made that doleful noise, like a hog in a high wind, beneath the gates of the Castle.

"I come," replied the ambassador, in a high and shrill voice, and without any of the usual salutations or deferences,—"I come from the godly army of the Solemn League and Covenant, to speak with two carnal malignants, William Maxwell, called Lord Evandale, and Miles Bellenden of Charnwood."

"And what have you to say to Miles Bellenden and Lord Evandale?" answered the Major.

"Are you the parties?" said the Laird of Langcale, in the same sharp, conceited, disrespectful tone of voice.

"Even so, for fault of better," said the Major.

"Then there is the public summons," said the envoy, putting a paper into Lord Evandale's hand, "and there is a private letter for Miles Bellenden from a godly youth who is honoured with leading a part of our host. Read them quickly, and God give you grace to fructify by the contents, though it is muckle to be doubted."

The summons ran thus: "We, the named and constituted leaders of the gentlemen, ministers, and others, presently in arms for the cause of liberty and true religion, do warn and summons William Lord Evandale and Miles Bellenden of Charnwood, and others presently in arms, and keeping garrison in the Tower of Tillietudlem, to surrender the said Tower upon fair condition of quarter, and license to depart with bag and baggage—Otherwise to suffer such extremity of sword and fire as belong by the laws of war to those who hold out an untenable post. And so may God defend his own good cause."

This summons was signed by John Balfour of Burley, as quarter-master-general of the army of the Covenant, for himself, and in name of the other leaders.

The letter to Major Bellenden was from Henry Morton. It was couched in the following language:—

"I have taken a step, my venerable friend, which, among many painful consequences, will, I am afraid, incur your very decided disapprobation. But I have taken my resolution in honour and good faith, and with the full avowal of my own conscience. I can no longer submit to have my own rights and those of my fellow-subjects trampled upon, our freedom violated, our persons insulted, and our blood spilt, without legal cause or legal trial. Providence, through the violence of the oppressors themselves, seems now to have opened a way of deliverance from this intolerable tyranny, and I do not hold him deserving of the name and rights of a freeman, who, thinking as I do, should withhold his arm from the cause of his country. But God, who knows my heart, be my witness, that I do not share the angry or violent passions of the oppressed and harassed sufferers with whom I am now acting. My most earnest and anxious desire is, to see this unnatural war brought to a speedy end, by the union of the good, wise, and moderate of all parties, and a peace restored, which, without injury to the King's constitutional rights, may substitute the authority of equal laws for that of military violence, and, permitting to all men to worship God according to their own consciences, may subdue fanatical enthusiasm by reason and mildness, instead of driving it to frenzy by persecution and intolerance.

"With these sentiments, you may conceive with what pain I appear in arms before the house of your venerable relative, which we understand you propose to hold out against us. Permit me to press upon you the assurance, that such a measure will only lead to effusion of blood —that, if repulsed in the assault, we are yet strong enough to invest the place, and reduce it by hunger, being aware of your indifferent preparations to sustain a protracted siege. It would grieve me to the heart to think what would be the sufferings in such a case, and upon whom they would chiefly fall.

"Do not suppose, my respected friend, that I would propose to you any terms which could compromise the high and honourable character which you have so deservedly won and so long borne. If the regular soldiers (to whom I will ensure a safe retreat) are dismissed from the place, I trust no more will be required than your parole to remain neuter during this unhappy contest, and I will take care that Lady Margaret's property, as well as yours, shall be duly respected, and no garrison intruded upon you. I could say much in favour of this proposal; but I fear, as I must, in the present instance, appear criminal in your eyes, good arguments would lose their influence when coming from an unwelcome quarter. I will, therefore, break off with assuring you, that whatever your sentiments may be hereafter towards me, my sense of gratitude to you can never be diminished or erazed, and it would be the happiest moment of my life that should give me more effectual means than mere words to assure you of it. Therefore, although in the first moment of resentment you may reject the proposal I make to you, let that not prevent you from resuming the topic, if future events should render it more acceptable; for whenever, or howsoever, I can be of service to you, it will always afford the greatest satisfaction to

"HENRY MORTON"

Having read this long letter with the most marked indignation, Major Bellenden put it into the hands of Lord Evandale.

"I would not have believed this," he said, "of Henry Morton, if half mankind had sworn it! The ungrateful, rebellious traitor! rebellious in cold blood, and without even the pretext of enthusiasm that warms the liver of such a crack-brained fop as our friend the envoy there. But I should have remembered he was a presbyterian—I ought to have been aware that I was nursing a wolf-cub, whose diabolical nature would make him tear and snatch at me on the first opportunity. Were Saint Paul on earth again and a presbyterian, he would be a rebel in three months—it is in the very blood of them."

"Well," said Lord Evandale, "I will be the last to recommend surrender; but, if our provisions fail, and we receive no relief from Edinburgh, or Glasgow, I think we ought to avail ourselves of this opening, to get the ladies at least safe out of the Castle."

"They will endure all, ere they would accept the protection of such a smooth-tongued hypocrite," answered the Major indignantly; "I would renounce them for relatives were it otherwise. But let us dismiss the worthy ambassador—My friend," he said, turning to Langcale, "tell your leaders, and the mob they have gathered yonder, that, if they have not a particular opinion of the hardness of their own skulls, I would advise them to beware how they knock them against these old walls. And let them send no more flags of truce, or we will hang up the messenger in retaliation of the murder of Cornet Grahame."

With this answer the ambassador returned to those by whom he had been sent. He had no sooner reached the main-body than a murmur was heard amongst the multitude, and there was raised, in the front of their ranks, an ample red flag, the borders of which were edged with blue. As this signal of war and defiance spread out its large folds upon the morning wind, the ancient banner of Lady Margaret's family, together with the royal ensign, were immediately hoisted on the walls of the Tower, and, at the same time, a round of artillery was discharged against the foremost ranks of the insurgents, by which they sustained some loss. Their leaders instantly withdrew them to the shelter of the brow of the hill.

"I think," said John Gudyill, while he busied himself in recharging his guns, "they hae fund the falcon's neb a bit ower hard for them— It's no for nought that the hawk whistles."

But as he uttered these words, the ridge was once more crowded with the ranks of the enemy. A general discharge of their fire-arms was directed against the defenders upon the battlements. Under cover of the smoke, a column of picked men rushed down the road with determined courage, and, sustaining with firmness a heavy fire from the defenders, they forced their way, in spite of opposition, to the first barricade by which the avenue was defended. They were led on by Balfour in person, who displayed courage equal to his enthusiasm, and, in spite of every opposition, forced the barricade, killing and wounding several of the defenders, and compelling the rest to retreat to their second position. The precautions, however, of Major Bellenden, rendered this success unavailing, for no sooner were the Covenanters in possession of the post, than a close and destructive fire was poured into it from the Castle, and from those stations which commanded it in the rear. Having no means of protecting themselves from this fire, or of returning it with effect against men who were under cover of their barricades and defences, the Covenanters were obliged to retreat; but not until they had, with their axes, destroyed the stockade, so as to render it impossible for the defenders to re-occupy it.

Balfour was the last man that retired. He even remained for a short space, almost alone, with an axe in his hand, labouring like a pioneer amid the storm of balls, many of which were specially aimed against him. The retreat of the party he commanded was not effected without heavy loss, and served as a severe lesson concerning the local advantages possessed by the garrison.

The next attack of the Covenanters was made with more caution. A strong party of marksmen, (many of them competitors at the game of the popinjay) under the command of Henry Morton, glided through the woods where they afforded them the best shelter, and, avoiding the open road, endeavoured, by forcing their way among the bushes and trees, and up the rocks which surrounded it on either side, to gain a position, from which, without being exposed in an intolerable degree, they might annoy the flank of the second barricade, while it was menaced in affront by a second attack from Burley. The besieged saw the danger of this movement, and endeavoured to impede the approach of the marksmen, by firing upon them at every point where they shewed themselves. The assailants, on the other hand, displayed great coolness, spirit, and judgment in the manner in which they approached the defences. This was, in a great measure, to be ascribed to the steady and adroit manner in which they were conducted by their youthful leader, who showed as much skill in protecting his own followers as spirit in annoying the enemy.

He repeatedly enjoined his marksmen to direct their aim chiefly upon the red-coats, and to spare the others engaged in the defence of the Castle; and, above all, to spare the life of the old Major, whose anxiety made him more than once expose himself in a manner, that, without such generosity on the part of the enemy, might have proved fatal. A dropping fire of musketry now glanced from every part of the precipitous mount on which the Castle was founded. From bush to bush—from crag to crag—from tree to tree, the marksmen continued to advance, availing themselves of branches and roots to assist their ascent, and contending at once with the disadvantages of the ground and the fire of the enemy. At length they got so high on the ascent, that several of them possessed an opportunity of firing into the barricade against the defenders, who then lay exposed to their aim, and Burley, availing himself of the confusion of the moment, moved forward to the attack in front. His onset was made with the same desperation and fury as before, and met at first with less resistance, the defenders being alarmed at the progress which the sharp-shooters had made in turning the flank of their position. Determined to improve his advantage, Burley, with his axe in his hand, pursued the party whom he had dislodged even to the third and last barricade, and entered it along with them.

"Kill, kill—down with the enemies of God and his people!"—"No quarter"—"The Castle is ours!" were the cries by which he animated his friends; the most undaunted of whom followed him close, whilst the others, with axes, spades, and other implements, threw up earth, cut down trees, hastily labouring to establish such a defensive cover in the rear of the second barricade as might enable them to retain possession of it, in case the Castle was not carried by this coup-de-main.

Lord Evandale could no longer restrain his impatience. He charged with a few soldiers who had been kept in reserve in the court-yard of the Castle; and, although his arm was in a sling, encouraged them, by voice and gesture, to assist their companions who were engaged with Burley. The combat now assumed an air of desperation. The narrow road was crowded with the followers of Burley, who pressed forward to support their companions. The soldiers, animated by the voice and presence of Lord Evandale, fought with fury, their small numbers being in some measure compensated by their greater skill, and by their possessing the upper ground, which they defended desperately with pikes and halberds, as well as with the butt of the carabines and their broad-swords. Those within the Castle endeavoured to assist their companions, whenever they could so level their guns as to fire upon the enemy without endangering their friends. The sharp-shooters, dispersed around, were firing incessantly on each object that was exposed upon the battlements. The Castle was enveloped with smoke, and the rocks rang to the cries of the combatants. In the midst of this scene of confusion, a singular accident had nearly given the besiegers possession of the fortress.

Cuddie Headrigg, who had advanced among the marksmen, being well acquainted with every rock and bush in the vicinity of the Castle, where he had so often gathered nuts with Jenny Dennison, was enabled, by his local knowledge, to advance farther, and with less danger, than most of his companions, excepting some three or four who had followed him close. Now Cuddie, though a brave enough fellow upon the whole, was by no means fond of danger, either for its own sake, or for that of the glory which attends it. In his advance, therefore, he had not, as the phrase goes, taken the bull by the horns, or advanced in front of the enemy's fire. On the contrary, he had edged gradually away from the scene of action, and, turning his line of ascent rather to the left, had pursued it until it brought him under a front of the Castle different from that beneath which the parties were engaged, and to which the defenders had given no attention, trusting to the steepness of the precipice. There was, however, on this point, a certain window belonging to a certain pantry, and communicating with a certain yew-tree, which grew out of a steep cleft of the rock, being the very pass by which Goose-Gibbie was smuggled out of the Castle in order to carry Edith's express to Charnwood, and which had probably, in its day, been used for other contraband purposes. Cuddie, resting upon the butt of his gun, and looking up at this window, observed to one of his companions,—"There's a place I ken weel; mony a time I hae helped Jenny Dennison out o' that winnock, forby creeping in whiles mysel to get some daffin, at e'en after the pleugh was loosed."

"And what's to hinder us to creep in just now?" said the other, who was a lively, smart, enterprizing young fellow.

"There's no muckle to hinder us, an' that were a'," answered Cuddie; "but what were we to do neist?"

"We'll tak the Castle," cried the other; "here are five or six o' us, and a' the sodgers are engaged at the gate."

"Come awa' wi' you, then," said Cuddie; "but mind, de'il a finger ye maun lay on Leddy Margaret, or Miss Edith, or the auld Major, or ony body but the sodgers—cut and quarter amang them, I carena."

"Ay, ay," said the other, "let us once in, and we'll make our own terms with them all."

Gingerly, and as if treading upon eggs, Cuddie began to ascend the well-known pass, not very willingly; for, besides that he was something apprehensive of the reception he might meet with in the inside, his conscience insisted that he was making but a shabby requital for Lady Margaret's former favours and protection. He got up, however, into the yew-tree, followed by his companions, one after another. The window was small, and had been secured by stauncheons of iron; but these had been long worn away by time, or forced out by the domestics to possess a free passage for their own occasional convenience. Entrance was therefore easy, providing there was no one in the pantry, a point which Cuddie endeavoured to discover before he made the final and perilous step. While his companions, therefore, were urging and threatening him behind, and he was hesitating and stretching his neck to look into the apartment, his head became visible to Jenny Dennison, who had ensconced herself in said pantry as the safest place in which to wait the issue of the assault. So soon as this object of terror caught her eye, she set up a hysteric scream, flew to the adjacent kitchen, and, in the desperate agony of fear, seized on a pot of kail-brose which she herself had hung on the fire before the combat began, having promised to Tom Halliday to prepare his breakfast for him. Thus burthened, she returned to the window of the pantry, and still exclaiming, "Murder! murder!—we are a' harried and ravished—the Castle's ta'en—tak it amang ye—tak it amang ye!"—she discharged the whole scalding contents of the pot, accompanied with a dismal yell, upon the person of the unfortunate Cuddie. However welcome the mess might have been, if Cuddie and it had become acquainted in a regular manner, the effects, as administered by Jenny, would probably have cured him of soldiering for ever, had he been looking upwards when it was thrown upon him. But, fortunately for our man of war, he had taken the alarm upon Jenny's first scream, and was in the act of looking down, expostulating with his comrades, who impeded the retreat which he was anxious to commence; so that the steel cap and buff coat which formerly belonged to Serjeant Bothwell, being garments of an excellent endurance, protected his person against the greater part of the scalding brose. Enough, however, reached him to annoy him severely, so that in the pain and surprise he jumped hastily out of the tree, oversetting his followers, to the manifest danger of their limbs, and, without listening to arguments, entreaties, or authority, made the best of his way by the most safe road to the main body of the army whereunto he belonged, and could neither by threats nor persuasion be prevailed upon to return to the attack.

As for Jenny, when she had thus conferred upon one admirer's outward man the viands which her fair hands were preparing for the stomach of another, she continued her song of alarm, running a screaming division upon all those crimes, which lawyers call the four pleas of the crown, namely, murder, fire, rape, and robbery. These hideous exclamations gave so much alarm, and created such confusion within the Castle, that Major Bellenden and Lord Evandale judged it best to draw off from the conflict without the gates, and, abandoning to the enemy all the exterior defences of the avenue, confine themselves to the Castle itself, for fear of its being surprised on some unguarded point. Their retreat was unmolested, for the panic of Cuddie and his companions had occasioned nearly as much confusion on the side of the besiegers, as the screams of Jenny had caused to the defenders.

There was no attempt on either side to renew the action that day. The insurgents had suffered most severely; and, from the difficulty which they had experienced in carrying the barricaded positions without the precincts of the Castle, they could have but little hope of storming the place itself. On the other hand, the situation of the besieged was dispiriting and gloomy. In the skirmishing they had lost two or three men, and had several wounded; and though their loss was in proportion greatly less than that of the enemy, who had left twenty men dead on the place, yet their small numbers could much worse spare it, while the desperate attacks of the opposite party plainly showed how serious the leaders were in the purpose of reducing the place, and how well seconded by the zeal of their followers. But, especially, the garrison had to fear for hunger, in case blockade should be resorted to as the means of reducing them. The Major's directions had been imperfectly obeyed in regard to laying in provisions; and the dragoons, in spite of all warning and authority, were likely to be wasteful in using them. It was, therefore, with a heavy heart, that Major Bellenden gave directions for guarding the window through which the Castle had so nearly been surprised, as well as all others which offered the most remote facility for such an enterprize.

Chapter Thirteen

——The King hath drawn
The special head of all the land together.
Henry IV. Part 2

THE LEADERS of the presbyterian army had a serious consultation upon the evening of the day in which they had made the attack on Tillietudlem. They could not but observe that their followers were disheartened by the loss which they had sustained, and which, as usual in such cases, had fallen upon the bravest and most forward. It was to be feared, that if they were suffered to exhaust their zeal and efforts on an object so secondary as the capture of this petty fort, their numbers would melt away by degrees, and they would lose all the advantages arising out of the present unprepared state of the government. Moved by these arguments, it was agreed that the main body of the army should march against Glasgow, and dislodge the soldiers who were lying in that town. The council nominated Henry Morton, with others, to this last service, and appointed Burley to the command of a chosen body of five hundred men, who were to remain behind, for the purpose of blockading the Tower of Tillietudlem. Morton testified the greatest repugnance to this arrangement.

"He had the strongest personal motives," he said, "for desiring to remain near Tillietudlem; and if the management of the siege was committed to him, he had little doubt that he would bring it to such an accommodation as, without being rigorous to the besieged, would fully answer the purpose of the besiegers."

Burley readily guessed the cause of his young colleague's reluctance to move with the army; for, interested as he was in appreciating the characters with whom he had to deal, he had contrived, through the simplicity of Cuddie, and the enthusiasm of old Mause, to get much information concerning Morton's relations with the family of Tillietudlem. He therefore took the advantage of Poundtext arising to speak to business, as he said, for some short space of time, which Burley rightly interpreted to mean an hour at the very least, and seized that moment to withdraw Morton from the hearing of their colleagues, and to hold the following argument with him:

"Thou art unwise, Henry Morton, to desire to sacrifice this holy cause to thy friendship for an uncircumcised Philistine, or thy lust for a Moabitish woman."

"I neither understand your meaning, Mr Balfour, nor relish your allusions," replied Morton, indignantly; "and I know no right you have to bring so gross a charge, or to use such uncivil language."

"Confess, however, the truth, that there are those within yon dark Tower, over whom thou wouldst rather be watching like a mother over her little ones, than thou wouldst bear the banner of the Church of Scotland over the necks of her enemies."

"If you mean that I would willingly terminate this war without any bloody victory, and that I am more anxious to do so than to acquire any personal fame or power, you may be," replied Morton, "perfectly right."

"And not wholly wrong," answered Burley, "in deeming that thou wouldst not exclude from so general a pacification thy friends in the garrison of Tillietudlem."

"Certainly," replied Morton; "I am too much obliged to Major Bellenden not to wish to be of service to him as far as the interest of the cause I have espoused will permit. I never made a secret of my regard for him." ·

"I am aware of that," said Burley; "but, if thou hadst concealed, I should, nevertheless, have found out thy riddle. Now, hearken to my words. This Miles Bellenden hath means to subsist his garrison for a month."

"That is not the case," answered Morton; "we know his stores are hardly equal to a week's consumption."

"Ay, but," continued Burley, "I have since had proof, of the strongest nature, that such a report was spread in the garrison by that wily and grey-headed malignant, partly to prevail on the soldiers to submit to a diminution of their daily food, partly to detain us before the walls of his fortress until the sword should be whetted to smite and to destroy us."

"And why was not the evidence of this laid before the council of war?" said Morton.

"To what purpose?" said Balfour.—"What need to undeceive Kettledrummle, Macbriar, Poundtext, and Langcale, upon such a point? Thyself must own, that whatever is told to them escapes to the host out of the mouth of the preachers even at their next holding-forth. They are already discouraged by the thoughts of lying before the fort a week. What would be the consequence were they ordered to prepare for the leaguer of a month?"

"But why conceal it, then, from me? or why tell it me now? And, above all, what proofs have you of the fact?" continued Morton.

"These are my proofs," replied Burley; and he put into his hand a number of requisitions sent forth by Major Bellenden, with receipts on the back to various proprietors, for cattle, corn, meal, &c., to such an amount, that the sum total seemed to exclude the possibility of the garrison being soon distressed for provision. But Burley did not inform Morton of a fact which he himself knew full well, namely, that most of these provisions never reached the garrison, owing to the rapacity of the dragoons sent to collect them, who readily sold to one man what they took from another, and abused the Major's press for stores, pretty much as Sir John Falstaff did that of the King for men.

"And now," continued Balfour, observing that he had made the desired impression, "I have only to say, that I concealed this from thee no longer than it was concealed from myself, for I have only received these papers this morning; and I tell it unto thee now, that thou mayest go on thy way rejoicing, and work the great work willingly at Glasgow, being assured that no evil can befall thy friends in the malignant party, since their fort is sufficiently victualled, and I possess not numbers sufficient to do more against them than to prevent their sallying forth."

"And why," continued Morton, who felt an inexpressible reluctance to acquiesce in Balfour's reasoning—"why not permit me to remain in the command of this smaller party, and march forward yourself to Glasgow? It is the more honourable charge."

"And, therefore, young man," answered Burley, "have I laboured that it should be committed to the son of my old friend Silas Morton. I am waxing old, and this grey head has had enough of honour where it could be gathered by dangers. I speak not of the frothy bubble which men call earthly fame, but the honour belonging to him that doth not the work negligently. But thy career is yet to run—thou hast to vindicate the high trust which was bestowed on thee through my assurance that it was dearly well-merited. At Loudoun-hill thou wert a captive, and at the last attack it was thy part to fight under cover, whilst I led the more open and dangerous attack; and, shouldst thou now remain before these walls when there is active service elsewhere, trust me, that men will say, that the son of Silas Morton hath fallen away from the paths of his father."

Stung by this last observation, to which, as a gentleman and soldier, he could offer no suitable reply, Morton hastily acquiesced in the proposed arrangement. Yet he was unable to divest himself of certain feelings of distrust which he involuntarily attached to the quarter from which he received this information.

"Mr Balfour," he said, "let us distinctly understand each other. You have thought it worth your while to bestow particular attention upon my private affairs and personal attachments. Be so good as to understand that I am as constant to them as to my political principles. It is possible, that, during my absence, you may possess the power of soothing or of wounding these feelings. Be assured, that whatever may be the consequences to the issue of our present adventure, my eternal gratitude, or my persevering resentment, will attend the line of conduct you may adopt on such an occasion; and, however young and inexperienced I am, I have no doubt of finding friends to assist me in expressing my sentiments in either case."

"If there be a threat implied in that denunciation," replied Burley, coldly and haughtily, "it had better have been spared. I know how to value the regard of my friends, and despise, from my soul, the threats of my enemies. But I will not take occasion of offence. Whatever happens here in your absence, shall be managed with as much deference to your wishes as the duty I owe to a higher power can possibly permit."

With this qualified promise Morton was obliged to rest satisfied.

"Our defeat will relieve the garrison," said he, internally, "ere they can be reduced to surrender at discretion; and, in case of our victory, I already see, from the numbers of the moderate party, that I shall have a voice as powerful as Burley's in determining the use which shall be made of it."

He therefore followed Balfour to the council, where they found Poundtext adding to his *lastly* a few words of practical application. When these were expended, Morton testified his willingness to accompany the main body of the army, which was destined to drive the regular troops from Glasgow. His companions in command were named, and the whole received a strengthening exhortation from the preachers who were present. Next morning, at break of day, the tumultuary army broke up from their encampment, and marched towards Glasgow.

It is not our intention to detail at length incidents which may be found in the history of the period. It is sufficient to say, that Claverhouse and Lord Ross, learning the superior force which was directed against them, entrenched, or rather barricaded themselves, in the centre of the city, where the town-house and old jail were situated, with the determination to stand the assault of the insurgents rather than to abandon the capital of the west of Scotland. The presbyterians made their attack in two bodies, one of which penetrated into the city in the line of the College and cathedral church, while the other marched up the Gallowgate, or principal access from the south-east. Both divisions were led by men of resolution, and behaved with great spirit. But the advantages of discipline and situation were too great for their undisciplined valour. Ross and Claverhouse had carefully disposed parties of their soldiers in houses, at the heads of the streets, and in the entrances of closes, as they are called, or lanes, besides those who were entrenched behind breast-works which reached across the street. The assailants found their ranks thinned by a fire from invisible opponents, which they had no means of returning with effect. It was in vain that Morton and other leaders exposed their persons with the utmost gallantry, and endeavoured to bring their antagonists to a close action. Their followers shrunk from them in every direction; and yet, although Henry Morton was one of the very last to retire, and exerted himself in bringing up the rear, maintaining order in the retreat, and checking every attempt which the enemy made to improve the advantage they had gained by the repulse, he had still the mortification to hear many of those in his ranks muttering to each other, that this came of trusting to latitudinarian boys, and that had honest, faithful Burley led the attack, as he did that of the barricades of Tillietudlem, the issue would have been as different as might

be. It was with burning resentment that Morton heard these reflections thrown out by the very men who had soonest exhibited signs of
discouragement. The unjust reproach, however, had the effect of
firing his emulation, and making him sensible that, engaged as he was
in a perilous cause, it was absolutely necessary that he should conquer
or die.

"I have no retreat," he said to himself. "All shall allow—even Major
Bellenden—even Edith—that in courage, at least, the rebel Morton
was not inferior to his father."

The condition of the army after this repulse was so undisciplined,
and in such disorganization, that the leaders thought it prudent to
draw off some miles from the city to gain time for reducing them once
more into such order as they were capable of adopting. Recruits, in the
meanwhile, came fast in, more moved by the extreme hardships of
their own condition, and more encouraged by the advantage obtained
at Loudoun-hill, than deterred by the last unfortunate enterprise.
Many of these attached themselves particularly to Morton's division.
He had, however, the mortification to see, that his unpopularity
among the more intolerant part of the Covenanters increased rapidly.
The prudence, beyond his years, which he exhibited in improving the
discipline and arrangement of his followers, they termed a trusting in
the arm of flesh, and his avowed tolerance for those of religious
sentiments and observances different from his own, obtained him,
most unjustly, the nickname of Gallio, who cared for none of those
things. What was worse than these misconceptions, the mob of the
insurgents, always loudest in applause of those who push political or
religious opinions to extremity, and disgusted with such as endeavour
to reduce them to the yoke of discipline, preferred avowedly the more
zealous leaders, in whose ranks enthusiasm in the cause supplied at
once the want of good order and military subjection, to the restraints
which Morton endeavoured to bring them under. In short, while
bearing the principal burden of command, (for his colleagues willingly relinquished in his favour every thing that was troublesome and
obnoxious in the office of general,) Morton found himself without
that authority which alone could render his regulations effectual.

Yet, notwithstanding these obstacles, he had, during the course of a
few days, laboured so hard to introduce some degree of discipline into
the army, that he thought he might hazard a second attack upon
Glasgow with every certainty of success.

It cannot be doubted that Morton's anxiety to measure himself
with Colonel Grahame of Claverhouse, at whose hands he had sustained such injury, had its share in giving motive to his uncommon
exertions. But Claverhouse disappointed his hopes; for, satisfied

with having had the advantage in repulsing the first attack upon
Glasgow, he determined that he would not, with the handful of
troops under his command, await a second attack from the insurgents with more numerous and better disciplined forces than had
supported their first enterprise. He therefore evacuated the place,
and marched at the head of his troops towards Edinburgh. The insurgents of course entered Glasgow without resistance, and without
Morton having the opportunity, which he so deeply coveted, of again
encountering Claverhouse personally. But, although he had not an
opportunity of wiping away the disgrace which had befallen his division of the army of the Covenant, the retreat of Claverhouse, and the
possession of Glasgow, tended greatly to animate the insurgent army
and to increase its numbers. The necessity of appointing new
officers, of organizing new regiments and squadrons, of making
them acquainted with the most necessary points of military discipline, were labours, which, by universal consent, seemed to be
devolved upon Henry Morton, and which he the more readily undertook, because his father had made him acquainted with the theory of
the military art, and because he plainly saw, that, unless he took this
ungracious but absolutely necessary labour, it was vain to expect any
other to engage in it.

In the meanwhile, fortune appeared to favour the enterprise of the
insurgents more than the most sanguine durst have expected. The
Privy Council of Scotland, astonished at the extent of resistance which
their arbitrary measures had provoked, seemed stupified with terror,
and incapable of taking active steps to subdue the resentment which
their measures had provoked. There were but very few troops in
Scotland, and these they drew towards Edinburgh, as if to form an
army for protection of the metropolis. The feudal array of the crown
vassals in the various counties was ordered to take the field, and
render to the King the military service due for their fiefs. But the
summons was very slackly obeyed. The quarrel was not generally
popular among the gentry; and even those who were not unwilling
themselves to have taken arms, were deterred by the repugnance of
their wives, mothers, and sisters, to their engaging in such a cause.
Meanwhile, the inadequacy of the Scottish government to provide for
their own defence, or to put down a rebellion of which the commencement seemed so trifling, excited at the English court doubts at once of
their capacity, and of the prudence of the severities they had exerted
against the oppressed presbyterians. It was, therefore, resolved to
nominate to the command of the army in Scotland, the unfortunate
Duke of Monmouth, who had by marriage a great interest in the
southern parts of that kingdom. The military skill which he had

displayed on different occasions abroad, was supposed more than adequate to subdue the insurgents in the field, while it was expected that his mild temper and the favourable disposition which he shewed to presbyterians in general, might soften men's minds, and tend to reconcile them to the government. The Duke was, therefore, invested with a commission, containing high powers for settling the distracted affairs of Scotland, and dispatched from London with strong succours to take the principal military command in that country.

Chapter Fourteen

——I am bound to Bothwell-hill,
Where I maun either do or die.

THERE was now a pause in the military movements on both sides. The government seemed contented to prevent the rebels advancing towards the capital, while the insurgents were intent upon augmenting and strengthening their forces. For this purpose, they established a sort of encampment in the park belonging to the ducal residence at Hamilton, a centrical situation for receiving their recruits, and where they were secured from any sudden attack, by having the Clyde, a deep and rapid river, in front of their position, which is only passable by a long and narrow bridge near the castle and village of Bothwell.

Morton remained here for about a fortnight after the attack on Glasgow, actively engaged in his military duties. He had received more than one communication from Burley, but they only stated, in general, that the Castle of Tillietudlem continued to hold out. Impatient of suspense upon this most interesting subject, he at length intimated to his colleagues in command his desire, or rather his intention,—for he saw no reason why he should not assume a licence which was taken by every one else in this ill-ordered army,—to go to Milne-wood for a day or two to arrange some private affairs of consequence. The proposal was by no means approved of; for they were sufficiently sensible of the value of his services to fear to lose them, and were somewhat conscious of their own inability to supply his place. They could not, however, pretend to dictate to him laws more rigid than they submitted to themselves, and he was suffered to depart on his journey without any direct objection being stated. The Reverend Mr Poundtext took the same opportunity to pay a visit to his own resid-ence in the neighbourhood of Milnewood, and favoured Morton with his company on the journey. As the country was chiefly friendly to their cause, and in possession of their detached parties, excepting here and there the strong-hold of some old cavaliering Baron, they travelled without any other attendant than the faithful Cuddie.

It was near sunset when they reached Milnewood, where Poundtext bid adieu to his companions, and travelled forward alone to his own manse, which was situated half a mile nearer Tillietudlem. When Morton was left alone to his own reflections, with what complication of feelings did he review the woods, banks, and fields, that had been familiar to him! His character, as well as his habits, thoughts, and occupations, had been entirely changed within the space of little more than a fortnight, and twenty days seemed to have done upon him the work of as many years. A mild, romantic, gentle-tempered youth, bred up in dependence, and stooping patiently to the controul of a sordid and tyrannical relation, had suddenly, by the rod of oppression and the spur of injured feeling, been compelled to stand forth a leader of armed men, was earnestly engaged in affairs of a public nature, had friends to animate and enemies to contend with, and felt his individual fate bound up in that of a national insurrection and revolution. It seemed as if he had at once experienced a transition from the romantic dreams of youth to the labours and cares of active manhood. All that had formerly interested him was obliterated from his memory, excepting only his attachment to Edith, and even his love seemed to have assumed a character more manly and disinterested, as it had become mingled and contrasted with other duties and feelings. As he revolved the particulars of this sudden change, the circumstances in which it originated, and the possible consequences of his present career, the thrill of natural anxiety which passed along his mind, was immediately banished by a glow of generous and high-spirited confidence.

"I shall fall young," he said, "if fall I must, my motives misconstrued, and my actions condemned by those whose approbation is dearest to me. But the sword of liberty and patriotism is in my hand, and I will neither fall meanly nor unavenged. They may expose my body and gibbet my limbs, but other days will come when the sentence of infamy will recoil against those who may pronounce it. And that Heaven, whose name is so often profaned during this unnatural war, will bear witness to the purity of the motives by which I have been guided."

Upon approaching Milnewood, Henry's knock upon the gate no longer intimated the conscious timidity of a stripling who has been out of bounds, but the confidence of a man in full possession of his own rights, and master of his own actions—bold, free, and decided. The door was cautiously opened by his old acquaintance, Mrs Alison Wilson, who started back when she saw the steel cap and nodding plume of the martial visitor.

"Where is my uncle, Alison?" said Morton, smiling at her alarm.

"Lordsake, Mr Harry, is this you?" returned the old lady. "In troth, ye garr'd my heart loup to my very mouth—But it canna be you your ainsel, for ye look taller and mair manly-like than ye used to do."

"It is, however, even my own self," said Henry, sighing and smiling at the same time; "I believe this dress may make me look taller, and these times, Ailie, make men out of boys."

"Sad times, indeed!" echoed the old woman; "and O that you suld be endangered wi' them! but wha can help it?—ye were ill aneugh guided, and, as I tell your uncle, if ye tread on a worm it will turn."

"You were always my advocate, Ailie, and would let no one blame me but yourself, I am aware of that.—Where is my uncle?"

"In Edinburgh," replied Alison; "the honest man thought it was best to gang and sit by the chimney when the reek rase—a vex'd man he's been and a fear'd—but ye ken the laird as weel as I do."

"I hope he has suffered nothing in health?" said Henry.

"Naething to speak of," answered the housekeeper, "nor in gudes neither—we fended as weel as we could; and, though the troopers of Tillietudlem took the red cow and auld Hackie, (ye'll mind them weel,) yet they sauld us a gude bargain of four that they were driving to the Castle."

"Sold you a bargain?" said Morton, "how do you mean?"

"O, they cam out to gather marts for the garrison," answered the housekeeper; "but they just fell to their auld trade, and rade through couping and selling a' that they gat, like sae mony west-country drovers. My certie, Major Bellenden was laird o' the least share o' what they lifted, though it was a' done in his name."

"Then," said Morton, hastily, "the garrison must be straitened for provisions?"

"Stressed aneugh," replied Ailie—"there's little doubt o' that."

A light instantly glanced on Morton's mind.

"Burley must have deceived me—craft as well as cruelty is permitted by his creed.—I cannot stay, Mrs Wilson, I must go forward directly."

"But, oh! bide to eat a mouthfu'," entreated the affectionate housekeeper, "and I'll mak it ready for ye as I used to do afore thae sad days."

"It is impossible," answered Morton. "Cuddie, get our horses ready."

"They're just eating their corn," answered Cuddie.

"Cuddie?" exclaimed Ailie, "What garr'd ye bring that ill-fa'ard, unlucky loon alang wi' ye?—It was him and his randie mither began a' the mischief in this house."

"Tut, tut," replied Cuddie, "ye should forget and forgi'e, mistress.

Mither's in Glasgow wi' her tittie, and sall plague ye nae mair, and I'm the Captain's wally now, and I keep him tighter in thack and rape than ever ye did;—saw ye him ever sae weel put on as he is now?"

"In troth and that's true," said the old housekeeper, looking with great complacence at her young master, whose mien she thought greatly improved by his dress. "I am sure ye ne'er had a laced cravat like that when ye were at Milnewood; that's nane o' my sewing."

"Na, na, mistress," replied Cuddie, "that's a cast o' my hand—that's ane o' Lord Evandale's braws."

"Lord Evandale?" answered the old lady, "that's he that the whigs are gaun to hang the morn, as I hear say."

"The whigs about to hang Lord Evandale?" said Morton, in the greatest surprise.

"Ay, troth are they," said the housekeeper. "Yesterday night he made a sally, as they ca' it, (my mother's name was Sally—I wonder they gi'e Christian folks names to sic unchristian doings)—but he made an outbreak to get provisions, and his men were driven back and he was ta'en, an' the whig Captain, Balfour, garr'd set up a gallows, and swore, (or said upon his conscience, for they winna swear,) that, if the garrison wasna gi'en ower the morn by daybreak, he would hing up the young Lord, poor thing, as high as Haman.—These are sair times!—but folk canna help them—sae do ye sit down and tak bread and cheese until better meat's made ready. Ye suldna hae kenn'd a word about it, an' I had thought it was to spoil your dinner, hinnie."

"Fed, or unfed, saddle the horses instantly, Cuddie. We must have no rest until we get before the Castle."

And, resisting all Ailie's entreaties, they instantly resumed their journey.

Morton failed not to halt at the dwelling of Poundtext, and summon him to attend him to the camp. That honest divine had just resumed for an instant his pacific habits, and was perusing an ancient theological treatise, with a pipe in his mouth, and a small jug of ale beside him, to assist his digestion of the argument. It was with bitter ill-will that he relinquished these comforts (which he called his studies) in order to recommence a hard ride upon a high-trotting horse. However, when he knew the matter in hand, he gave up, with a deep groan, the prospect of spending a quiet evening in his own little parlour; for he entirely agreed with Morton, that whatever interest Burley might have in rendering the breach between the presbyterians and the government irreconcileable, by putting the young nobleman to death, it was by no means that of the moderate party to permit such an act of atrocity. And it is but doing justice to Mr Poundtext to add, that, like most of his own persuasion, he was decidedly averse to any such acts of unnecessary violence; besides that, his own present feelings induced him to listen with much complacence to the probability held out by Morton, of Lord Evandale becoming a mediator for the establishment of peace upon fair and moderate terms. With this similarity of views, they hastened their journey, and arrived about eleven o'clock at night at a small hamlet adjacent to the Castle of Tillietudlem, where Burley had established his head-quarters.

They were challenged by the centinel, who made his melancholy walk in the entrance of the hamlet, and admitted upon declaring their names and authority in the army. Another kept watch before a house, which they conjectured to be the place of Lord Evandale's confinement, for a gibbet of such great height as to be visible from the battlements of the Castle, was erected before it, a melancholy confirmation of the truth of Mrs Wilson's report. Morton instantly demanded to speak with Burley, and was directed to his quarters. They found him reading the Scriptures with his arms lying beside him, as if ready for any sudden alarm. He started upon the entrance of his colleagues in office.

"What has brought ye hither?" said Burley, hastily. "Is there bad news from the army?"

"No," replied Morton; "but we understand that there are measures adopted here in which the safety of the army is deeply concerned—Lord Evandale is your prisoner?"

"The Lord," replied Burley, "hath delivered him into our hand."

"And you will avail yourself of that advantage, granted you by Heaven, to dishonour our cause in the eyes of all the world, by putting a prisoner to an ignominious death?"

"If the house of Tillietudlem be not surrendered by daybreak," replied Burley, "God do so to me and more also, if he shall not die that death to which his leader and pattern, John Grahame of Claverhouse, hath put so many of God's saints."

"We are in arms," replied Morton, "to put down such cruelties, and not to imitate them, far less to avenge upon the innocent the acts of the guilty. By what law can you justify the atrocity you would commit?"

"If thou art ignorant of it," replied Burley, "thy companion is well aware of the law which gave the men of Jericho to the sword of Joshua, the son of Nun."

"But we," answered the divine, "live under a better dispensation, which instructeth us to return good for evil, and to pray for those who despitefully use us and persecute us."

"That is to say," said Burley, "that thou wilt join thy grey hairs to his green youth to controul me in this matter?"

"We are," rejoined Poundtext, "two of those to whom, jointly with thyself, authority is delegated over this host, and we will not permit thee to hurt a hair of the prisoner's head. It may please God to make him a means of healing these unhappy breaches in our Israel."

"I judged it would come to this," answered Burley, "when such as thou wert called into the council of the elders."

"Such as I?" answered Poundtext.—"And who am I that you should name me with such scorn?—Have I not kept the flock of this sheep-fold from the wolves for thirty years? Ay, even while thou, John Balfour, wert fighting in the ranks of uncircumcision, a Philistine of hardened brow and bloody hand—Who am I, sayst thou?"

"I will tell thee what thou art, since thou wouldst so fain know," said Burley. "Thou art one of those who would reap where thou hast not sowed, and divide the spoil while others fight the battle—thou art one of those that follow the gospel for the loaves and for the fishes—that love their own manse better than the church of God, and that would rather draw their stipend under prelatists or heathens, than be a partaker with those noble spirits who have cast all behind them for the sake of the Covenant."

"And I will tell thee, John Balfour," returned Poundtext, deservedly incensed, "I will tell thee what *thou* art. Thou art one of those for whose bloody and merciless disposition a reproach is flung upon the whole church of this suffering kingdom, and for whose violence and blood-guiltiness, it is to be feared, this fair attempt to recover our civil and religious rights will never be honoured by Providence with the desired success."

"Gentlemen," said Morton, "cease this recrimination; and do you, Mr Balfour, inform us, whether it is your purpose to oppose the liberation of Lord Evandale, which appears to us a profitable measure in the present position of our affairs."

"You are here," answered Burley, "as two voices against one; but you will not refuse to tarry until the united council shall decide upon this matter?"

"This," said Morton, "we would not decline, if we could trust the hands in whom we are to leave the prisoner. But you know well," he added, looking sternly at Burley, "that you have already deceived me in this matter."

"Go to," said Burley, disdainfully,—"thou art an idle inconsiderate boy, who, for the black eye-brows of a silly girl, wouldst barter thy own faith and honour, and the cause of God and of thy country."

"Mr Balfour," said Morton, laying his hand on his sword, "this language requires satisfaction."

"And thou shalt have it, stripling, when and where thou darest," said Burley, "I plight thee my good word on it."

Poundtext, in his turn, interfered, to remind them of the madness of quarrelling, and effected with difficulty a sort of sullen reconciliation.

"Concerning the prisoner," said Burley, "deal with him as ye think fit. I wash my hands free from all consequences. He is my prisoner, made by my sword and spear, while you, Mr Morton, were playing the adjutant at drills and parades, and you, Mr Poundtext, were warping the Scriptures into Erastianism. Take him unto you, nevertheless, and dispose of him as you think meet.—Dingwall," he continued, calling a sort of aid-de-camp, who slept in the next apartment, "let the guard posted on the malignant Evandale give up their post to those whom Captain Morton shall appoint to relieve them.—The prisoner," he said, again addressing Poundtext and Morton, "is now at your disposal, gentlemen. But remember, that for all these things there will one day come a term of heavy accounting."

So saying, he turned abruptly into an inner apartment, without bidding them farewell. His two visitors, after a moment's consideration, agreed it would be prudent to ensure the prisoner's personal safety, by placing over him an additional guard, chosen from their own parishioners. A band of these happened to be stationed in the hamlet, having been attached, for the time, to Burley's command, in order that the men might be gratified by remaining as long as possible near to their own homes. They were, in general, smart, active young fellows, and were usually called, by their companions, the Marksmen of Milnewood. By Morton's desire, four of these lads readily undertook the task of centinels, and he left with them Headrigg, on whose fidelity he could depend, with instructions to call him, if any thing remarkable happened.

This arrangement being made, Morton and his colleague took possession, for the night, of such quarters as the over-crowded and miserable hamlet could afford them. They did not, however, separate for repose ere they had drawn up a memorial of the grievances of the moderate presbyterians, which was summed up with a request of free toleration for their religion in future, and that they should be permitted to attend gospel ordinances as dispensed by their own clergymen, without oppression or molestation. Their petition proceeded to require that a free parliament should be called for settling the affairs of church and state, and for redressing the injuries sustained by the subject; and that all those who either now were, or had been in arms, for obtaining these ends, should be indemnified. Morton could not but strongly hope that these terms, which comprehended all that was wanted, or wished for, by the moderate party among the insurgents, might, when thus cleared of the violence of fanaticism, find advocates even among the royalists, as claiming only the ordinary rights of Scottish freemen.

He had the more confidence of a favourable reception, that the Duke of Monmouth, to whom Charles had entrusted the charge of subduing this rebellion, was a man of gentle, moderate, and accessible disposition, well known to be favourable to the presbyterians, and invested by the king with full powers to take measures for quieting the disturbances in Scotland. It seemed to Morton, that all which was necessary for influencing him in their favour was to find a fit and sufficiently respectable channel of communication, and such seemed to be opened through the medium of Lord Evandale. He resolved, therefore, to visit the prisoner early on the morning, to sound his dispositions to undertake the task of mediator; but an accident happened which led him to anticipate his purpose.

Chapter Fifteen

Gi'e ower your house, lady, he said,—
Gi'e ower your house to me.
Edom of Gordon

MORTON had finished the revisal and the making out a fair copy of the paper on which he and Poundtext had agreed to rest as a full statement of the grievances of their party, and the conditions on which the greater part of the insurgents would be contented to lay down their arms; and was about to betake himself to repose, when there was a knocking at the door of his apartment.

"Enter," said Morton; and the round bullet-head of Cuddie Headrigg was thrust into the room. "Come in," said Morton, "and tell me what you want. Is there alarm?"

"Na, sir; but I hae brought ane to speak wi' you."

"Who is that, Cuddie?" enquired Morton.

"Ane o' your auld acquaintance," said Cuddie; and, opening the door more fully, he half led, half dragged in a woman, whose face was muffled in her plaid.—"Come, come, ye need na be sae bashfu' before auld acquaintance, Jenny," said Cuddie, pulling down the veil and discovering to his master the well-remembered countenance of Jenny Dennison. "Tell his honour now—there's a braw lass—tell him what ye were wanting to say to Lord Evandale, mistress."

"What was I wanting to say," answered Jenny, "to his honour himsel the other morning, when I visited him in captivity, ye muckle hash?—D'ye think that folk div na want to see their friends in adversity, ye dour croudy-eater?"

This reply was made with Jenny's usual volubility; but her voice quivered, her cheek was thin and pale, the tears stood in her eyes, her hand trembled, her manner was fluttered, and her whole presence bore marks of recent suffering and privation, as well as of nervous and hysterical agitation.

"What is the matter, Jenny?" said Morton, kindly. "You know how much I owe you in many respects, and can hardly make a request that I will not grant, if in my power."

"Mony thanks, Milnewood," said the weeping damsel; "but ye were aye a kind gentleman, though folk say ye hae become sair changed now."

"What do they say of me?" answered Morton.

"A'body says that you and the whigs hae made a vow to ding King Charles aff the throne, and that neither he, nor his posteriors from generation to generation, shall sit upon it ony mair; and John Gudyill says ye are to gi'e a' the kirk organs to the pipers, and burn the book o' Common Prayer by the hands of the common hangman, in revenge of the Covenant that was burned when the king cam hame."

"My friends at Tillietudlem judge too hastily and too ill of me," answered Morton. "I wish to have free exercise of my own religion, without insulting any other; and, as to your family, I only desire an opportunity to shew them I have the same friendship and kindness as ever."

"Bless your kind heart for saying sae," said Jenny, bursting into a flood of tears; "and they never needed kindness or friendship mair, for they arc famished for lack o' food."

"Good God!" replied Morton, "I heard of scarcity, but not of famine!—is it possible?—have the ladies and the Major"——

"They hae suffered like the lave o' us," replied Jenny; "for they shared every bit and sup wi' the whole folk in the Castle—I am sure my poor e'en see fifty colours wi' faintness, and my head's sae dizzy wi' the mirligoes that I canna stand my lane."

The thinness of the poor girl's cheek and the sharpness of her features bore witness to the truth of what she said. Morton was greatly shocked.

"Sit down," he said, "for God's sake!" forcing her into the only chair the apartment afforded, while he himself strode up and down the room in horror and impatience. "I knew not of this," he exclaimed, in broken ejaculations.—"I could not know of it.—Cold-blooded, hard-hearted fanatic—deceitful villain!—Cuddie, fetch refreshments—food—wine, if possible—whatever you can find."

"Whisky is gude eneugh for her," muttered Cuddie; "ane wadna hae thought that gude meal was sae scant amang them, when the quean threw sae muckle gude kail-brose scalding het about my lugs."

Faint and miserable as Jenny seemed to be, she could not hear this allusion to her exploit during the storm of the Castle, without bursting into a laugh which weakness soon converted into a hysterical giggle. Confounded at her state, and reflecting with horror on the distress which must have been in the Castle, Morton repeated his commands to Headrigg in a peremptory manner; and, when he had departed, endeavoured to sooth his visitor.

"You came, I suppose, by the orders of your mistress, to visit Lord Evandale?—Tell me what she desires; her order shall be my law."

Jenny appeared to reflect a moment, and then said, "Your honour is sae auld a friend, I must needs trust to you, and tell the truth."

"Be assured, Jenny," said Morton, observing that she hesitated, "that you will best serve your mistress by dealing sincerely with me."

"Weel, then, ye maun ken we are starving, as I said before, and have been mair days than ane; and the Major has sworn that he expects relief daily, and that he will not gi'e ower the house to the enemy till we have eaten up his auld boots,—and they are unco thick in the soles, as ye may mind weel, forby being teugh in the upper-leather. The dragoons, again, they think they will be forced to gi'e up at last, and they canna bide hunger weel, after the life they led at free quarters for this while by-past; and, since Lord Evandale's ta'en, there's nae guiding them, and Inglis says he'll gi'e up the garrison to the whigs, and the Major and the leddies into the bargain, if they will but let the troopers gang free themsels."

"Scoundrels!" said Morton; "why do they not make terms for all in the Castle?"

"They are fear'd for want o' quarter to themsels, having done sae muckle mischief through the country, and Burley has hanged ane or twa o' them already—sae they want to draw their ain necks out o' the collar at hazard o' honest folk's."

"And you were sent," continued Morton, "to carry to Lord Evandale the unpleasant news of the men's mutiny?"

"Just e'en sae," said Jenny; "Tam Halliday took the rue, and tauld me a' about it, and gat me out o' the Castle to tell Lord Evandale, if possibly I could win at him."

"But how can he help you? he is a prisoner."

"Well-a-day, ay," answered the afflicted damsel; "but maybe he could make fair terms for us—or, maybe, he could gi'e us some gude advice—or, maybe, he might send his orders to the dragoons to be civil—or"——

"Or, maybe," said Morton, "you were to try if it were possible to set him at liberty?"

"If it were sae," answered Jenny with spirit, "it wadna be the first time I hae dune my best to serve ane in captivity."

"True, Jenny, I were most ingrateful to forget it. But here comes Cuddie with refreshments—I will go and do your errand to Lord Evandale, while you take some food and wine."

"It willna be amiss ye should ken," said Cuddie to his master, "that this Jenny—this Mrs Dennison, was trying to cuittle favour wi' Tam Rand, the miller's man, to win into Lord Evandale without ony body kenning. She wasna aware, the gipsey, that I was at her elbow."

"And an unco fought ye gae me when ye cam ahint and took a grip on me," said Jenny, giving him a sly twitch with her finger and thumb —"if ye hadna been an acquaintance, ye daft gomeril"——

Cuddie, somewhat relenting, grinned a smile on his artful mistress, while Morton wrapped himself up in his cloak, took his sword under his arm, and went straight to the place of the young nobleman's confinement. He asked the centinels if any thing extraordinary had occurred.

"Nothing worth notice," they said, "excepting the lass that Cuddie took up, and two couriers that Captain Balfour had dispatched, one to the Reverend Ephraim Macbriar, another to Kettledrummle," both of whom were beating the drum ecclesiastic in different towns between the position of Burley and the head-quarters of the main army near Hamilton.

"The purpose, I presume," said Morton, with an affectation of indifference, "was to call them hither?"

"So I understand," answered the centinel, who had spoke with the messengers.

"He is summoning a triumphant majority of the council," thought Morton to himself, "for the purpose of sanctioning whatever action of atrocity he may determine upon, and thwarting opposition by authority. I must be speedy, or I shall lose my opportunity."

When he entered the place of Lord Evandale's confinement, he found him ironed, and reclining on a flock-bed in the wretched garret of a miserable cottage. He was either in a slumber, or in deep meditation, when Morton entered, and turned on him, when aroused, a countenance so much reduced by loss of blood, want of sleep, and scarcity of food, that no one could have recognized in it the gallant soldier who had behaved with so much spirit at the skirmish of Loudoun-hill. He displayed some surprise at the sudden entrance of Morton.

"I am sorry to see you thus, my lord," said that youthful leader.

"I have heard you are an admirer of poetry," answered the prisoner; "in that case, Mr Morton, you may remember these lines,

> Stone walls do not a prison make,
>   Or iron bars a cage;
> A free and quiet mind can take
>   These for a hermitage.

But, were my durance less endurable, I am given to expect to-morrow a total enfranchisement."

"By death?" said Morton.

"Surely," answered Lord Evandale; "I have no other prospect. Your comrade, Burley, has already dipped his hand in the blood of men whose meanness of rank and obscurity of extraction might have saved them. I cannot boast such a shield from his vengeance, and expect to meet it."

"But Major Bellenden," said Morton, "may surrender, in order to preserve your life."

"Never while there is one man to defend the battlement, and that man has one crust to eat. I know his gallant resolution, and grieved I should be if he changed it for my sake."

Morton hastened to acquaint him with the mutiny among the dragoons, and their resolution to surrender the Castle, and put the ladies of the family, as well as the Major, into the hands of the enemy. Lord Evandale seemed at first surprised, and something incredulous, but immediately afterwards deeply affected.

"What is to be done?" he said—"How is this misfortune to be averted?"

"Hear me, my lord," said Morton. "I believe you may not be unwilling to bear the olive-branch between our master the King, and that part of his subjects which is now in arms, not from choice, but necessity."

"You construe me but justly," said Lord Evandale; "but to what does this tend?"

"Permit me, my lord," continued Morton. "I will set you at liberty upon parole; nay, you may return to the garrison, and shall have a safe-conduct for the ladies, the Major, and all who leave it, on condition of its instant surrender. In doing this you will only submit to circumstances; for, with a mutiny in the garrison, and without provisions, it will be found impossible to defend the place twenty-four hours longer. Those, therefore, who refuse to accompany your Lordship must take their fate. You and your followers shall have a free pass to Edinburgh, or wherever the Duke of Monmouth may be. In return for your liberty, we hope that you will recommend to the notice of his Grace, as Lieutenant-General of Scotland, this humble petition and remonstrance, containing the grievances which have occasioned this insurrection, on redress of which being granted, I will answer, with my head, that the great body of the insurgents will lay down their arms."

Lord Evandale read over the paper with attention.

"Mr Morton," he said, "in my own simple judgment, I see little objection that can be made to the measures here recommended; nay, farther, I believe, in many respects, they may meet the private sentiments of the Duke of Monmouth—And yet, to deal frankly with you, I have no hopes of their being granted, unless, in the first place, you were to lay down your arms."

"The doing so," answered Morton, "would be virtually conceding that we had no right to take them up, and that, for one, I will never agree to."

"Perhaps it is hardly to be expected you should," said Lord Evandale; "and yet, on that point, I am certain the negociation will be wrecked. I am willing, however, having frankly told you my opinion, to do all in my power to bring about a reconciliation."

"It is all we can wish or expect," replied Morton; "the issue is in God's hands, who disposes the hearts of princes.—You accept then the safe-conduct?"

"Certainly," answered Lord Evandale; "and if I do not enlarge upon the obligation incurred by your having saved my life a second time, believe I do not feel it the less."

"And the garrison at Tillietudlem?"

"Shall be withdrawn as you propose. I am sensible the Major will be unable to bring the mutineers to reason, and I tremble to think of the consequences should the ladies and the brave old man be delivered up to this blood-thirsty ruffian Burley."

"You are in that case free," said Morton. "Prepare to mount on horseback; a few men whom I can trust shall attend you till you are in safety from our parties."

Leaving Lord Evandale in great surprise and joy at his unexpected deliverance, Morton hastened to get a few chosen men under arms and on horseback, each rider holding the rein of a spare horse. Jenny, who, while she partook of her refreshment, had contrived to make up her breach with Cuddie, rode on the left hand of that valiant cavalier. The tramp of their horses was soon heard under the window of Lord Evandale's prison. Two men whom he did not know entered the apartment, disencumbered him of his fetters, and, conducting him down stairs, mounted him in the centre of the detachment. They set out at a round trot towards Tillietudlem.

The moonlight was giving way to the dawn when they approached that ancient fortress, and its dark massive tower had just received the first pale colouring of the morning. The party halted at the lower barrier, not venturing to approach more nearly for fear of the fire of the place. Lord Evandale alone rode up to the gate, followed at a distance by Jenny Dennison. As they approached the gate, there was heard to arise in the court-yard a tumult which accorded ill with the quiet serenity of a summer dawn. Cries and oaths were heard, a pistol-shot or two were discharged, and every thing announced that the mutiny had broken out. At this crisis Lord Evandale arrived at the gate where Halliday was centinel. This man had given a reluctant consent to the conspiracy, and had indeed contrived the means by which Jenny escaped from the Castle to communicate the plot to his officer. On hearing Lord Evandale's voice, he instantly and gladly admitted him, and he arrived among the mutinous troopers like a man dropped from the clouds. They were in the act of putting their design into execution, of seizing the place into their own hands, and were about to disarm and overpower Major Bellenden, and Harrison, and others of the Castle, who were offering the best resistance in their power.

The appearance of Lord Evandale changed the scene. He seized Inglis by the collar, and, upbraiding him with his villainy, ordered two of his comrades to seize and bind him, assuring the others, that their only chance of impunity consisted in instant submission. He then ordered the men into their ranks. They obeyed. He commanded them to ground their arms. They hesitated; but the instinct of discipline, joined to their persuasion that the authority of their officer, so boldly exerted, must be supported by some forces without the gate, induced them to submit.

"Take away those arms," said Lord Evandale to the people of the Castle; "they shall not be restored until these men know better the use for which they are entrusted with them.—And now," he continued, addressing the mutineers, "begone—Make the best use of your time, and of a truce of three hours, which the enemy are contented to allow you. Take the road to Edinburgh, and meet me at the House-of-Muir. I need not bid you beware of committing violence by the way; you will not, in your present condition, provoke resentment for your own sakes. Let your punctuality shew you mean to atone for this morning's business."

The disarmed soldiers slunk in silence from the presence of their officer, and, leaving the Castle, took the road to the place of rendez-vous, making such haste as was inspired by the fear of meeting with some detached party of the insurgents, whom their present defence-less condition, and their former insolence, might inspire with thoughts of revenge. Inglis, whom Evandale destined for punishment, remained in custody. Halliday was praised for his conduct, and assured of succeeding to the rank of the culprit. These arrangements being hastily made, Lord Evandale accosted the Major, before whose eyes the scene had seemed to pass like the changes of a dream.

"My dear Major, we must give up the place."

"Is it even so?" said Major Bellenden. "I was in hopes you had brought reinforcements and supplies."

"Not a man—not a pound of meal," answered Lord Evandale.

"Yet I am blithe to see you," returned the honest Major; "we were informed yesterday that these psalm-singing rascals had a plot on your life, and I had mustered the scoundrelly dragoons ten minutes ago in order to beat up Burley's quarters and get you out of limbo, when the dog Inglis, instead of obeying me, broke out into open mutiny.—But what is to be done now?"

"I have myself no choice," said Lord Evandale, "I am a prisoner, released on parole, and bound for Edinburgh. You and the ladies must take the same route. I have, by the favour of a friend, a safe-conduct and horses for you and your retinue—for God's sake make haste—you cannot propose to hold out with seven or eight men and without provisions—Enough has been done for honour, and enough to render the defence of the highest consequence to government. More were needless as well as desperate. The English troops are arrived at Edinburgh, and will speedily move upon Hamilton. The possession of Tillietudlem by the rebels will be but temporary."

"If you think so, my Lord," said the veteran, with a reluctant sigh, "I know you only advise what is honourable—I must submit, for the mutiny of these scoundrels would render it impossible to man the walls.—Gudyill, let the women call up their mistresses, and all be ready to march—But if I thought my remaining in these old walls, till I was starved to a mummy, could do the King's cause the least service, old Miles Bellenden would not leave them while there was a spark of life in his body."

The ladies, already alarmed by the mutiny, now heard the determination of the Major, in which they readily acquiesced. Hasty preparations were made for evacuating the Castle; and long ere the dawn was distinct enough for discovering objects with precision, they were mounted on the led horses, and others which had been provided in the neighbourhood, and proceeded towards the north, still escorted by four of the insurgent horsemen. The rest of the party who had accompanied Lord Evandale from the hamlet, took possession of the deserted Castle, carefully forbearing all outrage or acts of plunder. And, when the sun arose, the scarlet and blue colours of the Scottish Covenant floated from the Keep of Tillietudlem.

Chapter Sixteen

And, to my breast, a bodkin in her hand
Were worth a thousand daggers.
                                        MARLOW

THE CAVALCADE which left the Castle of Tillietudlem halted a few
minutes, after passing the outposts of the insurgents, to take some
slight refreshments which the care of their attendants had provided,
and which were really necessary to persons who had suffered considerably by want of proper nourishment. They then pressed forward
upon the road towards Edinburgh. It might have been expected, during the course of their journey, that Lord Evandale would have been
frequently by the side of Miss Edith Bellenden. Yet, after his first
salutations had been exchanged, and every precaution solicitously
adopted which could serve for her accommodation, he rode in the van
of the party with Major Bellenden, and seemed to abandon the charge
of immediate attendance upon his lovely niece to one of the insurgent
cavaliers, whose dark military cloak, large flapped hat and feather,
which drooped over his face, concealed at once his figure and his
features. They rode side by side in silence for more than two miles,
when the stranger addressed Miss Bellenden in a tremulous and
suppressed voice.

"Miss Bellenden," he said, "must have friends wherever she is
known; even among those whose conduct she most disapproves. Is
there any thing that such can do to shew their respect for her, and their
regret for her sufferings?"

"Let them learn for their own sakes," replied Edith, "to venerate
the laws and to spare innocent blood—Let them return to their allegiance, and I could forgive them all that I have suffered were it ten times
more."

"You think it impossible then," rejoined the cavalier, "for any one
to serve in our ranks having the weal of his country sincerely at heart,
and conceiving himself in the discharge of a patriotic duty?"

"It might be imprudent while so absolutely in your power," replied
Miss Bellenden, "to answer that question."

"Not in the present instance, I plight you the word of a soldier,"
replied the horseman.

"I have been taught candour from my birth," said Edith; "and, if I
am to speak at all, I must utter my real sentiments. God only can judge
the heart—men must estimate intentions by actions. Treason, murder
by the sword and by gibbet, the oppression of a private family such as

ours, who were only in arms for defence of our own property, are actions which must needs sully all that have accession to them, by whatever specious terms they may be gilded over."

"The guilt of civil war," rejoined the horseman—"the miseries which it brings in its train lie at the door of those who provoked it by illegal oppression, rather than of such as are driven to arms in order to assert their natural rights as freemen."

"That is assuming the question," replied Edith, "which ought to be proved; each party contends that they are right in point of principle, and in doubt the guilt must lie with those who first drew the sword, as, in an affray, law holds those to be the criminals who are the first to have recourse to violence."

"Alas!" said the horseman, "were our vindication to rest there, how easy it would be to shew that we have suffered with a patience which almost seemed beyond the power of humanity, ere we were driven by oppression into open resistance!—But I perceive," he continued, sighing deeply, "that it is vain to plead before Miss Bellenden a cause which she has already pre-judged, perhaps as much from her dislike of the persons as of the principles of those engaged in it."

"Pardon me," answered Edith; "I have stated with freedom my opinion of the principles of the insurgents; of their persons I know nothing,—excepting in one solitary instance."

"And that instance," said the horseman, "has influenced your opinion of the whole body?"

"Far from it," said Edith, "he is—at least I once thought him, one in whose scale few were fit to be weighed—he is—or he seemed—one of early talent, high faith, pure morality, and warm affections. Can I approve of a rebellion which has made such a man, formed to orna- ment, to enlighten, and to defend his country, the companion of gloomy and ignorant fanatics, or canting hypocrites,—the leader of brutal clowns,—the brother-in-arms to banditti and highway mur- derers?—Should you meet such a one in your camp, tell him that Edith Bellenden has wept more over his fallen character, blighted prospects, and dishonoured name, than over the distresses of her own house,—and that she has better endured that famine which has wasted her cheek and dimmed her eye, than the pang of heart which attended the reflection by and through whom these calamities were inflicted."

As she thus spoke, she turned upon her companion a countenance whose faded cheek attested the reality of her sufferings, even while it glowed with the temporary animation which accompanied her lan- guage. The horseman was not insensible to the appeal; he raised his hand to his brow with the sudden motion of one who feels a pang shoot along his brain, passed it hastily over his face, and then pulled the shadowing hat still deeper on his forehead. The movement and the feelings which it excited did not escape Edith, nor did she remark them without emotion.

"And yet," she said, "should the person of whom I speak seem to you too deeply affected by the hard opinion of—of—an early friend, say to him, that sincere repentance is next to innocence;—that, though fallen from a height not easily recovered, and the author of much evil, because gilded by his example, he may still atone in some measure for the evil which he has done."

"And in what manner?" asked the cavalier, in the same suppressed, and almost choked voice.

"By lending his efforts to restore the blessings of peace to his distracted countrymen—to induce the deluded rebels to lay down their arms. By saving their blood, he may atone for that which has been already spilled—he that shall be most active in accomplishing this great end, will best deserve the thanks of this age, and an honoured remembrance in the next."

"And in such a peace," said her companion, with a firmer voice, "Miss Bellenden would not, I think, desire that the interests of the people were sacrificed unreservedly to those of the crown."

"I am but a girl," was the young lady's reply, "and I scarce can speak on the subject without presumption. But, since I have gone so far, I will freely add, I would wish to see a peace which should give rest to all parties, and secure the subjects from military rapine, which I detest as much as I do the means now adopted to resist it."

"Miss Bellenden," answered Henry Morton, raising his face, and speaking in his natural tone, "the person who has lost such a highly-valued place in your esteem, has yet too much spirit to plead his cause as a criminal, and, conscious that he can no longer claim a friend's interest in your bosom, he would be silent under your harsh censure, were it not that he can refer to the honoured testimony of Lord Evandale, that his earnest wishes and most active exertions are, even now, directed to the accomplishment of such a peace as the most loyal cannot censure."

He bowed with dignity to Miss Bellenden, who, though her language intimated that she well knew to whom she had been speaking, probably had not expected that he would justify himself with so much animation. She returned his salute confused and in silence. Morton then rode forward to the head of the party.

"Henry Morton!" exclaimed Major Bellenden, surprised at the sudden apparition.

"The same," answered Morton; "who is sorry that he labours

under the harsh construction of Major Bellenden and his family. He commits to my Lord Evandale," he continued, turning towards the young nobleman, and bowing to him, "the charge of undeceiving his friends both regarding the particulars of his conduct and the purity of his motives. Farewell, Major Bellenden—All happiness attend you and yours—May we meet again in better and happier times."

"Believe me," said Lord Evandale, "your confidence, Mr Morton, is not misplaced; I will endeavour to repay the great services I have received from you by doing my best to place your character on its proper footing with Major Bellenden, and all whose esteem you value."

"I expected no less from your generosity, my lord," said Morton.

He then called his followers, and rode off along the heath in the direction of Hamilton, their feathers waving and their steel caps glancing in the sun. Cuddie Headrigg alone remained an instant behind his companions to take an affectionate farewell of Jenny Dennison, who had contrived, during this short morning's ride, to re-establish her influence over his susceptible bosom. A straggling tree or two obscured, rather than concealed, their *tete-a-tete*, as they halted their horses to bid adieu.

"Fare ye weel, Jenny," said Cuddie, with a loud exertion of his lungs, intended perhaps to be a sigh, but rather resembling the intonation of a groan,—"Ye'll think o' puir Cuddie sometimes—an honest lad that lo'es ye, Jenny; ye'll think o' him now and then?"

"Whiles—at brose-time," answered the malicious damsel, unable either to suppress the repartee or the arch smile which attended it.

Cuddie took his revenge as rustic lovers are wont, and as Jenny probably expected,—caught his mistress round the neck, kissed her cheek and lips heartily, and then turned his horse and trotted off after his master.

"De'il's in the fallow," said Jenny, wiping her lips and adjusting her head-dress, "he has twice the spunk o' Tam Halliday, after a'.— Coming, my leddy, coming—Lord have a care o' us, I trust the auld leddy didna see us!"

"Jenny," said Lady Margaret, as the damsel came up, "was not that young man who commanded the party the same that was captain of the popinjay, and was afterwards prisoner at Tillietudlem on the morning Claverhouse came there?"

Jenny, happy that the query had no reference to her own little matters, looked at her young mistress, to discover, if possible, whether it was her cue to speak truth or no. Not being able to catch any hint to guide her, she followed her instinct as a lady's-maid, and lied.

"I dinna believe it was him, my leddy," said Jenny, as confidently as if she had been saying her catechism; "he was a little black man, that."

"You must have been blind, Jenny," said the Major; "Henry Morton is tall and fair, and that youth was the very man."

"I had ither thing ado than be looking at him," said Jenny, tossing her head; "he may be as fair as a farthing candle, for me."

"Is it not," said Lady Margaret, "a blessed escape which we have made, out of the hands of so desperate and blood-thirsty a fanatic?"

"You are deceived, madam," said Lord Evandale; "Mr Morton merits such a title from no one, but least from us. That I am now alive, and that you are now on your safe retreat to our friends, instead of being prisoners to a real fanatical homicide, is solely and entirely owing to the prompt, active, and energetic humanity of this young gentleman."

He then went into a particular narrative of the events with which the reader is acquainted, dwelling upon the merits of Morton, and expatiating on the risk at which he had rendered them these important services, as if he had been a brother instead of a rival.

"I were worse than ungrateful," he said, "were I silent on the merits of the man who has twice saved my life."

"I would willingly think well of Henry Morton, my Lord," replied Major Bellenden; "and I own he has behaved handsomely to your Lordship and to us; but I cannot have the same allowances which it pleases your Lordship to entertain for his present courses."

"You are to consider," replied Lord Evandale, "that he has been partly forced upon them by necessity; and I must add, that his principles, though differing in some degree from my own, are such as ought to command respect. Claverhouse, whose knowledge of men is not to be disputed, spoke justly of him as to his extraordinary qualities, but with prejudice, and harshly, concerning his principles and motives."

"You have not been long in learning all his good qualities, my Lord," answered Major Bellenden. "I, who have known him from boyhood, could, before this affair, have said much of his good principles and good-nature; but as to his high talents"——

"They were probably hidden, Major, even from himself, until circumstances called them forth; and, if I have detected them, it was only because our intercourse and conversation turned on momentous and important subjects. He is now labouring to bring this rebellion to an end, and the terms he has proposed are so moderate, that they shall not want my hearty recommendation."

"And have you hopes," said Lady Margaret, "to accomplish a scheme so capricious?"

"I should be, madam, were every whig as moderate as Morton, and every loyalist as disinterested as Major Bellenden. But such is the fanaticism of both parties, that I fear nothing will end this civil war save the edge of the sword."

It may be readily supposed, that Edith listened with the deepest interest to this conversation. While she regretted that she had expressed herself harshly and hastily to her lover, she felt a conscious and proud satisfaction that his character was, even in the judgment of his generous rival, such as her own affection had once spoke it.

"Civil feuds and domestic prejudices," she said, "may render it necessary for me to tear his remembrance from my heart, but it is no small relief to know assuredly, that it is worthy of the place it has so long retained."

While Edith was thus retracting her unjust resentment, her lover arrived at the camp of the insurgents, near Hamilton, which he found in considerable confusion. Certain advices had arrived that the royal army, having received the recruits which they expected from England, were about to take the field. Fame magnified their numbers and their high state of equipment and discipline, and spread abroad other circumstances which dismayed the courage of the insurgents. What favour they might have expected from Monmouth, was likely to be intercepted by the influence of those associated with him in command. His Lieutenant-general was the celebrated General Thomas Dalzell of Binns, who, having practised the art of war in the then barbarous country of Russia, was as much feared for his cruelty and indifference to human life and human suffering, as respected for his steady loyalty and undaunted valour. This man was second in command to Monmouth, and the horse were commanded by Claverhouse, burning with desire to revenge the death of his nephew, and his defeat at Drumclog. To these accounts was added the most formidable and terrific description of the train of artillery and the cavalry force with which the royal army took the field; and every rumour tended to increase the apprehension among the insurgents, that the king's vengeance had only been delayed in order that it might fall more certain and more heavy.

Morton endeavoured to fortify the minds of the common people by pointing out the probable exaggeration of these reports, and by reminding them of the strength of their own situation, with an unfordable river in front, only passable by a long and narrow bridge. He called to their remembrance their victory over Claverhouse when their numbers were few, and these much worse disciplined and appointed for battle than now, shewed them that the ground afforded, by its undulation and the thickets which intersected it, considerable protection against artillery, and even against cavalry, if stoutly defended; and that their safety, in fact, depended on their own spirit and resolution.

But while Morton thus endeavoured to keep up the courage of the army at large, he availed himself of these discouraging rumours to endeavour to impress on the minds of the leaders the necessity of proposing to the government moderate terms of accommodation, while they were still formidable as commanding an unbroken and numerous army. He pointed out to them, that, in the present humour of their followers, it could hardly be expected that they would engage, with advantage, the well-appointed and regular forces of the Duke of Monmouth; and that, if they chanced to be defeated and dispersed, the insurrection in which they had engaged, so far from being useful to the country, would be rendered the apology for oppressing it more severely. Pressed by these arguments, and feeling it equally dangerous to remain together, or to dismiss their forces, most of the leaders readily agreed, that if such terms could be obtained as had been transmitted to the Duke of Monmouth by the hands of Lord Evandale, the purpose for which they had taken up arms would be, in a great measure, accomplished. They then entered into similar resolutions, and agreed to guarantee the petition and remonstrance which had been drawn up by Morton. On the contrary there were still several leaders, and those men whose influence with the people exceeded that of persons of more apparent consequence, who treated every proposal of treaty which did not proceed on the basis of the Solemn League and Covenant of 1643, as utterly null and void, impious, and unchristian. These men diffused their feelings among the multitude, who had little foresight, and nothing to lose, and persuaded many that those timid counsellors who recommended peace upon terms short of the dethronement of the royal family, and the declared independence of the church with respect to the state, were cowardly labourers, who were about to withdraw their hands from the plough, and despicable trimmers, who sought only a specious pretext for deserting their brethren in arms. These contradictory opinions were fiercely argued in each tent of the insurgent army, or rather in the huts and cabins which served in the place of tents. Violence in language often led to open quarrels and blows, and the divisions into which the army of sufferers was rent served as too plain a presage of their future fate.

Chapter Seventeen

The curse of growing factions and divisions
Still vex your councils!——
                                        Venice Preserved

THE WITS of Morton were sufficiently occupied in stemming the furious current of these contending parties, when, two days after his return to Hamilton, he was visited by his friend and colleague, the Reverend Mr Poundtext, flying, as he presently found, from the face of John Balfour of Burley, who was not a little incensed at the share he had taken in the liberation of Lord Evandale. When the worthy divine had somewhat recruited his spirits, after the hurry and fatigue of his journey, he proceeded to give Morton an account of what had passed in the vicinity of Tillietudlem after the memorable morning of his departure.

The night march of Morton had been accomplished with such dexterity, and the men were so faithful to their trust, that Burley received no intelligence of what had happened until the morning was far advanced. His first enquiry was, whether Macbriar and Kettledrummle had arrived agreeably to the summons which he had dispatched at midnight. Macbriar had come, and Kettledrummle, though a more heavy traveller, might, he was informed, be instantly expected. Burley then dispatched a messenger to Morton's quarters to summon him to an immediate council. The messenger returned with news that he had left the place. Poundtext was next summoned; but he thinking, as he said himself, that it was ill dealing with fractious folk, had withdrawn to his own quiet manse, preferring a dark ride, though he had been on horseback the whole preceding day, to a renewal in the morning of a controversy with Burley, whose ferocity overawed him when unsupported by the firmness of Morton. Burley's next enquiries were directed after Lord Evandale; and great was his rage when he learned that he had been conveyed away over night by a party of the Marksmen of Milnewood, under the immediate command of Henry Morton himself.

"The villain!" exclaimed Burley, addressing himself to Macbriar; "the base, mean-spirited traitor, to curry favour for himself with the government, hath set at liberty the prisoner taken by my own right hand, through means of whom, I have little doubt, the possession of the place of strength, which hath wrought us such trouble, might now have been in our hands."

"But is it not in our hands?" said Macbriar, looking up towards the

Keep of the Castle; "and are not these the colours of the Covenant that float over its walls?"

"A stratagem—a mere trick," said Burley, "an insult over our disappointment, intended to aggravate and embitter our spirits."

He was interrupted by the arrival of one of Morton's followers sent to report to him the evacuation of the place, and its occupation by the insurgent forces. Burley was rather driven to fury than reconciled by the news of this success.

"I have watched," he said—"I have fought—I have plotted—I have striven for the reduction of this place—I have forborn to seek to head enterprises of higher command and of higher honour. I have narrowed their outgoings, and cut off the springs, and broken the staff of bread within their walls. And, when the men were about to yield themselves to my hand, that their sons might be bondsmen, and their daughters a laughing-stock to our whole camp, cometh this youth, without a beard on his chin, and takes it on him to thrust his sickle into the harvest, and to rend the prey from the spoiler! Surely the labourer is worthy of his hire, and the city, with its captives, should be given to him that wins it."

"Nay," said Macbriar, who was surprised at the degree of agitation which Balfour displayed, "chafe not thyself because of the ungodly. Heaven will use his own instruments; and who knows but this youth"——

"Hush! hush!" said Burley; "do not discredit thine own better judgment. It was thou that first badest me beware of this painted sepulchre—this lacquered piece of copper, that passed current with me for gold. It fares ill, even with the elect, when they neglect the guidance of such pious pastors as thou. But our carnal affections will mislead us—this ungrateful boy's father was mine ancient friend. They must be as earnest in their struggles as thou, Ephraim Macbriar, that would shake themselves clear of the clogs and claims of humanity."

This compliment touched the preacher in the most sensible part; and Burley deemed, therefore, he should find little difficulty in moulding his opinions to the support of his own views, more especially as they agreed exactly in their opinions of church government.

"Let us instantly," he said, "go up to the Tower; there is that among the records in yonder fortress, which, well used, as I can use it, shall be worth to us a valiant leader and an hundred horsemen."

"But will these be of the children of the Covenant?" said the preacher. "We have already among us too many who hunger after lands and silver and gold rather than after the word; it is not by such that our deliverance shall be wrought out."

"Thou errest," said Burley; "we must work by means, and these worldly men shall be our instruments; at all events, the Moabitish woman shall be despoiled of her inheritance, and neither the malignant Evandale, nor the Erastian Morton, shall possess yonder Castle and lands, though they may seek in marriage the daughter thereof."

So saying, he led the way to Tillietudlem, where he seized upon the plate and other valuables for the use of the army, ransacked the charter room, and other receptacles for family papers, and treated with contempt the remonstrances of those who reminded him, that the terms granted to the garrison had guaranteed respect to private property.

Burley and Macbriar, having established themselves in their new acquisition, were joined by Kettledrummle in the course of the day, and also by the Laird of Langcale, whom that active divine had contrived to seduce, as Poundtext termed it, from the pure light in which he had been brought up. Thus united, they sent to the said Poundtext an invitation, or rather a summons, to attend a council at Tillietudlem. He remembered, however, that the door had an iron grate, and the Keep a dungeon, and resolved not to trust himself with his incensed colleagues. He therefore retreated, or rather fled, to Hamilton, with an advice, that Burley, Macbriar, and Kettledrummle, were coming to Hamilton as soon as they could collect a body of Cameronians sufficient to overawe the rest of the army.

"And ye see," concluded Poundtext, with a deep sigh, "that they will then possess a majority in the council; for Langcale, though he has always passed for one of the honest and rational party, cannot be suitably, or preceesely, termed either fish, or flesh, or gude red-herring—whoever has the stronger party has Langcale."

Thus concluded the heavy narrative of honest Mr Poundtext, who sighed deeply, as he considered the dangers in which he was placed betwixt unreasonable adversaries amongst themselves and the common enemy from without. Morton exhorted him to patience, temper, and composure; informed him of the good hope he had of negotiating for peace and indemnity through means of Lord Evandale, and made out to him a very fair prospect that he should again return to his old parchment-bound Calvin, his evening pipe of tobacco, and his noggin of inspiring ale, providing always he would afford his strong support and concurrence to the measures which he, Morton, had taken for a general pacification. Thus backed and comforted, Poundtext resolved magnanimously to await the coming of the Cameronians.

Burley and his confederates had drawn together a considerable body of these sectaries, amounting to a hundred horse and about fifteen hundred foot, clouded and sour in aspect, morose and jealous in communication, haughty of heart, and confident, as men who

believed that the pale of salvation was open for them exclusively; that
all others, however slight were the shades of difference of doctrine
from their own, were in fact little better than outcasts and reprobates.
These men entered the presbyterian camp, rather as dubious and
suspicious allies, or possibly antagonists, than as men who were heartily embarked in the same cause, and exposed to the same dangers.
Burley made no private visit to his colleagues, and held no communication with them on the subject of the public affairs, otherwise than by
sending a dry invitation to them to attend a meeting of the general
council for that evening.

On the arrival of Morton and Poundtext at the place of assembly,
they found their brethren already seated. Slight greeting passed between them, and it was easy to see that no amical conference was
intended by those who convoked the council. The first question was
put by Macbriar, the sharp eagerness of whose zeal urged him to the
van on all occasions. He desired to know by whose authority the
malignant, called Lord Evandale, had been freed from the doom of
death justly denounced against him.

"By my authority and Mr Morton's," replied Poundtext, who,
besides being anxious to give his companion a good opinion of his
courage, confided heartily in his support, and, moreover, had much
less fear of encountering one of his own profession, and who confined
himself to the weapons of theological controversy, in which Poundtext
feared no man, than of entering into debate with the stern homicide
Balfour.

"And who, brother," said Kettledrummle, "who gave you commission to interpose in such a high matter?"

"The tenor of our commission," answered Poundtext, "gives us
authority to bind and to loose. If Lord Evandale was justly doomed to
die by the voice of one of our number, he was of a surety lawfully
redeemed from death by the warrant of two of us."

"Go to, go to," said Burley, "we know your motives; it was to send
that silkworm—that gilded trinket—that embroidered trifle of a
Lord, to bear terms of peace to the tyrant."

"It was so," replied Morton, who saw his colleague begin to flinch
before the fierce eye of Balfour—"it was so; and what then?—Are we
to plunge the nation in endless war, in order to pursue schemes which
are equally wild, wicked, and unattainable?"

"Hear him!" said Balfour; "he blasphemeth."

"It is false," said Morton; "they blaspheme who pretend to expect
miracles and neglect the use of the human means with which Providence has blessed them. I repeat it—Our avowed object is the re-
establishment of peace on fair and honourable terms of security to our

religion and our liberty. We disclaim any desire to tyrannize over those of others."

The debate would now have run higher than ever, but they were interrupted by intelligence that the Duke of Monmouth had commenced his march towards the west, and was already advanced half way from Edinburgh. This news silenced their divisions for the moment, and it was agreed that the next day should be held as a fast of general humiliation for the sins of the land; that the Reverend Mr Poundtext should preach to the army in the morning, and Kettledrummle in the afternoon; that neither should touch upon any topics of schism or of division, but animate the soldiers to resist to the blood, like brethren in the good cause. This healing overture having been agreed to, the moderate party ventured upon another proposal, confiding that it would have the support of Langcale, who looked extremely blank at the news which they had just received, and might be supposed reconverted to moderate measures. It was to be presumed, they said, that since the King had not entrusted the command of his forces upon the present occasion to any of their active oppressors, but, on the contrary, had employed a man of gentle temper, and of a disposition favourable to their cause, there must be some better intention entertained towards them than they had yet experienced. They contended, that it was not only prudent but necessary to ascertain, from a communication with the Duke of Monmouth, whether he was not charged with some secret instructions in their favour. This could only be learned by dispatching an envoy to his army.

"And who will undertake the task?" said Burley, evading a proposal too reasonable to be openly resisted—"Who will go up to their camp, knowing that Grahame of Claverhouse hath sworn to hang up whomsoever we shall dispatch towards them, in revenge of the death of the young man his nephew?"

"Let that be no obstacle," said Morton; "I will with pleasure encounter any risk attached to the bearer of your errand."

"Let him go," said Balfour, apart to Macbriar; "our councils will be well rid of his presence."

The motion, therefore, received no contradiction even from those who were expected to have been most active in opposing it, and it was agreed that Henry Morton should go to the camp of the Duke of Monmouth in order to discover upon what terms the insurgents would be admitted to treat with him. As soon as his errand was made known, several of the more moderate party joined in requesting him to make terms upon the footing of the petition entrusted to Lord Evandale's hands; for the approach of the King's army spread a general trepidation, by no means allayed by the high tone assumed by the

Cameronians, which had so little to support it, excepting their own headlong zeal. With these instructions, and with Cuddie as his attendant, Morton set forth towards the royal camp at all the risks which attend those who assume the office of mediator during the heat of civil discord.

Morton had not proceeded six or seven miles before he perceived that he was on the point of falling in with the van of the royal forces; and, as he ascended a height, saw all the roads in the neighbourhood occupied by armed men marching in great order towards Bothwell-muir, an open common, on which they proposed to encamp for that evening, at the distance of about two miles from the Clyde, on the farther side of which river the army of the insurgents was encamped. He gave himself up to the first advanced guard of cavalry which he met, and communicated his wish to obtain access to the Duke of Monmouth. The non-commissioned officer who commanded the party made his report to his superior, and he again to another in still higher command, and both immediately rode to the spot where Morton was detained.

"You are but losing your time, my friend, and risking your life," said one of them, addressing Morton; "the Duke of Monmouth will receive no terms from traitors with arms in their hands, and your cruelties have been such as to authorize retaliation of every kind."

"I cannot think," said Morton, "that even if the Duke of Monmouth should consider us as criminals, he would condemn so large a body of his fellow-subjects without even hearing what they have to plead for themselves. On my part I fear nothing. I am conscious of having consented to, or authorized no cruelty, and the fear of suffering innocently for the crimes of others shall not deter me from executing my commission."

The two officers looked at each other.

"I have an idea," said the younger, "that this is the young man of whom Evandale spoke"——

"Is my Lord Evandale in the army?" said Morton.

"He is not," replied the officer; "we left him at Edinburgh too much indisposed to take the field—Your name, sir, I presume, is Henry Morton?"

"It is, sir," answered Morton.

"We will not oppose your seeing the Duke, sir," said the officer, with more civility of manner; "but you may assure yourself it will be to no purpose; for, were his Grace disposed to favour your people, others are joined in commission with him who will hardly consent to his doing so."

"I shall be sorry to find it thus," said Morton, "but my duty requires that I should persevere in my desire to have an interview with him."

"Lumley," said the superior officer, "let the Duke know of Mr Morton's arrival, and remind his Grace that this is the person of whom Lord Evandale spoke so highly."

The officer returned with a message that the General could not see Mr Morton that evening, but would receive him by times on the ensuing morning. He was detained in a neighbouring cottage all night, but treated with civility, and every thing provided for his accommodation. Early on the next morning the officer he had first seen came to conduct him to his audience.

The army was drawn out, and in the act of forming column for march, or attack. The Duke was in the centre, nearly a mile from the place where Morton had passed the night. In riding towards the General, he had an opportunity of estimating the force which had been assembled for the suppression of this hasty and ill-concocted insurrection. There were three or four regiments of English, the flower of Charles's army—there were the Scottish Life Guards, burning with desire to revenge their late defeat. Other Scottish regiments of regulars were also assembled, and a large body of cavalry, consisting partly of gentlemen volunteers, partly of the tenants of the crown who did military service for their fiefs. Morton also observed several strong parties of Highlanders drawn from the points nearest to the lowland frontiers, a people particularly obnoxious to the western whigs, and who hated and despised them in the same proportion. These were assembled under their chiefs, and made part of this formidable array. A complete train of field-artillery accompanied the army; and the whole had an air so imposing, that it seemed nothing short of an actual miracle could prevent the ill-equipped, ill-modelled, and tumultuary army of the insurgents from being utterly destroyed. The officer who accompanied Morton endeavoured to gather from his looks the feelings with which this splendid and awful parade of military force had impressed him. But, true to the cause he had espoused, he laboured successfully to prevent the anxiety which he felt from appearing in his countenance, and looked around him on the warlike display as on a sight which he expected, and to which he was indifferent.

"You see the entertainment prepared for you," said the officers.

"If I had no appetite for it," replied Morton, "I would not have been accompanying you at this moment. But I shall be better pleased with a more peaceful regale, for the sake of all parties."

As they spoke thus, they approached the commander-in-chief, who, surrounded by several officers, was seated upon a knoll commanding an extensive prospect of the distant country, and from which could be easily discovered the windings of the majestic Clyde and the distant camp of the insurgents on the opposite bank. The officers of the royal army appeared to be surveying the ground with the purpose of directing an immediate attack. When Captain Lumley, the officer who accompanied Morton, had whispered in Monmouth's ear his name and errand, the Duke made a signal for all around him to retire, excepting only two general officers of distinction. While they spoke together in whispers for a few minutes before Morton was permitted to advance, he had time to study the appearance of the persons with whom he was to treat.

It was impossible for any one to look upon the Duke of Monmouth without being captivated by his personal graces and accomplishments, of which the Great Highpriest of all the Nine has since recorded—

> "Whate'er he did was done with so much ease,
> In him alone 'twas natural to please;
> His motions all accompanied with grace,
> And Paradise was opened in his face."

Yet, to a strict observer, the manly beauty of Monmouth's face was occasionally rendered less striking by an air of vacillation and uncertainty, which seemed to imply hesitation and doubt at moments when decisive resolution was most necessary.

Beside him stood Claverhouse, whom we have already fully described, and another general officer, whose appearance was singularly striking. His dress was of the antique fashion of Charles the First's time, and composed of shamoy leather, curiously slashed and covered with antique lace and garniture. His boots and spurs might be referred to the same distant period. He wore a breast-plate, over which descended a grey beard of venerable length, which he cherished as a mark of mourning for Charles the First, having never shaved since that monarch was brought to the scaffold. His head was uncovered, and almost perfectly bald. His high and wrinkled forehead, piercing grey eyes, and marked features, evinced age unbroken by infirmity, and stern resolution unsoftened by humanity. Such is the outline, however feebly expressed, of the celebrated General Thomas Dalzell, a man more feared and hated by the whigs than even Claverhouse himself, and who executed the same violences against them out of a detestation of their persons, or perhaps an innate severity of temper, which Grahame only resorted to on political accounts, as the best means of intimidating the followers of presbytery, and destroying that sect entirely.

The presence of these two generals, one of whom he knew by person, and the other by description, seemed to Morton decisive of

the fate of his embassy. But, notwithstanding his youth and inexper-
ience, and the unfavourable reception which his proposals seemed
likely to meet with, he advanced boldly towards them upon receiving a
signal to that purpose, determined that the cause of his country, and of
those with whom he had taken up arms, should suffer nothing from
being entrusted to him. Monmouth received him with the graceful
courtesy which attended even his slightest actions; Dalzell regarded
him with a stern, gloomy, and impatient frown; and Claverhouse, with
a sarcastic smile and inclination of his head, seemed to claim him as an
old acquaintance.

"You come, sir, from these unfortunate people," said the Duke of
Monmouth, "and your name, I believe, is Morton; will you favour us
with the purport of your errand?"

"It is contained, my Lord," answered Morton, "in a paper, termed,
a Remonstrance and Supplication, which my Lord Evandale has
placed, I presume, in your Grace's hands?"

"He has done so, sir," answered the Duke; "and I understand,
from Lord Evandale, that Mr Morton has behaved in these unhappy
matters with much temperance and generosity, for which I have to
request his acceptance of my thanks."

Here Morton observed Dalzell shake his head indignantly, and
whisper something into Claverhouse's ear, who smiled in return, and
elevated his eyebrows, but in a degree so slight as scarce to be percept-
ible. The Duke, taking the petition from his pocket, proceeded, obviously struggling between the native gentleness of his own disposition,
and his conviction that the petitioners demanded no more than their
rights, and the desire, on the other hand, of enforcing the king's
authority and complying with the sterner opinions of the colleagues in
office, who had been assigned for the purpose of controlling as well as
advising him.

"There are, Mr Morton, in this paper, proposals, as to the abstract
propriety of which I must now waive delivering any opinion. Some of
them appear to me reasonable and just; and, although I have no
express instruction from the King upon the subject, yet I assure you,
Mr Morton, and I pledge my honour, that I will interpose in your
behalf, and use my utmost influence to procure you satisfaction from
his Majesty. But you will understand, that I can only treat with
supplicants, not with rebels; and, as a preliminary to every act of
favour on my side, I must insist upon your followers laying down their
arms and dispersing themselves."

"To do so, my Lord Duke," replied Morton, undauntedly, "were to
acknowledge ourselves the rebels that our enemies term us. Our
swords are drawn for recovery of a birth-right wrested from us; your

Grace's moderation and good sense has admitted the general justice of our demand,—a demand which would never have been listened to had it not been accompanied with the sound of the trumpet. We cannot, therefore, and dare not, lay down our arms, even on your Grace's assurance of indemnity, unless it were accompanied with some reasonable prospect of the redress of the wrongs which we complain of."

"Mr Morton," replied the Duke, "you have sense enough to perceive that requests, by no means dangerous in themselves, may become so by the way in which they are pressed and supported."

"We may reply, my Lord," answered Morton, "that this disagreeable mode has not been resorted to until all others have failed."

"Mr Morton," said the Duke, "I must break this conference short. We are in readiness to commence the attack, yet I will suspend it for an hour, until you can communicate my answer to the insurgents. If they please to disperse their followers, lay down their arms, and send a peaceful deputation to me, I will consider myself bound in honour to do all I can to procure redress of their grievances; if not, let them stand on their guard and expect the consequences.—I think, gentlemen," he added, turning to his two colleagues, "this is the utmost length to which I can stretch my instructions in favour of these misguided persons?"

"By my faith," answered Dalzell, sullenly, "and it is a length to which my poor judgment durst not have stretched them, considering I had both the King and my conscience to answer to. But, doubtless, your Grace knows more of the King's private mind than we, who have only the letter of our instructions to look to."

Monmouth blushed deeply. "You hear," he said, addressing Morton, "General Dalzell blames me for the length which I am disposed to go in your favour."

"General Dalzell's sentiments, my Lord," replied Morton, "are such as we expect from him; your Grace's such as we were prepared to hope you might please to entertain; but I cannot help adding, that, in the case of the absolute submission upon which you are pleased to insist, it might still remain something less than doubtful how far, with such counsellors around the King, even your Grace's intercession might procure us effectual relief. But I will communicate to our leaders your Grace's answer to our supplication; and, since we cannot obtain peace, we must bid war welcome as well as we may."

"Good morning, sir," said the Duke. "I suspend the movements of attack for one hour, and for one hour only. If you have an answer to return within that space of time, I will receive it here, and earnestly entreat it may be such as to save the effusion of blood."

At this moment another smile of deep meaning passed between Dalzell and Claverhouse. The Duke observed it, and repeated his words with great dignity.

"Yes, gentlemen, I said I trusted the answer might be such as would save the effusion of blood. I hope the sentiment neither meets your scorn, nor incurs your displeasure."

Dalzell returned the Duke's frown with a stern glance, but made no answer. Claverhouse, his lip just curled with an ironical smile, bowed, and said, "It was not for him to judge the propriety of his Grace's sentiments."

The Duke made a signal to Morton to withdraw. He obeyed; and, accompanied by his former escort, rode slowly through the army to return to the camp of the non-conformists. As he passed the fine corps of Life Guards, he found Claverhouse was already at their head. That officer no sooner saw Morton, than he advanced and addressed him with perfect politeness of manner.

"I think this is not the first time I have seen Mr Morton of Milne-wood?"

"It is not Colonel Grahame's fault," said Morton, smiling sternly, "that he or any one else should be now incommoded by my presence."

"Allow me at least to say," replied Claverhouse, "that Mr Morton's present situation authorizes the opinion I then entertained of him, and that my proceedings only squared to my duty."

"To reconcile your actions to your duty, and your duty to your conscience, is your business, Colonel Grahame, not mine," said Morton, justly offended at being thus, in a manner, required to approve of the sentence under which he had so nearly suffered.

"Nay, but stay an instant," said Claverhouse; "Evandale insists that I have some wrongs to acquit myself of in your instance. I trust I shall always make some difference between a high-minded gentleman, who, though misguided, acts upon generous principles, and the crazy fanatical clowns yonder, with the blood-thirsty assassins who head them; therefore, if they do not disperse upon your return, let me pray you instantly come over to our army and surrender yourself prisoner, for, be assured, they will not stand our assault for half an hour. If you will be ruled and do this, be sure to enquire for me. Monmouth, strange as it may seem, cannot protect you—Dalzell will not—I both can and will; and I have promised to Evandale to do so if you will give me an opportunity."

"I should owe Lord Evandale my thanks," answered Morton coldly, "did not his scheme imply an opinion that I might be prevailed on to desert those with whom I am engaged. For you, Colonel Grahame, if you will honour me with a different species of satisfaction, it is probable, that, in an hour's time, you will find me at the west end of Bothwell Bridge with my sword in my hand."

"I will be happy to meet you there," said Claverhouse, "but still more so should you think better on my first proposal."

They then saluted and parted.

"That is a pretty lad, Lumley," said Claverhouse, addressing himself to the other officer; "but he is a lost man—his blood be upon his head."

So saying, he addressed himself to the task of preparation for instant battle.

END OF VOLUME

THE TALE OF
OLD MORTALITY

Chapter One

But, hark! the tent has changed its voice,
There's peace and rest nae langer.
BURNS

WHEN Morton had left the well-ordered outposts of the regular army, and arrived at those which were maintained by his own party, he could not but be peculiarly sensible of the difference of discipline, and entertain a proportional degree of fear for the consequences. The same discords which agitated their councils raged even among their meanest followers; and their picquets and patroles were more interested and occupied in disputing the true occasion and causes of wrath, and defining the limits of the Erastian heresy, than in looking out for and observing the motions of their enemies, though within hearing of their drums and trumpets.

There was a guard, however, posted at the long and narrow bridge of Bothwell, over which the enemy must necessarily advance to the attack; but, like the others, they were divided and disheartened; and, entertaining the idea that they were posted on a desperate service, they even meditated withdrawing themselves to the main body. This would have been utter ruin; for, on the defence or loss of this pass, the fortune of the day was most likely to depend; all beyond it was a plain open field, excepting a few thickets of no great depth, and, consequently, was ground on which the undisciplined forces of the insurgents, deficient as they were in cavalry, and totally unprovided with artillery, were altogether unlikely to withstand the shock of regular troops.

Morton, therefore, viewed the pass carefully, and formed the hope, that by occupying two or three houses on the left bank of the river, with the copse and thickets of alders and hazels that lined its side, and, by blockading the passage itself, and shutting the gates of a portal, which, according to the old fashion, was built on the central arch, the bridge of Bothwell might be easily defended against a very superior force. He issued directions accordingly, and commanded the parapets of the bridge, on the farther side of the portal, to be thrown down, that they might afford no protection to the enemy when they should attempt the passage. Morton then conjured the party at this important post to be watchful and upon their guard, and promised them a speedy and strong reinforcement. He caused them to advance videttes beyond the river to watch the progress of the enemy, which out-posts he directed should be withdrawn to the left bank as soon as they approached; finally, he charged them to send regular information to the main body of all that they could observe. Men under arms, and in a situation of danger, are usually sufficiently alert in appreciating the merit of their officers. Morton's intelligence and activity gained the confidence of these men, and with better hope and heart than they had before, they began to fortify their position in the manner he recommended, and saw him depart with three loud cheers.

Morton now galloped hastily towards the main body of the insurgents, but was surprised and shocked at the scene of confusion and clamour which it exhibited, at the moment when good order and concord were of such essential consequence. Instead of being drawn up in line of battle, and listening to the commands of their officers, they were crowding together in a confused mass that rolled and agitated itself like the waves of the sea, while a thousand tongues spoke, or rather vociferated, and not a single ear was found to listen. Scandalized at a scene so extraordinary, Morton endeavoured to make his way through the press to learn, and, if possible, to remove the cause of this so untimely disorder. While he is thus engaged, we shall make the reader acquainted with that which he was some time in discovering.

The insurgents had proceeded to hold their day of humiliation, which, agreeably to the practice of the puritans during the earlier civil war, they considered as the most effectual mode of solving all difficulties and waiving all discussions. A temporary pulpit, or tent, was erected in the middle of the encampment; which, according to the fixed arrangement, was first to be occupied by the Reverend Peter Poundtext, to whom the post of honour was assigned, as the eldest clergyman present. But as the worthy divine, with slow and stately steps, was advancing towards the rostrum which had been prepared for him, he was prevented by the unexpected apparition of Habakkuk Meiklewrath, the insane preacher, whose appearance had so much startled Morton at the first council of the insurgents after their victory at Loudoun-hill. It is not known whether he was acting under the influence and instigation of the Cameronians, or whether he was merely impelled by his own agitated imagination, and the temptation of a vacant pulpit before him, to seize the opportunity of exhorting so respectable a congregation. It is only certain, that he took occasion by the forelock, sprung into the pulpit, cast his eyes wildly round him, and, undismayed by the murmurs of many of the audience, opened the Bible, read forth as his text from the thirteenth chapter of Deuteronomy, "Certain men, the children of Belial, are gone out from among you, and have withdrawn the inhabitants of their city, saying, let us go and serve other gods which you have not known;" and then rushed at once into the midst of his subject.

The harangue of Meiklewrath was as wild and extravagant as his intrusion was unauthorized and untimely; but it was provokingly coherent, in so far as it turned entirely upon the very subjects of discord, of which it had been agreed to adjourn the consideration until some more suitable opportunity. Not a single topic did he omit which had offence in it; and, after charging the moderate party with heresy, with crouching to tyranny, with seeking to be at peace with God's enemies, he applied to Morton, by name, the charge that he had been one of those men of Belial, who, in the words of his text, had gone out from among them to withdraw the inhabitants of his city, and to go astray after false Gods. To him, and all who followed him, or approved of his conduct, Meiklewrath denounced fury and vengeance, and exhorted those who would hold themselves pure and undefiled to come up from the midst of them.

"Fear not," he said, "because of the neighing of horses, or the glittering of the breastplate. Seek not aid of the Egyptians, because of the enemy, though they be numerous as locusts, and fierce as dragons. Their trust is not as our trust, nor their rock as our rock; how else shall a thousand fly before one, and two put ten thousand to the flight! I dreamed it in the visions of the night, and the voice said, 'Habakkuk, take thy fan and purge the wheat from the chaff, that they be not both consumed with the fire of indignation and the lightning of fury.' Wherefore, I say, take this Henry Morton—this wretched Achan, who hath brought the accursed thing among ye, and hath made himself brethren in the camp of the enemy—take him and stone him with stones, and thereafter burn him with fire, that the wrath may depart from the children of the Covenant. He hath not taken a Babylonish garment, but he hath sold the garment of righteousness to the woman of Babylon—he hath not taken two hundred shekels of fine silver, but he hath bartered the truth, which is more precious than shekels of silver or wedges of gold."

At this furious charge, brought so unexpectedly against one of their most active commanders, the audience broke out into open tumult, some demanding that there should instantly be a new election of officers, into which office none should hereafter be admitted who had, in their phrase, touched of that which was accursed, or temporized more or less with the heresies and corruptions of the time. Such was the demand of the Cameronians, who vociferated loudly, that those who were not with them were against them,—that it was no time to relinquish the substantial part of the covenanted testimony of the Church, if they expected a blessing on their arms and their cause; and that, in their eyes, a lukewarm presbyterian was little better than a prelatist, an anti-covenanter, and a nullifidian.

The parties accused repelled the charge of criminal compliance and defection from the truth, with scorn and indignation, and charged their accusers with breach of faith, as well as with wrong-headed and extravagant zeal in introducing such divisions into an army, the joint strength of which could not, by the most sanguine, be judged more than sufficient to face their enemies. Poundtext, and one or two others, made some faint efforts to stem the increasing fury of the factions, exclaiming to those of the other party, in the words of the Patriarch,—"Let there be no strife, I pray thee, between me and thee, and between thy herdsmen and my herdsmen, for we be brethren."— No healing overture could possibly obtain audience. It was in vain that even Burley himself, when he saw the dissension proceed to such ruinous lengths, exerted his stern and deep voice, commanding silence and obedience to discipline. The spirit of insubordination had gone forth, and it seemed as if the exhortation of Habakkuk Meikle- wrath had communicated a part of his frenzy to all who heard him. The wiser, or more timid part of the assembly, were already withdraw- ing themselves from the field, and giving up their cause as lost. Others were moderating an harmonious call, as they somewhat improperly termed it, to new officers, and dismissing those formerly chosen, and that with a tumult and clamour worthy of the deficiency of good sense and good order implied in the whole transaction. It was at this moment when Morton arrived in the field, and found the army in total con- fusion, and on the point of dissolving itself. His arrival occasioned loud exclamations of applause on the one side, and of imprecation on the other.

"What means this ruinous disorder at such a moment?" he exclaimed to Burley, who, exhausted with his vain exertions to restore order, was now leaning on his sword, and regarding the confusion with an eye of resolute despair.

"It means," he replied, "that God has delivered us into the hands of our enemies."

"Not so," answered Morton, with a voice and gesture which com- pelled many to listen; "it is not God who deserts us, it is we who desert him, and dishonour ourselves by disgracing and betraying the cause of freedom and religion.—Hear me," he exclaimed, springing to the pulpit which Meiklewrath had been compelled to evacuate by actual exhaustion—"I bring from the enemy an offer to treat, if you incline to lay down your arms. I can insure you the means of making an honourable defence, if you are of more manly tempers. The time flies fast on. Let us resolve either for peace or war; and let it not be said of us in future days, that six thousand Scottish men in arms had neither courage to stand their ground and fight it out, nor prudence to treat for peace, nor even the coward's wisdom to retreat in good time and with safety. What signifies quarrelling on minute points of church-discipline, when the whole edifice is threatened with total destruction. O, remember, my brethren, that the last and worst evil which God brought upon the people whom he had once chosen—the last and worst punishment of their blindness and hardness of heart was the bloody dissensions which rent asunder their city, even when the enemy were thundering at its gates."

Some of the audience testified their feeling of this exhortation by loud exclamations of applause; others by hooting, and exclaiming,—"To your tents, O Israel!"

Morton, who beheld the columns of the enemy already beginning to appear on the right bank, and directing their march upon the bridge, raised his voice to its utmost pitch, and, pointing at the same time with his hand, exclaimed,—"Silence your senseless clamours, yonder is the enemy! On maintaining the bridge against him depend our lives, as well as our hope to reclaim our laws and liberties.—There shall at least one Scottishman die in their defence.—Let any who loves his country follow me!"

The multitude had turned their heads in the direction to which he pointed. The sight of the glittering files of the foot-guards, supported by several squadrons of horse, of the cannon which the artillery-men were busily engaged in planting against the bridge, and of the long succession of troops which were destined to support the attack, silenced at once their clamorous uproar, and struck them with as much consternation as if it were an unexpected apparition, and not the very thing which they ought to have been looking out for. They gazed on each other, and on their leaders, with looks resembling those that indicate the weakness of a patient when exhausted by a fit of frenzy. Yet when Morton, springing from the rostrum, directed his steps towards the bridge, he was followed by about an hundred of those young men who were particularly attached to his command.

Burley turned to Macbriar—"Ephraim," he said, "it is Providence points us the way, through the worldly wisdom of this latitudinarian youth.—He that loves the light, let him follow Burley!"

"Tarry," replied Macbriar; "it is not by Henry Morton, or such as he, that our goings-out and comings-in are to be meted; therefore tarry with us. I fear treachery to the host from this nullifidian Achan—Thou shalt not go with him. Thou art our chariots and our horsemen."

"Hinder me not," replied Burley; "he hath well said that all is lost, if the enemy win the bridge—therefore let me not—Shall the children of this generation be called wiser or braver than the children of the sanctuary?—Array yourselves under your leaders—let us not lack supplies of men and ammunition; and accursed be he who turneth back from the work on this great day!"

Having thus spoken, he hastily marched towards the bridge, and was followed by about two hundred of the most gallant and zealous of his party. There was a deep and disheartened pause when Morton and Burley departed. The commanders availed themselves of it to display their lines in some sort of order, and exhorted those who were most exposed to throw themselves upon their faces, to avoid the cannonade which they might presently expect. The insurgents ceased to resist or to remonstrate; but the awe which had silenced their discords had dismayed their courage. They suffered themselves to be formed into ranks with the docility of a flock of sheep, but without possessing, for the time, more resolution or energy; for they experienced a sinking of the heart, imposed by the sudden and imminent approach of danger, which they neglected to provide against while it was yet distant. They were, however, drawn out with some regularity; and as they still possessed the appearance of an army, their leaders had only to hope that some favourable circumstance would restore their spirit and courage.

Kettledrummle, Poundtext, Macbriar, and other preachers, busied themselves in their ranks, and prevailed on them to raise a psalm. But the superstitious among them observed, as an ill omen, that their song of praise and triumph sunk into "a quaver of consternation," and resembled rather a penitentiary stave sung on the scaffold of a condemned criminal, than the bold strain which had resounded along the wild heath of Loudoun-hill, in anticipation of that day's victory. The melancholy melody soon received a rough accompaniment, for the cannon began to fire on one side, and the musketry on both, and the bridge of Bothwell, with the banks adjacent, were involved in wreaths of smoke.

Chapter Two

As e'er ye saw the rain down fa',
    Or yet the arrow from the bow,
Sae our Scots lads fell even down,
    And they lay slain on every knowe.
                        Old Ballad

ERE Morton or Burley reached the post to be defended, the enemy
had commenced an attack upon it with great spirit. The two regiments
of Foot-Guards, formed into a close column, rushed forward to the
river, where one corps, deploying along the right bank, commenced a
galling fire on the defenders of the pass, while the other pressed on to
occupy the bridge. The insurgents sustained the attack with great
constancy and courage; and while one part of their number returned
the fire across the river, the rest maintained a discharge of musketry
upon the further end of the bridge itself, and every avenue by which
the soldiers endeavoured to approach it. The latter suffered severely,
but still gained ground, and the head of their column was already upon
the bridge, when the arrival of Morton changed the scene; and his
marksmen, commencing upon the pass a fire as well aimed as it was
sustained and regular, compelled the assailants to retire with much
loss. They were a second time brought up to the charge, and a second
time repulsed with still greater slaughter, as Burley had now brought
his party into action. The fire was continued with the utmost vehemence on both sides, and the issue of the action seemed very dubious.

Monmouth, mounted on a superb white charger, might be discovered on the top of the right bank of the river, urging, entreating,
and animating the exertions of his soldiers. By his orders, the
cannon, which had hitherto been employed in annoying the distant
main body of the presbyterians, were now turned upon the defenders
of the bridge. But these tremendous engines, being wrought much
more slowly than in modern times, did not produce the effect of
annoying or terrifying the enemy in the extent proposed. The insurgents, sheltered by copsewood along the bank of the river, or stationed in the houses already mentioned, fought under cover, while
the royalists, owing to the precautions of Morton, were entirely
exposed. The defence was so protracted and obstinate, that the royal
generals began to fear it might be ultimately successful. While Monmouth threw himself from his horse, and, rallying the Foot-Guards,
brought them on to another close and desperate attack, he was
warmly seconded by Dalzell, who, putting himself at the head of a

body of Lennox Highlanders, rushed forward with their tremendous war-cry of Loch-sloy. The ammunition of the defenders of the bridge began to fail at this important crisis; messages, commanding and imploring succours and supplies, were in vain dispatched, one after the other, to the main body of the presbyterian army, which remained inactively drawn up on the open field in the rear. Fear, consternation, and misrule, had gone abroad among them, and, while the post on which their safety depended required to be instantly and powerfully reinforced, there remained none either to command or to obey.

As the fire of the defenders of the bridge began to slacken, that of the assailants increased, and became more fatal. Animated by the example and exhortations of their generals, they obtained a footing upon the bridge itself, and began to remove the obstacles by which it was blockaded. The portal-gate was broken open, the beams, trunks of trees, and other materials of the barricade, pulled down and thrown into the river. This was not accomplished without opposition. Morton and Burley fought in the very front of their followers, and encouraged them with their pikes, halberts, and partisans, to encounter the bayonets of the Guards and the broadswords of the Highlanders. But those behind them began to shrink from the unequal combat, and fly singly, or in parties of two or three, towards the main body, until the remainder were, by the mere weight of the hostile column as much as by their weapons, fairly forced from the bridge. The passage being now open, the enemy began to pour over. But the bridge was long and narrow, which rendered the manœuvre slow as well as dangerous; and those who first passed had still to force the houses, from the windows of which the Covenanters continued to fire. Burley and Morton were near each other at this critical moment.

"There is yet time," said the former, "to bring down horse to attack them, ere they can get into order; and, with the aid of God, we may thus regain the bridge—hasten thou to bring them down, while I make the defence good with this old and wearied body."

Morton saw the importance of the advice, and, throwing himself on the horse which Cuddie held in readiness for him behind the thicket, galloped towards a body of cavalry which chanced to be composed entirely of Cameronians. Ere he could speak his errand, or utter his orders, he was saluted by the execrations of the whole body.

"He flies," they exclaimed—"the cowardly traitor flies like a hart from the hunters, and hath left valiant Burley in the midst of the slaughter!"

"I do not fly," said Morton. "I come to lead you to the attack.— Advance boldly, and we shall yet do well."

"Follow him not!—Follow him not!"—such were the tumultuous

exclamations which resounded from the ranks; "he hath sold you to the sword of the enemy."

And while Morton argued, entreated, and commanded in vain, the moment was lost in which their advance might have been useful; and the outlet from the bridge, with all its defences, being in complete possession of the enemy, Burley and his remaining followers were driven back upon the main body, to whom the spectacle of their hurried and harassed retreat was far from restoring the confidence which they so much wanted.

In the meanwhile, the forces of the King crossed the bridge at their leisure, and, securing the access, formed in line of battle; while Claverhouse, who, like a hawk perched on a rock, and eying the time to pounce on its prey, had watched the event of the action from the opposite bank, now passed the bridge at the head of his cavalry, at full trot, and, leading them in squadrons through the intervals and round the flanks of the royal infantry, formed them on the moor, and led them to the charge, advancing in front with one large body, while other two divisions threatened the flanks of the Covenanters. Their devoted army was now in that situation when the slightest demonstration towards an attack was certain to inspire panic. Their broken spirits and disheartened courage were unable to endure the charge of the cavalry, attended with all its terrible accompaniments of sight and sound;—the rush of the horses at full speed, the shaking of the earth under their feet, the glancing of the swords, the waving of the plumes, and the fierce shout of the cavaliers. The front ranks hardly attempted one ill-directed and disorderly fire, and their rear were broken and flying in confusion ere the charge had been completed; and in less than five minutes the horsemen were mixed with them, cutting and hewing without mercy. The voice of Claverhouse was heard, even above the din of conflict, exclaiming to his soldiers—"Kill, kill—no quarter—think on Richard Grahame!"—The dragoons, many of whom had shared the disgrace of Loudoun-hill, required no exhortations to vengeance as easy as it was complete. Their swords drank deep of slaughter among the unresisting fugitives. Screams for quarter were only answered by the shouts with which the pursuers accompanied their blows, and the whole field presented one general scene of confused slaughter, flight, and pursuit. About twelve hundred of the insurgents who remained in a body a little apart from the rest, and out of the line of the charge of cavalry, threw down their arms and surrendered at discretion, upon the approach of the Duke of Monmouth at the head of the infantry. That mild-tempered nobleman instantly allowed them the quarter which they prayed for; and, galloping about through the field, exerted himself as much to stop the slaughter as he had done to obtain the victory. While busied in this humane task he met with General Dalzell, who was encouraging the fierce Highlanders and royal volunteers to shew their zeal for King and country, by quenching the flame of the rebellion with the blood of the rebels.

"Sheathe your sword, I command you, General!" exclaimed the Duke, "and sound the retreat; enough of blood has been shed; give quarter to the King's misguided subjects."

"I obey your Grace," said the old man, wiping his bloody sword and returning it to the scabbard; "but I warn you, at the same time, that enough has *not* been done to intimidate these desperate rebels. Has not your Grace heard that Basil Olifant has collected several gentlemen and men of substance in the west, and is in the act of marching to join them?"

"Basil Olifant!" said the Duke, "who, or what, is he?"

"The next male heir to the last Earl of Torwood; he is disaffected to government from his claim to the estate being set aside in favour of Lady Margaret Bellenden; and I suppose the hope of getting the inheritance has set him in motion."

"Be his motives what they will," replied Monmouth, "he must soon disperse his followers, for this army is far too much broken to rally again. Therefore, once more, I command that the pursuit be stopped."

"It is your Grace's province to command, and to be responsible for your commands," answered Dalzell, as he gave reluctant orders for checking the pursuit.

But the fiery and vindictive Grahame was already far out of hearing of the signal of retreat, and continued with his cavalry an unwearied and bloody pursuit, breaking, dispersing, and cutting to pieces all the insurgents whom they could come up with.

Burley and Morton were both hurried off the field by the confused tide of fugitives. They made some attempt to defend the streets of Hamilton; but, while labouring to induce the flyers to face about and stand to their weapons, Burley received a bullet which broke his sword-arm.

"May the hand be withered that shot the shot!" he exclaimed, as the sword which he was waving over his head fell powerless to his side. "I can fight no longer."

Then turning his horse's head, he retreated out of the confusion. Morton too now saw that the continuing his unavailing efforts to rally the flyers could only end in his own death or captivity, and, followed by the faithful Cuddie, he extricated himself from the press, and, being well mounted, leaped his horse over one or two enclosures, and got into the open country.

From the first hill which they gained in their flight, they looked back, and beheld the whole country covered with their fugitive companions, and with the pursuing dragoons, whose wild shouts and halloo, as they did execution on the groups whom they overtook, mingled with the groans and screams of their victims, rose shrilly up the hill.

"It is impossible they can ever make head again," said Morton.

"The head's ta'en aff them as clean as I wad bite it aff a sybo," rejoined Cuddie. "Eh, lord! see how the broad-swords are flashing! —war's a fearsome thing—they will be cunning catches me at this wark again—but, for God's sake, sir, let us mak for some strength."

Morton saw the necessity of following the advice of his trusty squire. They resumed a rapid pace, and continued it without intermission, directing their course towards the wild and mountainous country, where they thought it likely some part of the fugitives might draw together for the sake either of making defence, or of obtaining terms.

Chapter Three

They require
Of Heaven the hearts of lions, breath of tigers,
Yea, and the fierceness too.
                              FLETCHER

EVENING had fallen; and, for the last two hours, they had seen none of their ill-fated companions, when Morton and his faithful attendant gained the moorland, and approached a large and solitary farmhouse, situated in the entrance of a wild and moorish glen, far remote from any other habitation.

"Our horses," said Morton, "will carry us no farther without rest or food, and we must try to obtain them here, if possible."

So speaking, he led the way to the house. The place had every appearance of being inhabited. There was smoke issuing from the chimney in a considerable volume, and the marks of recent hoofs were visible around the door. They could even hear the murmuring of human voices within the house. But all the lower windows were closely secured; and, when they knocked at the door, no answer was returned. After vainly calling and entreating admittance, they withdrew to the stable, or shed which served as such, in order to accommodate their horses, ere they used farther means of gaining admission. In this place they found ten or twelve horses, whose appearance of fatigue, as well as the military yet disordered appearance of their saddles and accoutrements, plainly indicated that their owners were fugitive insurgents in their own case.

"This meeting bodes gude luck," said Cuddie; "and they hae walth o' beef, that's ae thing certain, for here's a raw hide that has been about the hurdies o' a stot not half an hour syne—it's warm yet."

Encouraged by these appearances, they returned again to the house, and, announcing themselves as men in the same predicament with the inmates, clamoured loudly for admittance.

"Whoever ye be," answered a stern voice from the window, after long and obdurate silence, "disturb not those who mourn for the desolation and captivity of the land, and search out the causes of wrath and of defection, that the stumbling-blocks may be removed over which we have stumbled."

"They are wild western whigs," said Cuddie, in a whisper to his master, "I ken by their language. Fiend hae me if I like to venture on them."

Morton, however, again called to the party within, and insisted on admittance; but, finding his entreaties still disregarded, he opened one of the lower windows, and pushing asunder the shutters, which were but slightly secured, stepped into the large kitchen from which the voice had issued. Cuddie followed him, muttering betwixt his teeth, as he put his head within the window, "That he hoped there was nae scauding brose on the fire," and master and servant both found themselves in the company of ten or twelve armed men, seated around the fire on which refreshments were preparing, and busied apparently in their devotions.

In the gloomy countenances, illuminated by the fire-light, Morton had no difficulty in recognizing several of those zealots who had most distinguished themselves by their intemperate opposition to all moderate measures, together with their noted pastor, Ephraim Macbriar, and the maniac, Habakkuk Meiklewrath. The Cameronians neither stirred tongue nor hand to welcome their brethren in misfortune, but continued to listen to the low murmured exercise of Macbriar, as he prayed that the Almighty would lift up his hand from his people, and not make an end in the day of his anger. That they were conscious of the presence of the intruders only appeared from the sullen and indignant glances which they shot at them, from time to time, as their eyes encountered.

Morton, finding into what unfriendly society he had unwittingly intruded, began to think of retreating; but, on turning his head, observed with some alarm, that two strong men had silently placed themselves beside the window through which they had entered. One of these ominous centinels whispered to Cuddie, "Son of that precious woman, Mause Headrigg, do not cast thy lot farther with this child of treachery and perdition—Pass on thy way, and tarry not, for the avenger of blood is behind thee."

With this he pointed to the window, out of which Cuddie jumped without hesitation; for the intimation he had received plainly implied the personal danger he would otherwise incur.

"Winnocks are na lucky wi' me," was his first reflection when he was in the open air; his next was upon the probable fate of his master. "They'll kill him, the murdering loons, and think they're doing a gude turn; but I'se tak the road back for Hamilton, and see if I canna get some o' our ain folk to bring help in time of needcessity."

So saying, Cuddie hastened to the stable, and, taking the best horse he could find instead of his own tired animal, he galloped off in the direction he had proposed.

The noise of his horse's tread alarmed for an instant the devotion of the fanatics. As it died in the distance, Macbriar brought his exercise to a conclusion, and his audience raised themselves from the stooping posture, and louring downward look with which they had listened to it, and all fixed their eyes sternly on Henry Morton.

"You bend strange countenances on me, gentlemen," said he, addressing them. "I am totally ignorant in what manner I can have deserved them."

"Out upon thee! out upon thee!" exclaimed Meiklewrath, starting up; "the word that thou hast spurned shall become a rock to crush and to bruise thee; the spear which thou wouldst have broken shall pierce thy side; we have prayed, and wrestled, and petitioned, for an offering to atone the sins of the congregation, and, lo! the very head of the offence is delivered into our hand. He hath burst in like a thief through the window; he is a ram caught in the thicket, whose blood shall be a drink-offering to redeem vengeance from the church, and the place shall from henceforth be called Jehovah-Jirah, for the sacrifice is provided. Up then, and bind the victim with cords to the horns of the altar!"

There was a movement among the party; and deeply did Morton regret at that moment the incautious haste with which he had ventured into their company. He was armed only with his sword, for he had left his pistols at the bow of his saddle, whereas the whigs were all provided with fire-arms, and there was little or no chance of escaping from them by resistance. The interposition, however, of Macbriar protected him for the moment.

"Tarry yet a while, brethren—let us not use the sword rashly, lest the load of innocent blood lie heavy on us.—Come," he said, addressing himself to Morton, "we will reckon with thee ere we avenge the cause thou hast betrayed. Hast thou not," he continued, "made thy face hard as flint against the truth in all the assemblies of the host?"

"He has—he has," murmured the deep voices of the assistants— "he ever urged peace with the malignants," said one—"and pleaded for the dark and dismal guilt of the Indulgence," echoed another— "and would have surrendered the host into the hands of Monmouth," echoed a third, "and was the first to desert the honest and manly Burley, while he yet resisted at the pass. I saw him on the moor, with his horse bloody with spurring, long ere the firing had ceased at the bridge."

"Gentlemen," said Morton, "if you mean to bear me down by clamour, and take my life without hearing me, it is perhaps a thing in your power; but you will sin before God and man by the commission of such a murder."

"I say, hear the youth," said Macbriar, "for Heaven knows our bowels have yearned for him, that he might be brought to see the light, and exert his gifts in its defence. But he is blinded by his carnal knowledge, and has spurned the light when it blazed before him."

Silence being obtained, Morton proceeded to assert the good faith which he had displayed in the treaty with Monmouth, and the active part he had borne in the subsequent action.

"I may not, gentlemen," he said, "be fully able to go the lengths you desire, in assigning to those of my own religion the means of tyrannizing others; but none shall go farther in asserting our own lawful freedom. And I must needs aver, that had others been of my mind in counsel, or disposed to stand by my side in battle, we should this evening, instead of being a defeated and discordant remnant, have sheathed our weapons in an useful and honourable peace, or brandished them triumphantly after a decisive victory."

"He hath spoken the word," said one of the assembly—"he hath avowed his carnal self-seeking and Erastianism; let him die the death!"

"Peace yet again," said Macbriar, "for I will try him further.—Was it not by thy means that the malignant Evandale twice escaped from death and captivity? Was it not through thee that Miles Bellenden and his garrison of cut-throats were saved from the edge of the sword?"

"I am proud to say, that you have said the truth in both instances," replied Morton.

"Lo you," said Macbriar, "again hath his mouth spoken it—And didst thou not do thus for the sake of a Midianitish woman, one of the spawn of prelacy, a toy with which the arch-enemy's trap is baited?

Didst thou not do all this for the sake of Edith Bellenden?"

"You are incapable," answered Morton, boldly, "of appreciating my feelings towards that young lady; but all that I have done I would have done had she never existed."

"Thou art a hardy rebel to the truth—And didst thou not so act, that, by conveying away the aged woman, Margaret Bellenden, and her grand-daughter, thou mightest thwart the wise and godly project of John Balfour of Burley for bringing forth to battle the worldly Basil Olifant, who agreed to take the field if he were insured possession of Edith Bellenden's person and property?"

"I never heard of such a scheme," said Morton, "and therefore I could not thwart it—But does your religion permit you to take such uncreditable and immoral modes of recruiting?"

"Peace," said Macbriar, somewhat disconcerted; "it is not for thee to instruct tender professors, or to construe Covenant obligations; for the rest, you have acknowledged enough of sin and sorrowful defection to draw down defeat on a host were it as numerous as the sands on the sea-shore. And it is our judgment, that we are not free to let you pass from us safe and in life, since Providence hath given you into our hands at the moment that we prayed with godly Joshua, saying, What shall we say when Israel turneth their backs before their enemies?— Then camest thou, delivered to us as it were by lot, that thou mightest sustain the punishment of one that hath wrought folly in Israel. Therefore, mark my words. This is the Sabbath, and our hand shall not be on thee to spill thy blood upon this day. But, when the twelfth hour shall strike, it is a token that thy time on earth hath run! Wherefore improve thy span, for it flitteth fast away.—Seize on the prisoner, brethren, and take his weapon from him."

The command was so unexpectedly given, and so suddenly executed by those of the party who had gradually closed behind and around Morton, that he was overpowered and disarmed before he could offer any effectual resistance. When this was accomplished, a dead and stern silence took place. The fanatics ranked themselves around a large oaken table, placing Morton amongst them, in such a manner as to be opposite to the clock which was to strike his knell. Food was placed before them, of which they offered their intended victim a share; but, it will readily be believed, he had little appetite. When this was removed, the party resumed their devotions, Macbriar expostulating in prayer, as if to wring from the Deity a signal that the bloody sacrifice they proposed was an acceptable service. The eyes and ears of his hearers were anxiously strained, as if to gain some sight or sound which might be converted or wrested into a type of approbation, and ever and anon dark looks were turned on the dial plate of the time-piece, to watch its progress towards the moment of execution.

Morton's eye frequently took the same course, with the sad reflection, that there appeared no possibility of his life being expanded beyond the narrow segment which the index had yet to travel on the circle until it arrived at the fatal hour. Faith in his religion, with a constant unyielding principle of honour, and the sense of conscious innocence, enabled him to pass through this dreadful interval with less agitation than he himself could have expected, had the situation been prophesied to him. Yet there was a want of that eager and animating sense of right which supported him in similar circumstances, when in the power of Claverhouse. Then he was conscious, that, amid the spectators, were many who were lamenting his condition, and some who applauded his conduct. But now, among these pale-eyed and ferocious zealots, whose hardened brows were soon to be bent, not merely with indifference, but with triumph, upon his execution,—without a friend to speak a kindly word, or give a look either of sympathy or encouragement,—awaiting till the sword destined to slay him crept out of the scabbard gradually, and as it were by straw-breadths, and condemned to drink the bitterness of death drop by drop,—it is no wonder that his feelings were less composed than they had been on any former occasion of danger. His destined executioners, as he gazed around on them, seemed to alter their forms and features, like the spectres in a feverish dream; their figures became larger, and their faces more distorted; and, as an excited imagination predominated over the realities which his eyes received, he seemed surrounded rather by a band of demons than of human beings; the walls seemed to drip with blood, and the light tick of the clock thrilled on his ear with such loud, painful distinctness, as if each sound were the prick of a bodkin inflicted on the naked nerve.

It was with pain that he felt his mind wavering when on the brink between this and the future world. He made a strong effort to compose himself to devotional exercises, and unequal, during that fearful strife of nature, to arrange his own thoughts into suitable expressions, he had, instinctively, recourse to the petition for deliverance and for composure of spirit which is to be found in the Book of Common Prayer of the Church of England. Macbriar, whose family were of that persuasion, instantly recognized the words which the unfortunate prisoner pronounced half aloud.

"There lacked but this," said he, his pale cheek kindling with resentment, "to root out my carnal reluctance to see his blood spilt. He is a prelatist who has sought the camp under the disguise of an Erastian, and all, and more than all, that has been said of him, must needs be verity. His blood be on his head, the deceiver,—let him go down to Tophet with the ill-mumbled mass which he calls a prayer-book in his right hand."

"I take up my song against him!" exclaimed the maniac. "As the sun went back on the dial ten degrees for intimating the recovery of holy Hezekiah, so shall it now go forwards, that the wicked may be taken away from among the people, and the Covenant established in its purity."

He jumped on a chair with an attitude of frenzy, in order to anticipate the fatal moment by putting the index forward; and several of the party began to make ready their weapons for immediate execution, when Meiklewrath's hand was arrested by one of his companions.

"Hist!" he said,—"I hear a distant noise."

"It is the rushing of the brook over the pebbles," said one.

"It is the sough of the wind among the bracken," said another.

"It is the gallopping of horse," said Morton to himself, his sense of hearing rendered acute by the dreadful situation in which he stood; "God grant they may come as my deliverers!"

The noise approached rapidly, and became more and more distinct.

"It is horse," cried Macbriar. "Look out and descry who they are."

"The enemy are upon us," cried one who had opened the window, in obedience to his order.

A thick trampling and loud voices were heard immediately round the house. Some rose to resist, and some to escape; the doors and windows were forced at once, and the red coats of the troopers appeared in the apartment.

"Have at the bloody rebels!—Remember Cornet Grahame!" was shouted on every side.

The lights were struck down, but the dubious glare of the fire enabled them to continue the fray. Several pistol-shots were fired; the whig next to Morton received a shot as he was rising, stumbled against the prisoner, whom he bore down with his weight, and lay stretched above him a dying man. This accident probably saved Morton from the damage he might otherwise have received in so close a struggle, where fire-arms were discharged and sword-blows given for upwards of five minutes.

"Is their prisoner safe?" said the well-known voice of Claverhouse; "look about for him—and dispatch the dog who is groaning there."

Both orders were executed. The groans of the wounded man were silenced by a thrust with a rapier, and Morton, disencumbered of his weight, was speedily raised and in the arms of the faithful Cuddie, who blubbered for joy when he found that the blood with which his master was covered had not flowed from his own veins. A whisper in

Morton's ear explained the secret of the very timely appearance of the soldiers.

"I fell into Claverhouse's party when I was seeking for some o' our ain folk to help ye out o' the hands o' the whigs; sae being atween the de'il and the deep sea, I e'en though it best to bring him on wi' me, for he'll be wearied wi' felling folk the night, an' the morn's a new day, and Lord Evandale awes ye a day in ha'arst; and Monmouth gi'es quarter, the dragoons tell me, for the asking. Sae haud up your heart, an' we'll do a' weel aneugh yet."

Chapter Four

Sound, sound the clarion, fill the fife,
To all the sensual world proclaim,
One crowded hour of glorious life
Is worth an age without a name.
Anonymous

WHEN the desperate affray had ceased, Claverhouse commanded his soldiers to remove the dead bodies, to refresh themselves and their horses, and prepare for passing the night at the farm-house, and for marching early in the ensuing morning. He then turned his attention to Morton, and there was politeness, and even kindness, in the manner in which he addressed him.

"You would have saved yourself risk from both sides, Mr Morton, if you had honoured my counsel yesterday morning with some attention; but I respect your motives. You are a prisoner-of-war at the disposal of the King and Council, but you shall be treated with no incivility; and I will be satisfied with your parole that you will not attempt an escape."

When Morton had passed his word to that effect, Claverhouse bowed civilly, and, turning away from him, called for his serjeant-major.

"How many prisoners, Halliday, and how many killed?"

"Three killed in the house, sir, two cut down in the court, and one in the garden—six in all; four prisoners."

"Armed or unarmed?" said Claverhouse.

"Three of them armed to the teeth," answered Halliday; "one without arms—he seems to be a preacher."

"Ay—the trumpeter to the long-ear'd route, I suppose," replied Claverhouse, glancing slightly round upon his victims, "I will talk with him to-morrow. Take the other three down to the yard, draw out two files, and fire upon them; and, d'ye hear, make a memorandum in the orderly-book of Three rebels taken in arms and shot—with the date and name of the place. Drumshinnel, I think, they call it—Look after the preacher till to-morrow; as he was not armed, he must undergo a short examination. Or better, perhaps, take him before the Council; I think they should relieve me of a share of this disgusting drudgery.— Let Mr Morton be civilly used, and see that the men look well after their horses, and let my groom wash Wildblood's back with some vinegar, the saddle has touched him a little."

All these various orders,—for life and death, the securing of his prisoners, and the washing his charger's shoulder,—were given in the same unmoved and equable voice, of which no accent or tone intimated that the speaker considered one direction as of more importance than another.

The Cameronians, so lately about to be the willing agents of a bloody execution, were now themselves to undergo it. They seemed prepared alike for either extremity, nor did any of them shew the least sign of fear, when ordered to leave the room for the purpose of meeting instant death. Their severe enthusiasm sustained them in that dreadful moment, and they departed with a firm look and in silence, excepting that one of them, as he left the apartment, looked Claverhouse full in the face, and pronounced, with a stern and steady voice,—"Mischief shall hunt the violent man;" to which Grahame only answered by a smile of contempt.

They had no sooner left the room than Claverhouse applied himself to some food, which one or two of his party had hastily provided, and invited Morton to follow his example, observing, it had been a busy day for them both. Morton declined eating; for the sudden change of circumstances—the transition from the verge of the grave to a prospect of life, had occasioned a dizzy revulsion in his whole system. But the same confused sensation was accompanied by a burning thirst, and he expressed his wish to drink.

"I will pledge you, with all my heart," said Claverhouse; "for here is a black jack full of ale, and good it must be, if there be good in the country, for the whigs never miss to find it out.—My service to you, Mr Morton," he said, filling one horn of ale for himself and handing another to his prisoner.

Morton raised it to his head, and was just about to drink, when the discharge of carabines beneath the window, followed by a deep and hollow groan, repeated twice or thrice, and more faint at each interval, announced the fate of the three men who had just left them. Morton shuddered and set down the untasted cup.

"You are yet but young in these matters, Mr Morton," said Claverhouse, after he had very composedly finished his draught; "and I do not think the worse of you as a young soldier for appearing to feel them acutely. But habit, duty, and necessity, reconcile men to every thing."

"I trust," said Morton, "they will never reconcile me to such scenes as these."

"You would hardly believe," said Claverhouse in reply, "that, in the beginning of my military career, I had as much pain in seeing blood spilled as ever man felt—it seemed to me to be wrung from my own heart; and yet, if you trust one of these whig fellows, he will tell you I drink a warm cup of it every morning before I breakfast. But, in truth, Mr Morton, why should we care so much for death, light around us wherever it may? Men die daily—not a bell tolls the hour but it is the death-note of some one or other, and why hesitate to shorten the span of others, or take over-anxious care to prolong our own? It is all a lottery—when the hour of midnight came you were to die—it has struck—you are alive and safe, and the lot has fallen on these fellows who were to murder you.—It is not the expiring pang that is worth thinking of in an event that must happen one day, and may befal us on any given moment—it is the memory which the soldier leaves behind him, like the long train of light that follows the sunken sun—that is all which is worth caring for, which distinguishes the death of the brave or the ignoble. When I think of death, Mr Morton, as a thing worth thinking of, it is in the hope of pressing one day some well-fought and hard-won field of battle, and dying with the shout of victory in my ear —*that* would be worth dying for, and more, it would be worth having lived for!"

At the moment when Grahame delivered these sentiments, his eye glancing with the martial enthusiasm which formed such a prominent feature in his character, a gory figure, which seemed to rise out of the floor of the apartment, stood upright before him, and presented the wild person and hideous features of the maniac so often mentioned. His face, where it was not covered with blood streaks, was ghastly pale, for the hand of death was on him. He bent upon Claverhouse eyes, in which the grey light of insanity still twinkled, though just about to flit for ever, and exclaimed with his usual wildness of ejaculation, "Wilt thou trust in thy bow and in thy spear, in thy steed and in thy banner? And shall not God visit for innocent blood?—Wilt thou glory in thy wisdom, and in thy courage, and in thy might? And shall not the Lord judge thee?—Behold the princes, for whom thou hast sold thy soul to the destroyer, shall be removed from their place, and banished to other lands, and their names shall be a desolation, and an astonishment, and a hissing, and a curse. And thou, who hast partaken of the wine-cup of fury, and hast been drunken and mad because thereof, the wish of thy heart shall be granted to thy loss, and the hope of thine own pride shall destroy thee. I summon thee, John Grahame, to appear before the tribunal of God, to answer for this innocent blood, and the seas besides which thou hast shed."

He drew his right hand across his bleeding face, and held it up to Heaven as he uttered these words, which he spoke very loud, and then added more faintly, "How long, O Lord, holy and true, doest thou not judge and avenge the blood of thy saints?"

As he uttered the last word he fell backwards without an attempt to save himself, and was a dead man ere his head touched the floor.

Morton was much shocked at this extraordinary scene, and the prophecy of the dying man, which tallied so strangely with the wish which Claverhouse had just expressed. Two of the dragoons who were in the apartment, hardened as they were, and accustomed to such scenes, showed great consternation at the sudden apparition, the event, and the words which preceded it. Claverhouse alone was unmoved. At the first instant of Meiklewrath's appearance, he had put his hand to his pistol, but on seeing the situation of the wounded wretch, he immediately withdrew it, and listened with great composure to his dying exclamation.

When he dropped, Claverhouse asked, in an unconcerned tone of voice—"How came the fellow here?—Speak, you staring fool," he added, addressing the nearest dragoon, "unless you would have me think you such a poltroon as to fear a dying man."

The dragoon crossed himself, and replied with a faultering voice,— "That he had escaped their notice when they removed the other bodies, as he chanced to have fallen where a cloak or two had been flung aside, and covered him."

"Take him away now, then, you gaping idiots, and see that he does not bite you, to put an old proverb to shame.—This is a new incident, Mr Morton, that dead men should rise and push us from our stools. I must see that my blackguards grind their swords sharper; they used not to do their work so slovenly.—But we have had a busy day; they are tired with their bloody work, and I suppose you, Mr Morton, as well as I, are well disposed for a few hours repose."

So saying, he yawned, and taking a candle which a soldier had placed ready, saluted Morton courteously, and walked to the apartment which had been prepared for him.

Morton was also accommodated, for the evening, with a separate room. Being left alone, his first occupation was the returning thanks to Heaven for redeeming him from danger, even through the instrumentality of those who seemed his most dangerous enemies; he also prayed sincerely for the Divine assistance in guiding his course through times which held forth so many dangers and so many errors.

And having thus poured forth his spirit in prayer before the Great Being who gave it, he betook himself to the repose which he so much required.

Chapter Five

The charge is prepared, the lawyers are met,
The judges all ranged—a terrible show!
Beggar's Opera

SO DEEP was the slumber which succeeded the agitation and embarrassment of the preceding day, that Morton hardly knew where he was when it was broken by the stamp of horses, the hoarse voices of men, and the wild sound of the trumpets blowing the reveillie. The serjeant-major immediately afterwards came to summon him, which he did in a very respectful manner, saying the General (for Claverhouse now held that rank) hoped for the pleasure of his company upon the road. In some situations an intimation is a command, and Morton considered that the present occasion was one of these. He waited upon Claverhouse as speedily as he could, found his own horse saddled for his use, and Cuddie in attendance. Both however were disarmed of their fire-arms, though they seemed, otherwise, rather to make part of the troop than of the prisoners; and Morton was permitted to retain his sword, the wearing which was, in these days, the distinguishing mark of a gentleman. Claverhouse seemed also to take pleasure in riding beside him, in conversing with him, and in confounding his ideas when he attempted to appreciate his real character. The gentleness and urbanity of his general manners, the high and chivalrous sentiments of military devotion which he occasionally expressed, his deep and accurate insight into the human bosom, demanded at once the approbation and the wonder of those who conversed with him; while, on the other hand, his cold indifference to military violence and cruelty seemed altogether inconsistent with the social, and even admirable qualities which he displayed. Morton could not help, in his heart, contrasting him with Balfour of Burley; and so deeply did the idea impress him, that he dropped a hint of it as they rode together at some distance from the troop.

"You are right," said Claverhouse, with a smile; "you are very right —we are both fanatics; but there is some distinction between the fanaticism of honour and that of dark and sullen superstition."

"Yet you both shed blood without mercy or remorse," said Morton, who could not suppress his feelings.

"Surely," said Claverhouse, with the same composure; "but of what kind?—There is a difference, I trust, between the blood of learned and reverend prelates and scholars, of gallant soldiers and noble gentlemen, and the red puddle that stagnates in the veins of psalm-singing mechanics, crack-brained demagogues, and sullen boors;—some distinction, in short, between spilling a flask of generous wine and dashing down a cann-ful of base muddy ale."

"Your distinction is too nice for my comprehension," replied Morton. "God gives every spark of life—that of the peasant as well as the prince; and those who destroy his work recklessly or causelessly, must answer in either case. What right, for example, have I to General Grahame's protection now, more than when I first met him?"

"And narrowly escaped the consequences, as you would say," answered Claverhouse—"why, I will answer you frankly. Then I thought I had to do with the son of an old round-head Colonel, and the nephew of a sordid presbyterian laird; now I know your points better, and there is that about you which I respect in an enemy as much as I like in a friend. I have learned a good deal concerning you since our first meeting, and I trust you have found that my construction has not been unfavourable."

"But yet," said Morton——

"But yet," interrupted Grahame, taking up the word, "you would say you were the same when I first met you that you are now? True; but then, how could I know that? though, by the by, even my reluctance to suspend your execution may shew you how high your abilities stood in my estimation."

"Do you expect, General," said Morton, "that I ought to be particularly grateful for such a mark of your esteem?"

"Pooh! pooh! you are critical," returned Claverhouse. "I tell you I thought you a different sort of person. Did you ever read Froissart?"

"No," was Morton's answer.

"I have half a mind," said Claverhouse, "to contrive you should have six months' imprisonment to procure you that pleasure. His chapters inspire me with more enthusiasm than even poetry itself. And the noble canon, with what true chivalrous feeling he confines his beautiful expressions of sorrow to the death of the gallant and high-bred knight, of whom it was a pity to see the fall, such was his loyalty to his king, pure faith to his religion, hardihood towards his enemy, and fidelity to his ladye-love!—Ah benedicite! how he will mourn over the fall of such a pearl of knighthood, be it on the side he happens to favour, or on the other. But, truly, for sweeping from the face of the earth some few hundred of villain churles, who are born but to plough it, the high-born and inquisitive historian has marvellous little sympathy—as little, or less, perhaps, than John Grahame of Claverhouse."

"There is one ploughman in your possession, General, for whom," said Morton, "in despite of the contempt in which you hold a profession which some philosophers have considered as useful as that of a soldier, I would humbly request your favour."

"You mean," said Claverhouse, looking at a memorandum-book, "one Hatherick—Hedderick—or—or Headrigg. Ay, Cuthbert, or Cuddie Headrigg—here I have him.—O, never fear him, if he will be but tractable. The ladies of Tillietudlem made interest with me on his account some time ago. He is to marry their waiting-maid, I think. He will be allowed to slip off easy, unless his obstinacy spoils his good fortune."

"He has no ambition to be a martyr, I believe," said Morton.

"'Tis the better for him," said Claverhouse. "But, besides, although the fellow had more to answer for, I should stand his friend, for the sake of the blundering gallantry which threw him into the midst of our ranks last night, when seeking assistance for you. I never desert any man who trusts me with such implicit confidence. But, to deal sincerely with you, he has been long in our eye.—Here, Halliday; bring me up the black-book."

The serjeant, having committed to his commander this ominous record of the disaffected, which was arranged in alphabetical order, Claverhouse, turning over the leaves as he rode on, began to read names as they occurred.

'Gumblegumption, a minister, aged 50, indulged, close, sly, and so forth—Pooh! pooh!—H—H—I have him here—Heathercat; outlawed—a preacher—a zealous Cameronian—Keeps a conventicle among the Campsie hills—Tush!—O, here is Headrigg—Cuthbert; his mother a bitter puritan—himself a simple fellow—like to be forward in action, but of no genius for plots—more for the hand than the head, and might be drawn to the right side, but for his attachment to'——(Here Claverhouse looked at Morton, and then shut the book and changed his tone.) "Faithful and true are words never thrown away upon me, Mr Morton. You may depend on the young man's safety."

"Does it not revolt a mind like yours," said Morton, "to follow a system which is to be supported by such minute enquiries after obscure individuals?"

"You do not suppose *we* take the trouble?" said the General haughtily. "The curates, for their own sakes, willingly collect all these materials for our regulation in each parish; they know best the black sheep of the flock. I have had your picture for three years."

"Indeed?" replied Morton. "Will you favour me by imparting it?"

"Willingly," said Claverhouse; "it can signify little, for you cannot avenge yourself on the curate, as you will probably leave Scotland for some time."

This was spoken in an indifferent tone. Morton felt an involuntary shudder at hearing words which implied a banishment from his native land, but ere he answered, Claverhouse proceeded to read, 'Henry Morton, son of Silas Morton, Colonel of horse for the Scottish parliament, and nephew of Morton of Milnewood—imperfectly educated, but with spirit beyond his years—excellent at all exercises—indifferent to forms of religion, but seems to incline to the presbyterian—has high-flown and dangerous notions about liberty of thought and speech, and hovers between a latitudinarian and an enthusiast. Much admired and followed by the youth of his own age—modest, quiet, and unassuming in manner, but in his heart peculiarly bold and intractable. He is'——"Here follow three red crosses, Mr Morton, which signify triply dangerous. You see how important a person you are.—But what does this fellow want?"

A horseman rode up as he spoke, and gave a letter. Claverhouse glanced it over, laughed scornfully, bade him tell his master to send his prisoners to Edinburgh, for there was no answer; and, as the man turned back, said contemptuously to Morton—"Here is an ally of yours deserted from you, or rather, I should say, an ally of your good friend Burley—Hear how he sets forth—'*Dear Sir*,' (I wonder when we were such intimates,) 'may it please you, Excellency, to accept my humble congratulations on the victory'—hum—hum—'blessed his Majesty's army. I pray you to understand I have my people under arms to take and intercept all fugitives, and have already several prisoners,' and so forth. Subscribed Basil Olifant—You know the fellow by name, I suppose?"

"A relative of Lady Margaret Bellenden, is he not?"

"Ay," replied Grahame, "and heir male of her father's family, though a distant one, and moreover a suitor to the fair Edith, though discarded as an unworthy one; but, above all, an admirer of the estate of Tillietudlem, and all thereunto belonging."

"He takes an ill mode of recommending himself," said Morton, suppressing his own feelings, "to the family at Tillietudlem by corresponding with our unhappy party."

"O, this precious Basil shall turn cat in pan with any man! He was displeased with the government, because they would not overturn in his favour a settlement of the late Earl of Torwood which gave his own estate to his own daughter; he was displeased with Lady Margaret because she shewed no desire for his alliance, and with the pretty Edith, because she did not like his tall ungainly person. So he held a close correspondence with Burley, and raised his men with the purpose of helping him, if he needed no help, that is, if you had beat us yesterday—And now the rascal pretends he was all the while proposing the King's service, and, for aught I know, the Council will receive his pretext for current coin, for he knows how to make friends among them. And a dozen scores of poor vagabond fanatics will be shot, or hung, while this cunning scoundrel lies snug under his double cloak of loyalty, well lined with the fox-fur of hypocrisy."

With conversation on this and other matters they beguiled the way, Claverhouse all the while speaking with great frankness to Morton, and treating him rather as a friend and companion than as a prisoner; so that, however uncertain of his fate, the hours he passed in the company of this remarkable man were so much lightened by the varied play of his imagination, and the depth of his knowledge of human nature, that since the period of his becoming a prisoner of war, which relieved him at once from the cares of his doubtful and dangerous station among the insurgents, and from the consequences of their suspicious resentment, his hours flowed on less anxiously than at any time since his having commenced actor in public life. He was now, with respect to his fortune, like a rider who has flung his reins on the horse's neck, and, while he abandoned himself to circumstances, was at least relieved from the task of attempting to direct them. In this mood he journeyed on, the number of his companions being continually augmented by detached parties of horse who came in from every quarter of the country, bringing with them, for the most part, the unfortunate prisoners who had fallen into their power. At length they approached Edinburgh.

"Our Council," said Claverhouse, "being resolved, I suppose, to testify, by their present exultation, the extent of their former terror, have decreed a kind of triumphal entry to us victors and our captives; but as I do not quite approve the taste of it, I am willing to avoid my own part in the shew, and, at the same time, to save you from yours."

So saying, he gave up the command of the forces to Allan, (now a Lieutenant-colonel,) and, turning his horse into a by-lane, rode into the city privately, accompanied by Morton and two or three servants. When Claverhouse arrived at the quarters which he usually occupied in the Canongate, he assigned to his prisoner a small apartment, with an intimation, that his parole confined him to it for the present.

After about a quarter of an hour spent in solitary musing on the strange vicissitudes of his late life, the attention of Morton was summoned to the window by a great noise in the street beneath. Trumpets, drums, and kettle-drums, contended in noise with the shouts of a numerous rabble, and apprised him that the royal cavalry were passing in the triumphal attitude which Claverhouse had mentioned.

The magistrates of the city, attended by their guards with halberts, had met the victors with their welcome, at the gate of the city, and now preceded them as a part of the procession. The next object was two heads borne upon pikes; and before each bloody head were carried the hands of the dismembered sufferers, which were, by the brutal mockery of those who bore them, often approached towards each other as if in the attitude of exhortation or prayer. These bloody trophies belonged to two preachers who had fallen at Bothwell Bridge. After them came a cart led by the executioner's assistant, in which were placed Macbriar, and other two prisoners, who seemed of the same profession. They were bareheaded, and strongly bound, yet looked around them with an air rather of triumph than dismay, and appeared in no respect moved either by the fate of their companions, of which the bloody evidences were carried before them, or by dread of their own approaching execution, which these preliminaries so plainly indicated.

Behind these prisoners, thus held up to public infamy and derision, came a body of horse, brandishing their broadswords, and filling the wide street with acclamations, which were answered by the tumultuous outcries and huzzas of the rabble, who, in every considerable town, are too happy in being permitted to huzza for any thing whatsoever which calls them together. In the rear of these troopers came the main body of the prisoners, at the head of whom were some of their leaders, who were treated with every circumstance of inventive mockery and insult. Several were placed on horseback with their faces to the animal's tail; others were chained to long bars of iron, which they were obliged to support in their hands, like the galley-slaves in Spain when travelling to the port where they are to be put on shipboard. The heads of others who had fallen were borne in triumph before the survivors, some on pikes and halberts, some in sacks, bearing the name of the slaughtered person labelled on the outside. Such were the objects which headed the ghastly procession, who seemed as effectually doomed to death as if they wore the *sanbenitos* of the condemned heretics in an *auto-da-fe*.

Behind them came on the nameless crowd to the number of several hundreds, some retaining under their misfortunes a sense of confidence in the cause for which they suffered captivity, and were about to give a still more bloody testimony; others seemed pale, dispirited, dejected, questioning in their own minds their prudence in espousing a cause which Providence seemed to have disowned, and looking about for some avenue through which they might escape from the consequences of their rashness. Others there were who seemed incapable of forming an opinion on the subject, or of entertaining either hope, confidence, or fear, but who, foaming with thirst and fatigue, stumbled along like over-driven oxen, lost to every thing but their present sense of wretchedness, and without having any distinct idea whether they were driven to the shambles or to the pasture. These unfortunate men were guarded on each hand by troopers, and behind them came the main body of the cavalry, whose military music was resounded back from the high houses on each side of the street, and mingled with their own songs of jubilee and triumph, and the wild shouts of the rabble.

Morton felt himself heart-sick while he gazed on this dismal spectacle, and recognized in the bloody heads and still more miserable and agonized features of the living sufferers, faces which had been familiar to him during the brief insurrection. He sunk down upon a chair in a bewildered and stupified state, from which he was awakened by the voice of Cuddie.

"Lord forgi'e us, sir!" said the poor fellow, his teeth chattering like a pair of nut-crackers, his hair erect like boar's bristles, and his face as pale as that of a corpse—"Lord forgi'e us, sir! we maun instantly gang before the Council—O, Lord, what needed them send for a puir bodie like me, sae mony braw lords and gentles!—and there's my mother come on the tramp frae Glasgow to see to gar me testify, as she ca's it, that is to say, confess and be hanged; but de'il tak me if they mak sic a goose o' Cuddie, if I can do better. But here's Claverhouse himsel—the Lord preserve and forgi'e us, I say anes mair!"

"You must immediately attend the Council, Mr Morton," said Claverhouse, who entered while Cuddie spoke, "and your servant must go with you. You need be under no apprehension for the consequences to yourself personally. But I warn you that you will see something that will give you much pain, and from which I would willingly have saved you, if I had possessed the power. My carriage waits us—shall we go?"

It will be readily supposed that Morton did not venture to dispute this invitation however unpleasant. He rose and accompanied Claverhouse.

"I must apprise you," said the latter, as he led the way down stairs, "that you will get off cheap, and so will your servant, providing he can keep his tongue quiet."

Cuddie caught these last words to his exceeding joy.

"De'il a fear o' me," said he, "an' my mother doesna pit her finger in the pye."

At that moment his shoulder was seized by old Mause, who had contrived to thrust herself forward into the lobby of the apartments.

"O, hinny, hinny!" said she to Cuddie, hanging upon his neck, "glad and proud, and sorry and humbled am I, a' in ane and the saame instant, to see my bairn ganging to testifee for the truth gloriously with his mouth in council, as he did with his weapon in the field."

"Whisht, whisht, mother," cried Cuddie impatiently. "Odd, ye daft wife, is this a time to speak o' thae things?—I tell ye I'll testifee naething either ae gate or anither. I hae spoken to Mr Poundtext, and I'll tak the declaration, or whate'er they ca' it, and we're a' to win free off if we do that—he's gotten life for himsel and a' his folk, and that's a minister for my siller; I like nane o' your sermons that end in a psalm at the Grassmarket."

"O, Cuddie, man, laith wad I be they suld hurt ye," said old Mause, divided grievously between the safety of her son's soul and that of his body; "but mind, my bonny bairn, ye hae battled for the faith, and dinna let the dread o' losing creature-comforts withdraw ye frae the gude fight."

"Hout tout, mither," replied Cuddie, "I hae fought e'en ower muckle already, and, to speak plain, I'm wearied o' the trade. I hae swaggered wi' a' thae arms, and musquets, and pistols, buff-coats, and bandaliers, lang eneugh, and I like the pleugh-paidle a hantle deal better. I ken naething suld gar a man fight, (that's to say, when he's no angry,) by and out-taken the dread o' being hanged, or killed if he turns back."

"But, my dear Cuddie," continued the persevering Mause, "your bridal garment—Oh, hinny, dinna sully the marriage garment!"

"Awa', awa', mither," replied Cuddie; "dinna ye see the folks waiting for me?—Never fear me—I ken how to turn this far better than ye do—for ye're bleezing awa' about marriage, and the job is how we are to win by hanging."

So saying, he extricated himself out of his mother's embraces, and requested the soldiers who took him in charge to conduct him to the place of examination without delay. He had been already preceded by Claverhouse and Morton.

Chapter Six

My native land, good night.
LORD BYRON

THE PRIVY COUNCIL of Scotland, in whom the practice since the union of the crowns vested great judicial powers, as well as the general superintendence of the executive department, was met in an ancient, dark, Gothic room, adjoining to the House of Parliament in Edinburgh, when General Grahame entered and took his place amongst them at the council table.

"You have brought us a leash of game to-day, General," said a nobleman of high place amongst them. "Here is a craven to confess— a cock of the game to stand at bay—and what shall I call the third, General?"

"Without further metaphor, I will entreat your Grace to call him a person in whom I am specially interested," replied Claverhouse.

"And a whig into the bargain," said the nobleman, lolling out a tongue which was at all times too big for his mouth, and accommodating his coarse features to a sneer, to which they seemed to be familiar.

"Yes, please your Grace, a whig, as your Grace was in 1641," replied Claverhouse, with his usual appearance of imperturbable civility.

"He has you there, I think, my Lord Duke," said one of the Privy Counsellors.

"Ay, ay," returned the Duke, laughing, "there's no speaking to him since Drumclog—but come bring in the prisoners—and do you, Mr Clerk, read the record."

The clerk read forth a bond, in which General Grahame of Claverhouse and Lord Evandale entered themselves securities, that Henry Morton, younger of Milnewood, should go abroad and remain in foreign parts, until his Majesty's pleasure was further known, in respect of the said Henry Morton's accession to the late rebellion, and that under penalty of life and limb to the said Henry Morton, and of ten thousand marks to each of his sureties.

"Do you accept of the King's mercy upon these terms, Mr Morton?" said the Duke of Lauderdale, who presided in the Council.

"I have no other choice, my Lord," replied Morton.

"Then subscribe your name in the record."

Morton did so without reply, conscious that, in the circumstances of his case, it was impossible for him to have escaped more easily. Macbriar, who was at the same instant brought to the foot of the council table, bound upon a chair, for his weakness prevented him from standing, beheld Morton in the act of what he accounted apostacy.

"He hath summed his defection by owning the carnal power of the tyrant!" he exclaimed, with a deep groan—"A fallen star!—a fallen star!"

"Hold your peace, sir," said the Duke, "and keep your ain breath to cool your ain porridge—ye'll find them scalding hot, I promise you.— Call in the other fellow, who has some common sense. One sheep will leap the ditch when another goes first."

Cuddie was introduced unbound, but under the guard of two halberdiers, and placed beside Macbriar at the bottom of the table. The poor fellow cast a piteous look around him, in which were mingled awe for the great men in whose presence he stood, and compassion for his fellow-sufferers, with no small fear of the personal consequences which impended over him. He made his clownish obeisances with a double portion of reverence, and then awaited the opening of the awful scene.

"Were you at the battle of Bothwell Brigg?" was the first question which was thundered in his ears.

Cuddie meditated a denial, but had sense enough, upon reflection, to discover that the truth would be too strong for him; so he replied with true Caledonian indirection of response,

"I'll no say but it may be possible that I might hae been there."

"Answer directly, you knave—yes or no?—You know you were there."

"It's no for me to contradict your Lordship's Grace's honour," said Cuddie.

"Once more, sir, were you there?—yes or no?" said the Duke, impatiently.

"Dear, stir," again replied Cuddie, "how can ane mind preceesely where they hae been a' the days o' their life?"

"Speak out, you scoundrel," said General Dalzell, "or I'll dash your teeth out with my dudgeon-haft—Do you think we can stand here all day to be turning and dodging with you, like greyhounds after a hare?"

"Aweel, then," said Cuddie, "since naething else will please you, write down that I cannot deny but I was there."

"Well, sir," said the Duke, "and do you think that the rising upon that occasion was rebellion or not?"

"I am no just free to gi'e my opinion, stir, on what might cost my neck; but I doubt it will be very little better."

"Better than what?"

"Just than rebellion, as your honour ca's it," replied Cuddie.

"Well, sir, that's speaking to the purpose. And are you content to accept of the King's pardon for your guilt as a rebel, and to keep the church, and pray for the King?"

"Blithely, stir; and drink his health into the bargain, when the ale's gude."

"Egad," said the Duke, "this is a hearty cock.—What brought you into such a scrape, mine honest friend?"

"Just ill example, stir, and a daft auld jaud of a mither, wi' reverence to your Grace's honour."

"Why, God-a-mercy, my friend, I think thou art not likely to commit treason on thine own score.—Make out his free pardon, and bring forward the rogue in the chair."

Macbriar was then moved forward to the post of examination.

"Were you at the battle of Bothwell Bridge?" was, in like manner, demanded of him.

"I was," answered the prisoner, in a bold and resolute tone.

"Were you armed?"

"I was not—I went in my calling as a preacher of God's word, to encourage them that drew the sword in his cause."

"In other words, to aid and abet the rebels?" said the Duke.

"Thou hast spoken it," replied the prisoner.

"Well, then," continued the interrogator, "let us know if you saw John Balfour of Burley among the party?—I presume you know him?"

"I bless God that I do know him," replied Macbriar; "he is a zealous and sincere Christian."

"And when and where did you last see this pious personage?" was the query which immediately followed.

"I am here to answer for myself, and not to endanger others."

"We shall know," said Dalzell, "how to make you find your tongue."

"If you can make him fancy himself in a conventicle," answered Lauderdale, "he will find it without you.—Come, laddie, speak out while the play is good—you're too young to bear the burthen will be laid on you else."

"I defy you," retorted Macbriar. "This has not been the first of my imprisonments or of my sufferings; and, young as I may be, I have lived long enough to know how to die when I am called upon."

"Ay, but there are some things which must go before an easy death, if you continue obstinate," said Lauderdale, and rung a small silver bell which was placed before him on the table.

A dark crimson curtain, which covered a sort of niche, or Gothic recess in the wall, rose at the signal, and displayed the public executioner, a tall, grim, and hideous man, having an oaken table before him, on which lay thumb-screws, and an iron case, called the Scottish boot, used in these tyrannical days to torture accused persons. Morton, who was unprepared for this ghastly apparition, started when the curtain arose, but Macbriar's nerves were more firm. He gazed upon the horrible apparatus with much composure; and if nature called the blood from his cheek for a second, resolution sent it back to his brow with greater energy.

"Do you know who that man is?" said Lauderdale, in a low, stern voice, almost sinking into a whisper.

"He is, I suppose," replied Macbriar, "the infamous executioner of your blood-thirsty commands upon the persons of God's people. He and you are equally beneath my regard; and, I bless God, I no more fear what he can inflict than what you can command. Flesh and blood may shrink under the sufferings you can doom me to, and poor frail nature may shed tears, or send forth cries; but I trust my soul is anchored firmly on the rock of ages."

"Do your duty," said the Duke to the executioner.

The fellow advanced, and asked, with a harsh and discordant voice, upon which of the prisoner's limbs he should first employ his engine.

"Let him choose for himself," said the Duke; "I should like to oblige him in any thing that is reasonable."

"Since you leave it to me," said the prisoner, stretching forth his right leg, "take the best—I willingly bestow it in the cause for which I suffer."

The executioner, with the help of the assistants, inclosed the leg and knee within the tight iron boot, or case, and then placing a wedge of the same metal between the knee and the edge of the machine, took a mallet in his hand, and stood waiting for farther orders. A well-dressed man, by profession a surgeon, placed himself by the other side of the chair, bared the prisoner's arm, and applied his thumb to the pulse in order to regulate the torture according to the strength of the patient. When these preparations were made, the President of the Council repeated with the same stern voice the question, "When and where did you last see John Balfour of Burley?"

The prisoner, instead of replying to him, turned his eyes to Heaven as if imploring Divine strength, and muttered a few words, of which the last were distinctly audible, "Thou hast said thy people shall be willing in the day of thy power!"

The Duke of Lauderdale glanced his eye around the Council as if to collect their suffrages, and, judging from their mute signs, gave on his own part a nod to the executioner, whose mallet instantly descended on the wedge, and, forcing it about two inches downwards between the knee and the iron boot, occasioned the most exquisite pain, as was evident from the flush which instantly took place on the brow and on the cheeks of the sufferer. The fellow then again raised his weapon, and stood prepared to give a second blow.

"Will you yet say," repeated the Duke of Lauderdale, "where and when you last parted from Balfour of Burley?"

"You have my answer," said the sufferer resolutely, and the second blow fell. The third and fourth succeeded, but at the fifth, when a larger wedge was introduced, the prisoner set up a scream of agony.

Morton, whose blood boiled within him at witnessing such cruelty, could bear no longer, and, although unarmed and himself in great danger, was springing forward, when Claverhouse, who observed his emotion, withheld him by force, laying one hand on his arm and the other on his mouth, while he whispered, "For God's sake, think where you are!"

This movement, fortunately for him, was observed by no other of the counsellors, whose attention was engaged with the dreadful scene before them.

"He is gone," said the surgeon—"he has fainted, my Lords, and human nature can endure no more."

"Release him," said the Duke, and added, turning to Dalzell, "He will make an old proverb good, for he'll scarce ride to-day, though he has had his boots on. I suppose we must finish with him."

"Ay, dispatch his sentence, and have done with him, we have plenty of drudgery behind."

Strong waters and essences were busily employed to recal the senses of the unfortunate captive; and, when his first faint gasps intimated a return of sensation, the Duke pronounced sentence of death upon him, as a traitor taken in the act of open rebellion, and adjudged him to be carried from the bar to the common place of execution, and there hanged by the neck; his head and hands to be stricken off after death, and disposed of according to the pleasure of the Council, and all and sundry his moveable goods and gear escheat and inbrought to his Majesty's use.

"Doomster," he continued, "repeat the sentence to the prisoner."

The office of Doomster was in these days, and till a much later period, held by the executioner *in commendam* with his ordinary functions. The duty consisted in reciting to the unhappy criminal the sentence of the law as pronounced by the judge, which acquired an additional and horrid emphasis from the recollection, that the hateful personage by whom it was uttered was to be the agent of the cruelties he denounced. Macbriar had scarce understood the purport of the words as first pronounced by the Lord President of the Council; but he was sufficiently recovered to listen and to reply to the sentence when uttered by the harsh and odious voice of the ruffian who was to execute it, and at the last awful words, "And this I pronounce for doom," he answered boldly—"My Lords, I thank you for the only favour I looked for, or would accept at your hands, namely, that you have sent the crushed and maimed carcase which has this day sustained your cruelty to this hasty end. It were indeed little to me, whether I perish on the gallows or in the prison-house. But if death, following close on what I have this day suffered, had found me in my cell of darkness and bondage, many might have lost the benefit of seeing how a Christian man can suffer in the good cause. For the rest, my Lords, I forgive you what you have appointed and I have sustained—And why should I not?—Ye send me to a happy exchange —to the company of angels and the spirits of the just for that of frail dust and ashes—Ye send me from darkness into day—from mortality to immortality—and, in one word, from earth to heaven!—If the thanks, therefore, and pardon of a dying man can do you good, take them at my hand, and may your last moments be as happy as mine!"

As he spoke thus, with a countenance radiant with joy and triumph, he was withdrawn by those who had brought him into the apartment, and executed within half an hour, dying with the same enthusiastic firmness which his whole life had evinced.

The Council broke up, and Morton found himself again in the carriage with General Grahame.

"Marvellous firmness and gallantry!" said Morton, as he reflected upon Macbriar's conduct; "what pity it is that with such self-devotion and heroism should have been mingled the fiercer features of his sect!"

"You mean," said Claverhouse, "his resolution to condemn you to death?—to that he would have reconciled himself by a single text; for example, 'And Phineas arose and executed judgment,' or something to the same purpose—But wot ye where you are now bound, Mr Morton?"

"We are on the road to Leith, I observe," answered Morton. "Can I not be permitted to see my friends ere I leave my native land?"

"Your uncle," replied Grahame, "has been spoken with, and declines visiting you. The good gentleman is terrified, and not without reason, that the crime of your treason may extend itself over his lands and tenements—he sends you, however, his blessing and a small sum of money. Lord Evandale continues extremely indisposed. Major Bellenden is at Tillietudlem putting matters in order. The scoundrels have made great havoc there with Lady Margaret's monuments of antiquity, and have destroyed what the good lady called the Throne of his most Sacred Majesty. Is there any one else whom you would wish to see?"

Morton sighed deeply as he answered "No—it would avail nothing —but my preparations,—small as they are, some must be necessary."

"They are all made for you," said the General. "Lord Evandale has anticipated all you can wish. Here is a packet from him with letters of recommendation for the court of the Stadtholder Prince of Orange, to which I have added one or two. I made my first campaigns under him, and first saw fire at the battle of Seneff. There are also bills of exchange for your immediate wants, and more will be sent when you require it."

Morton heard all this, and received the parcel with an astounded and confused look, so sudden was the execution of the sentence of banishment.

"And my servant?" he said.

"He shall be cared for, and replaced, if it be practicable, in the service of Lady Margaret Bellenden; I think he will hardly neglect the parade, or go a-whigging a second time.—But here we are upon the quay, and the boat waits you."

It was even as Claverhouse said. A boat waited for Captain Morton with the trunks and baggage belonging to his rank. Claverhouse shook him by the hand, and wished him good fortune, and a happy return to Scotland in quieter times.

"I shall never forget," he said, "the gallantry of your behaviour to my friend Evandale, in circumstances when many men would have sought to rid him out of their way."

Another friendly pressure, and they parted. As Morton descended the pier to get into the boat, a hand placed in his a letter folded up in very small space. He looked round. The person who gave it seemed much muffled up; he pressed his finger upon his lip, and then disappeared among the crowd. The incident awakened Morton's curiosity; and when he found himself on board of a vessel bound for Rotterdam, and saw all his companions of the voyage busy making their own arrangements, he took an opportunity to open the billet thus mysteriously thrust upon him. It ran thus:—"Thy courage on the fatal day when Israel fled before her enemies, hath, in some measure, atoned for thy unhappy owning of the Erastian interest. These are no days for Ephraim to strive with Israel.—I know thy heart is with the daughter of the stranger. But turn from that folly; for in exile, and in flight, and even in death itself, shall my hand be heavy against that bloody and malignant house, and Providence hath given me the means of meting unto them with their own measure of ruin and confiscation. The resistance of their strong-hold was the main cause of our being scattered at Bothwell Bridge, and I have bound it upon my soul to visit it upon them. Wherefore, think of her no more, but join with our brethren in banishment, whose hearts are still towards this miserable land to save and to relieve her. There is an honest remnant in Holland whose eyes are still looking out for deliverance. Join thyself unto them like the true son of the stout and worthy Silas Morton, and thou wilt have good acceptance among them for his sake and for thine own working. Shouldst thou be found worthy again to labour in the vineyard, thou wilt at all times hear of my in-comings and out-goings, by enquiring after Quintin Mackell of Irongray, at the house of that singular Christian woman, Bessie Maclure, near to the place called the Howff, where Niel Blane entertaineth guests. So much from him who hopes again to hear from thee in brotherhood, resisting unto blood, and striving against sin. Meanwhile, possess thyself in patience. Keep thy sword girded, and thy lamp burning, as one that wakes in the night; for He who shall judge the Mount of Esau, and shall make false professors as straw, and malignants as stubble, will come in the fourth watch with garments dyed in blood, and the house of Jacob shall be for spoil, and the house of Joseph for fire. I am he that hath written it, whose hand hath been on the mighty in the waste field."

This extraordinary letter was subscribed J.B. of B.; but the signature of these initials was not necessary for pointing out to Morton that it could come from no other than Burley. It gave him new occasion to admire the indomitable spirit of this man, who, with art equal to his courage and obstinacy, was even now endeavouring to re-establish the web of conspiracy which had been so lately torn to pieces. But he felt no sort of desire, in the present moment, to sustain a correspondence which must be perilous, or to renew an association, which, in so many ways, had been nearly fatal to him. The threats which Burley held out against the family of Bellenden, he considered as a mere expression of his spleen on account of their defence of Tillietudlem; and nothing seemed less likely than that, at the very moment of their party being victorious, their fugitive and distressed adversary could exercise the least influence over their fortunes.

Morton, however, hesitated for an instant, whether he should not send the Major or Lord Evandale intimation of Burley's threats. Upon consideration, he thought he could not do so without betraying his confidential correspondence; for to warn them of his menaces would have served little purpose, unless he had given them a clew to prevent them, by apprehending his person; while, by doing so, he deemed he should commit an ungenerous breach of trust to remedy an evil which seemed almost imaginary. Upon mature consideration, therefore, he tore the letter, having first made a memorandum of the name and place where the writer was to be heard of, and threw the fragments into the sea.

While Morton was thus employed the vessel was unmoored, and the white sails swelled out before a favourable north-west wind. The ship leaned her side to the gale, and went roaring through the waves, leaving a long and rippling furrow to track her course. The city and port from which he had sailed became indistinguishable in the distance; the hills by which they are surrounded melted finally into the blue sky, and Morton was separated for several years from the land of his nativity.

Chapter Seben

Whom does time gallop withal?
SHAKSPEARE

I T IS fortunate for tale-tellers that they are not tied down like theatrical writers to the unities of time and place, but may conduct their personages to Athens and Thebes at their pleasure, and bring them back at their convenience. Time, to use Rosalind's simile, has hitherto paced with the hero of our tale; for, betwixt Morton's first appearance as a competitor for the popinjay, and his final departure for Holland, hardly two months elapsed. Years, however, glided away ere we find it possible to resume the thread of our narrative, and Time must be held to have galloped over the interval. Craving, therefore, the privilege of my cast, I entreat the reader's attention to the continuation of the narrative, as it starts from a new æra, being the year immediately subsequent to the British Revolution.

Scotland had just begun to repose from the convulsion occasioned by a change of dynasty, and, through the prudent tolerance of King William, had narrowly escaped the horrors of a protracted civil war. Agriculture began to revive; and men, whose minds had been disturbed by the violent political concussion, and the general change of government in church and state, had begun to recover their ordinary temper, and to give the usual attention to their own private affairs in lieu of discussing those of the public. The Highlanders alone resisted the newly-established order of things, and were in arms in a considerable body under the Viscount of Dundee, whom our readers have hitherto known by the name of Grahame of Claverhouse. But the general state of the Highlands was so unruly, that their being more or less disturbed was not supposed greatly to affect the general tranquillity of the country, so long as their disorders were confined within their own frontiers. In the Lowlands, the Jacobites, now the undermost party, had ceased to expect any immediate advantage by open resistance, and were, in their turn, driven to hold private meetings, and form associations for mutual defence, which the government termed treason, while they cried out persecution.

The triumphant whigs, while they re-established presbytery as the national religion, and assigned to the General Assemblies of the Kirk their natural influence, were very far from going the lengths which the Cameronians and more extravagant portion of the non-conformists under Charles and James loudly demanded. They would listen to no proposal for re-establishing the Solemn League and Covenant; and those who had expected to find in King William a zealous Covenanted Monarch were grievously disappointed when he intimated, with the phlegm peculiar to his country, his intentions to tolerate all forms of religion which were consistent with the safety of the state. These principles of toleration, which were espoused and gloried in by the government, gave great offence to the more violent party, who condemned them as diametrically contrary to Scripture; for which narrow-spirited doctrine they cited various texts, all, as it may well be supposed, detached from their context, and most of them derived from the charges given to the Jews in the Old Testament dispensation to extirpate idolaters out of the promised land. They also murmured highly against the influence assumed by secular persons in exercising the right of patronage, which they termed a rape upon the chastity of the Church. They censured and condemned as Erastian many of the measures by which government after the Revolution shewed an inclination to interfere with the management of the Church, and they positively refused to take the oath of allegiance to King William and Queen Mary, until they should, on their part, have sworn to the Solemn League and Covenant, the Magna Charta, as they termed it, of the Presbyterian Church.

This party, therefore, remained grumbling and dissatisfied, and made repeated declarations against defections and causes of wrath, which, had they been prosecuted as in the two former reigns, would have led to the same consequence of open rebellion. But as the murmurers were allowed to hold their meetings uninterrupted, and to testify as much as they pleased against Socinianism, Erastianism, and all the compliances and defections of the time, their zeal, unfann'd by persecution, died gradually away, their numbers became diminished, and they sunk into the scattered remnant of serious, scrupulous, and harmless enthusiasts, of whom Old Mortality, whose legends have afforded the ground-work of my Tale, may be taken as no bad representative. But in the years which immediately succeeded the Revolution, the Cameronians continued a sect strong in numbers and vehement in their political opinions, whom government wished to discourage while they prudently temporized with them. These men formed one violent party in the state; and the Episcopalian and Jacobite interest, notwithstanding their ancient and national animosity, yet repeatedly endeavoured to intrigue among them, and avail themselves of their discontents, to obtain their assistance in recalling the Stuart family. The Revolution government, in the meanwhile, was supported by the great bulk of the Lowland interest, who were chiefly disposed to a moderate presbytery, and formed, in a great measure, the party, who, in the former oppressive reigns, were stigmatized by the

Cameronians, for having exercised that form of worship under the declaration of Indulgence issued by Charles II. Such was the state of parties in Scotland immediately subsequent to the Revolution.

It was upon a delightful summer evening, that a stranger, well mounted, and having the appearance of a military man of rank, rode down a winding descent which terminated in view of the romantic ruins of Bothwell Castle and the river Clyde, which winds so beautifully between rocks and woods to sweep around the towers formerly built by Aymer de Valence. Bothwell Bridge was at a little distance, and also in sight. The opposite field, once the scene of slaughter and conflict, now lay as placid and quiet as the surface of a summer lake. The trees and bushes, which grew around in romantic variety of shade, were hardly seen to stir under the influence of the evening breeze. The very murmur of the river seemed to soften itself into unison with the stillness of the scene around. The path, through which the traveller descended, was occasionally shaded by detached trees of great size, and elsewhere by the hedges and boughs of flourishing orchards, now loaden with summer fruit.

The nearest object of consequence was a farm-house, or it might be the abode of a small proprietor, situated on the side of a sunny bank, which was covered by apple and pear-trees. At the foot of the path which led up to this modest mansion was a small cottage, pretty much in the situation of a porter's-lodge, though obviously not designed for such a purpose. The hut seemed comfortable, and more neatly arranged than is usual in Scotland; it had its little garden, where some fruit-trees and bushes were mingled with kitchen herbs; a cow and six sheep fed in a paddock hard by; the cock strutted and crowed, and summoned his family around him before the door; a heap of brushwood and turf, neatly made up, indicated that the winter fuel was provided; and the thin blue smoke which ascended from the strawbound chimney, and winded slowly out from among the green trees, shewed that the evening meal was in the act of being made ready. To complete the little scene of rural peace and comfort, a girl of about five years old was fetching water in a pitcher from a beautiful fountain of the purest water, which bubbled up at the root of a decayed old oak-tree, about twenty yards from the end of the cottage.

The stranger reined up his horse, and called to the little nymph, desiring to know the way to Fairy-knowe. The child set down its water-pitcher, hardly understanding what was said to her, put her fair flaxen hair apart on her brows, and opened her round blue eyes with the wondering "What's your wull?" which is usually a peasant's first answer, if it can be called one, to all questions whatsoever.

"I wish to know the way to Fairy-knowe."

"Mammie, mammie," exclaimed the little rustic, running towards the door of the hut, "come out and speak to this gentleman."

Her mother appeared,—a handsome young country-woman, to whose features, originally sly and espiegle in expression, matrimony had given that decent matronly air which peculiarly marks the peasant's wife of Scotland. She had an infant in one arm, and with the other hand she smoothed down her apron, to which hung a chubby child of two years old. The older girl, whom the traveller had first seen, fell back behind her mother as soon as she appeared, and kept that station, occasionally peeping out to look at the stranger.

"What was your pleasure, sir?" said the woman, with an air of respectful breeding, not quite common in her rank of life, but without any thing resembling forwardness.

The stranger looked at her with great earnestness for a moment, and then replied, "I am seeking a place called Fairy-knowe, and a man called Cuthbert Headrigg. You can probably direct me to him."

"It's my good-man, sir," said the young woman, with a smile of welcome; "will you alight, sir, and come into our poor dwelling?— Cuddie, Cuddie,"—(a white-headed rogue of four years appeared at the door of the hut)—"Rin awa', my bonnie man, and tell your father a gentleman wants him.—Or, stay—Jenny, ye'll hae mair sense—rin ye awa' and tell him; he's down at the Four-acres Park.—Winna ye light down and bide a blink, sir?—Or would ye take a mouthfu' o' bread and cheese, or a drink o' ale, till our good-man come? It's gude ale, though I should say sae that brews it; but pleughman lads work hard, and maun hae something to keep their heart aboon by ordinary, sae I aye pit a gude gowpin maut to the browst."

As the stranger declined her courteous offers, Cuddie, the reader's old acquaintance, made his appearance in person. His countenance still presented the same mixture of apparent dullness, with occasional sparkles, which indicated the craft so often found in the clouted shoe. He looked on the rider as on one whom he never had before seen; and, like his daughter and wife, opened the conversation with the regular query, "What's your wull wi' me, sir?"

"I have a curiosity to ask some questions about this country," said the traveller, "and I was directed to you as an intelligent man who can answer them."

"Nae doubt, sir," said Cuddie, after a moment's hesitation; "but I would first like to ken what sort of questions they are. I hae had sae mony questions speered at me in my day, and in sic queer ways, that if ye kend a', ye wadna wonder at my jealousing a' thing about them. My mother gar'd me learn the Single Carritch, whilk was a great vex; than I behoved to learn about my godfathers and godmothers to

please the auld leddy; and whiles I jummled them thegither and
pleased nane o' them; and whan I cam to man's yestate, cam anither
kind o' questioning in fashion, that I liked waur than Effectual Calling; and the 'did promise and vow' of the tane were yokit to the end of
the tother. Sae ye see, sir, I aye like to hear questions asked before I
answer them."

"You have nothing to apprehend from mine, my good friend; they
only relate to the state of the country."

"Country?" replied Cuddie; "ou, the country's weel aneugh, an' it
werena that dour devil, Claver'se, (they ca' him Dundee now) that's
stirring about yet in the Highlands, they say, wi' a' the Donalds, and
Duncans, and Dugalds, that ever wore bottomless breeks, driving
about wi' him, to set things a-stear again, now we hae gotten them a'
reasonably weel settled. But Mackay will pit him down, there's little
doubt o' that; he'll gi'e him his fairing, I'll be caution for it."

"What makes you so positive of that, my friend?" asked the
horseman.

"I heard it wi' my ain lugs," answered Cuddie, "foretauld to him by
a man that had been three hours stane dead, and came back to this
earth again just to tell him his mind. It was at a place they ca' Drumshinnel."

"Indeed?" said the stranger; "I can hardly believe you, my friend."

"Ye might ask my mither than, if she were in life," said Cuddie; "it
was her explained it a' to me, for I thought the man had only been
wounded. At ony rate, he spake of the casting out of the Stuarts by
their very names, and the vengeance that was brewing for Claver'se
and his dragoons. They ca'd the man Habakkuk Meiklewrath; his
brain was a wee agee, but he was a braw preacher for a' that."

"You seem," said the stranger, "to live in a rich and peaceful
country."

"It's no to complain o', sir, an' we get the crap weel in," quoth
Cuddie; "but if ye had seen the blude rinnin' as fast on the tap o' that
brigg yonder as ever the water ran below it, ye wadna hae thought it sae
bonnie a spectacle."

"You mean the battle some years since?—I was waiting upon Monmouth that morning, my good friend, and did see some part of the
action," said the stranger.

"Then ye saw a bonny stour," said Cuddie, "that sall serve me for
fighting a' the days o' my life.—I judged ye wad be a trooper by your
red scarlet lace-coat and your looped hat."

"And which side were you upon, my friend?" continued the
inquisitive stranger.

"Aha, lad!" retorted Cuddie, with a knowing look, or what he designed for such—"there's nae use in telling that, unless I kenn'd wha was asking me."

"I commend your prudence, but it is unnecessary; I know you acted upon that occasion as servant to Henry Morton."

"Ay!" said Cuddie, in surprise, "how came ye by that secret?—No that I need care a bodle about it, for the sun's on our side o' the hedge now. I wish my master were living to get a blink o't."

"And what became of him?" said the rider.

"He was lost in the vessel ganging to that weary Holland—clean lost —and a' body perished, and my poor master amang them. Neither man nor mouse was ever heard o' mair." Here Cuddie uttered a groan.

"You had some regard for him, then?" continued the stranger.

"How could I help it?—His face was made of a fiddle, as they say, for a' body that looked on him liked him. And a braw soldier he was. O, an' ye had but seen him down at the brigg there, fleeing about like a fleeing dragon to gar folk fight that had unco little will till't! There was he and that dour devil they ca'd Burley—if twa men could hae won a field, we wadna hae gotten our skins paid that day."

"You mention Burley—Do you know if he yet lives?"

"I kenna muckle about him. Folk say he was abroad, and our sufferers wad hold no communion wi' him, because o' his having murdered the archbishop. Sae he cam hame ten times dourer than ever, and broke aff wi' mony of the Presbyterians; and, at this last incoming of the Prince of Orange, he could get nae countenance nor command for fear of his devilish temper, and he hasna been heard of since; only some folks say, that pride and anger hae driven him clean wud."

"And—and," said the traveller, after considerable hesitation,—"do you know any thing of Lord Evandale?"

"Div I ken ony thing o' my Lord Evandale?—Div I no? Is not it my young leddy up by yonder at the house, that's as good as married to him?"

"And are they not married, then?" said the rider, hastily.

"No; only what they ca' betrothed—my wife and I were witnesses— it's no mony months by past—it was a lang courtship—few folk kenn'd the reason by Jenny and mysel.—But will ye no light down? I douna bide to see ye sitting up there, and the clouds are casting up thick in the west ower Glasgow-ward, and maist skeily folk think that bodes rain."

In fact, a deep black cloud had already surmounted the setting sun; a few large drops of rain fell, and the murmur of distant thunder was heard.

"The de'il's in this man," said Cuddie to himself; "I wish he would either light aff or ride on, that he may quarter himsel in Hamilton or the shower begin."

But the rider sate motionless on his horse for two or three minutes after his last question, like one exhausted by some uncommon effort. At length, recovering himself, as if with a sudden and painful effort, he asked Cuddie, "if Lady Margaret Bellenden still lived."

"She does," replied Cuddie, "but in a very sma' way. They hae been a sair changed family since thae rough times began; they hae suffered aneugh first and last—and to lose the auld Tower, and a' the bonny barony and the holms that I hae pleughed sae aften, and the Mains and my kale-yard that I suld hae gotten back again, and a' for nae-thing, as a body may say, but just the want o' some bits of sheep-skin that were lost in the confusion of the taking of Tillietudlem."

"I have heard something of this," said the stranger, deepening his voice and averting his head. "I have some interest in the family, and would willingly help them if I could. Can you give me a bed in your house to-night, my friend?"

"It's but a corner of a place, sir," said Cuddie, "but we'se try, rather than ye suld ride on in the rain and thunner; for, to be free wi' you, sir, I think ye seem no that ower weel."

"I am liable to a dizziness," said the stranger, "but it will soon wear off."

"I ken we can gi'e you a decent supper, sir," said Cuddie; "and we'll see about a bed as weel as we can. We wad be laith a stranger suld lack what we have, though we are jimply provided in beds rather; for Jenny has sae mony bairns, (God bless them and her,) that troth I maun speak to Lord Evandale to gi'e us a bit eik, or outshot o' some sort, to the onstead."

"I shall be easily accommodated," said the stranger, as he entered the house.

"And ye may rely on your naig being weel sorted," said Cuddie; "I ken weel what belangs to suppering a horse, and this is a very gude ane."

Cuddie took the horse to the little cow-house, and called to his wife to attend in the meanwhile to the stranger's accommodation. The officer entered, and threw himself on a settle at some distance from the fire, and carefully turning his back to the little lattice window. Jenny, or Mrs Headrigg, if the reader pleases, requested him to lay aside the cloak, belt, and flapped-hat which he wore upon his journey, but he excused himself under pretence of feeling cold; and, to divert the time till Cuddie's return, he entered into some chat with the children, carefully avoiding, during the interval, the inquisitive glances of his landlady.

Chapter Eight

What tragic tears bedim the eye!
What deaths we suffer ere we die!
Our broken friendships we deplore,
And loves of youth that are no more.
                    LOGAN

CUDDIE soon re-entered, assuring the stranger, with a cheerful voice, "that the horse was properly suppered up, and that the gude-wife should make a bed up for him at the house, mair purpose-like and comfortable than the like o' them could gi'e him."

"Are the family at the house?" said the stranger, with an interrupted and broken voice.

"No, stir; they're awa' wi' a' the servants—they keep only twa now-a-days, and my gude-wife, there, has the keys and the charge, though she's no a fee'd servant. She has been born and bred in the family, and has a' trust and management. If they were there, we behoved na to take sic freedom without their order; but when they are awa', they will be weel pleased we serve a sick stranger gentleman. Miss Bellenden wad help a' the haill warld an' her power were as gude as her will; and her grandmother, Leddy Margaret, has an unco respect for the gentry, and she's no ill to the poor bodies neither—And now, wife, what for are ye no getting forrit wi' the sowens?"

"Never mind, lad," rejoined Jenny, "ye sall hae them in gude time; I ken weel that ye like your brose het."

Cuddie fidgetted, and laughed with a peculiar expression of intelligence at this repartee, which was followed by a dialogue of little consequence betwixt his wife and him, in which the stranger took no share. At length he suddenly interrupted them by the question—"Can you tell me when Lord Evandale's marriage takes place?"

"Very soon, we expect," answered Jenny, before it was possible for her husband to reply; "it would hae been ower afore now, but for the death o' auld Major Bellenden."

"The excellent old man!" said the stranger; "I heard at Edinburgh he was no more—Was he long ill?"

"He couldna be said to haud up his head after his brother's wife and his niece were turned out of their ain house; and he hurt himsel sair borrowing siller to stand the law—but it was in the latter end o' King James's days—and Basil Olifant, who claimed the estate, he turned a papist to please the managers, and than naething was to be refused him, sae the law gaed again the leddies at last, after they had fought a weary sort o' years about it, and, as I said before, the Major ne'er held up his head again. And than cam the pitting awa' o' the Stuart line; and, though he had but little reason to like them, he couldna brook that, and it clean broke the heart o' him, and creditors cam to Charnwood and cleaned out a' that was there—he was never rich, the gude auld man, for he dow'd na see ony body want."

"He was, indeed," said the stranger, with a faultering voice, "an admirable man—that is, I have heard that he was so.—So the ladies were left without fortune as well as without a protector?"

"They will neither want the tane nor tother while Lord Evandale lives," said Jenny; "he has been a true friend in a' their griefs—E'en to the house they live in is his Lordship's; and never man, as my auld gude-minnie Mause used to say, since the days of the patriarch Jacob, served sae lang and sae sair for a wife as gude Lord Evandale has dune."

"And why," said the stranger, with a voice that quivered with emotion, "why was he not sooner rewarded by the object of his attachment?"

"There was the law-suit to be ended," said Jenny readily, "forby many other family arrangements."

"Na, but," said Cuddie, "there was another reason forby; for the young leddy"——

"Whisht, haud your tongue, and sup your sowens," said his wife; "I see the gentleman's far frae weel, and downa eat our coarse supper—I wad kill him a chicken in an instant."

"There is no occasion," said the stranger; "I shall want only a glass of water, and to be left alone."

"You'll gi'e yoursel the trouble then to follow me," said Jenny, lighting a small lantern, "and I'll shew you the way."

Cuddie also proffered his assistance; but his wife reminded him, "That the bairns would be left to fight thegither, and coup ane anither into the fire," so that he remained to take charge of the menage.

His wife led the way up a little winding path, which, after threading some thickets of sweet-briar and honeysuckle, conducted to the back-door of a small garden. Jenny undid the latch, and they passed through an old-fashioned flower-garden, with its clipped yew hedges and formal parterres, to a glass-sashed door, which she opened with a master key, and lighting a candle, which she placed upon a small work-table, asked pardon for leaving him there for a few minutes, until she prepared his apartment. She did not exceed five minutes in these preparations; but, when she returned, was startled to find that the stranger had sunk forward with his head upon the table, in what she at first apprehended to be a swoon. As she advanced to him, however, she could discover by his short-drawn sobs that it was a paroxysm of mental agony. She prudently drew back until he raised his head, and then shewing herself, without seeming to have observed his agitation, informed him, that his bed was prepared. The stranger gazed at her a moment, as if to collect the sense of her words. She repeated them, and only bending his head, as an indication that he understood her, he entered the apartment, the door of which she pointed out to him. It was a small bed-chamber, used, as she informed him, by Lord Evandale when a guest at Fairy-knowe, connecting, on one side, with a little china-cabinet which opened to the garden, and, on the other, with a saloon, from which it was only separated by a thin wainscot partition. Having wished the stranger better health and good rest, Jenny descended as speedily as she could to her own mansion.

"O, Cuddie!" she exclaimed to her helpmate as she entered, "I doubt we're ruined folk!"

"How can that be? What's the matter wi' ye?" returned the imperturbed Cuddie, who was one of those persons who do not easily take alarm at any thing.

"Wha d'ye think yon gentleman is?—O, that ever ye suld hae asked him to light here!" exclaimed Jenny.

"Why, wha the muckle de'il do ye say that he is? There's nae law against harbouring and intercommunicating noo," said Cuddie; "sae, whig or tory, what need we care whae he is?"

"Ay, but it's ane will ding Lord Evandale's marriage ajee yet, if it's no the better looked to," said Jenny; "it's Miss Edith's first joe, your ain auld master, Cuddie."

"The de'il, woman!" exclaimed Cuddie, starting up, "trow ye that I am blind? I wad hae kenn'd Mr Harry Morton amang a hunder."

"Ay, but, Cuddie lad," replied Jenny, "though ye are no blind, ye are no sae notice-taking as I am."

"Weel, what for needs ye cast up that to me just now? or what did ye see about the man that was like our Maister Harry?"

"I will tell ye," said Jenny; "I jaloused his keeping his face frae us, and speaking wi' a made-like voice, sae I e'en tried him wi' some tales o' lang syne, and when I spake o' the brose, ye ken, he didna just laugh —he's ower grave for that now-a-days,—but he gae a gledge wi' his e'e that I kenn'd he took up what I said. And a' his distress is about Miss Edith's marriage, and I ne'er saw a man mair tane down wi' true love in my days—I might say man or woman—only I mind Miss Edith when she first gat word that him and you (ye muckle graceless loon) were coming against Tillietudlem wi' the rebels.—But what's the matter wi' the man now?"

"What's the matter wi' me, indeed!" said Cuddie, who was again hastily putting on some of the garments he had stripped himself of, "am I no ganging up this instant to see my maister that my heart aye warmed to?"

"Indeed, Cuddie, but ye are ganging nae sic gate," said Jenny, coolly and resolutely.

"The de'il's in the wife," said Cuddie; "d'ye think I am to be John Tamson's man, and maistered by women a' the days o' my life?"

"And wha's man wad ye be? And wha wad ye hae to maister ye but me, Cuddie lad?" answered Jenny. "I'll gar ye comprehend in the making of a hay-band. Naebody kens that this young gentleman lives but oursels, and frae that he keeps himsel up sae close, I am judging that he's purposing, if he fand Miss Edith either married, or just gaun to be married, he'll just slide awa' easy and gi'e them nae mair trouble. —But if Miss Edith kenn'd that he was living, and if she were standing before the very minister wi' Lord Evandale when it was tauld to her, she wad say no when she suld say yes."

"Weel," replied Cuddie, "and what's my business wi' that? if Miss Edith likes her auld joe better than her new ane, what for suld she no be free to change her mind like ither folk?—Ye ken, Jenny, Halliday aye threeps he had a promise frae yoursel."

"Halliday's a liar, and ye're a gomeril to hearken till him, Cuddie. And then for this leddy's choice, lack-a-day!—ye may be sure a' the gowd Mr Morton has is on the outside o' his coat, and how can he keep Leddy Margaret and the young leddy?"

"Isna there Milnewood?" said Cuddie. "Nae doubt, the auld laird left his housekeeper the life-rent as he heard nought o' his nephew; but it's but speaking the auld wife fair, and they may a' live brawly thegither, Leddy Margaret and a'."

"Hout tout, lad," replied Jenny, "ye ken them little to think leddies o' their rank wad set up house wi' auld Ailie Wilson, when they're maist ower proud to tak favours frae Lord Evandale himsel. Na, na, they maun follow the camp, if she tak Morton."

"That wad sort ill wi' the auld leddy, to be sure," said Cuddie; "she wad hardly win ower a lang day in the baggage-wain."

"Than sic a flyting as there wad be between them a' about whig and tory," continued Jenny.

"To be sure," said Cuddie, "the auld leddy's unco kittle in thae points."

"And then, Cuddie," continued his helpmate, who had reserved her strongest argument to the last, "if this marriage wi' Lord Evandale is broken aff, what comes o' our ain bit free-house, and the kale-yard, and the cow's grass?—I trow that us and a' thae bonny bairns will be turned on the wide warld."

Here Jenny began to whimper—Cuddie writhed himself this way and that way, with one sleeve of his coat off and another on, the very picture of indecision. At length, "Weel, woman, canna ye tell us what we suld do, without a' this din about it?"

"Just do naething at a'," said Jenny. "Never seem to ken ony thing about this gentleman, and for your life say a word that he suld hae been here or up at the house.—An' I had kenn'd I wad hae gi'en him my ain bed, and sleepit in the byre or he had gane up by, but it canna be helpit now. The neist thing's to get him cannily awa' the morn, and I judge he'll be in nae hurry to come back agen."

"My puir maister!" said Cuddie; "and maun I no speak to him, then?"

"For your life, no," said Jenny; "ye're no obliged to ken him; and I wadna hae tauld ye, only I feared ye wad ken him in the morning."

"Aweel," said Cuddie, sighing heavily, "I'se awa' to pleugh the outfield then; for, if I am no to speak to him, I wad rather be out o' the gate."

"Very right, my dear," replied Jenny; "naebody has better sense than you when ye crack a bit wi' ane ower your affairs, but ye suld ne'er do ony thing aff hand out o' your ain head."

"Ane wad think it's true," quoth Cuddie; "for I hae aye had some carline, or quean or another, to gar me gang their gate instead o' my ain. There was first my mither," he continued, as he undressed and tumbled himself into bed—"than there was Leddy Margaret didna let me ca my soul my ain—than my mither and her quarrelled, and pu'ed me twa ways at ance, as if ilk ane had an end o' me, like Punch and the Deevil rugging about the Baker at the fair—and now I hae gotten a wife," murmured he in continuation, as he stowed the blankets around his person, "and she's like to tak the guiding o' me a' the-gither."

"And am na I the best guide ye ever had in a' your life?" said Jenny, as she closed the conversation by assuming her place beside her husband, and extinguishing the candle.

Leaving this couple to their repose, we have next to inform the reader, that, early on the next morning, two ladies on horseback, attended by their servants, arrived at the house of Fairy-knowe, whom, to Jenny's utter confusion, she instantly recognized as Miss Bellenden, and Lady Emily Maxwell, a sister of Lord Evandale.

"Had I no better gang to the house to put things to rights?" said Jenny, confounded with this unexpected apparition.

"We want nothing but the pass-key," said Miss Bellenden; "Gudyill will open the windows of the little parlour."

"The little parlour's locked, and the lock's spoiled," answered

Jenny, who recollected the local sympathy between that apartment and the bed-chamber of her guest.

"In the red parlour, then," said Miss Bellenden, and rode up to the front of the house, but by an approach different from that through which Morton had been conducted.

"All will be out," thought Jenny, "unless I can get him smuggled out of the house the back way."

So saying, she sped up the bank in great tribulation and uncertainty.

"I had better hae said at ance there was a stranger there," was her next natural reflection. "But then they wad hae been for asking him to breakfast. O, Lord! what will I do?—And there's Gudyill walking in the garden, too!" she exclaimed internally on approaching the wicket —"and I daurna gang in the back way till he's aff the coast. O, Lord! what will become of us?"

In this state of perplexity she approached the *ci-devant* butler, with the purpose of decoying him out of the garden. But John Gudyill's temper was not improved by his decline in rank and increase in years. Like many peevish people, too, he seemed to have an intuitive perception as to what was most likely to teaze those whom he conversed with; and, upon the present occasion, all Jenny's efforts to remove him from the garden served only to root him in it as fast as if he had been one of the shrubs. Unluckily, also, he had commenced florist during his residence at Fairy-knowe, and, leaving all other things to the charge of Lady Emily's servant, his first care was dedicated to the flowers which he had taken under his special protection, and which he propped, dug, and watered, prosing all the while upon their respective merits to poor Jenny, who stood by him trembling, and almost crying with anxiety, fear, and impatience.

Fate seemed determined to win a match against Jenny this unfortunate morning. So soon as the ladies entered the house, they observed that the door of the little parlour, the very apartment out of which she was desirous of excluding them on account of its contiguity to the room in which Morton slept, was not only unlocked, but absolutely ajar. Miss Bellenden was too much engaged with her own immediate subjects of reflection to take much notice of the circumstance, but, commanding the servant to open the window-shuts, walked into the room along with her friend.

"He is not yet come," she said. "What can your brother possibly mean?—Why express so anxious a wish that we should meet him here? And why not come to Castle-Dennan, as he proposed? I own, my dear Emily, that, even engaged as we are to each other, and with the sanction of your presence, I do not feel that I have done quite right in indulging him."

"Evandale was never capricious," answered his sister; "I am sure he will satisfy us with his reasons, and if he does not, I will help you to scold him."

"What I chiefly fear," said Edith, "is his having engaged in some of the plots of this fluctuating and unhappy time. I know his heart is with that dreadful Claverhouse and his army, and I believe he would have joined them ere now but for my uncle's death, which gave him so much additional trouble on our account. How singular that one so rational and so deeply sensible of the errors of the exiled family, should yet be ready to risk all for their restoration!"

"What can I say?" answered Lady Emily; "it is a point of honour with Evandale. Our family have always been loyal—he served long in the Guards—the Viscount of Dundee was his commander and his friend for years—he is looked on with an evil eye by many of his own relations, who set down his inactivity to the score of want of spirit. You must be aware, my dear Edith, how often family connections, and early predilections, influence our actions more than abstract arguments. But I trust Evandale will continue quiet, though, to tell you truth, I believe you are the only one who can keep him so."

"And how is it in my power?" said Miss Bellenden.

"You can furnish him with the scriptural apology for not going forth with the host,—'he has married a wife, and therefore cannot come.'"

"I have promised," said Edith, in a faint voice; "but I trust I shall not be urged on the score of time."

"Nay," said Lady Emily, "I will leave Evandale (and here he comes) to plead his own cause."

"Stay, stay, for God's sake," said Edith, endeavouring to detain her.

"Not I, not I," said the young lady, making her escape; "the third person makes a silly figure on such occasions. When you want me for breakfast, I will be found in the willow-walk by the river."

As she tripped out of the room, Lord Evandale entered—"Good-morrow, brother, and goodbye till breakfast-time," said the lively young lady; "I trust you will give Miss Bellenden some good reasons for disturbing her rest so early in the morning."

And so saying, she left them together without waiting a reply.

"And now, my Lord," said Edith, "may I desire to know the meaning of your singular request to meet you here at so early an hour?"

She was about to add, that she hardly felt herself excuseable in having complied with it; but, upon looking at the person whom she addressed, she was struck dumb by the singular and agitated expression of his countenance, and interrupted herself to exclaim—"For God's sake, what is the matter?"

"His Majesty's faithful subjects have gained a great and most decisive victory near Blair of Athole; but, alas! my gallant friend, Lord Dundee"——

"Has fallen?" said Edith, anticipating the rest of his tidings.

"True—most true—he has fallen in the arms of victory, and not a man remains of talents and influence sufficient to fill up his loss in King James's service. This, Edith, is no time for temporizing with our duty. I have given directions to raise my followers, and I must take leave of you this evening."

"Do not think of it, my Lord," answered Edith; "your life is essential to your friends; do not throw it away in an adventure so rash. What can your single arm and the few tenants or servants who might follow you, do against the force of almost all Scotland, the Highland clans only excepted?"

"Listen to me, Edith," said Lord Evandale. "I am not so rash as you may suppose me, nor are my present motives of such light importance as to affect only those personally dependent on myself. The Life-Guards, with whom I served so long, although new-modelled and new-officered by the Prince of Orange, retain a predilection for the cause of their rightful master and"—(here he whispered as if he feared even the walls of the apartment had ears) —"when my foot is known to be in the stirrup, two regiments of cavalry have sworn to renounce the usurper's service, and fight under my orders. They delayed only till Dundee should descend into the low country;—but, since he is no more, which of his successors dare take that decisive step, unless encouraged by the troops declaring themselves? Meantime, the zeal of the soldiers will die away. I must bring them to a decision while their hearts are glowing with the victory their old leader has obtained, and burning to avenge his untimely death."

"And will you, on the faith of such men as you know these soldiers to be," said Edith, "take a step of such dreadful moment?"

"I will," said Lord Evandale—"I must; my honour and loyalty are both pledged for it."

"And all for the sake," continued Miss Bellenden, "of a prince, whose measures, while he was on the throne, no one could condemn more than Lord Evandale?"

"Most true," replied Lord Evandale; "and as I resented, even during the plenitude of his power, his innovations on church and state, like a free-born subject, I am determined I will assert his real rights, when he is in adversity, like a loyal one. Let courtiers and sycophants flatter power and desert misfortune, I will neither do the one nor the other."

"And if you are determined, my Lord, to act what my feeble judgment must still term rashly, why give yourself the pain of this untimely meeting?"

"Were it not enough to answer," said Lord Evandale, "that ere rushing on battle, I wished to bid adieu to my betrothed bride?— surely it is judging coldly of my feelings, and shewing too plainly the indifference of your own, to question my motive for a request so natural."

"But why in this place, my Lord?" said Edith—"why with such peculiar circumstances of mystery?"

"Because," he replied, putting a letter into her hand, "I have yet another request, which I dare hardly proffer, even when prefaced by these credentials."

In haste and terror Edith glanced over the letter, which was from her grandmother.

"My dearest child," such was its tenor in style and spelling, "I never more deeply regretted the reumatizm, which hath disqualified me from riding on horseback, than at this present writing, when I would most have wished to be where this paper will soon be, that is at Fairy-knowe, with my poor dear Willie's only child. But it is the will of God I should not be with her, which I conclude to be the case, as much for the pain I now suffer, as because it hath not given way either to cammomile poultices or to decoxion of wild mustard, wherewith I have often relieved others. Therefore, I must tell you, by writing instead of word of mouth, that, as my young Lord Evandale is called to the present campaign, both by his honour and his duty, he hath earn-estly solicited me that the bonds of holy matrimony be knitted before his departure to the wars between you and him, in implement of the indenture formerly entered into for that effeck, whereuntill, as I see no raisonable objexion, so I trust that you, who have always been a good and obedient childe, will not devize any which has less than raison. It is trew that the contraxs of our house have heretofor been celebrated in a manner more befitting our Rank, and not in private, and with few witnesses, as a thing done in a corner. But it has been Heaven's pleasure to alter our state, whilk doubtless He can repare at His own free-will, as well as those of the kingdom where we live. And I trust He will yet restore the rightful heir to the throne, and turn his heart to the true Protestant Episcopal faith, which I have the better right to expect to see even with my old eyes, as I have beheld the royal family when they were struggling as sorely with masterful usurpers and rebels as they are now; that is to say, when his most sacred Majesty, Charles the Second of happy memory, honoured our poor house of Tillietudlem, by taking his disjune therein," &c. &c. &c.

We will not abuse the reader's patience by quoting more of Lady

Margaret's prolix epistle. Suffice it to say, that it closed by laying her commands on her grandchild to consent to the solemnization of her marriage without loss of time.

"I never thought till this instant," said Edith, dropping the letter from her hand, "that Lord Evandale would have acted ungenerously."

"Ungenerously, Edith?" replied her lover. "And how can you apply such a term to my desire to call you mine, ere I part from you perhaps for ever?"

"Lord Evandale ought to have remembered," said Edith, "that when his perseverance, and, I must add, a due sense of his merit and of the obligations we owed him, wrung from me a slow consent that I would one day comply with his wishes, I made it my condition, that I should not be pressed to a hasty accomplishment of my promise; and now he avails himself of his interest with my only remaining relative, to hurry me with precipitate and even indelicate importunity. There is more selfishness than generosity, my Lord, in such eager and urgent solicitation."

Lord Evandale, evidently much hurt, took two or three turns through the apartment ere he replied to this accusation. At length he spoke—"I should have escaped this painful charge, durst I at once have mentioned to Miss Bellenden my principal reason for urging this request. It is one which she will probably despise on her own account, but which ought to weigh with her for the sake of Lady Margaret. My death in battle must give my whole estate to my heirs of entail; my forfeiture as a traitor, by the usurping government, may vest it in the Prince of Orange, or some Dutch favourite. In either case, my venerable friend and my betrothed bride must remain unprotected and in poverty. Vested with the rights and provisions of Lady Evandale, Edith will find, in the power of supporting her aged parent, some consolation for having condescended to share the title and fortunes of one who does not pretend to be worthy of her."

Edith was struck dumb by an argument which she had not expected, and was compelled to acknowledge, that Lord Evandale's suit was urged with delicacy as well as with consideration.

"And yet," she said, "such is the waywardness with which my heart reverts to former times—that I cannot—" (she burst into tears,) "suppress a degree of ominous reluctance at fulfilling my engagement upon such a brief summons."

"We have already fully considered this painful subject," said Lord Evandale; "and I hoped, my dear Edith, your own enquiries, as well as mine, had fully convinced you that these regrets were fruitless."

"Fruitless indeed!" said Edith, with a deep sigh, which, as if by an unexpected echo, was repeated from the adjoining apartment. Miss

Bellenden started at the sound, and scarcely composed herself upon Lord Evandale's assurances, that she had heard but the echo of her own suspiration.

"It sounded strangely distinct," she said, "and almost ominous; but my feelings are so harassed that the slightest trifle agitates them."

Lord Evandale eagerly attempted to sooth her alarm and reconcile her to a measure, which, however hasty, appeared to him the only means by which he could secure her independence. He urged his claim in virtue of the contract, her grandmother's wish and command, the propriety of insuring her comfort and independence, and touched lightly on his own long attachment, which he had evinced by so many and such various services. These Edith felt the more the less they were insisted upon; and at length, as she had nothing to oppose to his ardour, excepting a causeless reluctance, which she was herself ashamed to oppose against so much generosity, she was compelled to rest upon the impossibility of having the ceremony performed upon such hasty notice, at such a time and place. But for all this Lord Evandale was prepared, and he explained, with joyful alacrity, that the former chaplain of his regiment was in attendance at the Lodge with a faithful domestic, once a non-commissioned officer in the same corps; that his sister was also possessed of the secret; and that Head-rigg and his wife might be added to the list of witnesses, if agreeable to Miss Bellenden. As to the place, he had chosen it on very purpose. The marriage was to remain a secret, since Lord Evandale was to depart in disguise very soon after it was solemnized, a circumstance which, had their union been public, must have drawn upon him the attention of the government as being altogether unaccountable, unless from his being engaged in some dangerous design. Having hastily urged these motives and explained his arrangements, he ran, without waiting for answer, to summon his sister to attend his bride, while he went in search of the other persons whose presence was necessary.

When Lady Emily arrived, she found her friend in an agony of tears, of which she was at some loss to comprehend the reason, being one of those damsels who think there is nothing either wonderful or terrible in matrimony, and joining with most who knew him in thinking, that it could not be rendered peculiarly alarming by Lord Evandale being the bridegroom. Influenced by these feelings, she exhausted in succession all the usual arguments for courage, and all the expressions of sympathy and condolence ordinarily employed on such occasions. But when Lady Emily beheld her future sister-in-law deaf to all those ordinary topics of consolation—when she beheld tears follow fast and without intermission down cheeks as pale as marble—when she felt that the hand which she pressed in order to enforce her arguments turned cold within her grasp, and lay, like that of a corpse, insensible and unresponsive to her caresses, her feelings of sympathy gave way to those of hurt pride and pettish displeasure.

"I must own," she said, "that I am something at a loss to understand all this, Miss Bellenden. Months have passed since you agreed to marry my brother, and you have postponed the fulfilment of your engagement from one day to another, as if you had to avoid some dishonourable or highly disagreeable connection. I think I can answer for Lord Evandale, that he will seek no woman's hand against her inclination; and, though his sister, I may boldly say, that he does not need to urge any lady further than her inclinations carry her. You will forgive me, Miss Bellenden; but your present distress augurs ill for my brother's future happiness, and I must needs say, that he does not merit all these expressions of dislike and dolour, and that they seem an odd return for an attachment which he has manifested so long and in so many ways."

"You are right, Lady Emily," said Edith, drying her eyes, and endeavouring to resume her natural manner, though still betrayed by her faultering voice and the paleness of her cheeks—"You are quite right—Lord Evandale merits such usage from no one, least of all from her whom he has honoured with his regard. But if I have given way, for the last time, to a sudden and irresistible burst of feeling, it is my consolation, Lady Emily, that your brother knows the cause; that I have hid nothing from him, and that he at least is not apprehensive of finding in Edith Bellenden a wife undeserving of his affection. But still you are right, and I merit your censure for indulging for a moment fruitless regret and painful remembrance. It shall be so no longer; my lot is cast with Evandale, and with him I am resolved to bear it; nothing shall in future occur to excite his complaints, or the resentment of his relations; no idle recollections of other days shall intervene to prevent the zealous and affectionate discharge of my duty; no vain illusion recal the memory of other days"——

As she spoke these words, she slowly raised her eyes, which had before been hidden by her hand, to the latticed window of the apartment, which was partly open, uttered a dismal shriek, and fainted. Lady Emily turned her eyes in the same direction, but saw only the shadow of a man, which seemed to disappear from the window, and, terrified more by the state of Edith than by the apparition she had herself witnessed, she uttered shriek upon shriek for assistance. Her brother soon arrived with the chaplain and Jenny Dennison, but strong and vigorous remedies were necessary ere they could recal Miss Bellenden to sense and motion. Even then her language was wild and incoherent.

"Press me no further," she said to Lord Evandale; "it cannot be—Heaven and earth—the living and the dead, have leagued themselves against this ill-omened union.—Take all I can give—my sisterly regard—my devoted friendship. I will love and serve you as a bondswoman, but never speak to me more of marriage."

The astonishment of Lord Evandale may easily be conceived.

"Emily," he said to his sister, "this is your doing—I was accursed when I thought of bringing you here—some of your confounded folly has driven her mad."

"On my word, brother," answered Lady Emily, "you're sufficient to drive all the women in Scotland mad. Because your mistress seems much disposed to jilt you, you quarrel with your sister who has been arguing in your cause, and had brought her to a quiet hearing, when, all of a sudden, a man looked in at window, whom her crazed sensibility mistook either for you or some one else, and has treated us gratis with an excellent tragic scene."

"What man?—What window?" said Lord Evandale, in impatient displeasure. "Miss Bellenden is incapable of trifling with me, and yet what else could have"——

"Hush! hush!" said Jenny, whose interest lay particularly in stifling further enquiry; "for Heaven's sake, my Lord, speak low; my lady begins to recover."

Edith was no sooner somewhat restored to herself than she begged, in a feeble voice, to be left alone with Lord Evandale. All retreated, Jenny with her usual air of officious simplicity, Lady Emily and the chaplain with that of awakened curiosity. No sooner had they left the apartment than Edith beckoned Lord Evandale to sit beside her on the couch; her next motion was to take his hand and press it, in spite of his surprised resistance, to her lips; her last was to sink from her seat and to clasp his knees.

"Forgive me, my Lord!" she exclaimed—"Forgive me!—I must deal most untruly by you, and break a solemn engagement. You have my friendship, my highest regard, my most sincere gratitude—You have more; you have my word and my faith—But, O, forgive me, for the fault is not mine—you have not my love, and I cannot marry you without a sin!"

"You dream, my dearest Edith!" said Evandale, perplexed in the utmost degree—"you let your imagination beguile you; this is but some delusion of an over-sensitive mind; the person whom you preferred to me has been long in a better world, where your unavailing regret cannot follow him, or, if it could, would only diminish his happiness."

"You are mistaken, Lord Evandale," said Edith, solemnly. "I am not a sleep-walker or a madwoman. No—I could not have believed from any one what I have seen—but, having seen him, I must believe my own eyes."

"Seen *him*?—seen whom?" asked Lord Evandale, in great anxiety.

"Henry Morton," replied Edith, uttering these two words as if they were her last, and very nearly fainting when she had done so.

"Miss Bellenden," said Lord Evandale, "you treat me like a fool or a child; if you repent your engagement to me," he continued, indignantly, "I am not a man to enforce it against your inclination; but deal with me as a man, and forbear this trifling."

He was about to go on, when he perceived, from her quivering eye and pallid cheek, that nothing less than imposture was intended, and that by whatever means her imagination had been so impressed, it was really disturbed by unaffected awe and terror. He changed his tone, and exerted all his eloquence in endeavouring to sooth and extract from her the secret cause of such terror.

"I saw him!" she repeated—"I saw Henry Morton stand at that window, and look into the apartment at the moment I was on the point of abjuring him for ever. His face was darker, thinner, and paler than it was wont to be; his dress was a horseman's cloak, and hat looped down over his face; his expression was like that he wore on that dreadful morning when he was examined by Claverhouse at Tillietudlem. Ask your sister, ask Lady Emily, if she did not see him as well as I.—I know what has called him up—he came to upbraid me, that, while my heart was with him in the deep and dead sea, I was about to give my hand to another. My Lord, all is ended between you and me— be the consequences what they will, she cannot marry whose union disturbs the repose of the dead."

"Good Heaven!" said Lord Evandale, as he paced the room, half mad himself with surprise and vexation, "her fine understanding must be totally overthrown, and that by the effort which she has made to comply with my ill-timed, though well-meant, request. Without rest and attendance her health is ruined for ever."

At this moment the door opened, and Halliday, who had been Lord Evandale's principal personal attendant since they both left the Guards on the Revolution, stumbled into the room with a countenance as pale and ghastly as terror could paint it.

"What is the matter next, Halliday?" cried his master, starting up. "Any discovery of the"——

He had just recollection sufficient to stop short in the midst of the dangerous sentence.

"No, sir," said Halliday, "it is not that, nor any thing like that; but I have seen a ghost!"

"A ghost! you eternal idiot!" said Lord Evandale, forced altogether out of his patience. "Has all mankind sworn to go mad in order to drive me so?—What ghost, you simpleton?"

"The ghost of Henry Morton, the whig captain at Bothwell Bridge," replied Halliday. "He passed by me like a fire-flaught when I was in the garden!"

"This is mid-summer madness," said Lord Evandale, "or there is some strange villainy afloat.—Jenny, attend your lady in her chamber, while I endeavour to find a clew to all this."

But Lord Evandale's enquiries were in vain. Jenny, who might have given him (had she chosen) a very satisfactory explanation, had an interest to leave the matter in darkness; and interest was a matter which now weighed principally with Jenny, since the possession of an active and affectionate husband in her own proper right had altogether allayed her spirit of coquetry. She had made the best use of the first moments of confusion hastily to remove all traces of any one having slept in the apartment adjoining to the parlour, and even to erase the mark of footsteps beneath the window through which she conjectured Morton's face had been seen while attempting, ere he left the garden, to gain one look at her whom he had so long loved, and was now on the point of losing for ever. That he had passed Halliday in the garden was equally clear; and she learned from her elder boy, whom she had employed to have the stranger's horse saddled and ready for his departure, that he had rushed into the stable, thrown the child a guinea, and, mounting his horse, ridden with fearful rapidity down towards the Clyde. The secret was, therefore, in their own family, and Jenny was resolved it should remain so.

"For, to be sure," she said, "although her lady and Halliday kenn'd Mr Morton by broad daylight, that was nae reason I suld own to kenning him in the gloaming and by candle-light, and him keeping his face frae Cuddie and me a' the time."

So she stood resolutely upon the negative when examined by Lord Evandale. As for Halliday, he could only say, that as he entered the garden-door, the supposed apparition met him walking swiftly, and with a visage on which anger and grief appeared to be contending.

"He knew him well," he said, "having been repeatedly guard upon him, and obliged to write down his marks of stature and visage in case of his escape. And there were few faces like Mr Morton's."

But what should make him haunt the country where he was neither hanged nor shot, he, the said Halliday, did not pretend to conceive.

Lady Emily confessed she had seen the face of a man at the window, but her evidence went no farther. John Gudyill deponed *nil novit in causa*. He had left his gardening to get his morning dram just at the time when the apparition had taken place. Lady Emily's servant was waiting orders in the kitchen, and there was not another being within a quarter of a mile of the house.

Lord Evandale returned perplexed and dissatisfied in the highest degree, at beholding a plan which he thought necessary not less for the protection of Edith in contingent circumstances, than for the assurance of his own happiness, and which he had brought so very near perfection, thus broken off without any apparent or rational cause. His knowledge of Edith's character set her beyond the suspicion of covering any capricious change of determination by a pretended vision. But he would have set the apparition down to the influence of an overstrained imagination, agitated by the circumstances in which she had so suddenly been placed, had it not been for the coinciding testimony of Halliday, who had no reason for thinking of Morton more than any other person, and knew nothing of Miss Bellenden's vision when he promulgated his own. On the other hand, it seemed in the highest degree improbable that Morton, so long and so vainly sought after, and who was, with such good reason, supposed to be lost when the Vryheid of Rotterdam went down with crew and passengers, should be alive and lurking in this country, where there was no longer any reason why he should not openly shew himself, since the present government favoured his own party in politics. When Lord Evandale reluctantly brought himself to communicate these doubts to the chaplain, in order to obtain his opinion, he could only obtain a long lecture on dæmonology, in which, after quoting Delrio, and Burthoog, and De L'Ancre, on the subject of apparitions, together with sundry civilians and common lawyers on the nature of testimony, the learned gentleman expressed his definite and determined opinion to be, either that there had been an actual apparition of the deceased Henry Morton's spirit, the possibility of which he was, as a divine and a philosopher, neither fully prepared to admit or to deny; or else, that the said Henry Morton, being still in *rerum natura*, had appeared in his own proper person that morning; or, finally, that some strong *deceptio visus*, or striking similitude of person, had deceived the eyes of Miss Bellenden and of Thomas Halliday. Which of these was the most probable hypothesis, the Doctor declined to pronounce, but expressed himself ready to die in the opinion that one or other of them had occasioned that morning's disturbance.

Lord Evandale soon had additional cause for distressful anxiety. Miss Bellenden was declared to be dangerously ill.

"I will not leave this place," he exclaimed, "till she is pronounced to be in safety. I neither can nor ought to do so; for whatever may have been the immediate occasion of her illness, I gave the first cause for it by my unhappy solicitation."

He established himself, therefore, as a guest in the family, which the presence of his sister as well as of Lady Margaret Bellenden, (who, in despite of her rheumatism, caused herself to be transported thither when she heard of her grand-daughter's illness,) rendered a conduct equally natural and delicate. And thus he anxiously awaited, until, without injury to her health, Edith could sustain a final explanation ere his departure on his expedition.

"She shall never," said the generous young man, "look on her engagement with me as the means of fettering her to a match, the idea of which seems almost to unhinge her understanding."

Chapter Nine

Ah, happy hills! ah, pleasing shades!
    Ah, fields beloved in vain!
Where once my careless childhood stray'd,
    A stranger yet to pain.
        Ode on a distant Prospect of Eton College

IT IS NOT by corporeal wants and infirmities only, that men of the most distinguished talents are levelled, during their lifetime, with the common mass of mankind. There are periods of mental agitation when the firmest must be ranked with the weakest of his brethren; and when, in paying the general tax of humanity, his distresses are even aggravated by feeling that he transgresses, in indulgence of his grief, the rules of religion and philosophy, by which he endeavours in general to regulate his passions and his actions. It was during such a paroxysm that the unfortunate Morton left Fairy-knowe. To know that his long-loved and still-beloved Edith, whose image had filled his mind for so many years, was on the point of marriage to his early rival, who had laid claim to her heart by so many services, as hardly left her a title to refuse his addresses, bitter as the intelligence was, yet came not as an unexpected blow. During his residence abroad he had once written to Edith. It was to bid her farewell for ever, and to conjure her to forget him. He had requested her not to answer his letter, yet he half hoped, for many a day, that she might transgress his injunction. The letter never reached her to whom it was addressed, and Morton, ignorant of its miscarriage, could only conclude himself laid aside and forgotten, according to his own self-denying request. All that he had heard of their mutual relations since his return to Scotland, prepared him to expect that he could only look upon Miss Bellenden as the betrothed bride of Lord Evandale; and, even if freed from the burthen of obligation to the latter, it would still have been inconsistent with his generosity of disposition to disturb their arrangement, by attempting the assertion of a claim, prescribed by absence and barred by a thousand circumstances of difficulty. Why then did he seek the cottage which their broken fortunes had now rendered the retreat of Lady Margaret Bellenden and her grand-daughter? He yielded, we are under the necessity of acknowledging, to the impulse of an inconsistent wish, which many might have felt in his situation.

Accident apprised him, while travelling towards his native district, that the ladies, near whose mansion he must necessarily pass, were absent, and, learning that Cuddie and his wife acted as their principal domestics, he could not resist pausing at their cottage, to learn, if possible, the real progress which Lord Evandale had made in the affections of Miss Bellenden—alas! no longer his Edith. This rash experiment ended as we have related, and he parted from the house of Fairy-knowe, conscious that he was still beloved by Edith, yet compelled, by faith and honour, to relinquish her for ever. With what feelings he must have listened to the dialogue between Lord Evandale and Edith, the greater part of which he involuntarily overheard, the reader must conceive, for we dare not attempt to describe them. An hundred times he was tempted to burst upon their interview, or to exclaim aloud—"Edith, I yet live!"—and as often the recollection of her plighted troth, and of the debt of gratitude which he owed Lord Evandale, (to whose influence with Claverhouse he justly ascribed his escape from torture and from death) withheld him from a rashness which might indeed have involved all in further distress, but gave little prospect of forwarding his own happiness. He repressed forcibly these selfish emotions, though with an agony which thrilled his every nerve.

"No, Edith!" was his internal oath, "never will I add a thorn to thy pillow—That which Heaven has ordained let it be, and let me not add, by my selfish sorrows, one atom's weight to the burden thou hast to bear. I was dead to thee when thy resolution was adopted; and never —never—shalt thou know that Henry Morton still lives!"

As he formed this resolution, diffident of his own power to keep it, and seeking that firmness in flight which was every moment shaken by his continuing within hearing of Edith's voice, he hastily rushed from his apartment by the little closet and the sashed door which led him to the garden.

But firmly as he thought his resolution was fixed, he could not leave the spot where the last tones of a voice so beloved still vibrated on his ear, without endeavouring to avail himself of the opportunity which the parlour window afforded to steal one last glance at the lovely speaker. It was in this attempt, made while Edith seemed to have her eyes unalterably bent upon the ground, that Morton's presence was detected by her raising them suddenly. So soon as her wild scream made this known to the unfortunate object of a passion so constant, and which seemed so ill-fated, he hurried from the place as if pursued by the furies. He passed Halliday in the garden without recognizing, or even being sensible that he had seen him, threw himself on his horse, and, by a sort of instinct rather than recollection, took the first by-road rather than the public route to Hamilton.

In all probability this prevented Lord Evandale from learning that he was actually in existence, for the news that the Highlanders had obtained a decisive victory at Killiecrankie, had occasioned an accurate look-out to be kept on all the passes, for fear of some commotion among the Lowland Jacobites. They did not omit to post centinels on Bothwell Bridge, and as these men had not seen any traveller pass westward in that direction, and as, besides, their comrades stationed in the village of Bothwell were equally positive that none had gone eastward, the apparition, in the existence of which Edith and Halliday were equally positive, became yet more mysterious in the judgment of Lord Evandale, who was finally inclined to settle in the belief that the heated and disturbed imagination of Edith had summoned up the phantom she stated herself to have seen, and that Halliday had, in some unaccountable manner, been infected by the same superstition.

Meanwhile, the by-path which Morton pursued, with all the speed which his vigorous horse could exert, brought him in a very few seconds to the brink of the Clyde, at a spot marked with the feet of horses who were conducted to it as a watering-place. The steed, urged as he was to the gallop, did not pause a single instant, but, throwing himself into the river, was soon beyond his depth. The plunge which the animal made as his feet quitted the ground, with the feeling that the cold water rose above his sword-belt, were the first incidents which recalled Morton, whose movements had been hitherto mechanical, to the necessity of taking measures for preserving himself and the noble animal which he bestrode. A perfect master of all manly exercises, the management of a horse in water was as familiar to him as when upon a meadow. He directed the animal's course somewhat down the stream towards a low plain, or holm, which seemed to promise an easy egress from the river. In the first and second attempt to get on shore, the horse was frustrated by the nature of the ground, and nearly fell backwards on his rider. The instinct of self-preservation seldom fails, even in the most desperate circumstances, to recal the human mind to some degree of equipoize, unless when altogether distracted by terror, and Morton was obliged to the danger in which he was placed for complete recovery of his self-possession. A third attempt at a spot more carefully and judiciously selected, succeeded better than the former, and placed the horse and his rider in safety upon the left-hand bank of the Clyde.

"But whither," said Morton, in the bitterness of his heart, "am I now to direct my course? or rather, what does it signify to which point of the compass a wretch so forlorn betakes himself? I would to God, could the wish be without a sin, that these dark waters had flowed over me, and drowned my recollection of that which was, and that which is."

The sense of impatience, which the disturbed state of his feelings had occasioned, scarcely had vented itself in these violent expressions, ere he was struck with shame at having given way to such a paroxysm. He remembered how marvellously the life, which he now held so lightly in the bitterness of his disappointment, had been preserved through the almost unceasing perils which had beset him since he entered upon his public career.

"I am a fool!" he said, "and worse than a fool, to set light by that which Heaven has so oft preserved in the most marvellous manner. Something there yet remains for me in this world, were it only to bear my sorrows like a man, and to aid those who need my assistance. What have I seen,—what have I heard but the very conclusion of that which I knew was to happen? They"—(he durst not utter their names, even in soliloquy)—"they are embarrassed and in difficulties. She is stripped of her inheritance, and he seems rushing on some dangerous career, of which, but for the low voice in which he spoke, I might have become the depositary. Is there no means to aid or to warn them?"

As he pondered upon this topic, forcibly withdrawing his mind from his own disappointment, and compelling its attention to the affairs of Edith and her betrothed husband, the letter of Burley, long forgotten, suddenly rushed on his memory, like a ray of light darting through a mist.

"Their ruin must have been his work," was his internal conclusion —"If it can be repaired, it must be through his means, or by information obtained from him. I will seek him out. Stern, crafty, and enthusiastic as he was, my plain and downright rectitude of purpose has more than once prevailed with him. I will seek him out, at least, and who knows what influence the information I may acquire from him may have on the fortunes of those whom I shall never see more, and who will probably never learn that I am now suppressing my own grief to add, if possible, to their happiness."

Animated by these hopes, though the foundation was but slight, he

sought the nearest way to the next high-road, and as all the tracks
through the valley were known to him since he hunted through them
in youth, he had no other difficulty than that of surmounting one or
two enclosures, ere he found himself on the road to the small burgh
where the feast of the popinjay had been celebrated. He journeyed in a
state of mind sad indeed and dejected; yet relieved from its earlier and
more intolerable state of anguish; for virtuous resolution and manly
disinterestedness seldom fail to restore tranquillity even where they
cannot create happiness. He turned his thoughts with strong effort
upon the means of discovering Burley, and the chance there was of
extracting from him any knowledge which he might possess favourable to her in whose cause he interested himself, and at length formed
the resolution of guiding himself by the circumstances in which he
might discover the object of his quest, trusting, that, from Cuddie's
account of a schism betwixt Burley and his brethren of the presbyterian persuasion, he might find him less rancorously disposed against
Miss Bellenden, and inclined to exert the power which he asserted
that he possessed over her fortunes more favourably than heretofore.

Noontide had passed away when our traveller found himself in the
neighbourhood of his deceased uncle's habitation of Milnewood. It
rose among glades and groves that were chequered with a thousand
early recollections of joy and sorrow, and made upon Morton that
mournful impression, soft and affecting, yet, withal, soothing, which
the sensitive mind usually receives from a return to the haunts of
childhood and early youth, after having experienced the vicissitudes
and tempests of public life. A strong desire came upon him to visit the
house itself.

"Old Alison," he thought, "will not know me, any more than the
honest couple whom I saw yesterday. I may indulge my curiosity, and
proceed on my journey, without her having any knowledge of my
existence. I think they said my uncle had bequeathed to her my family
mansion—Well—be it so. I have enough to sorrow, besides lamenting for such a disappointment as that; and yet methinks he has chosen
an odd successor in my grumbling old dame, to a line of respectable, if
not distinguished, ancestry. Let it be as it may, I will visit the old
mansion at least once more."

The house of Milnewood, even in its best days, had nothing cheerful about it, but its gloom appeared to be doubled under the auspices
of the old housekeeper. Every thing indeed was in repair; there were
no slates deficient upon the steep grey roof, and no panes broken in
the narrow windows. But the grass in the court-yard looked as if the
foot of man had not been there for years; the doors were carefully
locked, and that which admitted to the hall seemed to have been shut

for a length of time, since the spiders had fairly drawn their webs betwixt the door-way and the staple. Living sight or sound there was none, until, after much knocking, Morton heard the little window, through which it was usual to reconnoitre visitors, open with much caution. The face of Alison, puckered with some score of wrinkles, in addition to those with which it was furrowed when Morton left Scotland, now presented itself, enveloped in a *toy*, from under the protection of which some of her grey tresses had escaped in a manner more picturesque than beautiful, while her shrill tremulous voice demanded the cause of the knocking.

"I wish to speak an instant with one Alison Wilson who resides here," said Henry.

"She's no at hame the day," answered Mrs Wilson, *in propria persona*, the state of whose deranged head-dress, perhaps, inspired her with this direct mode of denying herself; "and ye are but a mislear'd person to speer for her in sic a manner. Ye might hae had an M under your belt for *Mistress* Wilson of Milnewood."

"I beg pardon, Madam," said Morton, internally smiling at finding in old Ailie the same jealousy of disrespect which she used to exhibit upon former occasions—"I beg pardon; I am but a stranger in this country, and have been so long abroad, that I have almost forgot my own language."

"Did ye come frae foreign parts?" said Ailie; "then maybe ye may hae heard of a young gentleman of this country that they ca' Henry Morton?"

"I think," said Morton, "I have heard such a name in Germany."

"Then bide a wee bit where ye are, friend—or stay—gang round by the back o' the house, and ye'll find a laigh door; it's on the latch, for it's ne'er barred till sunset.—Ye'll open't—and tak care ye dinna fa' ower the tub, for the entry's dark—and than ye'll turn to the right, and than ye'll haud straught forward, and than ye'll turn to the right again, and ye'll tak heed o' the cellar stairs, and then ye'll be at the door o' the little kitchen—it's a' the kitchen that's at Milnewood now—and I'll come down t'ye, and whate'er ye wad say to Mistress Wilson ye may very safely tell it to me."

A stranger might have had some difficulty, notwithstanding the minuteness of the directions supplied by Ailie, to pilot himself in safety through the dark labyrinth of passages that led from the back-door to the little kitchen, but Henry was too well acquainted with the navigation of these streights to experience danger, either from the Scylla which lurked on one side in shape of a bucking tub, or the Charybdis which yawned on the other in the profundity of a winding cellar-stair. His only impediment arose from the snarling and vehement barking of a small cocking spaniel, once his own property, but which, unlike to the faithful Argus, saw his master return from his wanderings without any symptom of recognition.

"The little dogs and all!" said Morton to himself, on being thus disowned by his former favourite. "I am so changed that no breathing creature that I have known and loved will now acknowledge me."

At this moment he had reached the kitchen, and soon after the tread of Alison's high heels, and the pat of the crutch-handled cane, which served at once to prop and to guide her footsteps, were heard upon the stairs, an annunciation which continued for some time ere she fairly reached the parlour.

Morton had, therefore, time to survey the slender preparations for housekeeping, which were now sufficient in the house of his ancestors. The fire, though coals are plenty in that neighbourhood, was husbanded with the closest attention to economy of fuel, and the small pipkin, in which was preparing the dinner of the old woman and her maid-of-all-works, a girl of twelve years old, intimated, by its thin and watery vapour, that Ailie had not mended her cheer with her improved fortune.

When she entered, the head which noddled with self-importance—the features in which an irritable peevishness, acquired by habit and indulgence, strove with a temper naturally affectionate and good-natured—the coif—the apron—the blue checked gown, were all those of old Ailie; but laced pinners, hastily put on to meet the stranger, with some other trifling articles of decoration, marked the difference between Mrs Wilson of Milnewood and the housekeeper of the late proprietor.

"What were ye pleased to want wi' Mrs Wilson, sir?—I am Mrs Wilson," was her first address; for the five minutes time which she had gained for the business of the toilette, entitled her, she conceived, to assume the full merit of her illustrious name, and shine forth on her guest in unchastened splendour. Morton's sensations, confounded between the past and present, fairly confused him so much, that he would have had difficulty in answering her, even if he had known well what to say. But as he had not determined what character he ought to adopt while concealing that which was properly his own, he had an additional reason for remaining silent. Mrs Wilson, in perplexity, and with some apprehension, repeated her question.

"What were ye pleased to want wi' me, sir? Ye said ye had kenn'd Mr Harry Morton?"

"Pardon me, madam," answered Henry; "it was of one Silas Morton I wished to speak."

The old woman's countenance fell.

"It was his father then ye kent o', the brother o' the late Milnewood, —ye canna mind him abroad, I wad think—he was come hame afore ye were born. I thought ye had brought me news of poor Maister Harry."

"It was from my father I learned to know Colonel Morton," said Henry; "of the son I know but too little; rumour says he has died abroad on his passage to Holland."

"That's ower like to be true, and mony a tear it's cost my auld e'en. His uncle, poor gentleman, just sough'd awa' wi' it in his mouth. He had been gi'eing me preceeze directions anent the bread and the wine, and the brandy, at his burial, and how aften it was to be handed round the company, (for, dead or alive, he was a prudent, frugal, pains-taking man) and than he said, said he, 'Ailie,' (he aye ca'd me Ailie, we were auld acquaintance) 'Ailie, tak ye care and haud the gear weel thegither; for the name of Morton of Milnewood's ga'en out like the last sough of an auld sang.' And sae he fell out o' ae dwam into anither, and ne'er spake word mair, unless it were something we cou'dna mak out, about a dippit candle being gude aneugh to see to die wi'.—He cou'd ne'er bide to see a moulded ane, and there was ane, by ill luck, on the table."

While Mrs Wilson was thus detailing the last moments of the old miser, Morton was pressingly engaged in diverting the assiduous curiosity of the dog, which, recovered from his first surprise, and combining former recollections, had, after much snuffing and exam-ination, begun a course of capering and jumping upon the stranger which threatened every instant to betray him. At length, in the urgency of his impatience, Morton could not forbear exclaiming, in a tone of hasty impatience, "Down, Elphin! Down, sir!"

"Ye ken our dog's name," said the old lady, struck with great and sudden surprise—"ye ken our dog's name, and it's no a common ane. An' the creature kens you too," she continued, in a more agitated and shriller tone—"God guide us! it's my ain bairn!"

So saying, the poor old woman threw herself around Morton's neck, clung to him, kissed him as if he had been actually her child, and wept for joy. There was no parrying the discovery, if he could have had the heart to attempt any further disguise. He returned her embrace with the most grateful warmth, and answered—

"I do indeed live, dear Ailie, to thank you for all your kindness, past and present, and to rejoice that there is at least one friend to welcome me to my native country."

"Friends!" exclaimed Ailie, "ye'll hae mony friends—ye'll hae mony friends; for ye will hae gear, hinny—ye will hae gear, Heaven mak ye a gude guide o't! But, eh, sirs!" she continued, pushing him back from her with her trembling hand and shrivelled arm, and gazing in his face as if to read, at more convenient distance, the ravages which sorrow rather than time had made on his face—"Eh, sirs! ye're sair altered, hinny, your face is turned pale, and your e'en are sunken, and your bonny red-and-white is turned a' dark and sun-burned. O weary on the wars! mony's the comely face they destroy.—And what cam ye here, hinny? And where hae ye been?—And what hae been doing?—And what for did ye na write till us?—And how cam ye to pass yersel for dead?—And what for did ye come creeping to your ain house as if ye had been an unco body, to gi'e poor auld Ailie sic a start?" she concluded, smiling through her tears.

It was some time ere Morton could overcome his own emotion so as to give the kind old woman the information which we shall communicate to our readers in the next Chapter.

Chapter Ten

————Aumerle that was,
But that is gone for being Richard's friend,
And, Madam, you must call him Rutland now.

THE SCENE of explanation was hastily removed from the little kitchen to Mrs Wilson's own matted room, the very same which she had occupied as housekeeper, and which she continued to retain as better secured against sifting winds than the hall, which she had found dangerous to her rheumatics, and more fitting for her use than the late Milnewood's apartment, honest man, which gave her sad thoughts; and as for the great oak parlour, it was never opened but to be aired, washed, and dusted, according to the invariable practice of the family, unless upon their most solemn festivals. In the matted room, therefore, they were settled, surrounded by pickle-pots and conserves of all kinds, which the *ci-devant* housekeeper continued to compound, out of mere habit, although neither she herself, nor any one else, ever partook of the comfits which she so regularly prepared.

Morton, adapting his narrative to the comprehension of his auditor, informed her briefly of the wreck of the vessel and the loss of all hands, excepting two or three common seamen, who had early secured the skiff, and were just putting off from the vessel when he leaped from the deck into their boat, and unexpectedly, as well as contrary to their inclination, made himself partner of their voyage and of their safety. Landed at Flushing, he was fortunate enough to meet with an old officer who had been in service with his father. By his advice, he shunned going immediately to the Hague, but forwarded his letters to the court of the Stadtholder.

"Our Prince," said the veteran, "must, as yet, keep terms with his father-in-law, and with your King Charles; and to approach him in the character of a Scottish malcontent would render it imprudent for him to distinguish you by his favour. Wait, therefore, his orders, without forcing yourself on his notice; observe the strictest prudence and retirement; assume for the present a different name; shun the company of the British exiles; and, depend upon it, you will not repent your prudence."

The old friend of Silas Morton argued justly. After a considerable time had elapsed, the Prince of Orange, in a progress through the United States, came to the town where Morton, impatient at his situation and the incognito which he was obliged to observe, still continued, nevertheless, to be a resident. He had an hour of private interview assigned, in which the Prince expressed himself highly pleased with his intelligence, his prudence, and the liberal view which he seemed to take of the factions of his native country, their motives and their purposes.

"I would willingly," said William, "attach you to my own person, but that cannot be without giving offence in England. But I will do as much for you, as well out of respect for the sentiments you have expressed, as for the recommendations you have brought me. Here is a commission in a Swiss regiment at present in garrison in a distant province, where you will meet few or none of your countrymen. Continue to be Captain Melville, and let the name of Morton sleep till better days."

"Thus began my fortune," continued Morton; "and my services have, on various occasions, been distinguished by his Royal Highness, until the moment that brought him to Britain as her political deliverer. His commands must excuse my silence to my few friends in Scotland; and I wonder not at the report of my death, considering the wreck of the vessel, and that I found no occasion to use the letters of exchange with which I was furnished by the liberality of some of them, a circumstance which must have confirmed the belief that I had perished."

"But, dear hinny," asked Mrs Wilson, "did ye find nae Scotch body at the Prince of Oranger's court that kenn'd ye? I wad hae thought Morton o' Milnewood was kenn'd a' through the country."

"I was purposely engaged in distant service," said Morton, "until a period when few, without as deep and kind a motive of interest as yours, Ailie, would have known the stripling Morton in Major-General Melville."

"Malville was your mother's name," said Mrs Wilson; "but Morton sounds far bonnier in my auld lugs. And when ye tak up the lairdship, ye maun tak the auld name and designation again."

"I am like to be in no haste to do either the one or the other, Ailie, for I have some reasons for the present to conceal my being alive from every one but you; and, as for the lairdship of Milnewood, it is in as good hands."

"As good hands, hinny!" re-echoed Ailie; "I am hopefu' ye are na meaning mine? The rents and the lands is but a sair fash to me. And I am ower failed to tak a help-mate, though Wylie Mactrickit the writer was very pressing and spak very civilly; but I am ower auld a cat to draw that strae before me. He canna whillywha me as he has dune mony a ane. And than I thought aye ye wad come back, and I wad get my pickle meal and my sowp milk, and keep a' things right about ye as I used to do in your puir uncle's time, and it wad be just pleasure aneugh for me to see ye thrive and guide the gear canny—Ye'll hae learned that in Holland, I'se warrant, for they're thrifty folk there, as I hear tell—But ye'll be for keeping rather a mair house than puir auld Milnewood that's gane; and, indeed, I would approve o' your eating butcher-meat maybe as aften as three times a-week—it keeps the wind out o' the stamack."

"We will talk of all this another time," said Morton, surprised at the generosity upon a large scale, which mingled in Ailie's thoughts and actions with habitual and sordid parsimony, and at the odd contrast between her love of saving and indifference to selfish acquisition. "You must know," he continued, "that I am in this country only for a few days on some special business of importance to the government, and therefore, Ailie, not a word of having seen me. At some other time I will acquaint you fully with my motives and intentions."

"E'en be it sae, my jo," replied Ailie, "I can keep a secret like my neighbours; and weel auld Milnewood kenn'd it, honest man, for he tauld me where he keepit his gear, and that's what maist folk like to hae as private as possibly may be.—But come awa' wi' me, hinny, till I show ye the oak-parlour how grandly it's keepit, just as if ye had been expectit hame everyday—I loot naebody sort it but my ain auld hands. It was a kind o' divertisement to me, though whiles the tear wan into my e'e, and I said to mysel, what needs I fash wi' grates, and carpets, and cushions, and the muckle brass candlesticks ony mair? for they will ne'er come hame that aught it rightfully."

With these words she hauled him away to this *sanctum sanctorum*, the scrubbing and cleansing whereof was her daily employment, as its high state of good order constituted the very pride of her heart. Morton, as he followed her into the room, underwent a rebuke for not "dighting his shoon," which shewed that Ailie had not relinquished her habits of authority. On entering the oak-parlour, he could not but recollect the feelings of solemn awe with which, when a boy, he had been affected at his occasional and rare admission to an apartment which he then supposed had not its equal save in the halls of princes. It may be readily supposed, that the worked worsted chairs, with their short ebony legs and long upright backs, had lost much of their influence over his mind, that the large brass andirons seemed diminished in splendour, that the green worsted tapestry appeared no master-piece of the Arras loom, and that the room appeared, on the whole, dark, gloomy, and disconsolate. Yet there were two objects, "the counterfeit presentment of two brothers," which, dissimilar as those described by Hamlet, affected his mind with a variety of sensations. One full-length portrait represented his father, in complete armour, with a countenance intimating his masculine and determined character; and the other set forth his uncle in velvet and brocade, looking as if he were ashamed of his own finery, though entirely indebted for it to the liberality of the painter.

"It was an idle fancy," Ailie said, "to dress the honest auld man in thae expensive fal-lalls that he ne'er wore in his life, instead o' his douce Raploch grey, and his band wi' the narrow edging."

In private, Morton could not help being much of her opinion; for any thing approaching to the dress of a gentleman sate as ill on the ungainly person of his departed relative as an open or generous expression would have done on his mean and money-making features. He now extricated himself from Ailie to visit some of his haunts in the neighbouring wood, while her own hands made an addition to the dinner she was preparing; an incident no otherwise remarkable than as it cost the life of a fowl, which, for any event of less importance than the arrival of Henry Morton, might have cackled on till a good old age, ere Ailie could have been guilty of the extravagance of killing and dressing it. The meal was seasoned by talk of old times, and by the plans which Ailie laid out for futurity, in which she assigned her young master all the prudential habits of her old one, and planned out the dexterity with which she was to exercise her duty as governante. Morton let the old woman enjoy her day-dreams and castle-building during moments of such pleasure, and deferred, till some fitter occasion, the communication of his purpose again to return and spend his life upon the continent.

His next care was to lay aside his military dress, which he considered as likely to render more difficult his researches after Burley. He exchanged it for a grey doublet and cloak, formerly his usual attire at Milnewood, and which Mrs Wilson produced from a chest of walnut-tree, wherein she had laid them aside, without forgetting carefully to brush and air them from time to time. Morton retained his sword and fire-arms, without which few persons travelled in these unsettled times. When he appeared in his new attire, Mrs Wilson was first thankful "that they fitted him sae decently, since, though he was nae fatter, yet he looked mair manly than whan he was ta'en frae Milnewood."

Next she enlarged on the advantage of saving old clothes to be what she called beet-masters to the new, and was far advanced in the history of a velvet cloak belonging to the late Milnewood, which had first been converted to a velvet doublet, and then into a pair of breeches, and appeared each time as good as new, when Morton interrupted her account of its transmigrations to bid her good-bye.

He gave, indeed, a sufficient shock to her feelings, by expressing the necessity he was under of proceeding on his journey that evening.

"And whare are ye ganging?—And what wad ye do that for?—And whare wad ye sleep but in your ain house, after ye hae been sae mony years frae hame?"

"I feel all the unkindness of it, Ailie, but it must be so; and that was the reason that I attempted to conceal myself from you, as I suspected you would not let me part from you so easily."

"But whare are ye ganging, then?" said Ailie, once more. "Saw e'er mortal e'en the like o' you, just to come ae moment, and flee awa' like a fire-flaught the neist!"

"I must go down," replied Morton, "to Niel Blane the piper's Howff; he can give me a bed, I suppose?"

"A bed?—I'se warrant can he," replied Ailie, "and gar ye pay weel for't into the bargain. Laddie, I dare say ye hae lost your wits in thae foreign parts, to gang and gi'e siller for a supper and bed, and might hae baith for naething, and thank to ye for accepting them."

"I assure you, Ailie," said Morton, desirous to silence her prudential remonstrances, "that this is a business of great importance, in which I may be a great gainer, and cannot possibly be a loser."

"I dinna see how that can be, if ye begin by gi'eing maybe the feck o' twal shillings Scots for your supper; but young folks are aye venturesome, and think to get siller that way. My puir auld maister took a surer gait, and never parted wi' it when he had anes gotten it."

Persevering in his desperate resolution, Morton took leave of Ailie, and mounted his horse to proceed to the little town, after exacting a solemn promise that she would conceal his return until she again saw or heard from him.

"I am not very extravagant," was his natural reflection, as he trotted slowly towards the town; "but were Ailie and I to set up house together, as she proposes, I think my profusion would break the good old creature's heart before a week were out."

Chapter Eleven

————Where's the jolly host
You told me of? 'T has been my custom ever
To parley with mine host.
                              Lovers' Progress

MORTON reached the burrow-town without meeting with any remarkable adventure, and alighted at the little inn. It had occurred to him more than once, while upon his journey, that his resumption of the dress which he had worn while a youth, although favourable to his views in other respects, might render it more difficult for him to remain *incognito*. But a few years of campaigns and wandering had so changed his appearance, that he had great confidence that in the grown man, whose brows exhibited the traces of resolution and considerate thought, none would recognize the raw and bashful stripling who won the game of the popinjay. The only chance was, that here and there some whig, whom he had led to battle, might remember the Captain of the Milnewood Marksmen; but the risk, if there was any, could not be guarded against.

The Howff seemed full and frequent, as if possessed of all its old celebrity. The person and demeanour of Niel Blane, more fat and less civil than of yore, intimated that he had increased as well in purse as in corpulence; for in Scotland a landlord's complaisance for his guests decreases in exact proportion to his rise in the world. His daughter had acquired the experienced air of a dexterous bar-maid, undisturbed by the circumstances of love and war, so apt to perplex her in the exercise of her vocation. Both shewed Morton the degree of attention which could have been expected by a stranger travelling without attendants, at a time when they were particularly the badges of distinction. He took upon himself exactly the character his appearance presented,—went to the stable and saw his horse accommodated,—then returned to the house, and, seating himself in the public room, (for to request one to himself would, in these days, have been thought an overweening degree of conceit,) he found himself in the very apartment in which he had some years since celebrated his victory at the game of the popinjay, a jocular preferment which led to so many serious consequences.

He felt himself, as may well be supposed, a much changed man since that festivity; and yet, to look around him, the groups assembled in the Howff seemed not dissimilar to those which the same scene had formerly presented. Two or three burghers husbanded their "dribbles o' brandy;" two or three dragoons lounged over their muddy ale, and cursed the inactive times that allowed them no better cheer. Their Cornet did not, indeed, play at backgammon with the curate in his cassock, but he drank a little modicum of *aqua mirabilis* with the grey-cloaked presbyterian minister. The scene was another, and yet the same, differing only in persons, but corresponding in general character.

"Let the tide of the world wax or wane as it will," he thought, as he looked around him, "enough will be found to fill the places which chance has rendered vacant; and, in the usual occupations and amusements of life, human beings will succeed each other, as leaves upon the same tree, with the same individual difference and the same general resemblance."

After pausing a few minutes, Morton, whose experience had taught him the readiest mode of securing attention, ordered a pint of claret, and, as the smiling landlord appeared with the pewter measure foaming fresh from the tap, (for bottling wine was not then in fashion,) he asked him to sit down and take a share of the good cheer. This invitation was peculiarly acceptable to Niel Blane, who, if he did not positively expect it from every guest not provided with better company, yet received it from many, and was no whit abashed or surprised at the summons. He sat down, along with his guest, in a secluded nook near the chimney; and, while he received encouragement to drink by far the greater share of the liquor before them, he entered at length, as a part of his expected function, upon the news of the country—the births, deaths, and marriages—the change of property—the downfall of old families, and the rise of new. But politics, now the fertile source of eloquence, mine host did not care to mingle in his theme, and it was only in answer to a question of Morton, that he replied, with an air of indifference, "Um! ay! we aye hae sodgers amang us, mair or less. There's a wheen German horse doun at Glasgow yonder; they ca' their commander Wittybody, or some sic name, though he's as grave and grewsome an auld Dutchman as e'er I saw."

"Wittenbold, perhaps?" said Morton; "an old man, with grey hair and short black moustaches—speaks seldom?"

"And smokes for ever," replied Niel Blane. "I see your honour kens the man. He may be a very gude man too, for aught I see, that is, considering he is a sodger and a Dutchman; but if he were ten generals, and as mony Wittybodies, he has nae skeel in the pipes; he gar'd me stop in the middle o' Torphichen's Rant, the best piece o' music that ever bag gae wind to."

"But these fellows," said Morton, glancing his eye towards the soldiers that were in the apartment, "are not of his corps?"

"Na, na, these are Scots dragoons; our ain auld caterpillars; these were Claver'se lads a while syne, and wad be again, maybe, if he had the lang ten in his hand."

"Is there not a report of his death?" said Morton.

"Troth is there—your honour is right—there is sic a fleeing rumour, but, in my puir opinion, it's lang or the de'il die. I wad hae the folks here look to themsels. If he makes an outbreak, he'll be doun here or I could drink this glass—and whar are they than? A' thae hell-rakers o' dragoons wad be at his whistle in a moment. Nae doubt they're Willie's men e'en now, as they were Jamie's a while syne—and reason good—they fight for their pay; what else hae they to fight for? They hae neither lands nor houses, I trow. There's ae gude thing o' the change, or the Revolution, as they ca' it, folks may speak out afore thae birkies now, and nae fear o' being haul'd awa' to the guard-house, or having the thumikins screwed on your finger-ends, just as I wad drive the screw through a cork."

There was a little pause, when Morton, feeling confident in the progress he had made in mine host's familiarity, asked, though with the hesitation proper to one who puts a question on the answer to which rests something of importance,—"Whether Mr Blane knew a woman in that neighbourhood called Elizabeth Maclure?"

"Whether I ken Bessie Maclure?" answered the landlord, with a landlord's laugh—"How can I but ken my ain wife's (haly be her rest) —my ain wife's first gudeman's sister, Bessie Maclure? an honest wife she is, but sair she's been trysted wi' misfortunes,—the loss o' twa decent lads o' sons, in the time o' the persecution, as they ca' it now-a-days; and doucely and decently she has bore her burthen, blaming nane, condemning nane. If there's an honest woman in the world, it's Bessie Maclure. And to lose her twa sons, as I was saying, and to hae dragoons clinked down on her for a month bypast—for, be whig or tory uppermost, they aye quarter thae loons on victuallers,—to lose, as I was saying"——

"This woman keeps an inn, then?" interrupted Morton.

"A public, in a puir way," replied Blane, looking round at his own superior accommodations—"a sour browst o' sma' ale that she sells to folk that are ower drouthy wi' travel to be nice, but naething to ca' a stirring trade or a thriving change-house."

"Can you get me a guide there?" said Morton.

"Your honour will rest here a' the night?—ye'll hardly get accommodation at Bessie's," said Niel, whose regard for his deceased wife's relative by no means extended to sending company from his own house to hers.

"There is a friend," answered Morton, "whom I am to meet with there, and I only called here to take a stirrup cup and enquire the way."

"Your honour had better," answered the landlord, with the perseverance of his calling, "send forward some ane to warn your friend to come on here."

"I tell you, landlord," answered Morton impatiently, "that will not serve my purpose; I must go straight to this woman Maclure's house, and I desire you to find me a guide."

"Aweel, sir, ye'll chuse for yoursel, to be sure; but de'il a guide ye'll need, if ye gae doun the water for twa miles or sae, as gin ye were bound for Milnewood-house, and then tak the first broken disjaskit-looking path that makes for the hills—ye'll ken't by a broken ash-tree that stands at the side o' a burn just where the roads meet, and than travel out the path—ye canna miss Widow Maclure's public, for de'il another house or hauld is on the road for ten lang Scots miles, and that's worth twenty English. I am sorry your honour would think of ganging out o' my house the night. But my wife's gude-sister is a decent woman and a kind of connection, and it's no lost that a friend gets."

Morton accordingly paid his reckoning and departed. The sunset of the summer day placed him at the ash-tree; where the path led up towards the moors.

"Here," he said to himself, "my misfortunes commenced; for just here, when Burley and I were about to separate on the first night we ever met, he was alarmed by the intelligence, that the passes were secured by soldiers laying in wait for him. Beneath that very ash sate the old woman who apprised him of his danger. How strange that my whole fortunes should have become inseparably interwoven with that man's, without any thing more on my part, than the discharge of an ordinary duty of humanity! Would to Heaven it were possible I could find my humble quiet and tranquillity of mind upon the spot where I lost them!"

Thus arranging his reflections betwixt speech and thought, he turned his horse's head up the narrow path.

Evening lowered around him as he advanced up the narrow dell which had once been a wood, but was now divested of trees, unless where a few, from their inaccessible situation on the edge of precipitous banks, or clinging among rocks and huge stones, defied the invasion of men and of cattle, like the scattered tribes of a conquered country, driven to take refuge in the barren strength of its mountains. These too, wasted and decayed, seemed rather to exist than to flourish, and only served to indicate what the landscape had once been. But the stream brawled down among them in all its freshness and vivacity, giving the life and animation which a mountain rivulet alone can confer on the barest and most savage scenes, and which the inhabitant of such a country misses when gazing even upon the tranquil winding of a majestic stream through plains of fertility, and beside palaces of splendour. The track of the road followed the course of the brook, which was now visible, and now only to be distinguished by its brawling heard among the stones, or in the clefts of the rock, that occasionally interrupted its course.

"Murmurer that thou art," said Morton, in the enthusiasm of his reverie,—"why chafe with the rocks that stop thy course for a moment? There is a sea to receive thee in its bosom, and an eternity for man when his fretful and hasty course through the vale of time shall be ceased and over. What thy petty fuming is to the deep and vast billows of a shoreless ocean, are our cares, hopes, fears, joys, and sorrows, to the objects which must occupy us through that awful and boundless succession of ages!"

Thus moralizing, he passed on till the dell opened, and the banks, receding from the brook, left a little green vale, exhibiting a croft, or small field, on which some corn was growing, and a cottage, whose walls were not above five feet high, and whose thatched roof, green with moisture, age, house-leek, and grass, had in some places suffered damage from the encroachment of two cows, whose appetite this appearance of verdure had diverted from their more legitimate pasture. An ill-spelled, and worse written inscription, intimated to the traveller that he might here find refreshment for man and horse;—no unacceptable intimation, rude as the hut appeared to be, considering the wild path he had trode in approaching it, and the high and waste mountains which rose in desolate dignity behind this humble asylum.

"It must indeed have been," thought Morton, "in some such spot as this, that Burley was likely to find a congenial confidante."

As he approached, he observed the good dame of the house herself, seated by the door; she had hitherto been concealed from him by a huge elder-bush.

"Good evening, mother," said the traveller. "Your name is Mistress Maclure?"

"Elizabeth Maclure, sir, a poor widow," was the reply.

"Can you lodge a stranger for a night?"

"I can, sir, if he will be satisfied with the widow's cake and the widow's cruize."

"I have been a soldier, good dame," answered Morton, "and nothing can come amiss to me in the way of entertainment."

"A sodger, sir?" said the old woman with a sigh, "God send ye a better trade."

"It is believed to be an honourable profession, my good dame. I hope you do not think the worse of me for having belonged to it?"

"I judge no one, sir," replied the woman, "and your voice sounds like that of a civil gentleman; but I hae seen sae muckle ill wi' sodgering in this puir land, that I am e'en content that I can see nae mair o't wi' these sightless organs."

As she spoke thus, Morton observed that she was blind.

"Shall I not be troublesome to you, my good friend?" said he, compassionately; "your infirmity seems ill calculated for your profession."

"Na, sir," answered the old woman; "I can gang about the house readily aneugh; and I hae a bit lassie to help me, and the dragoon lads will look after your horse when they come hame frae their patrole, for a sma' matter; they are civiller now than lang syne."

Upon these assurances, Morton alighted.

"Peggy, my bonny bird," continued the hostess, addressing a little girl of twelve years old, who had by this time appeared, "tak the gentleman's horse to the stable, and slack his girths, and tak aff the bridle, and shake down a lock o' hay before him, till the dragoons come back.—Come this way, sir," she continued; "ye'll find my house clean, though it's a puir ane."

Morton followed her into the cottage accordingly.

Chapter Twelve

Then out and spak the auld mother,
And fast her tears did fa'—
"Ye wadna be warn'd, my son Johnie,
Frae the hunting to bide awa!"
Old Ballad

WHEN he entered the cottage, Morton perceived that the old hostess had spoken truth. The inside of the hut belied its outward appearance, and was neat, and even comfortable, especially the inner apartment, in which the hostess informed her guest that he was to sup and sleep. Refreshments were placed before him, such as the little inn afforded, and, though he had small occasion for them, he accepted the offer, as the means of maintaining some discourse with the landlady. Notwithstanding her blindness, she was assiduous in her attendance, and seemed, by a sort of instinct, to find her way to what she wanted.

"Have you no one but this pretty little girl to assist you in waiting on your guests?" was the natural question.

"None, sir; I dwell alone, like the widow of Zarephtha. Few guests come to this puir place; and I haena custom eneugh to hire servants. I

had anes twa fine sons that lookit after a' thing—But God gives and
takes away—His name be praised!" she continued, turning her
clouded eyes towards Heaven—"I was anes better off, that is, worldly
speaking, even since I lost them; but that was before this last change."

"Indeed! But you are a presbyterian, good mother?"

"I am, sir; praised be the light that shewed me the right way,"
replied the landlady.

"Then, I should have thought the Revolution would have brought
you nothing but good."

"If," said the old woman, "it has brought the land gude, and freedom of worship to tender consciences, it's little matter what it has
brought to a puir blind worm like me."

"Still," replied Morton, "I cannot see how it could possibly injure
you."

"It's a lang story, sir. But ae night, sax weeks or thereby afore
Bothwell Brigg, when I had just dune milking the cow, a young gentleman stopped at this puir cottage, stiff and bloody with wounds, pale
and dune out wi' riding, and his horse sae weary he couldna drag ae
foot after the other, and his faes were close ahint him, and he was ane
o' our enemies—What could I do, sir?—You that's a soldier will think
me but a silly auld wife—but I fed him, and relieved him, and keepit
him hidden till the pursuit was ower."

"And who," said Morton, "dares disapprove of your having done
so?"

"I kenna—I gat ill-will about it amang some o' our ain folk. They
said I should hae been to him what Jael was to Sisera—But weel I wot I
had nae divine command to shed blood, and to save it was baith like a
woman and a Christian.—And than they said I wanted natural affection to relieve ane that belanged to the band that murdered my twa
sons."

"That murdered your two sons?"

"Ay, sir; though maybe ye will gi'e their deaths another name—
The tane fell wi' sword in hand, fighting for a broken national Covenant; the tother—O, they took him out and shot him to dead on the
green before his mother's face!—My auld e'en dazzled when the
shots were looten aff, and, to my thought, they waxed weaker and
weaker ever since that weary day—and sorrow, and heart-break, and
tears, might help on the disorder. But, alas! betraying Lord Evandale's young blood to his enemies' sword wad ne'er hae brought my
Ninian and Johnie alive again."

"Lord Evandale?" said Morton in surprise; "Was it Lord Evandale
whose life you saved?"

"In troth, even his. And kind he was to me after, and gae me cow and calf, malt, meal, and siller, and nane durst steer me when he was in power. But we live on an outside bit of Tillietudlem land, and the estate was sair plea'd between Leddy Margaret Bellenden and the present laird, Basil Olifant, and Lord Evandale backed the auld leddy for luve o her daughter Miss Edith, as the country said, ane o' the best and bonniest lassies in Scotland. But they behuved to gi'e way, and Basil gat the Castle and land, and on the back o' that came the Revolution, and wha to turn coat faster than the laird? for he said he had been a true whig a' the time, and turned papist only for fashion's sake. And than he got favour, and Lord Evandale's head was under water; for he was ower proud and manfu' to bend to every blast o' wind, though mony a ane may ken as weel as me, that, be his ain principles as they will, he was nae ill friend to our folk when he could protect us, and far kinder than Basil Olifant that aye keepit the coble-head doun the stream. But he was set by and ill looked on, and his word ne'er asked; and then Basil, wha's a revengefu' man, set himsel to vex him in a' shapes, and specially by oppressing and despoiling the auld widow, Bessie Maclure, that saved Lord Evandale's life, and that he was sae kind to. But he's mista'en, if that's his end; for it will be lang or Lord Evandale hears a word frae me about the selling my kye for rent or e'er it was due, or the putting the dragoons on me when the country's quiet, or ony thing else that will vex him—I can bear my ain burthen patiently, and warld's loss is the least part o't."

Astonished and interested at this picture of patient, grateful, and disinterested resignation, Morton could not help bestowing an execration upon the poor-spirited rascal who had taken such a dastardly course of vengeance.

"Dinna curse him, sir," said the old woman; "I have heard a good man say, that a curse was like a stone flung up to the heavens, and maist like to return on his head that sent it. But if ye ken Lord Evandale, bid him look to himsel, for I have heard strange words pass atween the soldiers that are lying here, and his name is often mentioned; and the tane o' them has been twice up at Tillietudlem. He's a kind of favourite wi' the Laird, though he was in former times ane o' the maist cruel oppressors ever rade through a country (out-taken Serjeant Bothwell)—they ca' him Inglis."

"I have the deepest interest in Lord Evandale's safety," said Morton, "and you may depend on my finding some mode to apprize him of these suspicious circumstances: And, in return, my good friend, will you indulge me with another question? Do you know any thing of one Quintin Mackell of Irongray?"

"Do I know *whom?*" echoed the blind woman, in a tone of great surprise and alarm.

"Quintin Mackell of Irongray," repeated Morton; "is there any thing so alarming in the sound of that name?"

"Na—na—" answered the woman with hesitation, "but to hear him asked after by a stranger and a soldier—Gude protect us, what mischief is to come next!"

"None by my means, I assure you," said Morton; "the subject of my enquiry has nothing to fear from me, if, as I suppose, this Quintin Mackell is the same with John Bal——"

"Do not mention his name," said the widow, pressing her lips with her finger. "I see you have his secret and his pass-word, and I'll be free wi' you. But, for God's sake, speak lound and low. In the name of Heaven, I trust ye seek him not to his hurt.—Ye said ye were a soldier?"

"I said truly; but one he has nothing to fear from. I commanded a party at Bothwell Bridge."

"Indeed?" said the woman. "And verily there is something in your voice I can trust—Ye speak prompt and readily, and like an honest man."

"I trust I am so," said Morton.

"But nae displeasure to you, sir, in thae waefu' times," continued Mrs Maclure, "the hand of brother is against brother, and he fears as mickle almaist frae this government as e'er he did frae the auld persecutors."

"Indeed?" said Morton, in a tone of enquiry; "I was not aware of that. But I am only just now returned from abroad."

"I'll tell ye," said the blind woman, first assuming an attitude of listening that shewed how effectually her powers of collecting intelligence had been transferred from the eye to the ear; for, instead of casting a glance of circumspection around, she stooped her face, and turned her head slowly around, in such a manner as to ensure that there was not the slightest sound stirring in the neighbourhood, and then continued—"I'll tell ye. Ye ken how he has laboured to raise up again the Covenant, burned, broken, and buried in the hard hearts and selfish devices of this stubborn people. Now when he went to Holland, far from the countenance and thanks of the great and the comfortable fellowship of the godly, baith whilk he was in right to expect, the Prince of Orange wad shew him no favour, and the ministers no godly communion. This was hard to bide for ane that had suffered and done mickle—ower mickle it may be—but why suld I be a judge?—He came back to me and to the auld place o' refuge that had aften received him in his distresses, mair especially before the great day of victory at Drumclog, for I sall ne'er forget how he was bending hither of a' nights in the year on that after the play when young

Milnewood wan the papinjay; but I warned him off for that time."

"What," exclaimed Morton, "it was you that sate in your red cloak by the high-road, and told him there was a lion in the path?"

"In the name of heaven! wha are ye?" said the old woman, breaking off her narrative in astonishment. "But be ye wha ye may," she continued, resuming it with tranquillity, "ye can ken naething waur o' me than that I hae been willing to save the life o' friend and fae."

"I know no ill of you, Mrs Maclure, and I mean no ill by you—I only wished to show you that I know so much of this person's affairs, that I might be safely entrusted with the rest. Proceed, if you please, in your narrative."

"There is a strange command in your voice," said the blind woman, "though its tones are sweet. I have little mair to say. The Stuarts hae been dethroned, and William and Mary reign in their stead, but nae mair word o' the Covenant than if it were a dead letter. They hae taen the indulged clergy, and an Erastian General Assembly of the ance pure and triumphant Kirk of Scotland even into their very arms and bosoms. Our faithfu' champions o' the testimony agree e'en waur wi' this than wi' the open tyranny and apostacy of the persecuting times, for souls are hardened and deadened, and the mouths of fasting multitudes are crammed wi' fizenless bran instead of the sweet word in season; and mony an hungry, starving creature, when he sits down on a Sunday forenoon to get something that might warm him to the great work, has a dry clatter o' morality driven about his lugs, and"——

"In short," said Morton, desirous to stop a discussion which the good old woman, as enthusiastically attached to her religious profession as to the duties of humanity, might probably have indulged longer —"In short, you are not disposed to acquiesce in this new government, and Burley is of the same opinion?"

"Mony of our brethren, sir, are of belief we fought for the Covenant, and fasted, and prayed, and suffered for that grand national league, and now we are like neither to see nor hear tell of that which we suffered, and fought, and fasted, and prayed for.—And anes it was thought something might be made by bringing back the auld family on a new bargain and a new bottom, as, after a', when King James went awa', I understand the great quarrel of the English against him was in behalf of seven unhallowed prelates; and sae, though ae part of our people were free to join wi' the present model, and levied an armed regiment under the Yearl of Angus, yet our honest friend, and others of purity of doctrine and freedom of conscience, were determined to hear the breath o' the Jacobites before they took part again them, fearing to fa' to the ground like a wall built with unslacked mortar, or from sitting between twa stools."

"They chose an odd quarter," said Morton, "from which to expect freedom of conscience and purity of doctrine."

"O, dear sir! the natural day-spring rises in the east, but the spiritual day-spring may rise in the north, for what we puir blinded mortals ken."

"And Burley went to the north to seek it?"

"Truly ay, sir; and he saw Claver'se himsel, that they ca' Dundee now."

"The devil he did!" exclaimed Morton, "I would have sworn that meeting would have been the last of one of their lives."

"Na, na, sir; in troubled times, as I understand, there's sudden changes—Montgomery, and Ferguson, and mony ane mair that were King James's greatest faes, are on his side now—Claver'se spake our friend fair, and sent him to consult with Lord Evandale. But than there was a break off, for Lord Evandale wadna look at, hear, or speak wi' him, and now he's anes wud and aye waur, and roars for revenge again Lord Evandale, and will hear nought of ony thing but burn and slay—and O thae sturts o' passion! they unsettle his mind, and gi'e the enemy sair advantages."

"The enemy?" said Morton, "What enemy?"

"What enemy? Are ye acquainted familiarly wi' John Balfour o' Burley, and dinna ken that he has had sair and frequent combats to sustain against the Evil One? Did ye ever see him alone but the Bible was in his hand, and the drawn sword on his knee? did ye never sleep in the same room wi' him, and hear him strive in his dreams with the delusions of Satan? O, ye ken little o' him, if ye have seen him only in fair day-light, for nae man can put the face upon his doleful trials and strifes that he can do. I hae seen him after sic a strife of agony tremble that an infant might hae held him, while the hair on his brow was drapping as fast as ever my puir thatched roof did in a heavy rain."

As she spoke, Morton began to recollect the appearance of Burley during his sleep in the hay-loft at Milnewood, the report of Cuddie that his senses had become impaired, and some whispers current among the Cameronians, who boasted frequently of Burley's soul-exercises, and his strifes with the foul fiend; which several circumstances led him to conclude that this man himself was a victim to those delusions, though his mind, naturally acute and forcible, not only disguised his superstition from those in whose opinion it might have discredited his judgment, but by exerting such a force as is said to be proper to those afflicted with epilepsy, could postpone the fits which it occasioned until he was either freed from superintendance, or surrounded by such as held him more highly on account of these visitations. It was natural to suppose, and could easily be inferred from the narrative of Mrs Maclure, that disappointed ambition, wrecked hopes, and the downfall of the party which he had served with such desperate fidelity, were likely to aggravate enthusiasm into temporary insanity. It was, indeed, no uncommon circumstance in these singular times, that men like Sir Harry Vane, Harrison, Overton, and others, themselves slaves to the wildest and most enthusiastic dreams, could, when mingling with the world, conduct themselves not only with good sense in difficulties, and courage in dangers, but with the most acute sagacity and determined valour. The subsequent part of Mrs Maclure's information confirmed Morton in these impressions.

"In the grey of the morning," she said, "my little Peggy sall shew ye the gate to him before the sodgers are up. But ye maun let his hour of danger, as he ca's it, be ower, afore ye venture on him in his place of refuge. Peggy will tell ye whan to gang in. She kens his ways weel, for whiles she carries him some little helps that he canna do without to sustain life."

"And in what retreat then," said Morton, "has this unfortunate person found refuge?"

"An awsome place," answered the blind woman, "as ever living creature took refuge in. They ca' it the Black Linn of Linklater—it's a dolefu' place; but he loves it abune a' ithers, because he has sae often been in safe hiding there, and it's my belief he prefers it to a tapestried chamber and a down bed. But ye'll see't. I hae seen it mysel mony a day syne. I was a daft hempie lassie than, and little thought what use was to come o't. Wad ye chuse ony thing, sir, ere ye betake yoursel to your rest, for ye maun stir wi' the first dawn o' the grey light?"

"Nothing more, my good mother," said Morton, and they parted for the evening.

Morton recommended himself to Heaven, threw himself on the bed, heard, between sleeping and waking, the trampling of the dragoon horses as the riders returned from their patrole, and then slept soundly after a day of such painful agitations.

Chapter Thirteen

The darksome cave they enter, where they found
The accursed man, low sitting on the ground,
Musing full sadly in his sullen mind.
SPENSER

As the morning began to appear grey on the mountains, a gentle knock was heard at the door of the humble apartment in which Morton slept, and a girlish treble voice asked him from without, "If he wad please gang to the Linn or the folk raise?"

He arose upon the invitation, and, dressing himself hastily, went forth and joined his little guide. The mountain maid tript lightly before him, through the grey haze, over hill and moor. It was a wild and varied walk, unmarked by any regular or distinguishable track, and keeping, upon the whole, the direction of the ascent of the brook, though without tracing its windings. The landscape, as they advanced, turned waster and more wild, until nothing but heath and rock encumbered the side of the valley.

"Is the place still distant?" said Morton.

"Nearly a mile off," answered the girl. "We'll be there belive."

"And do you often go this wild journey, my little maid?"

"When grannie sends me wi' milk and meal to the Linn," answered the child.

"And are you not afraid to travel so wild a road alone?"

"Hout na, sir," replied the guide; "nae living creature wad touch sic a bit helpless thing as I am, and grannie says we need never fear ony thing else when we are doing a gude turn."

"Strong in innocence as in triple mail!" said Morton to himself, and followed her steps in silence.

They soon came to a decayed thicket, where brambles and thorns supplied the room of the oaks and birches of which it had once consisted. Here the guide turned short off the open heath, and, by a sheep-track, conducted Morton towards the brook. A hoarse and sullen roar had in part prepared him for the scene which presented itself, yet it was not to be viewed without surprise and even terror. When he emerged from the devious path which conducted him through the thicket, he found himself placed on a ledge of flat rock, projecting over one side of a chasm not less than a hundred feet deep, where the dark mountain stream made a decided and rapid shoot over the precipice, and was swallowed up by a deep, black, yawning gulph. The eye in vain strove to see the bottom of the fall; it could catch but one sheet of foamy uproar and sheer descent, until the view was obstructed by the projecting crags, which on each side inclosed the basin of the waterfall, and hid from sight the deep dark pool which received its tortured waters; far beneath, at the distance of, perhaps, a quarter of a mile, the eye caught the winding of the stream as it emerged into a more open course. But, for that distance, they were lost to sight as much as if a cavern had been arched over them; and indeed the steep and projecting ledges of rock through which they wound their way in darkness, were very nearly closing and over-roofing their course.

While Morton gazed at this scene of tumult, which seemed, by the

surrounding thickets and the cleft into which the waters descended, to
seek to hide itself from every eye, his little attendant, as she stood
beside him on the platform of rock which commanded the best view of
the fall, pulled him by the sleeve, and said, in a tone which he could
not hear without stooping his ear near the speaker, "Hear till him! Eh!
hear till him!"

Morton listened more attentively, and out of the very abyss into
which the brook fell, and amidst the tumultuary sounds of the cataract, thought he could distinguish shouts, screams, and even articulate
words, as if the tortured demon of the stream had been mingling his
complaints with the roar of his broken waters.

"This is the way," said the little girl; "follow me, gin ye please, sir,
but tak' tent to your feet;" and, with the daring agility which custom
had rendered easy, she vanished from the platform on which she
stood, and, by notches and slight projections in the rock, scrambled
down its face into the chasm which it overhung. Steady, and bold, and
active, Morton hesitated not to follow her; but the necessary attention
to secure his hold and footing in a descent where both foot and hand
were needful for security, prevented him from looking around him,
till, having descended nigh twenty feet, and being still sixty or seventy
above the pool which received the fall, his guide made a pause, and he
again found himself by her side in a situation that appeared equally
romantic and precarious. They were nearly opposite to the water-fall,
and in point of level situated at about one-quarter's depth from the
point of the cliff over which it thundered, and three-fourths of the
height above the dark, deep, and restless pool which received its fall.
Both these tremendous points, the first shoot, namely, of the yet
unbroken stream, and the deep and sombre abyss into which it was
emptied, were full before him, as well as the whole continuous stream
of billowy froth, which, dashing from the one, was eddying and boiling
in the other. They were so near this grand phenomenon that they were
covered with its spray, and well nigh deafened by the incessant roar.
But crossing in the very front of the fall, and at scarce three yards
distance from the cataract, an old oak-tree, flung across the chasm in a
manner that seemed accidental, formed a bridge of fearfully narrow
dimensions and uncertain footing. The upper end of the tree rested
on the platform on which they stood—the lower or uprooted extremity
extended behind a projection on the opposite side, and was secured,
Morton's eye could not discover where. From behind the same projection glimmered a strong red light, which, glancing in the waves of
the falling water, and tinging them partially with crimson, had a
strange preternatural and sinister effect when contrasted with the
beams of the rising sun, which glanced on the first broken waves of the

fall, though even its meridian splendour could not gain the third of its full depth. When he had looked around him for a moment, the girl again pulled his sleeve, and pointing to the oak and the projecting point beyond it, (for hearing speech was now out of the question,) indicated that there lay his farther passage.

Morton gazed at her with surprise; for, although he well knew that the persecuted presbyterians had in the preceding reigns sought refuge among dells and thickets, caves and cataracts,—in spots the most extraordinary and secluded—although he had heard of the champions of the Covenant, who had long abidden beside Dobs-linn in the wild heights of Polmoodie, and others who had been concealed in the yet more terrific cavern called Creehope-linn, in the parish of Closeburn, yet his imagination had never exactly figured out the horrors of such a residence, and he was surprised how the strange and romantic scene which he now saw had remained concealed from him while a curious investigator of such natural phenomena. But he readily conceived, that, lying in a remote and wild district, and being destined as a place of concealment to the persecuted preachers and professors of non-conformity, the secret of its existence was carefully preserved by the few shepherds to whom it might be known.

As, breaking from these meditations, he began to consider how he should traverse the doubtful and terrific bridge, which, skirted by the cascade, and rendered wet and slippery by its constant drizzle, traversed the chasm above sixty feet from the bottom of the fall, his guide, as if to give him courage, tript over and back again without the least hesitation. Envying for the moment the little bare feet which caught a safer hold of the rugged side of the oak than he could pretend to with his heavy boots, Morton nevertheless resolved to attempt the passage, and, fixing his eye firmly on a stationary object on the other side, without allowing his head to become giddy, or his attention to be distracted by the flash, the foam, and the roar of the waters around him, he strode steadily and safely along the uncertain bridge, and reached the mouth of a small cavern on the farther side of the torrent. Here he paused; for a light, proceeding from a fire of red-hot charcoal, permitted him to see the interior of the cave, and enabled him to contemplate the appearance of its inhabitant, by whom he himself could not be so readily distinguished, being concealed by the shadow of the rock. What he observed would by no means have encouraged a less determined man to proceed with the task which he had undertaken.

Burley, only altered from what he had been formerly by the addition of a grizly beard, stood in the midst of his cave, with his clasped Bible in one hand and his drawn sword in the other. His figure, dimly ruddied by the light of the red charcoal, seemed that of a fiend in the lurid atmosphere of Pandemonium, and his gestures and words, as far as they could be heard, seemed equally violent and irregular. All alone, and in a place of almost unapproachable seclusion, his demeanour was that of a man who strives for life and death with a mortal enemy.

"Ha! ha!—there—there—there!" he exclaimed, accompanying each word with a thrust, urged with his whole force against the impassible and empty air—"Did I not tell thee so?—I have resisted, and thou fleest from me!—Coward as thou art—come in all thy terrors—come with mine own evil deeds, which render thee most terrible of all—there is enough betwixt the boards of this book to rescue me—there is enough in this good sword and arm to protect me —What mutterest thou of grey hairs?—It was well done to slay him— the more ripe the corn the readier for the sickle.—Art gone?—art gone?—I have ever known thee but a coward—ha—ha! ha!"

With these wild exclamations he sunk the point of his sword, and remained standing still in the same posture like a maniac whose fit is over.

"The dangerous time is by now," said the little girl who had followed; "it seldom lasts beyond the time that the sun's ower the hill; ye may gang in and speak wi' him now. I'll wait for you at the other side of the linn; he canna bide to see twa folk at anes."

Slowly and cautiously, and keeping constantly upon his guard, Morton presented himself to the view of his old associate in command.

"What! comest thou again when thine hour is over?" was his first exclamation, and flourishing his sword aloft, his countenance assumed an expression in which ghastly terror seemed mingled with the rage of a demoniac.

"I am come, Mr Balfour," said Morton, in a steady and composed tone, "to renew an acquaintance which has been broken off since the fight of Bothwell Bridge."

As soon as Burley became aware that Morton was before him in person,—an idea which he caught up with marvellous celerity,—he at once exerted that mastership over his heated and enthusiastic imagination, the power of enforcing which was a most striking part of his extraordinary character. He sunk his sword point at once, and as he stole it composedly into the scabbard, muttered something of the damp and cold which sent an old soldier to his fencing exercise, to prevent his blood from chilling. This done, he proceeded in the cold determined manner which was peculiar to his ordinary discourse.

"Thou hast tarried long, Henry Morton, and hast not come to the vintage before the twelfth hour has struck. Art thou yet willing to take the right hand of fellowship, and be one with those who look not to thrones or dynasties, but to the rule of Scripture for their directions?"

"I am surprised," said Morton, evading the direct answer to his question, "that you should have known me after so many years."

"The features of those who ought to act with me are engraved on my heart," answered Burley; "and few but Silas Morton's son durst have followed me into this my castle of retreat. Seest thou that drawbridge of Nature's own construction?" he added, pointing to the prostrate oak-tree—"one spurn of my foot, and it is overwhelmed in the abyss below, bidding foemen on the farther side stand at defiance, and leaving enemies on this at the mercy of one who never yet met his equal in single fight."

"Of such defences," said Morton, "I should have thought you would now have had little need."

"Little need?" said Burley impatiently, "What little need, when incarnate fiends are combined against me on earth, and Sathan himself—but it matters not," added he, checking himself—"Enough that I like my place of refuge—my cave of Adullam, and would not change its rude ribs of limestone rock for the fair chambers of the castle of the Earls of Torwood, with their broad bounds and barony. Thou, unless the foolish fever-fit be over, mayst think differently."

"It was of these very possessions I come to speak," said Morton, "and I doubt not to find Mr Balfour the same rational and reflecting person which I knew him to be in times when zeal disunited brethren."

"Ay," said Burley; "Indeed?—Is such truly your hope?—wilt thou express it more plainly?"

"In a word then," said Morton, "you have exercised, by means at which I can guess, a secret, but most prejudicial influence over the fortunes of Lady Margaret Bellenden and her grand-daughter, and in favours of this base, oppressive apostate, Basil Olifant, whom the law, deceived by thy operations, has placed in possession of their lawful property."

"Sayest thou?" said Balfour.

"I do say so," replied Morton; "and face to face you will not deny what you have vouched by your hand-writing."

"And suppose I deny it not?" said Balfour, "and suppose that thy eloquence were found equal to persuade me to retrace the steps I have taken on matured resolve, what will be thy meed? Doest thou still hope to possess the fair-haired girl with her wide and rich inheritance?"

"I have no such hope," answered Morton calmly.

"And for whom then hast thou ventured to do this great thing, to seek to rend the prey from the valiant, to bring forth food from the den of the lion, and to extract sweetness from the maw of the devourer?—For whose sake hast thou undertaken to read this riddle, more hard than Sampson's?"

"For Lord Evandale's and that of his bride," replied Morton firmly. "Think better of mankind, Mr Balfour, and believe there are some who are willing to sacrifice their happiness to that of others."

"Then, as thy soul liveth," replied Balfour, "thou art, to wear a beard, and back a horse, and draw a sword, the tamest and most gall-less puppet that ever sustained injury unavenged. What! thou wouldst help that accursed Evandale to the arms of the woman that thou lovest?—thou wouldst endow them with wealth and heritages, and thou thinkst that there lives another man offended even worse than thou, yet equally cold-livered and mean-spirited, crawling upon the face of the earth, and hast dared to suppose that one other is John Balfour?"

"For my own feelings," said Morton composedly, "I am answerable to none but Heaven—To you, Mr Balfour, I should suppose it of little consequence whether Basil Olifant or Lord Evandale possess these estates."

"Thou art deceived," said Burley; "both are indeed in outer darkness, and strangers to the light, as he whose eyes have never been opened to the day. But this Basil Olifant is a Nabal—a Demas—a base churl, whose wealth and power are at the disposal of him who can threaten to deprive him of them. He became a professor because he was deprived of these lands of Tillietudlem—he turned a papist to obtain possession of them—he called himself an Erastian that he might not again lose them, and he will become what I list while I have in my power the document that may deprive him of them.—These lands are a bitt between his jaws and a hook in his nostrils, and the rein and the line are in my hands to guide them as I think meet; and his they shall therefore be, unless I had assurance of bestowing them on a sure and sincere friend. But Lord Evandale is a malignant of heart like flint, and brow like adamant; the goods of the world fall on him like leaves on the frost-bound earth, and unmoved he will see them whirled off by the first wind. The heathen virtues of such as he are more dangerous to us than the sordid cupidity of those, who, governed by their interest, must follow where it leads, and who, therefore, themselves the slaves of avarice, may be compelled to work in the vineyard, were it but to earn the wages of sin."

"This might have been all well some years since," replied Morton; "and I could then understand your argument, although I could never acquiesce in its justice. But at this crisis it seems useless to you to persevere in keeping up an influence which can no longer be directed to an useful purpose. The land has peace, liberty, and freedom of conscience—and what would you more?"

"More!" exclaimed Burley, again unsheathing his sword with a vivacity which nearly made Morton start; "look at the notches upon that weapon; they are three in number, are they not?"

"It seems so," answered Morton; "but what of that?"

"The fragment of steel that parted from this first gap, rested in the skull of the perjured traitor who first introduced Episcopacy into Scotland;—this second notch was made on the rib-bone of an impious villain, the boldest and best soldier that upheld the prelatic cause at Drumclog;—this third was broken on the steel head-piece of the captain who defended the Chapel of Holyrood when the people rose at the Revolution. I cleft him to the teeth through steel and bone. It has done great deeds this little weapon, and each of these blows was a deliverance to the church. This sword," he said, again sheathing it, "has yet more to do—to weed out this base and pestilential heresy of Erastianism—to vindicate the true liberty of the Kirk in her purity—to restore the Covenant in its glory,—then let it moulder and rust beside the bones of its master."

"You have neither men nor means, Mr Balfour, to disturb the government as now settled," argued Morton; "the people are in general satisfied, excepting only the gentlemen of the Jacobite interest; and surely you would not join with those who would only use you for their own purposes."

"It is they," answered Burley, "that should serve ours. I went to the camp of the malignant Claver'se, as the future King of Israel sought the land of the Philistines; I arranged with him a rising, and, but for the villain Evandale, the Erastians had ere now been driven from the west—I could slay him," he added, with a vindictive scowl, "were he grasping the horns of the altar!" He then proceeded in a calmer tone. "If thou, son of mine ancient comrade, wert suitor for thyself to this Edith Bellenden, and wert willing to put thy hand to the great work with zeal equal to thy courage, think not I would prefer the friendship of Basil Olifant to thine; thou shouldst then have the means that this document (he produced a parchment) affords, to place her in possession of the lands of her fathers. This have I longed to say to thee ever since I saw thee fight the good fight so strongly at the fatal Bridge. The maiden loved thee, and thou her."

Morton replied firmly, "I will not dissemble with you, Mr Balfour, even to gain a good end. I came in hopes to persuade you to do a deed of justice to others, not to gain any selfish end of my own. I have failed

—I grieve for your sake, more than for the loss that others will sustain by your injustice."

"You refuse my proffer then?" said Burley, with kindling eyes.

"I do," said Morton; "would you be really, as you are desirous to be thought, a man of honour and conscience, you would, regardless of all other considerations, restore that parchment to Lord Evandale, to be used for the advantage of the lawful heir."

"Sooner shall it perish," said Balfour; and, casting the deed into the heap of red charcoal beside him, pressed it down with the heel of his boot.

While it smoked, shrivelled, and crackled in the flames, Morton sprung forward to snatch it, and Burley catching hold of him, a struggle ensued. Both were strong men, but although Morton was much the more active and younger of the two, yet Balfour was the most powerful, and effectually prevented him from rescuing the deed until it was fairly reduced to a cinder. They then quitted hold of each other, and the enthusiast, rendered fiercer by the contest, glared on Morton with an eye expressive of frenetic revenge.

"Thou hast my secret," he exclaimed; "thou must be mine, or die!"

"I contemn your threats," answered Morton; "I pity you, and I leave you."

But, as he turned to retire, Burley stept before him, pushed the oak trunk from its resting place, and as it fell thundering and crashing into the abyss beneath, drew his sword, and exclaimed, with a voice that rivalled the roar of the cataract and the thunder of the falling oak,— "Now thou art at bay!—fight—yield, or die!" and standing in the mouth of the cavern, he flourished his naked sword.

"I will not fight with the man that preserved my father's life," said Morton,—"I have not yet learned to say the words, I yield; and my life I will rescue as I best can."

So speaking, and ere Balfour was aware of his purpose, he sprung past him, and exerting that youthful agility of which he possessed an uncommon share, leaped clear across the fearful chasm which divided the mouth of the cave from the projecting rock on the opposite side, and stood there safe and free from his incensed enemy. He immediately ascended the ravine, and, as he turned, saw Burley stand for an instant aghast with astonishment, and then, with the frenzy of disappointed rage, rush into the interior of his cavern.

It was not difficult for him to perceive that this unhappy man's mind had been so long agitated by desperate schemes and sudden disappointments, that it had lost its equipoise, and that there was now in his conduct a shade of lunacy, not the less striking from the vigour and craft with which he pursued his wild designs. Morton soon joined his

guide, who had been terrified by the fall of the oak. This he represented as accidental; and she assured him in return, that the inhabitant
of the cave would experience no inconvenience from it, being always
provided with materials to construct another bridge.

The adventures of the morning were not yet ended. As they
approached the hut, the little girl made an exclamation of surprise at
seeing her grandmother groping her way towards them, at a greater
distance from her home than she could have been supposed capable of
travelling.

"O, sir, sir!" said the old woman, when she heard them approach,
"gin e'er ye loved Lord Evandale, help now or never!—God be
praised that left my hearing when he took my puir eye-sight—Come
this way—this way—And O! tread lightly. Peggy, hinny, gang saddle
the gentleman's horse, and lead him cannily ahint the thorny shaw,
and bide him there."

She conducted him to a small window, through which, himself
unobserved, he could see two dragoons seated at their morning
draught of ale, and conversing earnestly together.

"The more I think of it," said the one, "the less I like it, Inglis;
Evandale was a good officer, and the soldier's friend; and though we
were punished for the mutiny at Tillietudlem, yet, by——, Frank, you
must own we deserved it."

"D——n seize me, if I forgive him for it though," replied the other;
"and I think I can sit on his skirts now."

"Why, man, you should forget and forgive—Better take the start
with him along with the rest, and join the ranting Highlanders. We
have all eat King James's bread."

"Thou art an ass; the start, as you call it, will never happen; the
day's put off. Halliday's seen a ghost, or Miss Bellenden's fallen sick
of the pip, or some blasted nonsense or another; the thing will never
keep two days longer, and the first that sings out will get the reward."

"That's true, too," answered his comrade; "and will this fellow—
this Basil Olifant, pay handsomely?"

"Like a prince, man; Evandale is the man on earth whom he hates
worst, and he fears him beside about some law business, and were he
once rubbed out of the way, all, he thinks, will be his own."

"But shall we have warrant and force enough? Few people here will
stir against my Lord, and we may find him with some stout fellows at
his back."

"Thou'rt a cowardly fool, Dick," returned Inglis; "he is living
quietly down at Fairy-knowe to avoid suspicion. Olifant is a magistrate, and will have some of his own people that he can trust along with
him. There are us two, and the laird says he can get a desperate

fighting whig fellow, called Quintin Mackell, that has an old grudge at Evandale."

"Well, well, you are my corporal, you know, and if any thing is wrong"——

"I'll take the blame," said Inglis. "Come, another pot of ale, and let us to Tillietudlem.—Here, blind Bess! where the devil has the old hag crept to?"

"Delay them as long as you can," whispered Morton, as he thrust his purse into the hostess's hand, "all depends on gaining time."

Then, walking swiftly to the place where the girl held his horse ready, "To Fairy-knowe?—no; alone I could not protect them.—I must instantly to Glasgow. Wittenbold, the commandant there, will readily give me the support of a troop, and procure me the countenance of the civil power. I must drop a caution as I pass. Come, Moorkopf," he said, addressing his horse as he mounted him,—"this day must try your breath and speed."

Chapter Fourteen

> Yet could he not his closing eyes withdraw,
> Though less and less of Emily he saw;
> So, speechless for a little space he lay,
> Then grasp'd the hand he held, and sigh'd his soul away.
> *Palamon and Arcite*

THE INDISPOSITION of Edith confined her to bed during the eventful day on which she had received such an unexpected shock from the sudden apparition of Morton. Next morning, however, she was reported to be so much better, that Lord Evandale resumed his purpose of leaving Fairy-knowe. At a late hour in the forenoon, Lady Emily entered the apartment of Edith with a peculiar gravity of manner. Having received and paid the compliments of the day, she observed it would be a sad one for her, though it would relieve Miss Bellenden of an incumbrance—"My brother leaves us to-day, Miss Bellenden."

"Leaves us!" exclaimed Edith in surprise; "for his own house, I trust in Heaven!"

"I have reason to think he meditates a more distant journey; he has little to detain him in this country."

"Good Heaven!" exclaimed Edith, "why was I born to become the wreck of all that is manly and noble? What can be done to stop him from running headlong on ruin? I will come down instantly—Say that I implore he will not depart until I speak with him."

"It will be in vain, Miss Bellenden; but I will execute your commission;" and she left the room as formally as she had entered it, and informed her brother, Miss Bellenden was so much recovered as to propose coming down stairs ere he went away.

"I suppose," she added pettishly, "the prospect of being speedily released from our company has wrought a cure on her shattered nerves."

"Sister," said Lord Evandale, "you are unjust, if not envious."

"Unjust I may be, Evandale, but I should not have dreamt," glancing her eye at a mirror, "of being thought envious without better cause —But let us go to the old lady; she is making a feast in the other room might have dined all your troop when you had one."

Lord Evandale accompanied her in silence to the parlour, for he knew it was in vain to contend with her prepossessions and offended pride. They found the table covered with refreshments arranged under the careful inspection of Lady Margaret.

"Ye could hardly weel be said to breakfast this morning, my Lord Evandale, and ye maun e'en partake of a small collation before ye ride, such as this poor house, whose inmates are so much indebted to you, can provide in their present circumstances. For my ain part, I like to see young folks take some refection before they ride out upon their sports or their affairs, and I said as much to his most Sacred Majesty when he breakfasted at Tillietudlem in the year of grace saxteen hundred and fifty-one, and his most Sacred Majesty was pleased to reply, drinking to my health at the same time in a flagon of Rhenish wine, 'Lady Margaret, ye speak like a Highland oracle.' These were his Majesty's very words; so that your Lordship may judge whether I have not good authority to press young folk to partake of their vivers."

It may be well supposed that much of the good lady's speech failed Lord Evandale's ears, which were then employed in listening for the light step of Edith. They had not met since the strange incident which had interrupted their nuptials. His absence of mind on this occasion, however natural, cost him very dear. While Lady Margaret was playing the kind hostess, a part she delighted and excelled in, she was interrupted by John Gudyill, who, in the usual phrase for announcing an inferior to the mistress of a family, said "There was ane wanting to speak to her Leddyship."

"Ane! what ane? Has he nae name? Ye speak as if I kept a shop, and was to come at every body's whistle."

"Yes, he has a name," answered John, "but your Leddyship likes ill to hear't."

"What is it, you fool?"

"It's Calf-Gibbie, my Leddy," said John, in a tone rather above the

pitch of decorous respect, on which he occasionally trespassed, confiding in his merit as an ancient servant of the family, and a faithful
follower of their humbled fortunes—"It's Calf-Gibbie, an' your
Leddyship will hae't, that keeps Edie Henshaw's kye down yonder at
the Brigg's-end—that's him that was Guse-Gibbie at Tillietudlem,
and gaed to the wappinshaw, and that"——

"Hold your peace, John; you are very insolent to think I wad speak
wi' a person like that. Let him tell his business to you or Mrs Headrigg."

"He'll no hear o' that, my Leddy; he says, them that sent him bade
him to gi'e the thing to your Leddyship's ain hand direct, or to Lord
Evandale's, he wots na whilk. But, to say the truth, he's far frae fresh,
and he's but an ideot an' he were."

"Then turn him out," said Lady Margaret, "and tell him to come
back to-morrow when he is sober. I suppose he comes to crave some
benevolence, as an ancient follower o' the house."

"Like eneugh, my Leddy, for he's a' in rags, poor creature."

Gudyill made another attempt to get at Gibbie's commission, which
was indeed of the last importance, being a few lines from Morton to
Lord Evandale, acquainting him with the danger in which he stood
from the practices of Olifant, and exhorting him either to instant
flight, or else to come to Glasgow and surrender himself, when he
could assure him of protection. This billet, hastily written, he
entrusted to Gibbie, whom he saw feeding his herd beside the bridge,
and backed with a couple of dollars his request that it might instantly
be delivered into the hand to which it was addressed.

But it was decreed that Goose-Gibbie's intermediation, whether as
an emissary or as a man-at-arms, should be unfortunate to the family
of Tillietudlem. He unluckily tarried so long at the ale-house, to prove
if his employer's coin was good, that, when he appeared at Fairy-
knowe, the little sense which nature had given him was effectually
drowned in ale and brandy, and instead of asking for Lord Evandale,
he demanded to speak with Lady Margaret, whose name was more
familiar to his ear. Being refused admittance to her presence, he
staggered away with the letter undelivered, perversely faithful to Morton's instructions in the only point which it would have been well had
he departed from.

A few minutes after he was gone Edith entered the apartment. Lord
Evandale and she met with mutual embarrassment, which Lady
Margaret, who only knew in general that their union had been
postponed by her grand-daughter's indisposition, set down to the
bashfulness of a bride and bridegroom, and, to place them at ease,
began to talk to Lady Emily on indifferent topics. At this moment

Edith, with a countenance as pale as death, muttered, rather than whispered, to Lord Evandale a request to speak with him. He offered his arm, and supported her into the small anti-room, which, as we have noticed before, opened from the parlour. He placed her in a chair, and, taking one himself, awaited the opening of the conversation.

"I am deeply distressed, my Lord," were the first words she was able to articulate, and those with difficulty; "I scarce know what I would say, nor how to speak it."

"If I have any share in occasioning your uneasiness," said Lord Evandale mildly, "you will soon, Edith, be released from it."

"You are determined then, my Lord, to run this desperate course with desperate men, in spite of your own better reason—in spite of your friends' entreaties—in spite of the almost inevitable ruin which yawns before you?"

"Forgive me, Miss Bellenden; even your solicitude on my account must not detain me when my honour calls. My horses stand ready saddled, my servants are prepared, the signal for rising will be given so soon as I reach Kilsythe—If it is my fate that calls me, I will not shun meeting it. It will be something," he said, taking her hand, "to die deserving your compassion, since I cannot gain your love."

"O, my lord, remain," said Edith, in a tone which went to his heart; "time may explain the strange circumstance which has shocked me so much; my agitated nerves may recover their tranquillity. O do not rush on death and ruin! remain to be our prop and stay, and hope every thing from time!"

"It is too late, Edith; and I were most ungenerous could I practise on the warmth and kindliness of your feelings towards me—I know you cannot love me; nervous distress, so strong as to conjure up the appearance of the dead or absent, indicates a predilection too powerful to give way to friendship and gratitude alone. But were it otherwise, the dye is now cast."

As he spoke thus, Cuddie burst into the room, terror and haste on his countenance. "O, my Lord, hide yoursel! they hae beset the outlets o' the house," was his first exclamation.

"They? Who?" said Lord Evandale.

"A party of horse, headed by Basil Olifant," answered Cuddie.

"O, hide yourself, my Lord!" echoed Edith, in an agony of terror.

"I will not, by Heaven!" answered Lord Evandale. "What right has the villain to assail me or stop my passage? I will make my way were he backed by a regiment; tell Halliday and Hunter to get out the horses— And now farewell, Edith." He clasped her in his arms, and kissed her tenderly; then, bursting from his sister, who, with Lady Margaret, endeavoured to detain him, rushed out and mounted his horse.

All was in confusion—the women shrieked and rushed in consternation to the front windows of the house, from which they could see a
small party of horsemen, of whom two only seemed soldiers. They
were on the open ground before Cuddie's cottage, at the bottom of the
descent from the house, and shewed caution in approaching it, as if
uncertain of the strength within.

"He may escape, he may escape," said Edith; "O, would he but take
the bye-road!"

But Lord Evandale, determined to face a danger which his high
spirit undervalued, commanded his servants to follow him, and rode
composedly down the avenue. Old Gudyill ran to arm himself, and
Cuddie snatched down a gun which was kept for the protection of the
house, and, although on foot, followed Lord Evandale. It was in vain
his wife, who had hurried up on the alarm, hung by his skirts, threatening him with death by the sword or halter for meddling wi' other
folk's matters.

"Haud your peace, ye b——," said Cuddie, "and that's braid
Scotch, or I wot na what is; is it other folk's matters to see Lord
Evandale murdered before my face?" and down the avenue he
marched. But considering on the way that he composed the whole
infantry, as John Gudyill had not appeared, he took his vantage
ground behind the hedge, hammered his flint, cocked his piece, and,
taking a long aim at Laird Basil, as he was called, stood prompt for
action.

As soon as Lord Evandale appeared, Olifant's party spread themselves a little, as if preparing to enclose him. Their leader stood fast,
supported by three men, two of whom were dragoons, the third in
dress and appearance a countryman, all well armed. But the strong
figure, stern features, and resolved manner of the third attendant,
made him seem the most formidable of the party; and whoever had
before seen him could have no difficulty in recognizing Balfour of
Burley.

"Follow me," said Lord Evandale to his servants, "and if we are
forcibly opposed, do as I do." He advanced at a hand gallop towards
Olifant, and was in the act of demanding why he had thus beset the
road, when Olifant called out, "Shoot the traitor!" and the whole four
fired their carabines upon the unfortunate nobleman. He reeled in the
saddle, advanced his hand to the holster, and drew a pistol, but,
unable to discharge it, fell from his horse mortally wounded. His
servants had presented their carabines. Hunter fired at random, but
Halliday, who was an intrepid fellow, took aim at Inglis, and shot him
dead on the spot. At the same instant a shot, from behind the hedge,

still more effectually avenged Lord Evandale, for the ball took place in the very midst of Basil Olifant's forehead, and stretched him lifeless on the ground. His followers, astonished at the execution done in so short a time, seemed rather disposed to stand inactive, when Burley, whose blood was up with the contest, exclaimed, "Down with the Midianites!" and attacked Halliday sword in hand. At this instant the clatter of horses' hoofs was heard, and a party of horse, rapidly advancing on the road from Glasgow, appeared on the fatal field. They were foreign dragoons, led by the Dutch commandant, Wittenbold, accompanied by Morton and a civil magistrate.

A hasty call to surrender, in the name of God and King William, was obeyed by all except Burley, who turned his horse and attempted to escape. Several soldiers pursued him by command of their officer, but being well mounted, only the two headmost seemed likely to gain on him. He turned deliberately twice, and discharging first one of his pistols, and then the other, rid himself of the one pursuer by mortally wounding him, and of the other by shooting his horse, and then continued his flight to Bothwell Bridge, where, for his misfortune, he found the gates shut and guarded. Turning from thence, he made for a place where the river seemed passable, and plunged into the stream, the bullets from the pistols and carabines of his pursuers whizzing around him. Two balls took place when he was past the middle of the stream, and he felt himself dangerously wounded. He reined his horse round in the midst of the river, and returned towards the bank he had left, waving his hand, as if with the purpose of intimating that he surrendered. The troopers ceased firing at him accordingly, and awaited his return, two of them riding a little way into the river to seize and disarm him. But it presently appeared that his purpose was revenge, not safety. As he approached the two soldiers, he collected his remaining strength, and discharged a blow on the head of one, which tumbled him from his horse. The other dragoon, a strong lusty man, had in the meanwhile laid hands on him. Burley, in requital grasped his throat, as a dying tiger seizes his prey, and both losing the saddle in the struggle, came headlong into the river, and were swept down the stream. Their course might be traced by the blood which bubbled up to the surface. They were twice seen to rise, the Dutchman striving to swim, and Burley clinging to him in a manner that showed his desire that both should perish. Their corpses were taken out about a quarter of a mile down the river. As Balfour's grasp could not have been unclenched without cutting off his hands, both were thrown into a hasty grave, still marked by a rude stone, and a ruder epitaph.*

While the soul of this stern enthusiast flitted to its last accompt, that of the brave and generous Lord Evandale was also released. Morton had flung himself from his horse upon perceiving his situation, to render his dying friend all the aid in his power. He knew him, for he pressed his hand, and, being unable to speak, intimated by signs his wish to be conveyed to the house. This was done with all the care possible, and he was soon surrounded by his lamenting friends. But the clamorous grief of Lady Emily was far exceeded in intensity by the silent agony of Edith. Unconscious even of the presence of Morton, she hung over the dying man; nor was she aware that fate, who was removing one faithful lover, had restored another as if from the grave, until Lord Evandale, taking their hands in his, pressed them both affectionately, united them together, raised his face, as if to pray for a blessing on them, and sunk back and expired in the next moment.

Conclusion

I HAD determined to waive the task of a concluding chapter, leaving to the reader's imagination the arrangements which must necessarily take place after Lord Evandale's death. But as I was aware that precedents are awanting for a practice which might be found convenient, both to readers and compiler, I confess myself to have been in a considerable dilemma, when fortunately I was honoured with an invitation to drink tea with Miss Martha Buskbody, a young lady who has carried on the profession of mantua-making at Gandercleugh, and in the neighbourhood, with great success, for about forty years.—Knowing her taste for narratives of this description, I requested her to look over my loose sheets the morning before I waited upon her, and enlighten me by the experience which she must have acquired in reading through the whole stock of three circulating libraries in Gandercleugh and the two next market-towns. When, with a palpitating

*Note. Gentle reader, I did request of mine honest friend, Peter Proudfoot, travelling merchant, known to many of this land for his faithful and just dealings, as well in muslins and cambrics as in small wares, to procure me, on his next peregrination to that vicinage, a copy of the Epitaphion alluded to. And, according to his report, which I see no ground to discredit, it runneth thus:

> Heir lyes ane Saint to prelates surley,
> Being John Balfour, sometime of Burley,
> Who stirred up to vengeance take,
> For Solemn League and Cov'nant's sake,
> Upon the Magus-moor, in Fife,
> Did tak James Sharpe's the apostate's life;
> By Dutchemen's hands was hacked and shot,
> Then drowned in Clyde nigh this saam spot.

heart, I appeared before her in the evening, I found her much disposed to be complimentary.

"I have not been more affected," said she, wiping the glasses of her spectacles, "by any novel, excepting the sweet tale of Jemmy and Jenny Jessamy, which is indeed pathos itself; but your plan of omitting a formal conclusion will never do. You may be as harrowing to our nerves as you will in the course of your story, but, unless you had the genius of the author of Julia de Roubigné, never let the end be altogether overclouded. Let us see a glimpse of sunshine in the last chapter; it is quite essential."

"Nothing would be more easy for me, madam, than to comply with your injunctions; for, in truth, the parties in whom you have had the goodness to be interested, did live long and happily, and begot sons and daughters."

"It is unnecessary, sir," she said, with a slight nod of reprimand, "to be particular concerning their matrimonial comforts.—But what is your objection to let us have, in a general way, a glimpse of their future felicity?"

"Really, madam, you must be aware, that every volume of a narrative turns less and less interesting as the author draws to a conclusion, just like your tea, which, though excellent hyson, is necessarily weaker and more insipid in the last cup. Now, as I by no means think the one improved by the luscious lump of half-dissolved sugar usually found at the bottom of it, so I think a history, growing already vapid, is but dully crutched up by a detail of circumstances which every reader must have anticipated, even though the author exhaust on them every flowery epithet in the language."

"This will not do, Mr Pattieson," continued the lady; "you have, as I may say, basted up your first story very hastily and clumsily at the conclusion; and, in my trade, I would have cuffed the youngest apprentice who had put such a hurried and bungled spot of work out of her hand.—And if you do not redeem this gross error by telling us all about the marriage of Morton and Edith, and what became of the other personages of the story, from Lady Margaret down to Goose-Gibbie, I apprize you, that you will not be held to have accomplished your task handsomely."

"Well, madam," I replied, "my materials are so ample, that I think I can satisfy your curiosity, unless it descend to very minute circumstances indeed."

"First, then," said she, "for that is most essential,—Did Lady Margaret get back her fortune and her castle?"

"She did, madam, and in the easiest way imaginable, as heir, namely, to her worthy cousin, Basil Olifant, who died without a will;

and thus, by his death, not only restored, but even augmented, the fortune of her, whom, during his life, he had pursued with the most inveterate malice. John Gudyill, reinstated in his dignity, was more important than ever; and Cuddie, with rapturous delight, entered upon the cultivation of the mains of Tillietudlem, and the occupation of his original cottage. But, with the shrewd caution of his character, he was never heard to boast of having fired the lucky shot which repossessed his lady and himself in their original habitations. 'After a',' he said to Jenny, who was his only confidante, 'he was my Leddy's cousin, and a grand gentleman; and though he was acting again the law, as I understand, for he ne'er shewed ony warrant, or required Lord Evandale to surrender, and though I mind killing him nae mair than I wad do shooting a muir-cock, yet it's as weel to keep a calm sough about it.' He not only did so, but ingeniously enough counten-anced a report that old Gudyill had done the deed, which was worth many a gill of brandy to him from the old butler, who, far different in disposition from Cuddie, was much more inclined to exaggerate than suppress his exploits of manhood. The blind widow was provided for in the most comfortable manner, as well as the little guide to the Linn; and"——

"But what is all this to the marriage—the marriage of the principal personages?" interrupted Miss Buskbody, impatiently tapping her snuff-box.

"The marriage of Morton and Miss Bellenden was delayed for several months, as both went into deep mourning on account of Lord Evandale's death. They were then wedded."

"I hope, not without Lady Margaret's consent, sir? I love books which teach a proper deference in young persons to their parents. In a novel they may fall in love without their countenance, because it is essential to the necessary intricacy of the story, but they must always have the benefit of their countenance at last. Even old Delville received Cecilia, though the daughter of a man of low birth."

"And even so, madam, Lady Margaret was prevailed on to countenance Morton: the old Covenanter, his father, stuck sorely with her for some time, but Edith was her only hope, and she wished to see her happy. Morton, or Melville Morton, as he was now more generally called, stood so high in the reputation of the world, and was in every other respect such an eligible match, that she put her prejudice aside, and consoled herself with the recollection, that marriage went by destiny, as was observed to her, she said, by his most Sacred Majesty, Charles the Second of happy memory, when she shewed him the portrait of her grandfather Fergus, third Earl of Torwood, the hand-somest man of his time, and that of Countess Jane, his second lady, who had a hump-back and only one eye. This was his Majesty's observation, she said, on one remarkable morning when he deigned to take his *disjune*"——

"Nay," said Miss Buskbody, again interrupting me, "if she bring such authority to countenance her acquiescing in a mesalliance, there was no more to be said.—And what became of old Mrs What's-her-name, the housekeeper?"

"Mrs Wilson, madam," answered I; "she was perhaps the happiest of the party; for once a year, and not oftener, Mr and Mrs Melville Morton dined in the great wainscotted-chamber in solemn state, the hangings being all displayed, the carpet laid down, and the huge brass candlestick set on the table, stuck round with leaves of laurel. The preparing the room for this annual festival employed her mind for six months before it came about, and the putting matters to rights occupied her the other six months, so that single day found her business for the whole year round."

"And Niel Blane?"

"Lived to a good old age, drank ale and brandy with guests of all persuasions, played whig or jacobite tunes as best pleased his customers, and died worth as much money as married Jenny to a cock-laird. I hope, ma'am, you have no other enquiries to make, for really"——

"Goose-Gibbie, sir—Goose-Gibbie, whose ministry was fraught with such consequences to the personages of the narrative?"

"Consider, my dear Miss Buskbody, (I beg pardon for the familiarity,)—but pray consider even the memory of the renowned Scheherazade, that Empress of Tale-tellers, could not preserve every circumstance. I am not quite positive as to the fate of Goose-Gibbie, but am inclined to think him the same with one Gilbert Dudden, alias Calf-Gibbie, who was whipped through Hamilton for stealing poultry."

Miss Buskbody now placed her left foot on the fender, crossed her right leg over her knee, lay back in the chair, and looked towards the ceiling. When I observed her assume this contemplative mood, I concluded she was studying some farther cross-examination, and therefore took my hat and wished her a hasty good-night, ere the Demon of Criticism had supplied her with any more queries. In like manner, gentle Reader, returning you my thanks for the patience which has conducted you thus far, I take the liberty to withdraw myself from you for the present.

THE END

𝔓eroration

*It was mine earnest wish, most courteous Reader, that the "Tales of my
Landlord" should have reached thine hands in one entire succession of tomes,
or volumes. But as I sent some few more of manuscript quires, containing the
continuation of these most pleasant narratives, I was apprised, somewhat
unceremoniously, by my publisher, that he did not approve of novels (as he
injuriously called these real histories) extending beyond four volumes, and,
if I did not agree to the first four being published separately, he threatened to
decline the article (O, ignorance! as if the vernacular article of our mother
English were capable of declension!) Whereupon, somewhat moved by his
remonstrances, and more by heavy charges for print and paper, which he
stated to have been already incurred, I have resolved that these four volumes shall be the heralds or avant-couriers of the Tales which are yet in my
possession, nothing doubting that they will be eagerly devoured, and the
remainder anxiously demanded, by the unanimous voice
of a discerning public. I rest, esteemed Reader,
thine as thou shalt construe me,*

Jedidiah Cleishbotham
Gandercleugh,
Nov. 15, 1816.

HISTORICAL NOTE

Much of the action of *The Tale of Old Mortality* takes place in the summer of 1679, a time of violent political upheaval in Scotland. The storm had been long a-brewing; indeed, it can be regarded as the latest manifestation of a sequence of events set in motion more than a century earlier by the Reformation of 1560.

At the time of the Reformation the young Mary Queen of Scots was in France, where her first husband reigned as Francis II from 1559 until his death in December 1560. Meantime in Scotland, French troops supporting the cause of the Catholic royal family were unable to maintain military opposition to the forces of the Protestant Lords of the Congregation and their English allies; and as a result the Queen acquiesced in a religious settlement under which the shape and nature of the new reformed church was dictated by her Protestant opponents. The weakness of royal power in Scotland in the years following 1560 allowed the reformed church to steer its own course; and many Scots began to regard their church as the best and purest reformed church in the world. It was felt to be a church shaped by God's will and not by the will of princes; a church worthy of the special approval of God, and a beacon and example to reformers everywhere.

In 1603 Mary's son James VI, who had already ruled Scotland in person as an adult king since the mid-1580s, inherited the English throne on the death of Queen Elizabeth of England. James moved to London and in his absence Scotland was ruled by the Scottish Privy Council, operating on his behalf and in frequent contact with him by letter. James's policy was to move the smaller and poorer kingdom towards conformity with English practice in religion and other matters. Naturally enough, this did not always commend itself to the Scots; but James was wise enough to move cautiously, and he was prepared to pause or even retreat when particularly fierce opposition was aroused by particular manifestations of his policy of anglicisation.

James VI died in 1625. His successor, Charles I, continued his father's policy of anglicisation, but pushed it on more quickly, more rigorously, and in more extreme form. Charles also reformed the Scottish Privy Council in ways which weakened its position as a separate power centre, seeking to make it merely an instrument of the King's will. In 1637 he sought to impose a new Scottish Prayer Book, based on its English counterpart; but the first use of the new book for public worship produced a riot at St Giles Cathedral in Edinburgh. The response of the Privy Council, weakened by Charles's reforms, was ineffective. The King himself, far away in London, was out of touch with the situation in Scotland and underestimated its seriousness; and the upholders of the royal cause allowed events to move beyond their control. The result was the Scottish Revolution of 1638–1651.

This period of Scottish history was ushered in by the signing of the National Covenant in 1638. Those signing the Covenant asserted that they were upholding legitimate royal power as well as true religion and the liberties of the country; but the reality clearly was that, if it came to a choice, they believed fighting for religion and liberty had priority over obedience to the crown. The central concern of the National Covenant was religious rather than political; and its signing on 28 February 1638 was felt to be nothing short of 'the glorious marriage day of the Kingdom with God'.[1] As Scott puts it in *Tales of a Grandfather*, 'a species of engagement, or declaration, was drawn up, the principal object of which was, the eradication of Prelacy in all its modifications, and the establishment of Presbytery on its purest and most simple basis. This engagement was called the National Covenant, as resembling those covenants which, in the Old Testament, God is said to have made with the people of Israel.'[2] Signed first by many of Scotland's noblemen at Greyfriars Church in Edinburgh, the Covenant was later signed by very large numbers of people in various parts of the country. Through possession of what they regarded as the best-reformed church on earth, many Scots felt themselves to be the natural successors to the Jews as a nation chosen by God for a unique role in the revelation of his will to humanity. Through the National Covenant the Scots accepted this role, and bound themselves to resist to the uttermost the efforts of Charles I to adulterate the purity of the Scottish church by forcing what were felt to be corrupt religious practices upon it. This is the reason why the Covenanters of *The Tale of Old Mortality* draw so very many parallels between their own experiences and those of that earlier chosen people, the Jews of the Old Testament.

The King responded to the National Covenant by raising a mainly English army in an attempt to restore his rule and authority in Scotland. However, Charles's troubles in the late 1630s were not confined to his northern kingdom, and he did not possess enough support in England to allow him to gather together the resources necessary to bring his planned expeditions into Scotland to a successful conclusion. A Scottish invasion of England followed in 1640, and enabled the Scots to impose a peace treaty on Charles. One result of this was the calling of an English parliament, which provided a focus for English opposition to the King; and England began to move into civil war.

Clearly, a royalist victory in the English Civil War would leave Charles in a position to impose his will on Scotland. In an attempt to prevent this outcome the Scots entered into a Solemn League and Covenant with the English parliament in 1643. Under this treaty the English parliament agreed that Presbyterianism—the form of church government favoured by the Covenanters—would become the established form of religion throughout the British Isles; and by a separate treaty, the Scots undertook in return to provide military assistance to the parliamentary side in the English Civil War.

In Scotland, the Solemn League and Covenant provoked a royalist response: the Marquis of Montrose's brilliant campaign of 1644–1645 produced a series of stunning victories against the odds before final defeat by the Covenanters at Philiphaugh. In England, the presence of the Scottish army helped tip the scales towards defeat for the royalists. But the victorious English parliament failed to honour the promises through which it had obtained Scottish military assistance. In response some of the Scottish nobles under the leadership of the Duke of Hamilton negotiated a treaty with the King, the Engagement of 1647, raised a new army and invaded England, only to be routed by the English parliamentary forces under Oliver Cromwell at Preston in 1648. Argyll and the extremist Kirk Party then seized power in Scotland with Cromwell's help.

In 1649 Charles I was executed by the triumphant English parliamentarians. In Scotland the ruling Kirk Party was genuinely horrified at this English execution of the King of Scots. The heir to the throne was immediately proclaimed King as Charles II, and was brought back to Scotland from the Netherlands. In *Tales of a Grandfather*, Scott points out that 'Scotland was at this time divided into three parties, highly inimical to each other':[3] the ruling Kirk Party of extreme Presbyterians led by the Marquis of Argyle; the moderate Presbyterians or Engagers under the Duke of Hamilton; and what Scott calls the Absolute Loyalists, followers of the Marquis of Montrose. These three strands of opinion might be said to be represented in *The Tale of Old Mortality* by the figures of Burley, Morton, and Claverhouse. Attempts were made by Argyll and his followers to force Charles into the role of a godly covenanted monarch; and in due course he did commit himself to the Covenant and was enthroned as King of Scots in January 1651. Even before the coronation, however, Scottish support for the new King provoked an English invasion during which Cromwell routed the Scots at Dunbar in September 1650. In the national crisis which resulted from this defeat most of Scotland, both royalists and moderate Presbyterians, rallied (as 'Resolutioners') to the King (only the extreme Covenanters—the 'Protesters'—remained aloof) but yet another Scottish invasion of England ended in defeat, at Worcester in 1651. This decisive battle opened the way for an English conquest of Scotland, and an incorporating union with the republican English Commonwealth.

The Cromwellian union lasted until 1660, when the Restoration returned Charles II to power in both England and Scotland. Like his father and grandfather before him Charles was resident in London, and ruled Scotland through the Scottish Privy Council. Under the new regime the Episcopal or prelatic form of church government was restored, bringing Scotland into line with England, and the King was declared to be 'supream Governour of this Kingdome over all persones and in all causes'.[4] In 1662 the Privy Council required ministers to take the oath of allegiance or supremacy, to accept presentation to their charges by lay patrons, to submit themselves to their bishops, and to recognise holy days, especially the anniversary of the King's birthday and restoration on 29 May. It was expected that all but a few of the existing parish ministers would be retained under the new dispensation; but in the end about 270, mainly in the West, refused to conform on conscientious grounds, and as a result were removed from their charges and replaced by much-resented Episcopal curates. The ejected ministers retained the loyalty of a substantial proportion of their congregations. These people, who considered themselves the heirs of the Covenants, met for worship in conventicles held in remote country areas; and this practice continued in spite of the regime's attempts to break up the conventicles by military force. Tension in the West on this issue erupted into rebellion in the brief Pentland Rising of 1666, in which an advance on Edinburgh ended in decisive defeat at Rullion Green. The regime then sought to tempt the conventiclers' clergymen back into the national church on easy terms by means of the Indulgences of 1669 and 1672; this met with some limited success. But persecution of the Covenanters then intensified; the reaction became increasingly embittered and fanatical; and the assassination of Archbishop Sharp in 1679 by a group of extreme Covenanters sparked the convulsion with which *The Tale of Old Mortality* deals.

After focusing on a sequence of events in summer 1679, the novel turns its attention to the summer of 1689. The years between 1679 and 1689 brought momentous changes to Scotland. In 1685 Charles II died, to be succeeded by his brother James VII (James II in England). The Catholic James was dethroned in England in 1688, in the 'Glorious Revolution' that brought the Protestant William and Mary to the throne. James also lost power in Scotland: the Scots Parliament declared on 11 April 1689 that James 'being a profest papist' and having by 'the advyce of wicked and evill Counsellors' invaded 'the fundamentall Constitution of this Kingdome' had forfeited the throne.[5] An army under Claverhouse was raised to fight for James—the first of a number of Jacobite[6] risings in Scotland over the next half century or so. This Jacobite army won a notable victory over William's forces at Killiecrankie in 1689, but the rising collapsed as a result of Claverhouse's death in the battle.

The 'Glorious Revolution' was a crucial factor in the establishment of the Scottish political and religious settlement under which Scott and his generation lived in the early years of the nineteenth century. When Scott was writing *The Tale of Old Mortality* in 1816 there was a constitutional rather than an absolute monarchy; the Jacobite cause was irrecoverably lost; the Hanoverian succession was secure; and Presbyterianism was the firmly established form of church government in the national church. Scotland, while retaining her own distinctive institutions and practices in law, education and religion, was nevertheless joined with England in a parliamentary union dating from 1707. In spite of the stability of these arrangements, the fear of revolution was strongly present. Scott and his circle, appalled and fascinated, had watched the progress of the French Revolution and the rise in its aftermath of a dangerous and threatening absolute ruler in Napoleon. Napoleon's escape from Elba and his final defeat at Waterloo took place in 1815, less than two years before the publication of *The Tale of Old Mortality*. Furthermore, revolution seemed a real and immediate possibility at home in Scotland. In 1815 thousands of 'democrats', mainly textile workers from the West, assembled on the battlefield of Loudoun-hill to celebrate the victory there in 1679 of their ancestors the Covenanters against the established government of the day; and also to celebrate the news of the escape of Napoleon from Elba. The seventeenth-century conflicts described in *The Tale of Old Mortality* were of much more than antiquarian concern in 1816.

The Tale of Old Mortality is fiction, not history. It does not set out to give a detailed and exact account of what actually happened in Scotland in the seventeenth century. Rather, it finds fictional means to demonstrate and enact Scott's view of the nature of the forces in conflict in seventeenth-century Scotland; his view of the ways in which these forces interacted; and his view of the nature of the eventual outcome of the struggle. For the purposes of the fiction, Scott makes use of real events—notably the battles of Loudoun-hill and Bothwell Bridge, both fought in the summer of 1679. However, much of the action (for example, the siege of Tillietudlem in Volume 2) is entirely fictional. Tillietudlem, the royalist citadel containing what Lady Margaret calls the throne of Charles II, is besieged by both kinds of Presbyterian—the fanatical Burley and the moderate Morton. Burley's brutal methods fail; but Morton's enlightened, reasonable tolerance allows him to win control of Tillietudlem's throne. Morton embodies Scott's view of the virtues of the 'Glorious Revolution'; and the siege of Tillietudlem allows Scott to include within his novel a demonstration of the nature of the forces that cost James VII the crown.

Even when making use of real events and characters, Scott adjusts details to suit his fictional purposes. Claverhouse is the most important royalist character in *The Tale of Old Mortality*; and Scott therefore finds it convenient to make the Claverhouse of the novel a more senior officer in 1679 than the Claverhouse of history was in that year. Many examples of this process could be cited: Scott takes history as his raw material, and shapes a great historical novel.[7]

NOTES

1   See David Stevenson, *The Covenanters: the National Covenant and Scotland* (Edinburgh, 1988), 1.
2   Scott, *Tales of a Grandfather*, second series, in *Prose Works*, 23.358. Scott is somewhat misleading here, however: the Covenant talks about trying the existing bishops for their crimes, but makes no mention whatever of abolishing prelacy as such (even though many of those involved ultimately aimed at this). Similarly, Scott in the novel exaggerates the extent to which Episcopalian forms of worship differed from Presbyterian practice in 17th-century Scotland.
3   Scott, *Tales of a Grandfather*, second series, in *Prose Works*, 24.83.
4   *Acts of the Parliaments of Scotland*, 7 (1820), 45.
5   *Acts of the Parliaments of Scotland*, 9 (1822), 38.
6   'Jacobus' is the Latin form of 'James'.
7   In drafting the above note I was greatly assisted by David Stevenson's lucid work, *The Covenanters*; and my debt of gratitude to Dr Stevenson was further increased when he read the note in draft form, and suggested a number of corrections and improvements.

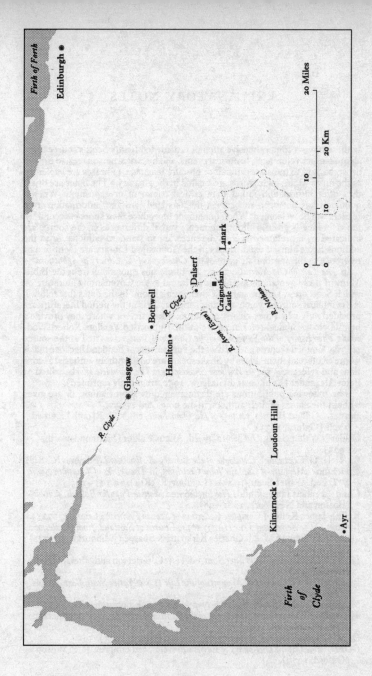

EXPLANATORY NOTES

In these notes a comprehensive attempt is made to identify Scott's sources, and all quotations, references, historical events, and historical personages, to explain proverbs, and to translate difficult or obscure language. (Phrases are explained in the notes while single words are treated in the glossary.) The notes are brief; they offer information rather than critical comment or exposition. When a quotation has not been recognised this is stated: any new information from readers will be welcomed. When quotations reproduce their sources accurately, the reference is given without comment; verbal differences in the source are indicated by a prefatory 'see'. References are to standard editions, or to the editions Scott himself used. Books in the Abbotsford Library are identified by reference to the appropriate page of the *Catalogue of the Library at Abbotsford*.

In *The Tale of Old Mortality* there are numerous quotations from the Bible. Many of these quotations are also to be found in the Covenanting literature on which Scott drew, and are part of Covenanting idiom. In the notes that follow it is the biblical sources which are cited, and parallels in the period literature are provided only when they clearly constitute the source or where they provide a helpful gloss. Biblical references are to the Authorised Version. Robert Wodrow's *The History of the Sufferings of the Church of Scotland* is cited as the source of Privy Council records and Acts of the Parliaments of Scotland because that is where Scott read them. Plays by Shakespeare are cited without authorial ascription, and references are to *William Shakespeare: The Complete Works*, edited by Peter Alexander (London and Glasgow, 1951, frequently reprinted).

The following publications are distinguished by abbreviations, or are given without the names of their authors, in the notes and essays:

Burnet   Gilbert Burnet, *History of His Own Time*, ed. M. J. R[outh], 2nd ed., 6 vols (Oxford, 1833).
Calder   Walter Scott, *Old Mortality*, ed. Angus Calder (Harmondsworth, 1975).
CLA   [J. G. Cochrane], *Catalogue of the Library at Abbotsford* (Edinburgh, 1838).
Creichton   *Memoirs of Captain John Creichton*, in *The Works of Jonathan Swift, D. D.*, ed. Walter Scott, 19 vols (Edinburgh, 1814), 10.101–195.
Child   Francis James Child, *The English and Scottish Popular Ballads*, 5 vols (Boston and New York, 1882–98).
Kelly   James Kelly, *A Complete Collection of Scotish Proverbs* (London, 1721).
Kirkton   *The Secret and True History of the Church of Scotland, from the Restoration to the Year 1678*, ed. Charles Kirkpatrick Sharpe (Edinburgh, 1817); *CLA*, 3.
Letters   *The Letters of Sir Walter Scott*, ed. H. J. C. Grierson and others, 12 vols (London, 1932–37).
Lockhart   J. G. Lockhart, *Memoirs of the Life of Sir Walter Scott, Bart.*, 7 vols (Edinburgh, 1837–38).
Magnum   Walter Scott, *Waverley Novels*, 48 vols (Edinburgh, 1829–33).
Minstrelsy   Walter Scott, *Minstrelsy of the Scottish Border*, ed. T. F. Henderson, 4 vols (Edinburgh, 1902).
OED   *The Oxford English Dictionary*, 12 vols (Oxford, 1933).
ODEP   *The Oxford Dictionary of English Proverbs*, 3rd edn, rev. F. P. Wilson (Oxford, 1970).

Prose Works   *The Prose Works of Walter Scott, Bart.*, 28 vols (Edinburgh, 1834–36).

Ramsay   'A Collection of Scots Proverbs', in *The Works of Allan Ramsay*, 6 vols, Scottish Text Society, vol. 5, ed. Alexander M. Kinghorn and Alexander Law (Edinburgh, 1972), 59–133.

Ray   J[ohn] Ray, *A Compleat Collection of English Proverbs*, 3rd edn (London, 1737); *CLA*, 169.

Russell   James Russell, 'An Account of the Murder of Archbishop Sharp', in Kirkton, 395–482.

SND   *Scottish National Dictionary*, ed. William Grant and David D. Murison, 10 vols (Edinburgh, 1931–76).

Walker   Patrick Walker, *Some Remarkable Passages of the Life and Death of Mr. Alexander Peden* (1724), in *Six Saints of the Covenant*, ed. D. Hay Fleming, 2 vols (London, 1901); *CLA*, 73.

Wodrow   Robert Wodrow, *The History of the Sufferings of the Church of Scotland*, 2 vols (Edinburgh, 1721–22); *CLA*, 11. In this edition the appendixes are numbered separately from the text; references to the text are in the form 1.449 (i.e. Vol. 1, p. 449), while references to appendixes are in the form 1. Ap.175.

Manuscripts referred to in the notes are in the National Library of Scotland. Information derived from the notes of the late Dr J. C. Corson is indicated by '(Corson)'. The following editions of *Old Mortality* have proved helpful: The Dryburgh Edition, 25 vols (London, 1892–4), vol. 6; ed. Arthur T. Flux (London, 1900); ed. A. J. Grieve (London, 1907); ed. Alexander Welsh (Boston, MS, 1966). But the Penguin edition edited by Angus Calder surpasses all predecessors, and the editors must acknowledge their indebtedness.

title-page   Jedidiah Cleishbotham   Jedidiah ('beloved of the Lord') is the name given to Solomon in 2 Samuel 12.25. 'Clashbottom' was a facetious name used by one of Joseph Train's 'Parish Clerks and Schoolmasters of Galloway'. The name is 'derived . . . from his using the Birch' (MS 3277, pp. 22–23); *clash* in Scots means 'strike' or 'flog'. For further discussion of the name, its origins, and Train's role in supplying it to Scott, see *The Black Dwarf*, ed. P. D. Garside, 129–30.

title-page   Parish-clerk   clerk to the kirk session, the lowest church court in the Presbyterian system. The position was very often given to the schoolmaster.

title-page   Gandercleugh   in Scots, *cleugh* is a gorge or ravine; hence 'goose-hollow'. In the first volume of *Tales of My Landlord*, Gandercleugh is said to be situated at the centre (or 'navel') of Scotland.

title-page   Hear, Land o' Cakes . . . prent it   Robert Burns, 'On the Late Captain Grose's Peregrinations thro' Scotland, collecting the Antiquities of that Kingdom' (1789), lines 1–6.

epigraph   for the translated passage, see *The Life and Exploits of the ingenious gentleman Don Quixote De La Mancha Translated from the original Spanish of . . . Cervantes . . . by Charles Jarvis, Esq.*, 2 vols (London, 1742), 1.204. The incident occurs in Part 1, Bk 4, Ch. 5 ('Which treats of what befel *Don Quixote*'s whole company in the inn').

5 motto   see John Langhorne (1735-79), 'The Wall-Flower', one of the 'Fables of Flora' (1771); in *Works of the English Poets from Chaucer to Cowper*, ed. Alexander Chalmers, 21 vols (1810), 16.447 (*CLA*, 42). The motto is appropriate to Peter Pattieson and his tales, for in 'The Wall-Flower' the person who seeks 'through death's dim walks to urge his way' is a 'letter'd sage' who explores 'the o'ergrown paths of time'.

5.10   Manuscript of Mr Pattieson   *Tales of My Landlord* was published anonymously, but presented as if the work of Peter (or Patrick) Pattieson. Pattieson's first name suggests that he is a Gael; the Celtic 'Patrick' was commonly anglicised as Peter in parish registers, and 'Patie' is a diminutive of Patrick. One of Scott's chief sources was Patrick Walker, also known as Peter, and called that name in *The Heart of Mid-Lothian*. (On the other hand, *paiter* in Scots means to patter, or chatter on endlessly.) We learn in the first volume of *Tales* that Pattieson has died young, and that his papers are presented for publication by his patron Jedidiah Cleishbotham.

5.21-22 himself against a host it was common to have 50 or 60 pupils or more in a class in a parish school.

5.26 flowers of classic genius literature in Latin.

5.29 Virgil 70–19 BC; his *Eclogues* were written *c.* 45–37 BC.

5.30 Horace 65–8 BC; his *Odes* were written *c.* 30–23 BC.

6.16-17 lone vale of green bracken Robert Burns, 'Their groves o' sweet myrtle let Foreign Lands reckon' (written 1795), line 3 (Corson). To Burns, the 'lone glen o' green breckan' which characterises Scotland is symbolic of freedom.

6.43 superior and patron in the Scottish system of landholding, a 'superior' is someone who has made grants of land in return for certain services or payments; the 'patron' appointed the minister of the parish.

7.4 dew of heaven Genesis 27.28.

7.19 armorial bearings coat of arms.

7.20 Dns. Johan *Latin abbreviations* Dominus Johanus, Lord John.

7.27 Presbyterians those who believe in Presbyterian church government, whereby the church is ruled by a system of courts: kirk session (the lowest), presbytery, synod, and general assembly.

7.29 the battle of Pentland Hills see 'Historical Note', 357, for the rising of 1666 which was decisively defeated by government forces at Rullion Green in the Pentland Hills.

7.32 rebels taken with arms in their hands armed insurgents could be shot without further enquiry or trial.

8.3 Hampden...Hooper or Latimer John Hampden (1594–1643) was an English parliamentarian celebrated for his opposition to the autocratic rule of Charles I. John Hooper (1495?–1555) and Hugh Latimer (1485?–1555) were English Protestant reformers burnt at the stake for heresy during the reign of Mary Tudor, Queen of England.

8.35 blue bonnet man's flat-topped, round cap. The cap indicates a respectable countryman and its colour a Covenanter.

8.37 heritable property land and houses etc. (as distinct from movable property), to be inherited by the heir specified by law.

8.38 Gussdub *guss* is Scots for a 'pig'; and *dub* is Scots for a 'stagnant, muddy pool'.

8.40 cespite viridi *Latin* with a piece of green turf. The phrase occurs several times in Classical authors, for example in Virgil's description of Hector's cenotaph at *Aeneid*, 3.304: *tumulum viridi...caespite inanem*, an empty mound of green turf.

8.42 Judges of the Land...Assembly of the Nobles Judges of the Court of Session, the supreme civil court of Scotland, and the House of Lords in London. As a result of the Union with England in 1707, it became possible to appeal to the House of Lords against decisions of the Court of Session.

8.44 adhuc in pendente *Latin* still pending. A recognised legal term.

9.10 pair of branks kind of bridle for horses or cows, used by country people.

9.18 Old Mortality in the Magnum Scott writes: 'The remarkable person, called by the title of Old Mortality, was well known in Scotland about the end of the last century. His real name was Robert Paterson. He was a native, it is said, of the parish of Closeburn, in Dumfries-shire, and probably a mason by profession—at least educated to the use of the chisel.' Scott goes on to tell of his own meeting with Old Mortality in the churchyard of Dunnottar in Kincardine-shire 'about thirty years since, or more'; and of how this meeting had been 'recalled to my memory by an account transmitted by my friend Mr Joseph Train, supervisor of excise at Dumfries, to whom I owe many obligations of a similar nature'. Scott says that at Dunnottar Old Mortality's 'appearance and equipment were exactly as described in the Novel'; and he gives many other details concerning the life and death of Robert Paterson. (Magnum, 9.221, 222, 227, 226).

9.28   the language of Scripture   compare Genesis 12.1 and Mark 10.29–30: Abram leaves his kindred and his father's house to answer God's call, and Jesus tells his followers that those who leave 'house, or brethren' for his sake will receive 'eternal life'.

9.31-32   regulated his circuit   jocular re-application of legal terminology; the High Court, the highest criminal court in Scotland, went on circuit to various fixed places at fixed times of year.

9.34   the two last monarchs of the Stuart line   Charles II, and James VII and II.

9.39   wanderers   word regularly used of the Covenanters, especially those outlawed and forced to hide in the period 1661–1688.

10.9   beacon-light   there was formerly a system of beacons sited on prominent hills to warn of invasion from England, and in Scott's period to warn of invasion from France.

10.14   some Cameronian of his own sect   the Cameronians were the extreme wing of the Presbyterians, named after Richard Cameron (d. 1680).

10.29   generation of vipers   Matthew 3.7; 23.33: the phrase is used by John the Baptist and by Jesus of the religious establishment.

10.35   the maxim of Solomon   see Proverbs 13.24: 'he that spareth his rod hateth his son: but he that loveth him chasteneth him betimes', one of the proverbs of Solomon.

11.11   the only true whigs   the only true followers of the Covenanters of the west of Scotland who rose against Charles II and James VII. The term 'Whig' was originally a nickname for the supporters of the National Covenant but came to be applied in England to those who in 1679 opposed the succession of James to the throne because he was a Roman Catholic. At the Revolution of 1688, when James was deposed, the word was used of those who favoured the Protestant succession, and thus it became the name of the dominant political party of the 18th century.

11.12-13   him whose kingdom is of this world   the devil: see Matthew 4.8; John 18.36; Revelation 11.15.

11.15   ne'er a hair   not the slightest bit.

11.16   blude-thirsty tories   supporters of the crown who persecuted the Covenanters. The word 'Tory' was taken into English from Irish Gaelic and was used in the 17th century as a name for the dispossessed Irish, who plundered and killed Protestant settlers from England and Scotland. By extension, it later came to be used of any Irish Roman Catholic or royalist in arms. After the Revolution of 1688 it became the name of the Jacobite political party, which supported the restoration of the exiled House of Stuart.

11.18-19   mighty men ... wrath   see Ezekiel 22.30; Revelation 6.17. Old Mortality applies the text metaphorically to the Covenanters.

11.21   Mr Peden   Alexander Peden (1626?–86). Peden was one of the ministers ejected from their charges in 1663; he took part in the rising of 1666, and was imprisoned on the Bass Rock from 1673 till 1678. His final days were spent in a cave near Sorn in Ayrshire. He was revered by the Covenanters, and gained a reputation as a prophet.

11.22   the French monzies ... broken covenant   Old Mortality implies that the French will be a scourge, punishing a self-seeking nation for its sins. He paraphrases some of Peden's prophecies. See Walker, 91–93: 'In the morning, they enquired what he meant by the Monzies; he said, "Oh, sirs, ye'll have a dreadful day by the French Monzies ...; they'll run thicker in the water of Air and Clyde than ever the Highland men did."' Upon another occasion, he said he had been allowed to '"see the Franchies marching with their armies thorow the breadth and length of the land, marching to their bridle-reins in the blood of all ranks, and that for a broken, burnt and buried covenant"'.

11.22-23   the Glens of Ayr, and the Kenns of Galloway   hilly districts in the west of Scotland, on the River Ayr and around Loch Ken.

11.23-24   Highlandmen ... in 1678   in 1677 a proclamation of the Scottish Privy Council commanded landowners to require their households and tenants to sign a bond promising to attend the parish church and not to go to conventicles. The penalties for non-compliance were severe: servants and tenants who refused to sign were to be turned out, and landowners who did not ensure compliance were to be subject to heavy fines; see Wodrow, 1.449, 1. Ap.173. Landowners, particularly in the western counties, protested vigorously, and, to enforce the law, the government sent Highland regiments (the 'Highland Host') to Ayrshire in February 1678, authorising them to take free quarters and horses as needed, and indemnifying them against 'all Pursuits civil and criminal' (Wodrow, 1. Ap.175). Wodrow comments that the 'particular Relation of the Oppressions, Depredations, Exactions, and Cruelties committed by them, would fill a Volume' (1.487).

11.24   the bow and ... the spear   see Psalm 46.9 and Jeremiah 6.23.

11.31   Wallace Inn   in the first volume of Tales of My Landlord Cleishbotham says that travellers from every corner of the country frequent 'my landlord's' Wallace Inn in Gandercleugh (Sir William Wallace being the greatest Scottish hero, the emblem of the national spirit).

11.38-39   her banner upon the mountains   see Isaiah 13.2: God is gathering together the army of his people to fight a holy war.

11.41   prophet's chamber   see 2 Kings 4.9–10: the prophet Elisha, in his travels, frequently received hospitality from a rich woman at Shunem, and was allocated 'a little chamber'.

12.8   latter harvest   compare Matthew 13.39.

12.11   colour in your cheek   the observation suggests that Pattieson was suffering from tuberculosis. See 12.20–21: 'my span of life may be abridged in youth'.

12.12–13   labour ... his master calleth   see Mark 13.34–35.

12.14   gane hame to your ain place   i.e. died and gone to heaven or hell, whichever is appropriate.

12.15   stane of memorial   see Exodus 28.12 and Joshua 4.7.

12.41   Smackawa   in Scots to smack means to 'kiss', and awa ('away') implies a continuous action.

12.42   chamber of dais   the best room in the house, the best bedroom.

13.9–10   authentic sources of tradition ... either party   Pattieson imitates Patrick Walker in his life of Alexander Peden in gathering verbal testimony, but where Walker spoke to the 'martyrs, sufferers, and other worthy Christians' (Walker, 3), Pattieson talked to 'the representatives of either party'.

13.13–14   the late general change of property   agrarian 'improvements' were a notable feature of Scotland in the late 18th and early 19th centuries; small tenant farmers frequently lost their grazing rights on common land, and thus their livelihood. For instance, in the account of the Parish of Avondale in the 1790s the minister reports 'The diminution of inhabitants in the country is owing to the moor farms having gone into fewer hands, and there being now almost no cottagers in the parish' (*The Statistical Account of Scotland*, ed. Donald J. Withrington and Ian R. Grant, 20 vols (Wakefield, 1973), 7.5–6).

13.20–21 our more wealthy neighbours the English.

13.22 winter web cloth woven during the winter months.

13.23 tailors it was customary for tailors to travel round country districts, making clothes to measure in the houses they visited.

13.38 right reverend the style of a bishop.

13.39 non-juring bishop non-swearing bishop, i.e. an Episcopalian bishop who refused to take oaths of loyalty to the government after the Revolution of 1688–89, and as a result lost his position. His income would therefore be as low as that of Jesus's first followers, the apostles (see Mark 6.8). During the 18th century the small remnant of the Scottish Episcopal Church was strongly Jacobite and so feared and suspected by the government.

14.3 Earlshall and Claverhouse Andrew Bruce of Earlshall (dates unknown) and John Graham of Claverhouse (*c.* 1649–89) were noted royalist military leaders, active against the Covenanters.

14.13 zeal for God's house did not eat up see Psalm 69.9.

14.14 the phrase of Dryden untraced. Scott edited a major edition of Dryden: *Life and Works of John Dryden*, 18 vols (Edinburgh, 1808).

14.20 the heroine of our only Scottish tragedy Lady Randolph, in [John Home,] *Douglas: A Tragedy* (Edinburgh, 1757), 10 (Act 1). *CLA*, 10, 209.

14 motto *Douglas: A Tragedy*, 43 (Act 4).

14.32 feudal institutions maintaining and producing a specified number of men for military service was a common obligation of the feu charters by which landowners held land as a grant from the crown.

15.1 resisting an Act of Council there was no historical act of Council of exactly the kind indicated, but a 1661 act of the Scottish Parliament ordered that 29 May be kept as a holy day to mark the King's birthday and the anniversary of his Restoration: prayers, preaching, and thanksgiving were to be followed by 'lawful Divertisements' (Wodrow, 1.28). The Scottish Privy Council was re-established in 1661; Wodrow (1.87) says that 'in the Intervals of Parliaments, they had all the executory power in their Hand, and assumed little less than a Parliamentary Power'. The members of the Council were appointed by the King, and in the course of his reign Charles II came to rely increasingly upon proclamations as a means of promulgating new law. For the Privy Council as a judicial body see 277.37.

15.6 Calvinists followers of the Frenchman John Calvin (1509–64), the most distinguished theologian of the Reformation. Calvin's *Institutes* (published in Latin 1536, and in French 1541) was widely read in Scotland from the 16th to the 19th centuries. The word *Calvinist* is used of those who followed Calvin's thought, particularly his doctrine of grace, but is often applied loosely to those with narrow moral and theological views.

15.7–8 Judaical observance of the Sabbath strict and literal interpretation of the fourth commandment, 'Remember the sabbath day, to keep it holy ... in it thou shalt not do any work'. See Exodus 20.8–11.

15.16–18 crown vassal ... high statutory penalties to improve the security of Scotland, crown vassals or barons (see notes to 14.32 and 17.28) had to turn out with their due number of men for county exercises, the militia and the King's host, which was an army of all able-bodied men. The penalties for non-attendance were severe: e.g. in November 1679 the King said it was his 'will and pleasure' that the penalty of death for absence from the host should be waived and that fines should be substituted. The fines were proportional to means and were heavy: Wodrow (2.114–15) gives examples ranging from £6000 Scots (£500) to 1000 merks (£55).

15.19   lord-lieutenants and sheriffs   representatives of the crown, with responsibility for administering and policing a county.

15.30   esprit de corps   *French* group spirit.

16.6−7   meddling with the accursed thing   see Joshua 6.18; 7.1. Before the capture of Jericho, the Israelites are told: 'keep yourselves from the accursed thing, lest ye make yourselves accursed, when ye take of the accursed thing'. See also note to 251.31−39.

16.7   abomination . . . Lord   see 2 Kings 21.2.

16.9   Upper Ward of Clydesdale   Lanarkshire was divided for administrative purposes into three parts, known as wards. The Upper Ward was administered from Lanark, the Middle from Hamilton, and the Lower from Rutherglen.

16.10   a royal borough   a royal burgh derives its charter, lands, and privileges directly from the crown.

16.11   5th of May, 1679   the date was determined by the murder of Archbishop Sharp on 3 May 1679.

16.14   shoot at the popinjay   in the Magnum (9.268−69), Scott says that the description of the shooting at the popinjay was suggested by a passage in James, eleventh Lord Somerville's *Memorie of the Somervilles* (2 vols (Edinburgh, 1815), 2.144−46; *CLA*, 231), which he had edited. The passage describes a shooting-match in Dalserf, a village in the Clyde Valley between Lanark and Hamilton.

16.30−31   a personage of ducal rank   Scott originally wrote 'The Duke of Hamilton' in the manuscript but deleted this and made the reference less specific. The then Duke (the 3rd) was William Douglas (1635−94), a moderate royalist but opposed to the measures taken to enforce Episcopacy on Scotland.

16.40   tie-wigs with three tails   wigs having the hair gathered behind into three tails and tied with ribbons.

17.5   title to precedence over the untitled gentry   Lady Margaret Bellenden is the widow of a knight. The order of precedence was the monarch, the various grades of peer, the various orders of knighthood, and the landed gentry.

17.6−7   Lady Margaret Bellenden   a fictional character, although Scott seems to have got some hints (see note to 273.27) from the career of the historical Sir William Bellenden (*c.* 1604−71) who was a noted anti-covenanter. 'Bellenden' is an appropriate name for a warlike royalist: in Scots a *bellandine* is a 'fight', and 'Bellendaine' was the war-cry of the Scotts of Buccleuch.

17.9−10   Montrose   James Graham (1612−50), fifth Earl and first Marquis of Montrose, a soldier and poet who achieved a brilliant series of royalist victories against Presbyterian armies in 1644 and 1645 before being heavily defeated at Philiphaugh in September 1645: see 'Historical Note', 355−56.

17.28   barony   in Scots law, a *barony* is an estate created by direct grant from the Crown. A grant of barony carried with it both civil and criminal jurisdiction, and usually required the baron to maintain and produce a specified number of men for military service. See also note to 14.32.

17.36   commination   formal 'denouncing of God's anger and judgements against sinners', usually used on the first day of Lent. See *The Book of Common Prayer*, and note to 94.18.

18.2   bring round   bring about, accomplish.

18.6   Kilsythe and Tippermoor   two of Montrose's victories in his campaign of 1644−45.

18.10   life-rentrix   the female holder of a life rent, which gives the right for life to the use of property and the income rising from it, but without ownership.

Scott does not explain how Lady Margaret comes to have a life-rent of Tillie-tudlem: the estate was inherited from her father, not her husband, and as the only child of the Earl of Torwood she was heir-at-law, i.e. the heir specified by Scots law. The most likely explanation is that the Earl entailed his property; this may be what is meant by his 'settlement' (273.39). Any landowner could entail heritable property, specifying which descendants could inherit, and in doing so preventing heirs from selling or giving away either the whole or any part of it. Thus the practical effect of entailing Tillietudlem would have been to make Lady Margaret life-rentrix.

18.12 troupe doree *French, literally* gilded troop.

18.18 in sair straits in a bad way.

18.23 domiciliary visit visit to a private dwelling, by an official person, to search or inspect it.

18.30 What for no why not.

19.5 her husband and two promising sons it is not literally possible for Edith's father to have been killed in the Civil War which ended in 1652 and yet to be the father of a young woman of about 20, but the imaginative time-scheme of the novel reduces the gap between the events of 1638–1652 and 1679.

19.8 the unfortunate field of Worcester the defeat of Charles II in 1651; see 'Historical Note', 432.

19.26 kick the beam *proverbial* the image is of a balance in which one side is very light and rises to hit the beam from which the balance is suspended (see *ODEP*, 422 and *Paradise Lost*, 4.1004).

19.42–20.2 romances of Calprenede and Scuderi ... Cyrus, Cleo-patra Gauthier de Costes de La Calprenède (1614–63), author of the multi-volume *Cléopâtre* (1647–56); Madeleine de Scudéry (1607–1701), author of *Artamène ou le Grand Cyrus (1649–53)*.

20.1–2 vessels of the first rate vessels of the highest of the classes into which warships are divided according to size and equipment.

20.3 small craft small trading vessels or lighters.

20 motto see Thomas Campbell, *The Pleasures of Hope* (1799), Part 2, lines 181–82.

20.33 follies the term has the biblical force of a reckless disregard of God's law.

20.40 palpable hit *Hamlet*, 5.2.273.

21.15 Evandale a fictitious title. Lord Evandale takes his name from the parish of Evandale which included Strathaven and Loudoun Hill in the western part of Lanarkshire. Scott uses the 17th-century spelling 'Evan', rather than the form 'Avon' adopted in the late 18th century.

21.36 good old cause phrase frequently used in England in the later 1650s to refer to the radical religious and political policies, betrayed (as many saw it) by Cromwell's becoming Lord Protector. The phrase was also used in England, and less frequently in Scotland, by opponents of the restored Stuart monarchy, 1660–89. See Milton, *The Ready and Easy Way to Establish a Free Commonwealth* (1660), final paragraph: 'What I have spoken is the language of that which is not called amiss "The good old Cause"'.

23.7 obedient start ... poor Malvolio see *Twelfth Night*, 2.5.53.

23.22–23 Dunbar and Inverkeithing battles of 1650 and 1651. After the execution of Charles I, majority opinion in Scotland swung behind Charles II, and royalists and moderate Presbyterians unsuccessfully joined forces against the English parliamentary army under Cromwell. Colonel Morton was fighting for the King as well as for the Covenant.

23.26 Marston-Moor and Philiphaugh battles of 1644 and 1645. Fol-lowing the signing of the Solemn League and Covenant in 1643, the combined forces of the English parliament and the Scottish army defeated the royal forces

at Marston Moor. The victory of the Covenanters at Philiphaugh brought
Montrose's brilliant royalist campaign of 1644–45 to a disastrous conclusion.

23.35   suit and service   offering 'suit and service' was one of the obligations
of barons or crown vassals, discharged by turning up when summoned to appear
at court or for military exercises. See notes to 14.32 and 17.28.

23.39–40   broad piece   £1 coin, called 'broad' because broader than the
guinea (£1.05).

24.30   hand gallop   slow gallop.

24.36   wiped away from the tablets of his memory   see *Hamlet*,
1.5.98–99.

25.2   martial tune of the Gallant Græmes   the music sounds appropriate:
the name associates it with Montrose (a Graham), and the royalist cause. But
the 'ballad' entitled 'The Gallant Graemes' (*Minstrelsy*, 2.222–241) is a
lament, and those versions of a tune of the same name that have been located are
plaintive rather than martial.

25.16–17   celebrated thrust of Orlando . . . frogs   see Ludovico Ariosto,
Orlando furioso (1532), canto 9, stanzas 68–69; *CLA*, 42, 55, 185.

25.33–34   stripped of his lion's hide   compare *King John*, 3.1.123–129.

25.43   gens d'armerie   *French* cavalry or men-at-arms.

26   motto   see Sir Robert Sempill of Beltrees (1595?–1660?), 'The Life
and Death of Habbie Simson, the Piper of Kilbarchan', lines 25–30.

26.21–22   five merks   £3. 6s. 8d. Scots; 28p. The pound Scots was worth
one twelfth of the English pound.

26.23   a dollar   in Charles II's second coinage of 1676 there was a series of
silver coins described as dollars or fractions thereof; see I. H. Stewart, *The
Scottish Coinage* (London, 1955), 157–58. A dollar was worth 4 merks (22p).

26.33   Gaius the publican   Romans 16.23 speaks of 'Gaius mine host',
whose house was a meeting-place of the Church.

27.12–13   baith up the street and doun the street   throughout the town.

27.18   keepit unco short by the head   kept on a short rein.

27.19   curate   a minister in the Scottish Church in the period 1662–1688;
curates were appointed by a patron, unlike Presbyterian ministers who were
called by a congregation.

27.19   Cornet   commissioned officer equivalent to second lieutenant, who
carried the colours.

27.21   dragoons   horse soldiers. In 1675 garrisons of a 'Company of Foot
and Twelve Horse' (Wodrow, 1.391) were posted throughout lowland Scotland
to prevent conventicles.

27.25   ten pund Scots   83p.

27.34   hill-folk   those who worshipped at the illegal conventicles in the hills
under ministers who had been ejected from their parishes in 1662 for refusing to
take the oath of allegiance.

27.35   red-coats   soldiers; although military uniforms in the 18th century
were generally red, only some regiments wore red in the 17th.

27.43   aff hands is fair play   proverbial (see *ODEP*, 348). Niel Blane is
telling Jennie that, provided nothing becomes physical, accepting banter is part
of the business.

28.1–2   when the malt gets aboon the meal   *proverbial* when people get
drunk (see Ray, 69; *ODEP*, 503).

28.8   cry on   shout for.

28.9   At no hand   by no means.

28.11   tak the tangs and poker   *literally* take the tongs and poker; i.e. start
fighting.

28.13   bag o' wind   bagpipes.

28.15   sma' drink   low-alcohol or non-alcoholic drink.

28.17 anes in a day once upon a time.

28.37 Claverhouse's regiment of life-guards in 1679 the historical Claverhouse was only a captain of a troop of horse. He was promoted Colonel in 1682, and took command of a newly-formed regiment, which, although separate from the troop of horse in the Scots army known as the Lifeguard, was granted the style of 'His Majesty's Own Regiment of Horse' in 1685.

28.40 mousquetaires part of the French king's household troops; the mousquetaires were all of noble birth.

29.3–4 Francis Stuart . . . Bothwell great-great grandson of James V. John Stuart, Prior of Coldingham, was one of the illegitimate children of James V. John Stuart's son, Francis Stuart Hepburn, was the 5th Earl of Bothwell, inheriting the title through his mother, Lady Jane Hepburn. The 5th Earl caused much trouble in the early part of the reign of James VI, and as a result the Bothwell estates were forfeited. The 5th Earl died in poverty in Naples *c.* 1612. His son Francis (d. 1639) regained part of his father's lands from Charles I, but poverty forced him to sell them; the title was never restored. The novel implies that the Bothwell of the novel was this Francis's son, but he was probably a nephew. The historical character features in Creichton (123–25), but, as Scott says in his note in the Magnum, 'The character of Bothwell, except in relation to the name, is entirely ideal' (9.297).

29.5–6 the infamous lover of the unfortunate Queen Mary James Hepburn (*c.* 1535–78), fourth Earl of Bothwell. He was the uncle of the fifth Earl (see previous note). The fourth Earl was deeply involved in the troubles of the reign of Queen Mary (1542–87), and was generally suspected of complicity in the murder of the Queen's husband Darnley at Kirk o' Field in 1567. Bothwell married the Queen two months after Darnley's murder. He died, insane, after a long imprisonment in Denmark.

29.24 levying fines, exacting free quarters very substantial fines were imposed for non-conformity and attendance at conventicles. Both fines and regular taxes were collected by the military, who, although forbidden to levy money or to quarter themselves on people without specific authorisation, frequently acted for themselves.

30.4–5 colt foaled of an acorn in the Magnum (10.18) Scott writes: 'The punishment of riding the wooden mare was, in the days of Charles and long after, one of the various and cruel modes of enforcing military discipline'. He may have got his information from the transcript of the diary of John Nicoll (1580?–1668) which he commissioned (*Letters*, 8.434, and *CLA*, 282), which was later published as *A Diary of Public Transactions . . . 1650–1667* (Edinburgh, 1836). For the description of the wooden mare see 33.

30.7 blue-bonnet a Cameronian; see note to 8.35.

30.18 the comfortable creature *comfortable* that which strengthens or sustains; *creature* brandy or whisky.

30.33 practical application punning reference to the section of a sermon which contains the practical lesson or 'moral' of the exposition.

30.39 James Sharpe James Sharp (1613–79) was a member of a group of Presbyterian leaders sent to London in 1660 to secure the position of the Scottish Church after the Restoration. Sharp played a dexterous and decisive part in the negotiations which produced not the confirmation of Presbyterianism Sharp was professedly seeking, but the restoration of Episcopalianism with Sharp himself as Archbishop of St Andrews.

30.40 the test the Test Act was only passed in 1681, and whether the term 'the test' was in use in Scotland before 1681 is not clear, although it is possible as the English Test Act was passed in 1673. However, the oath of allegiance (see 'Historical Note', 356) was certainly used as a test: 'their way was, whenever any suspected person was cited before them, to offer them this oath, and if they took it, whatever were objected against them they were absolved; but, if they were so scrupulous as to refuse, . . . they were condemned without mercy' (Kirkton, 91).

30.42   crop-eared   having the hair cut short, and thus showing the ears. Those who used the phrase intended to associate whigs with people who had their ears cut off as a criminal punishment.

31.16–17   pitch . . . axle-tree   games of strength: in *pitch the bar* the winner was whoever tossed a thick rod of wood or iron furthest; in *putt the stone* whoever putted a heavy stone furthest; and in *throw the axle-tree* whoever threw the wooden axle of a coach furthest.

31.23   good cause   see note to 21.36.

31.29–30   all such railing Rabshekahs   see 2 Kings Chs 18–19. The Assyrian leader Rabshakeh declaims blasphemously as an immensely powerful Assyrian army lays siege to Jerusalem, but the Jews keep their trust in the power of God, and Jerusalem is saved.

32.41   boot and saddle   the signal to cavalry to mount; from French *boute-selle*, 'place saddle'.

33.5–6   the Archbishop . . . assassinated   Archbishop Sharp (see note to 30.39) was assassinated, as described, on 3 May 1679.

33.12   thousand merks   £666 Scots; £55 sterling.

33.17   double-chested   the phrase is obscure, but probably means 'with a powerful chest'.

33.20–22   Haxtoun of Rathillet . . . John Balfour, called Burley   David Hackston of Rathillet (d. 1680) and John Balfour of Kinloch (d. 1688) were brothers-in-law, and the leaders of the party that assassinated Sharp. Balfour was sometimes 'called Burley' through confusion with John Balfour, 3rd Baron Balfour of Burleigh, but in the *Minstrelsy* Scott suggests that 'Burley' is a nick-name 'signifying *strong*' (2.263).

34   motto   untraced.

34.17–18   blood of God's saints . . . water   see Revelation 16.5–6. The early Christians are frequently called 'saints' in the New Testament, and the term is applied to the Covenanters, particularly the Covenanting martyrs, because of their special sense of being God's people.

34.20   wine-bibbing   see Proverbs 23.20.

34.21   with his fan . . . chaff   see Matthew 3.12.

34.28–29   thy master . . . obey   biblical formulations rather than specific echoes.

34.36   this Indulgence   see 'Historical Note', 357.

35.6   days of blood and darkness   see Revelation 6.12.

35.7–8   smiting . . . mountains   compare Ezekiel Ch. 34.

35.10   the children of light   the followers of Jesus: see John 12.36.

35.15–17   least lamb . . . whole Christian flock   ironic echo of Luke 15.4.

35.17–19   the golden calf . . . the waters   see Exodus 32.20; the children of Israel set up a golden calf, a false God, while Moses was absent on Mount Sinai. But it was Jeroboam who set up a golden calf at Bethel (1 Kings 12.28–29).

35.35   a lion in the path   see Proverbs 26.13 and 1 Peter 5.8.

35.37   Hamilton and Dingwall   in May 1679 an armed body of Coven-anters assembled in the west, one of the leaders being Sir Robert Hamilton of Preston (1650–1701). This group was joined by some of those involved in the assassination of Sharp, including Haxtoun, Balfour, and William Dingwall of Caddam.

35.38   drawn to any head   gathered in any numbers.

36.6   the Drake Moss   to *drake* is to drench or soak; a *moss* is boggy ground.

36.8   scattered remnant   see Jeremiah 40.15.

36.14   men of Belial   phrase used in the Old Testament of reprobate, dissol-ute or uncouth persons.

36.20 blessings of the promise the promise of everlasting life to all true believers. See Hebrews 9.15.

36.28–29 laws . . . inter-communed persons letters of intercommuning were issued in August 1675, forbidding people from contact with those who had been outlawed for persistent attendance at conventicles. The royal proclamation commands subjects not to 'reset, supply, or intercommune with any of the foresaid Persons our Rebels, . . . nor furnish them with Meat, Drink, House, Harbour, Victual, nor no other Thing useful or comfortable to them, nor have Intelligence with them by Word, Writ, or Message' (Wodrow 1. Ap.168).

36.34–35 a tabernacle . . . planks of cedar the tabernacle was a sacred tent. It was divided in two, and the inner sanctuary, in which the ark of the Covenant was kept, was decorated with rich curtains, shittim wood, silver and gold. See Exodus Ch. 26; 1 Kings 6.9 and 15; Song of Solomon 6.9.

37.1 the battle of Longmarston-Moor see note to 23.26.

37.4 Avenger of Blood see Numbers 35.12. According to Jewish law, when someone was killed, the deceased person's kinsman had to become the Avenger of Blood, and claim a life for a life. In cases of accidental homicide the killer could find asylum by going to a City of Refuge.

37.6 like a thief in the night see 1 Thessalonians 5.2 and 2 Peter 3.10.

37.9 perverse generation see Matthew 17.17.

37.16 Resolutioners and Protesters see 'Historical Note', 432.

37.35 the punishment . . . as in justice it should although 'in justice' the punishment should fall upon Henry, in practice the effects of the punishments and fines were not confined to the individual.

37.43 court of offices square of stables, barns, sheds etc.

38.10–11 implements i.e. flint and steel.

39.1–2 for as sair a hoast as I hae in spite of having as bad a cough as I have.

39.6 sae fair-fashioned as we are how well-mannered we are.

39.6–7 Mistress Wilson in his 'Memoirs', Scott speaks of 'old Alison Wilson, the house keeper' at his grandfather's farm of Sandyknowe. ('Memoirs', in *Scott on Himself*, ed. David Hewitt (Edinburgh, 1981), 11.)

39.12 what for do ye no why don't you.

39.18 ye're ill to serve you are hard to look after; i.e. you are very demanding.

39.21 atween and between now and.

39.23 scaff and raff riff-raff.

39.33 blawing in a woman's lug flattering a woman.

39.38–39 the Duke . . . lost his head James Hamilton (1606–49), 3rd Marquis and 1st Duke of Hamilton. His career included service in Europe in the Thirty Years' War, but his military shortcomings contributed to his decisive defeat by Cromwell at Preston in 1648. He was executed in London by the English parliamentarians in March 1649.

40.2 not very chancy not to be relied on, dangerous.

40.23 see ye mind about make sure you remember.

40.24 clow-gillieflower water wine made from the clove-scented pink.

40.34 take an account of his ways evaluate his conduct (in the course of the preceding day), as before God.

41 motto see *2 Henry IV*, 1.1.60–61.

41.25 indulged minister see 'Historical Note', 357.

42.31 my hour is not yet come see John 2.4, 7.30 and 8.20.

42.33 saints . . . slaughtered compare Milton, 'On the Late Massacre in Piemont' (1655), line 1.

43.2–3 righteous judgments of Heaven see Psalm 19.9, Revelation 16.7 etc.

43.3   in the body   2 Corinthians 12.2 and Hebrews 13.3.

43.13–14   Truth himself . . . delusion of the enemy   i.e. confuse messages from God with the promptings of the devil.

43.22–23   the dungeon-house of the Law   Burley means that Morton still holds the erroneous view that salvation comes from obedience to the law of God. He believes that salvation comes from faith alone.

43.23–25   a pit . . . mire   see Jeremiah 38.6.

43.25   seal of the covenant upon your forehead   see Revelation 7.3. Burley punningly implies both that Morton is the recipient of God's promise of salvation and that he will join in the defence of the Scottish Covenants.

43.26–27   banner . . . mountains   see Isaiah 13.2: God is gathering together the army of his people, to fight a holy war.

43.32   girded up our loins   see 1 Kings 18.46. Elijah girded up his loins and ran before Ahab to whom he had just demonstrated the truth of God and the powerlessness of Baal, the God of the Canaanites. See note to 45.21–22.

43.32   run the race boldly   compare Hebrews 12.1.

44.9   their heads on the Westport   the Westport was one of the gates of Edinburgh, over which the heads of those executed after Montrose's defeat at Philiphaugh were displayed.

44.10–11   reformers . . . tabernacle   those rebuilding the temple, i.e. those striving to re-establish godly government in Scotland.

44.13–17   We looked for peace . . . all that is in it   Jeremiah 8.15–16: because of Israel's faithlessness, the people of the Covenant will be overwhelmed by their enemies and Jerusalem will be destroyed.

44.26–28   When I put my hand . . . things I left behind me   see Luke 9.62: 'And Jesus said unto him, No man, having put his hand to the plough, and looking back, is fit for the kingdom of God'.

45.18   like bubbles in a late disturbed stream   *1 Henry IV*, 2.3.56.

45.20   Thou art taken, Judas   see Russell, 416.

45.21–22   a priest of Baal . . . at the brook Kishon   see I Kings 18.40: 'And Elijah said unto them, Take the prophets of Baal; let not one of them escape. And they took them; and Elijah brought them down to the brook Kishon, and slew them there.' Burley implies that he is like Elijah in removing corruption from the life of Israel. See note to 43.32.

45.22–23   Fire-arms will not prevail against him   Wodrow reports that having fired several shots without killing Sharp, the assassins 'began to imagine Shooting would not do' (Wodrow, 2. Ap.31) and so killed him with their swords. Scott embellishes this report by implying that Sharp was thought to be immune from shot, although he may have got a hint from Burnet (2.232); he elaborates yet further in *Tales of a Grandfather*, second series: 'when, conceiving, according to their superstitious notion, that their victim was possessed of a charm against gun-shot, they drew their swords, and killed him with many wounds, dashing even his skull to pieces, and scooping out his brains' (*Prose Works*, 24.237).

46.16–17   serve both God and Mammon   see Matthew 6.24 and Luke 16.13.

46.19–20   those who for the truth have forsaken all things   see Matthew 19.27: Peter says to Jesus 'Behold, we have forsaken all, and followed thee'.

46.20–21   touch pitch and remain undefiled   see Ecclesiasticus 13.1.

46.23–25   hold intercourse . . . the flood   see Genesis 6.1–7.

46.27   the accursed thing   see note to 16.6–7.

46.27–28   Touch not . . . handle not   Colossians 2.21.

46.30   snare to your feet   see Jeremiah 18.22.

46.30–33   the son of David . . . the text of Scripture   King Solomon, the son of David, was the reputed author of the canonical book Ecclesiastes; Burley, however, quotes from Ch. 40 of the apocryphal book Ecclesiasticus. This error is probably Scott's rather than the character's as there is a similar confusion in *Rob Roy*, 2.276.16–17.

47.3 has made wise men mad   see Ecclesiastes 7.7: 'Surely oppression maketh a wise man mad'. The phrase is used by Wodrow when discussing the Highland Host: 'the Oppression of the Savages would turn wise Men mad, and drive common People to a Tumult and Rebellion' (Wodrow, 1.460).

47.31–32 our Ruthvens . . . Protestant champion   Gustavus Adolphus (1594–1632), King of Sweden led the Protestant forces in the Thirty Years' War. Large numbers of Scots fought in Europe under him; those who achieved particular fame included Patrick Ruthven (*c.* 1573–1651), Alexander Leslie (*c.* 1580–1661), and Robert Monro (d. 1633).

48.24 his mess of porridge   see the chapter heading to Genesis 25 in the Geneva Bible (Geneva, 1560): 'Esau selleth his birth right for a messe of potage'.

48.40–41 if ye put . . . out o' ye   if you have caused me expense I shall make you work to pay me back.

48.41 haud the pleugh   drive the plough.

49.5 what for no?   why not?

49.9 I'll be your caution   I'll warrant you.

49.9 Haggie-holm   a *holm* is a stretch of low ground near a river, and *haggie* suggests it is pitted with marshy hollows.

49.10 keep the coulter down   the old plough had to be held down in the ground by the ploughman as it was pulled along by the oxen or horses.

49.33–34 serve a turn about the town   do some work around the farm

49.36 Hear till him   listen to him.

49.38–39 they maun either marry or do waur   compare 1 Corinthians 7.9.

50.1 Margrave   German title, originally given to the military governor of a border province, and later to princes of certain states of the Holy Roman Empire.

50.2 battle of Lutzen   an important Protestant victory (1632), but dearly bought, as Gustavus Adolphus was killed while leading a cavalry charge.

50.21 in a creel   mad.

50.25 curb his head ower sair in   control him too rigidly.

50.33 butter siller   the income from selling butter, which was traditionally the housewife's.

50.39 intercommuned rebels   see note to 36.28–9.

50.41 Raploch grey   garment made of coarse, homespun, undyed woollen cloth.

51.7 loop doun   remove the loops from.

51.7 lay by   lay aside.

51.8 at no hand   on no account.

51 motto   *As You Like It*, 2.3.71–74.

51.35–36 bed of justice   a sitting of the French parliament at which the king was present. As the king sometimes convened the parliament to enforce the registration of his own decrees, the term came to be applied chiefly to sessions held for this purpose. Lady Margaret is actually holding a somewhat comical baron court (see note to 17.28).

52.20 Earl of Torwood   a fictitious title. Most Scottish peerages could be held by women as well as men, but when this peerage was created the letters patent must have specified that it could be held only by heirs male, thus preventing Lady Margaret from succeeding.

52.32 curtesy   the way in which a kindly tenant (see note to 53.33) acknowledges the feudal relationship.

53.6 Malcolm Canmore Malcolm III (d. 1093), called Canmore, King of Scots, son of Duncan I.

53.25 ower boots in blude compare the proverb 'over shoes, over boots' (*ODEP*, 603).

53.28–29 hae nae broo o' them ava have no favourable opinion of them at all.

53.31 hunting, hosting, watching, and warding the supposed duties of tenants. *Hosting* involves attending the king's host when summoned (see note to 15.18), *watching* keeping watch, and *warding* keeping guard.

53.33 kindly tenants those having a right to the tenancy in consequence of long-continued occupation by the tenant in person, or the tenant's ancestors. They were in theory tenants at will; in practice they had considerable claims of the 'kindness' (kinship) entitling them to the land.

53.34 cow's grass enough pasturage for a cow.

53.34–35 brought farther ben treated more favourably.

53.38 ane canna serve twa maisters see Matthew 6.24.

54.13–25 Nebuchadnezzar ... Abednego see Daniel Ch. 3. Nebuchad-nezzar of Babylon set up 'an image of gold . . . in the plain of Dura', and commanded all and sundry to worship it. Shadrach, Meshach, and Abednego refused because they were Jews and faithful to the God of Israel. The King ordered them to be thrown into a 'fiery furnace', but God saved them, 'nor was a hair of their head singed'.

54.35–36 sixteen hundred and forty-twa the year the English Civil War began.

54.42 in another article on another matter.

55.14 windle-straes and sandy-lavrocks dog's grass and sea-larks. In *Tales of a Grandfather*, second series, Scott ascribes the same words to the Duke of Lauderdale: 'it were better that the west bore nothing but windle-straws and sandy-laverocks, than that it should bear rebels to the King' (*Prose Works*, 24.228).

55.19 error of your ways see James 5.20.

55.29 righteousness sake see Matthew 5.10: 'Blessed are they which are persecuted for righteousness' sake: for theirs is the kingdom of heaven'.

55.37 now lifted up her voice and wept aloud see Genesis 21.16. When Hagar and her son were cast out by Abraham, she 'lift up her voice, and wept'.

56.1 boarded bedstead box bed. It was entirely enclosed by wooden boards; when the doors were shut the occupant would be hidden, but would be able to hear what was going on.

56.6 The foul fa' ye may evil befall you.

56.8 let the leddy alane wi' leave the lady alone with.

56.13 within twa o't i.e. came third.

56.15 dung ower overwhelmed, done for.

56.16–17 plumb-damis-parridge porridge with raisins and prunes in it, eaten at Christmas. Presbyterians refused to keep the traditional feast-days of the church.

56.20–21 set days and holidays days prescribed for religious observance by the church.

56.34–35 the curates . . . ower again Cuddie associates the curates (see 'Historical Note') with the practice of reading prayers from a prayer book, but presbyterians believed that prayer should be the spontaneous outpouring of the soul to God. In fact, set prayers were not used by the curates at this period.

56.36 gude tale . . . twice tauld proverbial (see Ramsay, 65 and *ODEP*, 802).

57.3 ilka days weekdays.

57.7–9 nae neighbouring heritors daur tak us . . . non-enormity in

1677 an Act of Council required landowners to be the sureties for the bonds signed by their households and tenants promising to attend the parish church and not to go to conventicles (see note to 11.23–24), but because means were found to evade the requirements of the bond, a new proclamation of February 1678 required those moving from the service of one landlord to another to be furnished with certification that they 'lived orderly'. Non-conformity, i.e. the refusal to attend the churches of the curates or indulged ministers, was indicative of 'open and obstinate Contempt of all Authority' (Wodrow, 1. Ap.180).

57.20 Saint Johnstone's tippit *proverbial* hangman's noose (see *ODEP*, 694).

57.23 sae says the text see Psalm 37.25 : the Lord 'upholdeth the righteous'.

57.27 a cauld coal to blaw at *proverbial* a difficult task (*ODEP*, 132).

57.32–33 whiles convenience in looking a wee stupid compare Horace, 'misce stultitiam consiliis brevem': mix a little foolishness in your plans (*Odes* (*c.* 20 BC), 4.12.27).

58.4 by the lug and the horn by main force.

58 motto see *Twelfth Night*, 2.3.137.

58.28 For service ... at this time of the year the hire of farm workers began on term or quarter days; although the next Scottish term day would be Whitsunday, 15 May, Morton finds it strange that Cuddie would be moving in the agricultural 'busy' season.

59.1 it's ill sitting at Rome and striving wi' the Pope proverbial (see *ODEP*, 737).

59.18 Hamilton, or into ony sic far country Hamilton would be less than 10 miles away. A 'far country' is a common biblical phrase.

59.22 bring over win round.

59.25–26 in his own option of his own choosing.

59.38 the court of the Gentiles the outer area of the Temple in Jerusalem; Gentiles (non-Jews) were allowed to enter, but could go no farther. Mause means that the Milnewood people, having accepted the Indulgence, are not to be regarded as true people of the Covenant.

59.43 the strait path see Matthew 7.14 : 'strait is the gate, and narrow is the way, which leadeth unto life'.

60.3 Rumbleberry a fictitious character. To *rumble* is to 'knock violently' or 'beat severely'; to *berry* is to 'thrash'.

60.3–4 the Grassmarket the place of public execution in Edinburgh.

60.4–5 Erastianism doctrine which places the church under the authority of secular power.

60.13 single sodger a soldier of the lowest rank; a private.

60.14 the mair any more.

60.17 at a yoking at a stretch, at a time.

60.18 mair be taken moreover.

61.9 standing dish food of a stiff or thick consistency.

61.24 beneath the salt formerly a large salt-cellar was placed in the middle of the table; those of lower status sat 'beneath the salt', i.e. towards the bottom of the table.

62.31–32 them that deny the Word, the Word will deny the 'Word' is Jesus; see John Ch. 1. See also Matthew 10.32–33 : 'Whosoever therefore shall confess me before men, him will I confess also before my Father which is in heaven. But whosoever shall deny me before men, him will I also deny before my Father which is in Heaven.'

63.14 landward towns dwellings in the country. In Scots a *town* is a farm and its associated dwellings.

63.21–22 right juice of John Barleycorn i.e. not watered down or adulterated. John Barleycorn is the personification of malted barley.

63.37 tough ... hatched it the *devil's dam* (see *ODEP*, 179), was traditionally worse than the devil. See *The Comedy of Errors*, 4.3.45 : 'It is the devil. / Nay, she is worse, she is the devil's dam'. The precise meaning of the sentence is uncertain, but the general purport must be that 'the meat is so tough it must be from the offspring of the devil's mother'.

64.1 By the indulgence ... government i.e. Milnewood goes to Presbyterian worship as permitted by the Indulgences of 1669 and 1672. See 'Historical Note', 357.

64.2 out of law outside the law, unlawful.

64.9 crop-eared see note to 30.42.

64.13 took it off drank it up.

64.15–16 pledge me to the king's health Scott may have got the idea of a toast as a test of loyalty from Creichton (142).

64.28 Corra-linn a spectacular waterfall on the Clyde, near Lanark.

64.28–29 we canna make her hear day nor door we can't get her to hear anything.

64.39–40 the Covenant of Works, or the Covenant of Grace the Covenant of Works is the Old Testament dispensation, under which salvation is to be found through obedience to God's Law. In the New Testament, the old Covenant has been replaced by the new Covenant of Grace : sinful man can only be justified by faith in God's free grace, i.e. in his promise of eternal life to true believers. The story comes from Defoe's *Memoirs of the Church of Scotland* (1717), 247–48; *CLA*, 125. Scott quotes the relevant passage in his anonymous review of *Tales of My Landlord* for the *Quarterly Review* (*Prose Works*, 19.41–42).

65.13 relation published by government 'Proclamation, May 4th, for discovery of the murderers of the archbishop of St Andrews'. The phrases used by Milnewood (182.19–22) are largely derived from this proclamation: see Wodrow, 2. Ap.9.

65.41 cockade rosette or ribbon worn in the hat to indicate allegiance. Bothwell would have worn red (although Jacobite colours were later white), and the Covenanters blue. See John Spalding, *Memorialls of the Trubles*, Spalding Club, 2 vols (Aberdeen, 1850–51), 1.154.

65.42 Old Nol Oliver Cromwell (1599–1658), the outstanding general of the roundheads, the parliamentary forces in the English Civil War, and Lord Protector 1653–58.

66.1 Act of Council there were many such acts.

66.32–33 intercommuned rebel ... broke the law see note to 36.28–29.

67.5 barking and fleeing being spent in a prodigal way.

67.5 outfield and infield outlying pasturage or tillage of poor quality, and the nearer, cultivated, and better parts of a farm.

67.15 fine old Trojan merry old fellow, a good chap.

67.19 wink ... hard on overlook something improper.

67.20 thousand merks £55 sterling.

67.29–30 piece of lighted match see Wodrow, 2.77.

67.35–36 twenty ... punds would make up this ... matter there are stories in Creichton and Wodrow which indicate that the better off could bribe their way out of trouble: see e.g. Creichton, 118, 123.

67.39 [twenty] Punds Scotch £1.67 sterling.

67.43 look ower overlook.

68.6–7 the test-oath the words of the oath put by Bothwell recall the 1662 'Act against the Covenants', which declared that it was unlawful for subjects 'upon Pretext of *Reformation*, or any other Pretext whatsomever, to enter into *Leagues and Covenants*' (Wodrow, 1.120). See also note to 30.40.

68.12 like ... Dutch clock-work i.e. disjointed, broken down. Compare

Love's Labour's Lost, 3.1.179–82: 'I seek a wife—/ A woman, that is like a German clock,/ Still a-repairing, ever out of frame,/ And never going aright'. 'Dutch' is a form of 'Deutsch'.

68.12–13   set at liberty his imprisoned angels   *King John*, 3.3.8–9. An angel was a gold coin worth 10s. (50p), and last issued in the reign of Charles I.

68.27–28   the scarlet man   as well as referring to the soldier's uniform, there is a suggestion of the scarlet woman, the whore of Babylon of Revelation Ch. 17. See note to 27.35.

68.28–29   freed from the net of the fowler   see Psalm 124.7, which gives thanks to God for Israel's escape from dangerous and angry enemies.

68.30   has her leg ower the harrows   has got out of hand, has become unmanageable (*SND*).

68.34   horse and foot   *proverbial* completely (see *ODEP*, 386).

68.39–40   soul-killing . . . bands   Covenanters considered oaths to be damning because of Jesus's injunction 'But I say unto you, Swear not at all' (Matthew 5.34).

68.41–42   it is in vain that a net . . . any bird   see Proverbs 1.17. This verse is one of a series on the theme 'my son, if sinners entice thee, consent thou not' (Proverbs 1.10).

69.13   Philistines . . . Edomites   enemies of the Israelites.

69.13–14   leopards . . . evening-wolves   see Habakkuk 1.8: 'Their horses also are swifter than leopards, and are more fierce than the evening wolves'.

69.14   evening-wolves, that gnaw not the bones till the morrow   see Zephaniah 3.3: 'Her princes within her are roaring lions; her judges are evening wolves; they gnaw not the bones till the morrow'. Zephaniah pronounces impending judgment on Jerusalem, because the city's officials are licentious and profane, and have not followed the way of the Lord.

69.14–15   wicked dogs, that compass about the chosen   see Psalm 22.16: 'For dogs have compassed me; the assembly of the wicked have inclosed me: they pierced my hands and my feet'.

69.15–16   crushing kine, and pushing bulls of Bashan   the rich women of Samaria are condemned in Amos 4.1 as 'kine of Bashan . . . which oppress the poor, which crush the needy'; and in Psalm 22.12 'strong bulls of Bashan' typify the fierce enemies that beset the righteous man.

69.16   piercing serpents   see Isaiah 27.1: 'the Lord shall punish the piercing serpent'.

69.17   the great Red Dragon   see Revelation 12.3–4: 'And there appeared another wonder in heaven; and behold a great red dragon, having seven heads and ten horns, and seven crowns upon his head. And his tail drew the third part of the stars of heaven, and did cast them to the earth: and the dragon stood before the woman which was ready to be delivered, for to devour her child as soon as it was born.' There is also a play on 'dragon' and 'dragoon', both of which are red.

69.27   ducking stool   chair into which disorderly women were tied and ducked in water as a punishment.

69.33   deil be on't   *literally* may the devil be on it.

69.36   cows bursting on clover   the sugars in clover can react with the digestive juices of cattle to produce gas which blows the cattle up.

69.36   testify with your hands   i.e. fight.

70.3–4   nest of yellow boys   guineas, gold coins worth £1 1s. (£1.05).

70.36   mammon of unrighteousness   worldly wealth: see Luke 16.9.

70.36   sons of Belial   see note to 36.14.

70.38   the evil that Menaham did   see 2 Kings 15.18–20: Menaham, King of Israel, who 'did that which was evil in the sight of the Lord', removed an invading Assyrian army through payment of a thousand talents of silver.

70.41 the evil deed of Ahab see 2 Kings 16.8. Mause means Ahaz, not Ahab. Ahaz, King of Judah, under attack from Aram and Israel, sought safety, not by trusting in the Lord as the prophet Isaiah advised, but by becoming a vassal of the pagan King of Assyria, Tiglath-pileser.

70.43 backsliding even in godly Hezekiah see 2 Kings 18.14–15. Hezekiah, King of Judah, reformed the worship of his people, and destroyed objects that had become the focus of idolatry. He was thus a favourite of the Covenanters, who believed themselves to be upholders of a Reformation that had accomplished a similar task. His backsliding was to buy off an invasion led by Sennacherib, King of Assyria.

71.4–5 localities…cess…publicans *localities* were levies for maintaining troops in quarters; *cess* was the land tax; *publicans* were tax-gatherers who operated in Israel on behalf of the Roman Empire, and were considered 'unrighteous' because in serving the empire they were felt to be on the side of the heathen.

71.6–7 dumb dogs … loving to slumber see Isaiah 56.10. The prophet denounces the leaders of Israel for failing to fulfil their proper functions. They are greedy and self-indulgent, and have abandoned Israel's true worship.

71.8–9 casters of a lot compare the casting of lots for Jesus's garments at the crucifixion: Matthew 27.35, Mark 15.24, and John 19.24.

71.9–10 the preparing of a table … the furnishing a drink-offering see Isaiah 65.11–12. It is prophesied that Israel though exiled and defeated will again come to enjoy the promised land, but that those who have forsaken the Lord will be destroyed.

71.14 kylevine pen and a pair of tablets pencil and a pocket notebook.

71.43 dinna murmur at the cross do not complain about the sufferings that come to those who follow Jesus. See Matthew 16.24–25.

72.2–3 mark on their threshold … should pass by see Exodus 12.13. Moses instructs the Israelites to mark the lintel and doorposts of their houses with blood; God promises that 'when I see the blood, I will pass over you, and the plague shall not be upon you to destroy you, when I smite the land of Egypt'. For Mause, the inhabitants of Milnewood are not to be counted among the people of the Covenant.

72.3 back cast unexpected blow.

72.8 the elect those chosen by God for salvation and eternal life.

72.12 deserts, mountains see Hebrews 11.38. The passage deals with those who suffered for their faith.

72.13 bread eaten in secret Proverbs 9.17.

72.24–25 pressed the best in Milnewood's stable although illegal, it was standard practice for the soldiery to help themselves to horses.

73.1–2 bonds of sin, … gall of iniquity see Acts 8.9–23. Peter tells a man who has tried to buy 'the gift of God' to repent, for 'I perceive that thou art in the gall of bitterness, and in the bond of iniquity'.

73.5 bear testimony in the Grassmarket i.e. bear witness to their faith by being executed in the Grassmarket in Edinburgh.

73.8–9 the bloody Doegs see 1 Samuel 22.17–19. Saul commands his servants to 'slay the priests of the Lord; because their hand also is with David, and because they knew when he fled, and did not show it to me'. When his servants refuse, the King commands Doeg the Edomite to undertake the task: 'and he fell upon the priests, and slew on that day fourscore and five'.

73.9 the flattering Ziphites see 1 Samuel 26; the Ziphites come to King Saul and seek to betray David, who is hiding in the wilderness from the King.

73.13 cry as a woman in labour see Isaiah 42.14: 'I have long time holden my peace; I have been still, and refrained myself: now will I cry like a travailing woman; I will destroy and devour at once'.

73.14 stumbling-block a biblical word used of anything which causes someone to stumble and fall, and used figuratively in the sense of testing someone's faith. Compare 1 Corinthians 1.23, 8.9.

73.19 city of refuge see note to 37.4.

73.22 he likes as ill to quit wi' he likes so little to lose.

73.22 haud sae restrain yourself.

73.23 up a ladder ... tow i.e. up a ladder [to the scaffold to be hanged from] a rope.

74 motto Robert Burns, 'Love and Liberty—a Cantata' (written 1785–86), lines 29–32.

74.10 strapping up hanging.

74.20 Scottish regiments many such regiments were in the service of European princes in the 17th century; e.g., Hepburn's Regiment (which ultimately became the Royal Scots) served Sweden, France and England. See also note to 74.30.

74.30 Scotch French guard Scots fought in French armies in the Hundred Years' War, and in the early 15th century a Scots Guard was formed, some of whom were charged with the personal protection of the king (see *Quentin Durward*). This continued, and under a treaty of 1642 a regiment was formed with precedence in the French army immediately after the French and Swiss Guards.

74.36 Port Royale Port Royal in Jamaica. Britain captured Jamaica from Spain in 1655.

74.38 drum-head used as an improvised table in camp.

75.9–10 Huguenots French Calvinists. Although toleration for their religion was promised by the Edict of Nantes (1598), they were destroyed as a political force by the civil war of 1621–1628, and from 1655–1685 they suffered continuous harassment under Louis XIV ('le Grand'). The Edict of Nantes was revoked in 1685.

75.12 buon camerado *Spanish* good comrade.

75.14 cutter's law rogue's or highwayman's law. The suggestion is that professional 'colleagues' will share and share alike.

75.26 boot and saddle see note to 32.41.

75.31 best affected most favourably disposed, most loyal. See glossary under 'well-affected'.

76.18 trot on a horse of wood see note to 30.4–5.

76.23 Monk General George Monk (1608–70) was a commander of a regiment under Cromwell during the conquest of Scotland 1651–52, when, presumably, the gate of Tillietudlem was 'broken down'. He was commander of Cromwell's forces in Scotland 1654–60.

76.38 Sir Ralph de Bellenden unless the family name of the Earls of Torwood is also Bellenden this is a slip, for Tillietudlem was inherited from Lady Margaret's father, not her husband: see note to 18.10.

77.6–7 the great Marquis Montrose: see 'Historical Note', 431–32.

78.22 Francis Stewart see note to 29.3–4.

78.22 James I., his cousin-german that is, James VI, who was James I of England. See note to 29.3–4.

78.34 Rochester John Wilmot (1647–80), 2nd Earl of Rochester, English poet and libertine.

78.34 Buckingham George Villiers (1628–87), 2nd Duke of Buckingham, poet and playwright, one of the most prominent figures at the court of Charles II.

78.34–35 fought at Tangiers side by side with Sheffield John Sheffield (1648–1721), 3rd Earl of Mulgrave and later 1st Duke of Buckingham and Normanby. In 1680 he commanded an expedition for the relief of Tangiers, at that time besieged by the Moors. Tangiers became an English possession in 1661 as part of the dowry of Catherine of Braganza when she married Charles II.

79.13 grafting scions of his own   i.e begetting his own children. Charles II was notorious for his extra-marital affairs.

79.41 Kilsythe   one of Montrose's victories in 1645.

80.6 the boots ... the thumbkins   instruments of torture used on Covenanters.

80.32–33 Davy ... Shallow   see 2 *Henry IV*, 5.3.

80.38 the Duke   3rd Duke of Hamilton. See note to 16.30–31.

81.1 not to lippen to   not to be trusted.

81.2–3 Duke James ... the Worcester man   for Duke James see note to 39.38–39; the 'Worcester man' is William Hamilton (1616–51), the 2nd Duke, who was mortally wounded at the battle of Worcester (see 'Historical Note', 432.

81.4–18 parallel ... zigzag ... lodgment   *military engineering* in a siege a *parallel* was a trench (usually one of three) parallel to the face of the place being attacked, serving as a line of communication between the different parts of the siege-works. A *zigzag* was a trench leading towards a besieged place but zigzagged to prevent defenders from looking and shooting straight into it. A *lodgment* was a temporary defensive work made in a captured portion of the enemy's fortifications.

81 motto   see Matthew Prior (1664–1721), 'Henry and Emma', lines 385–92.

82.22 kenning the folk by head-mark   recognising people by their individual facial characteristics. The term *heid-mark* was originally used of sheep.

82.23 at kirk and market   in all the public places of life.

82.26 Nethersheils   *nether* in place-names indicates the lower-situated of two places of the same name; a *sheil* is a small house.

82.31–32 Outerside-Muir   a *muir* is a moor: the name suggests somewhere remote and wild.

83.13 resetting   *Scots law* receiving, sheltering: one of the crimes specified in the letters of intercommuning (see note to 36.28–29).

83.23–24 auld deaf John Macbriar ... hearing   based upon the report of the summary execution of Robert Auchinleck, in Defoe, *Memoirs of the Church of Scotland* (London, 1717), 252 (*CLA*, 125).

83.30 guide us   exclamation of surprise or consternation. The phrase is a shortened form of 'God (or gude) guide us', may God (or good) direct us.

83.33 what maun be maun be   proverbial (see *ODEP*, 552).

84.5 act of Assembly against this use of the mantle   untraced.

84.19 the lively Scottish air   see the traditional song 'I'll make ye be fain to follow', in which 'a soger' courts 'a bonie young lass': in *Songs from David Herd's Manuscripts*, ed. Hans Hecht (Edinburgh, 1904), 148 (Corson). There are many versions of the words. The tune is 'Bonie Dundee': see *The Poems and Songs of Robert Burns*, ed. James Kinsley, 3 vols (Oxford, 1968), no. 157.

84.24–25 for as rough as he is   however rough he is.

85.16–19 Keek into the draw-well ... My joe Janet   for words and tune see *Scotish Songs*, ed. Joseph Ritson, 2 vols (London, 1794), 1.173–75.

85.26 My sarty!   Gracious!

85.35 cracking clavers   talking, having a chat.

85.43–86.1 have had him cast in my dish   *proverbial* to have been taunted with his name (see Ray, 185, and *ODEP*, 190).

86.1–2 law enough to bear us out   i.e. enough law to support them.

86.12 driving ower   passing the time, relaxing.

86.16 Birling the brown bowl   drinking.

86.27 a horse i.e. a gallows. This sense is probably derived from the proverb 'to ride on a horse was foaled of an acorn', meaning 'to be hanged' (see Ray, 197, and *ODEP*, 387).

89.2 a blunt and unvarnished defence see *Othello*, 1.3.90.

89.10 root and branch-work complete removal or destruction; see Malachi 4.1. The phrase was used in the London petition of 1640 and the bill of 1641, for the abolition of Episcopacy.

89.11–12 his intimate friend and early patron Scott exaggerates Claverhouse's links with Sharp.

89.39 make a clear garrison i.e. clear people out of the guarded place.

90.7–8 chit face baby face.

91.3–4 draw up wi' become friendly with.

91.12 their lane on their own.

91.13 stand for hesitate because of.

91.19 Cappercleuch Scott imports a place-name from the Borders into Lanarkshire: Cappercleuch is a remote forking of roads, where the valley of the Megget joins the valley of the Yarrow.

91.19 Whomlekirn-pule *whomle* means to 'capsize', to 'overwhelm', to 'drown'; *kirn* means to 'stir', to 'mix together with a churning motion'; and a *pule* is a 'pool'.

91.20 the De'il's Loaning the *De'il* is the 'Devil'; and a *loaning* is a grassy track through arable land.

91.20–21 the kittle staps at the Pass of Walkwary *kittle* means 'ticklish', 'tricky', and *staps* are 'steps'. In *Redgauntlet* Scott has a note on the Kittle Nine Steps in Edinburgh, a 'pass on the very brink of the Castle rock to the north, by which it is just possible for a goat, or a High School boy, to turn the corner of the building where it rises from the edge of the precipice' (1.35.6).

92.11 the second volume of the Grand Cyrus *Artamène, ou le Grand Cyrus* (10 volumes, 1649–53: see note to 19.42–20.2) was hugely popular in the later 17th century.

92.14–15 pacing nag horse trained to amble or to walk by lifting the legs on the same side together, thus giving a smooth ride.

92.43–93.1 a taste of the variation *1 Henry IV*, 1.1.64.

93 motto see Swift, 'The Grand Question Debated. Whether Hamilton's Bawn should be turned into a Barracks or a Malthouse' (1732), lines 99–100.

93.10 Gideon Pike Gideon was one of the great soldier-heroes of Israel: see Judges 6–8. The pike was the chief weapon of foot-soldiers in the 17th century.

93.25 Kilsythe named after one of the victories of Montrose, the Major's old leader, in 1645.

93.30 boot and saddle see note to 32.41.

93.35–36 mounted . . . Mark Antony see *Antony and Cleopatra*, 1.5.48. The meaning of 'arm-gaunt' is a matter of dispute but may be explained as 'worn thin with hard service in armour'.

94.15 devil of a discipline by 'discipline', the Major suggests not only military discipline, but also two important documents of the Scottish Reformation: the *Book of Discipline* of John Knox (1560); and the second *Book of Discipline* of Andrew Melville (1581).

94.16 Geneva print the Major is punning: Gudyill is bleary-eyed either because he has been drinking Geneva (that is, gin) or because he has been reading the print (notoriously hard on the eyes) used in Bibles printed in the centre of Calvinism, Geneva.

94.18 reading the Litany the form of 'general supplication' appointed for use in the Church of England's *Book of Common Prayer* (1662). Episcopalians such as the Bellendens would have read the prayer book of 1637 or 1662; but Presbyterian ministers who had taken the oath of allegiance in 1662, or who came in later under the Indulgences, would not have done so. Bishop Rattray (1684–1743) observed: 'The method of our ordinary Assemblies on the Lord's-day was almost the same with that of the Presbyterians.' See J. F. S. Gordon, *Scotichronicon*, 2 vols (Glasgow, 1867), 2.109.

94.20–21   flowers of the field … lilies of the valley   see Psalm 103.15 and Song of Solomon 2.1.

94.22   hardly   barely, only just.

95.3   sin' syne   since then.

95.34–35   the damnable dinner that Noll gave us at Worcester   see 'Historical Note', 356 for Cromwell's victory at Worcester in 1651.

96.13   Holyrood-house   the royal palace in Edinburgh.

96.14   the year 1642   first year of the English Civil War.

96.25   News-letter   the manuscript record of parliamentary and court news, sent twice-weekly to subscribers from the London office of Henry Muddiman (1629–??), who founded the *Oxford Gazette*, predecessor of the *London Gazette*, in 1665.

96.29   Artamenes   see note to 19.42–20.2. The spelling is derived from the English translation possessed by Scott (*CLA* 102).

96.32   old Corporal Raddlebanes   to *raddle* is to 'beat' or 'thrash'.

96.36   picquet   17th century military punishment; '*To stand upon the Picket*, is when a Horseman for some Offence, is sentenc'd to have one Hand ty'd up as high as it can reach, and then to stand upon the Point of a Stake with the Toe of his opposite Foot' (Edward Phillips, *A New World of English Words*, 6th edn, ed. J. Kersey, 1706).

96.39–40   Monsieur Scuderi … the Sieur D'Urfé   Georges de Scudéry (1601–67), dramatist and older brother of the author of the *Grand Cyrus* (see note to 47.4–10); and Honoré d'Urfé (1568–1625), author of *L'Astrée* (1607–27), a long pastoral romance extremely popular in the 17th century.

96.43   The Whole Duty of Man   Anglican devotional work, first published 1658 and enormously popular for more than a century, attributed to Richard Allestree (1619–81), Chaplain in ordinary to the King, and Provost of Eton.

97.1   Turner's Pallas Armata   Sir James Turner (1615–86?), a prominent royalist whose military activities in the west provoked the Pentland Rising of 1666. His *Pallas Armata: Military Essays of the Ancient Grecian, Roman, and Modern Art of War, Written in the Years 1670 and 1671* was first published in 1683.

97.25   cairn-gorm pebbles   quartz; yellowish, semi-precious stones, widely used for personal ornaments.

99.8   the great Enemy of mankind   the Devil.

99   motto   Matthew Prior (1664–1721), 'Down-Hall, a Ballad' (1723), lines 98–99.

99.40–100.1   priestly ham … venison pasty   it is possible that the ham is called 'priestly' in joking contrast to the Covenanters' Mosaic dislike of pork; the sirloin was said to have been knighted by Henry VIII; why a baron of beef (two sirloins left uncut at the backbone) should be lordly is self-evident; the venison pasty is called 'princely' because of the depredations of Charles II (see 95.13).

100.5   no boys' play   *proverbial* amusement for boys (compare Ray, 52). See also *1 Henry IV*, 5.4.75–76, and John Fletcher, *Bonduca* (performed 1613–14), 2.3, where the phrase describes hearty eating.

100.12   peine forte et dure   *French* severe and hard punishment, inflicted on a person charged with a felony who persisted in refusal to plead. The victim was pressed to death between boards with heavy weights. There is a play on 'pressing to eat' (100.12) and pressing to death.

100.20   loud as a trumpet with a silver sound Dryden, *Palamon and Arcite* (1690), 3.85, where the phrase is used of the voice of '*Emetrius* King of *Ind*' (Corson).

101.6   Machiavel Niccolò Machiavelli (1469–1527), Florentine statesman and author of *Il Principe* (*The Prince*, written 1513).

102.12   hundred merk £5.50.

102.25   resetted see note to 83.13.

103.9–10   Cornet see note to 27.19.

105.13   publicly burnt the Act of Supremacy . . . and some others on 29 May 1679 at Rutherglen, a group of Covenanters publicly burned this act and others, including the 1669 Act of Supremacy (which asserted the king's supremacy over all ecclesiastical causes), and the 1662 act 'for the Restitution and Re-establishment of the ancient Government of the Church by Archbishops and Bishops'. The act 'for observing the martyrdom of Charles I' was not among those burned on this occasion.

105.29–30   an old trumpeter of rebellion a Covenanting preacher, John King, was captured by Claverhouse prior to Loudoun-hill, and regained his liberty at the battle, as Kettledrummle does in the novel. See Creichton, 127.

105.38   the war-horse of scripture see Job 39.19–25: 'Hast thou given the horse strength? . . . He saith among the trumpets, Ha, ha; and he smelleth the battle afar off, the thunder of the captains, and the shouting.'

105.39   six negroes in the 17th century (and indeed even earlier) the inhabitants of Scotland included a small number of people of black African descent.

106.21   miss one of the responses i.e. the responses of the congregation in Anglican worship. See note to 94.18.

109   motto see *Othello*, 3.3.169.

110.3   the current of his soul was frozen see Thomas Gray, 'Elegy Written in a Country Church-Yard' (1751), line 52.

110.31   Uncle Toby the benignly innocent old soldier of Laurence Sterne's *Tristram Shandy* (1759–67).

111.39   Mrs Dennison in the 17th century 'Mrs', now used only of married women, was a title of courtesy; in Scotland it was pronounced 'mistress'.

111.41   Mrs Quickly *The Merry Wives of Windsor*, 3.4.103–04.

113.6   in trim into proper condition or order.

113.16   strike sail to lower sail as a sign of surrender.

113.39   what has entered into my very soul i.e iron; see the proverb 'the iron entered into his soul' (*ODEP*, 405).

114.40–41   the madman in the play . . . Mr Justice Overdo see Ben Jonson, *Bartholomew Fair* (performed 1614), 4.1: the madman Trouble-all 'will do nothing but by Justice Overdo's warrant . . . His wife, sir-reverence, cannot get him make his water or shift his shirt without his warrant.' There is a strong element of anti-Puritan satire in the play to which Claverhouse alludes.

114.43   the mace of the Justiciary the symbol of the authority of the supreme criminal court of Scotland.

115.43   I leave vengeance to God, who calls it his own see Romans 12.19: 'Dearly beloved, avenge not yourselves, but rather give place unto wrath: for it is written, Vengeance is mine; I will repay, saith the Lord'.

119   motto see 'Jamie Telfer of the Fair Dodhead', stanza 12 (*Minstrelsy*, 2.5; Child 190).

120.30–31   a warld's wonder one whose conduct is notorious and surprising (*SND*).

120.40–41   it's like it seems.

121.2   Gabriel Kettledrummle not a historical character. Gabriel is one of the seven archangels, a messenger from God; and Kettledrummle calls to mind

a kettledrum, as well as Butler's phrase 'drum ecclesiastic' (*Hudibras* (1663),
1.1.11–12), used by Scott at 151 motto and 224.20. *Drumle* means 'make or be
muddy or disturbed'.

121.2   De'il that   would that, if only.

121.9–10   Binna cast doun   see Psalm 42, especially verse 11.

121.11   the mount o' the Covenant   God's Covenant with Israel was sealed
at Mount Sinai (Exodus Ch. 19).

121.17   win to   begin eating.

121.19–20   Miry-sikes   a *sike* is a marshy hollow.

121.22   Ramoth Gilead   see 1 Kings Ch. 22; prophets urge Ahab, King of
Israel, and Jehoshaphat, King of Judah, to 'go up' and recapture Ramoth-gilead
from Syria, but they are misled by a 'lying spirit', and Ahab is killed.

121.24   mile down the wind   Creichton reports that at one conventicle the
voice of John King (see note to 105.29–30) could be heard from a quarter of a
mile, 'the wind favouring the strength of his lungs' (Creichton, 120).

121.24–25   routed like a cow in a fremd loaning   *proverbial* bellowed like a
cow in a strange field (*ODEP*, 150).

121.32   wearying for   wait wearily for, long for.

121.34   the Philistines   a neighbouring people, enemies of Israel.

121.35   sting and ling   without ceremony, forcibly.

121.36   five-a-hand   probably, one of a team of five oxen.

121.42   Lanrick   Lanark, the county town of the Upper Ward of Lanarkshire.

122.11–12   gar them as gude   retaliate, pay them back in their own coin.

122.15   hae a look after   have a regard for, have an interest in.

122.19   lang syne   long ago.

122.22–23   gae them their kale through the reek   *proverbial* gave them a
severe scolding (*ODEP*, 416).

122.23   the whore of Babylon   see Revelation 17.1–6. In 17th-century
Protestant polemics the whore of Babylon is taken to be the Roman Catholic
Church.

122.24   the best word in their wame   *proverbial* the pleasantest thing they
said; compare 'the worst word in one's wame' (*SND*).

122.24   the kiln was in a bleeze   *proverbial* trouble broke out again (*ODEP*,
424).

122.37   speak evil o' dignities   see Jude 8: 'Likewise also these filthy
dreamers defile the flesh, despise dominion, and speak evil of dignities'. This is
part of a denunciation of 'ungodly men' who deny 'our Lord Jesus Christ'.

122.41–42   a cup o' cauld water   see Matthew 10.42 and Mark 9.41.

122.42   thae lords   presumably the members of the Privy Council.

123.1   outlaws   people put outside the law and deprived of its benefit and
protection. Cuddie is aware of outlawry because various ministers and others
had been outlawed for repeated attendance at conventicles, and those who
assisted them in any way were made outlaws by means of letters of intercommuning (see note to 36.28–29).

123.22   wi' speaking the loon fair   by speaking nicely to the chap.

123.24–25   fee and bountith   servant's wages, usually paid half-yearly, and
the gratuity usually paid in addition to wages.

124.20   ony thing   at all.

124.21   lay on   apply myself energetically to the job.

124.34   every man who is free-born   see Acts 22.25–28. When Paul is
brought before the Roman military authorities, and threatened with whipping,
he asks if it is lawful 'to scourge a man that is a Roman, and uncondemned'. He
is released. The centurion tells Paul that he paid a lot for his Roman citizenship;
'And Paul said, But I was free born'.

124.38–39   giving tribute to Cæsar   see Matthew 22.15-21, where the Pharisees ask Jesus: 'Is it lawful to give tribute unto Cæsar, or not? But Jesus ... said, Why tempt ye me, ye hypocrites? Shew me the tribute money. And they brought unto him a penny. And he saith unto them, Whose is this image and superscription? They say unto him, Cæsar's. Then saith he unto them, Render therefore unto Cæsar the things which are Cæsar's; and unto God the things that are God's.'

124.43–125.1   house of bondage   see Exodus 13.3: 'And Moses said unto the people, Remember this day, in which ye came out from Egypt, out of the house of bondage'.

125.1   wally-de-shamle   see Tobias Smollett, *The Expedition of Humphry Clinker* (1771), Win. Jenkins to Mary Jones 18 July. To Cuddie's ear, the word *wally* will imply 'big', 'strong', 'thriving' rather than 'valet'.

125.9–10   for as massy as he's riding ahint us   in spite of the self-importance with which he is riding behind us.

125.19   Jock the Giant killer   the hero of the traditional story of Jack and the bean-stalk, who goes to 'pouss' his fortune by climbing the beanstalk and stealing from the giant.

125.19   Valentine and Orson   brothers in the early French romance who have many adventures together. Valentine is brought up as a knight at the court of King Pepin, while Orson is a wild man who is captured by Valentine, and becomes his servant. They subsequently find that they are brothers.

125.19–20   we wad come back to merry Scotland, as the sang says   not identified.

125.26   as broken a ship's come to land   *proverbial* (*ODEP*, 723).

125.27   never stir   exclamation of surprise.

125.27   at the preaching   started preaching.

125.41–126.1   a threefold woe ... pouring forth of vials   see Revelation Chs 5–11. A threefold woe is announced through the breaking of seven seals, the blowing of seven trumpets, and the pouring forth of seven vials. In Ch. 7 the church's martyrs are seen in glory before the throne of God, receiving their reward for their sufferings.

126.2   black cast   stroke of ill fate.

126.2–3   the outside o' the loof ... at the last day   *the outside o' the loof* is a phrase of defiance and derision; presumably the sense here is of waving away with the back of the hand at the last judgment.

126.3   counter-tenor   part higher than tenor, sung by alto male voice. Scott seems to think that the word refers only to pitch, as in *Waverley* (ed. Claire Lamont (Oxford, 1981), 205; Ch.42) he again uses it of a woman.

126.4   second part of a catch   the second voice imitating the first voice's melody, but often with different words and with comic effect.

126.8–9   oaths, soul-damning and self-contradictory   for 'soul-damning' see note to 68.39–40. Wodrow in his discussion of the declaration required of those in public office in Scotland talks of 'ensnaring and Con-science-debauching Declarations, Bonds, and Oaths, ... some of them evid-ently self-contradictory' (1.120–21).

126.10   the wrath to come   Matthew 3.7; Luke 3.7.

126.15   De'il gin   would that, if only.

126.25   a desperate Judas   see note to 45.20.

126.26–27   a sanctuary-breaking Holofernes   see the apocryphal Book of Judith 2.6. Holofernes, Nebuchadnezzar's general, is commissioned to subdue the 'whole west country'. With his powerful army he seeks to destroy all worship except that of his King; and he prevails everywhere, except against the children of Israel.

126.27–28   an ambitious Diotrephes   see 3 John 9: 'I wrote unto the church: but Diotrephes, who loveth to have the preeminence among them, receiveth us not'.

126.28–29 a covetous and warld-following Demas see 2 Timothy 4.10: 'For Demas hath forsaken me, having loved this present world, and is departed unto Thessalonica'.

126.35 besom of destruction see Isaiah 14.23.

126.36 the filth out o' the Temple—whips of small cords see John 2.13–15: 'and Jesus went up to Jerusalem, And found in the temple those that sold oxen and sheep and doves, and the changers of money sitting: And when he had made a scourge of small cords, he drove them all out of the temple'. For Mause, the soldiers are being used as God's instruments to inflict punishment on backsliders from the Covenant but are themselves 'castaways ... fit only to be flung into the fire'.

126.39 only meet to mak latchets to the de'il's brogues compare Luke 3.16: 'one mightier than I cometh, the latchet of whose shoes I am not worthy to unloose'. Compare also Mark 1.7; John 1.27; *ODEP*, 922.

126.40 Fiend hae me Devil take me.

127.12–13 a pelican ... a sparrow see Psalm 102.2, 6–7. Gabriel and Mause quote from a prayer for deliverance: 'Hide not thy face from me in the day when I am in trouble ... I am like a pelican of the wilderness: I am like an owl of the desert. I watch, and am as a sparrow alone upon the house top.'

127.16 I will not peace at the commands of the profane see Jonson, *The Alchemist* (performed 1610; published 1612), 3.2.108.

127.17–18 earthly potsherd see Isaiah 45.9. The verse uses the metaphor of the potter and his clay to stress the absolute sovereignty of God. Mause will obey the great Potter; the corporal is only a broken scrap of earthenware.

127.18 a brick of the Tower of Babel see Genesis 11.3. The Tower of Babel was built of bricks baked from clay, so Mause continues her theme of the corporal as earthly clay (see previous note).

127 motto see Samuel Butler, *Hudibras* (1663), 1.1.721–26.

127.30 quantum in nobis *Latin* as far as in us lies, to the best of our ability.

128.35 drove of black cattle the trade in exporting live cattle to England began in the late 17th century.

129.16 Through the help of the Lord I have leaped over a wall see Psalm 18.29: 'For by thee I have run through a troop; and by my God I have leaped over a wall'.

129.20–21 I am sunk in deep mire ... the floods overflow me Psalm 69.2, part of the cry of a servant of the Lord beset by many foes and in deep misery.

129.24 sable streams i.e. Kettledrummle is in a peat bog.

130.15 royal Life Guards see note to 28.37.

130.21–22 a natural gulley see Russell, 442.

131.24 the females of the ancient German tribes Tacitus (*Germania* (AD 98), Part 7) refers to the practice of some German tribes, who station their women and children fairly close to the site of battle: 'A man's dearest possessions are at hand; he can hear close to him the laments of his women and the wailing of his children. These are the witnesses that a man reverences most, to them he looks for his highest praise.'

131.35 destroying angel angel sent to punish the people for their sins; compare 1 Chronicles 21.12.

131.37 metrical version many writers in the 16th, 17th and 18th centuries produced metrical versions of the psalms. Scottish psalters were published in 1615, 1634 and 1635; they included versions of the psalms (some of them composite) from many sources. Until the 19th century only metrical psalms and paraphrases were sung in Scottish churches as they were considered to be God's word while hymns were written by men.

131.39–132.15   In Judah's land ... a dead sleep cast   metrical version of Psalm 76.1–6. The psalm celebrates God's nature as divine warrior and judge, and recalls events in Israel's history when he saved his people in time of war. Salem and Zion are alternative names for Jerusalem.

132.26–27   Hackstoun ... Cleland   for David Hackston of Rathillet see note to 33.20–22. James Paton of Meadowhead (d. 1684) was a Covenanter whose military experience included the battles of Kilsyth, Worcester, and Rullion Green, but he was not, in fact, present at Loudoun-hill. William Cleland (1661?–89) was a Covenanter, a soldier, and a poet. He sought refuge in Holland after Bothwell Bridge, and returned to Scotland in 1688, when he became lieutenant-colonel of the newly-raised regiment, the Cameronians. He died defending Dunkeld against the Jacobites in 1689.

133.13   Lord Ross   George Ross (d. 1682), 11th Lord Ross. He was a member of Charles II's first parliament, was commissioned captain in one of the newly raised troops of Horse in 1674, and commanded the government troops stationed at Glasgow when Claverhouse was defeated at Loudoun-hill.

133.25   the race of Dunbar   the battle of 1650 in which Cromwell utterly destroyed the Scottish army: see 'Historical Note', 356.

134.13   rebels having arms in their hands   see note to 7.32.

134.18   the battle of Pentland-hills   in the unsuccessful Pentland Rising of 1666 the western Covenanters were dispirited and isolated even before being confronted by a royal army at Rullion Green in the Pentlands. See 'Historical Note', 433.

134.22   laws of war   the most important codification of the 'laws of war' in the period was Hugo Grotius, *De jure Belli ac Pacis* (1625).

134.28–29   risked ... life   the contrast between *spilling* (meaning 'destroying') and *saving* was traditional: compare 'Thow may me saif, thow may me spill,/ Baith lyfe and deide, lyis in thy will' (*Gude and Godlie Ballatis*, ed A. F. Mitchell, Scottish Text Society (Edinburgh, 1897), 170).

134.33   brother's son   the family circumstances of the Claverhouse of the novel differ from those of the Claverhouse of history: see C. S. Terry, *John Graham of Claverhouse* (London, 1905), 54–57. However, there was a Cornet Robert Graham at Loudoun-hill, and Scott may have got the idea that he was Claverhouse's kinsman from the ballad 'The Battle of Bothwell Bridge', stanza 12 (*Minstrelsy*, 2.281; Child 206). See also note to 137.6.

134.40   Flanders lace   Flanders (roughly the western half of Belgium) was famous for the quality of its lace.

135.2   only son   see Genesis 22.2, 12 and 16. Abraham is tested by God who requires Abraham to sacrifice his only son, Isaac.

135.7   as the old Scotch blazon has it, God shaw the right   the motto given by the Protestant Earl of Morton, Regent of Scotland 1572–78, to his follower Thomas Crawfurd, after the defeat of the Catholic Earl of Huntly in 1571. 'God shaw the right' implies that, by giving victory to one side or another in a conflict, God will show who is right. The motto was also used by one of Scott's friends, James Edmondstoune of Newton.

135   motto   see Samuel Butler, *Hudibras* (1663), 1.2.831–32 (*CLA*, 42, 182, 242).

136.1–2   perjured Charles Stuart   while he was under the control of the Kirk Party in 1650, Charles II promised under oath to uphold the Covenants, but on his Restoration parliament passed acts declaring the Covenants to be false oaths: see Wodrow 1.120 and 'Historical Note', 432.

136.2   whom you call King   *Richard II*, 4.1.134.

136.9   the hideous Act of Supremacy   the Act was 'hideous' because it gave the King '*supreme Authority and Supremacy over all Persons, all Causes ecclesi-atical*' (Wodrow, 2.137), a position which Covenanters believed was God's alone. However, as the Act of Supremacy was passed in 1669 it cannot be considered the King's 'first step, after his incoming into these kingdoms'; the speaker probably refers to the oath of allegiance ('which they called only alleadgance, but was indeed supremacy': Kirkton, 89), formulated in the first act of the Scottish parliament in 1661. It acknowledges the King as '*Supreme Governor of this Kingdom, over all Persons and in all Causes*' (Wodrow, 1.92). Scott calls this act 'that of supremacy' in his review of Kirkton (*Prose Works*, 19.242).

136.10−11 expulsing ... preachers see 'Historical Note', 356−57. Wodrow argues that the Privy Council had usurped the powers of Parliament (Wodrow, 1.125).

136.10 summons, libel *Scots law* a 'summons' is a writ calling someone to court, and 'libel' the ground of a charge on which a prosecution is based.

136.11−12 the bread of life the Gospel.

136.13 saltless ... lukewarm see Matthew 5.13; Mark 9.50; Luke 14.34; Colossians 4.6; and Revelation 3.16.

136.14 fourteen false prelates the bishops of the Scottish Church, after the re-establishment of the Episcopal system.

136.15 curates see note to 27.19.

136.21−22 with our swords on our thighs, as men that watch in the night see The Song of Solomon 3.8.

136.24 his blood be on his own head see Joshua 2.19.

136.26 evil of your ways common biblical term.

137.6 Richard Grahame the Cornet Graham of history did not die like the Cornet of the novel. Contrasting royalist and Covenanting accounts of his death can be read in Creichton (128−29) and Russell (442). See note to 134.33.

137.13−14 thou shalt be zealous even to slaying see Jeremiah 48.10: 'cursed be he that keepeth back his sword from blood'. Compare Numbers 25.13: Phinehas is 'zealous for his God' and in killing an Israelite and his 'Midianitish woman' he saves Israel from a plague sent in punishment for Israel's lusting after foreign women and worshipping their gods. Phinehas's action is cited in Covenanting literature as an example of a just killing.

138.15 uncircumcised Philistines see 1 Samuel 17.36. Male circumcision was a sign of God's covenant with Abraham and his people: see Genesis 17.11.

138.16 Dagon god associated with the Philistines; see 1 Samuel 5.

139.35 God do so to me, and more also common Biblical expression: e.g. 1 Samuel 3.17; and 2 Kings 6.31.

139.39 The sword of the Lord and of Gideon the war cry of Israel's soldier-hero Gideon as he leads a successful night attack against the Midian-ites; see Judges 7.18.

142.9 white feather the white cockade, the Jacobite badge worn in the cap.

142.14 the Evil Spirit the devil.

142.17−18 dollar ... silver bullet for 'dollar' see note to 26.23; for the 'silver bullet' compare note to 45.22−23.

142.22 the auld enemy the devil.

143.41 wounded his horse see Creichton, 129.

144.6 Hector in Homer's *Iliad* Hector is represented as the ideal warrior.

144.7 devil take the hindmost proverbial (see *ODEP*, 133).

144 motto see Thomas Campbell, 'Lochiel's Warning', stanza 1, in *Gert-rude of Wyoming* (1809). These words are spoken by a Wizard to Lochiel, the chief of the Clan Cameron, who is warned not to join the Jacobite rising of 1745 because disaster will befall it at Culloden.

144.31 stand to their tackle stick to their weapons, hold their ground or position.

144.39–145.1 the blessed Elihu ... bottles see Job 32.19. During a debate on God's justice Elihu has sat silent but, unable to contain his anger any longer, he intervenes.

145.1–2 day of judgment and deliverance the day on which God will both judge his people and deliver them from their enemies.

145.3–6 a Nazarite purer than snow ... coal see Lamentations 4.7–8. A Nazarite was a person of special sanctity, a holy man. Presumably Kettle-drummle is 'blacker than a coal' having been covered with mud from the peat bog.

145.6 beauty is departed see Lamentations 1.6.

145.6–7 loveliness withered like a dry potsherd see Psalm 22.15. Mause allows various texts to infect each other. In Job 32.19 it is not Elihu's bowels but his belly that is about to burst; the bowels come from Psalm 22.14. In the next verse 'strength', not 'loveliness', is 'dried up like a potsherd' (a broken piece of earthenware). In Lamentations 4.7 the Nazarites are more 'ruddy in body than rubies, their polishing was of sapphire'. It is either Peter Pattieson or Jedidiah Cleishbotham who points out that Mause should have said 'sapphire' and not 'sulphur'.

145.7 up and be doing see 1 Chronicles 22.16.

145.7–8 to cry loudly, and to spare nought see Isaiah 58.1.

145.8 wrestle compare Ephesians 6.12: 'For we wrestle not against flesh and blood, but against principalities, against powers, against the rulers of the darkness of this world, against spiritual wickedness in high places'.

145.12 Boanerges, or son of thunder the surname given to James and John by Jesus: see Mark 3.17.

145.24 wrestlings ... wrestle see Genesis 30.8, and note to 145.8.

145.24 of a verity truly. The first citation of this phrase in *OED* (verity 3b) is 1850.

145.30–31 He'll never fill Rumbleberry's bonnet i.e. he will never take Rumbleberry's place satisfactorily, will never measure up to Rumbleberry. For Rumbleberry see 60.1–6 and note to 60.3.

145.32–33 cheat the woodie avoid the gallows.

146.20 an' they ne'er should they never.

146.24–25 false Egyptians ... Ishmaelites all rivals and enemies of Israel.

146.26 sharp swords common biblical collocation.

146.26–27 fowls ... field see Psalm 79.2.

146.29 pillar o' cloud and pillar o' flame see Exodus 13.21. God led the children of Israel out of Egypt, going before them 'by day in a pillar of a cloud ... and by night in a pillar of fire'.

146.30–31 deliverance to the righteous compare Proverbs 10.2.

146.31 pouring out of wrath in Revelation 15.7–16.19 the 'seven golden vials full of the wrath of God' are poured out on the unrighteous earth.

146.40–42 like Deborah ... prancings see Judges 5.20–22. Deborah defeated Sisera (who lived 'in Harosheth of the Gentiles'), then sings a song of triumph: 'They fought from heaven; the stars in their courses fought against Sisera ... Then were the horsehoofs broken by the means of the prancings, the prancings of their mighty ones.'

147.1–2 a sign and a banner a sign is a message from God and a banner is here God's standard which will encourage the righteous: compare Psalm 60.4 and Isaiah 13.2.

147.33 Thessalian witch in classical times Thessaly in northern Greece was regarded as pre-eminently the country of magicians.

147.38–39 Wilt thou na bide the afternoon preaching in his introduct-
ory note to the ballad 'The Battle of Loudon Hill' Scott says that John King (see
note to 105.29–30) 'hollowed to the flying commander, to "halt, and take his
prisoner with him"; or, as others say, "to stay, and take the afternoon's preaching"' (*Minstrelsy*, 2.260). The same story appears in notes to Creichton's *Memoirs*
(Creichton, 129) and to 'James Russell's Account of the Murder of Archbishop
Sharp. 1679' (Kirkton, 439). The source of the story has not been traced.
147.40 cut the houghs compare Joshua 11.6.
147.42–43 railing Rabshekah see note to 31.29–30.
147.43 cursing Shemei see 2 Samuel 16.5, 7: 'And when king David came
to Bahurim, behold, thence came out a man of the family of the house of Saul,
whose name was Shimei, the son of Gera: he came forth, and cursed ... And
thus said Shimei when he cursed, Come out, come out, thou bloody man, and
thou man of Belial'. Mause's speech here is a 'taunt song' in the Old Testament
manner, and calls to mind Deborah's song in Judges 5 (see note to 146.40–42).
147.43 blood-thirsty Doeg see note to 73.8–9
148.1 ride as fast as ye will however fast you ride.
148.24–25 the land of bondage ... tents of Ham both phrases refer to
Egypt. Egypt, where the Israelites were held in captivity, is the 'house of bondage' (see Exodus 13.3 etc.), and the Egyptians are said to be descended from
Ham the son of Noah (see Psalm 78.51 and 106.22).
148.25 brand snatched out of the burning see Amos 4.11 and Zechariah
3.2.
148.26 die the death Dr Johnson says that 'die the death' seems to be 'a
solemn phrase for death inflicted by law' (*The Plays of William Shakespeare*, 8
vols (London, 1765), 1.311; Scott possessed the 5th ed. of 1803: *CLA*, 210).
148.27 hip and thigh unsparingly. See Judges 15.8, where Samson kills the
Philistines 'hip and thigh with a great slaughter'. *OED* does not explain the
origin of the phrase other than to say it is 'Biblical'.
148.27 from the rising to the going down of the sun see Psalm 50.1.
148.28–29 slay them like Amalek ... infant or suckling see 1 Samuel
15.3: 'Now go and smite Amalek, and utterly destroy all that they have, and
spare them not, but slay both man and woman, infant and suckling, ox and
sheep, camel and ass'.
148.40–41 the court of the Gentiles see note to 59.38.
148.41–42 Strong meat is not fit for babes see Hebrews 5.14.
148.42 grinding the sense is 'exacting', with a specific allusion to Jesus's
apocalyptic words about himself: 'whosoever shall fall on this stone shall be
broken: but on whom it shall fall, it will grind him to powder' (Matthew 21.44
and Luke 20.18).
149.1 huts of clay see Job 4.19.
149.2–3 the righteousness that is as filthy rags see Isaiah 64.6: 'But we
are all as an unclean thing, and all our righteousnesses are as filthy rags'. Burley
uses the phrase to express his contempt for the notion that man can earn
salvation through good actions: see note to 43.22–23.
149.4 Tophet Hell. See Isaiah 30.33, and note to 153.11–14.
149.7–9 the Amalekites ... Shur see 1 Samuel 15.7 and note to
148.28–29. For 'consumed from the face of the land' see Exodus 32.12.
149.24 ne'er be in me i.e. devil take me.
149.25 killing every ane o' the wounded and prisoners in his 'Letter of
Self-vindication' (1684), Robert Hamilton, the commander of the Covenanters at Loudoun-hill, said: 'But I, being called to command that day, gave out
the word that *no quarter should be given*'. He had 'one or two' killed, and reckoned
the giving of quarter to five others without his knowing 'among the first
steppings aside' (Kirkton, 445). However, Wodrow says that prisoners were

released 'without any further Injury, having no Prison-house to put them in'
(Wodrow, 2.46).

149.40   passed current   been accepted as genuine.

150.1   effectual   in addition to its obvious meaning of 'effective', the word
'effectual' would recall the phrase 'effectual calling' in *The Shorter Catechism*
(1648): see note to 290.3–4.

150.4   great things   common biblical phrase normally used about the works
of God.

150.6–10   plentiful pouring forth . . . garden of Eden   terminology of
17th-century Puritan discourse. See glossary for specific words.

150.12   Judden   a Scots form of Gideon.

150.14–16   Is it not written . . . Numbers, fourth and seventh   Mause in
fact quotes Numbers 4.18. The sons of Kohath, part of the tribe of Levi,
performed service 'about the most holy things' in the tabernacle: and care was to
be taken to ensure that they were not killed by this contact with the power of the
divine.

150.26   prayed on the Mount of Jehovah Nisi . . . Aaron and Hur   see
Exodus 17.10–15. Kettledrummle refers to a battle in which Joshua led the
forces of Israel against the Amalekites: 'And it came to pass, when Moses held
up his hand, that Israel prevailed: and when he let down his hand, Amalek
prevailed. But Moses' hands were heavy; . . . and Aaron and Hur stayed up his
hands, the one on the one side, and the other on the other side; and his hands
were steady until the going down of the sun. And Joshua discomfited Amalek
and his people with the edge of the sword.'

150.41–42   Middle Ward   see note to 16.9.

151   motto   Samuel Butler, *Hudibras* (1663), 1.1.11–12 (*CLA*, 42, 182,
242).

151.20   general committee   the terminology implies that all members of the
Covenanting army formed part of the committee, and immediately connects the
Covenanters with radical agitation in 1815 and 1816.

151.27   call a new successor to the crown   the terminology reflects the
democratic procedures of Presbyterianism in which ministers are 'called' to a
parish by the people. But a call for a new king was also illegal (Act for preservation of his majesty's person, authority and government, Wodrow, 1. Ap.64), and
those who made it were 'rebellious and treasonable'; the government position
upheld the king's prerogative 'by which alone the Liberties of Our People can be
preserved' (Proclamation of 12 October 1660, Wodrow, 1.16).

151.28   free parliament of the nation   in the third act of the Scottish Parliament of 1661, the king's prerogative is said to be the 'calling, holding, pro-
roguing or dissolving all Parliaments, Conventions or Meetings of estates; and
that all Meetings, without his special Warrant, are void and null' (Wodrow,
1.23). During the reign of Charles II, parliament met infrequently, and what
were in essence new laws were often formulated by the Privy Council and
effected by royal proclamation.

151.29   free assembly of the Kirk   the General Assembly was (and is) the
supreme court of the Church of Scotland. In the reigns of James VI and Charles
I it met only at the king's command, although it effectively overthrew monarch-
ical control in 1638 and met freely thereafter. As a result of the restoration of
Episcopacy in 1662 there was no General Assembly, although synods, presby-
teries and kirk sessions, the lesser courts of the church, continued.

151.34   like a rope of sand   proverbial (*ODEP*, 684).

151.35   the original principles of combination and union   political
theorists in the later 17th and 18th centuries argued that men combined together in societies for security and self-preservation; this must be what is
referred to by 'the original principles of combination'. Scott talks of 'original'

principles to avoid confusion with the Combination Acts of 1799 and 1800, designed to suppress trade union activity.

152.3   improve   turn to account for spiritual profit or edification, preach with a view to edification.

152.4   word in season   word at the right or opportune time. See Isaiah 50.4: 'The Lord God hath given me the tongue of the learned, that I should know how to speak a word in season to him that is weary'.

152.11   at a breathing   without pausing for rest.

152.17   of the right leaven   of the right sort. There is an allusion to the biblical use of 'leaven' as a universal spiritual agency: see e.g. Matthew 13.33 and 1 Corinthians 5.6.

152.18   the forty-ninth chapter of Isaiah   verses 25 and 26.

152.25–29   discourse . . . deliverance   whether this sermon division is quotation, imitation, or invention is not known.

152.26–27   uses of application   the bringing of the import of the text to bear upon particular examples.

152.28   backsliding and of wrath   in the Old Testament the Israelites are said to backslide and to provoke the wrath of God when they fail to keep his law.

152.28–29   promised and expected deliverance   deliverance from sin and mortality *either* by the accepting of the word of God, *or* as a result of the second coming of Christ.

152.42   Erastians   those in favour of the subordination of the church to secular power.

152.42   Independents   Congregationalists: the power of the Independents in the English Parliament in the 1640s blocked the establishment of Presbyterianism in England as envisaged in the Solemn League and Covenant.

152.42–43   Socinians   followers of Lælius and Faustus Socinus, two 16th-century Italian theologians who denied the existence of the Trinity and the divinity of Christ.

153.2   the beauty of the sanctuary   *literally* the rebuilding of the Temple in Jerusalem after the exile in Babylon; see Isaiah 44.26. The phrase is used metaphorically to propose the re-establishment of the theocracy envisaged in the Solemn League and Covenant (see 'Historical Note', 355).

153.4–5   nursing father   foster-father; the phrase (derived from Isaiah 49.23) was frequently used in the 17th century to describe the king's relationship to the church.

153.5   bastards   Charles II was well-known for the number of his illegitimate children, the most notable of whom was James Scott (1649–85), Duke of Monmouth.

153.8–9   Jeroboam . . . Pekah   all kings of the northern kingdom, Israel. Like the other kings of the northern kingdom, they are condemned in Kings and Chronicles as being in rebellion against the true worship of God.

153.11–14   Tophet . . . kindle it   Isaiah 30.33. Tophet, originally a spot outside Jerusalem, is usually taken as a name for hell. The 'King' in this passage from Isaiah is the god Moloch, but Kettledrummle applies it to Charles II.

153.30   hectic blush   the phrase implies not just that Macbriar has flushed cheeks but that he is consumptive.

153.35–36   the heavenly manna   the food sent by God to the Israelites in the wilderness: Exodus 16.15.

154.1   Macbriar   not a historical character.

154.7   Hagar   Abraham's slave, by whom he had a son. See Genesis 21.14–19: 'And Abraham . . . took bread, and a bottle of water, . . . and sent her away: and she departed, and wandered in the wilderness of Beer-sheba. And the water was spent in the bottle, and she cast the child under one of the shrubs. And she went . . . a good way off . . . : for she said, Let me not see the death of the child. And she sat over against him, and lift up her voice, and wept. And God heard the voice of the lad; and the angel of God called to Hagar out of heaven, and said unto her, ... Arise, lift up the lad, and hold him in thine hand; for I will make him a great nation. And God opened her eyes, and she saw a well of water; and she went, and filled the bottle with water, and gave the lad drink.'

154.8 like Judah under Vespasian, after the fall of Jerusalem in AD 70, coins of the Roman Empire were struck at Antioch and other places bearing on the reverse a figure of a Jewess seated in a mournful attitude under a palm. They are known as the Judaea Capta type from the inscription on many. But Scott may also have in mind Psalm 137.1–2, where Judeans mourn their captivity in Babylon and the destruction of the temple: 'By the rivers of Babylon, there we sat down, yea, we wept, when we remembered Zion. We hanged our harps upon the willows in the midst thereof'.

154.9 like Rahel see Jeremiah 31.15–16: 'Rahel weeping for her children refused to be comforted ... Thus saith the Lord; Refrain thy voice from weeping, and thine eyes from tears: ... and they shall come again from the land of the enemy.' See also Matthew 2.18.

154.11–12 the great things which God had done for them see e.g. Samuel 12.24 and Psalm 126.2, 3.

154.14 garments ... wine-press see Isaiah 63.1–3. God promises judgment and salvation.

154.15–18 your swords ... Idumea see Isaiah 34.5–8. In this passage Macbriar echoes a prophecy of God's vengeance on the enemies of his people; the promised slaughter is presented as sacrifice to God: see the two following notes.

154.19 the firstlings of the flock see Exodus 13.12: 'and every firstling that cometh of a beast which thou hast; the males shall be the Lord's'.

154.19–20 small cattle of burnt offerings see Isaiah 43.23. By 'small cattle' is meant kids or lambs.

154.20 bodies lie like dung see Psalm 83.9–10. The Psalmist describes the fate of the enemies of Israel: 'Do unto them as unto the Midianites; as to Sisera, as to Jabin, at the brook of Kison: Which perished at En-dor: they became as dung for the earth'.

154.21–22 myrrh ... herbs see Song of Solomon 4.14 etc. The speaker describes the beauties of his beloved.

154.23–25 the bow and the lance ... as if to the battle see Jeremiah 6.23 and 50.42. The prophet warns the Israelites of an invading army.

154.26–27 mighty men of war ... deliverance see Exodus Ch.3 and 14.19–31. Pharaoh's troops were destroyed in the Red Sea as the Israelites escaped from Egypt. Jacob was also called Israel, and as father of his people represents the nation.

154.27 devouring fires the phrase implies the anger of God. See for example Isaiah 30.30: 'And the Lord shall cause his glorious voice to be heard ... with the flame of a devouring fire, with scattering, and tempest, and hailstones'.

154.29 sanctuary ... silver see notes to 36.34–35 and 154.32–33.

154.30 ministering priests ... censors Jewish priests swung incense in censers to create 'an odour of a sweet smell' (Philippians 4.18) in praise of God, and also to hide God, for those who looked on him would die (see Leviticus 16.13).

154.31 sword and the bow standard biblical collocation.

154.32–33 yet verily ... glory after Solomon built the Temple in Jerusalem (see 1 Kings Chs 6–7) he sacrificed 'sheep and oxen, that could not be told nor numbered for multitude' (1 Kings 8.5). The passage also echoes Jesus in the sermon on the Mount: see Matthew 6.29 and Luke 12.27.

154.33   sacrifice more acceptable   see Romans 12.1, 15.16; Philippians 4.18; 1 Peter 2.5.

154.37   Leave not, therefore, the plough   see note to 44.26–28.

154.37–38   turn not back from the path   compare Psalm 44.18: 'Our heart is not turned back, neither have our steps declined from thy way'.

154.39   worthies of old   many Old Testament heroes disobeyed the commandments of God; for example, the Lord tells Samuel that Saul is 'turned back from following me' (1 Samuel 15.11).

154.40   halt not in the race   compare Hebrews 12.1.

154.41   lest the latter end . . . beginning   see 2 Peter 2.20: 'For if after they have escaped the pollutions of the world through the knowledge of the Lord and Saviour Jesus Christ, they are again entangled therein, and overcome, the latter end is worse with them than the beginning'.

154.42–43   set up a standard . . . mountains   see Jeremiah 51.27. The prophet calls on the nations to destroy Babylon and liberate Israel.

155.1–2   make the watch strong . . . shields   see Jeremiah 51.11–12.

155.2–3   name ye the captains of thousands . . . and of tens   see Deuteronomy 1.15. Moses recalls the way in which he organised the Israelites for their journey to the Promised Land.

155.4–5   rushing of winds . . . the sound of many waters   compare Acts 2.2 and Isaiah 17.12–13.

155.5–7   the passages of the destroyers . . . turned to flight   compare Jeremiah 51.32: the prophet tells how God will destroy Babylon. In the Authorised Version it is 'reeds', not 'rods', which are burned. Scott originally wrote 'reeds' in the MS, but presumably could make little sense of this for he scored it out and substituted 'rods'. The Good News Bible reads: 'the enemy . . . have set the fortresses on fire'; all modern translations concur with the tenor of this reading.

155.7–8   broken the bow of the mighty   see 1 Samuel 2.4.

155.9   Maccabeus   Judas Maccabeus led the Jews in a war of independence against the Syrian Greeks during which he recaptured Jerusalem and purified the temple. His exploits are recorded in the apocryphal book 2 Maccabees.

155.10   Sampson   Jewish hero, who fought against the Philistines. See Judges Chs 13–16.

155.10   Gideon   Jewish hero, who fought against the Midianites. See Judges Chs 6–8.

155.11–12   the banner . . . is spread abroad on the mountains   see Isaiah 13.2 and note to 11.38–39. The phrase 'in its first loveliness' may have been prompted by Song of Solomon 2.4: 'his banner over me was love'.

155.12–13   the gates of hell shall not prevail against it   Matthew 16.18: 'upon this rock I will build my church; and the gates of hell shall not prevail against it'.

155.14–15   sell his garment for a sword   see Luke 22.36.

155.16   the fulfilling of the promise   that is, the promise enshrined in the Covenant. Scotland's Covenant, like Israel's, involved the making of promises to God by the Covenanted nation.

155.18–19   the bitter curse of Meroz   see Judges 5.23: 'Curse ye Meroz, said the angel of the Lord, curse ye bitterly the inhabitants thereof; because they came not to the help of the Lord, to the help of the Lord against the mighty'.

155.20   Up . . . and be doing   see note to 145.7.

155.20   the blood of martyrs   see Revelation 17.6. Over 100 people were executed after the Pentland Rising of 1666.

155.21–22   bones of saints . . . highways   victims of arbitrary execution.

155.23   desolate isles of the sea   many Covenanters were imprisoned on the Bass Rock, a small, bleak island in the Firth of Forth.

155.23–24 dungeons...high places i.e. the dungeons of castles like that in Tillietudlem: see 79.40.

155.25–27 dens...cloathing those outlawed for their religious beliefs and practices lived in caves and the open country. Similarly, the Israelites sheltered in dens during the supremacy of the Midianites. See Judges 6.2, and Hebrews 11.37–38.

155.30 the stars...Sisera see note to 146.40–42.

155.34–35 the blessing of the promise the New Testament promise, the promise of salvation and eternal life.

156.6–7 play the men act the part of men. Compare 1 Corinthians 16.13.

156.31 three kingdoms Scotland, England and Wales, and Ireland.

156 motto *2 Henry IV*, 5.3.77–78.

157.16–17 by the strong hand by force, by (illegal) violence.

157.32–35 seignorial rights...pit and gallows capital jurisdiction attached to a barony, by which barons could put to death criminals found within their lands; see note to 17.28. The phrase 'pit and gallows' reflects the traditional practice whereby female malefactors were drowned in a water-filled trench, while males were hanged.

157.38–39 common law...justified at his sight Lady Margaret is talking of the right of barons to try within their own jurisdictions; thus Morton should be delivered to her officer and executed ('justified') under his supervision.

158.3 fag end the last part or remnant of anything.

158.5–8 And what...cold not identified; probably by Scott.

158.13 in biggit wa's in comfort or safety.

158.15–18 For time...overthrow not identified; probably by Scott.

158.41–159.4 Kilsythe...Philiphaugh victories in Montrose's campaign of 1644–45 terminating with his defeat at Philiphaugh. See 'Historical Note', 355–56.

159.16–17 shadows of coming events see Thomas Campbell, 'Lochiel's Warning', stanza 5, in *Gertrude of Wyoming* (1809).

159.21–22 the siege and storm of Dundee another of Montrose's victories.

159.39–40 knock down kill.

160.18–19 my brother's house...den of thieves see Matthew 21.13: 'It is written, My house shall be called the house of prayer; but ye have made it a den of thieves'.

160.28 a' on the spur...first to all hurrying to see who will get first to.

161.18–22 Tower of Tillietudlem...heavy artillery this description exactly matches Craignethan.

162.1 round dozen complete dozen.

162.17 Babel of discord see Genesis 11.9: 'Therefore is the name of it called Babel; because the Lord did there confound the language of all the earth'.

162.23–26 no pigeon...deluge see Genesis 8.7–9. When the flood began to subside, Noah sent a raven out from the ark; when it did not return he sent out a dove.

162.38–39 devotional observances there were few holy days in the Restoration period but Scott heightens the contrast between Episcopal and Presbyterian practice. Compare note to 94.18.

163.11 a thought more a very little more.

163.27 brought them off rescued them.

164 motto *Hardyknute*, in *The Works of Allan Ramsay*, 6 vols, Scottish Text Society, vol. 4, ed. Alexander M. Kinghorn and Alexander Law (Edinburgh, 1970), 291 (stanza 36). *Hardyknute* (1719) was by Lady Elizabeth Wardlaw but these lines come from one of the additional 13 stanzas written by Allan Ramsay.

164.36 make good a breach against the devil i.e. successfully defend a hole in the defences against an attack by the devil.

165.20–21 my destined heir see note to 134.33.

165.42–43 my marriage bed is barren the historical Claverhouse did not marry until 1684; his only son was born in 1689.

167.26 the provost-marshall and cord the head of army police and the hangman's rope.

167.34 gilding all besmirched see *Henry V*, 4.3.110.

168.7–8 denunciation of fire and sword *Scots Law* a legal order authorising a sheriff to dispossess an obstinate tenant by burning his house or to proceed against a delinquent by any means in his power.

168.14 keep a calm sough *proverbial* keep quiet, keep calm (*ODEP*, 416).

168.27 blue low blue flame; alcohol burns with a blue flame.

168.33 pock-puddings *literally* steamed puddings cooked in a bag. The phrase was used as a pejorative nickname for the English, from their supposed fondness for steamed puddings, and carries an implication of stolidity.

168.40–41 ninth generation an exhaustive plural.

169 motto Ben Jonson, *The Alchemist* (performed 1610; published 1612), 3.1.4–5 and 33–34.

169.35 a lukewarm Laodicean see Revelation 3.14–15: 'And unto the angel of the church of the Laodiceans write; . . . I know thy works, that thou art neither cold nor hot: I would thou wert cold or hot. So then because thou art lukewarm, and neither cold nor hot, I will spue thee out of my mouth.'

169.35 an indifferent Gallio Roman proconsul in Achaia. See Acts 18.17: the Jews complained to him that Paul was persuading men to worship God in a way that was 'contrary to the law'; Gallio refused to intervene. Greeks then attacked 'the chief ruler' of the synagogue. 'And Gallio cared for none of those things' (Acts 18.17).

170.7–8 the rebuilding of the decayed sanctuary see note to 153.2.

170.8–9 gathering of the dispersed saints see Isaiah 11.12. The dispersed are Jews left behind in the lands where the Israelites were held captive. Here Burley is referring to the outlawed ministers and their congregations, and to the Presbyterian exiles in Holland.

170.9 the man of sin the King, Charles II.

170.22 Ephraim in Calvinist Scotland it was common for people to have names of biblical origin. Ephraim was the younger son of Joseph, and father of one of the tribes of Israel.

170.25–26 a babe in swaddling clothes compare Luke 2.7, 12.

170.41 I will not peace see Jonson, *The Alchemist* (performed 1610; published 1612), 3.2.108.

170.42 Erastian see note to 60.4–5.

171.1–2 master and governor of his household Presbyterians objected to the oath of allegiance and Act of Supremacy because in them the king is said to be 'supreme governor' of the church (Wodrow, 1.22), whereas they believed that only Christ could be head of the churches.

171.2 adulterous husband of his spouse Christ is the head of the church (Colossians 1.18); and the church is the bride of Christ (Revelation 21.2, 9). Macbriar believes that Charles II has usurped Christ's headship of the church, and thus entered into an adulterous relationship with Christ's spouse.

171.4–5 the scattered remnant see Jeremiah 40.15.

171.5–6 veil of separation the veil separated the Holy of Holies, which only the high priest could enter, from the rest of the temple. But when Jesus was crucified, 'the veil of the temple was rent in twain' (Matthew 27.51); everyone could now come freely to God.

171.6–7   **build a wall with unslacked mortar**   see Ezekiel 13.10–15 and 22.10.

171.7   **if a fox go up, it will breach it**   see Nehemiah 4.3. Burley quotes Tobiah the Ammonite, who ridiculed the rebuilding of the walls of Jerusalem under Nehemiah after the return from the exile in Babylon.

171.9   **zealous, even unto slaying**   see note to 137.13–14.

171.12   **fleshly arm**   see 2 Chronicles 32.6–8: 'Be strong and courageous, be not afraid nor dismayed for the king of Assyria, nor for all the multitude that is with him: for there be more with us than with him: With him is an arm of flesh; but with us is the Lord our God to help us, and to fight our battles.'

171.12–13   **The sanctified end ... sanctified means**   Jonson, *The Alchemist* (performed 1610; published 1612), 3.1.13–14.

171.15–16   **the Laodiceans and the Erastians**   see notes to 169.35 and 60.4–5.

171.17   **the sons of Zeruiah are yet too strong for us**   see 2 Samuel 3.39: 'And I am this day weak, though anointed king; and these men the sons of Zeruiah be too hard for me: the Lord shall reward the doer of evil according to his wickedness'. David's followers Joab and Abishai, sons of Zeruiah, killed Abner in a blood feud, but David was unable to take action against them. According to Scott in *Tales of a Grandfather*, second series, Sir Henry Vane used these words in 1645 when persuading the Independents to temporise to maintain Scottish support for Parliament in the English Civil War (*Prose Works*, 24.40).

171.18–19   **God ... multitude**   see Judges Chs 6–8.

171.20–22   **broken upon Pentland-hills ... Charles Stuart**   those taking part in the Pentland Rising of 1666 acknowledged Charles II as King but wished to end oppression and restore the Presbyterian Church. The extremists, especially after Loudoun-hill, came to deny that Charles II was a lawful king; for Macbriar he is simply 'Charles Stuart'.

171.25   **tender consciences**   see *Henry VIII*, 2.2.40–41.

171.28–29   **my soul travails for**   see Isaiah 53.11.

171.40   **John Balfour of Kinloch, or Burley**   see note to 33.20–22.

172.14   **motives of private revenge**   none of Scott's sources supplies substantial evidence for this although some such accusations were made at the time. See Wodrow, 2.32.

173.1   **Richard Cameron ... Cameronians**   see note to 10.14.

173.4   **Solemn League and Covenant**   see 'Historical Note', 355.

173.23–24   **commander-in-chief**   the historical commander-in-chief of the Covenanters at Loudoun-hill and Bothwell Bridge was Robert Hamilton, who does not feature in the novel, but the ballad 'The Battle of Loudon Hill' implies that Burley was leader.

174.39   **Indulgence**   see 'Historical Note', 357.

175.1   **high places**   a common biblical phrase.

175.2   **blood of the saints**   see Revelation 16.6.

175.17   **smitten him with the edge of the sword**   see Numbers 21.24 and Jeremiah 21.7.

175.15   **Judas ... fifty thousand merks a-year**   as Judas betrayed Jesus for 30 pieces of silver, so Sharp was felt to have betrayed the Church of Scotland for his archbishop's salary. The phrase comes from the last speech of Andrew Guillan, a weaver, who was executed in 1683 for his part in the murder of Sharp (Wodrow, 2.304). Fifty thousand merks was £2750, but Scott, in his review of Kirkton, says that Sharp's salary was £1000 (*Prose Works*, 19.244).

175.20   **deliver him into our hands**   see Russell, 414: 'there is the bishop's coach ... which they seeing ... said, Truly, this is of God, and it seemeth that

God hath delivered him into our hands'. The phrase is commonly used in the earlier books of the Bible about the victories of the Israelites over neighbouring peoples; however, David is twice urged by his followers to kill Saul because 'God hath delivered thine enemy into thine hand' (1 Samuel 26.8) and twice refuses on the grounds: 'The Lord forbid that I should stretch forth mine hand against the Lord's anointed' (1 Samuel 26.11). See also 1 Samuel Ch. 24.

175.21　inferior tools of persecution　the assassins were actually looking for William Carmichael who was very active against those who attended conventicles.

175.23　written ... with the point of a diamond　see Jeremiah 17.1.

175.24-26　Was not the tragedy ... great work　see Wodrow, 2.32: 'The Actors in this bloody Tragedy could not but wonder at their own Preservation, and that, when this Fact was a doing in the open Fields, at the Height of the Day, in this Season of the Year, and so many Pieces discharged, they were neither interrupted or discovered; and this was the more strange to them, that there were Soldiers lying upon every Hand of them'.

175.32-33　it is not mine to judge you　compare Matthew 7.1: 'Judge not, that ye be not judged'.

175.35　the slaughter of Cumming　John Comyn, Robert the Bruce's rival for the throne of Scotland, was murdered by Bruce in a church in Dumfries in 1306. Since 1303 Comyn had been acting in concert with Edward I of England; thus Bruce directly challenged Edward and the murder led to the liberation of Scotland.

175.41　the rules of civilized nations　the most important 17th-century codification of international law on the rules of war was Hugo Grotius, *De jure Belli ac Pacis* (1625).

176.11　the vail　the veil of the temple in Jerusalem. See note to 171.5-6.

176　motto　*Troilus and Cressida*, 1.3.79-80.

177.38　opened upon it　developed their views about it.

178.11-12　strife of tongues　see Psalm 31.20.

178.31　right hand of fellowship　see Galatians 2.9. Within Presbyterian churches the right hand of fellowship denotes a welcome to membership of the church, the eldership, or the ministry.

178.36　resolutioners　see 'Historical Note', 356.

178.40　put hand to the plough　see note to 44.26-28.

179.23　build a fort and raise a mount against it　see Ezekiel 4.2.

179.24　rebellious　term frequently used in the Old Testament of those who repudiate God and his ways; compare e.g. Psalm 78.8.

179.24-25　their hand has been heavy　see Job 33.7 and Psalm 32.4.

179.25　children of the Covenant　as the phrase is biblical (see Acts 3.25), it links the Covenanters with the Christians of the early church.

179.26-27　Their hook ... betwixt our jaws　see 2 Kings 19.28 and Isaiah 37.29. The hook controls a fish (in Job 41.1-2 the same image is used of leviathan), and the bridle, which in the 16th and 17th centuries could mean the bit, controls a horse.

179.28　men of defence　men capable of defending.

179.37-38　blood of the saints　see Revelation 16.6.

179.40　sword will not turn back from battle　compare Jeremiah 21.4.

179.41　stricken in years　a biblical phrase.

180.18　fetters of iron　see Psalm 149.8: the saints will execute vengeance upon the heathen, and 'bind their kings with chains, and their nobles with fetters of iron'.

180.22　Habakkuk　see note to 170.22.

180.25-26　the earth quakes, and the mountains are rent　compare Nahum 1.5. Nahum is a poem of exultation on the fall of the empire of Assyria.

This and the following five notes cite biblical passages on the power of the word of God.

180.26 **the rivers are changed into blood** see Exodus 7.20 and Psalm 78.44.

180.26–27 **the two-edged sword** see Hebrews 4.12: 'For the word of the Lord is quick, and powerful, and sharper than any two-edged sword'. See also Revelation 1.16.

180.27 **is drawn from the sheath** see Ezekiel 21.3, 4, and 5.

180.27–28 **drink gore . . . and devour flesh** see Deuteronomy 32.42.

180.28 **devours dry stubble** see Nahum 1.10.

180.32–33 **shepherd's plaid** long shawl or blanket worn by a shepherd, especially one of a black and white check pattern.

181.4 **Meiklewrath** Meiklewrath is not a historical character (although there was a Covenanter of the name), but may have been inspired by Alexander Peden, for whom see note to 11.21.

181.13 **take the infants . . . stones** see Psalm 137.9: 'Happy shall he be, that taketh and dasheth thy little ones against the stones'. The Psalmist talks of doing to Babylon what it did to Judah. Compare Hosea 13.16.

181.15–16 **as they did on that of Jezebel** see 2 Kings 9.30–37. Jezebel, who promoted the worship of Baal, was killed by forces set in motion by the prophet Elisha. She was thrown down from a window, and her body was eaten by dogs.

181.16–17 **carcases . . . field** see 2 Kings 9.37, Psalm 86.10, Jeremiah 8.2, 9.22 etc.

181.17 **in the portion of** i.e. on the land inherited from.

181.21 **make fair weather** curry favour.

181.29 **We judge of the tree by the fruit** see Matthew 7.15–20. This is the method by which the followers of Jesus are to detect false prophets.

181.31–32 **the latter days . . . signs and wonders** biblical phrases. The latter days, which come as this present world approaches its end, are discussed in Daniel, Revelation, and elsewhere.

181.37 **Magor-Missabib** *literally* terror on every side. See Jeremiah 20.3.

181.39 **the Bass** see note to 155.23.

182.1–2 **high peaks of Dumbarton** the town of Dumbarton is on the Clyde downstream from Glasgow. The high rock on which Dumbarton Castle is built has twin peaks, from which the hills of Argyll are clearly visible. The Castle was still used as a prison in the 17th century.

182.6 **garments rolled in blood** see Isaiah 9.5: 'For every battle of the warrior is with confused noise, and garments rolled in blood'.

182.7–10 **Slay, slay . . . fill the courts with the slain** see Ezekiel 9.5–7. The prophet, in exile in Babylon, urges the destruction of those defiling the temple.

182.21 **hand . . . put to the plough** see note to 44.26–28.

182.29–30 **days of wrath . . . deliverance** see Revelation 6.17.

182.31 **her parliament of 1642** the English parliament that waged civil war against Charles I.

182.33 **the anabaptists of Munster** anabaptism is the doctrine that persons baptised as infants should be rebaptised as adults. Anabaptists established a republic in Munster in Germany in 1534, where in addition to a new religious order they instituted polygamy and a system in which property was held in common. The new republic was destroyed by the prince-bishop of Westphalia in 1535. The anabaptists and Munster became bywords for excess.

183.5–6 **the Midianites . . . delivered into our hands** see Judges 7.2 and note to 138.39.

183.21 **the stubborn . . . generation** see Psalm 78.8.

183.21 chastized with scorpions see 1 Kings 12.11: 'my father hath chastised you with whips, but I will chastise you with scorpions'.

183.22–23 hearts be humbled ... iniquity see Leviticus 26.41–42: 'if then their uncircumcised hearts be humbled, and they then accept of the punishment of their iniquity: Then I will remember my covenant'.

183.23–24 I will bring a sword ... avenge the quarrel of my Covenant Leviticus 26.25.

183.26–27 James Melvin ... Cardinal Beaton Cardinal David Beaton (*c.* 1494–1546), Archbishop of St Andrews, was active against the reformers and was responsible for the execution of George Wishart (*c.* 1513–46). Wishart's death provided one motive for Beaton's murder by a group of Fife lairds. According to John Knox (*History of the Reformation in Scotland*, ed. W. C. Croft Dickinson, 2 vols (Edinburgh, 1949), 1.77–78), Beaton had been struck twice when James Melville objected because Beaton was being killed in hot blood. Holding the cardinal at the point of his sword, Melville made him a speech about his wicked ways, asserted that he bore him no personal grudge but was going to kill him for being an enemy of Christ, and then stabbed him two or three times.

184 motto *1 Henry IV*, 2.2.100.

184.40–185.1 Our folk ... loose amaist i.e. our people had stripped the dead dragoons as bare as babies before we were finished. *Bawbee* is one of Cuddie's malapropisms in which he confuses 'baby' with the copper coin 'bawbee', worth 6*d.* Scots, or ½*d.* sterling (0.21p).

185.3 at the lang trot quickly.

185.15 to hae turn about wi' him to have turn about with him, i.e. to treat him as he treated Cuddie. Compare the proverb 'Turn about is fair play' (*ODEP*, 846).

185.22 bide a wee wait a little, hold on.

185.31 Straven the town of Strathaven in Lanarkshire; the spelling in the text reflects the pronunciation.

185.33–34 neither gar them hup nor wind neither get them to turn right or left.

185.41 ilka dog has its day proverbial (see Ramsay, 76; Ray, 98; *ODEP*, 195).

185.41 the auld sang says not identified.

186.5 ye suld aye be taking compare the proverb 'a going foot is aye getting' (Kelly, 11; Ramsay, 64; Ray, 281; *ODEP*, 315).

186.6–7 I hae seen gay weel to mysel I've looked after myself quite well.

186.29 the forfeited Earl of Bothwell see note to 29.5–6.

186.33 Haud Immemor *Latin* not unmindful.

187.14–43 Thy hue ... to love me! apparently by Scott. The lines are a pastiche of 17th and 18th-century verse.

188.12–13 Thus far shall ye come, and no farther see Job 38.8, 11: the Lord answered 'who shut up the sea with doors, when it brake forth, as if it had issued out of the womb? ... And said, Hitherto shalt thou come, but no further: and here shall thy proud waves be stayed'.

188.30 tinkling in biblical usage denoting triviality: Isaiah 3.16, 18; 1 Corinthians 13.1.

188.28–29 slaughter-weapon see Ezekiel 9.2.

188.30–31 daughters of perdition compare the biblical 'son of perdition': John 17.22 and 2 Thessalonians 2.3.

188.31 Vanity Fair the place of worldly pride and folly in John Bunyan, *The Pilgrim's Progress* (1678).

189.9 Langcale not a historical character. The name means 'long kale' or 'cabbage'.

190 motto see John Finlay, 'Dirge', in *Wallace; or the Vale of Ellerslie* (1804), 122.

192.26 Castle-Brecklan apparently fictional.

192.40 She bound my wounds see Luke 10.34: the parable of the good Samaritan.

193.24–25 incorporation of Barber Surgeons the barber was formerly also a surgeon and dentist. The Incorporation of Barber-surgeons (i.e. the Medieval Guild) was incorporated in 1461.

193.42 friar's chicken chicken broth with eggs in it.

193.43 chamber of dais the best room in the house, the best bedroom.

194.32 soon as syne sooner rather than later.

195.7 like wha but him like a paragon, the 'cock of the walk'.

195.10 cockit hat *either* three-cornered hat with brim turned up, *or* some kind of military hat.

195.10 blue ribbands the colours of the Covenanters. See note to 65.41.

195.10 the auld cause o' the Covenant see note to 21.36.

195.43–196.1 on the eve of fainting about to faint, on the point of fainting.

196.1 burnt feathers because of the strong smell, formerly used to bring round someone who had fainted.

196.1 cutting of laces tight lacing of women's dresses round the waist and chest was a common cause of fainting, for which the immediate cure was to cut the laces to allow the patient to breathe and the blood to circulate more easily.

196.6 taking on getting excited or worked up.

196.8 my mouth had been blistered proverbial. See *ODEP*, 68: 'a blister will rise upon one's tongue that tells a lie', or 'report has a blister on her tongue'. Compare *Love's Labour's Lost*, 5.2.335; *Romeo and Juliet*, 3.2.90; and *The Winter's Tale*, 2.2.33.

196.33–34 sorrow maun hae its vent proverbial. See *ODEP*, 338 ('Grief pent up will break the heart') and compare *Macbeth*, 4.3.209: 'Give sorrow words'.

197.2 when the first flight's ower when the first agitation is past.

197.8–9 worth siller very useful.

197 motto *Henry V*, 3.1.1.

197.31 served ... Low Countries such military experience was common among Scots in the 17th century. See note to 47.31–32. The 'Low Countries' are Holland and Belgium.

198.10–11 contended ... down my very throat forced the opinion on me.

199.12 flee the falcon *falconry* set one falcon against another; here used punningly as the cannon is called a 'falcon'.

199.38 right pharasaical leaven see Matthew 16.6: 'Take heed and beware of the leaven of the Pharisees'. Jesus warns his disciples to resist the punctilious keeping of Jewish law which was characteristic of the Pharisees.

200.2 with a Stentorian voice with a powerful voice: from the Greek Stentor, herald in the Trojan War (Homer, *Iliad*, 5.785).

200.3–5 Ye gates ... Be lifted up see Psalm 24.9, in the metrical version.

200.8 like a hog in a high wind variant form of the proverb 'the devil is busy in a high wind': see *ODEP*, 181. Pigs are often associated with the devil (see Matthew 8.28–32).

200.31–32 sword and fire see note to 168.7–8.

200.34–35 quarter-master-general officer with the rank of general responsible for finding provisions and quarters for the troops.

202.14 St Paul ... rebel even the greatest evangelist would be a rebel if he were a Presbyterian.

202.32–33 an ample red flag ... edged with blue see 'The Battle of

Bothwell Bridge', stanza 9 (*Minstrelsy*, 2.280): 'Then he set up the flag o' red,/ A' set about wi' bonny blue'. Blue was the Covenanters' colour, but it is not clear why the base colour should be red.

202.42 It's no for nought that the hawk whistles proverbial: see Kelly 199, and *ODEP*, 305, under 'gled'. But Gudyill applies the proverb literally: his cannon bears the name of a kind of hawk; the cannon-ball would sing in the air, and on landing damage the enemy.

203.20 labouring like a pioneer Burley is a leader, and yet is 'labouring' like an ordinary soldier. A *pioneer* was 'one of a body of foot-soldiers' who preceded an army or regiment, and had 'spades, pickaxes, etc. to dig trenches, repair roads, and perform other labours in clearing and preparing the way for the main body' (*OED*).

204.4 dropping fire irregular fire, the assailants shooting when they can.

204.16 turning the flank getting round the flank so as to attack from the side or the rear.

205.11 take the bull by the horns *proverbial* meet a difficulty rather than evade it. See *ODEP*, 800.

205.34 come awa' wi' you come along.

205.34 de'il a finger *emphatic* not a finger.

205.36 cut and quarter amang them, I carena i.e. I don't care whether you kill them or offer them terms.

206.28–29 buff coat ... endurance see *1 Henry IV*, 1.2.41–42.

206.39 outward man see 2 Corinthians 4.16.

206.40–41 running a screaming division executing shrilly a rapid melodic passage or descant.

206.41–42 the four pleas of the crown four serious criminal offences could not be tried in baron courts, but were reserved for the Justiciary court: murder (unless the murderer were caught red-handed when the offender could be tried by the sheriff), robbery, rape, and fire-raising.

207 motto *1 Henry IV*, 4.4.27–28.

208.26 uncircumcised Philistine see Judges 14.3: Samson goes 'to take a wife of the uncircumcised Philistines'. Male Jews were circumcised as 'a token of the covenant' between God and Israel (Genesis 17.11), and thus circumcision was the mark of being a Jew.

208.26–27 thy lust for a Moabitish woman see Numbers 25.1–2: 'And Israel abode in Shittim, and the people began to commit whoredom with the daughters of Moab. And they called the people unto the sacrifices of their gods: and the people did eat, and bowed down to their gods.'

208.33 little ones a standard biblical phrase.

208.34 necks of her enemies see Genesis 49.8, Joshua 10.24, 2 Samuel 22.14, and Ezekiel 21.29.

209.13–14 to smite and to destroy see Deuteronomy 7.2.

209.20–21 holding-forth 'The Phrase of *Holding-forth* was taken up by Non conformists about the year 1642 or 1643, . . . in contradistinction to the word *Preaching*' (John Wallis, *A Defence of the Christian Sabbath* (1692–94), 2.27).

209.30 distressed for running short of.

209.35–36 press for stores requisition of supplies of food.

209.35 as Sir John Falstaff did see *1 Henry IV*, 4.2.11–13: 'I have misused the King's press damnably. I have got, in exchange of a hundred and fifty soldiers, three hundred and odd pounds.'

209.41 go on thy way rejoicing see Acts 8.39.

209.41 work the great work see John 6.28, 9.4, and Acts 13.41.

209.42 no evil can befall see Psalm 91.10.

210.9 waxing old common biblical phrase.

211.2 at discretion unconditionally.

211.7 words of practical application see note to 30.33.

211.15–16 incidents ... history of the period the siege of Tillietudlem is fictional, but Scott's account of the attack on Glasgow is based on historical events.

211.29 entrances of closes Scott seems to combine 'entry', a public covered alley or passage in or between houses, and 'close', the Edinburgh word for the same.

212.4 firing his emulation arousing his ambition and determination.

212.5–6 conquer or die a standard antithesis: compare 'I maun either do or die' in the motto at 214.

212.21–22 trusting in the arm of flesh see note to 171.12.

212.24 Gallio see note to 169.35.

213.29–30 feudal array of the crown vassals see notes to 17.28 and 15.16–18.

213.42–43 Monmouth ... southern parts James Scott (1649–85), Duke of Monmouth and Duke of Buccleuch, was the natural son of Charles II and Lucy Walters. He took the surname Scott after his marriage in 1663 to Anne Scott, Countess of Buccleuch, who was made Duchess in her own right, and whose lands were in the Borders of Scotland. After the death of his father, Monmouth led a rising against his uncle, the Roman Catholic James VII and II, but defeat at Sedgemoor was followed by his execution at the Tower of London.

214 motto see 'The Battle of Bothwell Bridge', stanza 2 (*Minstrelsy*, 2.279; Child 206).

214.16–17 encampment ... ducal residence at Hamilton Wodrow records that after the first attempt to capture Glasgow Robert Hamilton fell back to Hamilton 'where they formed a Kind of Camp; the People not being unfriendly and the Duke and Dutchess at *London*, they took the Liberty to put their Horses into their Parks' (Wodrow, 2.47). Thereafter they moved about ten times before settling on Hamilton Muir for about three days before the battle of Bothwell Bridge.

215.8–9 little more than a fortnight Scott reduces the period over which the historical events took place: Sharp was murdered on 3 May; the shooting at the popinjay was on 5 May; Loudoun-hill was on 1 June; and Bothwell Bridge was on 22 June.

215.12 rod of oppression see Isaiah 9.4.

215.30–31 expose my body and gibbet my limbs in this period the hands of those convicted of treason were chopped off, the victim half-hanged, the heart removed, and the body dismembered and exhibited in various places. This appears to have been a comparatively recent innovation in Scotland, reflecting the influence of English practice. See note to 282.19–20.

216.3 your ainsel yourself.

216.9 if ye tread on a worm it will turn *proverbial* even the humblest will resent extreme ill-treatment (see Ray, 172; *ODEP*, 837).

216.13 best ... sit by the chimney when the reek rase *proverbial* safest to be close to the source of annoyance or danger (see *ODEP*, 738).

216.24–25 west-country drovers see note to 128.35.

216.25 My certie expression of surprise.

216.43 forget and forgie proverbial (see *ODEP*, 281).

217.2 thack and rape the thatch of a house, and the ropes tying it down; here used figuratively to imply that Cuddie keeps Morton better supplied and maintained than Alison did.

217.3 weel put on finely dressed.

217.8 a cast o' my hand my helping hand.

217.19 for they winna swear zealous protestants would not swear either

profanely or on oath because of Christ's teaching in the sermon on the mount.
See Matthew 5.34, 37.

217.20 gi'en ower surrendered.

217.21 as high as Haman see Esther Ch. 7. Haman is hanged on his
own gallows, which are 50 cubits (83 feet) high, because he tried to destroy
the Jews.

217.35 high-trotting horse fast-trotting horse; in a high or fast trot all four
feet are off the ground momentarily.

218.12 gibbet of such great height according to Creichton, such a gallows
was erected in the Covenanters' camp before Bothwell Bridge 'in order to hang
up the king's soldiers' (Creichton, 136).

218.24 The Lord ... hath delivered him into our hand the phrase is
commonly used in the earlier books of the Bible about the victories of Israel over
neighbouring peoples.

218.29 God do so to me and more also see note to 139.35.

218.36 the men of Jericho to the sword of Joshua see Joshua 6.21. The
inhabitants of Jericho were killed by the Israelites under Joshua after the city
walls had miraculously fallen down.

218.38 a better dispensation see Matthew 5.43–44: 'Ye have heard that it
hath been said, Thou shalt love thy neighbour,and hate thine enemy. But I say
unto you, Love your enemies, bless them that curse you, do good to them that
hate you, and pray for them which despitefully use you, and persecute you.'

219.3 these unhappy breaches in our Israel see Judges 21.15. The
moderate Poundtext, like the Cameronian Burley, shows the characteristic
Presbyterian identification with the Israelites of the Old Testament.

219.7–8 flock of this sheep-fold from the wolves in the Bible the flock is
commonly identified with the people of God, the sheep-fold with the church,
and the wolves with false pastors and the persecutors of the church. Poundtext
does not quote a specific text, but see the parable of the good shepherd, John
10.11–18.

219.9 the ranks of uncircumcision, a Philistine see note to 208.26.
Poundtext suggests that at an earlier period of his life Burley had fought abroad
for France or another Catholic power.

219.12–13 reap where thou hast not sowed see Matthew 25.24. Burley
misapplies Jesus's words in the parable of the talents, where the lord (who
represents God) says 'thou knewest that I reap where I sowed not, and gather
where I have not strawed' (verse 26).

219.13 divide the spoil common Old Testament phrase.

219.14 follow the gospel ... fishes see John 6.5–14: Jesus feeds the five
thousand on 'five barley loaves, and two small fishes'. Burley is accusing Poundtext of following the gospel for material reward.

219.16 draw their stipend under prelatists or heathens Poundtext was
an indulged clergyman (see 'Historical Note', 357) and thus received his stipend (ministerial salary) from those who acknowledged bishops. He would
particularly object to this charge because no General Assembly had ruled on the
status of the Indulgence.

219.23 blood-guiltiness the word is used once in the Authorised Version,
in a well-known passage from Psalm 51; used here it thus evokes the whole
context: 'Deliver me from bloodguiltiness, O God, thou God of my salvation:
and my tongue shall sing aloud of thy righteousness. . . . For thou desirest not
sacrifice; else would I give it: thou delightest not in burnt offering. The sacrifices of God are a broken spirit: a broken and a contrite heart, O God, thou wilt
not despise' (Psalm 51.14–17).

219.37 Go to come, come!

220.7 Erastianism see note to 60.4–5.

220.31–32 memorial of the grievances of the moderate Presbyterians there were extended disagreements between the moderate and the Covenanting wings of the insurgent army about their objectives and demands: see Wodrow, 2.55–61. However, the memorial drawn up by Morton and Poundtext paraphrases Wodrow's summary of the demands made by the Covenanters when they met Monmouth on 22 June 1679: 'That they might be allowed the free Exercise of Religion, and to attend Gospel Ordinances dispensed by their own faithful Presbyterian Ministers, without Molestation: That a Free Parliament, and a free General Assembly, without the Clogs of Oaths and Declarations, should be allowed to meet, for settling Affairs both in Church and State; and that all those who now are, or have been in Arms, should be indemnified' (Wodrow, 2.66).

220.34 gospel ordinances religious worship in accordance with the Gospel.

221.11 early on the morning i.e. the next day.

221.11–12 sound his dispositions find out how willing he might be.

221 motto see 'Edom of Gordon', in Percy's *Reliques of Ancient English Poetry*, stanza 9 (*CLA*, 172; Child 178D).

222.15 kirk organs most 17th-century Presbyterians disapproved of the use of organs in church. Pipers provided popular entertainment: see the description of Niel Blane as piper at 26.14–28.

222.15–16 book o' Common Prayer see note to 94.18.

222.17 the Covenant that was burned when the king cam hame although two 'seditious' books were burned in Edinburgh in October 1660, neither the National Covenant nor the Solemn League and Covenant seem to have been treated in this way. It was not until 1662 that they were declared to be 'unlawful oaths'.

222.31 my lane alone, unaided.

223.16 gi'e ower surrender.

223.20 free quarters see note to 11.23–24.

223.27 fear'd for afraid of.

223.33 took the rue repented, changed his mind.

223.35 win at get to.

224.6 cuittle favour wi' curry favour with.

224.7 win into get to.

224.20 beating the drum ecclesiastic thumping the pulpit: see note to 151 motto.

225.1–4 Stone walls . . . a hermitage see Richard Lovelace (1618–57/8), 'To Althea, from Prison'. Lovelace is supposed to have written these words while in the Gatehouse Prison in 1642.

225.41–42 humble petition and remonstrance see 220.31–32 and note. For the text of the supplication to Monmouth see Wodrow, 1.65.

226.7–8 unless . . . lay down your arms this was the condition stipulated by Monmouth before he would undertake to procure 'Satisfaction' for the Covenanters' grievances from the King: see Wodrow, 2.66.

226.10 no right to take them up the right to take up arms to rectify intolerable grievances is one of the rights repeatedly claimed by the Scots, and repeatedly declared unlawful by King and Parliament in the period. The declaration approved by Parliament in 1662 and required of all in positions of 'public trust' opens: 'I . . . do sincerely affirm and declare, that I judge it unlawful to subjects upon Pretext of *Reformation*, or any other Pretext whatsoever, to enter into *Leagues and Covenants*, or to take up Arms against the King, or those commissioned by him' (Wodrow, 1.120). The supplication to Monmouth presented before the battle opens: 'That whereas we the Presbyterians of the Church and Kingdom of *Scotland*, being, by a long continued Tract of Violence and Oppression upon us, in our Lives, Liberty, Fortune, and Conscience, and without all Hope of Remedy, cut off from all Access of Petitioning, and that by an Act of Parliament, and discharged to pour out our just Grievances and Complaints; and our Lives being made so bitter by cruel Bondage, as Death seemed more eligible than Life, the Causes whereof we have partly mentioned in our Declaration; and being, by an unavoidable Necessity, driven unto the Fields in Arms, in our own innocent Self-defence . . . ' (Wodrow, 2.65).

227.30 the House-of-Muir a common on the eastern slopes of the Pentlands; its situation would make it a convenient meeting point for troops retreating from Lanarkshire to Edinburgh.

228.9 beat up arouse, disturb, visit unceremoniously.

229 motto not identified: the words do not appear to be by Marlowe.

229.38–39 God . . . actions see 1 Samuel 16.7: 'for man looketh on the outward appearance, but the Lord looketh on the heart'.

230.2 have accession to are accessories to.

230.27–29 one of early talent . . . his country compare Ophelia on Hamlet, *Hamlet*, 3.1.150–161.

232.1 under the harsh construction see *Twelfth Night*, 3.1.112.

234.22–23 General Thomas Dalzell Scott's portrait of Dalzell (1599?–1685) follows his sources. He had fought for Charles I, for Charles II at Worcester (1651), became a general in Russia, and returned to Scotland in 1665. He was responsible for the brutal suppression of the Pentland Rising (1666). He was not present at Bothwell Bridge, but presumably Scott wished a fanatical royalist to balance the picture of the opposing sides.

234.27–28 Claverhouse . . . revenge the death of his nephew see 'The Battle of Bothwell Bridge', stanza 12: 'But wicked Claver'se swore an oath,/ His Cornet's death reveng'd sud be' (*Minstrelsy*, 2.281).

235.24–25 the Solemn League and Covenant see 'Historical Note', 355.

235.31 withdraw their hands from the plough see note to 44.26–28.

236 motto Thomas Otway, *Venice Preserved* (1682), Act 4, lines 263–64.

236.8 flying . . . from the face see Genesis 35.1.

237.11–12 narrowed . . . springs echoing Joshua 17.9, 18, and 10.40. *Narrowed their outgoings* means either 'harrassed their excursions' or 'restricted their exits'.

237.12–13 broken the staff of bread diminished or cut off the supply of food. See Leviticus 26.26 etc.

237.16–17 thrust his sickle into the harvest see Joel 3.13, Mark 4.29 and Revelation 14.15. Each context refers to the final judgment and harvest.

237.17–18 the labourer is worthy of his hire Luke 10.7.

237.25–26 painted sepulchre outwardly attractive, but in reality corrupt. See Matthew 23.27: 'Woe unto you, scribes and Pharisees, hypocrites! for ye are like unto whited sepulchres, which indeed appear beautiful outward, but are within full of dead men's bones, and of all uncleanness'.

237.26 lacquered piece of copper lacquer is a gold-coloured varnish used chiefly as a coating for brass; the image of lacquered metal is often used to imply deceit or falsehood.

238.1–2 the Moabitish woman see note to 208.27.

238.7 charter room room in which 'charters' (often royal documents granting land), title deeds, and other documents relating to the property, were kept.

238.25–27 cannot be . . . termed either fish, or flesh, or gude red-herring *proverbial* neither one thing nor another (see Ray, 190 and *ODEP*, 264).

238.35 Calvin i.e. Calvin's *Institutes*: see note to 15.6.

239.1 **pale of salvation** a 'pale' is a district or territory within which a particular jurisdiction operates. The 'pale of salvation' is thus an ironic image which suggests that God's gift of salvation is only available in some places and under particular rules or laws.

239.17–18 **doom of death** Scottish legal terminology.

239.29 **to bind and to loose** see Matthew 16.19.

240.7–8 **fast of general humiliation** see Russell, 461 : a council of war 'appointed Thursday to be a day of humiliation, and chose 4 old men, elders of the church, and 4 ministers, to draw up and to condescend upon the causes of the Lord's wrath'. Like the Israelites of the Bible, the Covenanters explain the approaching attack on them as the expression of God's wrath for their sin, and so decide on a 'general humiliation'. However, the objections of another faction prevented it.

241.9–10 **Bothwell-muir** Bothwell is on the north bank of the Clyde; at this point the Clyde flows from east to west in its generally north-westerly course. The royal forces approached Bothwell from the north and east, while the Covenanters were on the south and west side of the river.

241.21 **traitors with arms in their hands** see note to 7.32.

241.41 **joined in commission** i.e. other officers received direct instructions from the crown, and were responsible directly to the crown as well as to their general.

242.6 **by times** betimes, early.

242.21 **military service for their fiefs** see note to 14.32.

242.22–24 **Highlanders ... western whigs** see note to 11.23–24.

243.13 **the Great Highpriest of all the Nine** John Dryden (1631–1700). The nine are the Muses, daughters of Zeus and Mnemosyne, inspirers of poetry, drama, music, etc.

243.15–18 **Whate'er he did ... opened in his face** see Dryden, 'Absalom and Achitophel' (1679), lines 27–30. The Absalom of the poem represents Monmouth.

243.35 **General Thomas Dalzell** see note to 234.22–23. The description of his dress and appearance is partly derived from Creichton, 157–59.

244.9–10 **smile ... old acquaintance** see Wodrow, 2.66: the three appointed to take the supplication to Monmouth 'went in Disguise: Yet *Claverhouse*, ... having got some Hint of them, saluted them by their Names'.

244.15 **Remonstrance and Supplication** see 220.31–32 and note.

244.29–30 **controlling as well as advising him** the historical Monmouth was regarded as being pro-presbyterian, and thus in need of 'advice'.

244.33–37 **reasonable ... Majesty** see Wodrow 2.66: 'The Duke heard their Demands very patiently, and told them, "That the King had given him no express Instructions concerning these Matters, but assured them, upon his Honour, he would interpose, and use his Interest to the utmost with his Majesty for granting their Desires; and he was very confident he would be able to procure from his Majesty Satisfaction to them, for he reckoned their Desires reasonable and just."'

245.14–15 **suspend it for an hour** Scott does not follow his principal sources on the length of time the Covenanters were given or on the motivation for delaying the attack; for instance, Wodrow says half an hour (2.66), and Creichton says that the delay was used to get artillery into position (133).

247.6 **pretty lad** fine fellow.

247.7–8 **his blood be upon his head** biblical phrase meaning 'he himself will be responsible for the shedding of his own blood'. See Joshua 2.19.

249 **motto** Robert Burns, 'The Holy Fair' (1786), lines 118–19.

249.13 **true occasion and causes of wrath** i.e. the reasons for God's anger.

249.33–35 blockading ... the bridge of Bothwell these preparations, and the account given of the battle and its aftermath, accurately reflect the broad shape of the historical events.

250.28 day of humiliation see note to 240.7–8.

250.37–38 he was prevented by ... Meiklewrath see Kirkton, 459–60: on 15 June 'Mr Hume came where Mr Kid was going to preach, and commanded him out of the place as one that had been a troubler of the church'. Hume was a moderate; Kid was one of the preachers executed after Bothwell Brig.

251.1–2 took occasion by the forelock proverbial (see *ODEP*, 822). The Greek God Kairos (Opportunity) was represented as having a forelock but as wholly bald behind.

251.4 read forth as his text Deuteronomy 13.13. The text comes in a passage where Moses warns the children of Israel against those who will seek to tempt them to worship false gods. For 'children of Belial' see note to 36.14.

251.22 come up from the midst of them see 2 Corinthians 6.14, 17: 'Be ye not unequally yoked together with unbelievers ... come out from among them, and be ye separate'.

251.24 Seek not the aid of the Egyptians see Isaiah 31.1: 'Woe to them that go down to Egypt for help; and stay on horses, and trust in chariots, because they are many; and in horsemen, because they are very strong; but they look not unto the Holy One of Israel, neither seek the Lord!' The verse comes from Isaiah's account of Judah's ill-fated attempt to seek the aid of the Egyptians against the Assyrians.

251.25 numerous as locusts compare Exodus 10.5 and 15.

251.26–28 Their trust ... to the flight see Deuteronomy 32.30–31. Moses tells the children of Israel that they will face defeat, but that God will ultimately sustain his people against their enemies.

251.28 visions of the night standard biblical phrase.

251.29 fan ... chaff see Matthew 3.12.

251.30–31 fire of indignation and the lightning of fury see Isaiah 30.27 and 30.

251.31–39 this wretched Achan ... wedges of gold see Joshua Chs 6 and 7. Before the capture of Jericho, the Israelites are told 'keep yourselves from the accursed thing, lest ye make yourselves accursed, when ye take of the accursed thing' (6.18). But Achan took as spoil 'a goodly Babylonish garment, and two hundred shekels of silver, and a wedge of gold of fifty shekels weight' (7.21). The Israelites thus attract the anger of God, and to purge their contempt stone Achan to death.

251.36 garment of righteousness see Matthew 22.2–14. The wedding garment was known as the 'garment of righteousness'. The parable teaches that sinful man needs to be covered by the righteousness of Christ when final judgment comes.

251.37 the woman of Babylon see note to 122.23.

251.42–43 new election of officers see Wodrow, 2.64: 'At this meeting their Debates run higher than ever, even when the Enemy was within their view. ... 'twas urged, that all Places in the Army be declared vacant, and Officers now harmoniously chosen, that they might be intirely one when the Engagement came'.

252.1 that which was accursed see note to 251.31–39.

252.1–2 temporized ... with conformed to.

252.3–4 those who were not with them were against them see Matthew 12.30.

252.16–17 the words of the Patriarch see Genesis 13.8; Abraham is addressing his nephew Lot.

252.27 moderating an harmonious call to moderate a call is, properly, to preside over the election and induction of a minister to a parish. A moderator chairs meetings of the courts of Presbyterian churches; a 'harmonious call' is a unanimous one. See also note to 251.42–43.

252.28 formerly chosen see Russell, 463–64.

252.39 delivered us into the hands standard biblical phrase.

253.12 the last and worst evil the destruction of Jerusalem by Nebuchadrezzar, King of Babylon. See Jeremiah Chs 37–39, and 52.

253.19 To your tents, O Israel see 1 Kings 12.16: this was the cry of the northern tribes when rejecting King Rehoboam at the ending of the united kingdom. See also note to 183.21.

253.43 the light i.e. God; compare John 1.1–14.

254.2 our goings-out and comings-in see Ezekiel 43.11, part of a passage describing the return of the presence of God to a purified Temple.

254.4 Achan see note to 251.31–39.

254.4–5 our chariots and our horsemen the prophets Elijah and Elisha are both called 'the chariot of Israel, and the horsemen thereof': see 2 Kings 2.12 and 13.14.

254.7–9 the children of this generation ... the children of the sanctuary see Luke 16.8: Burley quotes the conclusion of Christ's parable of the unjust steward, which praises the nimble wits of an unscrupulous man.

254.10–11 accursed ... great day compare Luke 9.62.

254.32 a quaver of consternation Robert Southey, 'A Ballad, Shewing how an old woman rode double, and who rode before her' (1799), line 146 (Corson).

254.33 a penitentiary stave a verse of one of the penitential psalms. Newspaper reports show that Psalm 51 was certainly sung at executions in Scott's time, but how many of the other penitential psalms (6, 32, 38, 102, 130, and 143), if any, were used is not known.

255 motto see 'The Battle of Bothwell Bridge', stanza 11 (Minstrelsy, 2.281; Child 206).

255.30 tremendous engines the guns of this period were muzzle-loaded, and were much slower to operate than the breech-loaders of Scott's period.

256.1–2 Lennox Highlanders ... war-cry of Loch-sloy Loch Sloy, the war-cry of the MacFarlanes, is the name of a loch in their traditional territory in the district of Lennox, to the west of Loch Lomond.

256.9 none either to command or to obey Scott here follows those accounts which imply muddle and indecision, but Wodrow writes: 'Several of the Soldiers were killed, the Country Men stood their Ground near an Hour, making a brisk Resistance, till their Ammunition failed them. [New paragraph] When they found their Powder and Ball falling short, they dispatched up to their General, either to send them down Ammunition, or a fresh Body of Troops well provided. Instead of this he sent back Orders to them, forthwith to quit the Bridge, and retire to the Body of the Army' (2.66).

256.38–39 hart from the hunters see Proverbs 6.5.

257.19–20 demonstration towards an attack sign of an attack.

258.10 enough has not been done Dalzell, who had been replaced as commander-in-chief by Monmouth, was not present at the battle, but was reinstated on 24 June. 'The commander ... heartily wished his commission had come a day sooner; for then, said he, "these rogues should never have troubled his majesty or the kingdom any more"' (Creichton, 136–37).

258.14 Basil Olifant not a historical character. However, more recruits to the covenanting cause had been on their way: see Wodrow, 2.67–68.

258.16 his claim to the estate see note to 273.27.

258.26 the ... vindictive Grahame see Wodrow, 2.75: 'we shall find

Claverhouse raging in the West and South, this and several following Years, and committing many grievous Oppressions. He could never forgive the Baffle he met with at *Drumclog*, and resolved to be avenged for it; and yet we shall meet with some others more bloody and barbarous than he.'

258.32 face about turn round.

258.35 May the hand be withered see Russell, 474 note: 'In the deposition of witnesses respecting those concerned in Bothwell Insurrection, as quoted by Wodrow, one person depones, "that when Balfour was fleeing, he heard him say that he had received a shot, *the devil cut off the hands that gave it*."' The quotation has not yet been traced in Wodrow.

259.7 make head advance.

259.11 strength stronghold *or* body of soldiers.

259 motto John Fletcher and Shakespeare, *Two Noble Kinsmen* (performed 1613; published 1634), 5.1.38–40. This scene is by Shakespeare.

260.11–12 the desolation and captivity of the land standard biblical phraseology.

260.13 the stumbling-blocks may be removed see Isaiah 57.13–14: 'he that putteth his trust in me shall possess the land, and shall inherit my holy mountain; And shall say, Cast ye up, cast ye up, prepare the way, take up the stumblingblock out of the way of my people'.

260.16–17 Fiend hae me . . . them may the devil take me if I am likely to approach them.

260.29 zealots as well as the common meaning, Scott may allude to the Zealots, a Jewish sect which sought to establish a Jewish theocracy, and which fiercely resisted the Romans until the fall of Jerusalem in AD 70.

260.36 day of his anger standard biblical phrase.

261.3 child of . . . perdition see John 17.12 and 2 Thessalonians 2.3.

261.4 the avenger of blood see note to 37.4.

261.25–26 the word . . . to bruise thee see Matthew 21.44: 'And whosoever shall fall on this stone shall be broken: but on whomsoever it shall fall, it will grind him to powder'. The 'word' and the 'rock' are signs and metaphors for God. The word *bruise* means 'break in pieces, destroy', and is used in this sense when God condemns Satan (Genesis 3.15; Romans 16.20). Thus the meaning is that those who reject God will be destroyed by him.

261.26–27 spear . . . pierce thy side see Psalm 46.9: 'He maketh wars to cease unto the end of the earth; he breaketh the bow, and cutteth the spear in sunder'. See also John 19.34: 'But one of the soldiers with a spear pierced his side'.

261.27–28 offering . . . congregation see Leviticus 10.17: 'God hath given it [the sin offering] you to bear the iniquity of the congregation, to make atonement for them before the Lord'. Sacrifice as a means of atonement for the sins of the congregation is the central theme of Leviticus: compare Ch. 16.

261.28–29 very head of the offence see Matthew 18.7: 'woe to that man by whom the offence cometh!' The reference is to Judas who betrayed Christ.

261.29–30 like a thief through the window see John 10.1: 'He that entereth not by the door into the sheepfold, but climbeth up some other way, the same is a thief and a robber'.

261.30–32 a ram caught in the thicket . . . Jehovah-Jirah see Genesis 22.13–14: God tests Abraham by commanding him to kill his only son Isaac as a sacrifice. As Abraham prepares to obey, an angel intervenes, and Abraham is supplied with 'a ram caught in a thicket' instead of his son. Abraham named the place 'Jehovah-jireh'. 'Drink-offering' is a common biblical word for wine poured out as an offering to God.

261.33–34 bind . . . altar see Psalm 118.27. In the Jewish temple there were projections like horns at each corner of the altar. See also note to 340.32.

262.3 **thy face, as hard as flint** see Isaiah 50.7.
262.11 **bloody with spurring** *Richard II*, 2.3.58 (Corson).
262.13 **bear me down** overthrow me in debate.
262.17–18 **our bowels have yearned for him** see Genesis 43.30 and 1 Kings 3.26.
262.19–20 **carnal knowledge** worldly wisdom, understanding of temporal rather than spiritual matters.
262.41 **hath his mouth spoken it** see Psalm 66.14.
262.42 **Midianitish woman** see Numbers 25.6. When the men of Israel 'began to commit whoredom with the daughters of Moab' (Numbers 25.1), God ordered Moses to hang the transgressors. But even after this 'one of the children of Israel came and brought unto his brethren a Midianitish woman'. Outraged, Phinehas killed both the man and the woman.
262.43 **the arch-enemy's trap** the devil's trap.
263.10 **Edith Bellenden's person and property** see note to 273.27.
263.17–18 **numerous as the sands on the sea shore** standard biblical comparison.
263.20–23 **Joshua . . . folly in Israel** see Joshua 7.8, 15. As a result of Achan's sin at the fall of Jericho (see note to 251.31–39) 'the anger of the Lord was kindled against the children of Israel' and Israel's army was heavily defeated at Ai. After this defeat Joshua prays in the words quoted by Macbriar, and God tells him how to identify the guilty party. Achan confesses, is executed, and 'the Lord turned from the fierceness of his anger' (Joshua 7.26).
263.22 **as it were by lot** the use of lots to make decisions implied 'an appeal to chance or the divine agency supposed to be concerned in the results of chance' (*OED*).
263.24 **This is the Sabbath** Sunday, 22 June 1679.
263.40 **bloody sacrifice . . . acceptable service** compare 1 Peter 2.5: 'Ye also . . . are built up a spiritual house, an holy priesthood, to offer up spiritual sacrifices, acceptable to God by Jesus Christ'.
264.19 **bitterness of death** see 1 Samuel 15.32.
264.34–35 **petition . . . spirit** it is not clear what Scott refers to; three possibilities are the General Confession, the Litany, and the Collect for Peace, which ends: 'Defend us thy humble servants in all assaults of our enemies; that we, surely trusting in thy defence, may not fear the power of any adversaries, through the might of Jesus Christ our Lord'.
264.43–265.1 **go down to Tophet** see notes to 149.4, 153.11–14.
265.1 **ill-mumbled mass . . . prayer-book** in *Tales of a Grandfather*, Scott attributes these words to James VI: 'King James himself, when courting the favour of the Presbyterian party, had called the English service an ill-mumbled mass' (*Prose Works*, 23.354). In the 16th century protestants objected to the mass because it involved the empty repetition of Latin that none could understand. Later, the non-episcopal churches came to object to any kind of scripted worship, as they felt it prevented a direct response to God. See 'Historical Note', 355.
265.3–4 **the sun went back on the dial ten degrees** see 2 Kings 20.8–11. The going back of the sun was God's sign that King Hezekiah would recover from an illness thought to be fatal.
266.4–5 **being atween the de'il and the deep sea** *proverbial* being between two difficulties equally dangerous (see *ODEP*, 179).
266.6 **the morn's a new day** proverbial (see *ODEP*, 829).
266.7 **awes ye a day in ha'arst** *literally* owes you a day's work at the harvest; i.e. is under an obligation to you.
266 **motto** Thomas Osbert Mordaunt (1730–1809), in *The Bee*, 12 October 1791.

266.37 the long-ear'd route   the asinine rabble.

267.1 orderly book   book kept by a regiment or each company within a
regiment for the entry of general or regimental orders.

267.2 Drumshinnel   apparently fictional: a 'shin' is a ridge or steep face of
a hill.

267.3 as he was not armed   unarmed rebels had to be tried whereas rebels
taken with arms in their hands could be shot on the spot.

267.8 vinegar   used as an antiseptic.

267.22 Mischief shall hunt the violent man   see Psalm 140.11: 'evil shall
hunt the violent man to overthrow him'. The Psalmist begins by asking God to
deliver him from 'the violent man', and ends by asserting 'I know that the Lord
will maintain the cause of the afflicted'. See also Psalm 7.16: 'His mischief shall
return upon his own head'. The phrase as quoted by Scott is used by both
Walker and Howie about James Irvine who captured the Rev. Donald Cargill
in 1681 (Calder).

267.33 black jack   large leather jug for beer.

268.34–35 Wilt thou trust . . . in thy banner   see Psalm 44.6–7 and
Hosea 1.7. The people of the Covenant are saved through trust in God, not
through human power and weapons.

268.36 shall not God visit for innocent blood   i.e. will not God come to
judge and punish you for shedding the blood of the innocent. 'Innocent blood' is
a standard biblical phrase; see e.g. Proverbs 6.17 where the Lord hates 'hands
that shed innocent blood'.

268.36–37 glory . . . might   see Jeremiah 9.23: 'Let not the wise man glory
in his wisdom, neither let the mighty man glory in his might, let not the rich man
glory in his riches'.

268.37–38 shall not the Lord judge thee   the Old and New Testaments
repeatedly promise that God will judge; see e.g. Psalm 7.8: 'the Lord shall judge
the people'.

268.38–40 the princes . . . to other lands   Meiklewrath prophesies the
exile of the Stuarts after the 'Glorious' Revolution of 1688–89. The devil is the
'destroyer' to whom Claverhouse is said to have sold his soul (see 1 Corinthians
10.10). The latter's supposed immunity to lead bullets was taken as a sign of
their pact; see note to 142.17–18.

268.40–42 their names . . . drunken and mad   see Jeremiah 25.15–18:
God tells Jeremiah that after 70 years of the Jews' exile he will punish the King of
Babylon, and he tells Jeremiah: 'Take the wine-cup of fury at my hand, and
cause all the nations, to whom I send thee, to drink it. And they shall drink, and
be moved, and be mad'. Jeremiah takes the cup and 'made all the nations to
drink . . . to make them a desolation, an astonishment, an hissing, and a curse'.

268.43–269.1 the wish of thy heart . . . destroy thee   Claverhouse died at
Killiecrankie in 1689 in the very circumstances he hopes for at 268.21–25:
'with the shout of victory' in his ear.

269.6–7 How long . . . thy saints   see Revelation 6.9–10: 'I saw under the
altar the souls of them that were slain for the word of God, and for the testimony
which they held: And they cried with a loud voice, saying, How long, O Lord,
holy and true, dost thou not judge and avenge our blood on them that dwell on
the earth?'

269.29 an old proverb   i.e. 'dead men don't bite' (see *ODEP*, 171).

269.30 and push us from our stools   *Macbeth*, 3.4.82.

270 motto   John Gay, *The Beggar's Opera* (1728), 3.11.68–69.

270.13 General . . . Claverhouse   Claverhouse was made colonel only in
1682 and general in 1686.

271.28 Froissart   Jean Froissart (*c.* 1337–*c.* 1410). A French writer
and historian, he was of noble birth, and after 1369 had various church

appointments: hence 'the noble canon' (271.33). He travelled widely not just in France, but in Flanders, England, Scotland, and Italy, and met both Chaucer and Petrarch. His *Chroniques* is a brilliant account of the chivalric exploits of the nobles of England and France 1325–1400, but also reports the suppression of the Jacquerie, the peasants of northern France who rebelled in 1357–58, and to whom Claverhouse refers at 271.39–41. See *CLA*, 28, 29, 51.

272.2–4   profession ... soldier   a common view in literature through the ages; e.g. 'For right and wrong are confused here, there's so much war in the world,/ Evil has so many faces, the plough so little/ honour' (Virgil, *Georgics* (36–29 BC), trs. Cecil Day Lewis (1940), 1.505–7).

272.8   made interest   brought their personal influence to bear.

272.14   stand his friend   act the part of a friend to him.

272.19   the black-book   the traditional name for a book recording the names of persons who have made themselves liable to censure or punishment.

272.27   the Campsie hills   range of hills a little N of Glasgow.

272.32   Faithful and true   see Revelation 22.6: 'And he said unto me, These sayings are faithful and true'.

272.39   curates ... parish   see Wodrow 2.91.

273.27   Basil Olifant   the threat posed by Basil Olifant to Lady Margaret Bellenden and her grand-daughter is four-fold. 1] He tries an offer of marriage, but is rejected by both Edith and her grandmother. 2] As reported by Claverhouse, he tries to get the settlement of the Earl of Torwood judged void (see note to 18.10). 3] A common punishment for rebellion was the forfeiture of title and property; Olifant believes that in the event of a Covenanting victory Lady Margaret and Edith would be dispossessed, and that he would be rewarded with the estate. 4] He goes to law (after 1679) to claim the estate of Tillietudlem. The nature of his claim is not made clear, and, as Scots law specifies who may inherit heritable property, it is difficult to see the grounds for it. There were only two ways of circumventing the requirement of the law of inheritance: one, open only to those who held land as a fief of the crown, was to return the lands to the crown and to get a regrant in favour of different successors. The basis for Olifant's claim must be that a male line of inheritance for the barony had originally been specified, and that he is the 'next male heir to the last Earl of Torwood' (258.15). But he has been prevented from inheriting because Lady Margaret's grandfather or an earlier ascendant must have returned his estates to the crown, and been given a regrant that changed the original requirement that the barony be held by male heirs. Presumably it is the charter offering documentary proof of the regrant of the estate of Tillietudlem that Burley looks for, finds (see 284.30), and uses to bribe Olifant to join the Covenanters. Without this proof of their title, Lady Margaret and Edith cannot substantiate their claims, and so lose the law-case (293.40). It happens that in 1671 the historical Sir William Bellenden, Lord Bellenden of Broughton, resigned his title and estates to the crown, and had a regrant in favour of his first cousin twice-removed and his heirs male; in so doing he disinherited his only sister.

273.37   turn cat in pan   *proverbial* change sides for motives of interest (see *ODEP*, 847). The phrase is used in 'The Vicar of Bray', an anonymous 18th-century song about a vicar who manages to accommodate himself to the politics and religion of all five monarchs from Charles II to George I: 'When William our Deliverer came,/ To heal the Nations Grievance,/ I turned cat-in-pan again,/ And swore to him Allegiance' (lines 25–28).

274.6–7   double cloak   lined cloak.

274.22–25   number of his companions ... fallen into their power   see Wodrow 2.77: 'About twelve or thirteen Hundred were carried in from the Place of Action to *Edinburgh* ... Two Hundred more were brought in ... from *Stirling*;

some whereof were apprehended as coming from the North and *Fife* ... others of them were taken at and about *Glasgow*'.

274.27–29   Our Council ... triumphal entry   this does not seem to be historical, but see 275.1–26 and 275.24–25.

274.36   the Canongate   street in Edinburgh, leading from the Palace in the direction of the Castle.

275.1–26   The magistrates ... two heads borne upon pikes ... on horse-back ... long bars of iron   see Wodrow 2.141.

275.2   the gate of the city   probably the Water Gate (see previous note), which cut off the road leading north from the Canongate at Holyrood.

275.24–25   invective, mockery and insult   see Wodrow 2.77–78.

275.27   galley-slaves   galleys, ships rowed by long oars which took several men to work, were usually crewed by slaves or criminals. The way in which galley-slaves were secured on the way to their ships is not known.

275.29–30   heads ... in sacks   this detail comes from Hackston's own account of his capture. See Wodrow, 2. Ap.49–50.

275.33–34   sanbenitos ... auto-da-fe   under the Inquisition a *sanbenito* was a black garment, ornamented with flames and devils, worn by an impenitent confessed heretic at an *auto-da-fé*, the public burning of a heretic. Scott uses the Portuguese 'da' rather than the Spanish 'de' because 'auto-da-fe' entered English earlier.

276.22   confess and be hanged   proverbial: see *ODEP*, 139.

276.39–40   pit her finger in the pye   *proverbial* take part or meddle in the business (see Ray, 190; *ODEP*, 258).

277.7   the declaration   prisoners who were taken to Edinburgh after Bothwell Bridge were released if they pledged themselves not to take up arms again. See Wodrow, 2.79.

277.7–8   win free off   get off free.

277.9–10   psalm at the Grassmarket   see notes to 254.33 and 60.3–4.

277.14–15   the gude fight   see 1 Timothy 6.12 'Fight the good fight of faith, lay hold on eternal life'.

277.21   by and out-taken   besides and excepting

277.24   bridal garment   see Matthew 22.11–14: 'And when the king came in to see the guests, he saw there a man which had not on a wedding garment: And he saith unto him, Friend, how camest thou in hither not having a wedding garment? And he was speechless. Then said the king to the servants, Bind him hand and foot, and take him away, and cast him into outer darkness; there shall be weeping and gnashing of teeth. For many are called, but few are chosen.' The parable is about being prepared for the Last Judgment.

277.27   bleezing awa'   speaking in an exaggerated fashion.

277.28   win by   escape, avoid.

277   motto   Byron, *Childe Harold's Pilgrimage*, Canto 1 (1812), lines 125, 197.

277.38–39   ancient, dark, Gothic room   the Privy Council met in a first-floor room in a building adjacent to the east side of Parliament Hall, in Parliament Close (now called Parliament Square).

278.1   leash of game   *field sports* brace and a half, i.e. three.

278.2–3   craven ... cock of the game   *cock-fighting* cock that is cowardly or acknowledges defeat; fighting cock.

278.11   a whig, as your Grace was in 1641   John Maitland (1616–82), first Duke of Lauderdale, was 'for many years a zealous covenanter' (Burnet, 1.185): he signed the National Covenant in 1638, and was one of the Scottish commissioners who negotiated the Treaty of Ripon with Charles I in 1641 (in which Charles agreed among other things to the abolition of Episcopacy), and the Solemn League and Covenant with the English Parliament in 1643. But in 1647 he sided with the King, was captured at Worcester in 1651 and spent 1651–1660 in prison. He was Secretary for Scottish Affairs from the Restoration until his resignation in 1680, and as Secretary spent most of his time in London, formulating Scottish policy and conveying the King's commands to the Privy Council in Scotland. 'He made a very ill appearance: he was very big: his red hair, hanging oddly about him: his tongue was too big for his mouth, which made him bedew all that he talked to: and his whole manner was rough and boisterous, and very unfit for a court.' (Burnet, 1.186). He did not interrogate prisoners after Bothwell Bridge.

278.37   A fallen star!—a fallen star!   see Revelation 8.10: 'and there fell a great star from heaven, burning as it were a lamp'. This is part of a description of the fall of Lucifer.

278.39–40   keep your ain breath to cool your ain porridge   proverbial: see *ODEP*, 418.

278.41–42   one sheep will leap the ditch when another goes first   proverbial: see *ODEP*, 722, and compare 'One sheep follows another', 721.

279.35–36   to keep the church   to attend (or do your duty by) the established church.

280.1   Make out his free pardon   it seems that although those who signed the bond (see note to 277.7) were pardoned, they were not given a piece of paper to that effect ('They had no Pass given them': Wodrow 2.80).

280.11   Thou hast spoken it   see Mark 15.2: 'And Pilate asked him, Art thou the King of the Jews? And he answering said unto him, Thou sayest it'.

280.22   while the play is good   *proverbial* before the situation becomes serious or unpleasant. See *ODEP*, 453

280.33–34   thumb-screws ... the Scottish boot   instruments of torture.

281.5   the rock of ages   God. See the alternative (marginal) translation of Isaiah 26.4: 'Trust ye in the Lord for ever: for the Lord Jehovah is the rock of ages'. The use of the phrase seems to have started in the 17th century, in religious poetry and in sermons. See Edgar C. S. Gloucester, 'The Rock of Ages', in *Church Quarterly Review*, 90 (April 1920), 72–90.

281.12   take the best   the words are those of James Mitchell who was examined and tortured by the Privy Council in 1678 for his participation in the Pentland Rising of 1666. See Wodrow, 1.512.

281.26–27   thy people ... thy power   Psalm 110.3.

282.10–11   he'll scarce ride today, though he has had his boots on   perhaps a form of the proverb 'They that are booted are not always ready' (*ODEP*, 75).

282.14   Strong waters   alcoholic spirits.

282.19–20   his head and hands to be stricken off after death   see Wodrow 2.143, where he describes the execution of Hackston of Rathillet.

282.21   moveable goods and gear escheat   in Scots law, money, furniture, etc., as distinct from heritable or real property, i.e. land and houses. The escheat (forfeiture) of moveable goods to the crown occurred automatically whenever someone was sentenced to death by a royal court; the wording here is therefore formulaic.

282.25   in commendam   *ecclesiastical law* a benefice held in trust, particularly by a layman, until a proper incumbent was appointed was said to be held *in commendam*. The term is derived from the Latin *commendare*, to give into one's charge. By Scott's day the office of doomster had been abolished and the sentence was read over by the clerk; Scott himself was Clerk to the Court of Session.

283.2   company of angels and spirits of the just   compare Hebrews 12.22–23.

283.3 dust and ashes words used in Genesis 18.27 and Job 30.19 to indicate the frailty and impermanence of man.

283.3–4 mortality to immortality compare 1 Corinthians 15.53.

283.19 And Phineas arose and executed judgment see Psalm 106.30 which refers to Numbers 25.1–11. Macbriar did have Phineas in mind when condemning Morton to death: see note to 262.42. Calder (578) has an interesting note on a contemporary controversy about the interpretation and application of the Phineas story.

283.22 Leith the port of Edinburgh.

283.39 the Stadtholder Prince of Orange the chief magistrate of the Dutch Republic. A hereditary office, it was held at this time by the future King William II (of Scots) and III (of England).

283.41 the battle of Seneff Claverhouse was a volunteer in the army of the Prince of Orange which fought at Seneff on 11 August 1674.

283.41–42 bills of exchange written orders instructing the person addressed to pay stated sums of money to the person named on the bill.

284.24–25 the fatal day when Israel fled before her enemies see Joshua 7.4 and note to 263.20–23.

284.26–27 Ephraim to strive with Israel see Judges Ch. 12 for the conflict between the tribe of Ephraim and the other tribes of Israel. Burley is saying that the aftermath of Bothwell Bridge is no time for the different factions of the modern people of the Covenant to be struggling against each other.

284.27–28 thy heart is with the daughter of the stranger see note to 208.26–27.

284.29 my hand be heavy a biblical phrase.

284.29–30 bloody . . . house see 2 Samuel 21.1.

284.30 given me the means i.e. Burley has the charter giving a regrant of Tillietudlem; see note to 273.27.

284.30–31 meting unto them with their own measure see Matthew 7.1–2: 'Judge not, that ye be not judged. For with what judgment ye judge, ye shall be judged: and with what measure ye mete, it shall be measured to you again'.

284.33 bound it upon my soul vowed, bound myself absolutely.

284.40–41 to labour in the vineyard to work for the advancement of God's kingdom. See Matthew 20.1–16.

285.2–3 resisting unto blood, and striving against sin see Hebrews 12.4.

285.3–4 possess thyself in patience see Luke 21.19.

285.4–5 Keep . . . waits in the night see Matthew 25.1–13, the parable of the wise and the foolish virgins. As they await the bridegroom (who is Christ), the wise virgins have enough oil to keep their lamps burning, but the foolish virgins let their lamps go out, and are not ready to greet the bridegroom when he comes.

285.5 He who shall judge the Mount of Esau see Obadiah 21: 'And saviours shall come up on mount Zion to judge the mount of Esau; and the kingdom shall be the Lord's'.

285.6–8 false professors as straw . . . house of Joseph for fire see Obadiah 18: 'And the house of Jacob shall be a fire, and the house of Joseph a flame, and the house of Esau for stubble'.

285.7 in the fourth watch see Matthew 14.25. When his disciples were in trouble in a boat on the Sea of Galilee, Jesus came 'in the fourth watch of the night'.

285.7 garments dyed in blood see Isaiah 9.5: 'For every battle of the warrior is with confused noise, and garments rolled in blood'.

285.11 J. B. of B. after Bothwell Bridge the historical Burley evaded arrest and spent only a short time in Scotland before escaping to the Netherlands. He died in 1688, just before the Revolution.

286 motto see *As You Like It*, 3.2.292

286.5 the unities of time and place principles of dramatic construction derived from the *Poetics* of Aristotle (384–322 BC). The action (or events) of a play should be confined to a single limited area and take place within twenty-four hours.

286.7 to use Rosalind's simile i.e the simile in the motto above which is from a speech by Rosalind in *As You Like It*.

286.14–15 the year immediately subsequent to the British Revolution 1689. For the Revolution of 1688–89 which brought William and Mary to the thrones of England and of Scotland see 'Historical Note', 357. Scott offers what is in general an accurate sketch of the main features of the 'new æra'.

286.19 Agriculture began to revive 1688 was a year of scarcity, and Scott refers specifically to 1689.

287.2–3 the phlegm peculiar to his country i.e. the want of enthusiasm said to be characteristic of the Dutch.

287.13 the right of patronage the right of the chief landowner in a parish to select the minister of the parish. Patronage was abolished on the establishment of Presbyterianism in 1690 and the right of choosing their own minister given to congregations. It was restored by the British Parliament in 1712, and remained a source of fierce controversy throughout the 18th and 19th centuries in Scotland, leading to many schisms, and culminating in the Disruption of 1843, when a third of the ministers and members of the Church of Scotland left to form the Free Church.

287.13–14 rape upon the chastity of the Church the church is the bride of Christ, and in assuming to control the church secular authority was said to be raping it.

287.19 Magna Charta the agreement between King John and the barons of England in 1215, which, it was thought, defined the liberties of the subject in England in opposition to the rights of the sovereign.

287.26 Socinianism see note to 152.42–43.

288.6–7 the romantic ruins of Bothwell Castle see Introduction, xiv.

288.9 Aymer de Valence Earl of Pembroke (d. 1324) and leader of the English forces in Scotland during the Wars of Independence of the early 14th century. Bothwell Castle became his headquarters after its capture by the English in 1301, and its donjon or keep came to be known as the 'Valence Tower'.

288.9 Bothwell Bridge not actually visible from Bothwell Castle.

288.17–18 boughs of flourishing orchards the Clyde valley from Lanark to Bothwell was and remains a noted fruit-growing district.

289.26 keep their heart aboon by ordinary keep them in above-average good spirits.

289.31 the craft . . . in the clouted shoe *proverbial* the intelligence or cunning to be found in the patched shoe, i.e. in someone of low income or humble status. See *ODEP*, 153.

289.42 Single Carritch Shorter Catechism. Drawn up by the Westminster Assembly which first met in 1643, it was adopted by the Church of Scotland in 1648, and from then was much used to teach, in question and answer form, a summary of religious principles as expounded by the Assembly.

289.43 godfathers and godmothers in the Episcopalian baptismal service, godparents promise to supervise the religious upbringing of the child (see note to 290.4), whereas in Presbyterian practice the whole congregation accepts this role.

290.2 and whan I cam to man's yestate see *Twelfth Night*, 5.1.379.

290.3–4 Effectual Calling see *The Shorter Catechism*, question 31: 'Effectual calling is the work of God's spirit, whereby, convincing us of our sin and misery, enlightening our minds in the knowledge of Christ, and renewing our wills, he doth persuade and enable us to embrace Jesus Christ, freely offered to us in the Gospel'.

290.4 did promise and vow see 'A Catechism', in *The Book of Common Prayer* (1662). This series of questions and answers is 'to be learned of every person, before he be brought to be confirmed by the Bishop'. The candidate, on being asked about his godfathers and godmothers, is to reply: 'They did promise and vow three things in my name. First, that I should renounce the devil . . . Secondly, that I should believe all the Articles of the Christian Faith. And thirdly, that I should keep God's holy will and commandments'.

290.4–5 'did promise and vow' . . . yokit to the end of the tother Cuddie remembers the bond that he signed when before the Privy Council and which he feels combines elements of the Episcopalian and Presbyterian catechisms. See Wodrow, 2.79, for the words of the bond.

290.11–12 Donalds, and Duncans, and Dugalds typical Highland names, here used disparagingly.

290.12 bottomless breeks kilts.

290.14 Mackay Hugh Mackay (1640?–92), commander of the government forces which shadowed Claverhouse and his Jacobite army before the battle of Killiecrankie in 1689.

290.31 It's no to complain o' it is not to be complained about.

291.6 the sun's on our side o' the hedge now proverbial: a form of 'the sun does not shine on both sides of the hedge at once' (see *ODEP*, 786).

291.10–11 Neither man nor mouse proverbial: see *ODEP*, 506.

291.14 His face was made of a fiddle *proverbial* to be irresistibly charming (see *ODEP*, 237).

291.31 up by up there; often used of a place higher or more exalted than the speaker's.

291.34 betrothed . . . witnesses i.e. a formal contract of marriage, with witnesses, has been signed by Edith and Evandale.

291.36 light down dismount.

291.37 casting up gathering for a storm.

291.38 ower Glasgow-ward over in the direction of Glasgow.

292.1 light aff dismount.

292.7 very sma' way very humbly, in much reduced circumstances.

292.9 first and last all; i.e. they have all suffered enough.

292.12 the want o' some bits of sheep-skin see 284.30 and note.

293 motto John Logan, 'Ode on the Death of a Young Lady' (1781), stanza 8.

293.8 suppered up given its evening feed and bedded down for the night.

293.19 a' the haill warld *literally* all the whole world; i.e. the whole world.

293.21–22 what for are ye no why aren't you.

293.37 stand the law meet the legal expenses.

293.38–39 managers 'managers' is Wodrow's word for those in charge of the administration of government.

293.40–294.1 a weary sort a considerable number.

294.13 the patriarch Jacob Jacob had to serve two periods of seven years to win Rachel as his wife (see Genesis 29 and 30).

294.28 You'll gi'e yoursel the trouble you'll be good enough.

295.21 the muckle deil an expression of irritation.

295.21–22 nae law against harbouring and intercommunicating now letters of intercommuning which outlawed specific people and prevented anyone from harbouring them, were issued in 1675 and 1677; in June

1679, a proclamation declared that all who were in the Covenanting army at Bothwell Bridge were traitors, and prohibited anyone from helping or harbouring the leaders.

295.31 cast up that to me reproach me with that, cast that in my teeth.

295.38 tane down weakened, enfeebled.

296.6–7 John Tamson's man *proverbial* a man guided by his wife (see *ODEP*, 413). Here 'John' stands for 'Joan', both names coming from the same Latin root.

296.9–10 in the making of a hay-band in an instant.

296.11 frae that from the fact that.

296.26 life-rent see note to 18.10.

296.27 speaking ... fair addressing the old woman courteously or kindly.

296.32 maun follow the camp i.e. follow soldiers on their military duties. It was common for wives to accompany their husbands when on military service.

296.33 sort ill wi' would not suit, would not be agreeable to.

296.34 win ower recover from.

296.42 cow's grass enough pasturage for a cow.

297.8 up by up there.

297.9 the morn tomorrow.

297.15–16 outfield see note to 67.5.

297.20 aff hand on your own initiative.

297.26–27 Punch and the Deevil the popular puppet-show drama of Punch and Judy, introduced into the British Isles from the Continent towards the end of the 17th century. The story has taken many forms, and has many variations.

297.38 Lady Emily Maxwell Lord Evandale is called William Maxwell at 200.13, but his sister is called Emily Hamilton in both MS and Ed1. The use of 'Hamilton' reveals the underlying family identity of Lord Evandale, an identity which Scott originally wished to hide.

298.1 local sympathy *physiology* relationship between two organs whereby disorder in one induces disorder in the other.

298.13 he's aff the coast he's out of the way, the coast is clear.

298.22 commenced florist began to cultivate flowers.

298.40 Castle-Dennan apparently fictional.

299.15 set down ... to the score of attributed to.

299.22 he has married a wife, and therefore cannot come see Luke 14.20.

299.24 on the score of time on the grounds of.

300.1 victory near Blair of Athole Killiecrankie, 27 July 1689. Claverhouse was buried at the church of Blair Athol following his death in the battle.

300.17–19 Life-Guards ... rightful master for an account of disaffection in the army and of the problem of securing its support for the new regime, see Creichton, 173–85.

300.24 the low country Lowlands of Scotland.

300.39 real rights royal rights.

301.13–14 letter ... from her grandmother the spelling of Lady Margaret's letter is an imitation of what might be expected of a Scotswoman educated early in the 17th century.

301.27–28 implement of the indenture in fulfilment of the deed of agreement. See note to 291.34.

301.33 a thing done in a corner see Acts 26.26.

302.11 wrung from me a slow consent see *Hamlet*, 1.2.58.

302.24 heirs of entail an entail specified which descendants could inherit heritable property, and prevented heirs from alienating by gift or sale any part of it. Because an entail in effect transferred ownership of a property to future heirs, the property could not be forfeited as a punishment for rebellion. Evandale has no heirs of the kind specified in the deed; but were he married, his widow would have her widow's rights, and his child would succeed.

305.4–5   bondswoman   slave, servant. The term is biblical and used of Abraham's slave and concubine Hagar (see Genesis Ch. 21), but there were serfs in Scotland in the 17th century. See T. C. Smout, *A History of the Scottish People* (London, 1969), 181–83.

306.28   disturbs the repose of the dead   in a Magnum note Scott says that 'this incident is taken from a story in the History of Apparitions written by Daniel Defoe' (Magnum, 10.47). But the story is not a true parallel and is an unconvincing source; its real origin must be the folk motif of excessive grieving preventing the repose of the dead: compare the ballad 'The Unquiet Grave' (Child, 78). Belief in ghosts and spirits was general in the 17th century, as the citing of three European experts (308.26) implies.

307.7   mid-summer madness   *Twelfth Night*, 3.4.53.

307.42–43   deponed nil novit in causa   *Scots law* to *depone* means to testify on oath. Witnesses who knew nothing about the matter being investigated deponed *nil novit in causa* (*Latin* he knows nothing about the action).

308.19   Vryheid   *Dutch* vrijheid, freedom, liberty.

308.26   Delrio, and Burthoog, and De L'Ancre   Martin Antoine Delrio (1551–1608), Belgian biblical commentator and jurist; Richard Burthooge (*c.* 1638–*c.* 96), English theological writer; Pierre de Lancre (d. 1630), French writer on demonology.

308.27   civilians and common lawyers   'civilians' are those learned in the *ius civile*, i.e. the Roman law as developed in medieval and modern Europe; 'common lawyers' are those learned in the common law of England.

308.33   in rerum natura   *Latin* in the natural course of events. However, the meaning here must be 'in the natural or physical world' or 'the physical world', although it does not occur in this sense in the Classical period.

308.34   deceptio visus   *Latin* optical illusion (literally, deception of sight).

309   motto   Thomas Gray, 'Ode on a Distant Prospect of Eton College' (1742), lines 11–14.

309.28–29   his long-loved ... rival   the motif of the lost lover who returns unexpectedly to find his beloved on the point of marriage to another is common in traditional literature: see the ballad 'Hind Horn' (Child 17) and Child's notes. It recurs frequently in Scott. See *Waverley*, ed. Claire Lamont (Oxford, 1981), 16; 'The Noble Moringer' (*Poetical Works*, 6.345–59); and Magnum, 37.iii–xvi.

311.7   the furies   *Greek mythology* three supernatural beings who avenged crime, especially crime against the laws of kinship. They were often represented as winged women with snakes in their hair.

311.17–19   westward ... eastward   although the Clyde actually flows westwards at Bothwell and Hamilton, its general course is towards the north-west; thus Scott sees Bothwell as being on the east bank and Hamilton on the west rather than on the north and south banks respectively. Scott places Fairy-knowe on the Bothwell side of the river. As Morton does not cross the river by the bridge at Bothwell, and does not leave Bothwell on the east (or north), he is not seen by the sentinels. He crosses on to the left-hand bank (312.5), i.e. the south bank.

312.9   could the wish be without sin   compare *Hamlet*, 1.2.131–32.

312.9–11   these dark waters ... drowned my recollections   overtones of Lethe, the river of forgetfulness in the underworld.

312.19   set light by   despise, undervalue.

313.4   small burgh   i.e. Lanark.

314.13   the day   today.

314.13–14 **in propria persona** *Latin* in her own person.
314.16–17 **might hae had an M under your belt** *proverbial* might have used a respectful prefix (Mrs, Mr) when addressing a person (see *ODEP*, 497).
314.39–40 **Henry…navigation** Henry the Navigator (1394–1460) was a Portuguese prince noted for his patronage of voyages of discovery.
314.41–42 **Scylla… Charybdis** a rock and a whirlpool in the Straits of Messina between Sicily and Italy. A mariner who tries to avoid the one is in danger of coming to grief on the other, but Odysseus avoided the twin perils during his long journey home from the Trojan War.
315.2 **Argus** Odysseus's dog. On his return home from Troy after many years, Odysseus is recognised by Argus.
315.4 **The little dogs and all** *King Lear* 3.6.61–62.
315.14 **coals are plenty** coal was plentiful in the area round Hamilton, and was being mined in the 17th century.
316.9 **sough'd awa'** breathed his last.
316.15–16 **the last sough of an auld sang** proverbial; see *ODEP*, 220–21. These were the words of the Chancellor of Scotland, the Earl of Seafield, on the confirmation of the parliamentary union with England in 1707. See *Tales of a Grandfather*, second series: Seafield, 'on an occasion which every Scotsman ought to have considered as a melancholy one, behaved himself with a brutal levity, which in more patriotic times would have cost him his life on the spot, and said that "there was an end of an auld sang"' (*Prose Works*, 25.93).
316.18 **dippit candle** one made by repeatedly dipping a wick in melted tallow.
317.5–6 **weary on** devil take.
317.10 **an unco body** a stranger, a ghost.
317 **motto** *Richard II*, 5.2.41–43.
317.38 **Flushing** Vlissingen, at the mouth of the Schelde in the Netherlands.
318.1 **the Stadtholder** Prince William of Orange.
318.2 **keep terms with** keep on good terms with.
318.2–3 **his father-in-law, and … Charles** William's father-in-law was James Duke of York, later James VII and II. Fighting for his country's survival against the threat of Louis XIV's France, William needed the support of the British royal family.
318.11–12 **the United States** i.e. the United Provinces, the federal states of the Netherlands.
318.32 **letters of exchange** see note to 283.41–42; had Morton used them Claverhouse and Evandale would have known he was alive.
319.8 **Wylie Maetrickit the writer** *wylie* means 'clever', 'sagacious'; *maetrickit* implies 'tricked more' or 'tricked many'; *writer* is an old name for a solicitor.
319.9–10 **ower auld a cat to draw that strae before me** *proverbial* too old to be imposed on (see Kelly, 180; *ODEP*, 632).
319.14 **guide the gear canny** look after the moveable property carefully.
319.38 **sanctum sanctorum** *Latin* holy of holies.
320.4–5 **worsted-chairs … backs** i.e they are Jacobean.
320.8 **Arras** town in north-east France famous for the rich tapestry produced there.
320.9–10 **the counterfeit presentment of two brothers** *Hamlet*, 3.4.54.
320.19 **Raploch grey** see note to 50.41.
320.19 **band wi' the narrow edging** kind of neck-tie: two short white linen strips hanging from the collar, worn in the 17th century by Puritans and Presbyterians.

321.7   beet-masters to the new   from 'beet a mister', to fulfil a need, make good a deficiency.

321.32–33   feck o' twal shillings Scots   best part of 1s. (5p) sterling.

322   motto   John Fletcher and Philip Massinger, *Lovers' Progress* (1623), 3.1.

322.40–323.1   dribbles o' brandy   not traced. A 'dribble' is a small quantity, especially of liquor.

323.4   aqua mirabilis   *Latin* defined by Samuel Johnson in his *Dictionary* (1755) as 'the wonderful water prepared of cloves, galangals, cubebs, mace, cardomums, nutmegs, ginger, and spirit of wine, digested twenty-four hours, then distilled'.

323.34   Wittenbold   not a historical character.

323.40   Torphichen's Rant   a 'rant' is a lively tune used in an energetic dance; 'Torphichen's Rant' was a popular tune; it was collected by Robert Riddell in *A Collection of Scotch Galwegian & Border Tunes* (Edinburgh, 1794).

324.1   caterpillars   compare *Richard II*, 2.3.166 and 3.4.47. 'Caterpillars' are pests which feed off the country without contributing anything themselves.

324.3   the lang ten   the ten of trumps in 'Catch the ten', a card-game once played in Scotland 'in which the ten of trumps can be taken by any honour-card and counts ten points, the game being a hundred' (*OED*, 'ten' 4).

324.6   it's lang or the de'il die   proverbial; Kelly says that it is 'spoken when we are told that some wicked person is like to die' (230). See also Ramsay, 93; *ODEP*, 712.

324.10   e'en now   at the present time.

324.30   clinked down   quartered.

324.30   for a month bypast   for the last month.

324.35   sma' ale   low or non-alcohol drink.

325.1   stirrup cup   a drink given to a person already on horseback, setting out on a journey; a parting glass.

325.10   gae doun the water   follow the river.

325.15   lang Scots miles   Scots miles were about 1 1/8 English miles; they were proverbially long, and that is the way in which Blane is thinking of them.

325.18–19   it's no lost that a friend gets   proverbial: see Kelly, 198; Ramsay, 94 and *ODEP*, 487.

325.21   placed him   brought him to.

326.38–39   the widow's cake and the widow's cruize   see 1 Kings 17.8–16. In the reign of Ahab, a widow from Zarephath sustained the prophet Elijah by giving him 'a little cake' made of the meal from her almost-empty barrel, and the oil from her almost-empty cruse (bottle or jar).

327   motto   'Johnie of Breadislee', stanza 22 (*Minstrelsy* 3.145; Child 114).

327.40   Zarephtha   the Vulgate form of Zarephath; compare Sarepta (Luke 4.26) and see note to 326.38–39.

328.1–2   God...praised   see Job 1.21: 'the Lord gave, and the Lord hath taken away; blessed be the name of the Lord'.

328.6   the light   God. Compare John 8.12: 'Then spoke Jesus again unto them, saying, I am the light of the world: he that followeth me shall not walk in darkness, but shall have the light of life'.

328.12   worm   see Job 25.6, and Psalm 22.6: 'But I am a worm, and no man; a reproach of men, and despised of the people'.

328.15   sax weeks   Loudoun-hill was actually fought on 1 June 1679 and Bothwell Bridge on 22 June.

328.18   dune out   exhausted, worn out.

328.21   fed...keepit   compare Luke 10. 30–36.

328.26   what Jael was to Sisera   see Judges 4.21. Sisera was defeated by Israel (see note to 146.40–42); after the battle he sought refuge with Jael and fell asleep in her tent. 'Then Jael...took a nail of the tent, and took an hammer in her hand, and went softly unto him, and smote the nail into his temples, and fastened it into the ground: for he was fast asleep and weary. So he died.'

328.35 before his mother's face Scott has adapted the stories of two women from Walker's *Life and Death of Mr Alexander Peden*. Isobel Brown's husband was summarily shot by Claverhouse with her looking on. Walker continues: 'The said Isobel Weir [i.e Isobel Brown], sitting upon her husband's gravestone, told me that . . . [she] was helped to be a witness to all this without either fainting or confusion, except, when the shotts were let off, her eyes dazled'. After the event, the first person to help her was Jean Brown, who had herself been 'tried with the violent death of her husband at Pentland, afterwards of two worthy sons'; one died at Loudoun-hill and the other was killed by a party of soldiers (Walker, 1.84–86). See also Creichton, 154–56, 159–60.

329.3 estate was sair plea'd see note to 273.27.

329.7 on the back o' that shortly after that.

329.10–12 head . . . wind reverse forms of the proverbs 'keep one's head above water' (*ODEP*, 418), and 'better bend than break' (*ODEP*, 52).

329.14–15 aye keepit the coble-head doun the stream i.e. he always sailed with the stream. This a form of the proverb 'it is ill striving against the stream' (*ODEP*, 782).

329.15 set by and ill looked on rejected and held in disfavour.

329.17 in a' shapes in every way.

329.23 warld's loss worldly loss, loss of temporal things.

329.29–30 a curse . . . sent it the 'good man' who said that 'a curse was like a stone flung up to the heavens' has not been identified, but for 'like to return on his head that sent it' see Psalm 7.16.

329.36 Inglis not a historical character, but there was a Captain Inglis who served under Claverhouse. In a note in the Magnum edition, Scott says 'The deeds of a man, or rather monster, of this name, are recorded upon the tombstone of one of those martyrs which it was Old Mortality's delight to repair' (Magnum, 11.88).

330.21 the hand of brother is against brother see Mark 13.12. After the Revolution, some Covenanters supported the new government, and others stood out for the restoration of the Solemn League and Covenant. See note to 331.16.

330.33 hard hearts common biblical collocation, used to suggest minds that are closed to the truth; e.g. compare Mark 8.17: 'perceive ye not yet, neither understand? have ye your heart yet hardened?' See also *King Lear*, 3.6.77.

330.34 stubborn people a people who resist the truth of God. Compare Psalm 78.8.

330.36 baith whilk he was in right to expect both of which he had a justifiable cause to expect.

330.38–39 ane that had suffered and done mickle see Galatians 3.4: 'Have ye suffered so many things in vain?'

331.3 lion in the path see note to 35.35.

331.12 strange command in your voice compare *King Lear*, 1.4.28–30.

331.15 dead letter statute which is practically without force, or inoperative although not formally repealed.

331.16 General Assembly Presbyterian government in the church was re-established by act of Parliament in 1690, and the first General Assembly of the Church of Scotland since 1653 met later that year. But Parliament did not repeal the Act Rescissory of 1661 which had annulled all legislation passed after 1637, and thus it prevented the re-creation of a 'Covenanted Church', i.e. the church as envisaged in the Solemn League and Covenant of 1643.

331.20–21 fasting multitudes see Mark 8.2–3: the hunger of the people which Jesus satisfies with the loaves and fishes is normally understood to be a spiritual hunger which is met through the sacraments and the preaching of the word.

331.21   sweet word   see Psalm 119.103: 'How sweet are thy words unto my taste! yea, sweeter than honey to my mouth'. See also Psalm 141.6.

331.24   a dry clatter o' morality   Bessie Maclure in common with all Covenanters believes that people are saved by faith alone; see Ephesians 2.8: 'For by grace are ye saved through faith; and that not of yourselves: it is the gift of God'. Thus she objects to sermons that concentrate on morality, for to her salvation is not earned by good behaviour. The word *clatter* can mean 'gabble'.

331.34–35   on a new bargain and a new bottom   on new conditions and a new footing.

331.37   seven unhallowed prelates   a focus for English opposition to James was provided by the Archbishop of Canterbury and six bishops of the Church of England who sought to obstruct the King's attempts to promote toleration for Roman Catholics and other dissenters. They were tried in 1688 but were acquitted.

331.38   were free to join wi' the present model   felt free in conscience to support the present system of government in church and state.

331.38–39   armed regiment under the Yearl of Angus   the regiment later known as the Cameronians was raised from among the Cameronians by James Douglas, Earl of Angus (1671–92), in 1689. It successfully defended Dunkeld 22 August 1689 after the Jacobite victory at Killiecrankie, and thus kept civil war from lowland Scotland.

331.41   the breath o' the Jacobites   i.e. Burley was determined to hear what the Jacobites had to say for themselves before fighting against them. See note to 332.12.

331.42   a wall built with unslacked mortar   see Ezekiel 13.10–16: Ezekiel prophesies against false prophets.

331.43   sitting between twa stools   proverbial: see *ODEP*, 57.

332.3–4   the spiritual day-spring   see Luke 1.78, where the coming of Christ is called 'the day spring from on high'.

332.12   Montgomery, and Ferguson   Sir James Montgomerie of Skelmorie (d.1694) was imprisoned in 1684, was fined for harbouring rebels, and went into exile in Holland. After the Revolution he felt he had not been rewarded by William as he deserved and intrigued with the Jacobites. He fled to France in 1690 when his plotting was revealed. Robert Ferguson (1637–1714) was known as 'Ferguson the Plotter'. Possibly educated in Aberdeen, he spent his career in England. A leading figure in the Rye House Plot against the succession of the Roman Catholic James, Duke of York to the throne, Ferguson was outlawed in 1683. He accompanied William of Orange to England in 1688, but when his services to the new King were not rewarded as he had hoped, he became an enthusiastic and active Jacobite.

332.15   break off   severing of relations.

332.16   anes wud and aye waur   getting madder and madder.

332.35   the foul fiend   the devil; see *King Lear*, 3.6.9.

332.35   which several   each and all of which.

332.40   proper to   characteristic of.

333.5   Sir Harry Vane, Harrison, Overton   Vane (1613–62), a leading English parliamentarian and religious enthusiast, was executed after the monarchy was restored. Thomas Harrison (1606–60), a lawyer who rose high in the parliamentary armies in the English Civil War, and was a strong supporter of the trial of Charles I, was also executed as a regicide. Robert Overton (d. 1668) was a prominent and high-ranking English parliamentary soldier who became a Fifth-monarchy man, i.e. a zealot who, expecting the immediate second coming of Christ, repudiated all other government.

333.20 the Black Linn of Linklater apparently fictional.

333 motto see Spenser, *The Faerie Queene* (1590), 1.9.35.

334.19 Strong in innocence as in triple mail compare Milton, *Paradise Lost* (2nd edn, 1674), 2.268–69: 'arm th'obdured breast/ With stubborn patience as with triple steel'. The phrase probably originates with Horace in *Odes* (23 BC), 1.3.9: 'æs triplex circa pectus erat' (there was triple brass around the breast).

335.5 Hear till him listen to him.

335.13 tak' tent to pay attention to, be careful about.

336.1 meridian splendour ... depth i.e. the sun at midday only lit one third of the cave.

336.10–12 Dobs-linn ... Polmoodie ... Creehope-linn actual hiding-places in Peeblesshire and Dumfriesshire used by the Covenanters after the battle of Bothwell Bridge.

336.43–337.2 dimly ruddied ... Pandemonium compare Milton, *Paradise Lost* (2nd edn, 1674), 1.180–83: 'Seest thou yon dreary Plain, forlorn and wild,/ The seat of desolation, void of light,/ Save what the glimmering of these livid flames/ Casts pale and dreadful?' *Pandemonium* is the parliament in hell.

337.15 the corn ... the sickle see Mark 4.28–29.

337.27 thine hour see Luke 22.53.

337.43–338.1 the vintage ... the twelfth hour see Matthew 20.1–16: in the parable of the labourers in the vineyard, Jesus speaks of people who come to the work late, 'about the eleventh hour'. Burley means that Morton has arrived very late in the day in order to make his contribution to the work of the kingdom of God.

338.2 the right hand of fellowship see note to 178.31.

338.19 cave of Adullam a hiding-place of David: see 1 Samuel 22.1.

338.31–32 in favours of *Scots* in favour of.

339.2–5 to bring forth food ... Sampson's see Judges 14.14 where Samson 'puts forth' his riddle about honey from a lion's carcass.

339.9 as thy soul liveth a common biblical expression.

339.9–10 to wear a beard ... sword i.e. for one who has a beard, controls a horse and uses a sword.

339.10–11 and 339.15 gall-less ... cold-livered see *Hamlet*, 2.2.572: 'it cannot be/ But I am pigeon-liver'd and lack gall/ To make oppression bitter'.

339.15–16 crawling upon the face of the earth see *Hamlet*, 3.1.128.

339.22–23 outer darkness see Matthew 8.12: Israelites unworthy of heaven 'shall be cast into outer darkness'.

339.23 the light God.

339.24 a Nabal—a Demas for Nabal see 1 Samuel 25: Nabal was wealthy, and disclaimed any knowledge of David, asking 'Who is David?' For Demas, see note to 126.28–29.

339.31 bitt ... nostrils see note to 179.26–27.

339.40–41 work in the vineyard i.e. work to advance God's kingdom. See Matthew 20.1–16.

339.41 the wages of sin see Romans 6.23: 'the wages of sin is death'.

340.10–12 the perjured traitor ... impious villain i.e. Archbishop Sharp, and Sergeant Bothwell.

340.14–15 Chapel of Holyrood ... the Revolution in December 1688, troops were unable to protect the Chapel Royal which had been established by King James VII and II as a Catholic foundation in Holyrood Palace in Edinburgh. The chapel was sacked, but Balfour was not present (see note to 285.11) and Captain Wallace who led the defending troops was not killed, although it seems that about a dozen on each side lost their lives.

340.28–29 the future King of Israel ... Philistines see 1 Samuel

27.1–6: David, frightened that Saul would kill him, took refuge with the Philistines.

340.32 horns of the altar see note to 261.33–34. A criminal who held the horns of the altar was usually safe (compare 1 Kings 2.28: 'And Joab fled unto the tabernacle of the Lord, and caught hold on the horns of the altar'). But Burley, like Solomon, would execute nonetheless.

340.34 put thy hand to the great work see Luke 9.62.

340.39 fight the good fight see 1 Timothy 6.12.

341.7 lawful heir i.e. Edith Bellenden; see note to 273.27.

342.24 sit on his skirts *proverbial* punish him severely (see *ODEP*, 738).

342.25 forget and forgive proverbial: see *ODEP*, 281.

342.25 take the start decamp.

342.29–30 sick of the pip applied vaguely (often humorously) to various diseases in human beings.

342.36 rubbed out of the way eliminate, kill; perhaps a metaphor from bowls.

343.14–15 Moorkopf *Dutch* Moor head, i.e. black head.

343 motto John Dryden, *Palamon and Arcite* (1700), 3.840–43.

345.4 that keeps Edie Henshaw's kye Gibbie is herding cows: 'This employment, the worst and lowest known in our country, I was engaged in for several years under sundry masters, till at length I got into the more honourable one of herding sheep' (James Hogg, *The Mountain Bard* (Edinburgh, 1807), iv).

345.12 far frae fresh far from sober, i.e. drunk.

345.15 dollars see note to 26.23.

346.19 Kilsythe significant as the site of Montrose's victory in 1645.

346.32 the dye is now cast proverbial: see *ODEP*, 186.

347.16–17 meddling wi' other folk's matters *proverbial* 'Meddle not with another man's matters: see *ODEP*, 523.

347.18–19 that's braid Scotch that's plain speaking.

347.35 a hand gallop an easy gallop.

348.6 the Midianites enemies of Israel.

348.42 a hasty grave . . . rude stone the account of Balfour's death is fictional. The historical circumstances of his death are not known, but he is said to have been drowned while returning to Scotland from Holland in 1688.

349.22 Miss Martha Buskbody see Luke 10.40: 'Martha was cumbered about much serving'. To busk is to 'dress', to 'adorn', to 'deck', to 'dress up'.

349.28 circulating libraries libraries in which books were circulated among subscribers; they were much used by novel-readers in the early 19th century.

349.32 small wares small textile articles.

350.4–5 Jemmy and Jenny Jessamy Eliza Haywood (*c.* 1693–1756), *The History of Jemmy and Jenny Jessamy* (1753). Scott did not think highly of it; in his 'Memoirs' he writes of his taste in novels: 'The whole Jemmy and Jenny Jessamy tribe I abhorred' (*Scott on Himself*, ed. David Hewitt (Edinburgh, 1981), 32).

350.8 Julia de Roubigné novel by Henry Mackenzie (1745–1831), published in 1777.

350.28–30 Pattieson . . . conclusion i.e. Peter Pattieson, nominal author of *Tales of My Landlord* (see note to 5.10) of which the first tale was *The Black Dwarf*. Scott himself said in his anonymous review of *Tales of My Landlord* that the explanation of the dwarf's real circumstances had been 'huddled up . . . hastily' (*Prose Works*, 19.28).

351.13–14 to keep a calm sough *proverbial* to keep quiet, to hold one's tongue (see *ODEP*, 416).

351.31–32 Delville . . . Cecilia characters in *Cecilia* (1782), by Fanny Burney (1752–1840).

351.34 stuck sorely with her   was painfully unacceptable to her.
352.26–27 Scheherazade   the teller of the thousand tales of the *Arabian
Nights Entertainments*.
353.9 decline the article   Cleishbotham punningly comments on an alternative meaning of the phrase, and exclaims that in English one cannot decline
the definite article, i.e. 'the'.
353.17 construe   the word has several potentially relevant senses: 'construct', 'analyse', 'translate', 'explain', 'interpret', 'understand', and even 'mis-
construe'.

GLOSSARY

This selective glossary defines single words; phrases are treated in the Explanatory Notes. It covers Scottish words, archaic and technical terms, and occurrences of familiar words in senses that are likely to be strange to the modern reader. For each word (or clearly distinguishable sense) glossed, up to three occurrences are normally noted; when a word occurs four or more times in the novel, only the first instance is normally given, followed by 'etc.' Orthographical variants of single words are listed together, usually with the most common use first. Often the most economical and effective way of defining a word is to refer the reader to the appropriate explanatory note.

a' all titlepage etc.

abhorrent showing abhorrence 110.17

abide wait for, face 130.31, 136.19

abjure reject upon oath 306.19

a' body, a'body everybody 196.9, 222.12, 291.15

aboon above 28.2; in good cheer 289.26

abuilyiements warlike accoutrements 53.2

abune above 50.28, 333.21

accession see note to 230.2

accommodation supplying of things appropriate or necessary 197.11

accommodations room, suitable provision for reception of people 324.35

accompt account, reckoning 349.1

accoutre equip, array 18.38, 77.17

accoutrements clothes, trappings 18.14, 260.1

acquent acquaint 194.43

address skill, dexterity, adroitness 20.24, 124.26

advice information given, news 238.20

ae one, a single 27.29 etc.

aff off 27.43 etc.

affect pretend, assume 30.14, 58.31, 64.43

affection passion, disposition 43.31

affront position of hostility 203.33

afore before 49.30 etc.

aften often 39.8 etc.

again against 126.43 etc.; in preparation for when 184.23

agee, ajee disturbed, disordered 290.28; aside, to one side 295.24

agen again 297.10

agger Latin mound, dyke 8.38

ahint behind 57.37 etc.

ail have some thing the matter with one 145.2, 145.3, 145.5

ain own 12.14 etc.

ainsel see note to 216.3

air early 126.43

aitmeal oatmeal 168.16, 168.24, 168.32

alane alone 56.8, 85.27

alang 39.14, 216.41

amaist, almaist almost 38.43

amang among, in the middle of, in title-page etc.

amenable liable 62.41

amical friendly 239.13

an, an' if 56.24 etc.

anathematize curse 8.34

ance, anes once 54.13 etc.

ancient sometime 237.29

andirons fire-dogs 320.6

ane one 27.23 etc.

anent concerning, about 183.35, 316.10

anes see ance

aneugh, aneuch enough 91.30 etc.

angel English gold coin 68.13

anither another 290.2, 294.31

antinomianism belief that the moral law is not binding on Christians 73.12

antiquary one who studies the monuments of the past 7.16

apostrophize address rhetorically 48.24

apothegm pithy maxim 40.7

apprise, apprize inform 8.36 etc.

aquent acquainted 90.36

arch slily saucy 17.20, 232.26; chief, pre-eminent 188.24

ark chest 168.29

arles money given to confirm the engagement of a servant 59.31, 155.32, 184.31

arm-gaunt see note to 93.35−36

armlet oramental band worn round the arm 105.40

arsenal store for weapons and ammunition 74.34

assemblage assembly, number of persons gathered together 15.19

associate unite 42.32

a-stear in a commotion 290.13

asylum place of refuge 73.29, 326.27

a' thing everything 289.41

atone make amends for 72.19

attaint condemned to death with forfeiture of estate, etc. 66.35

attest be evidence of 230.40

atween between 27.31, 39.21 (see note) etc.

auditor listener, hearer 177.3, 317.32

aught¹ anything 91.2 etc.

aught² own, possess 319.37

aught³ eight 70.42

aughteenth eighteenth 70.41, 71.2

augur foretell 152.32; bode 304.12

augury omen 176.32

august venerable, revered 79.10

auld old 12.14 etc.

auspices propitious influence, favouring lead 16.24, 313.38

auto-da-fe *Spanish* see note to 275.34

ava, ava' at all 53.29, 120.38

avant-courier herald 353.13

aver assert, affirm 7.23, 142.14, 262.27

avouch acknowledge, confess to 45.30

avow acknowledge, admit 104.7 etc.

awa, awa' away 50.23 etc.

await wait 309.7

awe owe 52.43, 266.7 (see note)

awee, a wee slightly, a little 27.34, 290.28

aweel well 27.32 etc.

bab bunch 195.10

bacchante female follower of Bacchus, or one inspired by him 147.33

back mount, ride on 339.10

backslide fall away from religious faith 59.42 etc.

backsword sword with only one cutting edge 31.14

baff hit, shot 56.12

baggage-wain baggage-wagon 296.34

baillie magistrate 28.11; officer of a barony 157.38

bairn child 18.20 etc.

baith both 27.12 etc.

band covenant 68.40; see note to 320.19

bandelier, bandalier bandoleer, shoulder-belt for carrying musket-charges 84.33, 277.19

bang beat 84.34

bannock round flat cake made of meal and cooked on a griddle 28.21, 61.8, 61.16, 121.15, 168.20

bark see note to 67.5

barnsman thresher 61.29

barony lands held directly of the Crown 17.28 etc.

barouche type of four-wheeled carriage 16.29

bartizan battlemented parapet 96.16

basket-hilted *of a sword* provided with a defence for the hand, made of a narrow plate of steel curved into the shape of a basket 62.37

baste up tack or sew together loosely or roughly 350.29

bather annoy, pester 124.40

batts colic 53.18, 60.16

bawbee see note to 184.40−185.1

be by 28.16

bear barley 168.16

bedral beadle 8.41

beet-master see note to 321.7

behadden beholden 123.29

behint behind 68.31

behoved, behuved were obliged, had (to) 27.36 etc.

beild refuge, shelter 8.41, 59.9

bein, bien comfortable, cosy 59.34, 185.32

belang belong 50.14, 124.29, 328.28

Belial see note to 36.14

belie misrepresent 53.24, 63.1, 327.30

belive soon 334.11

belle pretty girl, beauty 26.18

ben see note to 53.34−35

bend proceed, direct one's way 330.42

benedicite *Latin* may you be blessed,

good gracious! 271.37

bennison blessing 55.25

bent[1] *adjective* wrinkled, furrowed 21.37, 185.13, 264.15

bent[2] *noun* course, direction 25.18

beset occupy 35.36, 37.33, 346.34, 347.36; surround 150.19; encompass 312.17

beside besides 342.35

besom *abusive* woman 73.32; broom, sweeping brush 126.35

besought entreated, implored 59.23

bespeak ask for 107.29

best-looked best-looking 82.17

bestial livestock 27.31

bethink ye *imperative* reflect, recollect 62.31

betoken be a token or sign of 104.29, 180.39

bicker drinking-cup 64.13; bowl 145.34

bide endure, bear 58.38 etc.; await, stay for 147.38, 160.1, 342.15; wait, stay 185.22 etc.

bien *see* bein

biggit built 158.13 (see note)

bilbo good-quality sword 32.8

billet letter, note 59.4, 284.23, 345.23

binn bottle-stand in wine-cellar 81.13

binna be not, are not 39.32; do not be 121.9

birding-piece hand-gun for shooting birds 31.11

birkie fellow 324.14

birl drink, carouse 39.23, 86.16 (see note)

bit[1] *goes with following word* indicating smallness, familiarity or contempt 57.28 etc.; some 57.43, 59.9; bite, something to eat 222.29

bit[2] provide (a horse) with a bit 19.35, 22.15

bittock little, short distance 90.43, 93.4

black unfortunate 90.17; dark 27.24, 233.1

black-a-vised dark-complexioned 95.6

black-cock male black grouse 10.20

black-fishers night poachers 18.9

black-jack, black jack leather beer-jug 61.14, 267.33

blatant clamorous, bellowing 125.32

blate bashful, hesitant 28.20

blaw blow 39.33 (see note), 54.34,

57.27 (see note), 125.28

blazon armorial bearings, coat of arms 135.7 (see note)

bleeze blaze 39.20, 122.24 (see note); proclaim 56.32, 277.27 (see note)

blink[1] glance 85.25; short time, moment 168.30, 289.23; gleam 291.7

blink[2] *verb* shine dimly or unsteadily 177.9

blown out of breath 129.33

blude blood 11.16 etc.

blunderbuss short gun with a large bore, firing many balls or slugs with limited range and inaccurate aim 16.40

boddle, bodle small coin; something of little value 125.13, 291.6

bode portend, foretell 260.4, 291.39

body, bodie person, man 28.19 etc.

bondsman, bondswoman slave, servant 237.14, 305.4

bonnie, bonny pretty, lovely, fine, dear 38.41 etc.

bonny-dye trinket, pretty thing 85.21

booby bumpkin 116.41

boor peasant 166.19, 271.4

boot 80.6 (see note), 280.34, 281.15, 281.32

bore hole, hiding-place 121.7

bottom[1] *noun* hollow 144.27

bottom[2] *verb* base, found 170.4

bounds territory, district 55.12, 57.8, 338.21

bountith gratuity 123.25

bow[1] *measure* boll, 140lb (*c.* 63kg.) of meal 168.16

bow[2] arched front (of a saddle) 261.38

braid broad 347.18

branks see note to 9.10

bravo hired soldier 79.1

braw, bra' fine, splendid 18.29 etc.

brawly very well 18.30, 57.32, 86.5, 296.27

braws fine clothes 40.22, 217.9

breaker submerged rock on which waves break 42.24

brear produce, yield 58.22

brearing sprouting 58.22

breast-works temporary defensive barrier a few feet high 211.30

brecham draught-horse collar 144.32

breeks breeches, trousers 290.12

brickle delicate, awkward 57.4

brigg, brig bridge 159.3 etc.
brither brother title-page
broach stab, thrust through 25.17
broadsword cutting sword with broad blade 31.14
brogue leather shoe 126.39
broo see note to 53.28–29
brook endure, bear 99.38, 112.43, 294.3
brose oat- or pease-meal mixed with boiling liquid 145.34 etc.
browst brewing, brew 26.35, 28.5, 289.27, 324.34
bucking-tub tub used for bleaching yarn, cloth or clothes 314.41
budget leather gun-rest, holster 77.5
buff yellowish leather, used for military coats 18.14 etc.
buon *Spanish* good 75.12
burn stream 57.34, 325.13
busk set up, fix 40.20; dress 185.7
by¹ *adverb* past 337.20 etc.; see note to 291.31
by² *preposition* apart from 277.21, 291.36
byre cowshed 27.24, 297.8
ca, ca' call 39.6 etc.; drive 49.6
cairn heap of stones, often marking a boundary or hill-top 132.34 etc.
cairngorm semi-precious stone found on the mountain Cairngorm 97.25
callant, callan fellow 18.29, 66.28, 91.29
cam *past tense* came 57.31 etc.
cambric fine white linen 349.32
camerado *Spanish* companion, comrade 75.12
Cameronian see note to 10.14
canary from the Canary Islands 63.17
Candlemas 2 February, a Scottish quarter-day 18.1, 39.21, 60.4, 93.19
canna cannot 27.17 etc.
canny¹ *adjective* careful 27.37, 297.9, 342.14; skilful 40.17; comfortable 73.18; clever 89.25
canny² *adverb* carefully 319.14
cant peculiar language of a religious sect repeated mechanically 199.30, 192.15
caparisons saddle-cloths, trappings 146.10
capricious subject to change or irregularity, so as to appear ungoverned by law 233.42
carabine carbine, short gun used e.g.

by cavalry 16.18 etc.
carcage carcase, corpse 185.8
career short gallop at full speed 25.18; rapid course of action 312.27
carle fellow 17.42 etc.
carline old woman 62.27, 121.14, 297.22
carnal unregenerate, unspiritual 11.12 etc.
carritch catechism 289.42 (see note)
case plight 260.3
casque helmet 25.10
cassock long tunic worn by Episcopalian clergy 323.4
cast 'dash' 10.30; a twist to one side 30.22; tinge, overlay 42.21; chance, opportunity 59.11; type, caste 286.13; see notes to 72.3, 217.8, 291.37
castaway someone who is rejected; a reprobate 126.34
catacomb recess for storing wine in a cellar 80.35
caterpillar plunderer, despoiler 324.1
cates provisions, delicacies 100.8
catterin Highland marauders 44.8
causeway *verb* pave 48.27, 76.25
caution word of warning, admonition 15.26 etc.; surety, bail 49.9 (see note), 82.33, 290.15
centrical central 214.17
certie, sarty (my) word! 39.18, 85.26, 199.13, 216.25
cess tax 71.5 (see note), 71.15, 102.13
chainzie chain 51.10
chancy see note to 40.2
change-house inn 16.22, 26.31, 32.10, 324.37
chanter pipe on which the bagpipe melody is played 26.17
chapter subject 59.16
charger large soup-plate 61.4
chasseur huntsman 21.33
cheek side 27.33
cheer food 315.18
chield, chiel fellow epigraph, 27.23 etc.
chimley-neuck chimney-corner 54.37
china-cabinet small room for the display of china 295.10
chirurgeon surgeon 193.26
chit see note to 90.7–8
choppin Scots half-pint (*c.* 0.85 litre) 28.24

church-discipline system for regulating a church's practice (not its doctrine) 253.10

churl, churle peasant rogue 132.23, 140.23, 271.40, 339.25

ci-devant *French* former 28.26, 120.28, 298.15, 317.29

circumstantiality attention to details 11.10

civilty-money money given in anticipation of securing favourable treatment 70.7

clachan village 50.31

claes clothes 56.24

clairet claret 63.17

claiths clothes, clothing 185.7, 186.8

clang harsh cry of certain birds 181.41

clash chattering 62.29

clatter see note to 331.24

claver talk foolishly 146.33

clavers nonsense 56.13, 60.10; see note to 85.35

cleugh gorge 121.37

clink dump 324.30

close¹ *noun* a closing in fight, struggle 31.42

close² *noun* passageway, alley 211.29

closeness stuffiness 5.20

clouted repaired with a metal patch 9.5; see note to 289.31

clow-gillieflower clove-pink 40.24

clowr batter, thump 122.3

coble type of rowing-boat 329.14

cock-boat small ship's-boat 20.4

cock-laird small landowner who farmed his own land 352.20

cockade rosette or ribbons worn in hat as badge of office 65.41

cockernony, cocker nonny woman's starched cap 40.20, 123.16

cocking cocker (spaniel) 315.1

cockit see note to 195.10

coif close-fitting cap 315.23

colewort cabbage 61.5

collation light meal 158.21, 344.18

comfits preserves 317.31

comfort *verb* relieve, assist 50.39

comfortable strengthening, cheering, sustaining 64.34, 330.36

comforter that which cheers or sustains 76.8

commination recital of Divine denunciation against sinners 17.36

commons rations, fare 100.7

communing discussion 68.24

communion fellowship 330.38

compassionate *verb* treat with compassion, pity 102.8, 148.41

complacence satisfaction 217.5

complaisance desire to please, courtesy 322.22

compound put together, mix 317.29

comprehending inclusive 171.24

conduct a piece of behaviour 309.7

confide trust, feel assured 169.28

confort *noun* comfort, encouragement, support 51.38

congenial sympathetic 110.14

conjure entreat earnestly 250.3, 309.33; trick 89.5

consciousness knowledge of one's own state of innocence or guilt 52.24

conserves confections, preserves 317.28

considerate deliberate, prudent 322.13

contemn despise 341.20

conterminous having a common boundary 8.37

contingent uncertain 308.6

contumacy perverse disobedience 102.1

conventicle Presbyterian field-preaching 55.33 etc.

conventicler one who attends conventicles, a Covenanter 14.13

conversation behaviour, sexual intimacy 153.6

converse familiar occupation 10.22

convincing producing a moral conviction of sinfulness 150.8

convoke summon 239.14

cope cover with a sloping top-course 8.40

cornet commissioned officer in cavalry 27.19 (see note)

corse body 72.42

cot, cot-house farmworker's cottage 53.33, 54.5,

coulter cutting blade on a plough 49.10

countenance patronage 291.25

coup¹ barter, trade 216.24

coup² overturn 294.31

coup-de-main *French* sudden vigorous attack 204.22

court courtyard 37.43 etc.

cousin-german first cousin 78.23

Covenanter 15.18 (see 'Historical Note') etc.

crack talk, have a chat 58.18, 85.35 (see note), 297.19

crap crop 290.31

craven see note to 278.2–3

creature-curates curates owing their position to patrons 136.15

creel see note to 50.21

criminate incriminate 67.2

cripple crippled 61.26

crop-eared, crop-ear for 30.42, 32.8, 64.9, 75.4, 192.20 see note to 30.42

cross affliction 71.43; to thwart, obstruct 112.12

cross-grained difficult, contrary 41.2

croudy raw oatmeal and water 221.39

cruize see note to 326.38–39

crutch prop (up) 350.25

crutch-handled with a cross-bar handle like crutches 315.8

cry call, shout 27.22 etc.; call (on someone) for help 28.8, 28.10, 28.11, 28.12

cuittle see note to 224.6

culverin large cannon 161.26

curch kerchief, cap 129.19

curmurring rumbling 63.26

curney grainy, coarse 168.32

curvet leap of a horse with all four feet off the ground 135.15

cutter see note to 75.14

cuttie *contemptuous* girl 91.5

cuttit *past participle* cut 196.5

cypher do arithmetic 125.7

daffing, daffin teasing, smutty talk 27.41; courting 205.26

daft crazy, stupid 55.6 etc.; thoughtless 333.24

daidling ineffectual 145.30

dais 12.42 (see note), 193.43

dam mother 63.37

daur dare 57.7, 58.35

daurna daren't 89.30, 298.13

deave annoy, be a nuisance to 73.17

declivity downward slope 97.23, 130.17

decoxion liquid in which a substance has been boiled 301.22

deer's-hair rushes 12.23

defalcation defection, shortcoming 19.29, 126.18

deil, de'il, deevil devil 48.23 etc.

dejeuné breakfast 99.37

delation denouncement 70.18

dennty dainty 49.14

denounce promulgate 239.18

depone testify, declare on oath 307.42

depository person to whom something is confided 312.28

deprecate express disapproval of 36.40

depreciate underrate, belittle 8.1

derogation detracting from one's honour or reputation 23.6

descry discover, find out 265.20

devoted doomed 257.19

dight sift, winnow 55.1; wipe 319.42

dignity person holding high office or position 122.38; honourable or high office 351.3

din fuss, loud talk, disturbance 27.38 etc.

ding knock, push 222.12, 295.24

dinna don't 27.38 etc.

dirdum problem, punishment 56.15

dirk short dagger worn in the belt 26.16

discomposed disquieted, agitated 62.40

discover sight 255.25

disjaskit neglected 325.11

disjune breakfast 24.11 etc.

dismission discharge from service 40.40

disna doesn't 85.24, 86.6

dissension, dissention disagreement in matters of religious belief 83.6, 252.20, 253.15

distaff stick used in hand-spinning 76.32

distracted disturbed 214.6

div do 68.35, 68.38, 291.30

divertisement entertainment, light relief 319.34

Dns. *Latin abbreviation for* Dominus, Sir 7.20

dogmata *plural* beliefs, principles 178.1

dollar 1670s silver coin worth 4 merks 26.23 (see note) etc.

dolour suffering, sorrow 304.14

domiciliary for 18.23 and 62.39 see note to 18.23

dooms dashed 185.30

doomster court-officer who pronounced sentence 174.41, 282.23, 282.24

dotage feebleness of mind, senility 117.12

doublet close-fitting body-garment

with or without sleeves worn by men 320.40

doubt suspect, fear 40.19 etc.

douce, douse pleasant, respectable, decent 27.11 etc.

doudle play 28.13

doun down 50.26 etc.

dour stern 27.32; obstinate, stubborn, unyielding 67.43, 122.20, 290.10, 291.18, 291.23; gloomy, miserable 221.39

dow *term of endearment* dove, dear 51.14

dowless feeble 69.35

downa, douna cannot, be unable or unwilling 291.37, 294.6, 294.24

dragooner horse ridden by a dragoon 122.19

dram small measure of alcoholic drink 122.39, 122.41, 307.43

drammock oatmeal and cold water 136.13

drap drop 57.43, 81.9; drip 332.30

drave *past tense* drove 27.28

draw see note to 319.9–10

draw off withdraw 207.2, 212.12

draw out draw up, set in array 242.11, 254.25; detach 266.39

draw thegither close in sleep 40.22

draw up become friendly (with) 91.3; compose, arrange 199.29

draw-well deep well from which water is drawn by a bucket on a rope 85.16

dree endure, suffer 11.18

dreel drill 195.8

dribble drop 322.40

drink-offering see note to 261.30–32

drive rush 290.12

drive ower idle the time away 86.12

dropping desultory, not continuous 204.4

drouthy thirsty 28.4, 324.36

dry-stane-dike stone wall without mortar 8.39

ducking-stool see note to 69.27

dudgeon-haft dagger hilt 279.23

duds clothes 48.43, 123.31

dune done 57.1 etc.

dung *past participle of* ding see note to 56.15

durance imprisonment 225.5

dwalling dwelling 289.18

dwam swoon, fainting fit 316.16

dykeside ground beside a boundary wall 57.19

easter eastern 83.38

e'e eye 85.26, 86.6, 295.37, 319.35

e'en[1] *adverb* simply, just 36.7 etc.; even 177.41

e'en[2] *noun* eyes 40.22 etc.

e'en[3] *noun* evening 57.33 etc.

e'en now at the moment, just now 49.6, 324.10

e'enow enough 68.25

effeck effect 301.28

effectual effective 110.5; see note to 290.3–4

efficacy 150.8

egad *oath* by God! 69.1, 76.31, 117.43, 279.39

eident attentive 27.19

eik addition 292.27

elect for 72.8 and 237.27 see note to 72.8

elf-locks tangled mass of hair, tangles 180.36

embarrass hamper, make difficult 29.7

eneugh, enow enough 17.42 etc.

engineer designer of military works for attack or defence 81.6

entertain show hospitality to 92.5, 115.6, 285.1

entertainment hospitable provision of food and drink 48.37, 48.39, 326.40

enthusiasm (fancied) divine inspiration, wild religious emotion 145.38

episcopacy government of the church by bishops 13.41 etc.

epitaphion *Greek* epitaph 349.33

equipage get-up, accoutrements 9.15, 95.20, 131.18; carriage 16.41, 21.18, 25.13, 25.19

equipoize, equipoise equilibrium 311.43, 341.41

Erastian, Erastianism for 60.4 etc. see note to 60.4–5

escalade the scaling of walls with ladders 161.23

escheat *past participle* forfeit 282.21

espiegle sprightly, roguish 289.4

eve see note to 195.43–196.1

evil-disposed 158.26

evince display, show 20.6 etc.; prove 303.11

ewhow goodness!, gracious! 20.32, 35.41

exercise act of (private) worship

184.16 etc.

exercitation exercising 61.27

exigencies dire straits 151.38

exordium introduction 199.43

expatiate expand (in words) 233.15

expiation atonement, making amends 14.24

expulse drive out 136.10

extenuated emaciated 180.37

fa' fall 91.19 etc.; for 56.6 see note

faes foes 332.13

fail collapse, grow weak 125.15

failed infirm, worn out with age 319.8

fain glad, obliged 29.16; gladly 219.11

fair civilly, kindly 62.22 etc.

fair-fashioned well-mannered 39.6

fairing a present; one's deserts 290.15

fairly completely, quite, actually 25.27 etc.; candidly 74.11; properly 159.7

fal-lall piece of finery or frippery 320.18

falcon, falconet light cannon 161.26, 161.26

famish die 121.17

fand found 185.40, 296.12

fard paint 170.38

fash trouble, bother, fuss 27.21

fauld-dyke wall round a sheep-fold 75.33

faut, fau't, fault fault 50.25; want, lack 125.16, 200.19

fear'd, feared frightened, afraid 185.14, 216.14, 223.27

fearless impious, wicked 20.32

febrifuge medicine to reduce fever 197.40

feck greater part 321.32

feckless feeble, unimportant, helpless 70.27, 115.34; incompetent, stupid 185.21

fee wages 123.24

fee'd hired, engaged for wages 293.15

feifteen fifteenth 70.40, 71.3

fend provide (for) 35.41, 57.2, 57.4; support oneself, scrape by 216.17

fiat decree 100.21

fief feudal tenure 15.17, 213.31, 242.21

fiend (the) devil 85.34 etc.

fille-de-chambre *French* maidservant 82.43, 196.4

fire-flaught flash of lightning, thunderbolt 307.5, 321.22

firelock musket in which the powder was ignited by sparks; soldier armed

with a firelock 95.22

firstling first offspring, firstborn 154.19

fissenless, foisenless, fizenless spiritless, lacking in nourishment 36.16, 136.13, 331.21

fit-ba' football 125.8

five-a-hand see note to 121.36

flanker projecting fortification 76.36

flapped-hat, flapped hat hat with ear flaps 229.17, 292.13

flee fly 49.33 etc., and see note to 67.5; set one bird flying against another 199.12

fleech coax, chat up 157.22

flit move house, leave 55.11, 59.2

flock-bed bed stuffed with tufts of wool etc. 224.32

flyte scold, shout abuse 145.31, 149.39, 296.35

foisenless see fissenless

foment rouse, stir up 111.27

fond foolish 13.1

for for fear of 91.13

forage food for horse 77.10

forby, forbye in addition (to), besides 54.17 etc.

fore-hand leading 57.36

forenoon morning 331.23

forgather fall in with one another 122.22

forgi'e forgive 196.4

forrit forward 393.22

fortalice fortress 97.13

fought *noun* fight, struggle 224.9

foul for 56.6 and 71.38 see note to 56.6

foumart polecat, ferret, or weasel 185.14

frae from 2.70 etc.

frae that from the fact that, since 296.11

fraim, fremd strange 91.12, 121.25

frequent crowded, full 322.19

fresh sober 345.12

friend relative, kinsman 67.25

fructify bear fruit 60.31, 181.8, 200.23

fu' full, very 53.16

fule fool 123.28, 123.30; foolish, silly 53.42, 54.21

fume water or vapour arising from the sea 42.25

fur furrow 125.21

furl roll (up) 93.17

fusee light musket 16.18, 20.27

gae[1] go 73.1 etc.

gae[2] *past tense* gave 121.23 etc.

gaed, ga'ed went 27.28 etc.

ga'en see **gane**

gait way 321.35

gall bitterness, rancour 73.2

galless free from malice 339.10

galling irritating, harassing, offensive 88.16, 114.8, 255.12

galloway small sturdy horse 26.16

gane, ga'en gone 12.14 etc.

gang go 18.20 etc.

gar, gaur make 56.16, 122.11–12 (see note) etc.

garner granary 12.9

garniture trimming 243.33

gat got 27.23 etc.

gate way 27.23 etc.

gaun going 217.11

gauntrees gantry, stand for barrels 63.34

gaur see **gar**

gay rather, pretty, quite 57.35 etc.

gear property, possessions 17.42; armour 26.7

gie, gi'e give 69.11 etc.

gifted miraculously endowed with spiritual power 184.17

gilpey tomboy 39.38

gin[1] snare, trap 68.41

gin[2] if 126.15 (see note) etc.

gipscy hussy 93.21

girnel storage chest for meal 168.15, 168.29

gittern old type of guitar 188.30

Glasgow-ward in the direction of Glasgow 291.38

glass-sashed having one or more panes of glass 294.37

gledge squint 295.36

gleg quick, active 56.38, 59.12, 125.5

gliff short while 158.27

gloaming twilight 307.30

glowr stare 82.23

goad pointed stick used for driving cattle 121.36, 130.41

goadsman ploughboy, ploughman's assistant 49.7

gomeril fool 56.9, 224.11, 296.21

good-man see **gudeman**

governante housekeeper 50.10, 63.31, 320.33

gowd gold 50.3 etc.

gowk fool 73.30

gowpin the fill of the two hands held together 289.27

grace-cup parting drink 26.4

graith equip, array 26.8

gramoches leggings, gaiters 9.5

grane groan, grumble 68.33, 72.42, 124.38, 125.14

grass for 53.34, 54.5, 56.27, 296.42 see note to 53.34

grate door of interlaced iron bars 18.13, 238.17

gratuitous provided without payment, free 53.32

greaves armour for the lower leg 25.28

greet cry, weep 157.25

grewsome ugly 323.33

griping 139.28

grit great 55.24, 121.19, 123.30; proud 123.29

ground-officer official of a barony 55.11

grund ground 48.34, 57.6, 57.40, 127.4

gude[1] good 27.12 etc.

Gude[2] God 49.21, 330.4

gudeman, good-man husband 289.17, 289.24, 324.24

gudeminnie mother-in-law 294.13

gude-sister sister-in-law 325.17

gudewife, gude-wife mistress (of a farm, etc) 27.28; landlady of an inn 168.20; wife 293.8, 293.14

guide see note to 83.30; manager 316.43; manage 319.14

guse goose 49.29, 91.17

ha' hall 60.8

ha'arst harvest 266.7 (see note)

hadna hadn't 73.33, 95.6, 121.40, 224.11

hae, ha'e have 21.27 etc.; take 126.40, 260.16

haena haven't 168.25, 185.29, 327.41

haft become settled or established 73.20

haill, hail whole 58.36 etc.; (the) whole of the 168.29

halberdier soldier armed with a halberd 278.43

halbert, halberd weapon combining spear and battle-axe 32.38 etc.

haly holy 324.23

hame home 12.14 etc.

hamely homely, familiar 64.4, 98.18

hantle a great deal 277.20

hap luck 92.42

hardiness audacity 117.1

hardy presumptuously bold 263.5

harle drag, haul 69.37, 120.30

harmonious see note to 252.27

harness defensive equipment for horse and/or rider 24.6

harns brains 146.36

harrow see note to 68.30

harry plunder, lay waste, ruin 62.22, 62.23, 206.17

hash term of contempt for a person 221.37

haud¹ see note to 48.41

haud² hold, keep 39.14 etc.; see notes to 48.41, 73.22; continue 314.31

haugh level ground on the banks of a river 16.9, 54.15, 98.21

hauld habitation 325.15

hause neck 57.20; throat 81.9

havings behaviour, manners 85.1

hay-band see note to 296.9–10

head-mark see note to 82.22

heading beheading 72.10

hear till listen to 49.36, 335.5, 335.6

hearing scolding 122.40

heart-exercise training for spiritual improvement 150.8

hegh goodness! gracious! 39.6

hellicat good-for-nothing 123.11

hem clear the throat 199.39

hempie wild, mischievous 333.24

hen-wife woman who looks after the poultry 18.32, 91.30

herborage harborage, lodging, entertainment 12.39

heritage *Scots law* property in the form of land and houses 339.13

heritor proprietor, landowner 57.7, 72.18, 169.8

het hot 222.43, 293.24

heugh rough ground, steep bank 67.5; glen, ravine 163.19

hickery-pickery medicine of bitter aloes 60.17

hill-folk Covenanters 27.34 (see note), 30.11, 82.31

hinder-end backside 73.20

hing hang 185.23, 217.20

hinny, hinnie honey, dear 28.23 etc.

hoast cough 39.2, 126.42

hocus-pocus trickery 89.6

hoddin-grey undyed homespun woollen cloth 9.2, 58.10

holding-forth see note to 209.20–21

holm, holme low-lying land beside a river 49.9 etc.

horn drinking vessel made of horn 267.35

horning proclamation as an outlaw or rebel 72.8

host army 167.36

hosting attending the king's host 53.31

hostler innkeeper 27.42

hough hock, hind-leg joint 147.40

hout, hout tout tut-tut! oh dear! 50.24 etc.

howff meeting-place, public house 26.36

huff order (about) 111.38

humle-cow hornless cow 27.23

hunder hundred 295.28

hup see note to 185.33–34

hurcheon hedgehog; sloven, layabout 56.10

hurdies haunches 260.6

husbandman man who tills the soil 124.30, 154.21

huz us 149.39

hyson China tea 350.21

ilk each, every 28.6, 126.35, 297.26

ilka each, every 40.25, 54.3, 54.36, 185.41; ordinary, week (day) 57.3

ill difficult 39.18, 59.1, 185.35, 236.23; bad, unsatisfactory 168.31; harm 124.14, 124.19

ill-fa'ard, ill-fa'ar'd ugly, hateful 73.30, 91.5, 126.2, 216.40

impassible incapable of suffering pain or injury 337.9

importunate persistent, pertinacious 80.41

importunity troublesome pertinacity 104.43, 302.15

inbrought seized and confiscated 282.22

incident naturally appertaining 147.22, 153.25

incoming arrival 291.24

index minute hand of a clock 264.4

indulge grant as a favour or indulgence 61.16

indulged, indulgence for 35.12 etc. and 34.36 etc. see 'Historical Note'

infield see note to 67.5

ingle fireside 27.33, 30.7, 123.10

inhibit *law* prohibit 56.21

injurious wilfully inflicting wrong 48.14

insurgent rebel, one who rises in revolt against authority 7.29 etc.

intelligence understanding 137.40

intercommune communicate with (e.g. an outlaw) 66.32

intercommuned proscribed, outlawed 36.28, 50.39, 66.32, 115.6 see note to 36.28–29

intercommunicate see note to 295.21–22

intermit suspend 10.41

invest beseige 201.22

involve envelop 254.38

ironed in shackles 108.38, 113.11, 224.32

irons fetters, shackles 113.12, 113.38, 119.19

I'se I shall 48.40 etc.

ither other 28.7 etc.

jalouse, jealouse suspect, be suspicious of 27.35, 80.43, 289.41, 295.33

jaud *abusive* woman 71.35, 279.41

jealous zealous or vigilant in preserving 145.21

jennet small Spanish horse 17.14

jilt whore 64.35

jimp scanty, barely adequate 292.25

jocosely playfully 12.43

joe, jo sweetheart, dear 56.14 etc.

Judaical Jewish 15.7

jummle jumble 290.1

justify convict, condemn, execute 157.39

jute, jut any insipid drink, dregs 28.5, 63.24

kail-brose meal mixed with boiled cabbage water 206.13, 222.43

kail-worm caterpillar 29.43

kaisar emperor 53.41

kale curly cabbage 56.27; soup 57.43, 122.22–23 (see note), 122.40, 122.41

kale-yard kitchen-garden 53.34 etc.

kebbie stick 122.11

kebbock a whole cheese 61.20

keek peep 85.16

ken know 27.17 etc.

kenn'd, kend, kent *past tense* knew 57.35 etc.

kenna don't know 184.30, 291.21, 328.25

kent¹ see **kenn'd**

kent² staff 122.16

kettle large cooking pot 121.3

kindly see note to 53.33

kintra country 121.7

kintra-side country-side 121.29

kirk church 11.38 etc.

kirk-ganging churchgoing 59.35

kittle ticklish, tricky 91.20, 168.13; difficult to deal with 296.37

knap talk, chatter 54.37

knowe knoll, little hill 255.5 etc.

kye cows, cattle 329.20, 345.4

kylevine lead (pencil) 71.14

laddie boy, young fellow 50.21, 280.21, 321.26

laigh low 314.28

laird lord, landowner 8.37 etc.

laith loath, reluctant 277.11, 292.24

landau type of four-wheeled carriage 16.29

landward country 63.14, 125.4

lane *with possessive pronoun* by oneself 91.12 (see note), 222.31

lang long 56.7 etc.; tall 82.26; for 324.3 see note

Lanrick Lanark 121.42

Laodicean for 169.35 and 171.15 see note to 169.35

lapsarianism belief in the doctrine of the fall of man from innocence 73.12

lassock girl 39.38

latchet loop, fastening 126.39

latitudinarian *derogatory* liberal in opinion especially in religious matters, not insisting on adherence to standard rules or practice 18.8 etc.

lave (the) rest 50.33, 222.28

lawing reckoning, bill 27.17, 58.27

leaguer camp 135.32; siege 209.23; beleaguer 34.3

leash set of three 278.1

leasing-making *Scots law* making false accusations, verbal sedition 96.36

leddy lady 51.12 etc.

leggins leggings, gaiters 9.6

lenity mildness, mercifulness 105.4

let hinder, obstruct 254.7

lick blow 28.9

liege (vassal) bound to render feudal service 53.31

liege-lord superior to whom feudal allegiance is due 14.33

life-rent *Scots law* right to receive income from a property till death,

but not to dispose of the capital
296.26

life-rentrix female who has a life-rent 18.10

light, light aff, light down dismount
289.22, 291.35, 292.1, 295.20

like *adjective* likely 316.8

like *verb* be likely to 260.16

limbo prison, confinement 228.9

limner portrait-painter 100.39

line note, letter 59.3

lineally in direct line of descent 9.23,
29.5, 29.17

ling see note to 121.35

linn waterfall 333.20

lippen to trust, depend on 81.1

list please 339.29

livery-coat part of the distinctive uniform worn by the male servants of a
great house 26.22

loaning grassy cattle-track 91.20,
121.25

locality see note to 71.4–5

lock bundle, handful 327.19

lodgment see note to 81.4–18

lo'e love 232.24

long-ear'd asinine 266.37

long-winded not soon out of breath
26.19

loof hand 126.3 (see note to 126.2–3)

loon fellow, rascal 27.27 etc.

loot *past tense* let 123.16, 319.33

looten *past participle* let 328.35

Lordsake exclamation expressing
surprise 125.29

lound quietly, softly 330.11

lounder fight with, punch 28.7

loup leap, jump 216.2

lour frown 261.19

low flame 168.27

lucubrations literary work resulting
from nocturnal study 6.11

lug ear 28.16

lum-head chimney-top 123.9

made-like contrived, assumed 295.34

main in the game of hazard, number
(from 5 to 9) called before the dice
are thrown 78.34

mains home-farm, i.e. principal farm
of an estate 57.5

mair more 28.4 etc.; superior 319.16

maist[1] most 27.43 etc.

maist[2] almost 296.31

maister master 39.25 etc.

major strut, swagger 39.21

mak make 56.43 etc.

malignant applied by Covenanters to
their religious opponents 16.28 etc.;
ill-disposed 20.18

manse minister's house 215.4,
219.15, 236.26

man-sworn forsworn, perjured
194.25

manteau loose gown 77.11

mantled with foaming head, brimming over 100.2

mantua woman's loose gown 349.23

march-dike boundary wall 8.26

Margrave *German title* prince 50.1
(see note)

mark see **merk**

Mars Roman god of war 74.2

mart cow fattened for slaughter
216.22

martingale strap joining horse's noseband to girth 126.32, 127.15

marvedie maravedi, Spanish coin
worth about 1/6 penny sterling
99.22

mashlum mixed grain and pulses
168.20

mask mash, brew 86.19

masque mask, disguise 63.5

massy bumptious, self-important
125.9

maun must 21.28

mauna, maunna must not 27.22 etc.

maunder mutter, grumble 40.10

mausoleum stately tomb 7.34

maut malt 289.27

maw stomach; jaws 339.3

mawkin hare 57.19

meal-ark chest for storing oatmeal
126.30

mechanic manual labourer 271.3

meed reward 338.40

menage members of a household
294.32

menial servant 41.3

mensefu' seemly, proper 50.41

merk, mark silver coin worth 13s. 4d.
Scots (13 1/3d. sterling in late 17th
century) 26.22 etc.

merrily briskly 54.36

mess portion of food 48.24, 206.21

mickle see **muckle**

minch mince 56.18

mind remember 40.23 etc.

minnie *term of affection* mother
84.30

mirligoes vertigo, light-headedness 222.31

miscarriage misconduct, failure, disaster 51.30

misdoubt distrust, doubt 57.22, 80.43, 144.32

misericordé *Spanish/Italian* mercy 98.20

mislear'd rude, unmannerly 314.15

mista'en mistaken 329.19

mither mother 56.31 etc.

money-broking money-dealing 72.18

monument written document, record 283.30

mony many 18.29 etc.

morass bog, marsh 42.40 etc.

morn (the morn) tomorrow 217.11, 217.20, 266.6, 297.9

moss bog, moor 36.6, 72.12, 138.24

moss-flow wet bog 72.12

moss-hags dangerous boggy moorland 60.16

mousquetaire see note to 28.40

moveable see note to 282.21

muckle[1] *adjective* much 39.20 etc.; great, great big 221.37, 295.21 (see note), 295.40, 319.36

muckle[2] *adverb* much 18.19 etc.

muckle[3], mickle *noun* much, a lot 27.42 etc.

Mucklewhame *imaginary placename* great hollow 57.5

muir moor 36.4 etc.

muir-cock male red grouse 351.13

mummery play-acting, performance 34.13

murgeon contortion, posturing 54.27

murus *Latin* wall 8.39

mutchkin *measure of capacity* 1/4 pint Scots, i.e. 3/4 pint Imperial (0.426 litre); sometimes 1 Imperial pint (0.568 litre) of spirits 12.43, 28.24

na, na' not 11.15 etc.; no 49.22 etc.

nae no 11.19 etc.; not 56.19, 82.42

naebody nobody 57.34 etc.

naething nothing 27.30 etc.

naig horse 122.18, 185.33, 292.31

nane none 121.19 etc.

nash-gab talkativeness, garrulousness 69.33

natheless nevertheless 73.11

neb beak 202.41

needcessity necessity 261.12

needna needn't 28.21

neist next 121.7 etc.

neuter neutral 201.32

nevoy nephew 48.28, 62.17

nice fastidious, difficult to please 324.36

niece grand-daughter 77.15, 77.15, 111.19, 113.24; great-niece 92.17 etc.

no not 39.12 etc.

noble gold coin worth 6s. 8d. (33p) 31.15, 185.34

noddle nod 40.32, 315.20

nomenclator one who announces or tells someone other people's names 23.34

non-conformity 57.9 (see note to 57.7–9), 336.19

non-juring see note to 13.39

noo now 295.22

Odd God 56.11, 145.31, 197.2, 277.4

o'er-drive see over-drive

offices outhouses 37.43, 98.28

ohon ochone! exclamation expressing sorrow 53.22

onstead farm building 292.28

ony any 17.42 etc.

or before 121.16; until 324.6, 329.20; rather than that 62.30, 297.8

orderly-men non-commissioned officers or privates who attend on superior officers to carry orders or messages 119.16

other another 257.18

ou *exclamation* oh! 55.23, 184.34, 197.7, 290.9

out[1] finished 31.9

out[2] along, up 325.14

outbreak *noun* breaking out 217.17, 324.7

outfield for 67.5, 297.16 see note to 67.5

outshot extension 292.27

outside outlying 292.2

out-taken with the exception of 277.21, 329.35

over-drive, o'er-drive drive too hard, overwork 49.7, 276.2

ower too 27.36 etc.; over 39.41 etc.

owsen oxen 49.8

pacification appeasement, conciliation, treaty of peace 208.40

paduasoy heavy silk garment 92.8, 93.20

paid beaten 291.19

palfrey small saddle-horse for ladies

17.6, 17.23

pantomime significant gestures without speech 104.26

papa-prelatist supporter of **prelates** who act like a pope 46.21

papinjay see popinjay

papist adherent of the Pope, Roman Catholic 46.21 etc.

parallel see note to 81.4–18

park field 58.21, 289.22

parley call for a conference 199.40

parole word of honour 201.31

parricide murder of one regarded as particularly sacred 65.22

parritch porridge 48.25 etc.

part duty, allotted portion of a task 210.15

parterre flat area with ornamental flower-beds 294.37

particular individual, special 104.19

partisan long-handled spear 256.18

party-coloured of various colours 16.16

pass¹ *noun* strategic passage 255.11, 262.10

pass² *verb* pledge 266.28

passage incident, occurrence 11.8

pat *past tense* put 83.23

peace keep silent 170.41

pearlins, pearlings lace edgings 77.14, 123.25

pease-meal flour made of ground pease, used in a wide variety of dishes in country areas 61.7, 168.16, 168.19

peat-hag a cut peat-working 72.12

peddling petty, pettifogging 94.9

peel-house fortified house 168.42

pendulous suspended 21.30

penny-fee wages 57.41, 59.13, 59.16

perdue hidden 55.39

phrase song and dance, fuss 86.7

pickle small amount 58.17, 319.12

picquet for 96.36 see note; picket, small body of troops 249.12

piddle pick at one's food 100.5

piece gun 20.23 etc.

pike weapon with long shaft and sharp spear-like point 25.7 etc.

pinners streamers, ribbons 123.25; long flaps attached to a **coif** 315.24

pint strip of cut corn 125.22

pioneer see note to 203.20

pip see note to 342.29–30

pipkin small cooking pot 315.16

pit put 27.43 etc.

pit down defeat 290.14

plack small coin; money, one's worldly wealth 126.30

plaid woollen wrap 58.9 etc.

plea contest 329.3

pledge toast 11.36, 267.32

plenishing household equipment 59.10

pleugh plough 48.41 etc.

pleugh-paidle tool for scraping earth from a plough-coulter 277.19

plight pledge 6.39

plumb-damis-parridge porridge containing prunes, raisins etc., formerly eaten at Christmas 56.16

pock-puddings see note to 168.33

pockmankle portmanteau, travelling bag 185.39

popery Roman Catholicism 73.11, 172.40

popinjay parrot 16.14 etc.

popish Roman Catholic 44.3

pose heap, cache, hoard 185.8

postillion each of the riders on the near horses of a carriage 16.39

potation drink 76.9

potch mash or churn (up) 129.6

potsherd fragment of broken earthenware pot 127.17, 145.7

pouch pocket 185.16

pouss push 125.18

pouther, powther powder, gunpowder 39.20, 48.43

powder gunpowder 86.31, 142.22

preceese, preceeze precise 195.1, 238.26, 279.20, 316.10

precious used by Puritans of someone of high spiritual worth or standing 145.2

precision precise thought or definition 30.13

prelacy authority of **prelates**; church government by **prelates** 7.33 etc.

prelate high-ranking ecclesiastic, e.g. bishop, archbishop 30.38 etc.

prelatic Episcopalian 54.2, 340.12

prelatist supporter or adherent of **prelacy**, Episcopalian 59.40 etc.

prent print title-page

presbytery the Presbyterian system; the ecclesiastical court above the Kirk Session and below the Synod 145.18

prescribe *Scots law* lapse, become invalid because of the passage of time 310.4

presently immediately or shortly afterwards 152.38

presentment representation 320.10

press crowd 250.25; thick of the fight 143.43, 258.41; cupboard 92.9

pretend claim 239.40

pretty fine, manly, brave 23.36 etc.

prim close primly 52.30

primate archbishop, principal bishop 30.20 etc.

primitive old-fashioned 17.7

privy for 15.38 etc. see note to 15.1

professor one who makes open profession of religious faith 73.15

prognostic prognostication 51.15

proper own 6.41, 308.32; for 332.40 see note

proselyte convert, one who has transferred from one party or belief to another 15.25, 171.34

prosing 298.26

protester see 'Historical Note'

province business 258.23

provost Scottish equivalent of mayor 26.24, 32.37, 125.16

provost-marshal head of army police 167.26

psaltery ancient stringed instrument like a dulcimer but plucked 54.20

public public-house, tavern 324.34, 325.14

publicans see note to 71.4–5

puir poor 35.36 etc.

pule pool 91.19

pund 27.25 (see note) etc.

purpose-like neat 293.9

putten up comfortably lodged 184.35

quaigh shallow bowl-shaped drinking-cup 64.13

quarter cut into quarters 205.36

quarter-master-general staff-officer in charge of quartering of troops 200.34

quarterings division of the body into four quarters 72.10

quarters lodgings, billet 10.13

quean girl 39.35, 123.21, 222.43, 297.22

querist interrogator 65.25

quick alive 72.11

quotha indeed! 62.1

rade *past tense* rode 164.3, 216.23, 329.35

raff see note to 39.23

rag-weed ragwort 94.23

raillery banter, joking 30.31, 84.28

raise rise 334.1

raison reason 301.29, 301.31

randie foul-mouthed woman 71.37; loud-voiced 216.41

ranking roaring 126.5

rant lively tune 323.40 (see note)

ranting noisy, boisterous 123.6

rape see note to 217.2

Raploch for 50.41 and 320.19 see note to 50.41

rascally wretched, mean 32.10

rase *past tense* rose 216.13

rax stretch, hang 62.28

re-edify rebuild, restore 153.1

real royal 300.39

reckoning payment in settlement of an account 32.22

recreant confessing oneself beaten, defeated 192.22

recruited refreshed 32.23

rectilinear forming a straight line 8.28

recusancy refusal to obey authority 51.37, 101.36, 172.8

recusant one who refuses to obey authority, especially in religious matters 17.35 etc.

redder person who tries to stop a fight 28.9

rede advise title-page

red-herring see note to 238.25–27

reduce compel to surrender 189.23

reduction surrender 237.10

reek smoke 122.22–23 (see note), 123.8, 216.13

refection refreshment 344.21

regale feast, entertainment 242.40

reive steal, rob 27.27

relict widow 26.35

religionist religious zealot 199.42

reliques remains 7.10

rencontre chance meeting 110.39

rent-mail rent 102.12

repining discontented, complaining 16.6

repossess reinstate 351.8

requisition written demand by the military for supplies etc. 209.27

reset *Scots law* receive, shelter 66.35, 83.13, 102.25

resolutioner for 37.16, 178.36 see

'Historical Note'

reversionary leftover 158.25

revulsion sudden violent change of feeling 267.29

Rhenish from the Rhine 344.25

rheumatize rheumatism 38.43

ribband ribbon 26.17

rid remove 284.15

rigs land 50.22, 55.13, 125.21

rin run 66.28

ripe turn out the contents of 185.15

rood a square measure 8.40

roof-tree the main beam of a roof, often the subject of toasts in Scotland 72.21

round[1] *adjective* large, considerable 74.12; brisk 226.39

round[2] *noun* part of a building, having a circular form 83.38

rout roar, rumble 121.24, 126.43

route common herd, rabble 266.37

row wrap 89.26

rue see note to 223.33

ruffle disturbance, vexation 192.18

rug[1] *noun* rough woollen material 80.11

rug[2] *verb* pull, tug 297.27

ruth pity 89.17

sack general name for a class of white wine from Spain and the Canaries 65.27

sackbut obsolete musical instrument like a trombone 54.20

saddle-bow arched front of saddle 16.41 etc.

sae so 21.28 etc.; so long as, provided that 39.34; see notes to 39.6, 73.22

sair[1] *adjective and adverb* sore, painful, severe, terrible 18.18 etc.

sair[2] *adverb* terribly, greatly 27.36 etc.; harshly 50.25; hard, laboriously 294.14; vehemently, fiercely 122.19, 329.3

saker small cannon 161.26

sall shall 11.22 etc.

saloon large reception room 100.43, 295.11

sanbenitos *Spanish* see note to 275.33–34

sanctum sanctorum *Latin* holy of holies 319.38

sandy-lavrock ringed plover 55.14

sang song 125.20 etc.

sark shirt 195.11

sarty see **certie**

satellite servant, agent 63.10

saul soul 27.42, 56.42

sauld sold 216.19

saut salt 28.15

sax six 73.18 etc.

saxteenth sixteenth 70.42

scaff see note to 39.23

scale clean the bore of (a gun) 161.28

scauld scald 260.24

scaur precipice, sheer rock 91.20

scion descendant 79.10, 79.13

Scotch Scottish 64.9, 74.30, 135.7, 318.35; Scots, the language of Lowland Scotland 98.19, 347.19

Scotchman, Scottishman Scotsman, Scot 47.2 etc.

Scots Scottish 255.4, 324.1; of money value 27.25, 321.33; of measures, bigger than the English equivalents 325.15 (see note)

scrape awkward bow including scraping the foot back across the ground 6.19

screak screech, grate shrilly 125.35

screed long rigmarole 121.23

scrupulous troubled with scruples of conscience 14.37, 114.40, 287.29

sectary member of a dissenting sect 55.42 etc.

sedulously assiduously 21.9

seek resort 171.12

sell self 85.18

seneschalship administration of justice and of domestic arrangements 161.7

sensible sensitive 237.32

'septing excepting 125.7

sepulture burial 6.42

serun surround 58.9

service employment, job, work as a servant 53.32 etc.

set suit, be suitable or fitting for 48.42, 195.12

set by reject, disregard 329.15

set up pretend, claim (to be) 73.31

setting fitting 22.1

shamoy chamois, soft pliable leather 243.26

shaw[1] *noun* wood, thicket 342.14

shaw[2] *verb* show 135.7

sheeling-hill rising ground where grain was winnowed by the wind 55.5

sheugh shoo! go away! 147.41

shoon shoes 319.42

shoulder-knot braid hanging from
the shoulder as part of military uniform 114.42
shouther shoulder 147.9
shute shoot 123.26
sic such 18.21 etc.
siccan such 40.17
sifting searching 317.22
siller money 28.20 etc.
sin' see note to 95.3
single see notes to 60.13 and 289.42
sirs God preserve us! 20.32 etc.
skaith harm, damage 122.3
skeel skill 144.33, 323.39
skeily skilled, expert 291.38
skellie squint, be cross-eyed 33.24
skelp smack, spank 90.6; scamper,
gallop 121.43
skill knowledge 36.23
skinker toper, drunkard 94.26
skirl shriek, screech 49.32, 189.32
skirl-in-the-pan fried onions and
oatmeal 40.17
skirl up screech out 121.41
skirts coat-tails 342.24 (see note),
347.15
slops inferior garments 50.42
sma, sma' small; of alcohol, weak 28.5
etc.
small-craft small trading vessels 20.3
socinians see note to 152.42–43
sodger soldier 27.38 etc.; see note to
60.13
somegate somewhere 36.4; somehow
58.17
something somewhat 225.21
sorn *Scots law* taking meat or drink by
force or menaces 48.40
sorrow *verb* lament 313.32
sort[1] *verb* feed and litter (a horse)
292.27; for 296.33 see note; tidy,
arrange 58.2, 319.33
sort[2] *noun* considerable number 294.1
sough sound, whine 125.28, 265.14;
see notes to 168.14, 316.15–16,
351.13–14
sough awa' breathe one's last 316.9
sowens oatmeal steeped and fer-
mented in water 56.18, 293.22,
294.23
sowp sup, drink 122.39
spak spoke 319.9, 327.24
spang leap 56.25
spark smart young fellow 23.20,
67.14, 79.28

speel climb 91.9
speer ask 27.38 etc.
spence inner room 28.14
spill destroy, kill 134.28 (see note)
split be shipwrecked 103.6
sponsible reliable, respectable 72.17
springald youth 114.31
spurn kick 25.27
Stadtholder chief magistrate of the
United Provinces of the Netherlands 283.39, 318.1
stamach, stamack stomach 40.5 etc.
stamp character, kind 35.20
stand hesitate, stop to think 91.13
stane stone 8.39 etc.
stap[1] step 91.20
stap[2] thrust 123.23
staple post, pillar 314.2
start[1] *verb* force (hare) out of its form
187.36
start[2] *noun* sudden display of energy
23.7
stauncheon stanchion, bar 206.2
stave verse, stanza 254.33
staves staffs, sticks 166.21
staw satiate, disgust 11.14
stay detain 32.20
steek shut 121.8
steer molest, pester 329.1
Stentorian loud 200.2
stick hesitate, be reluctant 28.21
stilts plough-handles 49.8, 125.20
sting see note to 121.35
stipend salary 59.42, 71.6, 219.16
stir[1] *noun* sir 58.26 etc.
stir[2] *verb* raise as an issue 177.37
stir about be active or on the move
290.11
stirring brisk, busy 324.37
stot bullock 260.6
stoup tankard, decanter 28.24, 94.41
stour[1] commotion 290.38
stour[2] grim 27.32
strae straw 319.10
strait narrow 59.43, 121.38; difficulty,
dilemma 18.18, 36.26
strap string (of onions) 90.34
strapping up hanging 74.10
Strath wide valley 133.15
straught straight 314.31
streak stretch 38.6
streights narrows, narrow passages
314.40
strength strong place, place of refuge
259.11 (see note)

stress emergency 50.39

stressed distressed 216.29

stricture critical remark 112.19

strife competition 16.26

stripe blow, lash 102.2, 124.32

stude *past participle of* **stand** stopped to think twice 85.40

study meditate 352.35

stumbling-block obstacle to belief 73.14

sturt strife, violent behaviour 332.18

sublapsarianism doctrine that God's election of some to everlasting life came after his knowledge of the fall 73.12

subsist maintain, furnish with provisions 209.5

substantial essential 252.5

succours *military* reinforcements 214.7

sufferer martyr 72.43

suit 23.35 (see note); petition, entreaty 108.26; courtship 302.33

suivante confidential maid 111.28

suld, sud should 11.25 etc.

sum bring to completion or perfection 278.36

summon call upon to surrender 189.19

summons summon 200.25

sune soon 82.16, 146.36, 147.8

sunk straw pad 9.10

superscribe address (a letter) 91.38

surcease cease 101.29

surcingle band round a horse's body to keep a pack etc. in place 126.32

surmount extend over and across 291.40

suspiration sigh 303.3

sward turf, grass 127.10

sweal splash, splutter 39.14

sybo spring onion 259.7

syke small stream, especially in a bog 185.4

sync ago 38.43 etc.; in the past 333.24; see notes to 95.3, 194.32

tablets notebook 24.36, 71.14 (see note)

tabor drum 14.39

tae (the) one of two 122.2, 123.24, 157.27

ta'en down, tane down weakened, impaired in health 126.13, 295.38

ta'en on wi' taken a liking to 194.26

ta'en, taen taken 52.42 etc.

tail end 121.32

tak on start 124.41

tak, tak', take take 11.15 etc.; make for, resort to 57.17, 86.4

take off drink off, knock back 64.13

take place take effect, succeed 348.22

take up arrest, seize 224.18; understand 295.37; make one's way 185.4

talent in biblical times, gold or silver of a talent weight 70.39

tane[1] (the) one of two 124.38 etc.

tane[2] see **ta'en down**

tangs tongs 28.11

tap top 146.40, 290.32

tarry wait 261.42

tass cup, goblet 168.27, 195.28

tauld told 56.25 etc.

taupie foolish girl 27.30

temporize see note to 252.1–2

tender piously sensitive 170.37, 171.25, 263.15, 328.11

tent[1] care, attention 40.1, 49.7, 127.3, 335.13; attend to title page

tent[2] movable pulpit with steps and canopy 249.5, 250.31

test, test-oath see note to 68.6–7

testifee testify 277.2, 277.5

tether hangman's noose 121.28

teugh tough 223.18

thack see note to 217.2

thae those, these 27.21 etc.

than then 127.1 etc.

theeking a roof 58.1

thegither together 40.22 etc.

themsels themselves 11.16 etc.

thereby thereabouts 328.15

thir these 53.28, 168.13

thowless feeble, ineffectual 36.16

thrang busy 27.14; pressing or crowding of people 164.4

thrapple throat 48.27

thraw oppose, cross 62.22

threep assert, insist 296.20

thumbkins, thumikins 80.6 (see note), 324.15

thunner thunder 292.19

tie-wig see note to 16.40

tight neat, smart 26.18, 217.2; vigorous, brisk 90.6; vague, perhaps ironical, expression of approval 70.32

tilbury light open two-wheeled carriage 16.29

till to 49.36 etc.

tippit stole, scarf 57.20 (see note)

tirailleur *French* sharp-shooter 22.29

tirl strip 184.40

tither see **tother**

tittie sister 125.14, 217.1

to for 122.40

tolbooth town hall, containing the jail 68.32, 91.22

tory 11.16 (see note) etc.

tother, t'other, tither (the) other of two 122.2 etc.

touch chafe, graze 267.8

touzle tousle, rumple 123.16

tow rope 73.23

town estate, farm, village 39.7, 49.34, 63.14

toy a worthless trifle 262.43; a cap worn by elderly women 314.7

tract track 42.39

transpire become known 23.5

travail labour, toil (for) 171.29

travailed weary, tired 27.36

trencher plate, platter; food 28.27, 95.8

trick-track old variety of backgammon 158.36

Trojan merry fellow, good chap 67.15

troth indeed 39.36 etc.; truth 121.1, 216.1, 217.4; pledge, promise 310.24

trow believe, feel sure 11.14 etc.

truculent fierce, cruel, savage 146.23

trumpet trumpeter 135.28

trysted visited (with misfortune) 324.25

tumultuary irregular, undisciplined 144.14, 189.5, 211.13, 242.29; turbulent 335.8

twa two 27.27 etc.

twal twelve 57.11, 321.33

umqhile late 23.37

unblenched which has not gone pale 117.27

unce ounce 168.21

unco *adjective* great, extraordinary, awful 27.18 etc.; odd, peculiar 40.20; see note to 317.10

unkindness hostility 37.15

unslaked *used of lime* lacking or without water 171.6

uphauden beholden 49.1

upon in the course of, in the middle of 68.24

uptak uptake, understanding 125.6

urge direct forcibly 337.8

valet, valet-de-chambre personal manservant 61.2, 93.10, 125.2

van foremost division of an army when advancing 142.6

very true 64.37

viands food, provisions 99.39, 206.39

vicinage vicinity, neighbourhood 349.32

victual provisions 61.39, 66.37, 197.6; supply with provisions 159.36, 168.3, 197.6

victualler inn-keeper 324.31

vidette mounted sentry placed in advance of an army to observe the movements of the enemy 167.39, 250.6

visit take vengeance, inflict punishment 112.42, 268.36

vivers food 344.28

wa' away 73.1

wad would 11.14 etc.

wadna wouldn't 57.6 etc.

wae woe 59.37, 147.39; sad 55.26

waefu' woeful, sad 330.20

wait await, wait for 104.8, 299.35

wally, wally-de-shamle valet 125.1 (see note), 217.2

walth plenty, abundance 260.4

wame see note to 122.24

wan *past tense* won 39.41, 331.1; found its way 319.34

want do without 27.22

wappen-schaw, wappin-schaw, wappinshaw, wappen-shawing muster or review of those able to bear arms in a district 15.14 etc.

ward division of a shire 16.9 etc.

warder watchman 96.6, 190.10

warding see note to 53.31

ware spend 123.25, 123.31

wark work 54.36 etc.; fuss, palaver, "business" 39.19, 83.21

warld world 49.37 etc.

warn summon, give notice to 54.16, 54.18, 55.11, 200.27

warrant writ empowering arrest 54.11 etc.; scriptural authority 53.29 etc.; be sure, guarantee 47.8 etc.

warse worse 35.41

warst worst 28.9, 123.5

wa's walls 158.13 (see note)

wassail merrymaking, riotous drinking 74.40

wat wet 60.16

water-broo oatmeal mixed with boiling water 121.15

water-side river-side 39.24
waught swig 28.21
waur worse 49.38 etc.
wax grow 54.4 etc.
weal well-being 229.31
wean child 49.31
weary wearisome 87.43, 121.16, 196.11, 294.1; wretched, confounded 291.9; sad, hard to endure 328.36; see note to 317.5–6
weary for wait wearily for, long for 121.32
web see note to 13.22
wee little 57.32 etc.; a short while, a moment 185.22
weeds garments 17.8
weel well 28.19 etc.
well-a-day alas 223.37
well-affected, well affected favourably disposed towards the authorities, loyal 18.42 etc.
well-timbered well-built 26.18
wersh tasteless, insipid 81.3
we'se we shall 292.18
wha, whae who 26.11 etc.; see note to 195.7
whar where 321.15, 321.20, 324.8
whare'er wherever 57.2
whase whose 53.39, 147.40
what how much 168.15
wheen few 72.6, 185.25, 323.31
whig 17th-century Scottish Presbyterian 11.11 (see note) etc.; act the whig 121.18
whigamore =whig 67.20 etc.
whiggery whig principles or practice 55.31 etc.
whiles sometimes, from time to time 40.25 etc.
whilk which 57.22 etc.
whilly-wha, whillywha flattery 39.33; cajole, soft-soap 319.10
whinger short stabbing sword 122.2
whirry carry off 69.32

whisht quiet! sh! 27.30 etc.; be quiet 68.24 etc.
wi' with 27.12 etc.
wier-man soldier, warrior 26.11
wife woman 54.21 etc.
wight human being, person 158.17
win get (away, into, off, etc.) 122.20, 223.35, 224.7, 277.7; reach 59.39, 121.27
win by avoid 277.28
win ower survive, get through 296.34
win to set to, begin eating 121.17
wind see note to 185.33–34
windle-strae tall thin stalk of grass 55.14
window-bole window-opening 56.11
window-shut shutter 298.36
wine-bibbing tippling 34.20
winna won't 27.22 etc.
winnock window 205.25, 261.8
wiselike sensible 124.37
wish hope 39.30
without outside, beyond 99.19 etc.
wives *plural* women 39.34 etc.
woodie gallows rope 145.33
wot know, be aware 34.30 etc.
wow gracious! 56.28
wrang wrong 59.14 etc.
writ letter 66.36
writer lawyer, solicitor 319.8
wud mad 291.27, 332.16 (see note)
wull will 288.41, 289.34
wyte blame 69.35
yaird kitchen-garden 56.26
yard wooden spar 20.15
yersell yourself 39.36
yestate estate 290.2
yill ale 28.24
yoke attach, connect 185.2, 290.4
yoking stint, stretch 60.17
Yule-eve Christmas Eve 56.17
zigzag see note to 81.4–18
Zounds *oath* by God's wounds 31.16

READ MORE IN PENGUIN

In every corner of the world, on every subject under the sun, Penguin represents quality and variety – the very best in publishing today.

For complete information about books available from Penguin – including Puffins, Penguin Classics and Arkana – and how to order them, write to us at the appropriate address below. Please note that for copyright reasons the selection of books varies from country to country.

In the United Kingdom: Please write to *Dept. EP, Penguin Books Ltd, Bath Road, Harmondsworth, West Drayton, Middlesex UB7 ODA*

In the United States: Please write to *Consumer Sales, Penguin Putnam Inc., P.O. Box 999, Dept. 17109, Bergenfield, New Jersey 07621-0120.* VISA and MasterCard holders call 1-800-253-6476 to order Penguin titles

In Canada: Please write to *Penguin Books Canada Ltd, 10 Alcorn Avenue, Suite 300, Toronto, Ontario M4V 3B2*

In Australia: Please write to *Penguin Books Australia Ltd, P.O. Box 257, Ringwood, Victoria 3134*

In New Zealand: Please write to *Penguin Books (NZ) Ltd, Private Bag 102902, North Shore Mail Centre, Auckland 10*

In India: Please write to *Penguin Books India Pvt Ltd, 210 Chiranjiv Tower, 43 Nehru Place, New Delhi 110 019*

In the Netherlands: Please write to *Penguin Books Netherlands bv, Postbus 3507, NL-1001 AH Amsterdam*

In Germany: Please write to *Penguin Books Deutschland GmbH, Metzlerstrasse 26, 60594 Frankfurt am Main*

In Spain: Please write to *Penguin Books S. A., Bravo Murillo 19, 1° B, 28015 Madrid*

In Italy: Please write to *Penguin Italia s.r.l., Via Benedetto Croce 2, 20094 Corsico, Milano*

In France: Please write to *Penguin France, Le Carré Wilson, 62 rue Benjamin Baillaud, 31500 Toulouse*

In Japan: Please write to *Penguin Books Japan Ltd, Kaneko Building, 2-3-25 Koraku, Bunkyo-Ku, Tokyo 112*

In South Africa: Please write to *Penguin Books South Africa (Pty) Ltd, Private Bag X14, Parkview, 2122 Johannesburg*

READ MORE IN PENGUIN

A CHOICE OF CLASSICS

Walter Scott	**The Antiquary**
	Heart of Mid-Lothian
	Ivanhoe
	Kenilworth
	The Tale of Old Mortality
	Rob Roy
	Waverley
Robert Louis Stevenson	**Kidnapped**
	Dr Jekyll and Mr Hyde and Other Stories
	In the South Seas
	The Master of Ballantrae
	Selected Poems
	Weir of Hermiston
William Makepeace Thackeray	**The History of Henry Esmond**
	The History of Pendennis
	The Newcomes
	Vanity Fair
Anthony Trollope	**Barchester Towers**
	Can You Forgive Her?
	Doctor Thorne
	The Eustace Diamonds
	Framley Parsonage
	He Knew He Was Right
	The Last Chronicle of Barset
	Phineas Finn
	The Prime Minister
	The Small House at Allington
	The Warden
	The Way We Live Now
Oscar Wilde	**Complete Short Fiction**
Mary Wollstonecraft	**A Vindication of the Rights of Woman**
	Mary and **Maria** (includes Mary Shelley's **Matilda**)
Dorothy and William Wordsworth	**Home at Grasmere**